ALONE TOGETHER IN THE WILDERNESS

Heather told herself that what she felt for Captain Ian Brooks was not real. Her feelings came only from being so lonely, and having only him as company in this untamed land where every day might be her last.

But now he held her close, demanding, "Don't you care for me, Heather? What does your heart tell you?"

"No, no. It's not true," she protested, yet her voice distant even to herself.

"Maybe this will convince you," said Ian. He bent down, kissing her, his lips caressing hers over and over, until she was on fire, all thoughts of her husband, Cole, fading in the flames. And Heather knew then she was lost not only in the wilderness— but in the wildness of her own heart. . . .

WILD WINDS CALLING

D1570849

Ø

Fabulous Fiction by June Lund Shiplett from SIGNET

WILD WINDS CALLING

JUNE LUND SHIPLETT

A SIGNET BOOK

NEW AMERICAN LIBRARY

PUBLISHER'S NOTE

This novel is a work of fiction. Names, characters, places, and incidents either are the product of the author's imagination or are used fictitiously, and any resemblance to actual persons, living or dead, events, or locales is entirely coincidental.

NAL BOOKS ARE AVAILABLE AT QUANTITY DISCOUNTS
WHEN USED TO PROMOTE PRODUCTS OR SERVICES.
FOR INFORMATION PLEASE WRITE TO PREMIUM MARKETING DIVISION,
NEW AMERICAN LIBRARY, 1633 BROADWAY,
NEW YORK, NEW YORK 10019.

SIGNET TRADEMARK REG. U.S. PAT. OFF. AND FOREIGN COUNTRIES
REGISTERED TRADEMARK—MARCA REGISTRADA
HECHO EN CHICAGO, U.S.A.

SIGNET, SIGNET CLASSIC, MENTOR, PLUME, MERIDIAN AND NAL BOOKS
are published by New American Library,
1633 Broadway, New York, New York 10019

First Printing, June, 1984

1 2 3 4 5 6 7 8 9

PRINTED IN THE UNITED STATES OF AMERICA

This book is dedicated to my dear friend and part-time secretary Louise Smith, without whose help I wouldn't have had time to begin the first page. She not only takes care of all the little nitty-gritty things that come up, but is willing to go above and beyond the call of duty when I need her most. I couldn't do without her, and she knows it. Bless you Louise, I love you.

Heather and Cole

1

It had stopped raining only a short time before, and the furled sails were still wet, water dripping from the rigging as the *Interlude* inched its way into the harbor, joining the myriad of ships already anchored there. The afternoon air was heavy, with overcast skies still threatening more rain as Cole Dante, wearing worn buckskins, straightened, putting both hands on the railing of the sleek three-masted ship and watched it make its way to its moorings. He hadn't really wanted to come to New Orleans; it was too dangerous. Even though the paper pardoning him was tucked securely into the money pouch hanging from the leather thong around his neck, there were still wanted posters with his name on them in all the major cities throughout the territories, and too many people were prone to act first, then ask questions later. Besides that, he had spent enough time in New Orleans during the war so that he was no stranger to the city or its people.

He'd rather have headed north, but winter was on its way. He had to take a chance on coming here. As his friend and frontier companion Eli Crawford had reminded him, shortly after they'd set sail, they didn't have just themselves to worry about anymore. There was Heather, her maid Tildie, and the baby.

He drew his eyes from the waterfront buildings that were getting closer with each minute, and glanced back across the deck to where his wife had just emerged from belowdecks carrying their sleep-tousled eleven-month-old son, who had just awakened from a much-needed nap. Heather's titian locks weren't as bright as they would have been with the sun on them, and dampness had kinked them into wayward curls she was trying unsuccessfully to subdue with a frayed ribbon, but they framed her face stubbornly, making her violet eyes look wide and innocent.

The trip had been hard on Heather, what with the baby to take care of, along with the seasickness that had plagued her. She

9

wasn't used to sailing, and had spent a great deal of the trip nursing a queasy stomach, leaving a lot of the responsibility of caring for young Case to Tildie, whose smiling black face showed more than once her appreciation for being able to come along. Tildie was still in her mid-teens and it was an exciting adventure for her. She didn't even seem to mind the fact that the baby was hard to handle and didn't like sailing any more than his parents. That, and the fact that he was still teething, had upset his usual good-natured temperament, and now, with a quick flip of his head, he rested a cheek on his mother's shoulder, listening to her trying to reassure him they'd soon be off the ship. His lower lip pushed into a pout, and Cole frowned, watching him.

"I told you it wouldn't be easy," Eli said from behind him.

Cole turned, facing his friend. Eli's sandy hair was generously saturated with silver, his gray eyes darkening.

"What worries me," Cole said hesitantly, "is will she be able to keep up?"

Eli's eyes shifted from Cole's troubled face, and he watched Heather heft the baby higher onto her shoulder, letting him rest his head a little longer.

"She's never been on a trail, Cole," he reminded him.

"But she's tracked with me, I've taught her to shoot, and she really took to the woods."

"Carrying a baby?"

"We have the horses."

"Thank God." Eli watched Heather start toward them, picking her way carefully across the deck. He hadn't blamed Cole for wanting her with him. She was a lovely woman, a little shy and unworldly, but very much in love with the man she could finally call her husband. Eli looked first at one, then the other, noting the intense warmth in their eyes when they met.

Cole and Heather were first cousins and that's where all their troubles had started. There were no government laws against their loving one another, but society had refused to accept it. Therefore, when Heather realized she was carrying Cole's child, knowing marriage to him was impossible, she had married De-Witt Palmer, whose father owned a neighboring plantation. Unfortunately, her husband hadn't been as naive as Heather had hoped, and when he realized he'd been duped into marrying a woman who was to present him with another man's child, he'd become furious.

But that was all behind them now. At least Eli hoped it was

over and done. DeWitt was dead and Cole had been exonerated for the part he'd played in the man's death. And now Captain Casey, the captain of their grandfather's ship, had married them on orders from their grandparents, and it looked like things were going to work out after all. Only, for some reason, Eli wished the young couple had stayed in South Carolina. As he watched Heather approach, he had a feeling their newfound happiness had come too easily. He'd learned long ago that life was full of more than one nasty surprise.

He took a deep breath, trying to shake the unsettled feeling that gripped him, and greeted his companion's young wife with a hearty grin. "Well, what do you think of New Orleans?" he asked as she wrenched her deep violet eyes from her husband's face and began to scan the waterfront.

Heather frowned, hugging the baby closer to her as she took in the activity on shore. The city was bigger than she had expected, but then, she had only seen three other port cities—Beaufort, Port Royal, and Charleston—and she was more used to Beaufort and Port Royal, which were small in comparison. Men were loading and unloading ships, carts and wagons were everywhere, and the place was bustling with people. It was frightening to her.

"Maybe we should have gone to the Florida territories after all," she said, shifting her eyes back from the busy waterfront to search her husband's face.

Cole shook his head. "I'm afraid the Spanish have no love for Americans," he replied reluctantly. "No, to stay in the South, New Orleans was our best bet. But I don't intend to stay long." His eyes narrowed slightly, the intense feelings he was harboring showing clearly in their green depths. "Now, remember, from here on in, until we're certain it's safe, our last name is Avery, and you'll have to remember to call me Duke."

"Is that really necessary, Cole?" she asked, frowning.

"More than you realize," he answered. "As far as most people know, there's still a reward on my head, dead or alive, and I wouldn't relish getting a bullet in the back by some overly zealous bounty hunter."

"He's right," agreed Eli. "Until we're far enough into the back country for it not to matter, he'd better stay Duke Avery."

Heather didn't like it. She was certainly bound to forget and call him Cole. It had been her insistence that they leave South Carolina, but now she wasn't sure her decision had been the right one. There were so many bad memories back there, along with her dead husband's brother, Carl, and his father, Everett Palmer. And even with Cole's name cleared, there was too much chance something else might go wrong if they stayed. Once more her eyes moved to the waterfront, as the ship stopped and the men began to tie up, dropping anchor and lowering the gangplank. Well, there was no going back now. They were committed to the course they'd chosen and she prayed it was the right one.

It took a while for them to disembark, getting the horses off and bidding good-bye to Captain Casey. The old sailor had been torn inside by the orders his employers had given him. Being Irish, and brought up as a Catholic, he had been reluctant at first to marry the two young lovers. But after the ceremony, which took place once they were out to sea, as the days went by, he realized that not to have married them would have been the tragedy. They were as committed to one another as their grandparents Loedicia and Roth Chapman were. Now they had even named the baby after him, dropping the "y" from the name, since Case Dante sounded better then Casey Dante. He was proud of that.

As he said good-bye to them, his warm eyes smiling from his deeply freckled face, he reached up, ruffling the child's deep auburn hair, watching the slanted green eyes filling with big tears as they stared at him. Cole Dante could never deny this son, he thought to himself as the baby wiped a hand across his runny nose. Cole's father was three-quarters Indian, and Cole had inherited his Indian grandfather's handsomely chiseled features, and now the child reflected those features.

"You make sure you take good care of my namesake," said the captain as he reached out to shake Cole's hand.

Cole nodded, gripping Captain Casey's hand firmly.

"What do I tell them back at the Château?" the captain queried hesitantly.

Cole took a deep breath. "Thank our grandparents, Casey," he offered. "And tell them I'll try to send word as soon as we find the end of the road."

Casey smiled. "Good luck to all of you."

Heather and Eli both accepted his farewell, then watched as members of the crew finished bringing their belongings off the ship. Cole and Eli fastened everything on the four horses, including the baby, who rode in a blanket twisted and tied Indian fashion to Cole's saddle horn; then with a long backward glance and a hesitant wave, the four of them melted off into the crowd that was thickening now that the rain had stopped.

Once away from the waterfront, they moved on through the narrow streets toward the Vieux Carré. As they rode along, the wet, littered streets soon became wider until the old houses were adorned with wrought-iron balconies, their front doors opening onto well-kept streets, and it was here in the French quarter where they found a small inn with a livery and spent the next two days.

Heather kept to their rooms, with Tildie helping her, while Eli and Cole arranged passage for them on one of the new steamboats that had been introduced on the Mississippi since the end of the war. She hated the thought of another ship, but Cole assured her steamboat travel was nothing like bucking the high seas.

Having left South Carolina hurriedly, they had brought few possessions with them, and after leaving the inn for the last time, Heather watched apprehensively as Cole and Eli once more tied the bundles onto the horses, again securing a squirming Case into the improvised cradle made out of the blanket. Once fastened tightly, the baby usually settled down to enjoy his ride, but until the horse started to move, he fussed and fumed, his sloe eyes sparkling like emeralds as he waited for someone to rescue him.

"That black woman who took care of him had him spoiled," Eli said as he watched Cole trying to quiet his son.

Cole smiled. "Something we'll have to undo," he said, then turned to Heather. She was no longer wearing the black dress she'd been wearing when they arrived the day before yesterday, but had on a pair of buckskins Cole had found for her, as did the young black girl Tildie. Heather felt strange in them. It was the first time she'd been in public with pants on. She had worn some of Cole's old clothes when she'd followed him into the woods, learning how to track and shoot at his parents' plantation, Tonnerre, but now she was hesitant, wondering what people would think of a woman in buckskins. She felt terribly out-of-place.

"It can't be helped," Cole had told her when he'd handed them to her to put on. "We're only taking the packet as far as the Arkansas River, and from there on the going's rough. No place for dresses and kid shoes."

She had understood, and reluctantly agreed he was right, and now she smiled back at him as he reached over, picking her up, putting her astride the horse.

Eli helped Tildie onto the roan mare Cole's grandfather had given them for the young girl to ride; then both he and Cole mounted and the foursome headed toward the river, where the *Bonnie Belle* was scheduled to leave around ten o'clock.

The day was warm, the sun out by the time they reached the riverfront, and Heather stared in awe at the conglomeration of boats tied along its banks—everything from keelboats and barges to the fancier steamboats with their lightweight, powerful high-pressure engines. There was one other steamboat besides the *Bonnie Belle* tied up on the river, but it was some distance away and Heather was unable to see the name. She turned to her husband, watching as he studied the crowd; then suddenly she saw his eyes narrow as they settled on a group of men some hundred feet or so along the riverbank where they were unloading boxes from a barge.

"Eli?" Cole said hurriedly.

"What is it, Cole?" asked Heather.

"Shh!" he cautioned her. "Remember, my name's Duke." He turned to his friend. "See those men over there?" he asked.

Eli followed the direction where Cole was staring. "The ones working with those two big blacks?"

Cole nodded. "The tall one with the dark fringe of hair circling his bald spot, and the scar on his cheek, is named Rafe Turner. He used to live in Beaufort and was in my regiment while I was stationed here. He and I didn't get along too well. He must have stayed around after he was mustered out."

"Maybe he won't recognize you with the beard," suggested Eli.

Cole's hand raised to the clipped beard he'd been wearing while on the run. "Maybe, maybe not," he mumbled; then he turned once more to his friend as he reined his horse toward the *Bonnie Belle*, his back toward the half-loaded barge. "Come on, let's get aboard before he spots us," he said.

Heather's heart was in her throat as Cole made all the arrangements, led the horses up the gangplank, then came back for her while Eli helped Tildie, who was holding the baby. Young Case had been reluctant to leave his jostling ride tied to the saddle horn, and Heather kept glancing back as Cole helped steady her up the gangplank. She hoped the baby's cries wouldn't attract too much attention. But the men at the barge kept up their work, unloading and stacking boxes, and she sighed as her feet hit the main deck of the strange-looking vessel. She stood for a minute staring up at the high smokestacks on the steamboat, unaware for a brief moment that some of the other women passengers, dressed in all their finery, were staring at her, unaccustomed to seeing a woman in buckskins.

Cole glanced about, unsure which side of the ship to move to, since they'd be making the ride without benefit of a cabin. It was the only way he could get passage, so they joined a group of other people who had either booked passage after the cabins were full, as they had, or didn't have money for one, and as he led Heather to some boxes where he and Eli made them comfortable, then tied the horses to a support post nearby, he hoped the weather would hold out, because they'd be riding out in the open, their only cover being the balcony above them on the upper deck.

Heather moved back on the box where Cole had deposited her and reached out, taking the baby from Tildie so Eli could help Tildie up beside her; then she settled back against the side of another box, plopping the baby onto her lap, giving him a small wooden toy to play with while she watched Cole make sure the horses were secure. When he was finished, he and Eli joined the two women on the boxes of cargo, settling back for their journey upriver on the stern-wheeler.

The men Cole had been watching earlier had just finished unloading the barge, and the man with the scar on his cheek straightened, wiping his forehead, beginning to look around. The *Bonnie Belle* was preparing to shove off and he watched as her crew cast off, her smokestacks beginning to send a curl of dark swirls into the azure sky. The paddle wheel began turning slowly at first, then easing into a steady rhythm and the bow began to turn, heading upriver, away from the shore. The man's gaze scanned the passengers, watching them wave from the balcony above the main deck; then his eyes dropped to the deck passengers, mostly farmers, immigrants, and a few rivermen who plied the river looking for jobs. Suddenly he hesitated, moving his eyes back along the deck toward where the cargo was stacked, and rested them on two men and two women in buckskins. It was strange seeing a young black woman in such garb, and the redhead beside her looked like she would have been more at home in satins and silk. He saw the redhead lean down, kissing a baby who was squirming in her lap; then he looked over toward the tall buckskin-clad stranger who sat on the other side of her.

But was he a stranger? Rafe Turner frowned, squinting in the morning sun. There was something familiar about him, the tilt of the head, the line of the jaw. The stern-wheeler was close enough so he could see the frontiersman's features clearly. The slanted green eyes, high cheekbones . . . If it weren't for the beard . . . His face screwed into a puzzled scowl; then suddenly recognition came. By God, it was! Cole Dante! The man's scowl deepened. Now, what the hell was he doing in New Orleans? Suddenly he shoved the soiled handkerchief he'd been wiping his forehead with into his hip pocket, remembering an old poster he'd seen somewhere just last week. Cole Dante was a wanted man with a sizable reward on his head dead or alive. He stared, frowning, and watched as the steamboat headed upstream, fading in the distance.

Meanwhile, on board the *Bonnie Belle,* Cole, who had been keeping his eye on Rafe Turner, pursed his lips, cursing silently to himself as he saw Rafe's eyes settle on him, then saw the look of recognition light the man's dark eyes. Damn! All he needed was for someone to carry the tale back to the Palmers in Beaufort. Even though he was no longer a wanted man, he had a feeling the Palmers wouldn't agree with the governor, and he hadn't stuck around Beaufort and Port Royal long enough, after the pardon, to learn their reaction to the events that had taken place. One thing for certain, though, they sure as hell weren't going to be happy about the fact that Heather had run off with him, bringing the baby with her. Every time he thought of how they had tried to deceive her by making her think the baby was dead, his stomach tied in knots.

As the paddle wheel began churning faster, pushing the boat farther into midstream, until faces on the riverbank became only a blur, he heaved a sigh, turning to his wife and son. He loved them both so much, but did he have a right to ask this of them? The journey was going to be a hard one, and with the baby along . . . Just then Heather looked over at him, a smile lighting her eyes, transforming her face, and he suddenly knew that even if their decision had been a wrong one, it was the only one they could make. He had to have her with him, and besides, it had been her decision too. All he could do now was pray that Rafe Turner didn't suddenly decide to return to South Carolina.

Their first day on the steamboat was an adventure for Heather.

When she had boarded the *Interlude* it had been only her second time on a sailing ship; this was her first ride on a steamboat, and she was certain she was going to experience a lot of other firsts before this trip was over. She had been raised in Columbia, South Carolina, by a doting aunt and a strict mother, but her life since she had met Cole and her newfound grandparents had changed so completely that there was little resemblance anymore to the shy, naive young girl she had once been. Now, at twenty, she was a wife and mother, although the latter role was a new one for her. Her husband, DeWitt, had accidentally been killed in a fight with Cole the night her baby was born, and that evening her father-in-law, knowing the child wasn't his son's, and knowing that everyone would take one look at the child's distinctly Indian features and know who the child's father really was, had told her the child had died, sending the newborn out to the slave quarters to be raised by one of his darkies. She tried to put those horrible weeks and months, before she had learned the truth, out of her thoughts now, but it wasn't all that easy. She had suffered terribly, first from the beating DeWitt had subjected her to, then from thinking her child dead, and also from the knowledge that Cole was on the run, accused of murdering her husband. As they sat on deck at the end of the first day aboard the *Bonnie Belle*, enjoying the cool evening breeze, she stared into Cole's face, seeing the warmth and love that filled his eyes, and the memory of the pain she had endured became just that, a bad memory, and she hugged her son to her, trying to lull him to sleep before nestling him between a couple of boxes so he wouldn't crawl away or roll overboard. When he was finally bedded down for the night with Tildie beside him, she turned to Cole, moving close into his arms as he leaned against one of the boxes, watching the vague outline of the trees drifting past onshore. The moon was full, turning the landscape to silver, shining off the water, shimmering it to a pale luster.

"Sometimes I think I'm dreaming," she said softly as he drew her close against him.

He brushed her hair with his lips, feeling her soft warm body against him, remembering last night at the inn when he'd made love to her and wishing he hadn't been too late to get a cabin for their trip. And yet, if he had, they wouldn't be sharing the magic of such a beautiful evening. Water lapped at the sides of the boat, and the shush-shush of the paddle wheel slapping it seemed to be in rhythm with the beating of his heart.

"It's hard on you, I know," he said softly as his arm tightened around her. "But I'll make it up to you someday, I promise, Heather."

She reached up, touching his face, looking deeply into his eyes, so vibrant and alive. "Have I complained?" she asked.

He shook his head. "You don't have to for me to see how rough it's been for both you and Tildie," he said. "And I'm afraid it's going to get even worse before it gets better."

"I'll manage," she said playfully. Then grew more serious. "I know I told you once that I wouldn't be able to survive on the frontier, darling," she whispered softly. "But I've learned since then that I'd rather face the wilderness with you than live in luxury without you."

"There sure won't be any luxuries where we're going, love," he offered.

"I never asked for any."

"And we may not even come out of this alive."

"Nothing's worth life without you, Cole," she said passionately.

He stared at her hard. It was dark and they were sitting in the shadows of the overhead promenade, where the moonlight couldn't reach, and his hand moved up beneath her buckskin shirt, slipping inside the chemise she wore under it, cupping her breast, feeling the soft mound of flesh, letting it arouse him just enough to send shivers through him.

"I love you, Heather," he whispered huskily.

She smiled, lips parting seductively. "And I love you."

As his mouth covered hers in a slow lingering kiss, Eli, sitting close by, drew his eyes from the two young lovers and stared out across the river toward the bank some distance away, bathed in moonlight, remembering another time and another woman and a promise he had made that he'd been unable to keep, and he hoped to God Cole's low murmured sentence about not getting through this alive had no truth to it, because he knew what it was to lose someone you loved and he wouldn't wish that kind of pain on his worst enemy, let alone a young friend he'd grown so fond of. Eli sighed, shutting his eyes, and let the magic of dreams transport him back to the memories he kept so close inside him, while the night closed around him and soon all that could be heard on deck was an occasional snore, or some scuffling as someone moved position, and the deep breathing of sleep.

Heather awoke with the sun in her face and a stiff back from having lain on an uneven board. Cole was nowhere in sight, nor was Eli, but Tildie was busy already, on her knees, bent over a wooden bucket, a bar of lye soap sudsing her hands as she washed out the soiled diapers Case had dirtied the day before. They had only eight changes for him and he kept her busy every morning and sometimes evenings keeping caught up. She already had three of them spread out on top of some of the boxes to dry. Behind her, Case was gurgling while he chewed happily on a piece of crusty bread, his two bottom teeth softening it as he drooled. The black woman who'd been caring for him had still been breast-feeding him when they'd had to snatch him from her, and at first he had weaned reluctantly. But now he seemed to enjoy learning how to drink from a mug and using his new teeth. They'd had no milk for him, but he took to the broths and mashed foods and seemed little affected by his change of diet. In fact, he was so full of vigor that Tildie had used a leather thong fastened about his middle and tied him to a post so he wouldn't crawl away and fall into the water.

"Where's Cole . . . I mean Duke?" asked Heather, lowering her voice as she stretched, realizing her mistake and correcting it quickly as she looked about to make sure her error hadn't been heard.

Tildie nodded toward the galley. "Said they'd bring back some breakfast."

Heather moved over to the baby and reached out, touching his arm, still awed by the wonder of knowing he was really alive.

"He's a cute little fella," said a voice from behind her, and Heather whirled around.

The woman who had spoken and her family had settled down for the night some few feet from where Heather and Cole had slept, but this was the first any of the family had tried to be friendly.

"He'll be a year old in November," Heather said, staring up at the older woman.

The woman frowned as she studied the baby's face, then looked at Heather. "I noticed your husband . . . he's a half-breed?" she asked.

Heather's eyes narrowed. "My husband's an American," she answered curtly.

"Oh, don't take me wrong, dear." The woman was apologetic. "I didn't mean nothin' by what I said. It don't matter to me, but I heard some of the other passengers talkin'. Can't help but hear sometimes." She drew her eyes from Heather's face and perused the deck, then looked back at the young red-haired woman. "Only there's some as would make trouble for you and your young man if you let them," she said. "Thought maybe I'd let you know, just in case."

"What kind of trouble?" asked Heather as she stood up, feeling the engines' vibrations through the wooden deck beneath her moccasined feet.

The woman glanced back to where her own family was waiting for her return. The two girls, barely in their teens, were watching curiously, but her son, along with her husband, was walking off toward the galley.

"I don't know," she said, shrugging. "But you hear a word here, there . . . ." She turned and watched as Tildie rinsed a diaper and began to spread it out to dry. "Does she belong to you?" she asked.

Heather glanced over to Tildie, knowing Tildie had heard every word. "In a way," she answered. "But Tildie's more a friend than anything else."

Tildie wiped some beads of sweat from her forehead and her dark eyes shone in her young face.

"Then she is your slave?" the woman questioned.

"She was a present from my grandparents," Heather explained, then saw Cole and Eli heading toward her carrying breakfast. "Now, if you'll excuse me," she said quickly. "My husband . . ."

The woman turned and Cole and Eli stopped for a minute, staring at her, then stepped forward.

"I really should introduce myself," the woman said, tucking a strand of dark hair beneath the faded blue bonnet she was wearing. "My name's Taylor, Bessie Taylor." She smiled uneasily as Cole's eyes raked over her.

"Mrs. Taylor was telling me that some of the people have been talking about us," Heather offered.

"She's right," said Cole. "But I don't think we'll have any problems."

"What happened?" asked Heather.

"Nothing, really," answered Cole. "But I could tell by some of the looks directed our way that Eli and I had been the topic of more than one conversation." He studied Bessie Taylor. She was apparently somewhere in her late thirties, a bit plump and pleasant, but not too pretty, with a round face and warm brown eyes. "I presume you, like most people aboard, think I'm a half-breed, Mrs. Taylor. Am I right?" he asked.

Her face reddened.

"My mother was English, my father French and part Tuscarora Indian," Cole went on. "But I was raised as a southern gentleman, and am, in fact, legally a titled Englishman if I cared to acknowledge the heritage. I have, perhaps, seen more drawing rooms and been educated far beyond most of the men aboard the *Bonnie Belle*, and the thought amuses me. Now"—he glanced down at the food in his hands—"if you don't mind, I'm sure my wife is quite hungry, and since the biscuits I've brought are still warm, I think perhaps she'd like to start eating."

Bessie Taylor was still flushing as she moved slowly toward where her daughters were sitting, and tried to smile self-consciously. "I didn't mean to intrude Mr. . . ."

"Duke Avery!" Cole answered. "My wife, Heather"—he nodded toward Heather, then toward Eli and Tildie—"my best friend, Eli Crawford, and the baby's nurse, Tildie."

Bessie acknowledged all three; then her eyes wavered for a moment before she spoke, but when she did, her voice was a little unsteady. "I didn't mean to frighten your wife, Mr. Avery," she cautioned hesitantly. "But some folks ain't as tolerant as others, and I thought it best you knew so you could sort of keep your eyes open." She glanced around at all of them. "I'd sure hate to see anythin' happen to folks who don't seem to have done no harm to no one. I hope I'm wrong, but you just take care," and she hurried away quickly, beginning to admonish her daughters for staring.

Heather watched Cole's face as his eyes followed the woman the short distance to where her family had spent the night.

"She's right, isn't she, Cole?" Heather asked softly.

"Shh!" Cole reminded her not to call him Cole, then asked, "Did she say who was doing most of the talking?"

"No. Just that folks were talking." Heather's eyes saddened. "Why can't they just leave us alone?" she asked.

He took a deep breath. "Because people are people. But let's forget it for now." He handed her some of the food. "I think the baby's about ready for something besides that dried-up crust from last night's supper."

She took the food from Cole and Eli, realizing that Cole had managed to find a cup of milk for the baby, and Cole was rewarded by a warm smile from Heather, along with the satisfac-

tion of watching Case devour most of it. Between swallows of
milk, Heather broke off small pieces of biscuit, dipped them in
honey, and popped them in the baby's mouth, watching him gum
them hungrily.

While feeding him, Heather also fed herself. Besides the
biscuits and honey, Cole and Eli had brought some hard-cooked
eggs and deep-fried salt pork. Heather told Tildie to finish the
diapers later and handed her some of the food as soon as her
hands were dried, and the four of them sat on the deck along
with everyone else, enjoying their breakfast.

Cole watched Heather with the baby. Although Tildie took
care of him a great deal, Heather too seemed to be enjoying him.
He was starting to put together some of the words he'd discovered in the past few weeks, and the results were hilarious,
making them all laugh harder than they had ever laughed before.
And too, he was trying desperately to use his little legs and
imitate his father's strong stride, only to plop down time after
time with tears of frustration that soon turned to laughter when
he realized all those watching him were laughing too.

As the days went by and the steamboat made its way slowly
up the meandering Mississippi, there was little for them to do to
keep busy. Daylight hours were spent sitting on deck watching
the scenery go by, playing with the baby, and trying to keep to
themselves as much as possible. Cole and Eli saw to it that the
horses had feed and made the trips to the galley for food, while
Tildie and Heather made sure all of Case's needs were cared for,
and more than once the baby fell asleep in Heather's arms. Then
at night she and Cole would cuddle close, falling asleep beneath
the stars when the weather permitted. Other nights they'd huddle
close, trying to keep dry as rain pelted down, churning the river
to mud, and the wind brought chilly gusts that made them shiver.

Heather had learned early on the voyage that it was best not to
wander about the fancy steamboat. For one thing, Cole had
warned her that steamboats weren't as safe as their owners liked
to make people believe, and he liked knowing where she was,
just in case the engines blew.

And then there was Bessie Taylor's warning. So far, no one
had done anything more than talk, but with each passing day
Cole felt an undercurrent of bitterness spreading, and no matter
how hard he tried to tell himself nothing would come of it, he
still didn't like it.

They were a few days past the small town of Walnut Hills,

where the Yazoo River flowed into the Mississippi. The boat had hung up on the edge of a sandbar that morning and things had been in a turmoil until they had finally managed to clear it, and on top of that, the baby had been cranky most of the day. His top teeth were pushing through and all he wanted to do was chew on his fist or anything else he could grab, and Heather was worn out from holding him while he fussed.

Now the sun was setting as Tildie took Case from Heather and began humming, rocking him in her arms, hoping to put him to sleep.

"You look tired," said Cole as he took Heather's hand.

She smiled wearily. "Not really tired, just not used to motherhood, I guess."

"Do you think maybe you might enjoy a stroll?"

Her eyes lit up. "Oh, could we?"

"Why not?" He glanced about. "It'll do us both good. You've been practically glued here, what with the baby to look after." He helped her to her feet, glancing toward the stairs that led to the promenade deck above them.

He knew the view of the sunset from the upper deck would be beautiful and ushered Heather toward it, threading their way between people who were lounging about. Besides the Taylors, an assortment of riverhands, immigrants, and a few lone travelers on the open deck, there were some ten to fifteen Indians who had settled in a small group near the stairs leading to the upper promenade. They had boarded when the boat docked in Natchez. Cole had explained to Heather they were probably part of the Indians who had to relocate when the government took over their lands in Georgia and Alabama.

"Mostly Cherokee and Creeks," he'd said, and Heather reminded him he'd had a run-in with some Creeks on his way home from New Orleans after the war. But Cole had assured her two years made a big difference and the Creek nation wasn't what it once had been. In fact, now, as he and Heather moved toward the group of men who were staring at them sullenly, he felt a pang of regret, wishing the treaty that had been signed taking the land from these people could have been avoided, and wondering at the same time if his father's relatives, the Tuscarora, weren't perhaps suffering the same fate. The last they had heard, the Tuscarora too were heading west, hoping to find new lands they could call home.

He felt Heather's hand tighten on his arm as they drew closer to the Indians, and he knew she was instinctively afraid of them. He glanced toward one of the men, who seemed to be a leader, said something Heather couldn't understand, and she watched the Indian smile reluctantly as he motioned to the others and they cleared a path so he and Heather could ascend the stairs.

"What did you say to him?" Heather asked as they reached the promenade.

He glanced back down toward the tall man, whose scalp lock was peppered with gray, but whose eyes still held the fierceness of a young warrior. "Just passing the time of day like white folks do," he answered casually.

She stared up at him skeptically. "Is that why he had the others move aside to make a path for us?"

He smiled. "I told him I was taking the most beautiful woman on the boat, who just happens to be my squaw, for a walk so she could see what a truly lovely sight the sunset on the Mississippi is."

"You're incorrigible," she said, smiling up at him; then slowly her smile faded as they walked over and joined some of the other passengers who had also stopped to watch the sunset. But Heather's eyes were on Cole instead of the sky. "Cole?" she asked suddenly, but he stopped her with firm eyes that hardened in their intensity, reminding her silently that she wasn't supposed to call him by that name. "Why is it, Duke, darling," she went on correcting herself reluctantly, "that those Indians down there frighten me, yet you're part Indian and it doesn't bother me at all?"

He saw the bewilderment in her deep violet eyes and his own eyes softened. "Conditioning," he replied softly. "You have a right to fear them. At one time they'd have taken your scalp for no other reason than that you were white. If you look closely, you'll see that their eyes still mirror the hatred they feel toward the people who've driven them off their lands. They dress differently, act differently, and deep down inside they are different because they were born to be different. Their culture, their very existence, has no parallel with the way the white man lives, and most people are afraid of what they don't understand. If I had been raised by my father's people, perhaps you'd have been afraid of me too."

"Never!" she exclaimed softly. Her eyes were filled with love, and as his arm circled her waist, pulling her against him, they gazed out over the river toward the setting sun.

As they stood at the rail watching the sunset, neither of them noticed the small group of people beginning to cluster a few feet away, until suddenly Cole stiffened as one of the men looked over at them and said, "I said, take your hands off the white lady, you dirty Injun! Didn't you hear?"

Cole felt Heather tense against him. She couldn't help but hear what the man said.

"It isn't worth it, Cole," she whispered anxiously.

His eyes hardened. "I can't let it pass, Heather." His lips brushed her hair. "He's gone too far."

Heather wanted to protest, but knew once Cole made up his mind he wouldn't waver. "Be careful," she said hesitantly, and looked up at him for a brief moment, her eyes pleading with him to show restraint.

They turned slowly, Cole's arm dropping from about her and his eyes centered on the man he was certain had been the one who had spoken. Today wasn't the first time the man had made remarks, but it was the first time others had been close enough to hear, and the first time the remarks had been so derogatory. Cole stared at him, studying the man's whiskered face that was swollen from a chaw of tobacco in his cheek. His clothes were far from impressive and Cole was certain he was probably some sort of salesman, although it was apparent he hadn't been too well educated in the finer things of life.

"Excuse me, did you say something?" Cole asked, the timbre of his voice low and vibrant.

The man he addressed ignored the deadly look in Cole's eyes, confident there were enough people to back him up. After all, they'd been agreeing with him long enough. "I told you to take your hands off the lady," he repeated.

Cole's mouth curved into a half-smile. "Oh, then you do agree she's a lady," he said. "Good, because the lady happens to be my wife."

"Your wife?" The man sneered. "No white woman marries an Injun unless she's forced to!" he said angrily. "More like your captive, I'd say!" His eyes narrowed. "What'd you do, take her in a raid and spoil her for any decent man?"

Cole took a deep breath, trying to control the rage that was building inside him. He knew the people standing around were absorbing everything the man said.

"Contrary to your beliefs," Cole finally said, straightening to his full height and still managing to look calm, knowing that he should have called the man out, but not wanting to upset Heather any further, "I am not what you so crudely call an 'Injun.' My father's father was a Tuscarora chief, his mother French and Tuscarora, and my mother is English, the daughter of an earl. But even if I were a full-blooded Indian, what business is it of yours? Did I ask you to pay my way on this boat?"

"Hey, Harry, he talks like a reg'lar high-class gent," yelled one of the men in the crowd.

Harry straightened stubbornly. "Don't mean nothin'," he said, staring hard at Cole.

"Could be he's tellin' the truth," someone else piped in.

"The truth? You seen it," Harry said, then spit a long stream of tobacco juice, hitting a nearby spittoon dead center. "He was talkin' with them Injuns what got on at Natchez just as if they was old friends. I don't like havin' Injuns ridin' on no boat I'm on. Who's to say they won't try scalpin' a body while he's asleep?"

"Don't be ridiculous," said Heather, who had been watching the altercation with both anger and apprehension. She moved closer to Cole, needing his strength. "My husband's a civilized man. He wouldn't hurt anyone, nor would those poor Indians down below."

"Don't bother with him, Heather," said Cole. "The man's too ignorant to understand anything but what he wants to believe."

Harry blustered, trying to look important, and straightened arrogantly. "Who you callin' ignorant!" he yelled. "I don't take name-callin' from no damned Injun!" He started to step toward Cole, when suddenly Cole frowned.

Cole and Heather were both wearing moccasins, and as Harry stood facing them spouting off his venomous words, Cole had slowly but consistently felt a change to the vibrations beneath his feet. The constant throb of the engines had been reassuring, but now suddenly the throb had become a rumbling vibration that traveled to every nerve in his body.

"Wait!" he called, holding a hand up to ward off the man, at the same time cocking his head.

"Wait for what?" yelled Harry, hitting the spittoon again. "So you can get your friends up here to help? I say heave the whole lot of you overboard." He reached out.

Cole swung his arm out, deflecting the man's attempt to grab him. "You damn fool!" he yelled, facing the hostile crowd angrily. "Don't any of you know what's happening, can't you feel it?'' He stared at the blank faces glaring at him curiously, then turned quickly to Heather and began pushing her toward the stairs. "If we hurry, we might make it!" he yelled as the crowd behind him began to surge toward them, hoping to block their path.

But as he and Heather reached the top of the stairs, Cole suddenly realized it was too late. The boards beneath him shook violently, and as he stopped moving, pulling Heather back into his arms to shield her, the air was rent with a deafening explosion and both he and Heather felt themselves propelled backward against the rail, splintering it as they hit; then, seconds later, after being hurtled through the air, they both felt the impact of the water, and moments later there was a dead silence as the water entombed them.

Eli had felt the same stirrings beneath his feet only minutes before the high-pressured boilers blew. With quick, deft motions, he had untied the horses, and much to the surprise of everyone on deck, led them to the edge and forced them over the side, packs and all. Now, without hesitating, he grabbed Case and yelled to Tildie, "You know how to swim?"

Tildie nodded.

"Good!" he cried, shoving her toward the edge. Just as he started to push her over the side, the air was filled with the roar of the explosion and he felt himself hurtled into the air with a violence that was frightening. It was all he could do to fight the nauseating grip of panic that tried to take hold of him, and as his body hit the water, Eli's only thought was that he had to stay conscious to hold on to the baby, for his friends' sake, and his arms tightened about Case as he felt the water cover him, then felt himself sinking toward the muddy river bottom.

2

Fiery rays from the setting sun mingled with the flames that shot into the air from the still-burning wreckage as Heather lay on the riverbank gasping for air. She was leaning on one elbow breathing deeply, trying to get the taste of the river water from her mouth as she watched Cole struggling to pull more of the survivors from the water. Chilling screams still drifted across the water, and a sob wrenched from deep inside her as she thought of Case.

Gulping back a scream of terror, she pulled herself quickly from the rough grass and stumbled toward Cole, who was dragging the body of a half-conscious woman onto dry ground.

"Cole! The baby!" she screamed. "Where's Case?"

Cole lowered Bessie Taylor onto the grass, ignoring her half-conscious mumblings as he wiped the blood from her pale face; then he straightened, taking Heather's arm.

"She needs your help, Heather," he said hurriedly. "I've got to try to help the others."

"But Case . . . !"

"I'll find him!" He took her hands and squeezed them, gazing down into her tear-filled eyes. "I've got to find him," he groaned. "But while I'm looking, I can't let all these people die, and neither can you!"

Heather wanted to scream.

"I can't!" she cried hysterically. "Case is out there somewhere!"

Cole grabbed her shoulders. "Stop it!" he yelled desperately. "This isn't going to help." He shook her, hoping to calm her and stop her near-hysteria. "Heather, Mrs. Taylor could bleed to death unless something's done, and there are others out there."

Heather stared at him, tears running down her cheeks; then she looked out over the water, aware once more of the bodies floating amid the burning wreckage and the cries that sounded so agonizingly helpless.

"Don't worry, I'll find the baby," Cole assured her again.

Heather watched Cole turn from her and plunge back into the water, heading toward another half-submerged body, and her knees trembled. Only a few feet away, a man dragged himself onto the bank and dropped half in, half out of the water. His eyes were glazed with pain, and blood was quickly spreading over his clothes. Heather gasped, then looked down at the woman at her feet. Bessie Taylor's eyes were still closed, her body limp.

Suddenly, without thought, Heather stepped over Bessie's still body, ran to the struggling man, grabbed him beneath the arms, and began tugging until his feet were clear of the water; then she flipped him onto his back and knelt down, trying to find where all the blood was coming from. As she ripped the shirt from his stomach, she felt bile rise in her throat at the sight of the gaping hole, and knew within minutes he'd be dead. Her first thoughts

were that it would have been less painful had he drowned, and
she wondered how he had even managed to swim ashore. For a
brief moment the man's eyes flew open, but there was no look of
recognition and the mumbling was incoherent. Seconds later,
with a cry on his lips, the man's eyes closed, and Heather knew
there was nothing more she could do.

She stared down at him hesitantly for a few minutes, trying to
comprehend, hoping to see a flickering eyelid, any faint sign of
life; then, hearing a groan escape Bessie Taylor's lips, she
quickly hurried to the woman's side and lifted her head.

"My children!" Bessie screamed breathlessly.

"Shh! You're hurt," cautioned Heather, trying to keep the
woman still.

"But I don't know where they are!"

"Cole will find them," assured Heather, and tears ran down
her cheeks. "He'll find Case, and your children too. Now, lie
still, please." She had to stop the blood that was oozing from
Bessie's forehead. Quickly she reached down and tore a strip
from the woman's dress, from where it had already been ripped
in the explosion, and she used the rag to mop away any excess
blood to see how bad the cut was. Realizing it wasn't as bad as it
looked, she quickly tore off another strip of cloth and bound it
around the woman's head to help stop the bleeding, then helped
her to sit up as Cole returned, dragging another half-conscious
woman.

For the next half-hour Heather's world consisted of torn flesh,
broken bones, and blood as Cole dragged one body after another
onto the riverbank, where the grass was already stained red.
Those who hadn't drowned in the muddy waters more often than
not died on its banks in spite of their efforts, but still he kept on,
joined after a while by some of the other survivors.

Heather was bending over the man who had been harassing
them just before the explosion, tying a makeshift tourniquet
around the man's leg, when suddenly there was a shout from
behind her and she whirled around, staring in disbelief. Tears
that had been close to the surface blurred her eyes, and she
wiped them away quickly as she stumbled to her feet, half out of
her mind with joy at the sight of Cole supporting Eli as he
half-dragged him toward her, and in Eli's arms was Case. He
was dirty and frightened, clinging to the rough frontiersman with
tight little fists, his wet, soggy clothes plastered to him.

"Oh, my God, you're safe!" she cried as she reached them

and hugged both the baby and Eli at the same time, burying her head against the child, her face nuzzling his damp flesh.

"They'd been washed downriver a ways," explained Cole quickly as she drew her head back and began fussing with the baby, making sure he hadn't been hurt, thanking Eli for saving his life and worrying over him, making certain he was all right. She gave Case a big kiss, then straightened, looking deep into Eli's worried face.

"Tildie?" she asked.

He shook his head. "I don't know. We were getting ready to jump overboard when it happened. I haven't seen her since."

It was some ten minutes later when Heather, weary and trembling as she cuddled Case close to comfort him, stumbled over the unconscious body of the black slave girl. Her call to Cole and Eli, who were still trying to sort the dead from the living, almost went unheard amid the cries and sobbing that still filled the air as the first shadows of night began to replace the brilliant sunset that had blended with the flames from the burning ship.

It took Cole and Eli barely seconds to determine that Tildie was still alive, although they couldn't tell how badly she was hurt. It was only when she regained consciousness that her injuries were discovered to be a severe bump on the head, aches and pains all over from the force of the blast, especially in her left arm, and an upset stomach from swallowing too much muddy water. According to her story, she had evidently been unconscious before hitting the water, and when she came to, she grabbed hold of some floating debris. Her arm was hurt and she couldn't swim, so she hung on, floating and kicking toward shore until one of the Indians who had been aboard found her and began dragging her behind him. She wanted to relieve him and swim on her own, but couldn't. However, after making it to shore, he had left her to go after some others and she had become dizzy and sick, finally passing out.

Her enthusiasm at seeing all of them safe was surpassed only by their happiness that she was all right, but there was still work to be done. After propping the still-shaking Tildie to lean against a tree, Cole ordered Heather to stay with her and the baby and he and Eli stood up, looking about them.

There was no way of knowing how many people had been on board the steamboat; Cole guessed at somewhere near three or four hundred.

"What of the horses?" Cole asked Eli.

Eli watched the shadows getting deeper. "I managed to get them untied and over the side, but haven't seen hide nor hair of them since."

Cole frowned and both men gazed off toward the river, where the last few sputtering remnants of what was once the steamboat sank below the surface, leaving a deadly quiet behind, broken only by occasional sobs and wailing from the survivors sprawled along the riverbank. "Well, let's get it over with and make some kind of order out of this mess," said Cole, and walked off with Eli close at his heels. They were heading toward a lone figure standing at the edge of the riverbank.

"How many of your men have you counted, Lone Eagle?" Cole asked the Indian who had been the leader of the group aboard the steamboat.

Lone Eagle's face was hard, his eyes shadowed, and grim wrinkles etched his mouth into a tight line. "Four left," he answered, his voice deep and resonant. "All Cherokee. One have broken leg, one ribs and shoulder broken, other two not hurt much."

Cole nodded, then showed sorrow for the Indian's losses. "I'm sorry, Lone Eagle," he said. "They were brave warriors, and I know you valued their friendship."

The Indian straightened, trying to look dignified and ignore the fact that the buckskins he was wearing were soaked, muddy water dripping onto his moccasins. "You too have lost friends?" he asked.

Cole glanced about. "No, thank God," he answered, then realized the enormity of their predicament. He looked back to Lone Eagle. "Do you think you and your two warriors could give us a hand?" he asked. His eyes hardened. "It's going to take a miracle to straighten all this out."

Lone Eagle nodded, then turned 'and walked off toward where his two friends knelt, keening over the bodies of their companions, their eerie chanting hanging low on the night air.

By the time the moon was beginning to clear the trees that lined the riverbank, Cole and Eli had managed to take stock of the situation. Besides themselves, Heather, Tildie and the baby, Bessie Taylor, her daughter, and the five Indians, there were thirty-eight other survivors, including the man named Harry who had been harassing them just before the explosion. However, out of those thirty-eight, only thirteen were mobile.

The first thing they did was try to get some semblance of order out of the chaos. They put the uninjured Indians to work retrieving debris from the water so Heather and Bessie Taylor could sort through it for anything usable. Bessie's oldest daughter was the only other survivor from the Taylor family. She had been hysterical when they'd first found her, but now with tears still on her cheeks she helped her mother and Heather with a quiet strength that Heather was certain was still part shock.

The ridiculous calico bandage was still about Bessie's head, but the bleeding had stopped, and they went through crate after crate of debris, salvaging whatever they could. Much of the stuff was wet and unusable, but they did find most of the staples. Coffee, flour, sugar, and salt as well as utensils for cooking. It had undoubtedly been headed for trading posts far upriver. There were even gunpowder, some rifles, tools, a large box filled with bolts of material, another with blankets.

The men had built a fire using scattered brush from the area, and the women spread the wet goods around it, hoping to dry them out enough to be usable. Cole was hoping the fire would attract help for them, yet knew the idea was practically hopeless. Although traffic on the Mississippi was generally heavy, the explosion had occurred in rather isolated territory, and since the accident, few boats had passed. Those that had, had gone by after the last remnants of the *Bonnie Bell* had gone down beneath the water's surface, and in the dark it was impossible for someone, just happening on the scene, to recognize what had occurred. Even now, with a huge fire to attract attention, no boats were coming anywhere near the shore, and probably wouldn't until morning, when the results of the holocaust were revealed to them.

The banks of the Mississippi were spawning grounds for river pirates, and one of their ploys was to feign trouble, trying to get boats in close enough to rob without leaving witnesses, and at night no one in his right mind, with any experience on the river, would dare investigate a fire and people yelling for help.

Cole watched the lights from another boat disappearing in the distance, then cursed softly as he turned from the river, gazing at the flickering flames from the fire. He stared hard for a few minutes, then strode purposefully across the area to where Eli and some of the other men were hauling the dead, laying them out in even rows with blankets, robes, and canvases over them so that when morning came they could make identifications if possible.

It was toward the wee hours of the morning when Cole finally found a few minutes and walked over, dropping down beside Heather, who had just handed Case to Tildie so the young girl could sing him to sleep. The baby had been cranky all night, still unnerved by the frightening experience.

Cole sighed. "It's enough to make a body sick," he said softly, his slow drawl making the words even more significant. "Why the hell can't they make steamboats that won't blow!"

Heather reached over and touched his arm. His buckskins were still damp and she had forgotten how cool the night air could be this time of year. "You're going to catch cold," she said.

He glanced over at her. "How about you? Yours don't look any too dry."

"They're drier than yours. Sitting by the fire sorting all that stuff helped." She looked off toward the huge fire. One of the men was putting more wood on and a few sparks flew into the night sky. She watched until they disintegrated. "Cole, what happens when morning comes?" she finally asked.

He exhaled. "I wish I knew." He stared off toward the river. "We have to get someone to stop. These people need medical attention we can't give them." His hand went to his face and he rubbed his eyes wearily. "I haven't seen anything like this since the war," he went on. "If there was just something I could do for them."

Heather saw the pained look in his eyes. "You've done more than enough, Cole," she said. "Even that man who was so cruel on the boat . . . if it hadn't been for you, he'd have drowned before reaching shore."

"Maybe I should have let him," Cole said angrily. "It hasn't helped his attitude any. Did you hear the way he carried on when Lone Eagle's men began helping tend the wounded? He was yelling that everyone was going to be scalped!"

"I know." She looked off toward where the man named Harry was lying on the ground. "I guess it's hard to change some people." Her eyes softened as she looked back at Cole. "You should try to get some rest."

"Impossible. There's too much to do." He glanced about. "But I'd appreciate a cup of that hot coffee Bessie Taylor was parading around with before. I thought she might be with you.

When she comes back, tell her I'll be among the injured somewhere.''

He started to get up, but she reached out and touched his arm. "Cole, there are so few people," she said.

His hand covered hers on his arm. "And I thank God we're among them." He leaned over farther and kissed her lightly on the mouth. "Don't worry, we'll work it all out, love," he assured her. "It's just that for some reason these people seem to have picked Eli and me to run things until someone better comes along, and I don't like being put in a position like that. Especially under the circumstances. It's rather hard to be inconspicuous when you're shoved to the forefront. The fewer people who remember we came this way, the better.''

"I'm sorry, Cole.''

"Don't worry. It'll be all right." He glanced over to where Bessie Taylor had returned to the fire and was rummaging around at the edge of it, taking a pot from the hot coals.

"How's Bessie's head?" he asked. "Do you think maybe she might be doing too much?''

Heather shook her head. "You couldn't get her to rest if you tried. Once the bleeding stopped, she sort of took over. I think keeping busy helps take her mind off her husband and the other children who didn't make it.''

The fire was some twenty feet away from where Cole and Heather were talking, and Cole saw Bessie spot them, then head their way with a mug in one hand and the coffeepot in the other, using a wadded-up shawl to hold it with so the handle wouldn't burn her hand.

"Coffee?" she asked as Cole straightened.

He smiled wearily. "I was hoping you'd come over," he said.

She poured coffee into the mug and handed it to him. He took a sip of the hot beverage, as if inhaling it to savor the flavor without burning his tongue, then sighed and licked his lips as his eyes settled once more on Bessie.

"You look worn out, Mrs. Taylor," he said anxiously.

She shrugged. "No more'n anyone else. And I told you, the name's Bessie. Besides, I don't think I could sleep if I tried." Tears rimmed her eyes. "At least I have my Helene." Her voice trembled as she looked off toward where her daughter was caring for one of the injured men, trying to get some hot coffee into him to help him ward off a chill. "She's a good girl," she went on. "Nursed me through the fevers last year, and she'd barely turned thirteen.'' She bit her lip, and her voice lowered. "I hope she'll be able to forget all this someday.''

"Do you think any of us really will?" asked Cole.

Bessie shook her head. "Nope. But I'm certainly going to try.''

Cole held the mug out for a refill on the coffee. "Do you think you can do me a big favor, Bessie?" he asked as she finished filling it.

"What's that?"

"Do you think you and Heather salvaged enough from the wreckage that you could scrape up something to feed all the people in the morning? It's bad enough they have to contend with broken bones and all. I thought maybe if we could get some food down those who are able to eat, it might help.''

Bessie frowned, taking a mental inventory on the things they'd dragged ashore. "I think I could manage something," she said. "It won't be fancy, but it'll be edible.''

"Good.'' He gulped the last of the coffee, then handed her the mug. "Now I'd better go find out how Eli's doing. There's still a few hours till daylight.''

He reached down, squeezed Heather's hand and reassured her everything would be all right, then headed off into the darkness.

When he was out of sight Heather stood up, offering to help Bessie, and for the rest of the night, until the first few streaks of dawn began to creep into the shadows, the two women worked hard, managing to put together a nourishing if not tasty breakfast for the survivors.

Some of the survivors were able to feed themselves, but most could barely swallow, let alone hold a spoon, so Heather and Bessie recruited the only other woman who had escaped injury to help while Tildie took care of Case. The woman's name was Margaret Farrington. She had been on her way to St. Louis to meet her husband, who was a barrister there. Rather attractive, she was in her mid-thirties, with dark brown hair, pale blue eyes, and a generous mouth that almost didn't meet in front because of protruding teeth. On her it was an asset, as was the slight tilt to her nose. Unlike the three men who were also uninjured, she was more than willing to help and took orders from Bessie as if it was something she'd been used to doing for years, doing so without as much as a care to the fact that her blue traveling suit was ripped and filthy. Her only thought was the comfort of the poor souls who'd been hurt.

The men were more reluctant to take orders from Bessie, but evidently the woman wasn't used to being ignored, and when she asserted herself, it was surprising the respect she commanded. By the time the sun began to streak the sky with gold, she was giving orders to all three men, and having them carried out.

Reverend Jeremy Litchfield, the circuit rider, had been the hardest to get to fall into line. Every other phrase that came out of his mouth was a generous "Praise the Lord," yet he felt that taking orders from a woman was beneath him. He had helped Eli and Cole readily as they dragged bodies ashore and tried to restore order, but the first time Bessie handed him a mug and a spoon and told him to feed an elderly woman whose hands had been badly burned, he had straightened haughtily and looked at her in disbelief. It wasn't until she began quoting Scripture to him about the Good Samaritan, and how the Apostles emphasized taking care of widows and children, that he lost some of his pious arrogance and lent a hand.

The two other men were a little easier to convince. One was a man who rode the river regularly looking for work. He was a slim, muscular man, well into middle age. His name was Otis Calhoun. He'd been experienced enough on the river to know when pressure in the engines was getting dangerously high, and like Cole, he'd moved toward the end farthest away from the boilers and had come through unscathed. The other was one of the men who stoked the furnaces that fed steam to the boilers. He usually worked all night and had been asleep in the crew's quarters at the time of the accident. He was a free black, named Mose Wheatley, powerfully built across the shoulders, but short in stature compared to Cole. He had a partially bald head and whiskers growing in tufts on each side of his face, leaving his chin bare. Neither man was very anxious to play nursemaid, for various reasons, all of which Bessie declared were unfounded, and because of her expertise at getting her own way, both men soon joined her and the others, trying to get some of the cornmeal mush and molasses into their patients. Even Lone Eagle and his braves helped, much to the consternation of the man named Harry, who refused to let them near him and swore he'd starve to death before he'd let them touch him. Consequently Helene Taylor ended up caring for him.

While everyone else tended to the injured, Cole and Eli began the gruesome task of trying to identify the dead. Now that it was getting light enough to see, the full impact of what had happened was almost overwhelming.

Cole finished checking the body of another woman, then straightened in disgust. So many dead, and the worst part was that it was obvious more of the people had drowned than had been burned or hurt by the explosion. Especially the women, and he silently thanked God he had taught Heather to swim.

Suddenly he froze as he turned toward the river, staring upstream. The night had been cool, and now, with the warmth of the sun, misty fog hung low on the water, swirling eerily, and from somewhere in its depths the low wail of a foghorn could be heard.

Eli heard it too, as did the others, and they all stopped what they were doing, their eyes trying to penetrate the thick fog, waiting for what they hoped was help.

As they all stared, watching the fog swirl and begin to dissipate, the bow of a steamboat began slowly to emerge, and within seconds Cole was at the water's edge, waving his arms and yelling, with Eli at his side doing the same.

Clouds of dark smoke curled high, blending into the fog as the engines on the *Mississippi Queen* throbbed. Slowly the steamboat began to change its course, moving from the middle of the river, edging toward the bank. Aboard the steamboat, Captain Rankin hung over the rail, squinting, trying to get a better look at what he was getting into. At first he'd been apprehensive when he spotted the men in buckskins who were yelling and waving, but as the fog began to lift and the *Mississippi Queen* neared the shore, a feeling of dread swept over him. By now he could see the injured sprawled haphazardly about the fire, and as the early mists of morning filtered up, disappearing into the treetops, he recognized the canvas- and blanket-covered bodies for what they were. Then his eyes settled on the telltale signs of wreckage strewn along the bank. There was no mistaking what had happened.

Most of the passengers on the *Mississippi Queen* were still asleep, but as the boat neared the riverbank, people on deck began to stir and stretch and by the time they were tying up to a tree on the shore, there was a buzz of activity and commotion.

Cole's fingers itched anxiously as he watched the boat tie up; then he cupped his mouth and shouted an answer to the captain, who had called an urgent "Hello! Who are you?"

"The *Bonnie Belle* out of New Orleans," Cole yelled back,

then hurried to board. "Am I glad to see you," he said as he greeted the captain. "The name's Avery." Eli had followed him aboard. "My friend Eli Crawford."

"Where's the captain?" asked Captain Rankin as he shook hands with the men, while his eyes roved the riverbank.

"Never found him," answered Cole. "But we need help bad. There's some twenty-five injured, some in bad shape, and I have no idea what's to be done with the ones who didn't make it. Is there a town or anything around here?"

"Not along the river. You'd have to go inland, and then the most you'd find there is a few small settlements." The captain frowned. "I can take some of the injured back to Walnut Hills, but about all we can do with the dead is try to make a list to give to the authorities down in New Orleans when we get there, then bury them. My men can help." He looked beyond the immediate area. This stretch of the river, in fact most of this area the rest of the way north to St. Louis and south to the delta, was sparsely populated, the landscape wild and overgrown except where the keelboat paths led upriver, but that was on the opposite bank. Unlike the steamboats, keelboats, although descending the Mississippi in record time, often careening into anything in their way, made slow progress upriver, having to be pulled and poled inches at a time against the current.

After taking an overall survey of everything, and taking into account what had to be done, the captain spotted a small area just beyond the survivors that was clear enough, and within no time they were lowering the hapless victims Cole and the others had dragged from the water into shallow graves. Some had identification on them, but most of it was waterlogged and unreadable, and Cole shuddered as he thought of how many bodies must have floated downstream to snag up somewhere along the way and would never have a decent resting place.

As the morning wore on, activity on the river increased and keelboats and flatboats that would have passed unconcerned, had it been night, now stopped, hoping to help, and before long the bank of the river was teeming with people, boats lined up along its shores. Even some trappers in a canoe stopped, unable to squelch their curiosity.

It took most of the morning to bury the dead; then Cole, Eli, and the captain concentrated on the survivors. The captain was appalled at the extent of the injuries the survivors had sustained. A few let his men carry them aboard the steamboat, opting to ride it back to Walnut Hills, where they could get proper medical attention, but most were too frightened to ride on a steamboat again and argued against it, finally accepting offers from some of the flatboat and keelboat crews to ride downriver with them.

Then there were the others, along with Cole and his family and Bessie Taylor and her daughter, who hadn't even considered abandoning their journey. They refused everyone's offers to return to Walnut Hills or New Orleans. A few consented to be taken across the river to go north on whatever they could—keelboat, flatboat, anything but a steamboat—but Bessie wanted no part of the water. She had lost her husband, son, and a daughter. That was enough. When she found out Eli and Cole had decided to trek overland the rest of the way, she, along with a few others, decided to join them. Cole tried to talk the others out of it, especially the man named Harry, whose leg wasn't any too stable, but Harry refused adamantly, and became hysterical when they tried to haul him to one of the boats.

"I guess he'd rather take his chances on being scalped than drowned," Cole told the others as he watched Harry screaming at Captain Rankin's men to get their bloody hands off him.

The Indians had definitely decided to accompany Eli and Cole's group of travelers, and Harry knew it, but his fear of the water had become far more obsessive than his fear of the Cherokee and he was shaking all over when they finally let him be.

Captain Rankin tried to talk Cole out of his decision to go on foot, and occasionally his arguments against their going overland were logical, but shortly before noon they discovered their horses had survived and all the captain's arguments were forgotten.

Finding the horses had really been a boost to their morale. Cole had been helping fill in the last of the graves, when suddenly he froze. A faint, familiar sound had caught his ear, and he stood stock-still, hoping to hear it again. He stood quietly, then began to wonder if it had just been his imagination, because all he could hear now was the jumble of voices around him that carried over from where everyone else was. After standing for a full two minutes listening intently with no results, he was just ready to brush the thought aside, when he remembered the whistle. If she was around anyplace, there was no way she'd ignore that whistle.

He puckered his mouth, and the low, trilling sound cut the air like a knife, its high treble unfamiliar in these surroundings. As its shrill call floated through the trees, Cole waited anxiously for an answer. He didn't have to wait long. Seconds later, his heart warmed as he heard a crashing in the underbrush and his piebald mare slowly emerged, followed closely by the other horses, which seemed to have chosen her for their leader.

He dropped his shovel and ran to the mare, stopping to stroke her flanks and nuzzle her nose with his hand. There was a small cut near her mane, but other than that she didn't seem to have been hurt by the explosion. Nor had the other horses. Evidently they had just gotten lost, probably floating downriver a ways. Cole grabbed the bridle that was still on her and led her and the other three horses across the small clearing to the riverbank.

"I still think you're making a mistake, even with the horses," said Captain Rankin later that evening as he prepared the *Mississippi Queen* to cast off. He was still arguing about Cole's decision. "There's nothing between here and Arkansas Post except wilderness and swamps."

"We'll find our way," assured Cole. There was no use telling the good captain that he and Eli had been roaming the area just north of here quite freely only a few short months ago. After selling their furs in Cincinnati, they had ridden down the Ohio on a flatboat, sailed out onto the Mississippi, and followed it to the mouth of the White River. From there they had made their way to the Arkansas and Cole had fallen in love with the raw, rugged land.

"Cole Dante could lose himself in Arkansas County," he had told Eli the day he'd decided to go back to Beaufort for Heather and the baby, and now here he was standing on the banks of the Mississippi, his journey half over.

They were planning to start out first thing in the morning. The flatboats and keelboats had left shortly before dark, and now, as Cole, Heather, Eli, and the rest who had chosen to stay stood on the bank and watched the steamboat pull away from the shore and head out into the middle of the river, beginning to move downstream, each had mixed emotions. Lights from the *Mississippi Queen* flickered, reflecting off the water, and the rhythm of the paddle wheel could be heard swooshing and slapping in the darkness that was swiftly swallowing her up. Only a short time ago the riverbanks had been full of people, hurrying and scurrying. Now it was all but deserted, the bonfire, newly rekindled, turning their solemn figures to statues of yellow-orange in its light.

As the last flickering lights from the steamboat faded in the distance, accompanied by the long, low wail of the foghorn that was also quickly gone, leaving a deadly quiet in its wake, the people on the bank began to stir.

Cole straightened, turning slowly to look at those around him. Heather, Eli, Tildie, the baby—they had to be with him. And he didn't mind Bessie and her daughter, nor Lone Eagle and his men, but the rest . . . His eyes fell on Harry Ferguson.

He certainly could do without Harry Ferguson along. The man, besides being a bigot, was a chronic complainer. The fact that he was unable to walk didn't matter. They'd make a travois to haul him on. It was the man's personality that not only Cole but also the others resented. However, the rest, like Cole, didn't have the heart to force him to finish his trip by water, since he was so deathly afraid of it now.

Then there was the circuit rider. His constant preaching and pious, holier-than-thou attitude grated on Cole's nerves. He'd been hoping the wiry little man would decide to return to New Orleans or go on upriver by flatboat or keelboat, but no such luck. They were stuck with him. Cole didn't know if it was the man's short stature that made him so arrogant and haughty or the fact that he felt he was better than all the others and closer to God, but whatever it was, Jeremy Litchfield walked around like a proud bantam rooster and it rubbed everyone the wrong way. It wouldn't be so bad if he hadn't decided to try to convert what he considered the heathen Indians. Lone Eagle and his braves resented it. Already Cole had had to interfere when the Indians began their death chant and the reverend tried to stop them, insisting that he wasn't going to be a party to their pagan rites.

Of the other two men who'd been helping with the survivors, only the black man, Mose Wheatley, had elected to go the rest of the way by land, telling Cole he was tired of the heat and frustration in the boiler room of the steamboat. Cole had been hoping Otis Calhoun would come along, because he was a good worker and Harry Ferguson had taken a liking to him. It would make things a little easier, but Otis had decided to go back to Walnut Hills and catch the next steamboat heading upriver. Margaret Farrington also decided to continue upriver, but took one of the keelboats that came along during the day.

Off and on, all day, as flatboats and keelboats struggled upriver on the opposite bank, they reported finding some survivors the night before as well as bloated bodies floating in midstream and caught on tree roots and other debris along the banks.

Cole glanced about with trepidation. Thank God Eli was still

with them; he was going to need all the help he could get to keep
harmony along the way. He felt a movement close at his elbow
and looked down, capturing Heather's violet eyes, seeing the
anxiety in their depths.

"You could have refused to let them come along," she said
hesitantly.

He frowned. "Could I? I wonder . . ." He straightened,
putting his arm around her, pulling her hard against him. "One
thing for sure, I'm glad I have you with me this time."

"You said you and Eli had been here before?"

"Not this particular area, we were farther north, but I know
we can make it to Arkansas Post, only I wish there were just the
four of us and the baby. I don't like being responsible for the
others." He turned slightly so they could both look their companions over. "Rather a strange assortment, aren't they?" he said.

"I don't care." Her arm was about his waist and she snuggled
closer to him. "I'd rather be here with you, with a hundred
uncertainties ahead of us, than back in Beaufort in that horrible
house with Everett Palmer and his son Carl, knowing exactly
what each day held and dreading it."

He looked down at her, frowning. "You look so tired," he
said. His own voice was husky from loss of sleep.

"And what of you?"

"Maybe we can find someplace to collapse until morning,"
he said lazily, then sighed. "Where's Case?"

"Tildie has him. He should be asleep by now."

"Good." He inhaled, sighing. "Come on."

His arm was still about her shoulder and he led her away from
the others, where they'd be by themselves, then both of them
sank wearily to the ground, Cole with his back leaning against a
huge oak tree, with Heather cuddled close in his arms.

Cole closed his eyes, her soft warmth comforting him. He was
so exhausted, and every bone in his body ached. Suddenly he
realized how long they'd been without sleep. A cool breeze
caressed his brow, and he sighed.

"You're not cold, are you?" he asked.

"No." She took a deep breath. "Do you realize how lucky
we are, Cole?" she whispered against his throat where her face
was pressed. "Bessie lost most of her family . . . there are so
many dead, and injured . . . why were we spared?"

He took a deep breath. "Who knows?"

As she lay against him, slowly letting her weary body succumb to his nearness, her thoughts wandered back over everything that had happened. Why had they been spared? Was it coincidence or fate? One thing for certain, today had been a day she'd be long forgetting, and now, suddenly, as she thought of the wilderness ahead of them and the strange new direction her life was going, she thought back to the first time Cole had wanted her to go away with him, and how foolish she had been to think life without him would be better than the hardships and uncertainty of the frontier. She was still frightened. These vast forests and miles of wilderness were overwheming, but she'd make it. She had to, because without Cole, even the luxuries of civilization were meaningless.

Only one thing bothered her now. She was having such a hard time remembering to call him Duke. She had slipped up a number of times shortly after the explosion, and no one had seemed to notice, but now . . . As she closed her eyes and let her thoughts drift off, she made a promise to remember to call him Duke—in the morning . . . in the morning.

"Good night, love," Cole whispered, his body relaxing, but she didn't answer. He sighed, his arms tightening slightly about her, and within minutes he too was sound asleep.

3

It had been dark for well over an hour. Rafe Turner sat at a table in the corner of the tavern in New Orleans, a mug of ale in front of him, a piece of paper spread out near the mug. He stared at the paper, contemplating the recent turn of events. When he had first spotted the man he'd been certain was Cole Dante, a strange sense of power had filled him. Dante had always been one rung ahead of him, not only back in South Carolina but also in the army, and remembering the wanted poster he had seen only a few months before had momentarily filled him with anxiety.

The farther the *Bonnie Belle* moved upriver, the more apprehensive he had become. Had it really been Cole on board? Or had his imagination been playing tricks on him? After all, if it was Cole, why was he traveling out in the open as if nothing was wrong? Maybe it was just someone who looked a great deal like Dante. The more he thought about it, the more he'd talked himself into believing he'd been mistaken. After all, the man he had seen had been traveling with a woman and a small child. As far as he knew, Dante wasn't married.

That was weeks ago, and now here he was with the whole thing right back in his lap again.

He continued to stare at the wanted poster spread out on the table before him. Five thousand was a great deal of money. The poster stated that Cole Dante was wanted for the murder of one DeWitt Palmer. Rafe frowned, remembering the Palmers only too well. He had disliked them about as much as he had disliked the Dantes. "Resented" was a better word to describe his feelings. Both families had wealth and prestige. DeWitt and Cole had both been born into it, while he, Rafe Turner, had been born the middle son of the town drunk. His father was the man who was always given the odd jobs and dirty jobs because he was never quite sober enough to do anything on a steady basis. His father's drinking had put his mother in an early grave and relegated Rafe to the streets, where he had learned to survive.

Now his eyes sifted over the poster. Five thousand was a chance. With that kind of money he could do just about anything he wanted.

Strange how things happen. If he hadn't decided to go to the tavern that night, he wouldn't have run into the man with the poster and he wouldn't be sitting here now waiting for Carl Palmer to arrive.

He glanced up at the door as a group of men came in; then, recognizing none of them, and missing the last man who walked in the door, he looked back down to the poster, smoothing it lovingly with his callused hands before taking a swig of ale from the mug and wiping his mouth with the back of his hand.

Carl Palmer's hands were sweaty as he followed the small group of men into the taproom, then stood quietly gazing about. He wasn't a tall man, nor did he command attention for anything more than the fact that his hair was the kind of carrot red that accompanied pale skin and light eyes. Carl's eyes were hazel, hard and direct, the grim line of his mouth broadening his chin, making it appear more square, the jawline unyielding. His beaver hat was in his hand and he straightened the cloak on his shoulders as he studied the men in the room. It had been years since he'd seen Rafe Turner and he was afraid perhaps he wouldn't recognize him, but when his eyes fell on the bald spot atop the head of the man in the corner, then dropped down past the fringe clinging to its sides and perused the man's face, there was no mistaking the hard look.

Rafe was wearing dark clothes that emphasized the deep scar on his cheek and he looked up just as Carl Palmer began to make his way between the tables.

Carl was alone. His choice. When he'd received word that Roth Chapman's ship the *Interlude* had been seen rounding the coast of Florida, he'd been certain where it was heading, and he knew Cole and Heather had to be on it. The fact that word had come from the governor exonerating Cole didn't matter, not anymore. It wasn't just DeWitt's death that drove Carl on anymore. In fact, DeWitt's death had affected his father more than it had affected Carl. Except for the fact that DeWitt was his brother and any affront to DeWitt was a slur against the Palmer name, Carl couldn't care less if DeWitt was alive or dead. Carl had always hated DeWitt. His younger brother had been conceited, sarcastic, a virtual tyrant, and always his father's favorite, especially since Carl had made such a mess of his own life, marrying a woman who couldn't bear children, then watching her slowly go mad.

That was behind him now too, however. He had managed to obtain an annulment from his tragic marriage, and just when his dream of marrying his brother's lovely widow was so close to becoming a reality that he ached inside to possess her, she'd been stolen from him. Well, no one was going to ruin his life again.

He stopped before the table in the corner. "Rafe Turner?" he asked curtly.

Rafe had been watching the red-haired man approach. "Palmer?"

"It's been a number of years, but the resemblance is still there," said Carl as he pulled off his gloves, shoved his cloak back over his shoulder, pulled up a chair, and sat down.

Rafe watched him closely. There was a rough edge to Carl Palmer that showed in his eyes and the firm set of his shoulders as he sat across from him. "Have an ale?" asked Rafe.

Carl nodded and Rafe called for another mug of ale that was quickly brought over by a slim young woman, who looked Carl over cautiously, but smiled warmly at Rafe. She set it on the table, then quickly faded back into the crowd.

"My man said you had information," said Carl as he took a sip of the ale.

Both men became oblivious of the noise and confusion about them.

"It all depends," answered Rafe.

Carl nodded toward the wanted poster spread out in front of them. "Isn't that enough?" he asked.

"It could be, but then, I figure the information I've got could be worth more."

"How's that?"

"I know Dante was cleared by the governor."

"Oh!"

"That means he's not wanted for murder anymore, so you must have another reason for being after him. I'm hoping you want him badly enough to up the ante."

Carl's eyes narrowed. "A few questions first."

"Maybe."

"You saw him?"

"Maybe."

Carl's jaw tightened. "Was there a red-haired woman with him?"

"Maybe."

"All right!" Carl's eyes sparked dangerously. "Two thousand more, but that's all. Now . . ." He leaned forward. "I asked you if there was a woman with him."

Rafe took a deep breath. "There were two women with him. A black wench and a redhead. There was also a baby, and another man, a frontiersman from the looks of him. They were all wearing buckskins."

"Where did you see them?"

Rafe hesitated. "When do I get the money?"

"Half now, the other half when I have my hands on them."

"That means I'd have to go with you."

"You know your way around here. I need a guide. You'll do as good as any. Besides, with you along I won't have to worry about a double cross."

"What makes you so sure? I could lead you into the wilderness, take the money, and leave."

"I'm not that stupid, Turner," Carl sneered. "The money will be here in a bank in New Orleans. If you want it, you'll have to make sure I get back."

Rafe's eyes hardened. Palmer had thought of everything.

"You mentioned the wilderness," said Carl.

Rafe straightened. "I imagine that's where they were heading. They were dressed for it."

"Where did you see them?"

"On a steamboat heading upriver."

"Then they could have gotten off anywhere."

"That's right."

Carl was disgusted. "It'll take forever to locate them."

"Not if we catch up to the *Bonnie Belle*. I don't think her captain will forget them that easily. It isn't often you see two women traveling in buckskins, and one of them black."

Carl's jaw tightened. "How soon can you leave?"

"Whenever you're ready," answered Rafe. "The *Bonnie Belle* should be close to St. Louis by now. We'll probably meet her on the way back down."

"And if we miss her?"

"Then we backtrack by keelboat or flatboat until we catch her. Unless you'd rather just wait here until she gets back. It's up to you."

Carl shook his head. "Not on your life. I intend to find Dante, and as soon as possible."

"Then you'll make the arrangements?"

"What'll we need?"

They spent the next half-hour deciding they'd take the first steamboat leaving New Orleans, then buy supplies upriver wherever they left the boat.

"And it'll be just the two of us?" asked Rafe, confirming what he suspected.

Carl nodded.

Rafe finished the ale in front of him, then looked directly into Carl Palmer's hazel eyes, noting the way the light in the wall sconce gave them a yellow cast. "You never did say why you were still willing to pay to find Dante," he said huskily.

Carl hesitated. He wasn't used to confiding in people. Yet, if the plans were to work, maybe it was best the man did know.

"I want the woman!" he said arrogantly. "Cole Dante has no right to her."

Rafe contemplated Carl's answer. "Who is she?" he asked.

"My brother's widow," Carl answered bitterly; then his eyes narrowed. "And the woman I plan to marry."

"And the baby?"

Carl's face paled slightly as the muscle in his cheek twitched. "Forget the child," he said. "He's unimportant. The only thing you have to remember is that nothing's to happen to the woman, understand?''

Rafe nodded and Carl stood up.

"Good!" He twisted the brim of his beaver hat in his hands. "As long as there's no misunderstanding." He glanced about, conscious once more of the noise and confusion, aware that some of the other customers were staring at his fancy clothes. "Where do I reach you?" he asked.

Rafe leaned back in his chair. "I've got a room upstairs. Third door down on the left."

Carl gave a curt nod. "Then I'll be in touch," he said quickly, and turned, heading for the door.

Rafe watched Carl disappear out the front door of the tavern and he leaned forward, lifting the paper from the table where it had lain during their conversation. He studied it again for a long time, then smiled furtively, remembering the red-haired woman who was with Dante on board the *Bonnie Belle*. So that's why Carl Palmer had traveled all the way here from Beaufort, South Carolina. For a woman. And he thought it was for revenge. Well, he'd better keep an eye on Palmer, that's for sure. Any man who'd rather have his brother's wife than avenge his brother's death wasn't exactly the best man to trust. No, from here on in, he'd trust Carl Palmer no farther than his eyes could see him.

Rafe folded the wanted poster, shoved it into the pocket of his jacket, then called for another ale.

Carl was furious as he pounded on the door to Rafe's room. Of all the blamed luck.

"Turner, dammit! Open up!" he yelled, banging again.

It had been two days since their meeting downstairs. Rafe Turner stirred slowly at first, conscious of the ache in his head and the vile taste in his mouth. His eyes shot to the window, and he blinked, realizing the sun was well into the sky and it must be close to noon. He had really set one on last night, and now he glanced toward the door, calling out as he left the bed, fumbling for his pants.

"Hold on!" he yelled, slipping his feet into the pants, then shuffling to the door. "No need to break down the damn door!" He reached it, tripped the lock and swung it open, then stared hard at Carl Palmer, whose face was livid against the dark blue frock coat he was wearing. "Well, what's got into you?" he asked as Palmer straightened, then stepped into the room. Rafe closed the door behind him and Carl faced him.

"A keelboat and a couple flatboats hauled into the docks this morning," Carl blurted angrily. "Word is that the *Bonnie Belle* blew just north of a place called Walnut Hills."

"They're sure it was the *Bonnie Belle?*"

"No, they aren't sure. Not yet anyway, but how the hell are we going to find out for certain . . . and if it was, what then?"

Rafe sighed. "Well, if your lady's dead, there's not much use goin' upriver, is there?" he said.

Carl's lips tightened stubbornly. "She can't be dead," he said, and turned, walking over to look out the window, paying little attention to the sparse furnishings in the room.

Rafe watched him curiously. For a minute he thought he saw tears rimming the man's eyes, but then, he'd turned away so quickly it was hard to tell. Rafe hitched his pants up, then walked over and grabbed his shirt off the straight-backed chair next to the bed and continued getting dressed as he talked.

"It shouldn't take too long to find out one way or another," he assured Carl as he buttoned his shirt. "Rumors are followed pretty closely by fact around here. If she blew, there were bound to be a few survivors." He finished pulling on his boots, then stood up. "I suggest we go back to the docks and see what more we can find out."

Carl was torn up inside. She couldn't be dead. Not after all his planning. All this couldn't be for nothing. He closed his eyes to the sunshine and let the haunting warmth of her violet eyes fill his thoughts. She was so beautiful, so delicately sensual, and so many times he'd wondered what it'd be like to feel her body yielding to him. To touch her, caress her, bury his face in her fragrant hair and see her eyes light up with longing. That someone so alive, so vital, could be gone was beyond reasoning. His jaw clenched stubbornly. She had to be alive. God would never destroy anything so lovely. Rafe was right: they'd go back to the docks and ferret out the truth. It was the only thing they could do. He turned.

"Are you ready?" he asked, the anger from moments before replaced by a look of determination.

Rafe nodded. "Whenever you are."

It wasn't quite noon when they left the inn. The docks were a buzz of activity. Another keelboat had arrived, and with it came more rumors. It wasn't until late that evening that the first flatboat arrived to make fact out of the rumors, admitting they had dropped some of the survivors off at Walnut Hills. But it wasn't until the next afternoon, when the *Mississippi Queen* made her way to the river docks, that Carl and Rafe learned the whole truth.

"You say the man in buckskins, this Duke Avery, decided to go overland?" Carl confirmed as he talked to Captain Rankin on the deck of the steamboat.

Captain Rankin nodded. "I warned him about the swamps," he said. "But he didn't seem about to change his mind."

"And you're sure the lady with him wasn't hurt?" asked Carl.

The captain eyed him curiously. "They friends of yours, or what?" he asked.

Carl was undaunted. "Close friends," he said, then smiled congenially as he made plans for himself and Rafe to be aboard the *Mississippi Queen* when she left in two days, heading back upriver.

It had been raining since sunup, and everyone was soaked to the skin. Cole turned back and glanced up at Heather astride her horse, with Case tied to her saddle in his makeshift carrier. She looked tired, as did the others, and he didn't blame them. The baby was fussing, and he watched Heather lean forward, trying to quiet him. Cole frowned. Maybe he'd been pushing them too hard the past few days. But the weather had been extremely wet, and he wanted to get as far north as he could. As it was, the territory around Arkansas Post was swampy enough without having to worry about flooding.

They'd been following a river for days now, and its banks had been swollen when they'd first reached it. Ordinarily, if they'd been by themselves, Cole would have crossed the river and headed north to drier country, but because the others were along, he was compelled to go straight to Arkansas Post. He and Eli had purposely avoided going there earlier in the summer, and he was wary about going there now. There was too much chance a military post would have wanted posters on him, and there was a great possibility he might know some of the soldiers stationed there. Instead of going all the way to the White River on the *Bonnie Belle*, then taking the White River cutoff to the post, he had planned to leave the steamboat just this side of the Arkansas River and stay on the south side, following it up to the hot springs, then on up to the Verdigris. The explosion had changed those plans.

Bessie and her daughter were on Cole's horse, Tildie was on her horse, Harry Ferguson was on Eli's horse, and the rest of them were on foot. When they had first started out, their supplies had been carried on the horses, but now, with Harry able to ride astride instead of using the travois, they had piled their supplies on the travois, making room on the horses for the women to ride. Cole was glad. It was enough the men had to put up with ankle-deep mud and dense underbrush.

He turned back to the trail before him, if you could call it a trail. Eli and Lone Eagle, with his braves, were up ahead somewhere, out of sight, but their sign was fresh enough for Cole to follow. His feet sank in with each step, and the suction as he lifted them made a funny noise as he walked. Suddenly he stopped and wiped the rain from his face as he saw movement up ahead.

The horses halted behind him.

"What the devil's the holdup?" yelled Harry when Bessie reined to a halt in front of him.

"Shut up!" snapped Cole.

Harry pulled the hat he was wearing down farther to keep the rain from his eyes, as he gave Cole a dirty look. If there was anyone he could have done without on this trip, it was Duke Avery. He couldn't stand the self-appointed bully. Always telling him what to do, and acting like he was the only one who knew anything. Damn half-breed! And that mountain man with him! Stubborn, uncivilized, the man was a menace, the way he sneaked around all the time, watchin' over his shoulder, not missin' a thing goin' on. Harry's whiskers bristled as he clamped his mouth shut and watched Cole trying to keep the drizzling rain from his eyes as he studied the trail ahead.

Suddenly a slight movement to Cole's right caught his eye; then he exhaled as Eli's buckskin-clad frame emerged from some bushes that were starting to show a hint of fall color, made even more noticeable by the rain clinging to them.

Eli reached Cole in an easy gait, trying to avoid the worst of the water and mud that seemed to have become part of the riverbank. "We found a high place to camp," he said quickly. "Lone Eagle and his men are putting up makeshift shelters, since it doesn't look like it's going to stop raining."

Cole nodded. "Good." He glanced back again toward the

others. "I think we could all use some rest. There's about two hours of daylight left, but it'll do us good to get out of this rain. Lead the way."

Eli glanced quickly back over the line of people behind Cole, then turned abruptly and struck off in the direction where Cole had first spotted him, and Cole waved a hand, motioning for the rest to follow. Heather dug her horse in the ribs, and sighed, hoping the place Eli had picked wasn't too far away. She followed Cole, the rest of them trailing behind her.

Eli had chosen an ideal place to camp, and Heather breathed a sigh of relief as they rode in and she saw the leaf bowers the Indians had put up to keep off the rain. The leaves were turning, but still clung heavily to the branches, and their thickness not only held off the rain but also kept in the warmth from a fire Lone Eagle had started in the center of the encampment. She glanced up at the gray sky, then thanked God the rain wasn't hard enough to put the fire out. It looked so inviting.

The weary travelers straggled into the camp, and Cole came over, helping her down, then they both tended to the baby.

"I wish things could be better for you," Cole said as he released the baby from his confinement in the blanket, then held him close in his arms. "But it won't be much longer. Eli said we should reach the post by tomorrow afternoon. Maybe it'll stop raining before then."

Heather sighed, trying not to look too discouraged. "I won't melt," she said, and took the baby from him, heading toward one of the shelters.

All of the shelters had been set up in a large circle, with the fire in the center, and somewhere Lone Eagle's braves had managed to find fallen leaves that were fairly dry, lining the shelters with them. Heather bent down, setting Case far back under the shelter where the leaves were thickest and driest; then she knelt beside him, calling Tildie to bring a blanket from the canvas-covered travois. Taking it from the young black girl, she wrapped it about her son, trying to warm him. Although it wasn't bitter cold out, it was October and the temperature had dropped to the mid-forties with the rain, and the fear of sickness lingered at the back of her mind.

A short while later, when Case seemed to be settled comfortably, with a cup of broth warming his insides, Heather took a moment for herself. Tildie was with Case, so Heather moved closer to the fire, hoping to ward off the chill that had started her knees trembling. The fire felt so good against her hands, yet it seemed as if she'd never know what it was to feel dry again. Even her skin, beneath the buckskins, felt shriveled and waterlogged.

The shelters were placed at intervals some four to five feet apart and Heather glanced over, away from the fire, to where Cole and Eli were talking to some of the others, and as she stared at him, a warm tingling sensation began to ignite inside her. She loved him so very much. Those dark green eyes that gave away his Indian heritage, the lean face with a strength inherited from his forebears. His lanky body looked almost too lean, yet beneath the buckskins she knew every muscle was well-honed. It seemed like she could never get enough of looking at him and being near him. And sometimes, the wonder of knowing they were finally together for always was overwhelming.

Yet, as she stared, a flush of heat gripping her, she suddenly felt tears well up in her eyes. She had told Cole she'd rather brave the wilderness with him than try to live without him, but now that the reality was here, she was discovering it was far harder than she had ever imagined. Especially with the baby, and she even had Tildie to help. At first, just being with Cole was enough, but now they hadn't even had a chance to be alone since leaving New Orleans. Oh, they fell asleep in each other's arms at night, and it helped, but she needed more of him than just his arms and lips. She needed the love he had so often given her, needed it to help strengthen her and make it all worthwhile. And this was only the start.

She shifted her weight from one foot to the other, feeling the soreness in her hips and buttocks from so many hours in the saddle. She had always sat a horse well, but riding from sunup to sunset in the rain was far different from an hour's ride down the bridle trail.

Her stomach suddenly spasmed and she began to realize how hungry she was. Drawing her eyes from Cole, she moved to the other side of the fire, to where Bessie was stirring the broth she had made from some rabbits Eli and Lone Eagle had managed to shoot earlier in the day.

Bessie quit stirring the broth, then began dropping dumplings into the kettle as she glanced over at Heather.

"Don't worry, before long you'll be sleeping in a nice dry bed," Bessie said, trying to make Heather feel better. She had sensed Heather's misgivings.

Heather frowned. "Is it that noticeable?"

"Not really, but you look a little lost and forlorn."

"I'll just be glad when all this is over and we can find someplace to call home."

"Duke said you were heading for the Verdigris River area after you leave Arkansas Post." Bessie frowned. "You don't suppose you could use a good cook to help when you get there, do you?" she asked suddenly. "Helene and I don't have any special place to go now, what with the rest of the family gone." Her eyes saddened momentarily; then she went on. "You know I'm a good cook, and I can clean just as well, and Helene's good with a needle too, and she could help me. I wouldn't ask no wages, mind you, just a roof over our heads and food to eat."

"We don't even have a roof over our own heads yet, Bessie," Heather answered. "How can I promise you anything?"

"Oh, you'll get one," Bessie said firmly. "That man of yours is determined. Besides, I sort of got attached to the lot of you the past few days. Wouldn't seem right not to be around to make sure you was all all right. I'm used to lookin' after a whole brood. Don't seem right I should only have two people to worry about. I ain't used to doin' for just two."

Heather glanced over at Bessie and tried to smile, her mouth stiff from the cold that was beginning to settle with the growing darkness. "I'll talk to him about it, Bessie," she said. "But he may not go along with the idea."

Bessie winked. "Maybe you could give him a nudge." She chuckled conspiratorially. "Never hurts to try, 'specially with him lovin' you like he does. He'd probably do about anythin' to make you happy."

This time Heather did manage to smile, the flames from the fire helping redden the blush that crept into her face. "Why, Bessie, you're positively wicked," she gasped, pretending to be shocked. "But I'll see what I can do."

Bessie smiled back. "That's all I'm askin'." She nodded her head toward a spot across the fire, changing the subject. "Look who's gettin' chummy," she said, the smile fading.

Heather looked over the top of the fire to where Reverend Litchfield had just knelt down to say something to Harry Ferguson. Both men were talking in low tones, as if trying to make sure no one could overhear, and it wasn't the first time Heather had noticed it. She sighed, wondering what they were up to, but not really worrying about it. Right now, her first concern was her stomach and the gnawing hunger pains that were overtaking it.

She turned once more to Bessie, hoping perhaps the older woman might have something she could munch on until the stew was ready.

At the other side of the fire, Reverend Litchfield was clenching his jaw stubbornly.

"Why didn't you tell me about this earlier, Ferguson?" he asked as he turned his backside to the warming flames, rubbing his rear with gnarled hands.

"Because I wanted to be sure first. Besides, there ain't nothin' we can do about it until we reach the post, and I heard Crawford telling Avery we should get there sometime tomorrow."

"You're sure you heard her call him Cole, not Duke?"

"And each time, he gave her a funny look, like she was doin' somethin' she wasn't supposed to do."

"Maybe Cole's his real name and people just call him Duke," Jeremy Litchfield reasoned. "After all, Duke doesn't sound like a regular name."

"That's well and all," said Harry. "But if so, why would they make such an effort not to use it? It just ain't natural." He snorted irritably, the cold, damp weather making him even more miserable. "And another thing. He pretends to be a gentleman. In the first place, I ain't never heard of no Injun bein' one of the gentry."

"What about his wife?" countered Jeremy. "That little red-haired lady's no frontier woman. She's definitely one of the gentry. You can tell by the way she acts that she was reared with money. She's a lady if I ever saw one. And what about that slave they're totin' around? Poor folks don't own slaves."

"I told you," Harry said quickly. "There's somethin' that don't add up with them folks. I think they's runnin' from somethin' and I think when we reach Arkansas Post, one of us oughta say somethin' to the authorities about it."

Reverend Litchfield had to agree with Harry. In spite of the fact that Avery and Crawford were doing their best to see that the group arrived at Arkansas Post in one piece, there was something strangely mysterious about them.

"Well, which one of us is elected?" he asked Harry.

Harry shrugged. "Don't really matter, I guess." He spit a stream of tobacco into the red-hot ashes, watching it sputter. "But since you're a man of the cloth, they'd probably pay more attention to you."

Jeremy Litchfield studied his companion for a few seconds

while he debated the wisdom of his suggestion, then nodded. "Maybe you're right," he said. "After all, it's my duty to see that the sinful pay, and if they aren't who and what they say they are, then I'd be shirking my duty by not saying anything."

Harry smiled. "I thought maybe you'd see it my way," he said. "I'm glad you come along, Reverend. Makes a man feel better knowin' there's a man of God here among all these heathen." Harry glanced off to where Lone Eagle was in conversation with Cole and Eli, and his eyes narrowed. "And that's another thing, Reverend. Avery's too friendly with them redskins for me to sit easy on it. The sooner we get them out of our hair, the better I'll feel about it."

Jeremy Litchfield followed Harry's gaze, his own eyes settling on Lone Eagle. He and Harry had discussed Lone Eagle's status in the group more than once the past few days, and both had come to the conclusion that like all Indians, he couldn't be trusted. For now, the Indian seemed to be friendly enough, but he'd seen more than one man cut down by a so-called friend. Jeremy straightened and stood up, staring hard at the Indian for a few minutes longer, then jerked his attention toward the woods surrounding them, wondering if perhaps more Indians might be lurking in them, and realizing he was going to spend another restless night fitfully anxious about the attack he knew was bound to come. If only Avery would listen to him, but that too was understandable. After all, he was part Indian. It was logical he'd stick up for his own. If only he could have converted the heathen, but even that was denied him. All he could do now was pray for their souls and ask the good Lord to watch over everyone, since no one else seemed to care if they were murdered in their sleep.

He hitched his pants up higher onto his hips and quit gawking about, letting his eyes rest once more on Harry Ferguson. "Praise you, Brother Ferguson," he said, his voice hushed, almost inaudible amid the crackling from the fire. "The good Lord'll bless us both for speaking up. Who knows what evil those heathen may have planned? If not against us, then someone else, and it goes without saying that it looks like whatever it is, the man who calls himself Avery is right in the middle of it. Whatever he's headin' to or runnin' from, conniving with them Indians the way he's doing shows he isn't living for the Lord. First thing when we reach Arkansas Post, I'll see someone finds out why our mysterious leader's wife sees fit to call him by a different name than the one he claims is his, and maybe we'll find out just who Mr. Duke Avery really is, and why he's so anxious to take such a pretty little thing like his missus into the wilderness. One thing for sure, the man sure isn't up to any good. Now, if you'll excuse me, I've got some praying to do before I can rest easy tonight.''

Harry nodded, then watched Jeremy Litchfield stroll off toward the woods, knowing in a few minutes the whole camp would hear the man praying. That was one thing about Reverend Jeremy Litchfield: it was as if he was afraid the good Lord wouldn't hear him, and every night his voice rang out through the camp while he prayed for salvation for the heathen, exonerating his own soul, and condemning all nonbelievers to eternal hellfire and brimstone.

Sometimes Harry wondered, as he was sure the others did too: was the reverend so loud and conspicuous because he thought it was the proper way to pray, or had he just been to too many camp meetings and felt if he didn't pray out loud, people would think he wasn't praying at all? Oh, well, Harry didn't really care. All he cared about now was what was ahead of them for tomorrow, and as he burrowed back beneath the shelter the Indians had put up for him so he wouldn't have to sleep in the wet and cold, and sat waiting for Bessie Taylor to finish cooking the stew, his only thoughts were on tomorrow and the surprise Duke Avery was going to have in store for him when they finally reached Arkansas Post.

4

They had passed near a Choctaw village a few miles back, and had just managed to ford the Arkansas River, which, to their relief, was only some few hundred yards across at this point, and not overly deep. The rain that had made the past few days miserable had given way today to hot sunshine, and a searing heat that swirled through the forest warming the ground, and already beginning to dry out the muddy earth.

Heather sat astride her horse while Cole held its bridle, and they watched the last of their small group leave the river and join them on the bank; then they all turned, gazing toward the low bluffs some two hundred yards distant, where the settlement was spread out encompassing Arkansas Post. From here it looked much larger than Heather had imagined.

It was late afternoon as they began to make their way up a roadway that led from the river to the post, and Heather took time to look over the surroundings. A few houses were scattered here and there, with people moving about, and as they topped the ridge, leaving the sloping ascent to the bluff behind them, the fort itself came into view. The walls were high with fortified bastions set at intervals, the tips of cannon visible even from this distance. The walls looked thick and formidable in spite of years of abuse from wind and rain. Heather felt relieved at the sight. Except for the Indian village they had skirted earlier in the day, this was their first glimpse of civilization since starting their long trek.

The gates to the fort were open wide, a few people moving about, and occasionally a horse-drawn wagon passed them, the drivers gawking curiously, but for the most part, the road leading through the gates was all but deserted. Once inside, however, Heather was surprised to see a number of soldiers lounging about, and she glanced at Cole surreptitiously, knowing he had noticed them too.

A strange tightening had begun in the pit of Cole's stomach at the sight of the soldiers, and now he stopped, gazing about. The village inside the walls left much to be desired. Although the fort was of good size, there were only three stores, a few more houses and buildings—these, he supposed, housed the soldiers—along with a couple of small barns. Not really enough room for all the men lounging about. As he stood staring, with Eli close at his side, one of the soldiers broke away from a small group and wandered over, eyeing them curiously.

"You folks look a little the worse for wear," he said. "Anything I can help you with?"

Cole frowned, his hand tightening as he held the bridle of Heather's horse. "Where do I find someone in charge?" he asked.

The man's eyes continued to study them. "All depends on what you mean by 'in charge.' " He nodded his head toward one of the buildings. "If you listen to Notrebe and his cohorts over there at the trading post, you'd swear they was in charge." He paused, then went on, nodding toward another building. "But then if you were to talk to Lewis, the Indian agent, he'd tell you he's in charge. I guess rightly, though, the commandant's in charge. You'll find Major Stoddard in there," and he motioned with his head to another building farther down the line.

Cole thanked him and began leading Heather's horse toward the low-roofed building, with the others following close behind. When they reached it, he tied the horse's reins to the hitching post in front, cautioned everyone to wait, then took Eli with him and headed toward the commandant's office.

"Something I can do for you?" asked a soldier as they entered, and Cole faced a young man sitting at a small desk near a door at the back of the room.

"I hope so," said Cole. "One of the men outside said Major Stoddard was in charge."

"Yes, sir," answered the soldier. "But he's busy at the moment. If you'd care to wait?"

Cole hesitated. "Do you know how long he'll be?"

The man shrugged. "Never know. Could be five minutes to a half-hour."

Cole took a deep breath. He hated having to let everyone wait out front. They were all tired, the baby was fussing, and Harry Ferguson was complaining as usual.

"Is it possible you could interrupt the major?" he asked after a quick nod from Eli.

"Not likely."

"Even if it's urgent?"

"Everything around here's urgent," the soldier said quickly.

Cole straightened abruptly, but it was Eli who spoke. "Hey, look, sonny," he said quickly. "If that's Major Abel Stoddard you're referring to, he won't mind this interruption. Tell him Eli Crawford wants to see him."

"You know him?" the young corporal asked.

"Ran into him a few times over the years," answered Eli. "Don't worry, he'll know who I am."

The corporal frowned, then stood up and knocked on the door to the commandant's office. In answer to a quick command, he opened the door and entered.

Cole turned to Eli. "I didn't know you knew the man," he said, surprised.

"There's still a lot you don't know about me, friend," Eli said, smiling.

Cole smirked. "Maybe it's time I learned."

"Later," Eli said quickly. "Here comes the corporal."

The young soldier came back into the room and held the door to the inner office open for them. "The major will see you both now, sir," he announced importantly, then ushered them into the commandant's office.

Major Stoddard stood up and greeted Eli with a firm handshake. "My God, Crawford, how many years has it been?" he asked from across the huge oak desk.

Eli grinned. "Too many."

Major Stoddard straightened, then turned to the two men he'd been in conversation with when they'd interrupted him. "Major Long and Captain Brooks, I'd like to introduce one of the best scouts that ever broke trail for the army," he said. "Eli, Major Stephen Long, Corps of Engineers, Topographical Department, and his aide Captain Ian Brooks. Gentlemen, Mr. Eli Crawford."

Eli shook hands with the men, then introduced Cole. "Major Long, Captain Brooks, Major Stoddard, my traveling companion, Duke Avery."

Cole looked the three men over. Major Stoddard was a typical military man, curt, but hesitant, his eyes taking Cole in with one long penetrating look. Major Long was just the opposite. Although his expression was dour, his eyes seemed inquisitive as he studied Cole's face, noting the distinctive Indian features. Major Long looked to be in his early thirties, not extremely good-looking, but with dark hair, a rather long face, and narrow features. The captain was about the same age as Major Long, his hair a dusty blond, and he had dark brown eyes that hardened as they studied Cole. He was every bit as tall as Cole, and the tan that covered both men's faces led Cole to believe they spent most of their time outdoors.

When the introductions were over, Major Stoddard spoke first. "Major Long is with the Ninth Army out of Belle Fontaine up near St. Louis. He and Major William Bradford have been ordered to locate a good site on the upper river and set up a fort. Somebody's been selling whiskey to the Indians and stirring up trouble, and the only way we're going to be able to stop it is to be on top of it." His eyes narrowed shrewdly as he looked at Eli. "Which gives me an idea, Eli." His jaw set firmly. "You know your way up by the Verdigris, if I remember right, don't you?"

Eli nodded. "Some."

"That's what we were discussing," Stoddard said. "Major Bradford has about thirty men with him who are too sick to go any farther at this point, so Major Long's going to take some men and go on ahead. What he needs is a guide to go upriver with him, to help scout a good location." He hesitated a moment, then went on. "He needs a man he can trust, and someone who knows the territory."

"I know the territory," said Eli. "But I'm afraid things aren't quite that simple. That's why we're here," and he nodded toward Cole. "We were headed up the Mississippi on the *Bonnie Belle*, but she blew just north of Walnut Hills. We've got a bunch of survivors out there who refused to go back on the river, and something has to be done with them. We got them this far, but we were hoping somebody'd take them off our hands."

The major frowned. "How many?"

"Almost ten," answered Cole. "But I have my wife, son, and a young slave girl with us too."

"Where were you originally headed?" asked Major Long, joining the conversation.

"About the same place you are, I guess," Cole said. "We've been up there before."

Major Stoddard frowned. "You're planning to settle on the Verdigris?"

"A little south of the Verdigris. I've heard tell there's some good horseflesh out on the plains, and there's a market for them in the East."

"I hope you realize the danger you're putting your family in," said Captain Brooks. "The land's wild out there." He studied Cole. "But then, you're part Indian, Mr. Avery. Is your wife Indian too?"

"I'm not a half-breed," Cole said. "If that's what you were getting at. My father was three-quarters Indian and one-quarter French, my mother English. My wife has no Indian blood at all, but we'll manage."

"She knows what to expect?"

"She knows it won't be easy."

Eli interrupted the two men, addressing Major Long. "You going upriver by boat or horse?" he asked.

"By boat," replied the major. "I'm using a six-oared skiff. Since we've got only a few horses, they'll come up later with

Major Bradford in the keelboats we brought downriver with us. I'll have enough provisions with me for about twenty-four days, but if your friend has his family along . . . We hadn't counted on anything like that.''

"I didn't say we'd go," said Eli.

"You didn't say you wouldn't, either," Stoddard reminded him. "But I can see your situation." He sat back in his chair and leaned across the desk. "You're just what we've been looking for, Eli," he said. "But I don't know about your friend here. It's risky taking females along." He looked at Cole. "How old's your son?"

"Almost a year."

"A baby!" Major Long blurted. "God in heaven, what would we do with a baby along? This is a military expedition, Stoddard. We're not nursemaids."

"Don't worry," Cole said irritably. "Even if we did agree to go along, the baby's well taken care of."

Major Long exchanged a quick look with his captain, then glanced at Major Stoddard and shook his head. "Forget it, Stoddard," he said briskly. "I don't intend to make a fool of myself dragging a bunch of civilians along."

"You haven't much choice, Long," Stoddard countered. "Those two men the captain was planning to hire are as crooked as they come. I wouldn't trust them farther than I could see them."

"Then I'll go without scouts."

"And get lost?" Major Stoddard inhaled anxiously. "And remember, it isn't just the lay of the land that you have to contend with. There's the Osage and the Cherokee. As much as he's helped you out before, your captain here doesn't know their dialect, and if that isn't enough, some men out there don't care whose throat they slit when they think it's profitable enough."

"I'll have men with me," Long said. "Nobody's going to bother with us."

Cole was getting irritated. He didn't care whether they went with Major Long or without him. All he cared about was getting rid of Harry Ferguson and the others.

"Look," he said abruptly. "I don't care who the hell takes you upriver. All I care about is turning those people over to someone who can help them, because I don't intend to take them another foot farther. I've got my own family to take care of. I don't need the headaches.''

Major Stoddard was surprised. "They've given you problems?" he asked.

"That's not the half of it," answered Cole. "I've got a preacher out there who's trying to convert everybody to his way of believing, including three Cherokee Indians, and another man who thinks all Indians are eager to lift his scalp, and hates every damn one of them. Those two have caused me more trouble than all the others combined, with their stubbornness, prejudices, and complaining. I've had them up to here," and he touched his neck just beneath the chin.

"Where were they headed?" asked Stoddard.

"I guess the circuit rider was just traveling," answered Cole. "But from what I can make out, the other man is some sort of salesman, although he's never said what he was selling."

"Where was he headed?"

"Don't know that either. He rarely talks about himself. I guess he's too busy complaining."

Major Stoddard straightened in his chair, then stood up. "Maybe we'd better go outside and take a look," he said. "Gentlemen . . ." and he motioned toward the door, then followed them on outside.

Heather still sat her horse, but she was getting impatient. It seemed as if Cole had been gone forever. The baby was whimpering because the horse wasn't moving, and she had a premonition he might have filled his pants, making him twice as uncomfortable, and on top of it, Harry Ferguson was grumbling about Cole taking so long.

She glanced up suddenly as the door opened and Eli and Cole came out, followed closely by three men in uniform. Her hands gripped the horse's reins tighter and her eyes hardened warily as she watched them head toward where they were all waiting. When Cole reached her horse, he held his hands up and helped her dismount, then introduced everyone all around, including Lone Eagle and his two braves and the black man, Mose Wheatley, who had worked on the steamboat.

Mose had given them little trouble along the way. In fact, he'd been helpful more than once in setting up camp and helping with the horses.

Major Stoddard scrutinized the small group, noting the shifty gleam in Harry Ferguson's eyes every time he and the preacher exchanged glances, and he wondered what the two men were up to. They were a strange assortment, that was sure, and he couldn't help smiling at Bessie Taylor's warmhearted greeting.

"Mr. Avery here says you were on the *Bonnie Bell* when it blew. I can sympathize with you," he said. "But from here on your future's your own. There are always boats headed downriver and a few headed up, or if you want, you can try your luck here. But the ride's over. You're going to have to face it one way or another. Mr. Avery brought you this far, and what you do now is strictly up to you."

"You mean he's just going to dump us here?" complained Harry, who was still astride. "My leg ain't healed all the way yet."

"That," Cole said, "is your problem." He turned to the major. "Is there any place my family can stay, Major Stoddard?" he asked. "There must be an inn for travelers passing through, at least until we settle what's to be done."

The major frowned, rubbing his chin. "No inns, son, sorry," he answered. "But the Bergeracs often take strangers in who're passing through. They're a French couple who've been here for ages, and with their boys all gone, they have empty rooms."

"Would they have enough room for Mrs. Taylor and her daughter too?" asked Heather.

"I don't see why not."

"What about the rest of us?" asked Harry.

The major glanced toward Harry's bandaged leg. "We have a doctor on the post. Perhaps when you have him check your leg, you could ask him to put you up." He looked around at the others. "As for the rest of you, there's a few cots set up in a back room over at Notrebe's trading post. He's usually congenial."

"If we have money," said the reverend. "Which we don't have, since we lost everything in the explosion."

"I don't think Notrebe would be too demanding, told the circumstances," the major said, then stared hard at the reverend. "You planning to ride your circuit up the Arkansas, Reverend Litchfield?" he asked.

Jeremy Litchfield nodded. "What better way to convert the heathen? And there's white folks up there who need my services, too. I doubt they've seen a man of the cloth since settling hereabouts."

"Was the Arkansas your original destination? Or had you planned to go somewhere else?"

"Planned to go farther up the Mississippi, but since the good Lord decided to change things, I figure I'd better do what he wants rather than what I want."

"Well, remember one thing," Major Stoddard warned. "The Indians don't like anyone trying to run their lives for them. I'd advise you to concentrate on the settlers and leave the Indians alone, unless you really want to cause trouble."

"He probably won't take your advice, Major," Cole offered. "The reverend has a way of ignoring good advice."

"Mr. Avery," countered Jeremy Litchfield, "I am a man of God. It's my duty to save souls from hell, and that includes the Indians."

"See what I mean, Major?" Cole said, then turned to Heather's horse and began untying the baby from his makeshift cradle. "Now, if you'll direct us to the people you were talking about, we can discuss other matters after I get my family settled." He hefted Case into his arms, his nose verifying the fact that the baby desperately needed changing.

Major Stoddard and Major Long turned Cole, Heather, Tildie, and the Taylor women over to Captain Brooks, requesting that he introduce them to the Bergeracs, since that's where he too was staying; then they led the way for the others toward Notrebe's.

Captain Brooks glanced over at the couple next to him as they headed toward the Bergeracs' log house, near the west wall of the fort. Duke Avery was young, perhaps in his early twenties, but it was easy to see by his catlike walk, and the way his eyes shifted, taking in every detail of his surroundings, that he was an experienced woodsman. It was Mrs. Avery who brought the frown to Ian Brooks's forehead. She was lovely. In spite of the dirty buckskins and disheveled hair, she was delicately feminine and looked out of place here in the wilderness. Staying as close to her husband as possible, she gave the impression of being shy and reserved, and Ian began to wonder if her husband really knew what he was doing by bringing her here.

When they reached the house, he introduced all of them to their benefactors, then excused himself to return to the commandant's office, where he was surprised to find Major Stoddard and Major Long deep in thought as Major Stoddard stared at something on his desk.

"What now?" the captain asked both men, his dark eyes inquisitive.

Stoddard's jaw set hard as he nodded toward the paper before him. "We're not sure," he finally said as he leaned back in his chair. "But we think Crawford's young friend may have some explaining to do."

"How's that?"

Stoddard picked up the paper and handed it to the captain.

"At first we thought the reverend was just trying to get even with Avery for some imagined grievance," Stoddard said curtly. "But when the man named Ferguson confirmed it . . . And it does seem strange, him bringing a woman like Mrs. Avery into this godforsaken land."

Captain Brooks stared at the wanted poster, trying to put things together, then looked at Major Long.

"What the hell is he talking about, sir?" he asked. "Are you trying to tell me that the man called Duke Avery is really this . . . this Cole Dante?"

"That's just it," Major Long said, and his eyes hardened. "The man named Ferguson said he's heard Mrs. Avery call her husband Cole on more than one occasion, and each time, Avery acted like she was doing something wrong. He said she'd get all red, then call him Duke, as if it was awkward for her to use the name. At first we didn't think anything of it, but when the preacher pointed out how strange it was for them to be traveling with such a small baby, and her such a proper-brought-up lady and all . . . something bothered Major Stoddard. Then he happened to remember that wanted poster." He stared hard at the captain. "Take a good look at the description on that poster, Ian," he said. "Six feet tall, green eyes, black hair, part Indian, well-educated, can pass as a refined gentleman. The description fits."

"But it doesn't say a word about him being a family man."

"Maybe whoever wrote that description didn't know."

Captain Brooks's forehead wrinkled into a scowl as he remembered the beautiful woman Duke Avery had introduced as his wife. Would she be a part of something criminal? It didn't seem possible. Yet there was a sense of furtiveness, almost fear, in her mannerisms. He sighed.

"Maybe you'd better confront him," he said. "If the man's wanted for murder, he could be dangerous to have around."

"It could be a coincidence."

"Did Ferguson and the preacher mention the wanted poster?" Ian asked.

Stoddard shook his head. "Only that she called him Cole."

"Too much coincidence," insisted Ian. "I wonder if Crawford knows anything."

"You think it might be wise to talk to him first?" asked Major Long.

"Not really," answered the captain. "He could warn Avery that we're onto him."

"I think you're right," agreed Stoddard. "Much as I like Crawford as a scout, I know the man's loyalties are strong as far as his friends are concerned." He called for the orderly to come in.

"Yes, sir?" the corporal said, saluting.

"Have someone take a message to Mr. Avery, that as soon as he's settled, I want him to come to my office and to bring Eli Crawford with him."

The corporal saluted again and left.

Stephen Long took the wanted poster back from his captain, stared at it for a moment, then set it back on Major Stoddard's desk, while the captain began to wonder what would happen to Heather Avery and her young son if Major Long and Major Stoddard were right, and as he remembered her big violet eyes and the haunted, hesitant look that filled them when she looked at her husband, for some reason he hoped to God they were wrong.

Mrs. Bergerac was a small, well-rounded woman, adept at making strangers feel comfortable, her English well seasoned with a heavy French accent. She had raised five sons who had towered over her, yet not one had ever dared to cross her. Perhaps the reason was their father's strength rather than their mother's sharp tongue, for Leonce Bergerac was a bull of a man who brought up his children with a firm hand.

Cole and Heather watched Bessie Taylor and Helene start down the hall toward the rooms that would be theirs, then helped settle Tildie and the baby in one of the front bedrooms before moving down the hall to the other bedroom, where the Bergeracs had told them they could sleep. It was a simple room with solid cherry furniture, handmade rugs on the floor, a heavy patchwork quilt on the double bed, and a stone fireplace Cole lit as soon as they entered and set their few belongings down.

"Mrs. Bergerac said she'd heat some water and bring up a tub," Cole said as he used the bellows, making sure the fire had taken hold. When it was burning brightly, he stood up and watched Heather testing the softness of the bed.

"I hope Mrs. Bergerac won't take too long," she answered. "I feel so dirty." She looked down at the bed beneath her and frowned. "It feels like a corn-husk mattress."

"Probably is."

"I keep forgetting we're so far from civilization," she said. She sat up straighter, her hands in her lap, her eyes caressing the furniture. "I guess the furniture deceived me."

Cole knew what she meant. "They probably sent for it special from back east," he said. "I doubt there'd be a market for too much fancy furniture around here." He walked to the window and looked out across the parade grounds and buildings. His eyes spotted the top of the commandant's office some distance away. Just before coming upstairs, he'd received a message that the major wanted to see him and Eli as soon as they were settled. Frown lines creased his forehead, and his green eyes darkened warily. He turned back to Heather, who was still sitting on the edge of the bed. "I'd better go see Major Stoddard now," he said. "I suppose he wants to tell Eli and me that Major Long can find someone else to lead him up the Arkansas."

"Is that what you were talking about while we were waiting before?" she asked. "He wants you and Eli to go with him upriver?"

"Long doesn't, Stoddard does," Cole answered. "Stoddard knows Eli from some years back, and he knows we know our way upriver. Only Long doesn't like the idea."

"Because of me?" she asked.

"What makes you say that?"

She stood up. "I saw the strange way he stared at me when we were introduced. And he looked at Tildie and Case rather peculiarly too. I guess he figures we'd only be in the way."

Cole's eyes sifted over Heather. She looked so tired. Yet in spite of the weary eyes and dirty buckskins, she still had the power to stir him inside. He stepped over to stand in front of her, his hand moving out, touching her face, cupping her head so her eyes met his.

"You aren't going to let it bother you, are you, love?" he asked.

She sighed. "Why do you even have to discuss it?" she said

slowly. "Just tell him we're going by ourselves. That's the way we planned it."

"I would, except Major Stoddard's suggestion has merit. With Major Long and his men along, our chances of getting there in one piece are better. That's one thing that's been bothering me since we left Port Royal," he went on. "If it was just me and Eli, I wouldn't care. But with you and Case along . . ." His eyes searched hers. "If anything happened to you, I'd die inside," he whispered. "I love you so much, and if there's any way at all to make things safer for you and the baby . . ."

"But going with the army. What if one of his men recognizes you?"

"That's the chance I'll have to take."

"I don't like it."

He held her face between his hands and kissed her sensuously, the kiss warming them both inside. "Trust me, love," he said softly.

"I wouldn't have come if I didn't trust you, Cole," she said. "It's me I don't trust. I said I could put up with anything as long as we were together, but already I'm so tired of the mud and rain, and never feeling clean, and trying to cook over campfires." Tears rimmed her eyes. "I thought I could do it, Cole, but now I'm not so sure. I miss the comforts we had before."

"We'll have them again," he promised. "Someday you'll have a grand house with servants and all the comforts we left behind."

"You really believe that, don't you?"

"If I didn't, I wouldn't have brought you here." He kissed her again. "Now, you get your bath while I'm gone, and get some rest. Tildie's taking care of Case, and that'll give you enough free time for a nap."

"If I can sleep."

He kissed her again. "Try," he said, then headed for the door. "I'll tell Mrs. Bergerac to bring the water as soon as it's ready. And don't worry. Everything'll work out."

"I hope so," she said, and watched him leave.

Cole met Eli downstairs, and after a short conversation with the Bergeracs, they headed toward the commandant's office, where they were surprised to see four well-armed soldiers lounging around. At first Cole was apprehensive, but the corporal smiled, quickly assuring them Major Stoddard was waiting, and opened the door to the inner office after an abrupt knock and salutation from inside. After announcing the two visitors, the corporal shut the door and Cole frowned as sounds of scuffling could be heard coming from the room they'd just left.

"Come in," Major Stoddard said hurriedly, and motioned toward the front of his desk, where Major Long and Captain Brooks were already waiting.

"If this is about scouting for you, we haven't made up our minds yet," said Eli as he and Cole stopped next to Major Long.

"That's not why you're here," Major Stoddard said, leaning forward, picking up a piece of paper from his desk, holding it out for Cole to take. "I'd like an explanation of this."

Cole stared at the paper in the major's hand. He knew very well what it was. "What made you suspicious?" he asked, knowing full well Stoddard must have searched through a dozen wanted posters to come up with this one.

"The reverend and your Harry Ferguson," Stoddard answered. "They don't like you very much, Mr. Avery, or should I call you Mr. Dante?"

"That's why the men in the other room?"

"In case you decided to run." He stood up. "You *are* Cole Dante?"

"May I show you something?" asked Cole, and he began to reach inside his buckskin shirt.

All three officers tensed, their hands covering their gun butts.

"Don't worry, gentlemen," Eli interrupted, realizing the significance of their actions. "He's not going anywhere."

They relaxed slightly as Cole pulled the leather pouch from beneath his shirt, opened it, then took out a piece of paper and began unfolding it. When he finished, he handed it to Major Stoddard, then watched closely as he read it.

"How do I know this is genuine?" Stoddard asked when he'd finished.

"I'll vouch for it," said Eli.

"If you'll notice," said Cole, "it happens to be an official government document. Now, where would I get something like that except from the governor?"

Major Stoddard wasn't satisfied. "If you're no longer wanted, why the alias?"

"The wanted posters say 'dead or alive.' I'd be a fool to use my own name." He nodded toward the poster. "There are too many of those still around, and it's going to be a while before word gets this far that I'm no longer a wanted man. I don't relish a bullet in the back.''

Major Stoddard studied Cole for a few minutes, read the paper exonerating him once more, then handed it to Major Stephen Long. "What do you think, Major?" he asked as he leaned back again in his chair.

Major Long read the governor's statement, handed it to his aide when he'd finished, so he too could read it, then addressed Cole. "It appears to be genuine, but I think, under the circumstances, we deserve a full explanation, Mr. Dante. Why were you charged with murder in the first place?"

"Because DeWitt Palmer's father refused to admit his son was capable of doing anything wrong, and Everett Palmer had a lot of friends in Beaufort. It's a long story and rather personal, but the facts are that DeWitt Palmer was beating his wife, I intervened, trying to stop him, and he was accidentally killed. His father had all the slaves swear I'd purposely murdered him.''

"What made the governor intervene?" asked Major Long.

"DeWitt Palmer's wife sent a letter to the governor telling him what really happened." Cole purposely avoided explaining that his wife, Heather, was the dead man's widow. Why complicate matters? "The governor believed her," he finished simply.

Captain Brooks handed the paper exonerating Cole back to Major Stoddard. "Sounds plausible to me," he said, and looked at Major Long. "What do you think, sir?"

Major Long shrugged. "It certainly looks official."

Stoddard studied the paper a few minutes longer before handing it back to Cole, then stared at the wanted poster on his desk. He sighed thoughtfully. "Guess I can't argue with the governor of South Carolina," he said, and opened his desk, shoving the poster inside. "Now that that's taken care of, about the offer I presented to you two gentlemen earlier in the day . . ." He looked at Eli. "You say you haven't made up your minds. Maybe I can help. Besides being paid for your services, you'll have a military escort all the way. What more could you want? Especially you, Dante, with your family along and the situation as it is?"

"If you don't mind, Major, I'd like to stay Duke Avery for a while," Cole corrected him quickly. "There were a lot of those posters around.''

"Certainly," said Stoddard. "If that's what you want. But

you didn't answer. Will you two scout for Major Long up the Arkansas?''

Eli saw the way Cole's eyes flashed. He had learned to read that look over the past few months, and the slight nod of Cole's head confirmed it.

"All right," Eli said firmly. "Cole?"

"On one condition," Cole said as he folded the governor's paper again, stuffed it back into the small leather pouch, and dropped it beneath his shirt once more. "I want the major to remember we're not army. I don't care how he orders his men around, and if he's got a good suggestion, Eli and I'll listen to it, but out there where the wrong decision can mean life or death, I don't want someone else making mine for me."

Stoddard glanced over to Stephen Long. "Major?" he asked.

Long nodded reluctantly. "You're not the first man who's scouted for me, Avery," he said. "And you won't be the last, either of you. All I want is to find a good site to build a fort, and all I ask is your cooperation."

"That, you'll get," said Cole.

Stoddard smiled. "Then it's settled?"

They shook hands on it, then talked about Major Long's plans, deciding when the best time would be to leave and what all they'd need.

Night shadows were beginning to filter into the upstairs bedroom at the Bergeracs' by the time Cole finally returned, but Heather, deep in sleep, didn't stir. After taking a long, luxuriously warm bath, washing her hair, and slipping into her only nightgown, a pale lavender cotton she rarely had a chance to put on, she slid beneath the clean sheets covering the corn-husk mattress and, to her surprise, fell into a deep sleep.

Cole shut the door easily, then tiptoed across the room and stared down at her. He had run into Bessie, Helene, Tildie, and the baby a few minutes before. All of them had cleaned up, and Tildie was feeding Case downstairs in the kitchen while Bessie and Helene were helping Mrs. Bergerac with dinner, although Bessie was having a hard time understanding Mrs. Bergerac, shaking her head often in bewilderment at some of the woman's orders.

He was glad they had let Heather sleep, and now, as he stared at her, he felt a warmth creep through him. Her hair was spread across the pillow like flaming gossamer, its silken sheen caught by the golden sunset that still streaked the darkening sky. He wanted to wake her, to see her violet eyes light up as he made love to her, but one look down at his own dirty buckskins, mud ground into his moccasins and the feel of grit against his skin, and he knew this wasn't the time. Not just yet.

As quietly as he'd come in, he tiptoed to the glowing fireplace. The tub was still in front of it, the water in it cold, but that was the least of his worries. He undressed, then stepped into the cold bathwater. It smelled of lavender and he realized Mrs. Bergerac had given Heather a bar of special perfumed soap to use. He breathed in deeply, letting the sweet scent fill his nostrils, then with quick deft movements began to wash the dirt and grime from his long, lean body.

Although the water was cold enough to raise gooseflesh, he didn't seem to mind, and even ducked his head under, sudsing it up until it shone blue-black in the light from the fire.

When he was finished, he dried himself off, then wrapped the towel around his middle, leaving his chest bare, and walked to the bed, surprised to discover Heather awake and staring at him.

"How long have you been watching?" he asked.

She smiled, her eyes still heavy from sleep. "Only a few minutes. I heard the water splash." Her eyes lowered from his face to his chest and she saw the muscles ripple beneath the skin, strong and sinewy. "What did the major want?" she asked, her eyes moving again to his face.

Cole frowned. "He knows who I really am," he said as he sat down on the bed beside her. "It seems the reverend and Harry Ferguson told him they heard you call me Cole. He had a wanted poster and put two and two together."

"Oh, Cole."

"Don't worry," he replied. "I showed him the governor's paper."

"And he believed you?"

"Why shouldn't he?"

"I don't know, except . . . it's such a risk. What if he hadn't believed you?"

"But he did."

"And he knows about me?"

"Not exactly." Cole looked at her sheepishly. "He knows you're my wife, but he doesn't know you were once DeWitt Palmer's wife."

"And if he finds out?"

"He won't."

"What if he does? It could change everything."

He sighed. "What would it change? It wouldn't change the fact that the governor says I'm not guilty."

"It could make them start wondering. They might even think the paper from the governor was forged or something."

"Not in a million years," said Cole as he leaned over and began playing with her hair, then bent to kiss her.

"Cole, be serious," she said stubbornly, pushing him back; then her eyes narrowed suspiciously. "You told them we'd go with them, didn't you?" she suddenly said.

He nodded. "I told you before, it's the best way."

"But I don't like going with the army. I don't like having all those men staring at me and having to try to find some privacy. Besides, I wanted to ask you if Bessie and Helene could come with us."

"Bessie and Helene?"

"She asked me the other day," Heather said, trying to ignore the sensuous way he was toying with her, running his hand along the line of her shoulder and up into her hair, curling it about his fingers. "They don't have anyplace to go," she went on. "And besides, I want her along. I don't know how to cook, Cole. I'd never even boiled water until this trip. I don't know anything about taking care of a house."

"But Bessie? Major Long was furious enough about you, Tildie, and Case going. I can't ask him to take two more women."

"Why not? What's so terrible about two more women? You know Bessie'll make her own way. Why would Major Long object?"

"Because there won't be enough room. He's only taking his skiff, and they'll only slow him down all the more." He tensed. "We can't take them, Heather, it's out of the question."

It was the first time Cole had ever refused her anything, and suddenly tears threatened. "But we have to, Cole," she pleaded. "I can't do everything myself, I just can't!"

"You'll learn, love," he said. "It's not really so hard."

"How would you know?"

"I don't, but I've seen Liza cooking back home, watched Bessie on the way here, and I've seen Eli throw together a good meal out of practically nothing. I've even done it myself when I've had to."

"But it's more than just cooking, Cole," she protested. "It's all that goes with it. The baby, and cleaning, and making clothes. When we get there, I'm going to need help, I know I will. Please say you'll take her." Her lip thrust into an angry pout. "I won't go if you don't take her," she said angrily. "I'm not going to be stuck out there in the middle of nowhere with no one to help."

"Don't be silly, love," he said, trying to keep from losing his temper. "You have to go."

"No, I don't!"

"Heather!"

"Well, I don't! I can stay right here. I'm tired, Cole, and we aren't even there yet." Her eyes were glistening with tears. "I need Bessie, Cole. Please!"

"Heather . . ."

"I've never asked you for much, darling, please," she went on, her voice breaking. "You're taking Mose Wheatley upriver to help you and Eli. I heard you ask him the other day."

"But he's a man."

"So what?"

"So he can help."

"And Bessie won't? I see." His hand was caressing her earlobe and she reached up, brushing it away. "It's all right for you to have someone, but not me. Is that it?"

"It's not that, love. You know if it was just us I wouldn't say anything about Bessie coming along," he said, trying once more to touch her and soothe her anger. "But I'm not Major Long. He has a thing about civilians as it is, and when it comes to women, he thinks they're only in the way."

"You could talk him into it."

"But I won't."

"Why not?"

"Because he's touchy enough."

"Then I'll ask him myself."

"You can't."

"Why not? Maybe he'll understand. You don't seem to."

"I do, Heather," he answered. "But taking Bessie and Helene along . . . It's nonsense."

"It isn't, and if you don't ask him, I will."

Cole stared at her hard for a minute, realizing she wasn't about to give up. "All right," he conceded. "If you're going to be that stubborn about it, I'll ask him. But he'll only say no."

"Then you'll have to persuade him."

"And how do I do that?"

The anger left her eyes quickly, along with the tears that had mingled with it, and she suddenly became soft and inviting. "You'll find a way, don't worry," she whispered. "I have all the faith in the world in your powers of persuasion. After all, look what they do to me."

His laughter was low and husky as he lifted his feet from the floor and stretched out beside her on the bed. "You're a vixen, you know that, don't you, love?" he murmured against her ear. "You make me do things that I don't want to do, and wheedle and cajole until you have me right where you want me." He kissed her ear, his mouth brushing it as he found the soft warmth of her neck. "But just don't push me too far, Mrs. Dante," he whispered breathlessly. "Don't ever threaten to leave me again, because I'll never let you go. You can have anything you want, but don't ever leave me. Without you, I'm nothing," and with a groan from deep inside, his lips found hers and he kissed her long and hard.

Heather relaxed against him, her body yielding to his hands as the kiss deepened.

"They're waiting for us downstairs," she whispered breathlessly moments later as he raised his head and gazed down into her languid eyes.

"Let them wait," he murmured, his voice deep with emotion. "It's been a long time since I made love to my wife, and I don't intend to stop now," and with deft, sure hands he pulled up the nightgown that separated their flesh, moved over her and entered her slowly, savoring every moment as his lips sipped at her mouth. And as dark shadows crept into the room, leaving only the glow of the red coals in the fireplace to see by, the sounds of their passion mingled with the gentle friction emanating from the corn-husk mattress as Cole teased Heather's body, igniting it, thrusting into her over and over again until they were both carried to a peak of pleasure that left them trembling with contentment, and for a few minutes the journey upriver and all its dangers were easily forgotten.

5

It took a good two days to prepare everything for the long trek upriver, and Heather was glad, because it took almost that same amount of time to talk Major Long into letting Bessie and Helene go with them. It wasn't until after Heather had pleaded with him, almost tearfully, that he had finally consented, warning her, however, that the woman and her daughter would be hard pressed to keep up.

Heather had smiled inwardly at his statement. Major Long didn't know Bessie. Heather was certain Bessie would not only keep up but also prove her worth. So it was with mixed feelings that Heather sat now in the middle of the major's skiff and watched Cole, Eli, Captain Brooks, Major Long, and the few men he was taking with him saying good-bye to Major Bradford, who would be coming later, bringing not only the military equipment and the rest of the men but also all the horses. Because the women were going, Major Long couldn't take as many men with him as he would have liked, and it had taken a great deal of explaining before Major Bradford accepted what was going on.

Tildie sat beside Heather, with Case in her lap, and Bessie and Helene were farther toward the stern. Heather hated leaving the post. Although life here was rugged and far from what she was used to, it was the closest to civilization she would be for a long time to come, and the thought was frightening. Even having Bessie along couldn't still the butterflies that had settled in Heather's stomach.

When the supplies were all loaded and everything tied down, Major Long said a final farewell to Major Stoddard and Major Bradford, watched his men climb into the boat, and they shoved off. He was leaving the sick men and Major William Bradford behind with the promise that they follow as soon as they were able. With him he had thirteen men, all armed, including his aide, Captain Brooks, his two scouts, and a black man they'd insisted on bringing along, the four females, and a baby he could have done without. All he hoped was that the supply of food they had would be enough.

The trip up the Arkansas was an arduous one. Some days they left the boat only long enough to eat, then camped along the riverbank at night. Other days, some of the men were forced to wade waist-deep in the water, pulling the skiff over rough shallows. During the day, temperatures stayed in the high sixties, but at night, with the sun gone, the temperatures often dropped dramatically in only a few hours, bringing a wet cold that seemed to penetrate Heather's very bones.

Two days after leaving Arkansas Post, Case cut another tooth; five days after leaving, they almost capsized in a storm. Sometimes they rigged up a sail when the wind permitted, but most of the time it was a matter of hard work rowing against the current. At first, as they moved upriver, Heather tried to tell herself it didn't matter, that she didn't need all the frills and furbelows her former life had accustomed her to, but as the days wore on and the wilderness became more and more dense, she had to fight hard to enjoy the scenery, telling herself over and over again that all she needed to make her happy was Cole.

They passed a few scattered settlements and an occasional Indian village that reminded her of Lone Eagle and his two braves. The Indians had left Arkansas Post the morning after they arrived, heading across the great prairie north of the fort, toward Osage territory, a fact that had upset Major Stoddard. It seemed rumor had drifted down from the north that a band of Cherokee were gathering with the intention of running the Osage off the land the Cherokee felt should be theirs, and it looked like Lone Eagle was joining them. The major hoped he was wrong.

Farther on, the river wound through some of the most beautiful countryside Heather had ever seen. Huge trees hugged its banks, with fall flowers coloring the hillsides in purples and golds. Occasionally they'd see deer grazing at the edge of the forests, and once late at night Heather shuddered as the call of a wildcat filled the night air.

Each day brought something new, and each day she and the other women proved to Major Long he hadn't made the wrong choice by letting Cole bring them along. In fact, Heather noticed Major Long's aide, Captain Brooks, had become more than mildly attentive toward her, especially when Cole was off scouting with Eli. The captain was always asking her if she needed anything and if there were anything he could do for her to make the trip more comfortable. Bessie was the one who brought the matter to her attention one evening when they had camped on a huge sandbar in order to avoid the worst of the mosquitoes plaguing the fields near the river.

"Did you notice the way he looked at you, Heather?" Bessie asked as they stood at the edge of the sandbar and gazed off across the river. "I tell you, Captain Brooks isn't being nice to you just for something to do."

"Oh, Bessie," Heather said, "don't be ridiculous. I think Major Long gave him orders to be nice to me to make up for the major's being too stubborn about you and Helene coming with us."

"That's what you think? Child, you're naive," Bessie said. "I've seen the look in the captain's eyes when he's talking to you, and if he doesn't watch out, Duke's going to see it too, and I don't think he'll appreciate it." Bessie still hadn't been told Cole's true identity, and she still called him Duke.

"Bessie, I'm a married woman," Heather reminded her.

"And a beautiful young one. The only one within miles. Mark my words, Heather," she went on, as if the younger woman were her own daughter, "the man is a little too attentive. I'd be careful if I were you. The days are hard enough for all of us without complicating matters." She glanced over at Heather. "I know you wouldn't purposely lead him on, Heather," she continued. "I know you and Duke are very much in love, but we know very little about Captain Ian Brooks except that he's a rather moody, good-looking young man. Men like that don't always take love lightly. Be careful, Heather, please," she said.

Heather glanced over at Bessie and her eyes softened. "Don't worry, Bessie," she assured her. "I'm sure he's only trying to be nice," but two days later, she had reason to remember Bessie's warning.

They had had an encounter with some Quapaw Indians shortly before sundown while setting up camp, and Cole, with Eli at his side, accompanied the Indians back to their camp. Heather, Tildie, and Bessie carried on their normal routine, taking care of Case and fixing something to eat over the open campfire. The evening stretched on, darkness settled around them, and Heather began to worry. Cole had been gone so long. Although the Indians hadn't been too hostile, they had made Heather nervous and she hadn't wanted him to go.

Now, after settling Tildie and the baby for the night and making sure things were ready for morning, she strolled toward the edge of the woods, in the direction where Cole had disappeared, hoping with all her heart that any minute he'd come walking out from among the trees. She didn't hear the footsteps behind her until he spoke.

"Don't worry, Mrs. Avery, he'll be back," Captain Brooks said, and she whirled around.

"You frightened me."

"Sorry." He frowned. "I didn't mean to."

"I guess I'm just a little jumpy," she said quickly. "But it makes me nervous when he goes off like that. I've heard so many stories about scalping and the like."

"But your husband's part Indian himself."

"That doesn't guarantee his safety." She wrung her hands and sighed. "I will admit it helps, though, at least it's seemed to. He's almost been able to walk in both worlds. A feat not many people can accomplish."

"That bothers you, doesn't it?" he asked.

She stared at him curiously. "What do you mean?"

"I mean, I think you feel left out at times. Like now." His dark brown eyes studied her intensely. "You have no idea why he went off with those men, or what he's doing."

"He said he has to go with them to show we don't mean any harm to them, so there won't be any trouble."

"But you have no idea what he's doing while he's gone, and I think it bothers you."

"Why should it bother me?"

"Because you were born and raised in drawing rooms." His eyes met hers, and she blushed. "It's very obvious this is all new to you. It's a part of your husband's world you're not sharing; therefore you resent it."

She smiled reluctantly. "You make it sound terrible."

"I didn't mean to. But you haven't smiled all evening. I don't like to see you unhappy."

Her eyes flashed defiantly. "I'm not unhappy, just worried."

"I hope that's all," he answered. "But you seem so out of place out here." His eyes softened. "You're a beautiful woman, Heather Avery. Or should I say Heather Dante?"

She flushed again. "Cole insists on the former," she said, then added, "Do any of Major Long's other men know who we really are?"

"All they know is that Cole's one of our scouts. We all agreed with your husband that it wouldn't be expedient for him to use his real name. But we weren't talking about the past, we were talking about the future. Your future. You're not made for log cabins and all the hardships that go with it, Heather. You deserve better.''

"That's why we've brought Bessie Taylor along. She and Helene will be a big help." She tried to smile. "Besides, I'm not as helpless as I look. Cole has taught me a great deal. I can track and shoot. I'll survive."

"Oh, I don't doubt that. You look like a survivor, but there's more to happiness than just surviving."

Her eyes darkened and she tilted her chin up. "I think you're out of line, Captain Brooks."

He apologized. "Sorry again." His eyes studied her for a brief moment. "Perhaps you're right. No offense meant," he said. "It's only that sometimes, being with people every day, and especially in such close proximity, one has a hard time not becoming involved." He straightened, tugging on his uniform jacket. "If I've offended you, Heather, I'm sorry," he went on. "But I can't help what I see, and I wish to hell I could change things for you."

"There's nothing to change, Captain," she replied. "I know what I'm doing."

"Do you?" he asked. "I wonder."

"Good night, Captain Brooks," she said testily.

He frowned. "If that's the way you want it. Good night, Mrs. Avery," and he turned abruptly, leaving her standing at the edge of the woods, staring after him.

Heather watched him join the men about the campfire that had been built; then she turned, her eyes once more searching the dark woods, and a restless feeling made her nervous. The lines on her forehead deepened as she thought over the conversation she'd just had. What a strange man Captain Brooks was.

She glanced back again toward the fire and flushed. He was talking with one of the men, but his eyes were on her and she quickly looked away again. He had no right to say what he'd said to her. None whatsoever. A chill ran through her and she hugged her arms as she turned, talking toward the riverbank, looking out at the rushing waters. A crescent moon had already cleared the trees, and stars hung heavy in the midnight blue of the sky. The scent of the river water filled her nostrils, mingling with the faint fragrance of some fall flowers at her feet.

She sighed, trying to forget the past few minutes, but it wasn't that easy because the more Captain Brooks's words kept popping back into her head, the more she realized they were true. At least partially. Ever since Cole and Eli had left camp with the group of Quapaw Indians, Heather had been wondering what he was doing and why he was gone so long. It might not have been so bad if she hadn't heard comments here and there from some of the soldiers. She knew they'd had no idea she was within earshot of their conversations, but that still didn't lessen the effect their loose talk had on her.

It wasn't easy to hear men telling tales of Indians who offered virgins to their visitors and grew angry if their gifts were refused, and tribes who drank themselves into wild abandon, and Indian braves who challenged men to the death. How much of it was true, she had no idea, because Cole had never told her anything about these strange people.

Her frown deepened as she thought over the past few weeks they'd been traveling cross-country. Not only did he never talk about the Indians, but whenever she asked anything about them, he always changed the subject. It had been like that ever since he'd come home from the army. Even then he had shied away from talking about them when they'd asked about his run-in with the Creeks. All he had volunteered was that they'd made him prove he was the son of the son of a chief. This wasn't the first time she had wondered about Cole's excursions into the wilderness and his association with the Indians, but she had always managed to brush any negative thoughts aside. Tonight, for some reason, she couldn't seem to.

Captain Brooks was right. It did bother her. She tried to deny it, but the reality was there staring her in the face. It was a part of Cole's life she felt left out of, a part of him she couldn't share, and it hurt. She glanced back again toward the fire where Captain Brooks was talking to Major Long. It wasn't fair he should have guessed why she was so restless tonight, why she had been watching the woods so anxiously. If only Cole would come back. But he didn't, not until morning.

She had given up waiting and curled up alone near Case and Tildie, finally dropping off to sleep when her eyes grew too heavy to hold open anymore, and it was the damp fog of morning and chill from the dying fire that woke her as the rest of the camp also began to stir and Case's lusty squeals let her know he was awake.

Heather rubbed her eyes and glanced about, leaning on one elbow adjusting her eyes to the wakening dawn. Her mouth was dry, stomach empty, and a strange shiver ran down her spine as her eyes quickly took in her surroundings. Cole was nowhere in sight, nor was Eli. She shoved back the blanket she'd curled up in and sat up, stiff from the hard ground, and exhaled, on the verge of tears. He'd never been gone all night before. He'd scouted ahead many times in the evening, but had always managed to come back before dark.

She stood up, brushing grass from her buckskins, and untied the ribbon from her hair, pulling her auburn hair tighter toward the back of her head, then retying the ribbon to keep the hair out of her eyes.

"Have you seen Cole?" she asked Tildie hurriedly as the young black girl picked Case up and began cuddling him.

Tildie shook her head. "Wasn't around when I woke up," she answered.

Heather took a deep breath. "Where's Bessie?"

Tildie nodded with her head toward the river. "Down gettin' water so's she can get some coffee goin'."

Heather thanked her and headed toward the river, spotting Bessie carrying a wooden bucket up toward camp. She hurried up beside her and began measuring her stride for stride.

"Have you seen Duke this morning?" she asked.

"Nope," she answered. "Guess he and Eli are still with them Quapaws."

Heather bit her lip. "I'm worried, Bessie," she said as she kept pace with the woman. "What if something's happened? What if those Indians hurt him?"

Bessie glanced over at Heather, not wanting to upset her any more than she already was, yet aware that Heather could be right. "Don't worry, it's probably nothing," she said, trying to sound reassuring. "Why, he's probably on his way back now. No doubt figured it'd be too dangerous to travel after dark. You know the way men are. They figure women shouldn't worry. They can take care of themselves."

They reached the campfire, where the men were adding fresh wood so they could fix breakfast, and Heather stopped abruptly as Captain Brooks strolled toward them, stretching and blinking the sleep from his eyes.

"I hope your husband and his friend make it back here before long, Mrs. Avery," he said as his eyes settled on her worried face, "or Major Long said we'll be forced to pull out without them."

Heather straightened, trying to look self-assured, her heart pounding nervously. "Don't worry," she answered, a little louder than necessary, to keep her voice from trembling. "They'll be here," and she turned from him quickly, moving once more to where Tildie was changing Case, and brushed the young slave girl aside, ordering her to fix the baby some breakfast while she finished changing him, hoping the captain wouldn't see the tears that clung to the corners of her eyes.

Where was he? she cried frantically to herself. And where was Eli? Her hands were shaking as she tied the three-cornered diaper on the baby, then picked him up, pulling down his long shirt and taking him into her arms. She hugged him to her, shutting her eyes for a moment, then opened them and gazed around at the others, only it didn't help. All it did was start her to wondering all the more, especially when she noticed some of the soldiers who'd been talking about the beautiful, exotic Indian maidens last night. They were supposed to be breaking camp, but while they were taking down tents and putting things away, they kept laughing surreptitiously and glancing toward her and the baby, as if sharing a private jest, and she was certain she knew what it was. Her face reddened and she turned away, standing up, walking over to feel some of the warmth from the fire.

She wasn't going to cry. She was a grown woman and there was a logical explanation for Cole's absence, and it had nothing to do with those terrible things the soldiers had said. It couldn't. Cole would never do anything like that, not her Cole, no matter how angry those Indians got. He wouldn't, he just couldn't!

The fire was beginning to warm her, while the sick feeling inside was beginning to weaken her knees, when suddenly there was a shout from the other side of the clearing and she held her breath.

"Here they come now," said Bessie from behind her, and Heather turned hesitantly, staring off toward the edge of the woods, where Eli and Cole were emerging from among the trees, both men greeting Major Long's men.

Heather stood stock-still, waiting, her hand smoothing the back of her son's head, her heart fluttering wildly as both anger and relief fought to control her emotions. Her eyes were on Cole's face as he greeted Major Long, assuring him the Quapaws would give them no trouble for a while, and letting him know that the Indian camp was only a few miles inland and that the Indians had offered help if any was needed.

The major assured him they could do without the Indians' help, then asked if perhaps they weren't tired and might need some sleep.

"Nonsense," said Eli, grinning. "Had a right good sleep last night, Major. Them Indian gals have a way of lullin' a man off better'n bein' rocked in a cradle." Then his face suddenly reddened as he realized Heather was standing near the campfire and had heard his last remark.

Cole caught sight of Heather's face as she recoiled from Eli's remark, and he stopped abruptly, staring at the hard look in her eyes. It had been a long time since he'd seen that look, and the memory of it made his heart drop to his stomach. She was looking at him the way she'd looked at him the day he'd told her he'd been trying to forget her by making love to someone else, and the look was frightening.

"Heather?" he asked, his voice breaking as she turned suddenly and walked off toward where she and Tildie had spent the night. "What is it, love, what's wrong?" he asked, following her, completely ignorant of the worry she'd been through and the significance of Eli's casual remark.

Heather stopped, her arms tightening about her son, and her voice was unsteady as she turned to face him, her eyes dark with loathing. "Where were you all night, Cole?" she asked, anger making her forget she was supposed to call him Duke.

"You know where I was. I was with the Quapaws, at their camp," he answered. "That's my job."

"Your job? Sleeping with young Indian maidens is your job? How nice," she said sarcastically. "Not many men can have such a nice job. You enjoyed yourself, I presume?"

"Enjoyed myself? What are you talking about?"

"What am I talking about? That's what I'm talking about," she cried, trying to keep her voice to a whisper as she nodded toward some of the soldiers laughing and snickering near the fire. "I guess it doesn't matter to you that all the men in camp know you left your wife to sleep alone in the cold while you snuggled warm and cozy with some Indian."

"While I what?" he asked.

"You heard me," she spit savagely. "I heard Eli telling Major Long all about it!"

"Hey, wait," Cole shot back. "Don't confuse me with Eli,

love. Just because he likes anything that'll crawl into bed with him doesn't mean I do." His eyes flashed and his jaw clenched hard. "I don't like being accused of something I didn't do."

"Then where were you all night?"

"I told you. I was with the Quapaws."

"Doing what?"

"Sleeping!"

"Prove it!"

"Dammit, I don't have to prove it. I said that's where I was, and that's where I was."

"Why?"

"Why what?"

"Why didn't you come back? If there was no reason to stay, then why did you stay?"

"There was a reason to stay. I couldn't just leave. They had a feast and we were honored guests."

"And honored guests are presented with bed partners, I know, I've heard all about it."

"For God's sake, Heather," he yelled through clenched teeth. "I didn't sleep with anyone!"

Heather was crying now, her face pale, and the baby had begun whimpering. "I needed you last night, Cole," she cried tearfully, sniffling. "I was cold and alone and felt so left out. I don't know anything about your Indians or what you do when you go see them. And then Eli said—"

"Eli!" He shook his head. "Eli is not me, love," he said. His stomach constricted at the hurt in her eyes. "I stayed because it would have been an insult to them if I had left, and I knew Major Long didn't want any trouble."

"But they offered you someone?"

He flushed. "Yes, they offered. They usually do, but I didn't accept."

She sniffed again, trying to keep from crying, and gazed up at him suspiciously. "Weren't they insulted?"

"Not when I explained that I had a wife and she'd be upset if I were to accept their gift. They understand the white man's ways, love, believe me." He reached out and touched the baby's head, then let the back of his hand caress Heather's cheek. "I knew you were safe here, I didn't mean to frighten or hurt you in any way. That's the last thing I ever want to do is hurt you."

Tears flooded her eyes and she swallowed hard. "I thought you . . . I thought . . . when Eli said what he said . . ."

Cole shook his head, eyes shining as they caught hers, the warmth from them igniting the love he felt for her. "Don't you believe everything you hear, love," he whispered affectionately, "and only half of what you see, and remember, no matter what Eli does, I'm not Eli. Understand?"

She nodded hesitantly, then sniffed tears back again as Case turned in her arms and reached for his father.

"Now, let's put last night behind us," Cole went on as he took Case from her. "I should have explained when I left that I might not be back for some time." He hefted the baby in one arm, and put the other arm about Heather, hoping to reassure her. "I guess I'm not used to being a husband yet. I forget you might worry, wondering if I was all right."

"It might help if I knew something about the Indians and their ways," she said as they headed back toward the fire, where Bessie was fixing breakfast. "Maybe I could go with you the next time."

She felt him stiffen beside her as his steps slowed. "Go with me?" he echoed in surprise. "Heather, that's impossible," he said quickly. "You can't go on a scouting mission."

"I didn't say a scouting mission," she replied. "I said the next time we meet up with any Indians and you have to go off like that, maybe I could go along. It's better than staying here wondering what's going on, not knowing if you're alive or dead."

"Heather, be reasonable," he said. "You can't go."

"Why not?"

They had reached the fire, and Cole drew his arm from around her, trying to settle the baby more comfortably in his arms. "Because it just isn't done."

"What do you mean, it just isn't done? Why does it have to be something everybody else does? Why can't you do something on your own for a change? Why do you have to stick to other people's rules?"

"You don't understand," he tried to explain. "These aren't rules. It's just that it would be too dangerous. You don't know what you're asking."

"I know I want to go with you. I want to learn what you know, to be able to share that part of your life with you."

"No!" He tried to dissuade her. "There's nothing for you to learn, Heather. I'm sorry."

"But, Cole!"

"I said forget it," he insisted. "I won't take you with me and that's that." He handed the baby back to her. "Now, take Case I have to go explain a few more things to Major Long and put El straight about something. I'll be back in a few minutes," and he walked away, leaving her staring after him in surprise.

She held the baby for a few minutes longer, then turned him over again to Tildie, who was ready to feed him, and her eyes followed Cole as he headed toward Major Long and his men where they were packing up their equipment, and a gnawing suspicion made her bristle inside. Why had Cole suddenly become so insistent? Why the anger all of a sudden at her suggestion that she go along? He had assured her he'd done nothing wrong, yet the sharp edge of doubt was beginning to cut into her thoughts again, and she wondered. If he was so innocent, if nothing went on, then what was he trying to hide from her? Why wouldn't he let her go along? Once more the hurt that had claimed her earlier gripped her, and she had to gulp back the tears.

All the rest of the morning she went about helping Bessie and taking care of Case with her eyes veiled in tears, although she did a good job of hiding it from everyone, and as they finished breaking camp and climbed into the skiff to once more head upstream, she felt a sense of loss she hadn't felt for a terribly long time, not since that day so long ago when she had become DeWitt Palmer's wife.

Cole knew something was wrong. It was more than just sensing it. It was the way she looked at him, her eyes sad, as if she were dead inside. All day as the boat made its way upriver, she looked at him like that, until he wanted to scream, to shake her and force it from her, but every time he asked what was wrong, she brushed it off, refusing to admit anything, and it rankled him. How could he undo something when he didn't know what to undo? He hated seeing her so unhappy. Maybe tonight he could get to the bottom of it. He had an inkling of what might be the matter, and if that were the case, it was going to be harder to settle than he wanted to admit. He was certain it had to do with her request to go with him. She had been so anxious, but how could he tell her the reason he'd said no?

It wasn't easy for him to admit, even to himself, why he didn't want to take her along. Heather had been raised genteelly, she had no concept of what it was like to be an Indian and live in their culture. How could she be expected to understand what he himself had a hard time understanding? It wasn't that he was ashamed of them, but their lives were so different. She'd never understand children running around practically naked, and young girls of fourteen being married with babies of their own, and women who enjoyed inflicting pain on their enemies, enjoying it and purposely trying to make them suffer. And she'd never understand men who could scalp a man without flinching and kill a man with the same unconcern.

Heather recoiled at the thought of skinning a rabbit; what would she do in a primitive society that skinned their enemies as easily as they skinned their food? He cursed to himself softly. He should never have brought her out here. She was too soft, too civilized for life here.

He glanced back to where Bessie sat beside Heather in the stern of the boat. Thank God Bessie was along. At least that would help. But there was still Heather to contend with.

He turned back to the seat next to him, where Major Long and the captain were sitting, and pulled his thoughts back to the problems at hand as the men at the oars began to maneuver around another sandbar that had built itself up opposite the bend in the river.

It was almost nightfall by the time they made camp again not far from Cadron Creek. Cole was restless all evening, hoping to get a chance to talk to Heather alone, even though it seemed useless. She was always busy with something. If it wasn't Bessie, it was helping Tildie with the baby.

Finally, after the others had settled down for the night, there was no way she could avoid him, and he cornered her near the fire.

"We have to talk," he said as he took her arm.

She tried to pull away.

"Now!" he said irritably. She shrugged her shoulders and let him lead her away along the riverbank until they were completely out of sight of the others. It was a warm evening for a change, quite dark, the moon not up yet, and after following the course of the river around a bend where a flat prairie stretched out before them, he stopped, turning her to face him.

"All right, now, what's wrong?" he asked.

Her eyes fell before his steady gaze. "I told you, nothing," she answered, but he shook his head.

"Don't lie to me, Heather. I know damn well something's been eating at you all day. What is it?"

Her jaw tightened and she looked up at him defiantly. "I'm going with you the next time, Cole," she insisted, and he knew he'd guessed right.

He inhaled sharply. This was going to take some doing.

"Come here," he said softly, and took her hand, leading her to a fallen log, making her sit down; then he sat down beside her. "I have to make you understand," he said. "But I don't know how."

She was silent, and he glanced over at her. He had to find a way.

Reaching out, he picked up her hand, then knelt on the ground before her. "Heather, it's not what you think," he whispered huskily as he gazed into her eyes. "I'm not hiding anything from you. There's nothing to hide, I'm only trying to keep you from getting hurt."

She scowled.

His hand went to her hair and he touched a copper strand, its silky softness like velvet between his fingers. "There are things you wouldn't understand, and things that could hurt you," he went on. "Heather, do you remember the way those Indian braves stared at you when they first showed up in camp the other day?"

She was still reticent but answered, "Yes."

"Do you have any idea why?"

She shook her head.

"Because they aren't used to seeing anyone like you. Your hair, eyes . . . the sun was bright that day and they kept talking about you as if you were unreal, referring to you as the lady of fire. These people are simple and superstitious, Heather. Their world revolves around spirits and visions they take very seriously, and sometimes they can be dangerous."

"Like how?"

"As I said, they're very superstitious. They believe in dreams. You asked why I was gone all night. I was gone because their medicine man, Bear Who Walks Tall, had a dream the night before I arrived, of a woman whose face was pale like the moon, with big round purple eyes and tongues of flame leaping from her head. Instead of clothes, she was bound with heavy chains that suddenly began to move like snakes and cover all those around her, coiling around them and squeezing them until their flesh ran with blood. And as he watched, a young man came forward, kneeling before her, holding his hands up, offering a sacred bowl filled with precious stones and covered with eagle feathers, as if he were trying to appease her. But as the bowl reached her outstretched hands, it suddenly turned into a long sharp shaft that shone like the sun, and with it she pierced the warrior's heart, then pushed him down at her feet. As the young man sank to the ground, the shaft once more became a bowl, only this time it was filled with the sun that spilled out as the woman tipped it forward, covering the young man until he no longer breathed; then the woman began to cry tears that washed the ground before her, leaving in the place of the young man a lake of tears into which she dived, turning it to a lake of fire. With that, he woke up.''

Heather stared at him, frowning, and he went on.

''Bear Who Walks Tall listened to the young warriors who had brought Eli and me back with them, to your description, the lady with fiery hair, and insisted I couldn't leave until he had interpreted the dream.''

He paused, staring into her eyes, but she was still silent, waiting.

''If I had refused to stay, Bear Who Walks Tall would have considered it an insult, and to insult a medicine man is to court death, so I stayed.''

She took a deep breath, then exhaled. ''He told you?'' she asked softly.

He squeezed her hands. ''He said the woman in his dream is the woman his braves saw that morning in the camp with the long knives, and the warrior who knelt before her was me, and she and I have the same blood. Then he said, in spite of that blood, there is love between us, only because of that blood our love was chained for many moons. Then he said I gave her a gift of life that broke the chains, but also brought with it death and violence, and a danger I must be aware of at all times. One that could lead to more death. And only when the lady is consumed by the fire that lights her hair, the fire that comes from her heart and becomes one with another warrior with hair like the sun, will her heart, and the heart of the warrior who loves her and belongs to her, be out of danger.''

Heather frowned. ''What does it mean?''

''I wish I knew.'' His eyes darkened somberly. ''Some of it I can understand. The gift of life is Case; the blood and violence, DeWitt's death; but the rest . . .'' He shook his head. ''The point is, love,'' he went on, ''that there's never any way of knowing what might happen. What if he had interpreted the dream to mean that you should die? What then? If you had been with me, it could have been disastrous." His face was level with hers, and he reached up, cupping her face in his hands. "I shouldn't have brought you here," he whispered softly. "This is no place for you."

"It's where you are."

"Where I am!" He sighed. "Heather, I love you," he cried agonizingly. "I can't stand it when you look at me the way you have all day today. It isn't that I don't want you with me when I visit with the Indians. I'd like nothing better than to show you off to them, but I don't want you hurt. They're strange people, with weird customs."

"You're part Indian."

"Only part. That's what's so frightening. I know what could happen to you. Please, Heather, don't fight me when it comes to this. Just trust me. I love you, you know that. You're my life and I'd never do anything to hurt you. I'd die first." He caressed her face, his fingers burning her flesh where they touched. "I know you think you're being left out, but you're as much a part of my life when you're not with me as you are when we're together. My thoughts are always of you, and no matter how many Indian maidens they offer me, I'll never accept them. You're the only woman I want to make love to, the only woman I'll ever hold in my arms again." His hand cupped her face. "When I think of all those months without you, when I knew you were with DeWitt, and later, when I was on the run, I nearly went crazy."

She stared at him, seeing the love that flowed from his eyes, and a twinge of pain shot through her breast. Suddenly she felt ashamed. "Oh, Cole, I'm sorry," she cried helplessly. "I've been so foolish, but the way those men talked, and what Eli said, and then, when you refused to let me go with you . . . I got to thinking all sorts of things."

"I know." He leaned close, kissing her softly on the lips, then drew back, gazing into her eyes. "And I don't ever want to see that look in your eyes again, love," he whispered. "You have no reason to be jealous of anyone or anything. Someday I'll tell you what my grandfather's world is like, but not yet. You're not ready for it yet. You're still learning about our world. About living under the stars and coping with life out here. The other will come with time, when you're ready for it."

"If I ever am."

"You will be. Someday you're going to love the feel of the wind in your hair, and the rain in your face, and the smell of the spring flowers that are sweeter than any manmade perfume. This world, this land—you're going to grow with it, love, and one day you'll wake up and suddenly discover you're a part of it, just like I am, but it's going to take time." He kissed her again. "For now, just be patient with me, Heather, and trust me, trust our love, and don't ever doubt me again."

She reached out and touched his face, her fingers moving slowly, stroking the dark hair from his temples. "How can I not love you?" she whispered softly. "From the moment I first looked into your eyes, I've been a part of you. It's just that sometimes I feel like I'm competing with this world of yours, and I feel so inadequate. What if I fail, what if I never learn to belong?"

"Hush," he murmured, his mouth descending toward hers. "You'll always belong to me, no matter what." His mouth touched hers passionately, the strength in his lips sapping the strength from her body, and she groaned from deep inside.

The night was warmer than it had been for the past few days, and as Cole drew his head back, pulling her from the log so they were both standing, he sighed.

"Come swim with me," he said softly, his lips caressing her ear.

She inhaled. "Here?"

"Now!"

His eyes caught hers and held them mesmerized; then slowly she began to untie the leather thongs on her buckskin shirt. He helped her, kissing her softly as each garment was shed, then letting her help him until they stood naked, the night breeze caressing their flesh.

"Cold?" he asked.

She shook her head.

He smiled, then reached down, picking her up, cradling her in his arms, the feel of her against him warming him inside, making him tremble. He took a deep breath, then turned toward the river.

"Ready?" he asked.

She nodded shyly, overwhelmed by the vastness of the night around them.

His arms tightened, holding her even closer, and with deft

strides he walked to the river, stepping out onto the sandbar that clung close to the shore. Then, as the moon slowly began to climb above the treetops, turning the river to shimmering silver, he stepped into the water, carrying her with him, walking out from the sandbar until they were both submerged to their shoulders. The water was cold, but neither of them seemed to care, the heat of their love warming them deep inside. Heather couldn't take her eyes from his, and he began to stroke her gently, the water flowing against them as he held her so she wouldn't drift away in the strong current.

They kissed and loved, delighting in the wild feel of the rushing water as it swirled around them. The river wasn't deep here, the water barely to their shoulders, and Cole pulled her close, his mouth covering hers with all the violent emotions that poured from him. "I love you, Heather," he murmured against her mouth, and she clung to him desperately.

His arms closed about her, and he carried her with him to the edge of the sandbar, where he rolled over in the shallow water, pulling her down with him, until they lay stretched out, their bodies half in, half out of the water, Heather's head resting on the edge of the sand. Cole raised his head above her, looking down into her face. Water swirled her hair, mixing it with the sand, and her skin was pale in the moonlight. She looked like a water sprite, eyes dreamy with longing.

The cool night air washed over Cole's body, and he dropped down, his body covering hers, letting her warmth penetrate to him. And then she felt him, hard and searching, probing to find her beneath the water. She sighed, her body responding, arching upward to meet him, and the sensation as he entered brought a soft moan of delight from her.

Cole sighed, and as his mouth once more found hers, sipping at it passionately, he moved inside her, carrying her with him to an explosive climax that left them both breathless.

She trembled beneath him, the warmth of their lovemaking heating the water as it stroked their bodies, lifting them together, gently lifting their bodies, still fused together, to ride the current that lapped against the sandbar.

Cole stared down at her, his eyes glazed with the need to just look at her and lose himself in her love. "I need you, Heather," he whispered huskily. "Don't ever turn from me again."

She reached up, water dripping from her hand as she caressed his shoulder, feeling the strength rippling in the muscles beneath his bronzed skin. "Never," she answered breathlessly; then, as she stared up at him, her body still locked with his, he felt her tremble.

"What is it?" he asked.

She bit her lip.

"Heather, we promised . . . no more doubts."

She frowned, then took a deep breath, exhaling shakily. "Cole, what of that Indian's dream?" she asked suddenly.

He hesitated, his eyes searching hers as he continued to hold her close. "What of it?"

"His interpretation was right, wasn't it?"

"Partly."

"What of the rest of it?"

He watched the moonlight flood her face and saw the uncertainty in her eyes.

"Cole, he said you were still in danger," she went on. "What did he mean? And that dream . . . it was so frightening."

"Shhh . . . it was just an old man's dream," he answered.

"But how did he know? How could he know about us? And what did he mean? Cole, I'm frightened."

"Hush," he ordered firmly. "Don't worry about dreams, or Indians, don't think of anything but here and now. It was only a crazy man's dream." He kissed her softly. "Only a silly dream, love," and as he kept on kissing her, gently bringing her body back to life beneath him, Heather forgot not only the Indian's dream but also all the doubts and fears that had plagued her that day, and it was late when they finally returned to camp.

6

Some days later, in the middle of November, they rounded a bend in the river, and Major Long stared at the landscape ahead of them. The river stretched out for a good four miles in a straight line, with groves of cottonwoods edging the water; then the cottonwoods thinned out, dotting the grassy plains that stretched far into the distance on each side. They had passed the hills of Lee's Creek a few hours earlier, and now, as the major straightened, watching the horizon create a panorama against the blue sky, he felt a sense of elation.

Cole saw the look on his face and smiled. "The French call it La Belle Pointe," he offered.

Stephen Long exhaled dramatically. "It's perfect," he said. "What a view! And look there." He pointed ahead. "The main buildings could be spread out on that bluff above the river. Why, it must be at least fifty feet high, maybe more. From there nothing can pass either way without being seen. It's just what we've been looking for, Ian."

"That's what you said about the place we saw yesterday," said Ian Brooks.

"That was before I saw this."

"But we're still a long way from the Verdigris," Cole reminded him.

"How much farther?"

Cole frowned, looking over at his friend. "Eli?"

"A hundred-twenty, maybe a hundred-thirty miles or so," answered Eli.

"We can stop here if you want," said Cole.

Major Long thought for a minute as he listened to the splash of the oars in the water. "No," he said, shaking his head. "I'd better see it all first, just so there's no mistake."

He motioned for the men at the oars to keep rowing, but Cole saw the reluctance in his eyes a few minutes later as they passed beneath the high bluffs of La Belle Pointe.

Not quite a week later, after weathering a persistent storm that forced them in to shore, causing them to lose a full day, they landed at Three Forks, where the Verdigris and Grand rivers, also called the Six Bull by the French, converged with the Arkansas. Much to Heather's surprise, as they left the boat and waded ashore, she realized they weren't alone. A number of Indians were wandering about, as well as two trappers who were loading some canoes with supplies in preparation for winter trapping in the mountains to the north. The Indians stopped what they were doing and stared at the boatload of soldiers as they secured the skiff, then helped the women ashore.

"I don't think they see many soldiers this far north," said Eli as he and Cole watched Major Long step ashore, then they began to unload Cole and Heather's belongings.

"What are you doing?" asked Captain Brooks as he took one of the bundles from Eli and handed it to Heather, who was out of the water, standing on the water's edge.

"This is as far as we go," said Cole, handing Eli another

package. Then he lifted the last bundle out, headed toward shore with it. "If you'll remember right, I told Major Long we were going to the Verdigris, then south."

"But you promised to scout for us."

"To the Verdigris," reminded Cole.

"And if the major wants to go back to Belle Pointe?" asked Ian.

"He's decided?"

"From the way he talks, I think it's going to have to be Belle Pointe."

"Then Eli will take you." Cole set the last bundle down next to Heather, where the rest of their belongings were piled. "In fact, I've already talked it over with him. If you remember, our horses are with your Major Bradford, so Eli and I planned for Eli to take you to whatever site the major chose, then he'd stay till Bradford arrived. I'm heading out from here with my wife, son, and the others, and he'll meet us later with the horses."

Ian Brooks surveyed the group, his eyes coming to rest on Heather's sunburned face.

Even though the weather had been getting cooler every day, the sun had beat down on them relentlessly, and with only an old hat Leonce Bergerac's wife had given her to cover her face, Heather's nose and cheeks had taken the brunt of it. They were still peeling from the burn, and a smudge of dirt tipped the edge of her chin. She still looked so damn out of place in her buckskins with the floppy old hat on her head.

His eyes caught hers and for a few brief moments he remembered two nights ago when they'd made camp just north of where the Illinois River emptied into the Arkansas. Cole and Eli had heard, by way of a few stray Cherokee earlier in the day when they'd stopped for something to eat, that a party of Osage were camped along the river not too far ahead, bent on attacking the next boat heading upriver. So they had left camp to reconnoiter and see what they could find out, taking half a dozen soldiers with them this time.

Ian had watched the look on Heather's face intently as the small group of men melted into the woods early that evening. Every time her husband had left camp since that night some weeks ago when he hadn't returned until morning, her eyes had become apprehensive, and the lines about her mouth would deepen with a resentment he knew she was trying to hide. While Cole was in camp, there was never any doubt that everything seemed fine, but he could see the change in her every time Cole left, and it bothered him even though he tried to tell himself it was none of his business.

It had been cool that night, and although he'd avoided talking to her as much as possible since the night of their little altercation, he just couldn't seem to get her out of his mind, so when she'd left the baby with Tildie and wandered down to the water's edge to wash out a diaper Case had dirtied, he followed.

Heather was kneeling at the edge of the sandbar trying to swallow back the terrible feeling that had gripped her again as it always did whenever Cole left. She reached into the cold river water to swish away the mess from the diaper, watching it loosen and float off in the water. Tildie had done all the others earlier when they'd first made camp, but he'd dirtied again after eating, and since they still had only eight changes for him, she thought it best to wash it right away so it would give them another clean one for morning. She swirled the diaper back and forth, then laid it against a rock, where the water would wash over it, picked up a stone, and began beating the cloth, rubbing against it as the stone hit, pounding against the dark stains where she'd generously rubbed in some lye soap. Her hands were getting numb from the cold water and her fingers were sore from scraping them against the rocks, yet she kept at it.

Ian watched her for a few minutes as her hands turned first red, then white from the cold, her nails tinged with blue.

"Don't you think it's clean enough?" he asked as he stepped from the bank to the narrow sandbar, letting her know he was there.

She'd been staring off upriver, daydreaming as she'd flailed the diaper, and now her head jerked and she dropped the rock, shaking her numbed hands.

"I didn't hear you," she said, startled.

He inhaled and stooped down. "I know." He reached out, took the diaper from the rock, and began rinsing it in the water, while she stared at him dumbfounded.

Then suddenly she came to life and reached for the diaper, trying to take it from him.

"Here," she said, her voice breaking. "You don't have to do that."

"I know that too," he added.

She frowned.

"Your hands are almost blue," he went on, ignoring her

protest as he extricated her fingers from the other end of the diaper, swished it through the water one more time, then began wringing it out. "Why didn't you ask? I'd have carried a kettle of water back to camp for you and you could have washed it in warm water instead of freezing your hands."

"It was only one diaper," she said as she watched him unfold the three-cornered piece of absorbent cloth and shake it out.

"Shall we go hang it up?" he asked.

She stared at him and he stood up, holding the diaper in one hand, reaching out to help her with the other. She was hesitant at first, then took his hand, letting him pull her to her feet.

"Any bush will do, just so it's close to the fire," she said.

He nodded. "But first I think you could use a walk."

She opened her mouth to answer, but he shook his head.

"I won't brook any protest." He reached out, draping the diaper on a nearby bush. "We'll pick this up on the way back, along with the lye soap." Then he took her arm, turning her toward the riverbank, and helped her up the slight incline.

The sun had dipped below the horizon sometime earlier, and now a hush seemed to hover over everything as the birds found their roosting places for the night, and the first dark shadows of twilight began to ease their way in among the trees whose leaves were carpeting the floor with a blanket of color as winter drew nearer.

Ian gestured off downriver. They were on the north side, and although he knew it was Osage territory, Major Long had assured him earlier that he was sure there were none this close to camp. He glanced at Heather surreptitiously as they strolled along.

"You look tired," he said casually.

She sighed. "I am, but then, I think we all are, including you." She disliked the way he always seemed to know what she was feeling. "Do you think Major Long will be able to decide on any one place?" she asked.

"He already has, more or less. Only I think he feels compelled to make sure."

"That's why we're going all the way to the Verdigris?"

"That's his reason, but I'm glad we're going."

She glanced at him curiously. "You are?"

He stopped and she stopped beside him. "You have no idea why, do you?" he said hesitantly.

She flushed under the intensity of his gaze. "Am I supposed to?"

He stared at her for a minute longer, then sighed. "Knowing you as well as I've gotten to know you the past few weeks, no, I guess you wouldn't," he replied, then shrugged. "It doesn't matter, really, but I wanted to make sure. . . . You're still determined to follow your husband into the wilderness, aren't you?" he said.

She eyed him skeptically. "I'd follow him to the ends of the earth if I had to."

"Even if you died doing it?" He took a deep breath. "Heather, do you have any idea what it's going to be like out there?"

"It's going to be terrible," she said, then straightened stubbornly. "But I don't care. It's better than what we'd have back east. I love him, Captain Brooks, and I'm willing to put up with anything to be near him." She stared into his dark brown eyes. "Tell me, is it wrong to love so much?"

"Not wrong, but unwise." He began walking again, and she kept pace beside him, slow, meandering.

"Haven't you ever been in love, Captain?" she asked.

"What man hasn't?"

"Was she nice?"

"Who?"

"Your sweetheart."

"Which one?"

"Just like a man." She laughed softly. "The last one, Captain," she said. "What was she like?"

Again he stopped, but this time when she stopped beside him and looked up into his brooding face, the laughter left her eyes and she stared apprehensively.

"Do you really have to ask?" he half-whispered.

She swallowed hard. "What do you mean?"

"You want me to say it? Is that it?" His eyes darkened even more. "All right, Heather Dante or Heather Avery, whichever, I think I've been falling in love with you all the way up the damn Arkansas and fighting it every inch of the way," he said, his voice breaking slightly. "Because I know I don't mean a thing to you, and even if I did, nothing could ever come of it." He straightened, his dark eyes somber. "That's why I hate the thought of you being subjected to all the hardships I know are out there," he said. "Why I've tried to talk your husband into settling closer to civilization." His face reddened. "And why

'm glad Major Long didn't decide to just stay at Belle Pointe, so
I could keep you near me just a few days longer and maybe try
to persuade your husband to change his mind.''

Her hand covered her mouth as she stared at him; then slowly
she removed it. ''I had no idea.''

''I know you didn't.''

''But I haven't done anything . . .''

''You didn't have to.'' He tried to smile, and reached out,
touching her hair, watching the cool river breeze caress it. ''It's
not your fault, it's mine, but that doesn't make it any easier.''

''I'm sorry.''

''Don't be,'' he answered. ''I should have known better. All
my life I've prided myself on doing the right thing. If someone
had told me a month ago that in just a few short weeks I'd be
telling another man's wife I thought I was in love with her, I'd
have called him a liar, yet here I am.'' He sighed. ''I hate
myself for it, because I know morally it's wrong, yet I can't
ignore it, although I've tried to. You're not the easiest person in
the world to ignore, Heather Dante, you know that, don't you?''

''What can I say?''

He shook his head. ''Don't say anything, just listen to me.
Maybe it isn't love I feel for you, but it's something, and
whatever it is, whether it's just compassion or concern, I feel I
have to say something. Isn't there any way you can talk Cole
into forgetting this insane idea of taking you out into that
godforsaken country? Why, there are no other white women
within a hundred miles of where he's planning to go. There
aren't even any this far up the Arkansas, for that matter. I'm
afraid for you, Heather.''

''Don't be.'' She reached out and touched his arm, hoping the
gesture would let him know she wasn't upset with him and that
she cared about his opinion. ''I'll be all right, truly I will,'' she
said. ''And I thank you for caring.''

''But you won't try to change his mind?''

''I can't. Believe me, Cole knows what he's doing.''

He reached out, pulling her into his arms. ''Cole's a fool,'' he
said huskily.

She stared up at him, tears welling up in her eyes. ''You're
out of line again, Captain,'' she said unsteadily.

His arms eased around her, yet he didn't drop them. ''I'm
sorry.'' He saw the tears. ''I didn't mean to upset you, but

dammit, it's hard to stand aside and say nothing, especially when you feel deep down that someone's making a mistake.''

"Don't worry, I'll be all right," she said, trying to reassure him, but he did worry. He worried the rest of that evening while they walked back toward the campfire, and he apologized for his uncalled-for behavior, and he was worrying now as he stared into her sunburned face, watching her violet eyes fill with uncertainty.

He wrenched his eyes from her and turned to Cole. "You're sure I can't change your mind, Cole?" he asked, frowning. "There's plenty of land up toward St. Louis . . .''

Cole smiled lazily. "You don't give up easily, do you, Captain?" he said, then sighed. "I know exactly where I'm going, and so does Eli. Don't worry, we'll manage.'' Cole gazed about, spotting a building some distance back from the edge of the river. "You can tell the major we'll get the supplies we need from the trading post and head out in the morning.'' He glanced up at the sky. It was a hazy pink. "Looks like tomorrow might be a nice day.''

Ian nodded agreement, then turned to his men. "Major Long is going to want to leave in the morning too,'' he told them. "In the meantime, don't stroll too far. We want to set up camp before it gets too dark.''

They had arrived at what the trappers and Indians called Three Forks shortly after sunset, and now Cole gave Mose Wheatley orders to stay by their belongings while he took Heather's arm, calling for Bessie and Helene to follow, and they headed toward the trading post. The place was almost deserted this time of day, the only sign of life an Indian lounging on the steps and a lone trapper inside talking to the proprietor. Both of them stared as the women entered first, followed by Cole.

The building they had entered was made of rough-hewn logs with mud tucked into the cracks to keep the cold and wind out. To the right of them was a huge stone fireplace, the logs in it spouting tongues of orange flame that cast shadows about the darkening room. Tools, ropes, guns, and household implements hung all over the walls amid shelves stacked with boxes and crocks. A man behind a long plank counter was setting the chimney down over a whale-oil lamp he'd just lit.

"Evenin', stranger,'' he said as he finished, then set the lamp next to another that was already beginning to brighten the room with its light. "Somethin' I can do for you?" His eyes were on the women.

"We're going to need some staples," Cole said as he ushered Heather and the others ahead of him. "Not too much, just enough to last about two weeks."

Heather looked disappointed. "Is it going to take us that long to get there?" she asked.

"No," replied Cole. "But we have to have enough to last until Eli shows. He'll have the horses with him along with the rest of the supplies." He addressed the man behind the counter again. "And one other thing we need," he said. "Do you happen to have a cradleboard for the baby? We've got a long trek ahead of us."

The man frowned, his bushy gray eyebrows knit close. "Where you headin'?" he asked.

"South."

"Ain't nothin' south but empty land."

"That's what I want," said Cole. "Now, do you have what I need?"

The man's eyes rested again on the women. "Haven't seen a white woman for months," he said, making Cole think he hadn't heard the question. "Not since I was down by the post this past spring." His eyes settled on the baby in Tildie's arms as he finally gave Cole an answer. "Don't have any cradleboards at the post," he said matter-of-factly. "But seein' you need one pretty bad, I think I can get one for you. It won't come cheap, though, and may take a few days."

"We don't have a few days," Cole said. "We'll be leaving in the morning."

"Don't know as how I can help you, then," the man said. "Not with the cradleboard."

Cole frowned, then began to look at all the things hanging on the walls and on the shelves. He walked over and fingered a large piece of buckskin material, soft and pliable; then his eyes caught sight of some leather laces hanging on a nail. By the time they left the trading post to join Eli and Major Long's men, with whom they were planning to spend the night, they had not only the supplies needed, but Cole promised Heather that by bedtime he'd have a cradleboard.

Heather watched, fascinated, as Cole went into the woods and cut down a young sapling, then worked in the light from the campfire, making a frame, using the wood from the tree and the leather laces he'd bought at the trading post. After covering the frame on both sides with some of the buckskin and stitching the sides up with more lacing, he left a small hole open at the top, then had Helene, Bessie, and Heather help him gather as much dried grass as they could, which he stuffed into the opening, making a soft padding over the wooden frame that also had a footrest for the baby's feet. When this was done, he worked deftly, using the rest of the buckskin, lacing it onto the frame and fastening straps so the cradleboard could be carried on someone's back. It wasn't as expert as a squaw could have done, given the opportunity, but it was serviceable.

When it was finished, he handed it to Heather and she smiled hesitantly.

"It's a cradleboard," he explained, showing her how to secure Case in it. He saw the uncertain look on her face and smiled. "Don't worry. You won't have to carry him. Mose and I'll take turns." He set the cradleboard down. "All you have to do is come along, love," he said affectionately.

They were sitting near the campfire, with Case crawling all over them, going to first one, then the other as he jabbered noisily. Cole reached out, pulling the baby to him while Heather continued looking over the cradleboard.

"What about the supplies?" she asked. "Who carries them?"

"We all do. If each of us carries a little, it won't make it too hard on any one person." He studied her for a minute while Case played with his ear, trying to shove his finger inside. "Hey, there, fella, that's my ear," he scolded playfully. "Leave it in one piece," and he pulled Case's hand away, trying to get him interested in something else. When Case was thoroughly engrossed in the fringed collar of Cole's buckskin shirt, Cole once more turned his attention to Heather. She seemed restless.

"What's the matter, love?" he asked.

She shook her head and shrugged. "Nothing, I guess. It's just that . . ."

"That what?"

She took a deep breath, then gazed over at him. "Cole, that man in the trading post. He said we were the first white women he'd seen for months and they were at Arkansas Post, and the other night Captain Brooks said there weren't any white women this far north." Her eyes fell momentarily; then she looked back up at him. "Cole, you've asked me to trust you, and I have. You told me you were taking me to a wonderful place where we could live happily and no one would bother us. I know you said it wouldn't be easy for a while, and I guess I don't mind really—at least I'll have Bessie to help—but I'm frightened, Cole, and I can't help it. We'll be so isolated.''

Cole's heart constricted at the thought that she might not want to go. "Is that so bad?" he asked, hoping to ease her unrest. "People have caused us nothing but trouble so far. Where we're going, there'll be no one to hurt us."

"And no one to talk to. No doctor if Case gets sick. No place to buy anything."

"Case won't get sick," he said hopefully. "And we'll have each other to talk to. And as far as buying anything, we can make everything we need." Case was still playing with the collar of Cole's buckskin shirt, and Cole hugged the baby to him. "Where's your spirit of adventure?" he asked expectantly. "Remember the fun we had tracking through the woods at Tonnerre? It'll be fun again, love," he promised. "As long as we're together, we can make it work."

She didn't look too convinced.

"Please, Heather," he pleaded anxiously. "Don't give up now, when we're so close. You'll love it there."

Heather looked down at her hands. They were red, rough, and sore from scrubbing diapers, the nails chipped and uneven. Reaching up, she touched her nose, flaking off a bit of dry skin. It still hurt a little too. Her hands used to be so pretty, and her hair was never straggly like it was now. She knew she looked a mess, and yet . . . was it so important to look fancy and well groomed, or was she being selfishly vain to want to feel feminine again? She flushed self-consciously, feeling Cole's eyes on her. She loved him so very much.

"Don't worry, I'm not giving up," she said, her voice breaking. "It's only that . . . I hope I can do it. I'm not used to all this and I can't help but wonder if I'm strong enough for what's ahead. Captain Brooks said I'm not made for this kind of life."

Cole's eyes hardened momentarily; then he tried to reassure her. "You are, love, believe me," he said. "I know you, he doesn't. And it isn't going to be as bad as it sounds, either. I was going to surprise you and not tell you until we got there, but Eli and I put a cabin up when we were there this past summer. It has three rooms with a fireplace in each one. And there's a natural spring in the hill out back, so we won't have to carry water far. You'll love the hill. It's right behind the house about a hundred feet, with rock ledges wedged in among the wildflowers and trees. Then the valley spreads out with acres of tall prairie grass that's surrounded by forests so full of game we'll never go hungry. Wait till you see it, you'll fall in love with it just like I did.''

"I hope so," she said. "Because I want to like it and I want us to be happy there.''

"We will," he insisted, then pulled his head back as Case tried to stick his fingers in his mouth. "Now, don't worry your head over it. Once we're there, you'll see," he said firmly. "And you'll wonder why you even worried.''

"I hope you're right," she answered, then reached out for the baby, trying to relax, hoping Cole would forget she complained. "It's way past his bedtime," she said. "I'd better see if I can get him to sleep.''

Cole relinquished Case, then stood up. "I'll be back in a few minutes." His voice was a little more strained than usual. "There are some things I have to get settled before morning," and Heather watched him walk off toward where Major Long's men had pitched their tents.

Cole was furious. He'd managed to keep his anger in check until he'd left Heather, but now his jaw clenched and he inhaled, trying to contain himself as he bore down on Captain Brooks.

"Captain?" he said forcefully as he confronted him.

Ian was cleaning his rifle, and he glanced up as Cole approached. "Cole?''

"I hope you're not too busy to talk.''

"Not at all." He leaned back, flexing his shoulder muscles to ease the stiffness in his back. "What can I do for you?''

"You can tell me why you've been trying to scare my wife! That's what you can do," said Cole.

Ian frowned. He had been caught unawares, and for a few seconds didn't know what to say, then found his voice. "I didn't try to scare her," he said, trying to defend his actions. "But I do think you should have warned her ahead of time what she was getting into.''

"If I had wanted her to know, I'd have told her.''

"Instead you decided to let her find out the hard way, is that it?''

"That's not it at all! You just don't know Heather the way I know her," Cole said. "She's a worrier, and everything seems worse until it happens, but if she tackles things as they come, they don't seem so bad. But now, thanks to you telling her there are no white women out here and that she's not suited to living in the wilderness, and after some of the stories the rest of the major's men have let her hear, she's scared to death, imagining all sorts of things.''

"Is it imagination?" asked Ian irritably. "Or is she just using common sense? You know yourself she's too fragile for this life. She belongs back east with servants to wait on her, where life is simple and she doesn't have to be afraid of what each day will hold.''

"Is that why you've been trying to talk me into changing my mind? Because of Heather?''

"What do you think?" Ian stood up. "Cole, I know you think you're doing the right thing, but you're making a mistake, believe me. I've watched her on the trail. I've gotten to know her these past few weeks. She's not an Indian squaw, she's a delicate, well-bred woman. It's been hard on her all the way, and you'll kill her if you take her out there.''

Cole inhaled, his eyes blazing. "Never!" he exclaimed angrily. "I love her . . . and I know her, you don't.'' He straightened stubbornly. "I'd never hurt her ever, and she knows it. Now, just so you know where I stand. I didn't appreciate your interference one bit, and I don't want any more of it. Is that understood?''

Captain Brooks nodded. "She's your wife," he said. "Only I hope you know what you're doing.''

"I do!''

Ian stared at him hard. "I doubt it, but then, as you said, it's none of my business.''

"I'm sorry, Captain," Cole said. "But that's the way it is. Where I take my family is my business. I just wanted to make sure nothing more was said tonight or in the morning before we leave. As it is, now I have to try to undo all the damage that's already been done.''

"Don't worry," Ian said, wishing he didn't have to say it. "No more will be said, except that I wish you all the luck in the world, Cole. You're going to need it.''

Cole didn't answer, only stared at the captain for a long hard minute, then turned and stalked off, looking for Eli.

Heather had watched Cole walk off, then concentrated on changing the baby.

"You want me to put him to sleep?" asked Tildie as she dropped to the ground beside Heather.

Heather sighed. "Would you, Tildie?" she said, finishing tying his diaper on. "I'm not feeling too well, and Bessie said she wanted to see me."

Tildie took the baby from Heather, who stood up, then spotted Bessie and Helene near the edge of the water.

"Bessie?" she called, walking over to join her.

The older woman turned, watching her young friend approach, and her eyes studied her curiously.

"You said you had something to ask me?" questioned Heather as she reached them.

Bessie flushed. "I do, but I don't know how to bring it up." She bit her lip nervously.

"Bessie?" Heather was confused. Usually Bessie was anything but unsure of herself.

"Well," said Bessie more firmly, "I guess the only way is to come right out with it." She took a deep breath, then began. "When I first met you and your husband, you said his name was Duke and I believed it, but now . . ." She frowned. "If his name's Duke, why do you call him Cole so much? And Major Long too—sometimes he calls him Cole. Now, which is it, Duke or Cole? And once I heard Major Long call you Mrs. Dante."

Heather was taken by surprise. She stared at Bessie for a long time, not knowing quite what to say, then recovered her composure and tried to answer

"I guess you do deserve an explanation," she said hesitantly. She glanced off toward the others, then back to Bessie and Helene. "But the two of you must promise not to tell anyone, at least not until Cole gives you permission. And his name *is* Cole."

Bessie and Helene both promised, and Heather went on.

"His real name is Cole Dante and I'm Heather Dante," she said. "It's a long story, but the point is that he was falsely accused of killing a man and for almost a year there was a price on his head. He's been exonerated now and is no longer wanted, but there were so many posters around with his name and description, and he was wanted dead or alive, so we didn't want to take any chances."

Bessie nodded knowingly. "So that's why he's heading for the hills," she said. "I should have realized he was running from something. A man doesn't take a pretty thing like you into the wilderness unless there's a big reason." She smiled reassuringly. "But don't you worry, dear," she went on. "You won't be alone. I've homesteaded before, back east. We'll make out.''

"Then you don't blame us for using different names?" Heather asked.

"Heavens no." Bessie smiled. "I imagine there's more than one man on the frontier running from something or someone. And after knowing the two of you the way I do, I know Duke, or Cole, wouldn't hurt anyone without a reason. Only I hope he'll let me know what he wants me to call him. It seems funny for you to call him Cole and me to keep calling him Duke. Especially since we're more or less going to be by ourselves from here on.''

"Don't worry," Heather said, warming to Bessie's show of affection. "I'll talk to him about it tonight," and by the next morning when Cole and Heather stood on the bank watching Major Long and his men cast off, moving downstream once more in the skiff with Eli as their scout, Bessie was calling Cole by his real name and Helene was calling him Mr. Dante.

Before heading downstream, the major and his crew had ferried Cole and the others, along with all their new supplies, to the south side of the river, and now they stood on its bank, watching the boatload of soldiers disappear downriver until they were completely out of sight.

"Well, let's get going," Cole said as he glanced up at the sky, which was turning golden as the sun began to rise. "We've got a long walk ahead of us."

He and Mose had bundled everything into packs that could easily be carried on their backs, and after helping each other load up, with Cole carrying Case's cradleboard on his back, his rifle on one shoulder and another bundle in his arms, they started out.

At first Heather didn't mind it too much, but as the morning wore on, she realized the long days sitting in the boat, with no exercise, had given her little strength for what was ahead. By noon the muscles in her legs were aching, and she felt as if her back was about to break in two.

She glanced ahead to Cole. It didn't seem to bother him a bit, and he was still moving at the same pace he had been using since starting out. She took a deep breath and turned slightly, looking back to Bessie, Helene, and Tildie, wondering if they were as tired as she was. Mose was bringing up the rear, and as they moved single file, she noticed Cole was getting farther and farther ahead of her and the others were slowly catching up.

The sun was straight overhead now, with a slight breeze scattering leaves, now and then plucking a few from the trees as they plodded along, and Heather had to admit the scenery was lovely. Only she wished she could enjoy it more instead of having to keep her eyes on the ground so much so she wouldn't stumble.

When Cole finally called a halt for lunch, Heather didn't even take another step, but dropped in her tracks, breathing a big sigh.

Cole watched Heather sink to the ground, then frowned. They had been walking only half a day, and yet she looked exhausted. A tiny thread of guilt began to gnaw at him and he swung the rifle off his shoulder, put it down along with the bundle he'd been carrying, then hefted Case, cradleboard and all, from his back. He walked over and propped the cradleboard against a tree near where Heather was sitting on the ground, then sat down beside her.

"Here," he said, taking a piece of dried beef from the bundle he'd been carrying, handing her a piece. "It's not the greatest food, but it's nourishing."

She stared at the hunk of hard dried meat, then took it from him, bit off a piece, and began chewing.

He watched her closely as he gave Case a piece of bread to eat. "I've been going too fast, haven't I?" he finally said guiltily.

She shrugged. "I hadn't noticed."

"Come on, Heather." He glanced over at Mose, Tildie, Bessie, and Helene. They looked tired too. "Even they know I've been going too fast," he said. "Now, why on earth didn't all of you say something instead of half-killing yourselves trying to keep up? I'd have slowed down."

She tried to smile. "I guess we all hate to admit it. You move so effortlessly, while all we do is huff and puff, except for Mose. If he wasn't prodding us from behind, we'd probably drop in our tracks."

"Well, no more," Cole said firmly. "If I start going too fast, I want you to holler, understand?"

She nodded. "Yes, sir."

"And don't 'sir' me, either, love. We're in this together, remember."

This time the smile she gave him was broader and more relaxed, and for the first time that morning she began to think maybe Captain Brooks hadn't been right, maybe she'd make it after all.

Four days later, the endless miles of walking behind them, as Cole led them to the top of the hill where they could look down into the valley below, where the three-room cabin nestled serenely beneath the trees with the tall prairie grass stretched out before it, she was more certain than ever that everything would be all right. Because now that they were here, now that the danger was over, she could tell Cole the wonderful secret she'd been carrying with her these past few weeks, that if what she suspected was true, once more he was going to become a father, and this time he'd be right here to love her through the ordeal.

7

The weather was miserable, a light drizzle falling as Carl Palmer and Rafe Turner left the flatboat that had hauled them from the White River, through the cutoff, and over to the Arkansas. Now, as they approached the fort at Arkansas Post on foot, their boots sloshing in the mud, Carl cursed profusely.

"If it would only stop raining," he grumbled.

Rafe glanced up at the sky, his eyes squinting. "Won't last much longer," he said. "I bet it's over by nightfall."

"Hope you're right," Carl said as they moved down the main road and through the gates of the post, looking over the thick walls as they passed inside.

"Wonder what all the soldiers and horses are doing here?" Rafe asked as they stopped and stood gazing about. "I know it's a fort, but from what I've always heard, they don't even have a full company stationed here."

They were standing just inside the gates, and straight ahead was a group of thirty or forty soldiers wearing rain gear, and each one was leading a string of two or three horses, trying to line them up on the parade ground.

Rafe frowned. "Looks like they might be gettin' ready to leave," he said.

"My thoughts too," Carl agreed, and they began walking again until they reached one of the men.

"Excuse me," Carl said, addressing the first soldier they came to. "Could you tell me who's in charge?"

"Sure can." He pointed toward one of the buildings. "Major Stoddard's commandant."

"Thanks."

Carl nodded, and he and Rafe moved off toward the building, while Rafe speculated.

"You think all those keelboats and flatboats down by the river have anything to do with those soldiers?" he asked.

"Maybe." Carl hadn't thought too much about it. He had only one thing on his mind, and as they were introduced a few minutes later to Major Stoddard, he voiced the unspoken questions that had been gnawing away at him all the way up from the river.

"We're looking for two people, Major," he said sullenly. "Well, actually three people and a child. I've traced them up from New Orleans, and word has it they were headed cross country after their steamboat blew. They should have arrived here a short time ago." Carl saw a frown crease the major's brow and his eyes narrow warily. "I see you know what I'm talking about," he went on, jubilantly this time. "So I must ask. Where are they, sir?"

Major Stoddard hesitated, unwilling to commit himself just yet, because he wasn't sure what lay behind the gleam in his visitor's eyes.

"Tell me," he asked, avoiding the question. "Why are you looking for these people?"

"Because the man is wanted not only for murder but also for abducting my late brother's wife."

Abel Stoddard stared at him intently, trying to analyze his words and come up with a solution to the questions that were already forming in his mind.

"The man's name?" he asked cautiously.

"His name is Cole Dante, but he's been using the name Duke Avery."

The major took a deep breath, then opened the drawer in his desk, took out the wanted poster, which was still on top of the other posters, and flicked it onto the top of the desk, facing Carl. "Are you talking about this?" he asked.

Carl's eyes darkened. "You have him here?"

"He was here." Major Stoddard straightened authoritatively. "I don't know if you're aware of it or not, Mr. Palmer," he informed him, "but Mr. Dante has been pardoned by Governor Pinckney."

"You believed that?"

"He had the pardon with him, on official paper and signed by the governor."

"A governor who just happens to be a good friend of Senator Stuart Kolter, who just happens to be Cole Dante's sister's brother-in-law. Or didn't he tell you that? Ah, I see he didn't." Carl watched the major's eyes. "And I bet he didn't tell you that the woman posing as his wife is in reality the wife of the man he killed, my late brother, did he?"

"You're lying."

"Hardly."

"But they're married, they have a son."

"Oh, they have a son, all right," Carl said viciously. "A bastard son, but married? How can they possibly be married, Major? They're first cousins, and no one in South Carolina or anywhere else for that matter would dare perform the ceremony. They weren't married when they left Port Royal, they aren't married now."

Major Stoddard shook his head. "I can't believe that young woman would go along with such a blatant lie," he said. "I just can't believe it."

"Well, you're going to have to believe it, Major," Carl said. "Because it's true. Heather married my brother, DeWitt Palmer, when she discovered she was expecting Cole Dante's child. When the child was born and my brother realized he'd been duped, he confronted Cole with the truth and Cole murdered him. Everyone knew it was murder, including my brother's widow, but somehow Cole's sister had her brother-in-law use his influence with the governor to have Cole exonerated. Well, maybe the governor believed all the lies that were told, but I haven't. I may not be able to take Cole Dante back to any kind of justice, Major, but my father and I are responsible for my brother's widow, and I intend to see that she's released from that madman."

Major Stoddard stared at Carl Palmer, bewildered, not knowing quite what to believe. He had met Cole and Heather Dante, and liked them both. Not married? First cousins? It seemed absurd, yet . . . Was that why Cole Dante was so willing to risk the frontier, why he seemed so intent on going into territory that was so isolated, when he knew his wife was ill-suited to the experience?

"Just what do you intend to do, Mr. Palmer?" he asked after a long pause.

Carl straightened arrogantly. "I intend to follow Mr. Dante to where he's taken my sister-in-law and persuade her to return to Palmerston Grove with me, where she belongs."

"You'll leave the choice to her?"

"What do you mean?"

"Well, Mr. Dante is legally free of the murder charge, Mr. Palmer, so you have no right to interfere with him in any way. As for Heather Dante, or whatever you wish to call her, she's free to do as she wishes, and I won't tolerate any interference from you. From what I could see, the young woman has elected to stay with Mr. Dante, and brother-in-law or no brother-in-law, this is not South Carolina and I'll warn you, if you try to force her to return with you, you'll hold yourself subject to prosecution. Do you understand?"

"You're telling me I can't take her back with me?"

"I'm telling you, you might as well forget about your sister-in-law, Mr. Palmer," Major Stoddard explained. "Because I won't tolerate any violence in Arkansas County, nor will anyone else. My advice to you, and I suggest you take it, is to go back to South Carolina and forget the whole matter."

"Forget it? You can't be serious."

"I'm quite serious."

"Never," he replied angrily. "And if you won't help me, I'll find someone who will. Since I know now that they were here, there's bound to be someone who will tell me where they went. I'm sorry you won't cooperate, Major, but your advice is worthless. I intend to find Cole Dante."

"Just remember my warning, Mr. Palmer," the major said.

Carl stared at him, his hazel eyes narrowing; then with a curt command for Rafe to follow, he left the commandant's office.

"So what do we do now?" asked Rafe as they walked down the steps of the commandant's office to the main road again. "Where do we go from here?"

"We go after them," Carl said stubbornly. "Surely someone knows where they've gone." His eyes fell on the trading post a few buildings down. "Come on," he demanded, and Rafe followed.

It was still raining out and the rain had forced almost everyone inside. The trading post was crowded as they entered, and Carl told Rafe to see if they sold any ale or spirits, since there were a few tables set about at one end of the room; then he made his way over, trying to find an empty one. There were none available, however, and after looking the crowd over, Carl decided to ask two men at a table in the corner if he could sit with them. They were two of the few men in the place who were civilians, and they welcomed him readily, surprised to see a man of his apparent wealth, evident in the fancy clothes he wore, this far out on the frontier.

Carl introduced himself, then gazed about, studying the crowd while he waited for Rafe.

"Tell me," he asked the man at his left. "Why so many soldiers? I was told Arkansas Post was a small garrison with only a few men."

Harry Ferguson stared at the newcomer, anxious to make a good impression on him. "They're headed north," he answered importantly. "Seems the army's been ordered to build a fort up near Osage territory. Part of them left already a few days ago, but Major Bradford stayed behind with some of his men who've been sick. I guess they're plannin' to leave now, soon's the rain lets up enough."

Carl nodded, his mind sifting over the information. "You gents have been here for some time, then?" he asked.

"A few days." Harry was feeling talkative. "Came up on a steamboat that blew just north of Walnut Hills," he said importantly. "Me and the reverend was lucky we wasn't killed. Worst thing I've ever seen, with the smoke and fire and people dyin' all over the place. You should have seen it! Terrible, just terrible." He took a big swig of ale as Rafe made his way over to join them.

Carl introduced Mr. Ferguson and his companion, the Reverend Jeremy Litchfield; then his eyes narrowed shrewdly as Rafe sat down.

"Can you imagine, Rafe," he said smugly. "These two gentlemen were on that steamboat we heard about—you know, the *Bonnie Belle*—that blew up some weeks ago."

Rafe's eyebrows raised. "Were they, now?" he said, surprised. "How fortunate."

"Fortunate?" exclaimed the reverend, astonished. "My good fellow, it was the most unfortunate episode of my whole life. It's only by the grace of God that we were spared!"

"That's not what he meant," said Carl, trying to calm the excited man. "He meant it's fortunate for us. You see, we're looking for some people who were on that boat, who also survived. The trouble now is, we know they were here, but have no idea where they went when they left.''

Harry set his mug of ale on the table and glanced at the reverend, then back to' the pale redheaded man sitting beside him. ''Maybe we can help, maybe we can't,'' he said hesitantly. ''What's in it for us?''

''Mind you,'' interrupted the reverend, ''it ain't that we're greedy like some, but we lost everything we had when that boat blew, and a body can't live on air.''

Carl nodded. ''I understand,'' he said. ''And I'll make it worth your while. You tell me where a man calling himself Duke Avery has hied himself off to, and I'll give you each fifty dollars in gold.''

Both men sat motionless, staring at Carl; then slowly the reverend moved. ''Praise the Lord,'' he whispered softly. ''If it ain't our lucky day.''

''Then you know where he is?'' asked Carl hurriedly. ''And the woman with him? You know where he took her?''

''You mean his wife?''

''Wife!'' Carl sneered. ''She's no more his wife, gentlemen, than I am. How can she be, when she's his first cousin? No, gentlemen, the woman calling herself Heather Avery is my brother's widow, and the man claiming to be Duke Avery is in reality Cole Dante, the man who killed her husband.''

''God save us!'' gasped the reverend, clasping his hand to his breast in mortification. ''I knew they were sinnin'. I felt it in my bones. And they were sleepin' together at that Frenchman Bergerac's house while they were here. God help us!''

''I told you,'' said Harry, turning to the reverend. ''I knew I heard her call him Cole more'n once.''

Suddenly Harry frowned. ''But if that's so, then what're you doin' here? We should go see Major Stoddard and let him know the man's a killer.''

Carl shook his head. ''Hold it,'' he said as Harry started to get up. ''Sit back down. It won't do any good to tell the commandant. He knows.'' Carl's eyes hardened viciously. ''It seems Mr. Dante has convinced the authorities he had nothing to do with the killing. He has a paper from the governor,'' and Carl went on to explain to the two men about Cole's connection with Senator Kolter and all the rest. ''So you see,'' he said, finishing his tale, ''it's up to me personally not only to avenge my brother's death but also to take his widow back home, away from his evil influence.''

Harry and the reverend both inhaled at the same time, their eyes meeting, and each knew what the other was thinking. Harry emptied his mug of ale, wiped his mouth off, then leaned closer to Carl.

"They went up the Arkansas River with some of the soldiers," he said conspiratorially. "A Major Stephen Long, who's part of Major William Bradford's group, left here two days after we all arrived. There were about a dozen soldiers with them, and from what we learned, this Duke Avery and his friend Eli Crawford were to scout for the major."

"And the woman?" asked Carl.

"There were four women. The redhead, the one he said was his wife, a nigger slave who was takin' care of the kid, and a lady named Bessie Taylor and her daughter. Guess she planned to work for them once they got to where they was goin'.''

"And where was that?"

"Don't rightly know."

"One thing we do know," said the reverend. "I heard him say to Major Long that he was goin' all the way to the Verdigris." He shook his head. "Where he might have gone from there could be anybody's guess."

Carl leaned back in his chair and mulled everything over in his mind, then straightened as he took the money from his money pouch and paid the men.

"And you say this Major Bradford is heading up the Arkansas as soon as the rain clears?" he asked.

Both men nodded as they inspected the money he'd given them, then shoved it in their pockets.

Half an hour later, Carl Palmer was deep in conversation with Major Bradford and making no headway at all. Evidently Major Bradford had talked with Major Stoddard and both men were insistent about honoring the pardon, and no matter what Carl said, he couldn't sway Major Bradford to let him accompany him and his troops upriver. So once more Carl joined Harry Ferguson and the reverend in the trading post.

"If you could just help me find someone who knows the territory, someone who can talk to the Indians in case of any trouble . . ." he was saying. "Surely there's someone I could hire to take us upriver. Even by horseback, if need be," he said.

Harry frowned. "Where you gonna get the horses?"

"Buy them."

"How much you willing to pay?"

"For the horses?"

"For the man who takes you upriver."

"All depends," said Carl as he watched the eager gleam in Harry's eyes. "You been upriver before?"

"Might have."

"I thought you said you were new to this territory," the reverend cut in, but Harry brushed his protest aside.

"Never said no such thing."

"That's what you told Stoddard."

Harry's eyes held a warning. "And that's what I want Stoddard to keep thinkin', understand, Reverend?" he said.

Jeremy Litchfield grew a mite uneasy. He and Harry had become pretty good friends since they arrived at the post, but he didn't like this new turn of events. Lying was a sin, and he didn't like being a part of Harry's lying.

"Then you lied," insisted Jeremy.

"Look, Reverend," Harry said curtly, "he asked me if I'd ever been to this part of Arkansas territory, which I ain't. But he never asked if I'd ever been up near Belle Pointe or the Verdigris, so I wasn't lyin'. I just didn't tell him everything."

Jeremy wasn't sure he went along with this. He was going to have to think this over. But then quickly the conversation switched to the terrible crime perpetrated by Cole Dante, also known as Duke Avery, and the fact that he was going unpunished for that crime. And also the blatant way he and the woman he called his wife were living in sin, and before long Jeremy forgot his hesitancy at accepting Harry's lie. After all, next to the sins Cole Dante had committed, Harry's little lie was unimpressive.

"Anything north of Cadron Creek I know like the back of my hand, all the way down to the Red River," Harry was saying. "I could take you upriver, but not by boat. I don't want to set foot on another damn boat."

Carl stared at him in surprise. "But you'd be willing to take us?"

"For a price," said Harry.

For the next hour they made arrangements. Harry would see to the horses so Major Stoddard wouldn't get suspicious, and to keep the reverend from shooting off his mouth, he was to go along, to try to convert the sinners, so he decided.

Two days later, with the sun starting to dry up the wet ground, Major Bradford and his men boarded their keelboats with their

orses, equipment, and supplies, including two iron six-pounders
mounted on carriages along with small arms and almost twelve
hundred pounds of pig lead for casting musket balls. They had
been loading the keelboats since shortly before dawn, and now,
as they shoved off, beginning the arduous journey upriver, none
of them noticed the four riders heading west across the plains
north of town to where they'd pick up the river so they could
follow it.

Harry Ferguson's leg was still hurting a little as he reined his
horse away from the post, with Carl and Rafe following. But he
was getting a second chance, by God. He'd planned to make a
small fortune with the whiskey and guns that went down with the
Bonnie Belle. Well, now, with the money Carl Palmer had
promised, he could smuggle another load up from New Orleans,
and this time he wasn't going to miss out. He glanced back at the
reverend, bringing up the rear; if the reverend tried to stop him,
he'd take care of him too. The old coot was useful at times, but
right now he wished they could have left him back at the post,
and he wondered how long it'd be before the man's pious
exclamations of "Praise the Lord" got under his skin. Oh, well,
it was worth it, he guessed, especially when he thought of the
look that was going to be on Duke Avery's face when he
discovered they knew who he really was, and Harry began to
whistle a soft tune that blended in with the effervescent sounds
of the birds in the trees at the edge of the river as they greeted a
new day.

It hadn't taken as long for Eli, Major Long, and his men to
come back to Belle Pointe, because this time they rode with the
current instead of against it. They had arrived the day before,
and already Major Long's men had begun to put up shelters,
felling some of the trees close at hand. It was hard work, and
with so few men, the work went slowly, but by the end of their
second day they had a roof over their heads, even if the side
walls were missing. Major Long was pleased with the spot he'd
chosen. Not only was there enough wood in the area to furnish
the whole fort, but the plans he'd drawn up before leaving Belle
Fontaine earlier would need very little alteration to fit in with the
terrain. He spent his spare hours while waiting for Major Bradford working on the plans, making sure he'd left nothing out.

The outside walls were to be ten feet high and eight and a half
inches thick, with two blockhouses, one at each end, their

outside walls ten inches thick. The blockhouses would have two stories, plus an eight-by-eight-foot cupola on top, and would be at alternate ends of the garrison, which was to measure one hundred and thirty-two square feet in all. He had made provision for officers' and soldiers' quarters, surgeon's hospital and quarters, blacksmith and wheelwrights, carpenters, saddlery, tailor shop, sutlers, cooks' quarters, and a magazine for ammunition, which, unlike the rest of the rooms, would have walls three feet thick. All of this was to be poised atop the cliffs at Belle Pointe, where there was a natural command of both the Arkansas and Poteau rivers, with a four-foot-deep ditch surrounding it, the foundation of the walls made of stone quarried from the area, and a gate ten feet wide.

Major Long was quite proud of it, and as he made the last few alterations, he sighed. Now all they had to do was wait for Bradford and the rest of the men to arrive. He'd been sitting on his little folding stool beneath the crude shelter his men had put up, and as he stood up, stretching, he turned toward a commotion a short distance away.

There had been a few Indians camped nearby when they'd first arrived, but now a band of some fifteen to twenty had ridden in, jabbering excitedly, and Eli and Captain Brooks were right in the middle of the uproar, trying to calm them down. Suddenly Major Long saw Eli frown as he and Ian turned quickly and headed toward the shelter where he was standing.

"What is it?" Stephen asked as he slipped the plans for the fort into his attaché case and greeted them. "What are they raising such a fuss about?"

"It ain't good," answered Eli. "It seems while we were busy trying to locate a place for a fort to keep these redskins from each other's throats, close to six hundred Cherokee, reinforced with a few Indians from some of the other tribes and some white men, attacked the Osage up at Clermont and practically massacred the whole village. The town was burned, crops destroyed, and from what the men who just rode in said, the Cherokee are headed back east already with some of the prisoners. These braves managed to get away by the skin of their teeth. They've been riding for days, heading for the post, hoping to get some help. When they saw your men, they reined in."

Stephen Long winced. "What can I do?" he asked. "I only have thirteen men, and besides, I have no authority to act on my own. Major Bradford is the one who has to have the say-so on any reprisals. Did you tell them Major Bradford's on his way to Belle Pointe," he asked Ian; "and that I expect him any day now?"

"I had him tell them," Ian said, nodding to Eli. "He knows their language. They said they'd camp here and wait for him."

Stephen stared off at the warriors, who were making their way now to where the other Indians were camped. Ordinarily Osage warriors were strong, proud men, but as these braves rode off, they looked tired and worn.

"Their leader said no one had a chance," said Eli, "that the Cherokee sent a letter to the Osage assuring them they only wanted a friendly talk, and that there were barely a dozen of them who wanted to smoke the peace pipe, so plans were made to meet at the salt springs. Instead they murdered the Osage chief, then turned on the whole village. It seems most of the warriors were on a hunting trip. That left the village without any defense."

"I can imagine what happened," the major said angrily. "Why the hell can't they live in peace? Why can't they live side by side and share the land? No!" He shook his head. "They have to own it all. Damn them. And these white men who sell them whiskey and guns aren't helping matters either. I only hope Bradford can put a stop to it."

"I hear the men he has are all experienced fighters," Eli said.

"You heard right," said Ian. "Major Selden brought them up from Baton Rouge and Natchitoches. They're all crack troops."

Stephen stared off downriver. "And I wish to hell they'd hurry and get here, especially now with this going on." He sighed, turning to Ian. "Will you and Eli warn the men? There could possibly be trouble over this."

Ian nodded, and the two of them headed toward the woods, where the men were cutting down trees for more buildings.

"What if the Osage try to retaliate?" asked Ian as they walked along. "Your friends could be right in the middle of it, Eli."

Eli glanced at him curiously. "My friends? Seems you became pretty friendly with them yourself by the time we reached the Verdigris, Captain," he mused. "At least that's the way I saw it."

"You see too much," Ian said, then smiled. "But I guess I wasn't too discreet about my feelings, was I?"

Eli nodded knowingly. "You're a gentleman, Captain, and a conscientious one at that. A man like you has a hard time hiding how he feels, and an old expert like me doesn't let much get past him, although I didn't say anything to nobody about it, especially your major.''

"Good," said Ian, straightening stubbornly. "Because I'm not sure just how I felt about the young lady. I know it hurt to see her trying so hard to keep up with everything, and every time she didn't make it, I wanted to call Cole on it and ask him what the hell he was trying to prove by bringing her out here. I don't know." He shook his head. "It's hard to say exactly what I feel for her, but I know I wish to hell she was back east right now instead of out there somewhere."

"Don't worry," Eli assured him. "I know Heather looks fragile, but I think she'll make it. Right now I'm more worried about Major Bradford." He glanced at the sky. "The weather's turning, and if it gets too cold, he could really get into some trouble coming upriver."

Ian agreed, and both men frowned as they watched dark clouds rolling on the horizon.

It was four days before Christmas. Ian paced the dirt floor of the log hut the men had erected, blowing on his hands, which were cold in spite of the fire in the fireplace they had put in the south wall. Major Long was over by the Indian encampment talking with the Indians. He had sent a dispatch on to St. Louis on the third of December; that was almost three weeks ago, and Bradford should have been here already.

Ian straightened, walking to the fire, stirring it up, trying to get more heat from it, and thought back to that dispatch. The major had told him he probably should have mentioned the women in it, but just couldn't bring himself to do it. He said General Smith might not appreciate the fact that he let the women accompany his men. Ian had agreed; besides, he himself would rather forget the whole episode. More than once since they'd left the Verdigris he'd thought over his feelings for Heather Dante. She was at least ten years his junior, maybe more, and married, a fact that was the most damning of all. There were few women who had genuinely attracted him over the years, so what was it about this young woman that made her different? How does one pick out a certain trait, a reason for caring? How do you find an answer? It had been hard to say good-bye to her casually as he'd been forced to, but now he was glad he could get away from the temptation. In fact, the farther he got away from this territory, the better off he'd be, as far as his feelings for her were concerned. If he had to be stationed here permanently, it'd be too easy to try to keep abreast of what was happening to her. Damn! Why couldn't he have stayed unmoved by those big violet eyes of hers?

He turned, brought back to reality by a noise behind him.

"What is it, Private?" he asked as one of his men came through the door of the small cabin.

"It's Crawford, sir. He should be here in about ten minutes."

"I hope he's found out what's holding Bradford up," Ian said. "The major's been worried as all hell," and he followed the private outside to wait for Eli.

Major Long had told Captain Brooks to send Eli downriver a couple days before to see if he could find Bradford and his men. Now Ian waited, his eyes combing the edge of the woods.

Eli trotted toward the small camp that Major Stephen Long had hurriedly named Cantonment Smith—or Fort Smith, as the men were starting to call it—after the man who'd sent them here, General Thomas A. Smith. It wasn't much yet. Just a couple of log buildings, and not very expertly built ones at that, but Eli had seen the plans the major was working on, and the end result was going to be rewarding. He hailed Ian, who was waiting for him.

"Where's Long?" he asked as he reached him.

"Over by the Indian camp."

"Well, tell him they're about two, possibly three days downriver," he said. "I was going to hail them in to shore, but realized by doing that they'd only lose more time." He saw the look on Ian's face. "Don't worry, he'll be here by Christmas."

"I realize that. But the major's getting restless. He was planning to see what was down the Poteau River when he finished here, and all he's been doing the past couple of weeks is trying to keep himself busy so he doesn't go insane." He looked off toward where the Arkansas River flowed into the mouth of the Poteau River, and his eyes took on a faraway look. "I think you of all people should know what I mean, Eli," he said. "There's so much there to explore yet, and map. We all get itchy feet when we have to stay in one place too long."

Eli's solemn gray eyes followed Ian's gaze. "I'd love to go with you," he said longingly, "but I promised Cole I'd meet Bradford and bring the horses out. He's going to need them, and he'd kill me if I didn't show."

Ian took a deep breath. "You know, I have a feeling the

major's going to want to leave tomorrow," he said thoughtfully. "There's really no reason for him to stay anymore. He said as soon as he knows Bradford's close enough, he'll leave a couple of men here to meet him, and take off."

"You mean you don't want to celebrate Christmas with us?" Eli asked.

"Christmas?" Ian laughed. "I'd forgotten all about it. Unusual for me, too, because I always enjoyed the holiday." He gazed about quickly at the makeshift camp. "But then, I guess there hasn't been much around here to remind us of Christmas."

Eli agreed as both men left the cabin to go get the major so they could discuss his plans, and early the next morning Eli stood in front of the cabin shaking hands with Stephen Long and Ian.

"It's been a good trip, Major," he said firmly. "In spite of the weather," and he braced his head to keep the cold wind from whipping down the collar of his buckskin shirt.

Stephen reciprocated Eli's farewell. "When you reach your destination, give the Dantes my regards," he offered. "And make sure nothing happens to those plans I gave my men between now and when Major Bradford arrives. Everything depends on them."

"Don't worry, he'll get them."

"Good." Eli turned to Ian. "Take care of the major here, Captain Brooks," he said. "This country needs more men like him." Ian shook hands, then stared for a moment from the cliffs of Belle Pointe off across the river, trying to visualize what it would look like in the spring, with all the trees in full leaf, and the grasses high, wildflowers covering the hills. For a brief moment he wished they could stay and see it; then suddenly the thought of violets bursting forth reminded him of a pair of bewildered violet eyes and he knew he had to go with the major. Maybe someplace in the vast world out there he could find another pair of eyes to make him forget. At least he was going to try. "Take care, Eli," he said, then joined his men. They had secured some horses from some of the Indians and they all mounted, after making sure the packhorses were loaded properly.

Eli watched them move off, then stood on the hill until they were out of sight. He liked the major and he liked Captain Brooks, in spite of the fact that he knew the captain had begun to like Heather a little more than he should have. Ian was honest and forthright, a romantic at heart—maybe that's why he loved the land so much and seemed to enjoy working with the major, discovering new aspects of it. Yes, it was best Captain Brooks did leave with Major Long. Cole's valley was only a few days' ride from Fort Smith, and much as he liked Captain Ian Brooks, Eli knew the farther away the man was, the better for all concerned. He turned slowly and walked back to the cabin to wait for Major Bradford.

8

On December 25, 1817, with an icy rain driven by strong winds hampering their landing, Major Bradford and his detachment of rifle troops arrived at the newly christened Fort Smith, which was still referred to by most as Belle Pointe, and Eli was on hand to greet them, along with the two men Major Long had left behind. While the keelboats were safely secured and the men began unloading horses, equipment, and supplies, no one noticed four men watching from the nearby woods.

"Who's the man with the buckskins?" asked Carl Palmer as he tried to keep the sleet from stinging his face.

Harry snorted. "That's Avery's friend, Crawford."

"Then where's Dante . . . I mean, Avery?"

"How the hell should I know? Maybe he's in the cabin on the hill."

Carl had been watching the cabin closely since their arrival. "If he was there, he'd be outside by now, helping out."

"If you say." Harry pointed toward one of the keelboats where Eli was helping unload Cole's piebald mare and their other mounts. "But there's Avery's horse," he said. "The piebald mare they're unloading. Avery's got to be around somewhere."

Rafe had been watching too. He put a hand on Carl's back. "They don't know me," he offered. "Maybe I should go in, mosey around and see if I can find out what's going on."

Carl thought it over. Rafe was right. Major Stoddard had met Rafe, but when Carl had conferred with Major Bradford, trying to talk the major into letting him join him and his men, Rafe hadn't been with him, and he'd kept out of sight most of the time they were at Arkansas Post.

He straightened and turned to Rafe. "It might work at that," he said. "One thing's for certain, we haven't seen Dante anywhere." He motioned with his head toward the commotion at the river's edge. "Leave your horse here and go see what you can find out."

Rafe nodded, then turned the collar of his coat up to ward off the sleet, and left his companions.

Eli crooned softly to Cole's little piebald mare as he led the horse up the hill toward the crude lean-to he'd been using for shelter, where she joined the rest of their horses. Major Bradford's men had taken good care of them, but after the terror of surviving the steamboat explosion, their keelboat trip upriver had left all four horses a bit skittish around water. They seemed glad to be on dry land again, and the mare nuzzled against Eli as he tied her securely, then headed back toward the river's edge so he could help the major's men unload the rest of the things.

Men were moving back and forth steadily, and Eli joined a group who were complaining about the miserable weather.

"Well, at least it ain't two feet of snow," one of the men said. "Back home, Christmas ain't Christmas unless it snows, and we always get the worst of it."

"You couldn't get it any worse'n we get it," piped in another soldier; then he leaned forward to look around some of his companions. "How about it, Mr. Crawford?" he said, addressing Eli. "You've been around. Who has worse snows, Ohio or Pennsylvania?"

Eli laughed. "Son, there's no way you can calculate," he answered. "It all depends on who the good Lord decides to pick on at the time. I've seen waist-deep snow in both places." He felt the wind push against him and braced himself, turning his head to avoid the full onslaught of the icy rain. "But for what it's worth, I'd rather weather the winter out here any day. Nasty as this sleet is, it isn't as bad as diggin' yourself out of a ten-foot snowdrift."

"Then you're stayin' here with us all winter?" asked one of the men.

"Nope." Eli shook his head. "Plan to leave sometime tomorrow. My friends are waitin' for the horses."

"Where you headin'?" asked the same man.

"West."

They reached the boats and began helping some of the men who were still unloading equipment. Eli hadn't noticed the lone man who had asked the last two questions join the group as they walked, nor had the soldiers, possibly because of the biting sleet that was still making it hard for them to unload. Now the same man moved to within a few feet of Eli, keeping close to the other men so as not to be too noticeable.

"West is a big place," Rafe said, trying to be inconspicuous as they began forming a line down one of the gangplanks so they could unload a bunch of boxes. "Goin' anywhere in particular?"

Eli glanced toward the man. "Just a valley out south of Three Forks." He had a box in his hand and gave it to the soldier next to him as he watched the man. "I've been there before." Eli frowned as he studied the man. Strange, he thought, all the men with Bradford were soldiers. The man he was looking at definitely wasn't in uniform. Yet he seemed to know what he was doing, and the soldiers didn't seem to think it was odd, him being there. Eli shrugged as someone handed him another box, and he forgot the man momentarily until he spoke up again.

"You mentioned your friends," Rafe said cautiously. "You talkin' about the man and woman who was with you when you left the post with Major Long?"

Eli opened his mouth to answer, then suddenly hesitated. He didn't really know why, except that years of living dangerously had nurtured a built-in suspicion within him, and he frowned, squinting against the freezing rain to get a better look at the man who was asking so many questions. There didn't seem to be anything unusual about him. He was well built, with a scrubby beard on his face that was unable to cover what looked like a scar on one cheek, although that side of his face was almost hidden beneath his coat collar. Eli couldn't see the man's eyes because his beat-up old hat was pulled down too far in front to ward off the rain, but what he did see didn't seem to be out of the ordinary. Still, a sixth sense, something, told him to beware. He straightened, accepting a small wooden barrel from the man beside him as he spoke.

"Who wants to know?" he asked.

Rafe shrugged. "Just curious," he said, trying to pass it off as being unimportant. Eli's answer had alerted Rafe to the fact that the frontiersman was on guard. He was about to say something else, less incriminating, hoping to ease Eli's suspicions, when one of the soldiers from another keelboat started yelling, and all heads turned.

Within minutes, the conversation about Eli's departure was quickly forgotten as everyone joined the soldiers in the other keelboat, fighting to keep one of the iron cannon they'd had on board from sinking into the mud of the river bottom, and Rafe, certain there was nothing more to learn from Major Long's scout, and eager to get back to Carl Palmer with his news without being caught, took this opportunity to slip away unnoticed and head for the woods.

Eli was panting a short while later as he stepped out of the cold water and handed the rope he'd been hanging on to to one of the men, who immediately began tying it to a harness they'd put on one of the horses preparatory to hauling the cannon out from the muddy sand at the water's edge. They'd all been working hard, struggling with the cannon. Now, finally, everything seemed under control. Eli straightened, hands on his hips, and watched as the ropes tightened and the horse began to inch the carriage wheels the cannon was mounted on out of the water.

"I'm glad we didn't lose it," said a voice from behind him, and Eli turned abruptly to face Major William Bradford.

He was a solid man in his mid-forties who took his command very seriously and treated each man with consideration, a rarity with men in his position. Maybe it was because he'd worked his way up in the ranks and had been wounded near Fort Meigs in Michigan Territory during the War of 1812 and still carried a slight limp from the effects of those wounds. Whatever the reason, Eli didn't care; all he knew was that he liked the man.

"I had to do a lot of talking to get those six-pounders," Major Bradford went on as they stood watching. "And I have a feeling they're going to come in handy out here."

Eli wiped the icy rain from his face, then shivered. "Feels like the temperature's dropping again," he said.

Bradford nodded. "I came down to ask if you'd care to come up and have something hot to drink. I had one of my men put on a pot of coffee."

"I thought I'd finish helping your men," offered Eli, but the major shook his head.

"Nonsense, they can get the rest. Besides, when we arrived, you said you'd be leaving in the morning, and there's something I think you should know before you leave."

Eli nodded. "Let's go," he said, and they headed for the crude cabin on the hill.

A few minutes later, Eli was sitting on a box in the dimly lit cabin, sipping on a mug of black coffee and listening to the major tell him about the arrival of Carl Palmer at Arkansas Post.

"So you see, I thought perhaps I'd better let you know," Bradford finished, frowning. "I have a peculiar feeling the man isn't the type to give up easily, and a couple of my men said they were sure they saw riders a few times on our way upriver. Now, I'm not certain they followed us here, but there's always the chance."

Eli stared at the mug in his hands, then glanced up at the major, the incident earlier while they were unloading the boxes fresh in his mind.

"Major, tell me," he said. "Do you have any civilians working for you? Did you bring any upriver?"

"No, why?"

"Because there was a man down by the boats a short time ago asking questions, and he wasn't a soldier. Damn!" Eli exclaimed, and Major Bradford was startled.

"What is it?"

"I should have recognized him!" Eli shook his head. "How could I have been so stupid?" He scratched his graying hair irritably. "That man, the one asking all the questions, he's the same man Cole spotted down in New Orleans when we were getting ready to leave. It has to be. Let's see . . ." He tilted his head back, closing his eyes, trying to remember. "His name was . . . oh . . . Turner, that's it, Rafe Turner." Eli opened his eyes again, staring straight ahead. "He'd been in the army with Cole." He glanced over at Major Bradford. "You think he was the one who could have brought Carl Palmer to Arkansas Post?" he asked.

Major Bradford sighed. "I wouldn't doubt it. Mr. Palmer wasn't alone, but I didn't meet the man who arrived with him." The major stared hard at Eli for a few minutes. "Tell me, Mr. Crawford," he asked curiously, "is what Carl Palmer said the truth? Are Cole and Heather Dante first cousins, and was she Carl Palmer's brother's wife?"

Eli's eyes narrowed thoughtfully; then he took a deep breath. "It's true," he answered. "But Cole didn't murder DeWitt Palmer. It happened the way Cole told Major Stoddard and Major Long, and they are married, Major Bradford. I was there as a witness. The captain of their grandfather's ship the *Interlude* performed the ceremony after we left Port Royal." He finished the coffee, then stood up and took the mug over, setting it down on a rustic table near the fireplace. "So you see, there's no reason for anyone to be trailin' Cole unless they're up to no

good. I have a sneaky feelin' Carl Palmer intends to take up
where the authorities left off.'' He thought for a minute, then
made up his mind. ''I think I'd better change my plans, Major,'
he said abruptly, and shortly before midnight on December 25
warm skins protecting him from the cold sleet, Eli Crawford
slipped away from Belle Pointe, heading west, with his string of
horses following blindly in the darkness.

Jeremy Litchfield shivered as he leaned against the cottonwood
trying to steady himself as he finished taking a leak, then fastened his pants back again. It was so blamed cold his fingers felt
stiff as he shoved them back in his pockets, then started to turn
to go back to where Carl Palmer, Rafe, and Harry were huddled
together before a sputtering fire, trying to keep warm. Suddenly
he stopped, his eyes squinting hard in the darkness.

It had to be close to midnight, because the camp on the hill
had been quiet for some time. Only now, as the sleet began
turning into light snowflakes that brought far images into better
perspective, he frowned, watching movement that shouldn't be
going on. He rubbed his eyes, then stared again toward the
encampment some five hundred yards away, squinting, trying to
accustom his eyes to the darkness.

He hadn't been wrong, and now suddenly he was alert, every
muscle tense as he whirled, running back to the fire to wake Carl
Palmer and the others to tell them Eli Crawford had decided to
leave Belle Pointe now instead of in the morning as planned.

Eli was pleased with himself. He'd been making good time,
and as far as he could tell, he wasn't being followed. He had left
Belle Pointe four days ago, and now Cole's valley was about an
hour's ride to the southwest. His horse snorted restlessly as he
reined him down an incline, the other horses, tethered to a lead
line, following obediently. Suddenly he reined in, stopping the
string of horses as he squinted, watching the landscape.

A slight movement off to the right had caught his attention,
and as he stared ahead, the stealthy figure of a man moved
quickly across a small clearing, then disappeared again into a
cluster of trees. He waited, motionless, watching, his eyes intense.
The minutes went by; still he didn't move. Then suddenly another movement drew his attention and he stared hard as a big
buck sauntered slowly into the same clearing. He watched the deer
stop to sniff the wind, then hesitantly take another step, moving

farther into the clearing. The big buck was being cautious, aware there were predators in the area, and Eli could see a dark line across the deer's flank, probably the aftermath of an encounter with a bear or wildcat. The deer was edgy, still moving slowly out farther into the clearing.

Eli held his breath, watching; then suddenly a shot rang out, and he stared, fascinated, as the big buck jerked spasmodically. The deer's head flew up, his body hunching awkwardly, and then his legs buckled and he went down, first on all fours, then all the way to the ground. Seconds later a lone figure stepped out from the small cluster of trees into the open, and Eli grinned, watching the familiar stance on the man now staring down at the fallen animal. Eli raised a hand to his mouth, curling his fingers, and the mournful call of a whipporwill carried down to the clearing.

He saw the man in the clearing hesitate for a moment, cocking his ear to one side, then slowly raise a hand to his mouth, and Eli heard the echoing call float back to him. A few minutes later he had galloped into the clearing, slid from his horse, and was embracing Cole.

"My God, am I glad to see you," Cole said as he straightened, looking his friend over to make certain he was all in one piece. "What took you so long?"

Eli's arms dropped from about Cole and he straightened his buckskins, pulling at the sleeves. "It's winter, remember. For a while we thought Bradford and his men weren't going to make it at all." He gazed about him. "If they'd had weather like this, I might have been here a week earlier." The weather had warmed as he'd moved west, and now it almost felt like spring. "Doesn't it ever get cold here?" he asked.

"We had a few bad days about a week ago, but mostly those Indians we ran into last summer were right, the weather's been pretty mild."

They stepped over to the horses and Cole stroked the neck of his piebald mare affectionately. "Never realized how lost I was without my horse until now," he said, then glanced at the big buck deer he'd shot. "And looks like you showed up just in time."

"Come on, I'll help you," said Eli, and it took them only a few minutes to tie the animal's legs together, then throw the carcass on one of the packhorses.

Major Bradford had brought their saddles along with the horses, and Eli figured the best way to transport them was on the horses where they belonged, so all Cole had to do was climb into the saddle, joining Eli.

"How's Heather?" Eli asked as they reined away from the clearing, heading in a southwesterly direction.

Cole frowned. "I wish I knew."

"What does that mean?"

"Heather told me she was expecting another baby shortly after we arrived, and I'm afraid she doesn't look too well." He shrugged. "I guess it's just this sickness in the morning, but I'm a little worried about her."

Eli glanced over to his young companion. Cole looked fit as ever, and Eli knew it was hard for him to understand that everyone didn't thrive in the wilderness like he did. He felt sorry for Cole because he knew how much he loved Heather.

"Maybe she just needs time," he said. "After all, you've been here only a little over a month. She has to learn to adjust."

"But can she?" asked Cole. "Maybe Ian Brooks was right. Maybe I shouldn't have brought her out here."

"But you did, so it's too late for second-guessing. All you can do now, Cole, is try to make things a little easier for her. How're Bessie and everyone else?"

Cole smiled a little as he shifted in the saddle, looking back to check on the deer's carcass. "Bessie's been a lifesaver, Eli," he answered. "The woman's a veritable treasure. If it weren't for her and Helene, I don't think Heather could have made it so far. Bessie runs the place as if it were her own. Even Mose jumps when she starts giving orders."

Eli nodded. "Well, that's one thing in your favor." He hesitated a minute, then went on. "I have some bad news, Cole," he said, not wanting to change the subject but knowing it was best he mention it before they reached the cabin. "I hate having to tell you, but Carl Palmer trailed you all the way to Arkansas Post. In fact, Major Bradford and I are quite sure he and the men with him, which includes your friend Rafe Turner, have followed the major up to Belle Point."

"You saw them?"

"I saw Rafe. At least I think it was Rafe," and Eli told him about the man who'd asked so many questions the day Major Bradford and his men had arrived.

"Do you think they followed you here?" asked Cole when Eli had finished telling him.

Eli shook his head. "Lord, I hope not." He glanced behind

him surreptitiously, then went on. "I tried to cover my tracks, but with all these horses . . . I can't guarantee I wasn't followed, but if they have followed me, they sure as hell kept out of sight. Besides," he said, hoping to relieve Cole's anxiety, "they thought I wasn't leaving until morning. Instead I left in the middle of the night and the weather was bad. My tracks would have been washed out by morning."

"Well, we'll have to hope they were," said Cole, and he too glanced behind them quickly before settling steadily into the saddle for the ride the rest of the way to the cabin.

Heather was so tired. Her fingers were sore and sticky from twisting silk from the old milkweed pods they'd gathered into wicks tight enough to be used, and now the smell of the tallow filled the cabin with its pungent odor, turning her stomach. It smelled terrible, yet she knew they had to make candles. They'd been using the inside of pithy plants—Cole called them rushes—soaking them in grease and burning them for light, and he'd also managed to get some pine knots for them to use. But both were messy. Oh, how she longed for the clean scent of bayberry candles, only that was an impossibility. Well, at least these would be better than the smoky pine knots and rushes.

She glanced over to where Bessie was stirring the kettle with the tallow in it, ready to add the hot water so the tallow would float to the top so they could begin dipping again.

Cole and Mose had made straight-back chairs from some of the lumber they had cut, and Bessie had set two of the chairs so they were back to back about three or four feet apart, with poles across from one chair to the other for the wicks to hang, with an old hide beneath it to catch the drippings.

Heather finished tying the last wick on the rod in front of her, which was merely a fairly straight stick, then held it up for inspection. They'd dip three candles to a rod.

"Here, Helene," she said, handing it to Bessie's daughter. "Take this to your mother."

Helene blew an amber-colored curl from her sweaty forehead and handed the rod to Bessie, who set her stirring paddle down and began the dipping, while Heather began fastening more wicks onto the wooden rods. They were using deer tallow, and Cole was out now, hunting, hoping to find another deer.

It was hot in the cabin, and perspiration dampened Heather's skin, making her clothes stick to her. She was no longer wearing the buckskins, but had on the dress she'd been wearing when she'd run away from Palmerston Grove. It was a fancy black cotton with a high ruffled neck, bouffant sleeves to below the elbow, then tight to the wrists, with tiny buttons holding the bottom of the sleeve snug. Heather reached up, unfastening the buttons at her neck and partway down the front, trying to cool herself off. She had already rolled the sleeves up as high as she could, and still the heat was stifling.

They had almost twenty candles already made today, and Bessie said they should have over thirty by the time the day was over. Heather glanced over, watching Bessie dip the wicks, then set them to drip, and she thought back to the past weeks since they'd arrived.

She'd never forget her first look at the cabin. It had looked so inviting from the top of the hill that it was a shock when they reached it and entered. Although there was a door with a latch and latchstring, and shutters covering the windows, along with the spidery cobwebs and dirt they had chased out a family of raccoons, some squirrels, and mice that had evidently come in by way of the fireplace chimneys, and they had had to clean out the debris the animals had brought in with them. The place was a mess, and even though Cole had told her all three rooms of the cabin were the usual twenty by thirty feet, it was anything but impressive.

With Bessie's help and ingenuity they had managed to clean the place, using a broom she'd instructed Cole to make out of a hickory sapling, some lye soap Cole had bought at the trading post, and rags Heather had made by tearing up one of the petticoats she had been wearing before putting on the buckskins. And she'd never forget the first fire Cole built in the fireplace. Evidently some squirrels had decided to use the chimney for nesting, and within minutes of starting the fire, the cabin was full of choking smoke that drove them all outside. So they had spent their first night in the cabin in the dark, on the floor, with the smell of smoke heavy in the air.

It had taken Cole and Mose half the next morning to clean the chimney to the main room and make sure the others weren't blocked too, and in the next few days Heather really learned what wilderness living was all about. By the end of their first week, however, Cole, with Mose helping, had managed to make crude furniture for the place, kept them in fresh food, and taught Heather how to prepare and cure skins as well as how to make dishes out of clay he'd brought from a place he'd discovered when he'd been here during the summer.

Everything was so new to Heather, and at first she had accepted it cheerfully, trying to laugh off the little annoyances that crept up, but after a while the novelty seemed to wear off, and along with having an upset stomach most of the time, she began to miss terribly the relaxed hours she'd spent before, sewing or riding her horse Jezebel, or walking through the gardens at Palmerston Grove dressed in fancy dresses, or going into town on shopping sprees. The only thing that kept her from resenting the lack of leisure time and deprivation of all the comforts she had known before was the promise Cole had given her that someday she'd have all those things again, the fact that Bessie was here to help, and Heather's all-consuming love for Cole. Still, even loving him as much as she did, it was hard to have her life changed so drastically.

Now, as she gazed about her, watching Bessie and Helene, remembering the past few weeks, she felt guilty. Cole had been trying so hard to make things easier for her, and he worked so hard. It was strange the way he seemed to enjoy life so much here in the wilderness. He was never bored, and never complained how hard the work was. She felt lazy and worthless every time her thoughts rebelled against the constant work; then she'd flush, embarrassed at her guilt. After all, she had Bessie and Helene to help. It was ridiculous to be so discontented. She'd have to curb her thoughts more and fight against the selfish notions that tried so often to surface.

She stared down at her hands, then lifted the tips of her fingers, touching them with her tongue where they were sore, trying to soothe the pain a little, when suddenly the door opened and Tildie came in carrying the baby. She'd been calling Heather's name all the way to the cabin, but Heather hadn't heard because she'd been daydreaming.

"Miss Heather, didn't you hear me?" she asked as she came in, trying to keep the squirming baby in her arms. "I been calling loud as I could." She lost the battle and set Case down, then grabbed his hand to keep him from toddling into the room. "He's comin', Miss Heather," she went on. "Mr. Cole's comin', and Mr. Eli's with him, and they got all the horses."

Heather stared at Tildie and suddenly all thought of removing the pain from her fingers was gone. She stood up quickly. "Bessie, did you hear?" she asked, straightening her dress, pushing a stray strand of hair from her forehead. "Eli's back with the horses. That means he'll have brought the supplies Major Bradford was bringing up from Arkansas Post."

Bessie smiled, face flushed from the heat of the open fire. "You go greet them, honey," she said. "I'll finish here. And tell that old coot Eli that as soon as he unpacks some coffee and brings it in here, I'll fix a pot, 'less he wants some of that tea we been makin' out of dried clover blooms." She laughed. "That should get him to unpackin' the supplies in a hurry."

"I'll tell him," Heather said, and took a deep breath, then headed for the door. She stood outside, watching Cole and Eli approach. They were talking animatedly, and Eli, seeing her waiting, waved.

"Well, hello there, little gal," Eli said as they reached Heather and both men slid from their saddles. "Looks like you're all dandied up for my return," and his eyes sifted over the dress she was wearing.

She flushed self-consciously, her violet eyes darkening. When first she'd met Eli, she'd been afraid of his gruff manner and rough exterior, but she soon learned that he was warm and caring. "The dress is the only one I have, Eli," she said timidly. "And you've seen it before."

"You still look good in it," he said.

Cole smiled at the blush on her face. "Afraid she isn't used to compliments from anyone but me, Eli," he said as he came over and gave her a hurried kiss. "Look what I've got, love," he went on. "Now, with the supplies Eli's brought, we can have a real feast tonight." He walked over to the big buck deer. "Want to give me a hand, Eli?"

Eli nodded and turned to help Cole, when Mose walked up.

"I see you brought back mor'n a deer," Mose said to Cole, then grinned at Eli. "Glad to see you back, Eli. Cole was beginnin' to think somethin' happened to you."

"Just a slight oversight on the part of the weather," Eli replied as he shook the black man's hand. "I hear you've really been a big help, Mose."

Mose grinned. "It sure beats stokin' furnaces."

"Well, what's say we take this carcass to the shed and get it taken care of, then go in and have a bit to eat," suggested Cole. "Eli's been on the trail all day. I imagine by now he's ready for something solid."

Eli glanced off to where a small building stood a few feet from the house. Cole had told him that he and Mose had put up a combination smokehouse and lean-to, and now he and Mose helped Cole untie the deer and carry it to the lean-to, where they hung it up, skinned and butchered it, then sent Mose into the house with a haunch of venison for Bessie to put on to cook while they began cleaning everything.

"I notice you didn't say anything to Heather about Carl Palmer," Eli said as Mose left them. "I presume you've decided not to tell her?"

"I don't think it'd help," said Cole. "Things are rough enough for her as it is, without adding the worry of Carl Palmer to everything else."

"You think that's wise?" asked Eli. "What if they happen to find their way out here?" Eli glanced toward the house. "I'd hate for anything to go wrong, Cole," he said as he dipped his hands in a bucket of cold water to wash the blood off.

Cole nodded. "I feel the same as you. That's why tomorrow morning we're going to go out and scout back on your trail just to make sure."

Eli sighed, pleased. "Good," he said. "I'll feel better," and for the rest of the evening while they finished cleaning up, then went into the cabin to visit and eat a hearty meal, no more mention was made of Carl Palmer or anything else that had been haunting all of them since leaving Port Royal, while up in the hills that surrounded Cole's peaceful, snug little valley, Carl Palmer and the men with him saw the first faint lights come on in the log cabin and knew they'd finally reached the end of their search.

9

The next few days were busy in Cole's valley as the new year of 1818 came in warm and balmy. They had scouted the surrounding hills the day after Eli's arrival and found nothing, so after a quiet celebration on New Year's Eve, filled with small talk and hopes for the future, the work began again in earnest.

Cole and Mose had started building a corral for the horses shortly after their arrival, and now, with Eli's help, the rest of it went up quickly. It was going to be about a hundred feet from the cabin and big enough to hold not only the horses Eli had brought but also at least two or three dozen more, with good pasture for them and plenty of trees for shade. While the men worked on the corral, Bessie boiled down tallow from the big buck Cole had killed so she could set it to stand in one of the clay pots and make some soap with it later on, and Heather worked on the hide, scraping it so it could be softened. Helene helped Bessie, and Tildie, as usual, played with Case, keeping him out of mischief and making sure he didn't wander off.

For the first time in a long time, Heather didn't seem to mind the work. Maybe it was because for the first time in days they had sugar and flour and Bessie had made a small cake on New Year's Eve with some of it, and there were coffee and real tea. Cole had even bought a couple bolts of material and thread at Arkansas Post. It had been packed on the horses with the other things, and Bessie had promised to help Heather make herself a dress that would be suitable for her to wear, even while she was pregnant. And on top of everything else, Mose had promised to make a loom and spinning wheel so they could make their own cloth. Now the sun was shining, the weather fresh, and as she used the piece of sharp bone Cole had given her, scraping down the inside of the hide that was stretched taut, a strange sense of pleasure began to fill her.

Maybe things weren't going to be too bad `after all. Once everything was under control, the work wouldn't be so hard. She stared down at the hide and her nose wrinkled distastefully. Eventually maybe she wouldn't even have to cure any hides. Leaning back on her knees, she gazed across the way to where the men were working putting up the split-rail fence that would keep the horses in. Her hands rested on her lap for a few minutes as she watched Cole lifting the rails, helping to set them in place.

He had been so excited ever since they'd reached the valley. First about the expected baby, then about getting the cabin livable and making the furniture they could use. Luckily Mose had once worked as a joiner, and with the tools Eli and Cole had brought with them during the summer and left there when they'd built the cabin, they had tables and chairs to sit on, and Mose was making chests of drawers for all the clothes they'd have someday. About the only thing they didn't have so far was beds. There was plenty of wood and enough rawhide and leather for straps, but there was no cloth to use for ticking and nothing to stuff in a mattress if they had the cloth, so they were still sleeping on the floor wrapped up in furs and blankets.

It didn't matter really, though. As long as she was in Cole's arms, Heather didn't care too much where she slept, although a feather bed would sure come in handy about now. Or even one with a corn-husk mattress, and she thought back to their stay at Arkansas Post. That seemed so long ago.

She sighed, then shrugged and went back to her work on the deerskin, unaware that up in the surrounding hills, not too far from where they were all working, Carl Palmer was crouched behind some bushes, and he too was watching Cole, his hazel eyes studying him intently.

"So what happens now?" asked Rafe from over his shoulder as he too watched the men at work. "You said you wanted the woman, so how the hell do we get her out of there?"

"We take her."

"Be reasonable," said Rafe. "We were lucky the other day. They'd have discovered us for sure if that herd of deer hadn't wandered across our trail, hiding our tracks. Granted, Ferguson had us tie hides to our horses' hooves, but that was no guarantee those men down there wouldn't have been able to pick up on his little trick. Besides, for a man who hates Indians the way Ferguson does, how come he knows so much about them?"

"Use your head, Rafe," said Carl, half-whispering. "He's been running whiskey and guns to them. But just because he trades with them doesn't mean he has to like them."

"Well, it's certain he don't," replied Rafe. "Between him and the preacher, they make me nervous."

"Necessary evils," Carl said; then his eyes moved from where the men were working to where Heather was kneeling, working on the deerskin.

The sun was on her hair, turning it to a brilliant crimson, and he wished he could get closer to see her face. It had been months since he'd looked into those lovely violet eyes and watched her mouth curve sensuously as she smiled. Just remembering brought a hot flush to every nerve in his body, and he took a deep breath, trying to keep his voice from trembling as he spoke.

"I'm going to make Cole Dante pay, Rafe," Carl said as he watched Heather working on the deer hide. "She was to be mine. He had no right to her."

"You said we'd take her. How? We sure as hell can't just ride in and ride off with her."

"We watch and wait," Carl answered anxiously. "I'll know when the time's right." He took a deep breath. "Dante and

Crawford can't stay around all the time. We'll get our chance and I want to be ready at a moment's notice when we do." He turned abruptly and glanced behind them toward some cliffs ir the distance. "Where're Ferguson and the preacher?"

"Still in the cave. I told them to stay there until we get back."

"Good." Carl turned again to look out over the valley. "I don't want either one to blunder too far from camp and ge spotted by Dante." His eyes narrowed shrewdly. "This has to be done just right . . . just right," and he smiled to himself, dreaming of the revenge he was planning.

The weather stayed exceptionally warm for the next few days, and by the middle of the following week the corral was finished. It was late Friday evening. Cole and Heather had taken a walk before going to bed, and now they stood leaning on the top rail of the corral, watching the horses, and enjoying the warm breezes that filled the night.

Cole wrapped an arm about Heather's thickening waist and pulled her close against him, resting his head against hers. "Are you beginning to like the valley, love?" he asked tenderly.

She took a deep breath, mulling over his question. The valley was beautiful, she had to admit. And there were times, like now, when she almost felt a closeness with the place. But then she remembered the long days trying to take care of her little family. The heat of the cabin during candle dipping, the way her arms ached scrubbing the few clothes they had, trying to get them clean, and the awful smell of the drying hides. And now there'd be double the work when they started making their own clothes. She had to admit she was spoiled. If it weren't for Bessie, Helene, and Tildie . . . She sighed.

"It's beautiful, Cole," she whispered, then let the warmth of his nearness soothe her. "I guess I'll get used to it, after a fashion." She leaned away a bit and looked up into his face. "But there are times when I do miss the fancy parties, all the people, and the pretty clothes." She reached up, touching the lace at the throat of her black dress. "But those are only selfish things, the things Heather McGill, or rather Heather Chapman, would be concerned about, not Heather Dante."

"Have you changed that much, love?" he asked softly. "I hadn't noticed." He reached up, cupping her head in his hand, his thumb stroking her temple where small wispy curls ran rampant. "You'll always be my Heather, light of my life. You haven't changed. Not inside, or outside either. You're just as lovely as you ever were. And you're not spoiled. You deserve all those things, and someday I'm going to keep the promise I made to you back at Arkansas Post. Someday you're going to have a big house, servants, everything you've had to give up just for loving me.'' His green eyes were alive with passion. "I love you, Heather," he whispered huskily, and leaned down, his mouth covering hers.

The kiss was long and sweet, filled with all the warmth that filled his heart, and Heather trembled clear through, the love she felt for him echoing his words as her lips moved beneath his. Slowly he drew back, his breathing ragged, unsteady, his voice breaking as he spoke.

"I have to go away, love," he murmured hesitantly.

She inhaled, her eyes fearful.

"Not for long," he went on. "Only for a few days." He kissed her again, lightly, then explained. "I didn't tell you earlier because I didn't want to frighten you, but Eli said Major Bradford told him Carl Palmer was at Arkansas Post asking for us. And Eli has a suspicion he may have followed Bradford to Belle Pointe. We checked the day after Eli arrived, to make certain he hadn't been followed, but now I have to see if they're still about, and that means going back to Belle Pointe. It wouldn't do for them to find us. I don't want any more trouble from the Palmers."

"What if he is still there?"

"Don't worry. I'm taking Eli with me," he assured her. "Mose will take care of things here. He's gotten quite good at hunting, and he'll see to the heavy work for you and Bessie."

"It isn't that," she said softly, and reached up, touching his face, her fingers caressing him affectionately. "But I'm always so afraid when you leave me. If anything happened to you—"

"Hush!" His arms tightened about her and he studied her face in the darkness, drinking in every feature that was already indelibly printed on his mind. "I'll always come back to you, love," he whispered softly, and kissed her again, trying to assuage all her fears.

The next morning, with enough food to last for three or four days, Cole and Eli left for Belle Pointe. At first Heather did nothing but stare off into the hills where they'd disappeared; then, as if realizing nothing she could have said or done would have made Cole change his mind, she was once more swept into the everyday routine of keeping the place going. Actually, it was Bessie who kept things going, and Heather was grateful, although Bessie made sure Heather was always close by when she made decisions, trying to make Heather think she was running things. And Heather was learning. She had learned how to make candles, and Bessie had promised to teach her how to make soap and use the spinning wheel and loom, when Mose finished building them. Bessie had already told her how they were going to make the soap, but that wouldn't be until spring, when the lye was ready and they had enough grease. They were almost out of the bars of hard soap Cole had bought at Three Forks, but he promised to try to bring more back with him from Belle Pointe if he could talk Major Bradford into giving up part of his supply.

The first few days Cole was gone went by quickly. It was the nights that were the worst for Heather. The furs on the cabin floor in the room she and Cole shared were little comfort, especially when the nights grew cold and crisp. But the days were still warm, and she tried to fill them as best she could so the emptiness without him didn't overwhelm her.

It was the afternoon of the third day he was gone. The weather had cooled again, but the sun was out. Heather had been busy all day, but now suddenly found herself with some idle time. Case had been a little restless when he woke up from his nap, so wanting to give Tildie extra time to finish what she'd been doing while he was asleep, Heather decided to take him for a walk.

Case had turned a year old in November, and was now not only walking but trying to run every place he went. His little legs were still wobbly at times, but he was so inquisitive about everything that nothing seemed to hold him back.

There was a small stream at the southern end of the valley, and Heather, wearing her black dress and one of Cole's furs, headed for it. Mose and Cole fished there often, and Cole had taken Heather walking there occasionally, so that a path had already been worn through the dead winter grass. Heather had put warm clothes on Case before they'd left the cabin, and now she pulled the fur she was wearing tighter against the crisp January winds that tore through the valley, whipping her hair about, tangling it and blowing it into her eyes.

She watched Case toddling ahead of her, listening to his happy babbling as the wind caught it and carried it back to her. What a love he was, and the valley seemed to agree with him as much as it did his father. He loved the horses and was always begging someone to take him to the corral so he could see them up close. And he loved to wander all over outside, investigating everything. Even now. Heather smiled to herself as she watched him stop by a cluster of dried-up weeds and study a cocoon, fingering it, his pudgy little hand trembling with excitement at the thought of discovering something new.

"Don't break it off," Heather said quickly as she reached him and knelt down, putting an arm around him. "If we leave it until spring, we can watch it turn into a beautiful big butterfly."

"B-b-buttry?" Case stammered hesitantly.

"No, not buttry, butterfly, dear," she said distinctly. "But you wouldn't know what a butterfly is. Your daddy told me all about butterflies when we used to tramp the woods at Tonnerre, and I'll show you butterflies in the spring."

"Sping?" he asked, frowning.

"Yes, spring." She hugged him. "But for now, let's go see if Daddy and Eli left any fish in the stream. Then we'll head back to the cabin."

At the thought of seeing the fish that fascinated him as they swam in and out amid the rocks in the streambed, he quickly lost interest in the cocoon, grabbed his mother's hand, and once more headed down the path. They had gone only a few steps when Heather suddenly stopped, not knowing quite why.

Case tried to pull her on, but she knelt down again beside him, trying to hush his excited jabbering and trying to keep him from wrenching away from her.

"Be quiet, listen, dear," she cautioned him anxiously. "I think I heard a horse. Horsie!" she told him, hoping the word would make him quiet down and pay attention.

She put a finger to her lips, motioning for him not to say anything, then strained her ears, listening for the sound that had caused her to freeze on the spot only seconds earlier. She was certain she had heard the low nicker of a horse close by, and Cole and Eli had taken all the horses with them so they could bring back supplies.

She listened intently, cocking her head from side to side, but the only sounds were the echo of her own heartbeat and the wind as it whistled through the branches of the trees that edged the stream, scattering leaves across the ground and whirling them into the thick underbrush. A large outcropping of boulders was nestled in the middle of the underbrush, which would have been a solid mass of green if it were summer, but was now a tangle of dark branches and dried leaves, with a few twisted, scrubby pines vying with the boulders for space.

It was the only place anyone could be where she wouldn't be able to see him, yet it seemed illogical that anyone else would be around, unless . . .

Suddenly she remembered why Cole and Eli had gone to Belle Pointe, and she felt the hair at the nape of her neck prickle, her stomach tightening as fear settled into every nerve in her body. She swallowed hard, pulling Case closer against her, and stood up, holding him in her arms.

"Down!" He protested, beginning to squirm, but she held him all the tighter.

"No, Case, stop," she half-whispered. "Shhh . . . we can't go see the fish, not now. First we have to go get Mose."

Case stopped wriggling and stared at her, his big green eyes shining. "Mose?" he mimicked.

She nodded, trying to smile in spite of the way her legs were trembling. "Yes, Mose," she told him breathlessly, and turned to retrace her steps on the path, then once more froze. Not ten feet away, directly in the middle of the path behind her, stood the man Cole had pointed out to them in New Orleans, Rafe Turner.

Heather's mouth flew open, but nothing came out. It was dry, her throat constricting, and tears began to well up in her eyes. Clutching Case even harder in her arms, she turned, hoping to make a break toward the stream, where she might have a chance to get away, but the noise of crashing underbrush told her she was too late, and the tears that had only been rimming her eyes suddenly coursed down her cheeks as Carl Palmer stepped onto the path in front of her.

Instinctively knowing something was wrong, Case began whimpering. Heather tried to soothe him, but was shaking so badly all she could do was murmur, "Shhh . . . shhh . . ." while she cringed at the sight of the man standing in her way.

"Well, we meet again, Heather," Carl said abruptly, his eyes shining intently. He took a deep breath. "I knew I'd catch up with you."

Heather swallowed hard, finally finding her voice. "Wh-what do you want?"

"You don't know?" He laughed. "Come, my dear. You and I had talked over my plans enough times to know what I had in mind, and now that my annulment has been granted, there's nothing standing in our way."

"You're crazy!" she cried. "I'm married to Cole."

Again he laughed, but the laughter was strained. "I'll try to pretend I didn't hear that," he said curtly. "Now, if you'll kindly follow me . . ."

"I'll die first!"

"Rafe!" Carl nodded toward Rafe as Heather crashed into the brush, holding Case close against her, hoping to get away, but Rafe had moved up behind her while Carl was talking, and as Heather stepped off the path, his arm shot out, covering her mouth, strangling the cry that had begun to pierce the air, and his other hand gripped her arm, his fingers sinking into her flesh where the fur robe had slipped, and he held her firmly.

Heather tried to hang on to Case, but he began slipping as she fought to free herself from Rafe, and in seconds Harry Ferguson, who had been leading their horses out from behind the boulder, handed the reins to Carl and grabbed the baby as he hit the ground, trying to keep him from crying.

"Shhh . . ." he kept cautioning as he glanced back toward the cabin. "Be a good boy, don't cry, see?" and Harry reached in his pocket, pulling out a pocket watch that immediately caught the toddler's eye.

Heather was still struggling with Rafe, who pulled her hard against him. "You want your brat to stay healthy?" he asked viciously.

Heather stiffened as she stared down at Case, who was now engrossed in trying to chew Harry Ferguson's watch.

"That's better," he said, then looked at Carl.

"Get her on the horse," Carl said quickly as he led the horses toward them.

Heather started to struggle again, but Carl grabbed her hair, forcing her to look into his eyes. "I don't want to hurt you, Heather," he said angrily, "but I have no sympathies when it comes to your brat. Either you come willingly or your son will suffer the consequences, understand?"

Heather's eyes darkened as she stared at him, the sounds of Case's enthusiasm over Ferguson's watch the only sound that could be heard. Rafe's hand was still over her mouth, almost covering her nostrils, and she had to force the air out to keep breathing.

Carl's fingers tightened slightly in her hair. "Do you understand?" he asked again.

Unable to nod, she mumbled beneath Rafe's palm.

"Let go her mouth," he told Rafe, but cautioned, "easy . . ."

Rafe removed his hand slowly.

Heather took a deep breath, glad to be free of his hand, but his fingers were still dug into her arm, and Carl still held her hair.

"You understand?" he asked once more, his voice deadly serious.

"Yes," she gasped hesitantly. "I understand."

"Good." He let go of her hair and Rafe dragged her to the horse, lifting her into the saddle.

"What about the kid?" asked Harry as he took the watch from Case, making him cry again.

Carl glanced at Heather, then to the baby and back to Heather again. "Bring him," he ordered. "He's our insurance that she'll behave herself."

Harry picked Case up, ignoring his yelling, but a few yards back on the path, someone else was unable to ignore Case's cries.

Tildie was on her stomach in the tall, dry prairie grass, resting on her elbows, holding her head up enough so she could see. She had finished what she'd been doing and decided to join Heather and Case, and had approached just in time to see Rafe step onto the path behind Heather.

Her first instinct was to attack and help her mistress, but in the next moment she saw Carl, then Harry, and the preacher, Jeremy Litchfield, who was now joining the others, and she knew there was no way she could possibly fight off four men. So she had ducked off the path into the high grass and weeds, hoping to think of something.

She stayed low in the grass and watched Harry climb into the saddle with Case in his arms, his crying ceasing as he felt the horse beneath him. Then she watched Carl mount behind Heather, saying something to her that Tildie was certain was a warning, and as she watched, they reined their horses, starting to move off.

She wanted to run back and get Mose, but there wasn't time. Even if she took time to go hunt him up, without horses they'd never be able to track Heather's kidnappers. Her decision was made in a split second, and as the riders continued on the path that led to the stream, Tildie left her spot in the grass and began to follow slowly, yet as close as she could without being seen.

They were moving at a snail's pace, because of the terrain, Heather supposed. The hills surrounding Cole's valley were rocky, the footing unsteady, and Carl was smart enough not to want to end up with a crippled horse just when things were going his way.

Heather's heart was heavy, a dull ache settling in her breastbone, tears still clinging to her lashes, and she felt sick. The fur was still about her shoulders, but Carl's arm was about her waist and the feel of it made her tremble with loathing. If only she had stayed closer to the cabin, but it was too late now. Cole was miles away and she had no hope of being rescued. Bessie and the rest wouldn't even know what had happened to her and Case.

She tried to move her position so she could get a glimpse of Case on the horse behind her with Harry Ferguson, but Carl's words of warning settled her back down again, so she didn't see a few minutes later when Rafe cut off the trail they were following and fell back, hiding behind some boulders.

Tildie had been doing the best she could to keep out of sight, but occasionally they'd cross an area where there was nothing to hide behind and she'd have to crouch, scooting on her stomach sometimes to keep up and not be seen. She'd been following for over half an hour now, and with so many hills to climb, her legs were getting tired. Once she had lost sight of them for a few minutes and panicked; then they had emerged from a stand of trees ahead, so she moved on.

She had no idea what good she could do by following like this. It was getting colder as they moved higher into the hills, and the wool jacket she was wearing over her buckskins wasn't any too warm. It was one of the things Bessie had salvaged from the wreck of the *Bonnie Belle* and was the first thing Tildie had grabbed going out the cabin door. She pulled the collar up to keep the brisk wind off her neck, wishing she'd taken time to go to the room she shared with the baby and get the fur jacket Mose had made for her. The thought of Mose brought a sudden warmth flooding through her that defied the thin woolen jacket. She knew he'd taken notice of her while they were still on the *Bonnie Belle*, but it wasn't until the journey to Arkansas Post, then on upriver, that he'd let his feelings be known. Now she wished to God he was with her to tell her what to do.

She was huddled behind a tree, waiting, giving the horses up ahead time to disappear around some huge boulders before moving on. Although it wasn't raining, the sky was overcast and at times the trail ahead became shadowy, so she had to squint to see, especially where the trees were thickest. Peeking around the tree, she watched as the last horse disappeared around the boulder; then she waited a few minutes longer before gingerly stepping out onto the trail. She resumed following them, unaware that up ahead Rafe Turner had fallen back to hide behind the boulder, where he was waiting for her.

Rafe huddled, dark eyes alert. He'd ground-reined his horse, keeping it behind him so the black girl wouldn't see it; then he crouched, flattening himself hard against the rock.

Tildie was moving fast now, trying to make sure they wouldn't get too far ahead while they were out of sight. She was moving through the woods at a run, keeping the boulder in sight; then, as she rounded it, trying to check her forward speed so she wouldn't suddenly burst into the open, she tripped over Rafe, knocking into him with such force they almost hit the ground. Rafe grunted, cursing, then quickly pulled himself together and grabbed her, even though she was already screaming. He leaned close to her ear.

"Shut the caterwauling," he demanded through clenched teeth, and Tildie, realizing she'd never wrench herself free, inhaled, holding the scream in her lungs until her ragged breathing became more regular.

"That's better," he said, then straightened, keeping her arm twisted behind her back. He dragged her to the horse. "Get on," he ordered.

She stared over her shoulder at him, her eyes overly large in her dark face. "How's I gonna do that?" she argued, staring at the saddle of the horse, its stirrup way out of reach.

Rafe swore again, released her arm, lifted her into the saddle, then climbed on behind. He dug his horse in the ribs, reining the gelding in the same direction where his companions were still moving forward at a steady pace, and they followed.

Heather had heard Tildie's cries. At first Carl refused to let her see what was going on, but as Rafe approached, he suddenly reined to a halt, waiting for him.

"You were right," Rafe said as he reached them and reined in close. "Now"—he glanced quickly at the black woman sitting in front of him, then back to Carl—"what do we do with her?"

Carl stared at Tildie. "She must have been following us since we left the valley," he said, then hesitated, thinking for a minute. "But since she's alone," he finally went on, "it's reasonable to assume she didn't warn any of the others."

"If she did . . . ?"

"They'd be with her. No," he assured Rafe, "she's evidently by herself."

"Like I said," Rafe retorted, "do we kill her and leave her here or take her with us?"

Carl glanced at the sky. "Leave her here, and before nightfall the buzzards would warn the others back in the valley which way we went. Besides," he said, "I didn't plan on killing anyone. I told you that. No." His eyes narrowed shrewdly. "But they'll miss all three before long, so for now we'll take her with us. She can help Harry with the brat. Now, come on, I want to get as far from here as we can before dark, and that only gives us a few hours."

Rafe nodded, and Heather saw the fear in Tildie's eyes. She wished she could talk to her and reassure her, but it would do no good, because she was as frightened as Tildie. Instead, as the men reined their horses back onto the faint trail they were following, a lump lodged in Heather's throat and tears once more rolled down her cheeks. And while Case, unaware that he wasn't just taking a long horsie ride, laughed and giggled unconcernedly, they moved off again, putting more and more distance between them and the small cabin nestled in Cole's valley.

Dark shadows had already settled in among the trees by the time Carl finally decided to call the procession to a halt for the night. They had been traveling steadily and were a good four or five miles from the valley already. The place he picked was by a small stream, with huge trees all around and high cliffs only a short distance away shielding them from the sharp winds that had intensified since nightfall.

Heather cringed as Carl reached up to take her from the saddle. "I can get down by myself," she said, brushing his hands aside.

His eyes darkened. "Your son's crying already, Heather. Do you want me to have Harry give him a reason?" he asked.

She glanced a few feet away to where Harry Ferguson was trying to quiet Case. The baby had become disillusioned with his horsie ride about an hour earlier, and now he was tired, hungry, and sobbing. A band tightened about Heather's heart at the sight of his tear-streaked face. She wanted to ignore Carl's warning, but in the hopes that he might let her hold her son and quiet him, when he once more reached up to help her down, she let him.

Instead, as Heather's feet touched the ground, Carl called to Rafe to let the black girl see if she could get him to stop, while Carl took Heather's arm and ushered her toward a small clearing next to the stream.

"We'll make a fire here," he said, taking in the flat lay of the ground. "Sit down."

She glanced quickly toward where Tildie was trying to soothe Case. Darkness made it hard to see, but she could vaguely make out the young girl's silhouette and hear her voice as she cooed to him.

"I said, sit down," insisted Carl, knowing she was concerned about the baby, and anger at her concern hardening his feelings toward the child.

Heather drew her eyes back to Carl's shadowed face; then she slumped to the ground, pulling the fur closer about her. She didn't know whether the trembling inside was from cold or fear, but whatever, she was shivering clear through. Her eyes narrowed with hatred as she watched Carl and the other men setting up camp; then after a while she closed her eyes, trying to hold in her anger, fear, and frustration.

Suddenly she felt a movement beside her, and her eyes flew open again.

"Tildie," she gasped breathlessly, then fell against her, hugging Tildie and the baby both at the same time.

"Shhh, Miss Heather," cautioned Tildie, half-whispering. "If you fusses too much, they may not let me sit here."

Heather gulped back tears and inhaled quietly as she straightened a little and nuzzled her son, letting the baby bury his face in her hair.

"How are we going to take care of him, Tildie?" Heather asked as she pulled Case closer against her. "We don't have any changes for him, and no food."

"I'll think of somethin', Miss Heather," Tildie answered, keeping her voice low. "They's bound to have some biscuits with them, and I was thinkin', if you's got a petticoat on, maybe we could tear it up for diapers. He's awful wet and needs changin'."

Heather took a deep breath, handed Case back into Tildie's arms, then, her hands shaking, boosted herself into a crouch, reached up under her black dress, and pulled her petticoat down, stepping out of it, her legs still weak and shaky. She handed it to Tildie, took Case back from the black girl, and watched as Tildie ripped and tore the petticoat into squares large enough to use.

Tildie managed to get three diapers from the full petticoat, but before she was through, she made a handkerchief out of the scraps and handed it to Heather as she took the baby from her again to change him.

Heather was staring at the handkerchief, fighting the despair inside her, when Carl approached. The fire was going now, bringing light into the dark shadows, and she could see his face clearly as she looked up from the small square of white cloth in her hands. A frown creased her forehead, and she shuddered.

She had expected anger perhaps, or the same hard sharpness that had often masked her dead husband's face in those few months before his death, but Carl's face was completely transformed. The anger that had been in his eyes only a short time before when he'd lifted her from the horse was replaced by an intense warmth that seemed to sear her flesh as he stared at her.

He knelt down. "You look lovely in the firelight," he said softly, then reached out, touching her hair. "I'm sorry it has to be this way, Heather," he explained, his voice deep with emotion. "But you must have known I couldn't let you go."

She bit her lip, holding back tears, but didn't answer.

His finger fondled a curl, and the lines around his mouth softened as he spoke. "You do understand, don't you, my dear?" he went on. "And now, if you'll come, I'd like you to meet someone." He stood up and reached down for her to take his hand.

"I don't want to go with you," she said, but he shook his head.

"Heather, don't antagonize." He tensed momentarily, then took a deep breath, pulling himself together. "Now, take my hand and don't argue," he said. "Unless you don't really care as much for your son as you'd like me to believe."

Heather glanced toward Case, who by now was hugging Tildie while he whimpered. He was so tired he could hardly keep his eyes open.

"He's hungry and tired," Heather said as she let Carl pull her to her feet.

He smiled, pleased. "That's better," he said, then glanced over toward the fire. "I'll have Harry bring something so your girl can feed him." He began ushering her across the clearing to the fire. "Come."

Heather moved hesitantly, wishing she could have stayed by her son and Tildie, yet knowing it could be dangerous for all of them if she didn't go along with Carl.

Her face was flushed by the time they reached the fire, her stomach tightening into a twisted knot. She listened to Carl tell Harry to take food over to the baby; then he introduced Rafe.

"This is my bethrothed, Rafe," he said proudly. "My brother's widow, Heather Palmer. Heather, Rafe Turner."

Heather mumbled a timid greeting while Rafe said a quick hello, then left to tend to the horses.

"And I believe you'll remember the reverend," Carl said as he turned toward Jeremy Litchfield. "At first I was skeptical about bringing Jeremy along, but now I can see where he's going to come in quite handy."

Heather was startled as she stared at the minister, watching his fanatically alert eyes study her as he greeted her. Then Jeremy addressed Carl.

"You want the ceremony tonight?" he asked him.

Carl nodded. "Might as well." He tried to put an arm about Heather's waist. "After all, I've been waiting a long time to claim what's rightfully mine."

"Yours?" cried Heather, pulling away from him. "What ceremony are you talking about?"

"Our wedding, my dear," he answered. "Surely you knew my intentions were honorable."

"I can't marry you," she said. "I'm already married."

"Nonsense. First cousins can't marry." He grabbed her wrist, pretending it was an affectionate gesture, but his fingers held her like the jaws of a vise. "The reverend's right," he whispered. "Tonight would be a perfect night for a wedding."

"No!" She struggled against his grip, trying to pull away. "Let go of me!"

"Heather, please," he begged. "I don't want to hurt you."

"You're crazy," she yelled. "I'm having his baby!"

"You're what?" Carl's face was livid.

Her eyes were wild, frightened. "I'm having a baby," she repeated slowly. "Cole's baby."

He stared at her, eyes dancing dangerously, then reached out with his free hand and ripped the fur robe from her shoulders. His eyes dropped to the bulge at her thickened waistline. What a fool! He'd held her while they rode, and been so intoxicated by her nearness he hadn't noticed. "When?" he asked between clenched teeth.

She inhaled breathlessly. "The end of July, first part of August, I'm not sure."

"Bastard!" he cried, twisting her arm painfully. "Why'd you let him touch you?"

"He's my husband!"

"He's a son of a bitch! You were mine . . . always mine."

"Never!"

"She'll be yours again, Palmer," Jeremy cut in. "All it takes is a few words."

"Words?" he asked bitterly. "You think words will heal things?" He was still holding her wrist, forcing her to face him so he stared into her eyes. "You don't understand, Reverend," he hissed. "The ceremony's off now."

"Off?"

"That's right, off. I'll be damned if I'll marry her now and have another of Dante's bastards born to carry the Palmer name. No!" He straightened, forcing her to straighten with him, his eyes still glued to hers. "There'll be no ceremony tonight, Reverend," he said. "That'll have to wait until after the brat's born. But I'll have her, you can bet on that. I've waited a long time to make her mine. I may not be able to give her my name yet, but by God she'll be mine tonight in everything but name."

"No!" cried the reverend, realizing what Carl meant. His eyes were shining. "I'll not be a party to that," he said firmly. "I came with you to help free this poor woman from a life of sin. I won't tolerate you committin' further sin with her. There'll be no fornication as long as I'm with this party."

"Don't be ridiculous, old man." Carl laughed arrogantly. "You can't stop me from doing what I've a mind to."

"Oh, yes I can," countered Jeremy, and Heather held her breath as she heard the unmistakable click of a pistol hammer being pulled back. "Now, Mr. Palmer, in the name of God, take your hands off the lady," Jeremy demanded.

Carl's eyes narrowed viciously as he faced the barrel of the reverend's pistol. He studied it for a full minute; then his voice was steady as he spoke. "The Bible says, 'Thou shalt not kill,' Reverend," he reminded him.

Jeremy's eyes twinkled shrewdly. "The Bible also says that fornication's a sin—even Moses killed the idolaters." He shook his head. "No, Mr. Palmer, I came to stop the sinnin', not to be a part of it, condonin' it. If you want to marry this woman, I'll be glad to perform the ceremony, but until she's your wife, you ain't gonna be beddin' her."

"You're crazy," said Carl, but Jeremy shook his head.

"No, Mr. Palmer, I'm not crazy," he answered firmly. "I'm only statin' the way it is. Like I said, I'll be glad to marry the two of you, if you've a mind, but you'll have to kill me before I'll let you lie with her without her bein' your wife. Now, let the lady go before I decide the good Lord wants me to pull this trigger."

Carl cursed, throwing Heather's arm from him as if it were tainted. "The devil take you," he muttered angrily, then straightened, smoothing his hair back with both hands, pulling himself together as Rafe joined them again.

"What the hell's going on?" asked Rafe as Jeremy lowered his pistol just enough to let Carl relax.

"He was going to rape me, and the reverend stopped him," answered Heather breathlessly as she rubbed her wrist, where bruises were already darkening the skin.

Rafe sneered. "The hell you say." He looked at Carl. "You let him put a gun on you?"

Carl exhaled. "I told you before, Rafe, I don't believe in murder. Nor do I believe in rape, Heather," he said, addressing her. "I've never raped a woman in my life."

"Well, you'd have had to rape me," she answered furiously. "Because I'd never let you touch me willingly."

Carl laughed, his voice taunting. "Don't say never, my dear," he said, his hazel eyes intense. "None of us knows what the future holds, but for now, perhaps the reverend's right . . . I want our life together to be perfect, and to take you now would mean holding your son's safety over your head in order to make you cooperate. I'd rather wait until you realize the futility of fighting what we both know is inevitable. I've waited this long. I can wait awhile longer." His eyes moved once more to her waistline. "Go ahead, have your cousin's baby. The child can be easily disposed of. Then and only then will you become my wife, and by that time we'll be back at Palmerston Grove, where nothing will be able to separate us again, and the next child you conceive, my dear, shall be mine."

Heather trembled at the finality in Carl's words. He believed everything he was saying. The man was insane. She swallowed, as her head came up defiantly. "You'll never get away with this," she began. "Cole will find me."

Again he laughed, softly, ominously. "Cole won't even know you're gone, not for days yet," he said. "If I'm not mistaken, he and his friend were headed back toward the Arkansas when they left, am I right? That means they won't be back for days." He glanced up at the dark sky, sniffing the air. "There's rain in the air, my dear. Rain. Do you know what that means? It means our tracks will be washed away and not even your backwoods cousin can follow tracks that aren't there. No, my dear, by the time your precious cousin arrives back from his sojourn, we'll be long gone, and he'll never know where to look, or why."

"I hate you!" she cried furiously, her eyes glistening with tears. "Why didn't you leave me alone?"

"You know the answer to that," he said, looking calmer than she knew he was. "I made myself a promise when DeWitt died that someday you'd belong to me, and I intend to keep that promise. Now"—he inhaled, pleased with himself—"since the reverend has been kind enough to show me the error of my ways and helped me to keep from making a fool of myself, I suggest you let me offer you something to eat." He turned to the man beside him. "Rafe, will you pour the lady a tin of coffee, it'll help warm her up. And see she has some biscuits when they're finished." He held out his arm. "Shall we?" he asked, as if he were merely asking to escort her onto a dance floor.

Heather stared at him curiously. She had always felt there was something strange about Carl, even when she'd been married to DeWitt and had no reason to fear him. His behavior now only served to confirm her feelings. Carl was insane. Not the same kind of insanity his wife had suffered from. No. His was a diabolically clever insanity. One that brooked no opposition and warped the mind into believing that things existed only because he allowed them to exist, ignoring reality until it conformed to his wishes.

"I can walk back by myself," she said hesitantly.

He smiled, a warm smile that made her uneasy. "If you wish," he said, lowering his arm. "I'll send Rafe over with your food when it's ready. In the meantime, enjoy the evening and get some rest. We have a long day ahead of us tomorrow."

Heather stared at him curiously for a few seconds, then bent down, retrieving the fur robe from where it had dropped when he'd yanked it from her. She wrapped it about herself again, trying to find some comfort in its warmth. There was none. Instead a cold dread filled her, and without saying a word, knuckles white where she gripped the fur, praying for strength, she walked back toward where Tildie sat cradling Case in her arms.

For tonight it was over, but what of tomorrow? What if Carl decided to ignore the reverend's threats? As she glanced up toward the dark sky, praying God would watch over her until this nightmare was over, she felt the first few drops of rain that had been threatening all day, and her heart numbed. Carl was right: how could Cole possibly find them, when there'd be no trail to follow?

Once more the tears began.

10

Cole was pleased with the way things had gone at Belle Pointe. As he and Eli headed home, leading the two extra horses along the narrow trail through the hills toward his valley, he thought back with pleasure over the past few days. The fort was coming along beautifully. Major Bradford and his men had already erected a hospital, everything was under control, and the walls were taking shape. Most important, no one had seen anything of Carl Palmer, nor had Rafe Turner been spotted again anywhere near Belle Pointe.

On top of all this, not only had he managed to talk Major Bradford out of a supply of soap, but one of the men from Bradford's quartermaster outfit was heading back to Belle Fontaine with a dispatch ordering more supplies for the fort, and the major let him carry money and an order back with him to have someone send out a couple crates of chickens, a cow, a gaggle of geese, a few sheep, and household supplies Cole wasn't able to get from Bradford, as well as seeds for a garden. It was all supposed to arrive in time for spring planting.

With Mose to help, and Bessie and Helene, Heather would be feeling better in no time. There'd be eggs for her, fresh milk for Case, and they'd dig a root cellar in the hill out back. He had even ordered ticking for mattresses. All they had to do now was find something to stuff inside.

He breathed deeply, fresh air filling his lungs. The world was on his side for a change, and suddenly he could hardly wait to see Heather again and hold her in his arms. Lord, how he missed her.

"Don't worry, we'll be there in about half an hour," called Eli from behind him.

Cole turned in the saddle, glancing back as he rode along. "How did you know what I was thinking?"

Eli grinned. "When you ignore everything around you and stare off into space like that, there's usually only one thing on your mind."

"You're too observant."

"I'm your friend."

"I wish there was a way to warn her we were coming home today," Cole yelled back, frowning. "It almost seems cruel to just show up like this."

"She'll love it. Only, if you don't watch where you're going, we won't get home."

Cole turned quickly, reining his piebald mare to the right to keep her from stepping off the edge of a steep incline. He moved her ahead to where the hill had more of a slope to it. The trail widened here, and Eli dug his horse in the ribs, urging the other horse behind him until he caught up with Cole.

"What do you think about the report Bradford got from Belle Fontaine?" asked Eli as they moved easily down the slope.

"You mean about Brooks?"

"Seems a shame." Eli frowned. "When Major Long took off south, I was afraid he might be pushin' his luck a bit, especially with what happened at Clermont. And since they were riding Osage horses . . . The Quapaw and Osage never have gotten along, but I was hoping the uniforms might discourage them from trying anything."

"Did Bradford say how Long and his men got separated?"

Eli shook his head. "Only that they'd been scattered and everyone was accounted for except Ian Brooks. His horse came in with an empty saddle. The report said they searched the area for almost two days before giving up on him."

"Too bad," Cole said thoughtfully. "I didn't always see eye to eye with the man, but I wouldn't wish something like this on him, either."

"Maybe it was quick."

"Maybe," answered Cole. "If not, I'd hate to have been in his shoes. The poor devil didn't even know the language. He was more at home with tribes farther north." He sighed. "Don't say anything to the others, Eli," he cautioned as he began to see more and more familiar landmarks. "I don't want to scare Heather. She's skittish enough about being so isolated."

"Don't worry, I won't." Eli smiled as he saw a lone figure waiting near the edge of the corral some distance ahead on the floor of the valley. "Looks like we've been spotted." he said, his smile broadening, and both men waved a greeting.

Mose had been watching for them every day. One minute praying they'd hurry back, the next wishing he didn't have to face them when they did. He'd gone over the words again and again, trying to think of an easy way to tell them. There was none. Tears threatened, and he gulped them down. Cole, Heather, all of them—they were the first people ever to treat him like somethin' other than a workhorse. He owed them for the freedom of this valley. For the chance to be somethin' besides a steamboat hand. And now he owed Cole for Heather, the baby, and Tildie, and there was no way he could repay that debt. The thought of Tildie, not knowing where she was or whether she was even alive or dead, brought an empty feeling to his insides. She was such a little thing, so cute and laughin' all the time.

Furtively wiping tears from his eyes, and swallowing hard, he raised an arm and waved back, then waited for them to reach him.

Cole was whistling softly as he headed his mount toward the corral; then suddenly he slowed, holding a hand out, cautioning Eli.

"Wait. Something's wrong," he said quickly.

Eli reined up, staring at Mose. The sun was behind Mose, silhouetting him, and they couldn't see his face from this distance, only the way he was standing, the nervous way his hands kept returning to his pockets, his broad shoulders twitching and flexing.

"Indians?" Eli asked.

"No. Not Indians." Cole frowned. "If it was Indians, Mose wouldn't be alive." He glanced toward the cabin. It was quiet, yet nothing seemed amiss. Slowly he nudged his horse forward, Eli close beside him, but as he reached a point where they could see the black man's face, instinctivily Cole knew his first premonition had been right.

Slipping from the saddle in one fluid motion, he hurried forward, then stopped abruptly, staring at Mose.

"What is it?" he asked anxiously. "What's the matter?"

Mose tried to find the right words. "I didn't know," he mumbled. "I tried to track 'em, but it got dark, then the rain. If I'd knowed, I'd never let 'em outa my sight. You trusted me . . . I didn't mean to let you down—"

Cole grabbed Mose. "What the hell are you talking about?"

"Miss Heather, the baby, Tildie . . ."

"What about them?"

Mose took a deep breath, trying to pull himself together. "They's gone," he panted breathlessly. "The missus go for a walk with the boy, and Tildie tell Bessie she gon' go meet 'em, but they never come back. When I tried to find 'em, all I find is horse tracks." He took a nervous breath. "I tried to follow like you showed me with the deer, but it got too dark and I didn't have no torch. By mornin' there weren't no tracks left 'cause of the rain that started right after dark. It wasn't my fault!''

Cole's knees trembled, the happiness he'd felt moments ago replaced by a dread, weighing him down, numbing everything but his sense of loss.

"They couldn't!" he cried furiously. "Why? How?"

Eli grabbed Cole's arm. "That's why Palmer wasn't at Belle Pointe." Eli too was staring at Mose. "How long ago, Mose?" he asked.

Mose frowned. "You was gone three days."

"That means they have at least a week's head start." Eli turned to Cole. He was still in shock. "Cole?"

"No," Cole was saying softly to himself. Then his voice rose in volume. "No! No! No!" His hand covered his face and he choked, unable to hold back the tears. "Damn! This can't be!"

Eli's hand tightened on Cole's arm. "We'll find them, Cole." His eyes hardened. "Don't worry, we'll find them," but the next few days turned up nothing.

Cole was like a man possessed. The warm laughter was gone from his eyes, turning them to the deep murky green of troubled waters, and the smile, so often tilting his mouth, vanished, leaving behind a hard grim line. There was no laughter, no peace in him. After hearing the tragic news from Mose, and dredging from deep inside that one agonized outcry, he had straightened stiffly, led the extra horses to the cabin, where he greeted Bessie and Helene, told them to take care of the supplies he'd brought, then, without saying a word, mounted his little piebald mare and headed into the hills.

"Follow him," urged Bessie.

Eli shook his head. "He needs some time alone."

Two days later he was back at the cabin. During those two days while Eli too searched the hills, he spotted Cole now and then, yet never approached. They were both searching, not only for some sign that would show where Heather and Case had been taken, but Cole was searching for the strength he knew had to be his to see him through what lay ahead.

When Cole finally rode in on the second day, Eli knew he was ready and the two of them headed south, the direction Mose said the tracks had taken. However, there was no trail to follow. The land was wild, untamed, with a few Indians scattered here and there, but none could help. No one had seen any white men, although one small hunting party reported finding shod tracks the day before near a river they'd crossed. By the time Eli and Cole found the river, rain had once more washed away the sign, and there was nowhere they could turn. It was like looking for a will-o'-the-wisp. There were rumors, most of them unreliable, and as the days lengthened, so did Cole's anger and determination, and he vowed never to rest until he found Heather and Case again, even if it meant following Carl Palmer all the way back to Port Royal.

Meanwhile deep in the wilderness, the small party on horseback continued on their course toward the Red River. Carl's patience was wearing thin. Bringing Heather's son along had been the worst mistake they could have made. The baby was irritable, obnoxious, and thoroughly spoiled, screaming at the top of his lungs when not given his own way. And his nursemaid wasn't much better. Her whimpering and sniffling got on his nerves, as did her off-key singing when she was trying to quiet the brat at night. Oh, how he longed to stuff something in her mouth to keep her quiet. Only, if he did that, the baby'd start up again, and he didn't know which was worse, her singing or his squalling.

Not to be outdone, the reverend always made sure his prayers were said each night, and although he didn't seem to see any wrong in kidnapping Heather away from Cole, he still maintained that fornication was a sin and never let Carl, or Rafe for that matter, forget he'd tolerate no sinning while he was along.

And on top of everything else, Carl had to listen every night to Rafe complaining because he wouldn't just kill the reverend and to hell with his preaching.

"How many times do I have to tell you, Rafe," Carl was saying again as they rode along side by side, "I won't be a party to cold-blooded murder?"

Rafe cursed. "Jesus Christ, I suppose you believe all this about hellfire and brimstone he's preachin'."

"I believe in God, if that's what you mean," Carl retorted.

"Ha!" Rafe sneered. "If you really believed in God, you wouldn't be stealin' another man's wife."

Heather was still riding on the horse with Carl, his arm still holding her against him, and his cheek touched the back of her hair. "According to God's laws, first cousins aren't allowed to marry, so there is no marriage. Like the reverend says, I'm saving her from a life of sin. I've done nothing wrong." He glanced over toward Rafe. "But to kill the reverend for no reason except to justify my own desires . . . What sort of gentleman do you think I am?"

Rafe shook his head. "A stupid one. We could be rid of him, the brat, and that sniveling nigger."

"You'll do things my way, Rafe. Understand?" Carl cautioned him. "My way or there'll be no money when we reach New Orleans."

Rafe's eyes blazed angrily. "Have it your way," he said, sighing. "But I think she's right," and he nodded toward Heather, who'd been stoic through their whole conversation. "You're crazy," and he nudged his horse forward, taking his place behind Harry, who was still being nursemaid to Case and breaking trail at the head of the procession.

Carl's eyes bored into Rafe's back. Strange how you could hate a man, yet be dependent on him at the same time. And he did hate Rafe. The man was crude and animalistic, and Carl wished there had been another way, but there hadn't. Ah, well, one couldn't always choose one's friends. Sometimes necessity dictated the situation. Like now. He was still staring at Rafe's back when Harry held his hand up, warning those behind him to stop.

Carl reined his horse up past Rafe to where Harry sat astride, his bewhiskered face steady on the trail ahead of them, eyes squinting narrowly.

"What is it?" he asked.

Harry motioned forward. "Watch."

They were on a slight knoll, and as Carl's eyes settled to where the trail wound down the slope ahead, shadows began to move in and out among the trees, horsemen heading uphill, directly toward them.

"Indians?" he asked.

Harry nodded.

They had been traveling for a week already and had managed to stay clear of Indians until now. There was no way they could avoid the braves heading their way this time.

"Look like Comanche," Harry offered quickly.

Carl frowned. "You sure?"

"Hell no, I ain't sure. Won't be until they get up close, but from the looks of them I'd guess I'm right."

Carl felt Heather tense against him as the first Indian came into full view and reined his mount to a halt, staring at them.

"Comanche, all right," Harry said, and motioned for Rafe to come take the baby from him so he could palaver.

Tildie was riding with the reverend now. When Jeremy had discovered that Rafe was letting his hands wander to the wrong places while he and Tildie rode along, the result was a thorough scolding on the evils of a lustful heart, and the loss of the young black girl's companionship, much to Tildie's relief. She had never cared much for the reverend during their long trek to Arkansas Post, but would rather put up with his constant preaching than Rafe's pawing.

Rafe took Case from Harry, trying to quiet the baby as the Comanche slowly moved forward again and Harry waited. Finally the Indian in the lead stopped his mount, straightening boldly, his companions tense, alert.

Harry lifted his hand and made a wavy motion like a snake, then looked at the Comanche as if waiting for an answer. The Comanche nodded, his hands moving quickly in return.

For a few minutes their hands moved, first one, then the other. Finally Harry's hands stopped and he turned to Carl. "They want our horses," he said.

Carl felt a chill run through him as he glanced behind the lead Indian. They were outnumbered by three. His eyes met Harry's. "What do we do?"

"We don't give 'em the horses 'lessen we have to. I've got a notion." He began talking to the Indian again in sign language.

Heather watched both men closely, then frowned as the Indian quit talking with his hands long enough to study Tildie, Case, then herself, his eyes sifting over her appreciatively.

Once more his hands motioned, and this time he definitely pointed to her.

She held her breath while Harry said something in return; then Harry again addressed Carl.

"They'll take the black girl, the boy, and our rifles," he said, trying to keep his voice steady.

"Our rifles?" Carl's jaw clenched angrily. "We can't be out here unarmed."

"If we don't give them the rifles, we won't be out here at all," answered Harry. "As it is, I talked them out of the lady here. Told them she was evil medicine. That she's crazy in the head. Said we were takin' her back to the white man's city so she could be locked up and wouldn't cast no more evil spells."

"They believed you?"

"Let's say they do so far, so don't let her open her mouth."

Heather stared at him, his words suddenly sinking in, and a cold sick sensation spread through her. "Case?" she muttered, voice breaking. "God, no, Harry. Not my baby!" she cried.

"Shut 'er up!" ordered Harry.

Carl's hand tightened on her waist. "Shut up, Heather," he warned, but she struggled against him.

"Not Case! You can't!" Tears flooded her eyes. "I won't let you." Her elbows caught Carl in the stomach, and he exhaled, grunting, trying to quiet her while the Indians stared curiously.

"Do it!" Carl told Harry as he struggled with her. "Dammit, give them the girl and the brat before they get to thinkin' she isn't as crazy as you said."

Harry motioned for the reverend and Rafe to bring Tildie and Case forward.

Tildie cringed against the preacher, grabbing his jacket. "Don't let 'em take me, please, Mistuh Rev'rend," she pleaded. "I don't wanna go with no Injuns."

Jeremy's horse was moving forward, and he stopped by Harry. "There's no other way?" he asked.

Harry's eyes darkened. "Not if you expect to keep your hair."

Jeremy hesitated for a minute, then dismounted, dragged the whimpering black girl from his saddle, and shoved her toward the Indians.

Heather stopped struggling with Carl and stared horrified as the leader said something to one of the Comanche; then she watched as he rode forward, lifted a kicking, screaming Tildie to his horse, slapped her quickly, grunting at her, she assumed telling her to shut up, then returned to his position behind his leader with Tildie sitting in front of him, sniffling.

"Now the boy," said Harry, and Heather felt the tears gush, a sob wrenching from deep inside her, as Rafe rode forward with Case, who was staring at the Indian curiously, not aware of what was happening.

"Case, no!" Heather screamed again.

This time Carl's arm tightened so hard about her waist that the pain was almost unbearable. She didn't care. They were giving away her son, her life, the only part of Cole she had left. "God, help me!" she sobbed. "Please . . . not my son . . . not my baby . . ."

Rafe ignored her pleas as the leader of the Comanche reached out, taking the squirming baby from him, and handed him to one of his braves. Case had been kicking, but as the Indian brave settled back on his horse, the baby, sensing something wrong, looked at Heather and reached out his hands.

"Mommy . . . mommy . . ." he began to whimper.

Heather's heart tightened in her chest and she groaned miserably.

Tildie could barely see through her own tears, and her hands trembled as she watched the pain in Heather's tear-filled eyes. Was there nothing she could do?

"Don't worry, Miss Heather," she sobbed, voice breaking. "I'll watch after him. Don't you worry none."

Heather felt the salty tears in her mouth. "Tildie, no . . . don't let them . . . Oh, God . . . not this."

By now Harry was handing four rifles over to the leader of the Indians, who smiled, pleased as he looked them over, ignoring the cries that were still racking Heather.

When the Indian seemed satisfied nothing had been held back, he made sign with his hands to Harry, then reined his horse forward, riding between the four horses, and as Carl reined his horse about, the last Heather saw of Case was his little head bobbing along as he peeked around the brave whose horse he was on and tried to call to her, his small voice soon fading in the distance.

Heather couldn't breathe for a brief moment, her breath caught by the lump in her throat and the numbness that was settling into every nerve in her body, dazing her.

He was gone. Just like that, her son was gone, and Tildie too. She stared, transfixed. Her eyes never saw the trees or bushes where the Indians had disappeared, nor did they see the blue sky overhead filled with mammoth white clouds, nor did she feel the warm breeze that was caressing her wet cheeks, or the hot sun that had come from behind the clouds to turn her hair to fiery flame. All she saw was the face of her tiny son, pleading to stay with her, his green eyes misty with gathering tears.

"Let's get out of here," said Harry, and Carl nodded, reining his horse to the south again, following as Harry led the way. They must have ridden for almost a mile when Harry finally pulled up.

"Damn savages," he spat venomously, as he took a deep breath. "I was afraid they'd find this," and he pulled a pistol from the waistband at the back of his pants. He looked at Rafe. "You still got yours?"

Rafe nodded.

"Good." Harry glanced about. "I don't trust them Comanche," he went on. "First place, they're too far north. That means they been up to no good. Probably raiding the Osage and Quapaw, or having a go at the Caddo." He shook his head. "From here on we'd better move slow and keep our eyes peeled. Them Comanche'd been in a fight, that's for sure. Them was fresh scalps decorated their coup belts. That means there's other Injuns out there lookin' for blood." He glanced at Heather, still on the horse with Carl. "I see she quit her caterwaulin'," he said. "Fact is, she looks like she ain't even with us."

Carl tensed. "What the hell are you talking about?"

"Her," Harry said, studying Heather's face. "You sure she's all right?"

Carl released Heather's waist, reaching up, trying to turn her head so he could look into her face. Ferguson was right. Heather's eyes were lifeless, face pale, her breathing shallow.

She felt Carl's fingers on her chin, as if in a dream, and when he spoke, his voice was far away. All she could see in front of her were Case's green eyes pleading with her, and the only sound that penetrated the numbness that filled her was Tildie's voice promising she'd take care of him, while Case's tiny voice called her name. Over and over the sights and sounds of their parting echoed in her ears, blotting out everything else around her.

Carl swore. "Damn!"

"Don't worry, she'll pull out of it," said Rafe. "She's upset because we got rid of the kid, that's all."

Carl looked at Harry. "What will the Indians do with them?" he asked.

Harry shrugged. "Probably keep the girl as a slave and raise the boy Comanche. Or maybe sell both to the Spanish."

"They won't kill them, will they?"

"I doubt it." Harry glanced back to Jeremy, who was mumbling something to himself. "What's the matter with you?" he asked.

Jeremy shook his head. "We shouldn't of done it," he said nervously. "Those Indians are heathen. It wasn't right to give that young woman and the boy to heathen."

"And just what were we gonna do with them, Reverend?" Rafe asked. "Listen to that kid cry all the way to the Red River? Ask

Harry about that. He was the one had to put up with him snivelin' and wettin' all over him.''

"Amen," Harry cut in. "I smell like a slop jar." He took a quick look at Carl. "Besides, the good Mr. Palmer here wasn't any too fond of the brat. The Injuns just made it easier for him, that's all. He was gonna get rid of him anyway."

"Well, I don't like it."

Harry sneered. "It ain't what you like, Reverend. It's what saves our scalps." He glanced around quickly. "Now, let's put as much distance between us and them Comanche as we can before nightfall," and he spurred his horse forward, waving for them to follow.

By the time they reined up for the night, Carl was really worried. There hadn't been a sound from Heather all the rest of the afternoon, and when they stopped to make camp, she moved like someone in a daze as he lifted her from the saddle. He walked her to a nearby tree and helped her sit down, then reached up, brushing the hair from her forehead. The sunburn across her nose was peeling and her eyes were bloodshot; still she stared, unresponsive.

He touched her face, his palm resting on her cheek, the tips of his fingers tingling as a shudder went through him.

"Heather?" he asked softly. "Heather, can you hear me?"

She was silent, motionless.

"Please, Heather," he whispered softly. "Don't let this happen to me again." He let go of her cheek and waved his hand in front of her eyes. She didn't flinch. He watched her closely for a moment, then stood up, staring down at her, his face somber as Rafe walked over.

"Don't tell me she hasn't come out of it yet," he said. "What are you going to do?"

"I don't know. She's just staring, as if she doesn't see a thing."

"Harry said when he told those Indians she was crazy, he didn't think she'd really end up that way. Indians won't kill anyone who's crazy, did you know that? Their legend says if they kill a person who's possessed, the evil spirit comes out of that body and takes over theirs. Ain't that weird? Just as if a crazy person could—"

"Shut up!" yelled Carl, then rubbed his forehead wearily. "She's not crazy. She's just upset. You said so yourself. She's not crazy!"

Rafe glanced at Palmer. He sure was touchy. Then he remembered that Carl Palmer's first wife was insane. No wonder he was concerned. "Forget it," he said, shrugging. "I'll tell Harry to start huntin' for firewood," and he walked off, looking back over his shoulder at Carl Palmer, who was still standing staring down at Heather.

Carl knelt down again and tried to talk to her, but it still did no good, and finally, giving up, he stood up and walked to the fire, praying that she wouldn't end up like Charity. He couldn't stand that. She'd be all right. She had to be.

The next morning, Heather felt the sun on her face again, yet it meant nothing, just another day. Another day without Cole. Another day of riding, riding, riding. Another day with Carl's voice in her ear, Case's crying, Tildie's whimpering, and Rafe's vulgar remarks. No, that wasn't right, because Case wouldn't be there, nor would Tildie. It'd be just another day of torture and pain killing her from within. She swallowed, forcing the lump in her throat to give way. Her breathing was ragged yet strong as she rested against the tree while the others ate breakfast. She didn't want to eat. Food meant nothing to her anymore. Slowly, as the sun warmed her again after the chilling night, she began to remember more, and the pain was unbearable.

She closed her eyes, trying to wipe the memory of her son's eyes from her thoughts; then suddenly, as she held her breath, praying for release from the horror of losing Case, an eerie, bloodcurdling shriek pierced the early dawn, exorcising the pain swiftly like a wound being cauterized.

Her eyes flew open just in time to see Harry sprawl forward into the fire, his head smashed by a tomahawk, while Rafe fought, trying to keep from ending up beside him. There were Indians everywhere, grabbing at the horses, scattering the men. A shot rang out and she realized Carl had managed to reach the pistol Harry had dropped. An Indian went down. Another took his place. Carl threw the useless pistol into the Indian's face, then screamed, taking a tomahawk between the shoulder blades as another Indian pounced on him from behind.

Heather watched in horror as Carl hit the ground, the Indian jerking his tomahawk from Carl's back, grabbing the thatch of red-gold hair atop Carl's head, wielding the tomahawk again as a last cry froze on Carl's lips.

She wanted to yell, but no sound came out, only a choked cry that died when it hit the air. She could hear the reverend somewhere near the horses, shrieking and praying in the same breath; then even that suddenly stopped and all that was left were grunts, groans, and panting as Rafe still grappled with the Indian who'd tried to kill him.

Rafe's foot snaked around the Indian's leg, and he pushed, trying to topple him, but the warrior was too fleet-footed. Dancing out from the tangle of Rafe's legs, the Indian, having lost his tomahawk, slipped his knife from its sheath, and as Rafe tried to keep from losing his own footing, the knife slid between his ribs. Rafe went to his knees, face contorted in pain, eyes glazed. Then, as he started to topple facedown in the dirt, the Indian snatched the floppy old hat from Rafe's head, tossed it aside, and reached for the thatch of hair that should be there but wasn't.

Heather stared transfixed at the startled look on the Indian's face as his hand slipped across Rafe's bald pate, and suddenly the whole thing looked so ridiculous. Amid all the blood and commotion, the warrior's bewildered expression was so hilariously funny that Heather started to laugh. Her laughter was a low chuckle at first, softly vibrating through the clearing, then becoming more uncontrolled and hysterical as the full impact of the absurdity of the scene registered. It was so foolish, the way he was staring down at Rafe's dark-fringed bald spot, eyes like saucers, mouth open.

Ordinarily Heather would have been screaming and cringing from fear, but the shock of the past few days, and the trauma of trying to accept her son's fate, was more than she could bear, and that one moment of hilarity, so obviously out of place, was just too much. Her laughter rose, bubbling hysterically, until she was so convulsed all the Indians suddenly stopped, staring at her.

The leader of the small band of Cherokee stepped over the lifeless body of the man with no hair and frowned at the vision before him. They had seen the woman before attacking, and had watched her as she sat silently beneath the tree, knees drawn up to her chin, gazing at nothing in particular. The men around the campfire had been ignoring her; now suddenly he began to understand why. He motioned for his comrades to stand back, then slowly moved toward her, studying her intently.

Heather knew the Indian was closing in on her, but could care less. Her world was so torn apart already that nothing he did could make her feel any worse. In fact, death would take away the pain that seemed to be driving her hysteria on, and the effect, as the Indian looked first this way, then that, cocking his head, eyes squinting curiously as he closed in on her, only made her remember all the more how ridiculous he had looked only moments before, and the laughter convulsed her even worse. She tried unsuccessfully to stop, only nothing helped, and instead she shook all over, tears streaming down her face.

The Indian scowled, hesitating, not sure whether to get any closer to this madwoman or not, then stopped abruptly as one of his companions suddenly joined him, grabbing his arm. The other Indian said something to his leader, but the guttural sounds were lost in Heather's hysterical, high-pitched laughter. The leader of the Indians stood silently for a moment as if reflecting on what had been said; then, without warning, he straightened, giving Heather one last curious look before turning to the others and shouting. Within minutes everything salvageable was confiscated, and the warriors mounted, some riding double, and with the same eerie cries that had filled the forest at the start of their attack, they rode off, their war cries fading in the distance, leaving only the peal of Heather's laughter vibrating through the trees in their wake.

It was some minutes before Heather realized they were gone. The laughter was choking her, and she was gasping to catch her breath, to make her ribs stop hurting. It was ridiculous, so absolutely ridiculous.

Suddenly she took a deep breath, and with it came a light-headed feeling that brought her up short, making her hold the air in her lungs. She tensed, eyes blinking, washing away the tears that had blurred them, then looked around. The forest was silent, not even her shallow breathing to break the spell.

Then, slowly, once more the forest came to life as a small bird, perched on a limb in the tree overhead, began to sing.

Heather listened to the incongruously cheerful song of the little warbler as she stared in awe at what lay before her. As abruptly as she had closed the world out earlier, it suddenly came back to her in all its reality, and this time the reality was even more frightening than it had been before. They were dead, all dead. Carl, the reverend, Rafe, Harry. She exhaled with an agonized sob as her eyes fell on what was left of Carl's red-gold hair, then felt her stomach churn at the sight of the flames from the campfire roasting the side of Harry's bewhiskered face, a chew of tobacco still bulging his cheek.

Averting her eyes quickly, she leaned forward, looking at the dirt and grass at her side. She wouldn't look back, she couldn't, not again. It was too horrible even to imagine, and she gulped, trying to keep the nausea that was sweeping over her under control. She didn't want to think, yet knew she had to. She couldn't just sit here for the rest of her life staring at the ground.

Slowly, trembling all over, she forced herself to stand up, using the tree she'd been leaning against for support, and tried to breathe normally, trying to rationalize what to do next. What could she do? The Indians had taken everything. The horses, food, any blankets or bedding that had been lying around. She was still wrapped in the fur robe and pulled it tight around her, then straightened, feeling the soft breeze on her face.

The weather was warmer since they'd been moving south, and at least she wouldn't have to worry about freezing. What was she thinking? She glanced about curiously, purposely avoiding direct contact with the mutilated bodies of her four kidnappers, and began to weigh her alternatives.

She could stay here and watch scavengers converge on what was left of the men, taking a chance on the Indians coming back, or she could try to make it back home on her own. Home! Suddenly the valley seemed so dear to her. Tears threatened again, but she wiped them away, gazing up at the sky. Now, if she could just remember everything Cole had taught her those long-ago days back at Tonnerre. She concentrated hard. The sun would have been on her face if she hadn't been beneath the trees. That meant north was to her left. They'd been traveling south, so all she had to do now was go north. Good! Now she was using her head. Trying to get home was better than just standing here.

She made one more attempt to look around, but couldn't, and with a deep sigh she turned, so the sun was to her right, clenched her jaw in determination, and headed north, into the woods.

11

Rafe had no idea how long he'd been lying beside the campfire, but it must have been a long time. The ashes were barely warm, and it was close to sundown. His stomach was on fire and he knew he'd lost a great deal of blood.

Gingerly he raised himself up and looked around the clearing, but his eyes weren't any to steady. All he could see was blood and bodies. It was sickening. He turned away quickly. They were dead, all dead. He was the only one left alive. The horses were gone—that was easy to determine—and so were all their supplies.

Managing to get onto his knees, he grabbed a handkerchief from his pocket, shoved it against the hole in his stomach left by the Indian's knife, and tried to stop the bleeding. It didn't do much good, but it was the only thing he had. With a strength brought on by sheer determination, he managed to reach his feet, then lurched away from the fire, moving off toward the direction they'd all ridden the day before. There was no use staying here. Already scavengers were beginning to congregate, and he wasn't about to let them finish what the Indians started.

He winced, stopping to lean against a sapling, then swore softly as he stumbled forward again, almost falling amid the leaves and underbrush.

An hour and a half went by and he realized he was still moving. He wasn't on the trail anymore, and his legs had given way long before, but there was still life in him. He dragged himself along, feeling every bump of uneven ground, brushing aside sticks and stones that hindered his progress.

Then suddenly, when he felt the last shred of strength deserting him, the sound of someone moving close by brought new fear to him. He hesitated, holding his breath, his head pressed against the ground.

"Well, well, what have we got here?" said a low gravelly voice.

Rafe's eyes were only half-open, but it was enough. The man looking at him was grizzled, and dressed in dirty buckskins, his eyes dark, shining.

"Looks like you ain't gonna get much farther on your own fella," he said as he knelt down, staring at Rafe, who couldn't even muster enough strength to talk.

The old trapper gazed about, studying his surroundings, then shrugged. "Don't know where you come from, nor where you think you was goin'," he said wearily. "But one thing's for sure, you ain't gonna get no place in that condition, not all by yourself."

He straightened, whistled softly, and was joined by a roan horse with the rope from a shaggy old mule tied to its saddle horn, and with an ease brought about by years of conditioning, the old trapper easily lifted Rafe's half-conscious body, hefting him onto the mule; then the trapper mounted his horse and headed off toward his cabin on the Poteau River.

The sun was high in the sky. Heather had been walking for hours. It wouldn't have been so bad if she'd had a trail to follow, but Carl, Rafe, and the others hadn't been following a regular trail since the day before when they'd encountered the Comanche, so all she could do was try to keep to the places where there was less underbrush, where it was easier moving. She tried not to think where Case and Tildie might be, and forced them from her mind as she came to a steep hill and stood, looking up. There had to be a way around, or at least a better place to climb.

Glancing down at her feet, she realized how fortunate she'd been to be wearing moccasins with her dress the day they'd kidnapped her. She'd become so used to wearing them that anymore she hated to wear the fancy stiff shoes that society demanded be worn with dresses. Now it was a godsend. Fancy shoes would have hindered her and made walking impossible, especially now.

She moved forward, skirting the bottom of the hill. It was getting warmer as the day wore on, and the fur robe slipped from her shoulders, resting in the crook of her arm. She held it against her as she stepped over branches, rocks, and stubble that covered the ground; then suddenly she stopped. Up ahead, the hill leveled off more, and the ground was less rocky.

Making her way to the place she had chosen for climbing, she began moving up the hill, using an occasional tree for support. It was hot work, and a few times she slipped, going to her knees, but that didn't stop her. Nothing would. She was too determined, and by the time she reached the top, she was panting heavily, the muscles in her legs tired and wobbly.

No wonder. A person needed food to keep going, and she hadn't eaten since sometime the day before. She straightened, looking back down the hill. It was longer and steeper than she'd thought, and an endless sea of trees stretched out beyond it. Sighing, she turned back to the problems at hand. Somewhere, she had to find something to eat.

Her stomach grumbled, and for the first time since the Indian attack she remembered the baby. She pressed her hand on the small swelling at the waistline of her dress. Suddenly the thought that she might not live to have this new little one made her tremble. She glanced about. No, that wouldn't happen, she wouldn't let it. She was going to survive. She stood still, studying everything around her.

If it had been late summer or fall, there might be greens, or possibly wild fruit and berries, but it was late January. Nothing ripened in January. She studied the trees intently, trying to think of something, then frowned. Pecan trees left pecan nuts, and there was a cluster of them off to the left.

Eagerly she hurried to them and began to kick aside the brush, then stooped, finding some nuts the squirrels had overlooked. Fine, she had the nuts; now, what to do with them? She gathered more, using the skirt of her dress like a basket, until she had a whole skirtful, then made her way back to the edge of the hill where she'd seen some rocks, and piled nuts up beside them. Throwing the fur robe down, she searched the ground, coming up with a large enough rock to use, and for the next hour she cracked pecans and filled her stomach with nut meats until one more taste would have made her sick.

So far, so good. She wiped her mouth, then sat back on her heels and sighed. There were still nuts left over, and more under the trees. She needed those nuts, needed them desperately, because there was every chance she might not find any food later.

Standing up, she grabbed the fur robe, went back to the pecan trees, and began to fill it. When it was finally full, she added the nuts she had left over to what she had gathered, tied the ends together, hefted it onto her back, then took her directions once more from the sun before moving on.

The hours passed slowly as she plodded along. At first she was optimistic, happy with the nuts she'd found, and glad to be free from her kidnappers, but as the day wore on, the magnitude of what lay ahead began to overwhelm her.

She came to a small stream, put down her fur bundle, and knelt beside it, scooping the cold water up in her hands, quenching her thirst. She splashed the perspiration from her face, letting the cold water soothe it where small gnats had bitten her, then wiped the water off with the skirt of her black dress and pushed some stray strands of crimson hair out of her eyes as she stared off across the stream. She, Carl, the reverend, Rafe, and Harry had been traveling more than a week. That was such a long way. So many miles, and they had all been on horses. It was insanity to think she could make it back so far all alone and on foot. She had never even spent one night in the woods by herself, let alone trying to cope with everything else. She watched where the sun was lowering toward the treetops in the west. Nightfall had been the farthest thing from her mind as she'd trudged along, but now, suddenly, it loomed before her like a dark abyss. What was she going to do when it got dark?

A frown creased her sunburned forehead as she tried to think back to how Cole had showed her you could build a fire with the right rocks—rocks called flint. They worked on the same principle as the flints used back home to light the lamps. All she had to do was find some. But where?

She took one more long, cool drink, then stood up, hefting the fur bundle back to her shoulder, and moved on, crossing the stream, holding the hem of her dress up as best she could with one hand so it didn't get too wet. Her moccasins squished as she stepped out the other side, and she lifted her feet one at a time, shaking out the excess water. This done, she continued on her way.

All the rest of the afternoon as she made her way north, she searched every rock, every cliff, looking for flint. There was none, nor did she find any more food. Finally, as shadows began to filter in among the trees, bringing with them the ominous promise of darkness, she knew she had to do something. Wild animals roamed the woods. Earlier she had been able to keep downwind of a bear so he wouldn't find her, and about an hour ago she'd seen the tracks of a big cat.

If only she hadn't been so squeamish and had taken time to search the bodies back at the camp before leaving, she might have found a weapon the Indians overlooked. Something—a knife, a hatchet—anything would be better than no weapon at all.

She stopped suddenly and looked around. Up ahead was another cliff, only she wouldn't have to scale it. It was on the east, and the valley ran through it straight north. But the cliff was high, and a thought began to take shape as she stared at it. Halfway up, the earth had begun to slide away from the rest of the hill, but didn't make it all the way to the valley floor. Instead, a grassy ledge stretched about ten or fifteen feet from the floor of the valley, and it was only about eight or nine feet long. Just right for one person. However, getting there was another matter.

She studied the situation for a long time, once more trying to think how Cole would act, what he would do. The answer came quickly. Hurrying to the bottom of the cliff, she searched the ground until she found a fairly flat rock, then picked it up and began digging steps into the side of the cliff, scooping out dirt as fast as she could. It was getting darker by the minute, and she worked fast, hoping it wasn't all in vain.

It wasn't. Her idea worked. She stopped just long enough to prepare everything for when she reached her newfound perch, then went at her digging with new vigor. A short time later, her fingernails caked with dirt, her teeth gritty from the powdery earth falling back into her face, she gouged out the last couple of footholds, working steadily as she clung to the side of the cliff to keep from falling, then, minutes later, slid onto the grassy ledge, and gazed back down to the floor of the valley below.

Earlier in the day, she had ripped the very bottom part of her dress skirt off, torn it into strips and braided it into a rope so she could haul her cache of pecans up one of the steep hills she'd had to scale. Now she had tied the cloth rope about her wrist so she'd have it with her, and as she sat up, she hauled the fur bundle of pecans up so it too rested on the ledge. Good. She was high enough where bears, wolves, and other animals couldn't reach her, and defending such a small plot of ground would be easy if she had to.

She sat up, leaning back against the gritty dirt of the cliff, and stared at the sky as the first star began to shimmer in the vast midnight blue. Sighing, she wondered: was it worth it? What if all this was in vain? What if tonight was only a reprieve and she died tomorrow anyway? She mustn't think of that, she couldn't think of that. Tears threatened, and this time she let them come. Who was to see her? Who was to complain? The only thing was, now her nose began to run. She wiped it on her sleeve, then quit feeling sorry for herself and remembered she had to eat to keep up her strength. Opening the fur bundle, she took out her two rocks and began cracking pecans.

Heather woke to the sun in her face and a cold chill on her legs where the skirt of her dress no longer reached. Her drawers came only to her knees, leaving the rest of her legs bare, and it was disconcerting. Starting to stretch, she suddenly remembered where she was and moved more cautiously. The night had gone well. A few times she'd heard rustling below her, but nothing had tried to invade her little plot of ground and she'd fallen back to sleep quickly. Now she was wide-awake, stomach grumbling again for food.

She stared down at the few pecans left. It was enough for a small breakfast, but that was all. She was going to have to find more, or something else to keep her alive. She cracked the last few nuts, savoring them slowly, then gathered everything together and left her perch on the side of the cliff, wrapping the empty fur about her shoulders again and fastening the rope at her waistline.

It was colder today, and as she walked, she wished she hadn't had to rip off the bottom part of her skirt. Her legs were bare below the knees, and besides the cold, gnats kept at them, as well as scratchy branches and briars. By the time the sun was directly overhead, she knew she was in real trouble. There had been no new pecan trees, nor had she found any flint, and her stomach was already protesting the lack of food.

By late afternoon she began to limp. Her feet were sore from so much walking, and she knew she was going to have to rest them. She half-ran, half-limped down an incline, then skirted a small hill, avoiding a briar patch, her deep violet eyes searching the terrain. Arriving once more at a small stream, she sat down, took off her moccasins, and put her feet in the water. It felt so good, she didn't realize the numbing effect of the cold water until she pulled them back out and tried to wiggle her toes.

Drying her feet with what was left of her dress skirt, she put the moccasins back on, then stood up, looking around. That's when she saw the slope with layers of rock cascading down it. It was about a hundred yards west, but she headed for it anyway, hoping and praying all the way.

She was right. The dark color, the way it lay in shelves—it was flint. Now her only problem was to find enough pieces to strike together. It didn't take long, and she even had extra pieces in case something happened to the first two. She held all four pieces in her hand, then scratched her head, trying to figure out how she was going to carry them. This was ridiculous. Once more a piece was salvaged from her dress skirt on the left side and she wrapped the flintstone inside, tying the corners, then fastened the small packet about her waist with the braided rope. This done, she started out again, keeping her eyes peeled for anything that might be edible.

Sometime later, as the setting sun streaked the horizon, turning it to a golden pink, she discovered she was not only tired but also so hungry she had pains in her stomach, and she still hadn't found anything to eat. She picked a spot for the night and sat down, first administering to her sore feet. After rubbing them and trying to soothe the ache in them, she gathered kindling, dried leaves, and feathery dried weeds and sat down to start a fire.

On the fourth try, a tiny spark suddenly flew from the flint, landing in the center of one of the leaves, and she began to blow slowly, easily, her face so close to the ground she could smell the musty odor of the earth. It took just enough wind, yet not too much to fuel the tiny spark, making it spread, she remembered Cole saying, and she nursed it along carefully, watching anxiously as it took hold.

Within minutes she was piling more kindling onto a flaming fire, proud of her accomplishment and a little more optimistic than she had been earlier, at least about keeping animals away. But what of people? What if Indians were in the area? Well, she'd have to take that chance. As the shadows lengthened, the temperature dropping, bringing with it a crisp chill, she found a large stick and set it beside her to use as a club, just in case, then curled up as close to the fire as she could and tried to sleep.

It wasn't that easy. It hadn't been too bad the night before, perched on her narrow ledge where nothing could reach her, but down here she heard every sound, every rustle, and on top of that, her stomach was cramping from lack of food. She lay awake for a long time, her fingers around the club.

All day she had tried to avoid thinking of the predicament she was in. She had no one except herself to rely on. No one to furnish her with food, no one to protect her. Now, as she lay on the cold ground, letting the heat from the fire try to warm her, there was no way she could erase the doubts from her mind. She was alone, so terribly alone, and tonight, in spite of the fire, she was scared to death.

She ought to give up. If she just stayed here on the ground and let the fire go out, death would no doubt be quick. She was so tired and hungry, and it all seemed so useless. Cole had told her bears were known to kill with just one blow. Maybe it wouldn't hurt too much. But what if wolves found her? Being ripped to pieces by a pack of starving wolves wasn't a very pleasant thought. Her fingers tightened on the club as a rustling noise broke the stillness. She held her breath. Oh, God, if only Cole were here, she could face anything.

The rustling stopped, and she exhaled, relaxing again. Maybe if she tried harder, she could sleep. Her fingers eased on the club and she shut her eyes. She was so tired, so very tired. She had put enough wood on the fire to last the night, and now its warmth began to penetrate as she grew more and more drowsy, and the last thing she remembered before sleep overtook her was the image of Cole's face before her, telling her, as he had on those long treks through the woods at Tonnerre, to pay attention to what he was saying because it might come in handy someday.

It was late the next morning when Heather finally stirred, and even then she might not have awakened if a raccoon hadn't spotted her and crept out of the woods to investigate. She was lying on her stomach, soft moss beneath her, resting her head on her arm. The fire was only smoldering ashes and the sun high. Heather was exhausted, and even the raccoon's sniffing at first didn't register. She'd been dreaming about Cole, dreaming that he was making love to her and kissing her on the cheek and neck, so it was with mixed feelings that she began to waken.

At first the raccoon's warm breath against her skin was part of her dream; then suddenly reality flooded in as she opened her eyes

"Ahhh!" she yelled, scrambling for the club nearby, but it wasn't needed.

At the first scream, the frightened raccoon bolted for the woods, as frightened of her as she had been of him. Heather stared after him, panting breathlessly. Thank God it had been a raccoon and not a bear or wolf. Her heart pounded frantically, then settled down to a steady rhythm as she pushed the hair back from her face and lifted her eyes to the sun, trying to guess how late it might be. She gazed at the fire, almost burned out. Time to move on. If only she had something to eat.

She stretched, standing up, and tucked the fur robe tighter about her, then kicked dirt into the last of the ashes, putting the fire out. No use adding more wood; she had nothing to cook. She studied her surroundings. There were bushes, half-dried plants here and there, but absolutely nothing that could be cooked or even eaten raw. She sighed. If this had been South Carolina, she might find poke greens or any number of plants this time of year, but here, even though the weather wasn't that cold, she had no idea what was safe to eat and what wasn't. So many of the plants were new to her, and even those were dried up.

She swallowed back the nausea that occasionally swept over her and tried to think of something, then suddenly smiled, walking over to the edge of the small clearing she was in. Why hadn't she thought of this before? It wasn't much, and there was no water to brew it, but if Bessie could make dried-clover tea for them to drink, why couldn't she eat dried clover? She bent down, grabbing a handful of the clover, and stared at it. It looked terribly uninviting. She shrugged. If it would keep her alive, what did it matter what it looked like?

Closing her eyes, she shoved a handful into her mouth and began to chew. It had a strange flavor, similar to the tea Bessie had made, but stronger. She chewed slowly, accustoming herself to the taste so she wouldn't be as likely to gag when she tried to swallow, then forced it down and reached for another handful. There was a huge patch of clover here, and she gorged on it until she couldn't stand the thought of another mouthful. Now, if she only had some water.

She wiped her hands on what was left of her skirt, then stood staring at the rest of the clover, trying to figure out a way to take some with her. She didn't dare rip any more from her skirt; it was already in tatters. She studied her sleeve. It just might work. Slipping off the fur, she reached up and grabbed at the shoulder seam of her dress, pulling and tugging until she'd ripped the left sleeve free, then took it off her arm. Now what?

She stared at the sleeve, studying it intently. First she fastened the buttons that started near the wrist and ended just where the elbow would be. This done, she knew she'd need one more strip from her skirt. She tucked the sleeve under her arm and bent down, tearing a thin ribbon from the bottom of her skirt, then took the sleeve, tying the ribbon around one end, making a pouch out of it, into which she began to stuff more of the dried clover, until it was full, leaving just enough room to tie the other end. This she fastened onto the rope braid at her waist. It wasn't much, but it was food, and if she couldn't find any more, it would suffice for a while.

Now, to move on. Once more she took her directions from the sun and headed north.

For almost a week she plodded on, fighting her way through thick underbrush, taking advantage when she'd discover an open meadow or part of a trail, living on anything she could find. There were more dried clover blooms, dried mint leaves, acorns. The acorns made her sick, and for a while she thought her bowels would never stop. They finally did, but not until she found an old gourd, hollowed it out, filled it with water, then set it in the sun to brew, making a tea, using dried raspberry leaves and bayberry bark.

The soreness on her feet was turning into calluses, and the muscles of her legs, weak when she first started, had strengthened, until now they carried her up and down hills with little trouble. There were still days when she didn't know whether she could go on or not, yet something kept driving her. Use your head, Cole had always told her. Never panic. Well, she hadn't, and she was still alive. Yet there were so many miles to go. If only she had a horse.

The next afternoon she added something new to her diet. Some type of small crayfish or crab, some snails, and a couple of frogs. They weren't much, but roasted over a hot fire, they gave her a change from dried leaves and the few nuts she could gather. The worst part was going without water between streams and creeks. She had nothing to carry water in, so was forced to wait until a new source could be found, and at times her throat became so dry she felt as if she'd swallow her tongue.

The days wore on, and still she kept going—exhausted at times, sick when some of the leaves or nuts disagreed with her, and wearier with each passing day. Yet something inside wouldn't let her give up, although there were times when it would have been easy to just jump off a cliff or use the rope braid she'd made to end it quickly instead of prolonging it like this.

It was almost two weeks after her sojourn started that the biggest obstacle of all confronted her and she finally felt defeated. She had heard the river before seeing it, and now stood on its bank, gazing across to the other side, which was perhaps two hundred feet across. There was no way on earth she could swim it, because the current was too strong, and there was no other way to cross.

Dejected, she sat down cross-legged and stared at it, the heart pulled right from her. Was this what she'd traveled so far for, to be stopped by a river? It was close to noon, and she reached into her bag of dried clover, mint, and what-have-you, as she'd begun to refer to it, shoving a handful of the mixture into her mouth. At least she'd have water to wash it down. The bank of the river was high, and she tied her braided rope to her hollowed-out gourd, dropping it over the bank to get a drink. The water was cold and clear, as it should be, since there'd been no rain since she had been on her own.

She glanced at the sky. It didn't look like dry weather was

going to last much longer, however, because already dark clouds were tumbling about, and thunder rumbled in the distance.

She continued to sit, sipping from the gourd and contemplating, then once more remembered Cole's words. Most rivers and streams, besides running north to south, were never the same in any one long stretch, and if one followed a river far enough toward its source, one was bound to find a place to ford it. She gazed upriver, then sighed. It was better than sitting here doing nothing.

Once more she started out, this time following the river, moving more carefully along its bank than she had through the underbrush, because the farther she went, the more she became aware of small footpaths converging on it, and she didn't want to run into any more Indians or wild animals she'd be unable to handle.

Occasionally she startled a few deer, and once almost stepped on a snake, but she didn't stay around long enough to find out whether or not it was poisonous. Mostly, however, the trails along the river were deserted.

As the storm clouds gathered, the temperature dropping again to a cold chill, her tanned legs again began to feel the cold and she tried to move faster, hoping to keep warm.

Suddenly she stopped, cocking her head to one side. Something, a strange noise, seemed to be coming from behind her. She tensed, listening intently, then realized what she was hearing were voices. Quickly she turned, darting away from the river, leaping over the underbrush, trying to find a place to hide.

Suddenly, as she started by a huge tree, heading toward what looked like some tall grass where she could find cover, she was grabbed about the mouth and waist at the same time and thrown to the ground, where whoever held her shoved her against some clumps of dried brush and grasses, holding her down.

"Shhh," a voice cautioned in her ear, and although she wanted to scream and kick, something in the intense manner of her captor made her hesitate, and as he held her down, keeping his own head pressed against hers, she heard the excited jabbering of a number of Indians as they moved on foot, searching the riverbank.

Her heart was pounding, tears rimming her eyes, and she was so scared she could hardly breathe. For what seemed like an eternity, she lay on the ground, crushing the weeds and prairie grass, listening to the roar of the river mingling with the voices of the Indians. Then they began to fade, until all that was left was the sound of the river.

Slowly her captor's hand began to ease on her mouth, and once more he cautioned her.

"Now, when I let loose, don't scream, don't fight, or by God we'll have those Cherokee back down here searching again," he whispered. "Do you understand?"

Heather nodded hurriedly. If there was anything she didn't want, it was for the Indians to come back.

Her captor released her mouth, then moved away from her and sat up, waiting to see just whom he had helped from being caught.

Heather took a deep breath, filling her lungs, then slowly turned. Her face went pale beneath the sunburn, for staring straight at her was a blond-haired, bearded soldier, his uniform dirty and ragged.

"Captain?" she gasped unsteadily. "Captain Brooks?"

Ian scowled, staring into a pair of violet eyes he'd thought he would never see again. "Heather?" he asked hesitantly.

"My God, it is you," she blurted, and he shook his head, bewildered.

"How? What in hell are you doing here . . . and like this?" he asked, gesturing to her disheveled appearance. Her hair was unkempt, clothes filthy, and her fair skin was tanned where the blisters had dried, while some was still peeling.

She flushed beneath the deep tan, tears filling her eyes. "I don't believe it," she whispered incredulously. "I'm dreaming or something."

He glanced down at his own rough appearance. "No, I'm really here," he answered. "But what happened? Where's Cole?"

"Back at the valley." A tear ran down her cheek. "Carl kidnapped me, and Tildie and Case. Said he was taking me back to Port Royal."

"Who's Carl?"

"I'll explain later." She tried to smile through the tears. "All I know is I've never been so glad to see anyone in all my life." She sniffed, wiping her nose on her sleeve. "I've been all alone and scared half to death."

"How long have you been alone?"

"Over a week. The Indians killed Carl and the others. I guess they thought I was crazy or something, but they didn't touch me." She sniffed again, wiping the tears away, smearing her

ace. "I couldn't just stay there, so I decided to try to get
iome."

He was awed. His eyes took in her tanned legs, bare beneath
ier drawers. She had lost weight, but there was a strength about
ier, a sinewy, catlike grace. Her face was still as excitingly
ovely, in spite of the peeling and the dirt, but it no longer held
he softness and vulnerability that had been there the last time
ie'd seen her.

"But you . . ." she went on, realizing he was staring at her
:uriously. "What are you doing here?"

"Trying to stay out of the way of the Cherokee," he answered.
'Our expedition had a skirmish with them . . . let's see, it must
>e almost two weeks or more now, and I got separated from the
>thers. Lost my horse, and I've been dodging Indians ever since,
rying to make my way back to Belle Pointe."

"You mean they know you're out here?" she asked.

He nodded. "That's why I'm so far from the Poteau River,
vhere we were first hit. They had me once, but I got away." He
;azed about, making sure the Indians weren't coming back.
'But look, why don't we get away from here? It's getting close
o nightfall, and it sounds like there's a storm on the way. We'll
ind a place to hole up, then see if we can find a way to get
icross the river come morning. And in the meantime, you can
ell me everything that's happened, and I'll do likewise."

She stared at him hungrily. A human being. She was going to
iave someone to talk to. No more listening for night sounds and
umping at every shadow. And as she let him pull her to her feet,
eading her back toward the riverbank, watching the trail ahead
:arefully, eyes alert for any alien sounds, she prayed, thanking
;od for letting her run into Captain Ian Brooks.

12

Cole was anxious, yet he was tired and weary. For the second
:ime in his life the wilderness held no appeal for him. The last
time had been when he'd had to leave Heather back in Port
Royal because there was a price on his head, but at least then he
knew where she was. Now, as he rode along searching the

countryside, he not only had no idea where she might be but also
had no hint as to whether she was alive or dead.

His only hope was that the rumor he'd heard earlier back at
Fort Smith was true. Word had reached the fort that there was a
trapper on the Poteau River who'd found an injured man who fit
the description of Rafe Turner. The man was purported to be on
his deathbed, so time was of the essence. Cole and Eli had been
traveling fast since leaving Fort Smith, and now as they rounded
a bend in the river, sighting the old cabin they'd been looking
for, Cole sighed.

"I hope he's still alive, Eli," he said as they neared the place.
"And I hope it's Rafe."

"If it isn't?"

"Then we keep searching. Someone has to have seen her
somewhere." He reined up as a voice broke the afternoon
stillness.

"Hold to, gents." Morticae Beamer was a hard man, and he
was unsmiling as he stepped away from the cabin door.

Cole answered hurriedly. "Heard you got a sick man," he
said. "Thought maybe I might know him."

The old man studied Cole for a minute, then glanced at Eli.
"Seems I should know you," he said, squinting.

"If you're Mort Beamer, you should," answered Eli. "Last
time I saw you was nigh on six or seven years ago. Seems you
was workin' for the British then."

Mort nodded. "The money was good." His jaw tightened.
"No hard feelins'?"

"No hard feelins'." Eli nodded toward Cole. "Like my friend
says. We might know the gent you're nursin'."

Mort Beamer screwed his face thoughtfully. "Go ahead, but
won't do you much good. Be lucky if he lasts till sundown."

They dismounted, ground-reining their horses, and the old
trapper held the door open for them.

The cabin was dingy inside, and dim.

"You got a light?" Eli asked.

Mort snorted irritably but walked over to an old whale-oil
lamp, lit it, then carried it back to Eli. He motioned with his
head toward a corner near the fireplace. "He's over there," he
offered, and Eli held the lamp up, lighting the corner where Rafe
lay on the cabin floor, bundled in blankets, an old worn mattress
beneath him.

His face was pale and gaunt, and his eyes, once darkly

vibrant, were sunk into their sockets. They were dull and lifeless, and holding them open seemed an effort for him. He was barely breathing. Cole knelt down, touching his forehead. It was hot, and clammy with perspiration.

"Had his gut tore up with a knife," Mort explained as Cole lifted the blanket covering him and took a quick look at the festering wound. "I tried to cauterize it to stop the infection, but it was too deep."

Cole nodded that he understood, then put a hand up, touching Rafe's face again, hoping for a sign of recognition.

"Rafe . . . Rafe?"

Rafe heard his name and tried to respond, but it was like swimming through a thick, slippery fog.

"Rafe, it's Cole Dante. Do you understand?" He said his name again, slowly, effectively. "Cole Dante. Where are Heather and my son?"

Heather? Ah, yes, Heather! Rafe's mind began wandering again as it had off and on for days now. Everything was so mixed up. One minute he was back in New Orleans loading boats on the docks, the next he was wrestling with that goddamn Indian, and all the while the face of that redheaded wench kept dancing before his eyes.

For a moment the thick fog lifted from Rafe's eyes and his wandering mind began to focus on Cole, who was hovering over him. Dante? Was he still dreaming? He tried to talk, but it was so hard. "D-Dante?"

"Where is she, Rafe?" asked Cole again

"Heather?"

"Yes, Heather, my wife. Where is she?"

"Dead, all dead," he gasped weakly. "The Indians . . . they're all dead."

"Not Heather!" There was a lump in Cole's throat. "Rafe . . . tell me about Heather and the boy."

Already Rafe's mind was whirling again. It never seemed to want to stay in one place. There! Over there were the Indians, the Comanche riding off with the black girl and the kid . . . those purple eyes! She was staring at him again, accusing . . . Not the knife! God, how it hurt . . . dead, all dead.

Cole saw Rafe's lips move again.

"Dead, all dead!" Rafe whispered again; then suddenly he began to choke, the words gurgling in his throat. "All . . . dead."

Rafe's eyes closed and he shuddered, then lay still.

Cole felt for the pulse in his neck. "He's still alive," he said quickly.

Mort inhaled. "But not for long." He glanced at Cole. "Your wife?" he asked. "She was with him?"

"He and some other men kidnapped her, my son, and the baby's nurse, a young black girl. I've been searching for them for almost two weeks now."

"Might's well quit searchin' then, son," Mort said. "I been listenin' to him since I brung him here, and I don't think he's been talkin' with a clear head for days, but from what he's said, and the way he's said it, I don't think there's much chance of her bein' alive." He straightened, offering both Eli and Cole some coffee, then continued. "From what he's been muttering when he's out of his head, and from what I can put together, they musta been jumped by Comanche and he's the only one got away."

"You're sure?" asked Cole.

"Wish I could tell you different. But you heard yourself. If anybody else had been left alive, they'da probably been with him. When I found him, he was alone."

Cole sipped at his coffee, then glanced over to where Rafe lay bundled in the corner of the small cabin. If only he'd talk more rationally. Had Rafe really known he was here when he'd called his name? And what of his words? Were they really all dead? Cole closed his eyes, trying to strengthen himself for what lay ahead, and his hands tightened on the mug he was holding.

Rafe stirred again, and Cole was at his side in seconds.

"Rafe, please," Cole begged, bending close to his ear. "All I want to know is where Heather, Tildie, and the baby are. Please, Rafe, just long enough. I have to know the truth. Heather, Rafe . . . where is Heather?"

Rafe opened his eyes one more time, and this time there were no shadows in them and they seemed clearer as he looked directly into Cole's haunted green eyes.

"Dante?" he whispered softly. "Dante, never meant to hurt her. Palmer, . . . was his doin' . . . never hurt her."

"Eli, he's talking rationally," Cole said quickly, and all three moved closer, listening. "Where is she, Rafe?" Cole asked.

Rafe winced. He felt so weak. The knife, the Indians, he remembered, and it hurt. "She's dead. The Indians . . . They're all dead," he answered slowly, then suddenly felt the blackness beginning to creep up on him again. His feet felt numb, and his body was beginning to float again. He fought it, but it wasn't working. "Heather's dead . . . the others . . . all dead," he muttered again, and once more was lost in a gurgling choke that seemed to convulse his whole body. They all watched, frowning, and seconds later, when Cole felt for his pulse, there was none.

"He's gone," Cole whispered softly. "Damn!"

"He told you, friend." Eli was staring down at the dead man. "Be thankful he was lucid enough to tell you the truth."

"No!" cried Cole angrily. "She's not dead, Eli." He stared at Rafe's still face. "I can't believe him, I won't."

"You'd better." Eli was worried. "Cole, for God's sake, you heard him. He distinctly said Heather was dead."

"Not dead, Eli . . . not dead!" Cole moaned. "And Case . . . !"

Eli's hand rested on Cole's shoulder, then tightened, trying to reassure him. "You'll make it, Cole. There's a whole world out there," he said softly. "She would have wanted it that way."

Tears welled up in Cole's eyes as Rafe's last words filled him with a misery that hurt terribly deep down inside. What would he do without Heather? How could he go on living, never seeing her sweet face again, never hearing her warm laughter or seeing the tender beauty in her eyes? Never to kiss her lips again, or love her . . . God, it hurt.

"You have to go on, Cole," Eli said hopefully. "The world hasn't come to an end."

"Mine has." Cole turned, looking up at his friend. "Heather and Case were my whole life, Eli," he said, his voice breaking. "They were my reason for everything, for the valley, for the future. Without them it's all meaningless."

"You'll think differently someday."

"Maybe," Cole said, his heart breaking. "But right now I feel like nothing. Like one big hurt that'll never go away."

Eli nodded. "And you're gonna feel that way for a long time to come, I know firsthand," he said. "But then one day the hurt will heal, and . . . well, life won't ever be quite as good again, but it'll be there, and so will you, and you'll take it whenever you can, and live every moment you can, trying to find even a part of what used to be."

Cole stared hard at Eli, remembering how he'd told him about losing his own family. "But it's so hard, Eli," he said tearfully. "And we had so little time."

"I know."

Cole stood up and swallowed painfully, unable to say any more, then left the cabin.

"Will he be all right?" Mort asked.

Eli nodded. "I think so. He's strangely intense for one so young, and I just wish things could have been different for him."

"Well." Mort glanced back at Rafe. "You two gonna help bury him, or do I have to do it myself?"

"Afraid you'll have to do it yourself, Mort," Eli said as he headed for the door. "I think it'd be askin' too much for Cole to help give a decent burial to one of the men responsible for his wife's death." He stopped, looking back. "But we thank you for keepin' him alive long as you did. Like I said before, no hard feelin's."

Mort took a deep breath. "No hard feelin's," he echoed, and Eli left. He followed Cole, and they mounted up, riding off, heading back upriver.

All the way to Fort Smith, Cole wavered between anger and hurt. He cursed the night that hid his tears because Heather would never be there again to share it with him, and fought each day, because he knew there was no way he could change things. And all Eli could do was try to help hold together the pieces.

"We going back to the valley again?" Eli asked as they neared Belle Pointe.

Cole sighed. "Might as well, I guess. Bessie and Mose'll be waiting." He stared ahead dreamily. "I think Mose won't like hearing about Tildie."

"You saw it too?"

Cole tried to smile. "That big black may look rough, but he sure has one hell of a time trying to hide his feelings. They show all over his face."

Eli agreed. "There's still a lot can be done with the valley, you know, Cole," he said. "With the corral finished and spring close, we can still make a small fortune with just one trip west."

Cole straightened, gazing at the trail ahead, once more going over what he was going to do.

At first he'd planned to go back east, then changed his mind. There was nothing for him there. Then he'd decided to head north, St. Louis maybe, but he hadn't cared much for St. Louis. Too many people. He pondered the alternatives. Really, Eli was right. The valley was a good place, and the plan they'd decided on last summer was still a good one. It'd keep him busy and help keep his mind off everything, that's for sure.

"You're right, Eli," he said after a long pause. "Maybe we'll do just that, and I think maybe Major Bradford is the first man to do business with. What do you think?"

"Amen," said Eli, relieved. He was all right. Dammit, Cole was gonna be fine, and Eli was whistling softly as they rode into Belle Pointe.

The place had really changed over the past few months, and both Eli and Cole were pleased with it. Besides the hospital, storehouse, and provision house that had been completed the last time they were there, the men had built more log huts for shelter and the land was already being paced off and the ground dug for the walls of the fort, while the forests were being scouted for timber. By spring they expected to be in full swing.

Major Bradford greeted Cole and Eli enthusiastically, although the news of Cole's loss left him disturbed.

"If there's anything I can do . . ." he said as they sat in his office.

Cole shook his head. "Nothing as far as the kidnappers go," he said. "From what Rafe said, they've paid for what they've done, but there is something you can do," he said. "You can contract with Eli and me to buy fifty horses, healthy and saddle-broken. What do you say?"

"Fifty horses? Where are you going to get fifty horses out here?"

"Never mind where," said Cole. "Just tell me, can you use them?"

"Use them? Good Lord, Cole—or do you still want to be called Avery?"

"Cole will do fine."

"Well, you've seen what we have out there, Cole. I certainly could use some horses, but buying them from you?"

"I'll give you a good price. If you have them brought in from back east, it'll cost you a hundred a head for the horses plus another hundred apiece for someone to bring them out. Buy them from the Indians, they'll take advantage and you'll still be paying more than they're worth. I'll sell them to you for eighty a head and deliver them right here to the fort."

The major studied Cole thoughtfully. He needed horses badly. The battle at Clermont had stirred things into a hornet's nest and without horses his men were unable to be effective. However, what if he ordered the horses from Cole and Eli and they didn't deliver? "Can you guarantee arrival?" he asked.

Cole's eyes snapped. "You write up the contract, I'll guarantee arrival, but I need, let's see . . ." He contemplated. "I can have them to you by the end of May, but you'll have to furnish your own saddles."

Major Bradford looked pleased. "You get the horses, we'll find the saddles. There'll be a contract ready before you leave the fort. By the way," he asked, "when are you leaving?"

"I thought we'd leave tomorrow," Cole answered. "It takes at least four days to get back to the valley, and Eli and I'd like to get started on our little venture as soon as we can."

"What about the supplies you've got coming in?" Bradford asked. "Will you be around to pick them up?"

"With everything else, I forgot," Cole answered, then thought for a minute. "See if whoever brings them from St. Louis can take them on out to the valley." He glanced about. "You have a map?"

Major Bradford pulled a map from his desk and Cole showed him where the valley was.

"Good. You're not on Indian land," Bradford said. "You know, at first I was a little worried. Washington's been pretty upset about all them squatters that are starting to come out here. They don't bother to check to see where territory boundaries are and just put down claims, then expect us to protect them, and half those claims are in land treatied off to the Indians."

"Don't worry," Cole assured him. "Eli and I knew what we were doing when we picked the valley. Just make sure whoever brings the things out can find the way. I'd hate for the Osage or Cherokee to end up with my cow and chickens."

The major laughed. "Good luck to you, Cole, Eli," he said. "You can pick up your contract before leaving tomorrow, and if all goes well, I'll see you the end of May."

"Major . . ." Cole shook his hand, and Eli followed suit; then both men left.

"You think we can get all that done by the end of May?" Eli asked as they headed across what would one day be a parade ground.

"Why not?"

Eli took a deep breath. "Well, I don't rightly mind headin' out toward the plains and runnin' down those mustangs, that we planned on, Cole, but how the hell you gonna get all of 'em broke in time?''

Cole grinned. "Remember a long time ago when you told me about the Comanche and the way they tame a horse? Well, I'm going out there, find me a Comanche, and learn how."

"But I never saw it done, Cole," Eli protested. "I only heard about it by way of rumor."

"Well, there must be something to it, and by God, it's worth trying."

"What if the Comanche don't take rightly to you?"

"With this face, I think I can get by. Besides, I've got to keep busy or I'll go crazy, and this is the best way. Don't worry, Eli, we'll make it by the end of May."

"Or die tryin'. All right, I'll let you be the boss this time, Cole," Eli said hopefully. "But if we don't make good on that contract, I'll let you do the explainin' to Major Bradford—that is, if we get back in one piece." They headed toward their horses, then led them to the livery before finding a place to spend the night.

A few days later, when Eli and Cole rode down into Cole's valley, it was with heavy hearts because they knew how hard it was going to be to tell the others that Heather, Tildie, and Case were dead.

Bessie stood for a long time staring into the fireplace. She had known the minute they walked through the door, and now it was the moment of accepting.

"I hope you don't want Helene and me to go back east," she said tearfully.

Cole shook his head. "I'll need you more than ever now, Bess," he said. "Someone's got to keep this place going for me."

"It won't be the same without her," she said softly, then turned, straightening stubbornly. "But Helene and me, we'll try our best." Her eyes softened. "She was like one of my own," she whispered. "You know, sometimes we wonder . . ." She bit her lip. "But life still goes on." Glancing out the cabin window, she saw Mose off toward the corral walking by himself. He'd taken the news about Tildie hard. "I hope he's going to be all right," she said. "You know, he blames himself for all this. He keeps saying if he'd only kept a closer eye on things."

"He knows I don't blame him," Cole said. "And just to prove it, I'm leaving him in charge of the place again while Eli and I start rounding up some horses."

"You're leavin' again?" she asked.

"We have a contract with the army for fifty head of horses by the end of May, and I intend to deliver."

"Where you gonna get horses out here?"

Eli grinned. "He thinks the Comanche are gonna give them to him."

"I do not," Cole protested. "All I said was that I intended to find out how the Comanche tame a horse. Besides"—his eyes hardened—"Bessie doesn't need the two of us underfoot, especially since I'm not too good company lately." He nodded toward the bedroom door, where Helene had disappeared after learning about Heather, Tildie, and the baby. "Are you sure Helene's going to be all right?" he asked. "She didn't say much."

"It's her way," said Bessie, wiping a stray tear from her own eye. "She and Tildie spent a lot of time together with the baby, but she'll manage. She's a lot like her ma."

Cole stared at Bessie. She was right. She and Helene seemed to have the same kind of strength his grandmother had had when she survived the wilderness. A strength Heather hadn't had. Captain Brooks was right. He should never have brought Heather out here. If not, she'd still be alive today. She had been too fragile for this life, and he cursed Ian Brooks for being right.

The next afternoon, after making certain they had everything they needed, Cole and Eli said good-bye to Bessie, Mose, and Helene, making sure Mose knew they didn't expect miracles from him, then left, heading west into lands few white men had as yet traveled.

Heather glanced ahead at Ian as they made their way between the trees, keeping off the main trails, still heading north. This was their second day together now and she was pleased to have someone to talk to and help make the decisions. She studied him as they walked. It had quit raining yesterday and now the sun was shining, turning his hair to spun gold and adding golden highlights to his honey-colored beard.

Strange, she had never noticed before how light his hair was, but then, when they'd been together before, he'd usually been wearing his uniform hat, which he told her he'd lost along with his horse. He'd also lost his saber to the Indians when they'd captured him, but when he escaped he managed to take a hunting knife and tomahawk with him that had belonged to one of his captors. Now they hung at his waist, tucked into the belt that once held his sword. There were gold buttons missing from his uniform jacket as well as gold braid torn from one of the shoulders, and his pants were dirty, a tear in the left side, his boots covered with dust. Yet as he turned and smiled at her, his face was such a welcome sight.

He stopped, waiting for her to catch up. "Ready to find a place to stop for something to eat and for a little rest?" he asked.

"If you like. By the way," she said, "what are we having?"

His eyes twinkled mischievously. "How about some *pâté de foie de poulet* and perhaps we could have *petits fours* to go with it?"

She stared at him in surprise; then the corners of her mouth tilted slightly as the absurdity of what he just said made her smile.

"*Ah, oui,*" she said, going along with his playful mood. "And I can sprinkle the *pâté* with dried clover blossoms and we can find pecan nuts to put on the *petits fours*."

"That's the way," he said; then his smile broadened. "That's the first I've really seen you smile in a long time, and it looks good."

She flushed and he straightened, looking up ahead. "For our repast, my dear," he said, more seriously this time, "we'll have some of your clover blooms, naturally, and maybe I can dig up a few roots that are edible." He pointed to a small hill up ahead. "If we sit up there we can make sure no one sneaks up on us. Come along," and he started toward it, with Heather close behind.

After a sparse meal of dried clover and wild carrot roots washed down with water from a small flask Ian carried fastened to his belt, they once more set out.

It grew warm as the afternoon wore on, and soon Heather untied the braided rope that held her fur robe in place and slipped it from her shoulders, draping it lazily over her arm. It was then, the first time she'd removed the bulky fur, that he noticed the difference. They were walking through a meadow, the rough prairie grass dry and lifeless.

"Why didn't you tell me you were expecting a baby?" he asked as he moved closer beside her.

She shrugged. "I didn't think it was important."

"You've been tramping these woods, living on God-knows-what . . . and the way I've pushed you."

"Look, Captain, I'm not made of porcelain, I won't break."

He scowled. "You're not porcelain, no, Heather," he said. "But you are human, and you're not used to all this."

"And you are?"

"Yes, I am. Before joining Major Long on this expedition I was up north of St. Louis, mapmaking for the Ninth Army. That's why I was assigned to Major Long, because I knew enough about the wilderness to get by. But you . . ."

"Cole taught me a great deal when we were back at Tonnerre."

"Tonnerre?"

"His parents' plantation back in South Carolina."

"What were you, neighbors or something?"

"I was staying with my parents at my grandparents' plantation. I was born in Boston and raised in Columbia, South Carolina."

"Like I said before, you don't belong out here."

"I belong where Cole is."

"And where is he now?" he asked as they reached a wooded area and were forced apart by some small saplings. "Don't you see, he wasn't able to protect you all the time . . . and now . . ."

"Now I'm trying the best I can to get back to him."

"Look at you." He gestured toward her. "Your legs are full of scratches, you're hungry . . . it's a wonder you're still alive."

"But I am." Her fur caught on the branch of a small tree and she tugged it loose. "I'm surviving, Captain," she went on. "I didn't panic and I tried to remember everything."

"As I said once before, Heather, there's more to surviving than just being able to breathe."

"Well, right now that's good enough for me." She continued dodging her way through the trees, glancing over at him occasionally. "Just because I was brought up to be useless doesn't mean I have to stay that way. You know, before meeting Cole, all I knew how to do was embroider, play the piano, do the few lessons I learned at school and ride sidesaddle. He taught me how to fish, shoot, track game. You know, for some reason, I don't feel useless anymore."

Ian stared at her, watching closely as she made her way between the trees. She didn't look useless, either, but then, she never had. Not to him. Her hair was a riot of tangled curls, the sun highlighting it, brightening it to crimson, and although she hadn't had soap, she did mention being able to wash it in a stream a few days before. It was the only thing that even remotely reminded him of the woman he'd met back at Arkansas

Post. Her hair and her eyes. They were still the most dazzling color of violet he'd ever seen, with streaks of blue gentian running through them. But the woman walking with him now had lost the soft roundness that made her seem fragile, and had replaced it with a strength from somewhere deep inside, where she'd undoubtedly kept it hidden. The heart perhaps? Because it was obvious what was driving her. She was determined to get back to Cole.

He felt a twinge, remembering her husband, wondering if he was searching for her, and how long he'd keep searching before giving up. Brushing the thought aside, he once more brought up the subject of her pregnancy.

"Did Cole know you were pregnant before you were kidnapped?" he asked.

She had told him the whole story that first night while they'd huddled in a cave watching the rain outside. "Certainly," she answered. "Why wouldn't he?"

He shrugged. "I thought, maybe under the circumstances . . ."

"You mean because we'd settled so far into the wilderness?" She sighed. "He was very proud knowing he'd be a father again." Suddenly she thought of Case, and the thought was painful. "I only wish . . ." She stopped, staring at Ian. "You don't think those Comanche would hurt him, do you?" she asked.

"You mean Case?"

She nodded. "He's so young . . . they wouldn't hurt him, would they?"

"No, I'm sure they wouldn't," he tried to reassure her. She had enough problems. "They've probably adopted him into the tribe already. Don't worry. Someday you'll find him again." He glanced at the sky. "Look, we'd better change direction—we're heading a little too far west," and they turned slightly so the sun shining down through the trees was farther to their left, then resumed their steady pace.

They had found a place to cross the river the day before, right after the rain had stopped, and Heather was hoping they had left the Cherokee Indians on the other side, but suddenly as they reached the top of a hill and looked back, studying the landscape they'd just left behind them, Ian pointed, frowning.

"Look there," he said anxiously, and she held her hand over her eyes, shading them from the sun. About half a mile away, moving through a stretch of trees they'd traversed only a short time before, were ten, maybe twelve warriors.

"They've found our trail," Ian said, then glanced quickly at the sky. "And there's at least four or five hours till dark. That means we've got some fast moving to do. Come on!"

He grabbed her hand and they quickened their pace, almost at a run.

As the sun began to sink farther in the west, Ian's pace became not only faster but also more erratic as he tried to hide their trail, moving across huge boulders, and gravel whenever possible, running the length of fallen half-dead logs, leaping from one to another, trying anything to confuse the Indians he knew were still doggedly trailing them.

Heather was agile from her earlier days traveling alone, but she had never had to keep the pace she was forced to endure now. They'd stop occasionally so she could catch her breath, but the rests were brief, and the past mile, after hearing a loud whoop from one of their pursuers, Ian had begun to run as fast as possible, trying to put even more distance between them.

Heather was exhausted. They'd been moving for hours, and her mouth was dry even though she'd kept it closed while running, and now suddenly Ian halted, staring at the small river that was blocking their way.

"What do we do now?" she gasped breathlessly.

He stared intently, eyes searching for something, anything; then he looked at her abruptly. "Can you swim?" he asked.

"Yes."

"Well enough to swim to that beaver dam?" he asked, pointing downstream.

She nodded.

"Good, come on," and he grabbed her hand, pulling her into the water, dragging her toward the other side. The water was only waist-deep here. She had put the fur robe on again when they'd first spotted the Cherokee, tying it so she wouldn't lose it, and now the water reached it, wetting the edges. When they reached the other side, he pulled her onto the bank after him, water from their soaked bodies wetting the ground, leaving tracks in the mud. When he came to the edge where the grass started, he stopped her quickly.

"Back down into the water," he ordered hurriedly, and she stared at him, confused. "Like this," he said, and stepped backward, trying to step close to where he'd stepped before. "Come on, there's no time to explain."

She did as he said, walking backward into the water; then he splashed more water onto their tracks, making it harder for them to be seen.

"Now," he said. "Take my hand and don't let go, and we swim underwater to the beaver dam. Ready?"

"Ready," she answered, and as she took a deep breath, plunging in beside him, the cries from the pursuing Indians filled the air, closer than they'd ever been before.

When Heather's head finally broke the water, she took a huge gulp of air, then opened her eyes, trying to see. She was still holding Ian's hand, and using her free hand, she tried to grab something to hold her up. There were only sticks and branches, so thick she couldn't see out, and a minimum of light penetrated the tangle.

"Shhh," Ian cautioned close to her ear. "You can stand up easily here, but for God's sake, don't make a sound."

Heather felt the river bottom beneath her moccasins and steadied herself; then she heard it, some twenty feet or so away as the Cherokee reached the river.

Her body was trembling. The water was cold and it had been hard enough to shake off the initial shock when she had gone under, with the heat of running already flushed on her skin. Now the cold water burned the scratches and cuts on her legs, as well as numbing her to the bone. But she didn't move a muscle.

She felt a sudden pain, deep, near her groin, yet still didn't move. Seconds later, the pain intensified, yet all she did was bite her lip to hold back the cry. And all the while she could hear the Cherokee wading the river, calling to one another and shouting to the rest who'd already made it to the other side.

Soon the noise was gone and everything was quiet as she gazed about the inside of the beaver dam.

"Luckily no one's at home," Ian whispered.

She swallowed hard. "What if the Indians come back?"

"That's why we stay here awhile."

"Here?"

"I know it's cold—I feel like an icicle myself—but it won't be for too long. Only until we're certain they've lost our trail. Maybe this'll help," he said, and gently pulled her closer until her body was against his, his arm holding her tightly.

She was going to protest, then remembered Cole telling her that the heat from two bodies close together could often be the difference between freezing to death and staying alive, so instead of fighting him, she tried to relax.

If only the pains would stop, though. But suddenly she felt another. Not as bad this time, but longer, swirling up into her abdomen, and for a moment she felt nauseated.

Ian was listening hard. Strange, he could still hear a loud cry now and then, followed by more faint ones. All he could think was that they had discovered his ruse and were coming back. Still, the cries didn't seem to be coming any closer. He waited. The cries stopped after an unusually loud war whoop, and now he waited awhile longer.

Five, ten minutes. He had to be certain. Then he heard it, the unmistakable clomping of horses' hooves. White men?

A signal to halt by the leader as they reached the water left no doubt who they were. More Indians, and how many, he couldn't tell. He waited, listening as the Indians rode their horses into the water, crossed to the other side, and moved on, and after a while everything was silent once more. He guessed by how long they took to cross that there must have been at least twenty, and all mounted.

He waited another few minutes, just to be sure; then, just as one of the beavers whose home they had invaded returned to claim it for himself, Ian released Heather, then took her hand once more. They each took a deep breath and left the beaver dam, this time not bothering to swim all the way, but standing up, wading cautiously the rest of the way, leaving the waist-deep cold water.

Heather shivered as she reached the bank, and Ian was beside her in seconds. He reached out and began untying the fur. It was sopping and heavy. Then he saw her face.

"What is it?" Ian asked anxiously.

She swallowed hard. "The pain," she gasped helplessly, and leaned forward, suddenly doubling over.

Then he saw the blood on her legs, streaking the river water that dripped from her drawers. "My God," he exclaimed, and let loose of the ties that held the wet fur onto her. Reaching out, ignoring her protests, he picked her up, cradling her in his arms.

"I can walk," she said feebly.

He shook his head. "Not on your life."

His eyes scanned the area, while he held her safe in his arms; then he finally moved, not onto the trail they had pretended to follow earlier, but following the riverbank, pushing aside brush until he came to a small waterfall. Moving off to his right, he stopped beneath some trees at the side of a hill and bent over, setting her down.

"How do you feel?" he asked hurriedly.

She winced. "I'll be all right."

"Sure you will," he said, then knelt beside her, gazing about, trying to decide what to do next. Suddenly the decision was made for him as Heather let out another soft cry and grabbed his hand, her nails digging into him as the pain racked her body, and he knew his answer only moments ago had been only wishful thinking. The running, everything, had been too much for her. Heather was going to lose her baby.

13

It was over. Ian stood, bare to the waist, shivering slightly in the cool morning air, and stared down into Heather's face, pale even beneath the deep suntan, the paleness giving her skin a grayish hue. It had gone on for so long. At first he had had hopes, but then close to morning he knew there was no longer any reason to be optimistic. Now he had to stop the bleeding.

He had used his knife and the tomahawk to dig a shallow grave and buried what would have been Heather's second child, then piled rocks on the spot to keep scavengers away. Now his whole attention was centered on Heather. He tried to think back through his experiences. There had to be something that would help. He'd folded the drawers he'd taken off her and stuffed them between her legs to catch the blood, wadded the fur robe and tucked it beneath her head to make her more comfortable, then covered her legs with his uniform jacket. He had even used part of his shirt to mop the blood up last night. It was the best he could do. If he only had a dry blanket. The fire he'd started had helped warm her some, but he didn't even have anything to put under her to keep the dirt off except what was left of his shirt. Now it was soaked with blood and he couldn't leave it beneath her. He frowned, gazing up at the sky. Suddenly his attention was caught by a movement above the trees some distance away. He watched closely for a few seconds, then glanced back down at Heather. She was still sleeping, weak after the ordeal. He knelt down, making sure she wouldn't waken for a while; then, as the first faint rays of sunlight began to streak the gray dawn with gold, he moved off through the trees back to the trail near the creek. Following the trail cautiously, he headed in the direction of the circling buzzards.

He should have thought of this before, but he'd been so wrapped up in Heather. As he neared a bend in the trail, listening carefully, the distinct squawking of a number of buzzards and the occasional snapping and snarling of animals carried to him on the morning breeze. Now, more than ever, he was sure he'd guessed right, and the next few moments proved it to him.

As he rounded the bend and stopped, the scene before him was no surprise. A dozen bodies were strewn about the trail. It was what was left of the Cherokee who'd been pursuing him, and already scavengers were fighting over the remains. He took a deep breath, swallowing hard, and set to the task before him. Even though they'd been scalped, it wasn't too hard to identify the men who'd been after him for the better part of two weeks. They'd come a long way from their camp near the Poteau River and had become careless. This was Osage territory, and right now the Osage were the Cherokee's deadliest enemy.

Well, that solved one problem. The Osage had no idea the Cherokee had been after him. That meant he and Heather could travel the rest of the way without having to glance over their shoulder every few minutes. But if he didn't hurry, they wouldn't get to travel at all. He had to help Heather somehow.

The weather was still cool enough for the Cherokee to be wearing buckskins, and he needed a shirt as well as something other than the flimsy ragged dress for Heather to wear. Quickly he shooed some buzzards and crows away from a couple of the bodies, then stripped them right down to the moccasins. This done, he picked up one of the buckskin shirts. There was some blood on it and he used dirt and grass, rubbing it out, hoping Heather wouldn't be aware of what the stain was, slipped it on over his head, then rolled the rest of the things into a bundle to take with him. Now for something to cover her with. A few of the Cherokee had carried blankets folded and draped from their shoulders, wrapping them about their torsos, tying them with leather thongs at the waist. Most were gone now, but he found one under one of the bodies where it had been overlooked, and he thankfully folded it, setting it aside with the buckskins.

For a few minutes he stood, hands on hips, contemplating, his brown eyes trying to avoid the worst of the remains; then, certain there was nothing more he could use, and making sure the Osage hadn't forgotten to confiscate some of the weapons, he picked up the buckskins and blanket and headed back to where he'd left Heather.

Heather slowly began to stir. Not only was she weak from loss of blood, but her hips ached as if someone had beaten on them with hammers. At first she began to panic, wondering where she was and what had happened; then she began to remember, and with the remembrance, the pain began all over again. Not the physical pain she had been forced to endure during the miscarriage, but the pain of sorrow as she thought of the son or daughter that was no more.

The sun hurt her eyes as she lifted herself onto one elbow, looking for Ian. He was nowhere in sight. "Captain . . . Ian . . . where are you?" she called softly, half-choking, then dropped back again, burying her head in the damp fur robe rolled up beneath it.

He didn't answer. "Ian?" she called again, her eyes closed. Still there was no answer, and she began to get frantic. "Please, don't leave me now, Ian," she begged helplessly. "I can still go on, please, I have to go on. Don't leave me . . ."

Suddenly she felt a hand on her shoulder and opened her eyes.

"I thought you were gone."

"You weren't supposed to wake up yet," he said, comforting her. "Don't worry, I won't leave you. I just had to find a few things."

She stared up at him, realizing he wasn't wearing his uniform. "Your shirt . . . ?" she said softly.

He smiled. "I covered your legs with my jacket, and had to use my shirt last night, but here, I've got a blanket now," and he unfolded the blanket, slipped the jacket from her legs very discreetly, while covering her with the blanket; then he knelt down, and she held her breath as he rolled her toward him, slipped the bloody shirt from beneath her, tucked the blanket around her, and laid her back again so she was wrapped in it.

"How do you feel?" he asked as he set the shirt and jacket aside.

She closed her eyes. "Terrible."

He reached out, brushing a stray curl from her cheek. "You had a rough time of it."

"Captain?"

"I like Ian better."

She flushed. "I don't know what to say."

"Then don't say anything."

"But what you did . . . I couldn't have made it without you."
She remembered the way he'd held her hands, trying to give her
strength, and the way he'd bathed her forehead in cool water
while he talked to her, trying to ease the pain. But most of all
she remembered him kneading her abdomen, helping her to
expel everything, then trying to clean her as best he could
afterward, and it was embarrassing. How did you thank a man
for something so intimate? She couldn't put her thoughts into
words, so instead she changed the subject.

Reaching up, she put her hand on his arm, touching the
buckskin shirt he was wearing. "Where . . . ?" she asked, her
eyes questioning.

"Remember the Cherokee who were after us?" he asked, his
hand covering hers. "Well, they aren't anymore. Those were
Osage on the horses yesterday, and there's not much left of the
Cherokee."

"Oh, Ian."

His hand squeezed hers and his eyes warmed. "Don't worry,
they didn't need them anymore," he said. "So I have some
buckskins for you too. You'll need them when you're ready to
travel, only it won't be for some time yet, I'm afraid."

"But we can't stay here."

"We have to. You're in no condition to go on."

"I have to. I have to get back, Ian."

"You have to get back alive, Heather." He released her hand
and reached out, spreading his jacket over her shoulders, tucking
it under her chin. "It's a little cool today," he explained gently.
"Now, get some rest."

She gazed up at him, eyes misty with tears, and stared,
noticing that his hair was much lighter than his beard, which was
an amber gold. He was still wearing his uniform pants and boots,
and they looked strange with the buckskin shirt. He looked more
like a ruffian than a soldier, yet there was a calming strength
about him.

He left her and went over to the fire, putting some more wood
on it, then glanced back. "I'm going to have to leave you for a
while again," he said after a few minutes.

Tears still rimmed her eyes.

"I have to," he explained quickly. "You're bleeding heavily
and I'm going to see if I can find something to stop it."

"Do you know what you're looking for?"

"I think so. Let me worry about that. You just lie as quiet as you can. We're far enough off the trail here that I don't think you'll be bothered even if someone did happen to be passing by, which is unlikely, and I'm using special wood so there shouldn't be much smoke. Besides, I won't be gone long." He stood up and walked over, staring down at her. "Why don't you try to sleep some more," he suggested, and knelt down again, making sure she was tucked in all right. "It'll do you good."

"Maybe I will," she answered hesitantly. "If I can."

"I think you will," he assured her, then reached out, stroking her forehead. "Don't worry, all right?"

She nodded, unable to answer, the intense look in his eyes striking a chord deep inside, and she was reminded of the way Cole always looked at her.

"I'll be back," he said quickly, then left, and it wasn't until he was out of sight that the tears in her eyes rolled down her cheeks.

That first day was the worst for Heather. All the while Ian was gone, she heard every little sound, and with every noise, her heart would turn over inside her. The waiting seemed like an eternity, and just knowing she was unable to move if Indians did find her made it all the worse.

But true to his word, Ian wasn't gone long, and when he returned, he quickly brewed her some tea, using the dried lobelia leaves he'd found. She had questioned him as to how he was going to boil the tea, since they had no pan, but he only smiled, holding up a small piece of tree trunk he'd hollowed out. It was full of water, and as she watched, he heated stones until they were red hot, then using the tomahawk, lifted them, dropping them into the water after adding the lobelia leaves.

"It's supposed to help thicken the blood—so I was told by an old Indian woman," he said as he stirred the concoction with a stick.

She watched him curiously. He had also brought back a squirrel, and while he was waiting for the stones to heat to brew the medicine, he had skinned, cleaned, and skewered it, making a spit over the fire, and now, while he stirred the medicine, Heather watched the small carcass sizzle and spit as it browned, and in spite of the fact that she felt rather sick, her mouth watered. It had been ages since she'd eaten anything that looked so good, and as the aroma drifted her way, she sniffed eagerly.

"Is that our breakfast?" she asked.

He glanced over at her. "After the medicine," he said firmly; then, using the gourd she had made for drinking when she was by herself, he brought her some of the herbal tea.

"Here, let me help," he said, and put an arm beneath her, raising her enough so she could sip at it.

It tasted terrible, but it did work, and by the second day, after she had consumed an incredible amount of it, the heavy bleeding stopped, leaving only a normal flow. But it was four days before she was able to stand without her legs buckling beneath her, and another four days before the bleeding stopped completely. During that time Ian kept them alive with squirrels, rabbits, and anything he managed to, as he put it, accidentally hit with the hunting knife, along with roots from various plants he knew to be edible. The roots were hard to find, however, because spring was still a little way off, and he had to identify the plants by their dry winter foliage.

As each day went by, Heather grew stronger, but something else was also happening to her. Each day, she was becoming more and more dependent on Ian. Not for food, because she knew once her strength was back to normal she could survive alone, she had done it before. But Ian began to fill her moments with pleasure. When he smiled, pleased with something she said, or his deep laugh rang out when she did something funny, for some reason it made her feel good inside. And Ian laughed a lot, teasing her playfully as Cole often had.

Then there were nights they'd sit at the fire and talk. He was easy to talk to and never complained, no matter how badly the day went. In fact, the only time she ever saw anger in his eyes was when she talked about Cole; then they'd snap irritably and she knew he still blamed Cole for subjecting her to all this. Somehow, though, she understood, and forgave him his animosity toward Cole. How could she not forgive him? You couldn't spend almost every waking moment with a person, facing danger and starvation, relying on him as if he were a part of you, and not understand and be able to forgive. It was something she did without even questioning, and very naively accepted as the normal thing to do.

Two weeks and two days after losing her baby, Heather and Ian decided it was time to move on. The night before leaving, Heather sat in front of the fire, tired from the long day, yet anxious for tomorrow, for spring was coming to the Arkansas Territory, and with it, the first young shoots of green were beginning to appear, making her feel alive again. After Heather's bleeding had stopped, Ian took her back to the river, where he kept watch so she could bathe herself. Then she'd do the same for him. This evening she'd really been pleased when he'd found a soapwort plant and picked the new young leaves so she could crush them to make a lather and really get clean. The water was still cold, but it hadn't mattered. She was thankful to him for it, and she was also thankful for the buckskins she was wearing that he had confiscated from the dead Cherokee. Although they were too big, they felt more presentable than the raggedy dress. Now, sitting in front of the fire, although she was tired, it was a comfortable, clean tiredness.

Beside her, Ian sat motionless, contemplating the days ahead. They still had miles to go, and he wished they didn't even have to leave, because he knew every mile was going to be a painful one for him. He had only guessed at his feelings for Heather last year when they'd all traveled the Arkansas River together, because he'd never really been in love before, but now there was no mistaking the deep feelings that were tearing him apart inside. It had to be love. He had never felt like this about anyone in all his thirty years. He stared into the flames, wishing he'd never met her and tormented by the knowledge that she belonged to someone else.

If only things had been different. He drew his eyes from the flames, and looked over, studying her face in the firelight, wondering if she felt anything for him at all.

"Heather?" he said softly.

She turned, her eyes meeting his, and he felt a warmth rush through him, igniting a vibrant longing deep inside. He tried to squelch it, but the pain was so intense it actually hurt.

"You look lovely tonight," he said huskily.

She frowned. Now, why did he have to say that? She hesitated, holding her breath, then stared back into his searching eyes, suddenly realizing that she wanted him to say it. A sigh escaped her lips as she released her breath, still staring at him curiously.

"I think you've been in the woods too long," she finally said, trying to make light of what she couldn't understand.

He shook his head. "No, you forget, the woods are almost like home to me. No, it's not the woods, it's you, and you know it, Heather."

Her eyes fell before his gaze, and she looked away. "Please, Ian," she whispered softly. "Let it go."

"And if I can't?"

"You'll have to." She was afraid to look at him. Not afraid of Ian, but of the all-too-familiar feelings that were stirring deep inside her. Feelings she knew had nothing to do with love, although love intensified them, but feelings even DeWitt had managed to dredge from her when she'd been married to him, even though she hadn't loved him. She didn't want Ian to touch those feelings, yet he did and she despised him for it. "Don't do this to me, Ian, please," she begged, her voice breaking. "Don't spoil things."

"How would it spoil things?"

"Because I'd hate myself and you too, and I don't want to hate you."

"Nor do I want you to." He reached out, pulling her to him, cradling her in his arms. "I want you to love me, just a little, Heather," he whispered desperately, looking deep into her eyes. "Just a little," and suddenly his lips touched hers lightly, caressing, then sipping at them hungrily, and Heather felt desire, like a thief, stealing the will to resist from her, and she kissed him back, letting her feelings run free.

Ian's mouth took her passionately, drinking in the wonder of her response, giving as well as taking, until he felt her melt against him; then his lips trailed sensuously down her cheek to her throat, and she trembled. It felt so good, and she felt so alive again, the blood in her veins coursing like the surge of a mighty river. It had been so long since she had felt like this. So long since Cole had held her in his arms. Suddenly the thought of Cole made something snap inside her, a warning she couldn't ignore, and tears welled up in her eyes.

"Ian, no. I can't," she cried, fighting against the passion that was trying to consume her, and he lifted his head reluctantly at the agonized plea in her cry.

"Heather?"

She pushed him back, looking into his eyes, trying to escape the love she knew was there, and hoping to deny her body its fulfillment without hurting him. "Don't make me hate you, Ian," she whispered, her eyes begging him. "Don't take what I'm not free to give."

He stared at her, feeling her body quivering in his arms, and took a deep breath. "I could, you know, very easily."

"Yes, I know," she whispered, then swallowed hard. "That's

why I'm asking you not to. For me, for my sake. Please, Ian, let me go now while I can."

He studied her face for a long time, so close yet so far. Not his to hold, not his to touch, not his to love, yet he did love her, and because of that love he couldn't hurt her.

His arms eased from about her, and he released her, helping her to sit up straight; then he turned back to the fire, staring at it, his jaw set stubbornly. "We've got a long day ahead of us tomorrow," he said curtly. "You'd better get some sleep."

Heather saw the anger in his eyes, and felt the hurt he must be feeling. "I'm sorry," she murmured softly.

He flinched. "Good night, Heather."

"Ian?"

"Heather, for God's sake," he blurted recklessly, "will you go over to your blanket and go to sleep before I forget you're another man's wife!"

She bit her lip, trying to hold back the tears, and turned from him to where her blanket was spread with her fur robe rolled up for her to use as a pillow. She bunched the fur up, then settled down, but sleep was hard in coming because whenever she closed her eyes all she could see was Ian's face, anger and hurt mirrored in his eyes, and when she did finally fall asleep, her dreams were haunted by the memory of his kiss.

Ian stirred restlessly, the first gray streaks of dawn waking him. What a horrible night it had been. Not only had he ached physically with his need for Heather, but she'd haunted all of his dreams as she had for days now. He sat up, running a hand through his hair. It was getting so damn long. Already it lay in waves onto his shoulders.

He glanced over to where Heather was curled up with her head on the fur pillow. He wanted to hate her for what she'd done to him. For all the agony and hurt. But how did you hate someone who tore at your heart with just a look?

Taking a deep breath, he crawled over to where she was sleeping.

"Heather, come on," he said, nudging her awake. "We said we were going to get an early start."

She opened one eye and looked up at him, then closed it again and tried to scoot farther into her blanket.

"That won't get us out of here, Heather," he said briskly. "Besides, there's something I want you to do before we leave."

She opened her eyes lazily and stared up at him. "What?"

"Cut my hair."

"Your hair?"

"Yes, my hair. It's too damn long and keeps getting in my way."

She pulled herself into a sitting position, knees still under part of the blanket but drawn up in front of her. "What do I use?" she asked reluctantly.

He handed her the hunting knife.

"You want me to do it now?"

"Now's as good a time as any."

"But I've just barely opened my eyes."

He shrugged. "I'm a trusting soul."

"Ian!"

"Well, I am."

"What if I get it crooked?"

"Then you get it crooked. After all," he reminded her, "you'll be the only one who'll have to look at it. Hey, I don't give a damn how it looks, just so it doesn't keep falling in my face anymore."

"All right, it's your hair," she said skeptically, but he only turned his back, waiting for her to get started.

Cutting Ian's hair, especially now, was the last thing Heather wanted to do, but she knew she couldn't get out of it, and all the while she wielded the knife, slicing into his golden mane, she fought emotions she thought she had put to rest the night before. His nearness, the pleasurable feel of his silken hair beneath her fingers. Damn him anyway! There was a sensuous masculinity about him that frightened her, making her all too aware of her vulnerability, and she was never so glad to finish a task in all her life. She finally tossed the last hunk of hair away and breathed a sigh of relief.

"There," she said, surveying her handiwork critically. "If I must say so, I think I did a pretty good job."

He reached up, running a hand through his hair, then turned to her and smiled. "Now, was that so bad?" he asked.

"It was terrible." She handed him back his knife.

"No worse than last night was for me, dear lady," he retorted. Then his eyes softened as he said, "Now, let's pack up and get out of here before we lose the whole day trying to get even with each other for last night," and he stood up, leaving her staring after him in surprise.

After a quick breakfast they were well on their way again by the time the sun reached the treetops, but for the first few days things between them were rather strained. Then slowly, as the days wore on, they once again began to relax with each other, and by the end of the first week the very circumstances of their close existence and dependence on each other for comfort and companionship began to forge a bond between them again, although Heather would have been the first to deny it if anyone had been around to point it out.

One day blended into another, and still they moved on. Then one afternoon they caught a faraway glimpse of some Osage warriors riding the crest of a hill. Heather tensed, but Ian showed her they were going in the opposite direction, and she felt better. It was the first they had seen anyone since starting their journey again.

"Just so they keep going the other way," she said as they watched until they disappeared from sight.

It was two days later. They had been traveling through rugged territory that slowed their progress and made them change directions more than once because of sheer cliffs impossible to scale, and on top of that, the sky had been overcast all day, making it harder to calculate directions.

Ian was irritable. He hoped they could find water—another pond, lake, or even small stream where they could make camp—but as the day wore on, the possibility was becoming more and more remote. The only water they had seen all day was around noon, when they circled a small pond. Since then, it seemed like they had done nothing but climb, and now darkness was closing in, with no sign of water. Wisely they had used the water in the flask he carried sparingly, but without a new supply to replenish it, they'd have to continue using as little as possible, and he could already tell the night was going to be extremely warm.

They were walking along the side of a high ridge, trying to keep in the cover of the trees, when Ian suddenly stopped.

"It's going to be dark in about half an hour," he said as he stared at the terrain up ahead. "I was thinking that might be a good place to stop. What do you think?" and he pointed to a place a short distance away where the land had slid once and been stopped by some boulders; then trees had taken root, holding the soil in place, making a deep overhang.

"Looks about as good as any," she answered.

They began to pick up kindling and firewood while they headed toward it, and were glad they had, because by the time they reached the overhang, it was too dark to go hunting for much more. Ian soon had a fire going and they cooked a rabbit he'd killed earlier, along with some adder's-tongue bulbs he'd dug up shortly after breakfast and washed in the pond at noon. Besides the bag she had made from the sleeve of her dress, they had also made a pack from his uniform jacket. Ian had ripped it apart with his knife, and she had pieced it together by lacing it with narrow strips of cloth. It had kept her busy while she recuperated from the miscarriage, and now, as they journeyed, they'd fill it with bulbs and roots when they found them, so they'd always have something to eat, and they usually washed them in any streams along the way.

Heather savored the last of her adder's-tongue bulb, then licked her fingers contentedly. "I'm glad it's spring, or we'd probably never have found these," she said as she glanced over at Ian. "They were good for a change."

"They'll do," he answered, then sighed. "How do you like the mountains?"

She frowned. "The mountains? I thought you said the mountains were the other side of the Poteau River."

"Most of them are," he answered. "But I have a sneaky feeling we might have wandered a little too far east into the foothills." He stretched and stood up. "All I know is I feel like we've been climbing forever. Guess I'm getting too old for this sort of thing."

"You're not old."

"Well, right now I feel as old as Methuselah." He glanced over at her. She looked so pretty with the firelight dancing in her hair, turning it to a deep mahogany, the soft glow shining in her eyes. He wanted her so badly it hurt. If he didn't get out of here, and fast, he was going to make a fool of himself again. He hitched up his pants, making sure his knife was still in place. "I think I'll go say a last good night to the woods, then come back and get some sleep," he said curtly. "I have a premonition tomorrow's going to be a rough day."

She watched him leave, and smiled, amused at his delicate way of saying he was going to find a place to relieve himself. Ever the gentleman, she thought, then frowned slightly. He had been a gentleman, too, except for that one wayward kiss. Remembering it always brought a flush to her cheeks, and when he returned, she quickly excused herself, following his suit, leaving the overhang so she could find a place to go, hoping by the time she got back he'd have settled down for the night, because she didn't like remembering. It was unsettling.

The next morning they broke camp early and once more headed toward the top of the ridge. The sun was out again, and they had to change direction slightly, but were still headed uphill. The top of the ridge, unlike the terrain farther below, was rocky and uneven, huge boulders, broken rock, and gravel strewn about so they had to pick their way, trying to find the easiest route.

They were about a hundred yards from the top. Heather was following close behind Ian, grabbing his hand for help at times when the stretch from one rock to another was exceptionally wide, dangerously steep, or if the rock was slippery and covered with moss. But as long as she was able, she simply followed behind him, trying to duplicate his movements. She was doing that now, watching him ahead of her as she moved along. Ian's footing was deft and sure as he stepped from one rock to another, cleared a crevice about two feet wide, then started to scramble toward a small patch of grass that clung to the side of the hill.

Behind him, Heather started to imitate his brisk, sure movements, but as her foot cleared the crevice and touched the next rock, she suddenly felt her moccasined foot begin to slide. The rock beneath it felt more like gritty sand then solid stone, and there was no way she could keep her balance. She screamed, her hand striking out, hunting for something to grab onto, but Ian was too far ahead and there wasn't a tree or anything to break her fall.

There was a loud crack as her leg hit the rock; then she felt her skin being scraped viciously as her body bounced over the rest of the rocks and she slid awkwardly downward, landing in some gravelly dirt some ten feet below, the wind almost knocked out of her.

Ian stopped abruptly at her first cry, and whirled around just in time to watch in horror as she went down between the rocks. His heart jumped into his throat and with one leap he was at her side, eyes alert, face worried. "Don't move," he cautioned quickly, then brushed the hair from her face, his arm bracing her shoulders as she tried to sit up.

"My leg!" she gasped, tears already streaming down her face. "My God, Ian, my leg," and as the tears turned to deep sobs, he stared down at the buckskin breeches. Her legs were both tangled beneath her, and one was lying at a weird angle. As he started to ease her back against one of the rocks, trying to get her legs straightened in front of her, she let out a wild cry that tore into him, making him shudder.

Her arms flew around his neck and she clung to him desperately. "It hurts! Oh, God, please, it hurts," she screamed, burying her face against his shoulder, and he held her close, letting her cry until the deep sobs began to falter and she gulped back, trying to bear the pain.

Her head was cradled in his hand, and when she was no longer shaking from the sobs, he leaned back, staring into her tear-stained face, his eyes locked on hers.

"Heather, listen to me," he said, hoping she'd understand. "I have to find out just how bad it is."

"No," she groaned helplessly. "It hurts too much."

"I know it hurts, but it has to be done. If it's broken, it'll have to be set."

"Why?"

"So you won't be crippled. Now, come on, lean back against the rock, only this time I'm going to pull you part way up first so your legs will be dangling. Then I can lean you back and stretch your legs out."

"All right," she answered unsteadily, and as she clenched her teeth against the pain, he held her against him just long enough to untangle her legs, then stretched her out, so she was leaning back on the rock she'd slid down.

He released her, then took the knife from his belt and reached out, cutting away the leg of her buckskin breeches. One look was all he needed. He stared at the leg, his mouth set hard, knowing what was ahead of him. Procrastinating wouldn't help any. Reaching out with firm hands, he moved them gently over the spot where the cracked bone had punctured the skin, then sighed.

"You know what I'm going to have to do, don't you?" he asked as he looked back up at her face.

Heather's eyes were wild with fear. "You can't, Ian," she murmured. "Please. It'll hurt worse."

"If I don't, you'll never walk again."

"Oh, God!"

"Heather, look, you know I wouldn't hurt you unless I had to. You think I want this?" he said unhappily. "Lord, woman, it nearly kills me to see you in pain."

She reached out and touched his face. "I'm a coward, Ian," she whispered tearfully.

He shook his head. "Never," he answered, then caught her hand, opening the palm, kissing it tenderly. "I could never love a coward."

"Ian!"

"Shhh," he warned quickly. "Don't talk, just let me get on with it before I get too squeamish myself," and to her surprise, he leaned forward, kissed her salty lips affectionately, then leaned back again on his heels. "I'm going to leave you for a little bit," he said, frowning. "I have to find something to use for splints." While he was talking, he cut the rest of her pants leg off, then handed her what was left of the pants leg and his knife. "In the meantime, you can cut some strips from this to bind it with, and when I get back, we'll be ready to start."

He stood up, and she gazed up at him.

"Ian, I'm scared," she said, her voice breaking.

His eyes were hard, face troubled. "So am I," he answered hesitantly, then turned and started back down the hill to where they had passed a small stand of trees earlier, and she stared after him until he was out of sight.

The rest of the day was like a nightmare for Heather. When Ian returned, he pulled her over a few feet to a small boulder, and tied her to it, using the braid rope she'd made from her dress, fastening it about her waist to hold her down so he could set the leg. The break was a bad one, and the pain when Ian pulled it back into place was relieved only when she passed out. By the time she came to, he had wrapped the break to hold it together, put on the splints, and was fastening the last piece of buckskin around the splint, tying it off.

She moaned, and he let go the knot he'd just tied, hurrying to her, pulling the flask from where it hung at his belt. She was still leaning back against the rock, and he lifted the flask to her lips.

"Drink," he ordered.

She sipped at the water thankfully while he untied the rope that had been holding her. Her lips were parched, mouth even drier.

"Now what do we do?" she asked as she looked down at the bulky splints on her leg.

He tied the rope to his belt, took a swallow of the water himself, then sighed. "Well, we have a few things in our favor," he told her. "The break could have been worse. The bone could have shattered; then I couldn't have set it. Also, if you noticed, when I came back up the hill, I came from a different direction, and by going that way I not only found a small natural spring with plenty of water but also a cave we can hole up in until you're ready to travel on."

"Not again," she exclaimed disgustedly. "Will I never get home!"

He stared at her, his eyes intense. "Not for at least six weeks, maybe more," he answered curtly. "I guess you're stuck with me for a while yet."

"Oh, Ian, I didn't mean . . ." She reached out, grabbing his hand, holding it between both of hers as she studied his face. "It's just that . . ." She couldn't finish and left the words unsaid, but he seemed to understand.

"I know," he said bitterly. "Cole!" He stood up, then reached down and picked her up, cradling her in his arms, her bad leg sticking out awkwardly. "You'll like your new home," he said, trying to change the subject as he headed back down the hill, carrying her. "The cave's got plenty of room, there's grass near the door, and the closest neighbors are a pair of raccoons in a hollow tree about fifteen yards away. Now, how does that sound?"

Her arms were about his neck and she studied him thoughtfully. "Thank you, Ian," she whispered softly.

He smiled. "Forget it. I always take good care of my women," and she trembled at the deep timbre in his voice. His arms tightened about her, and as he held her close, making his way down the hill again toward the cave where he'd spend the next few weeks nursing her, once more Heather wished with all her heart that she could hate Captain Ian Brooks.

14

The afternoon sun shone down into Cole's valley, turning the sleek coats of the mustangs into a myriad of colors as Cole reined his horse first left, then right, maneuvering the last mare into the corral.

Eli, who'd been watching, grinned as Mose closed the gate.

"Now, what do you think of my idea, friend?" Cole asked as

he reined his horse over to where Eli was sitting in the saddle waiting for him. "Over fifty head and we didn't lose a one."

"Pure luck," retorted Eli.

"Luck, hell, it was brains. I remembered you telling me about the way those wild stallions keep a herd of mares with them and the way they follow him around as if he owned them, and it occurred to me that if I latched on to one or two stallions they could lead the mares right in for me, and it worked."

"After you almost got your head kicked in." Eli took a deep breath. "You take the damnedest chances. I could see you pickin' out some old mare or a young filly to make friends with on your first try, but buckin' up agin that big white stallion, and after you'd already riled him by chasin' him and his mares into that box canyon . . . only a fool'd try what you tried."

"It worked."

"God knows how."

"Just look at him," Cole said proudly as he gestured toward the corral, where a huge white stallion was prancing about, pawing the ground, his mares milling around him.

The corral was in three sections. They had put a stallion in each of the larger sections, the mares automatically following the stallion they belonged to, leaving the third part of the corral empty for breaking them in. Now that they were back, Cole made the whole adventure sound so easy, but it hadn't been. At first, out on the plains they had kept ropes only on the stallions, the mares docilely following behind. But when they reached timber country, the mares had a tendency to wander off and get lost among the trees, so they were forced to rope them into line and it wasn't easy leading a little over fifty horses strung out along a trail without trouble here and there along the way. Eli still claimed Cole was damn lucky.

They'd fought wolves, bears, and wildcats as well as almost getting scalped, but Cole had forgotten all that. All he could see now was what lay ahead, and Eli watched him as Cole reined his horse about, turning toward the cabin where Bessie and Helene had been standing watching in awe as they rode in.

Cole cantered to the hitch rail Mose had built in front of the cabin, with Eli close behind him, and both men dismounted easily.

"Well, how do you like them?" he asked Bessie as he nodded toward the corral.

She shook her head in amazement. "I ain't never seen so

many horses in all my life." She paused a minute, then looked at Cole, her eyes snapping. "And I was never so glad to see anyone show up alive. Why, you could have both been killed."

"And darn near was, some half-dozen times," complained Eli as he stared at Bessie. He'd been watching her closely ever since they'd reached the cabin. Funny, he'd never noticed before how full and velvety soft her mouth was and how the little bits of gray in her hair were more silver with the afternoon sun on them. His eyes sifted over her voluptuous figure, and he flushed, hoping she hadn't noticed his silent appraisal of her. Damn! If he didn't know better, he'd swear he'd missed her. But how could you miss someone with such a sharp tongue? And she was so bossy . . . He ignored the thought, and kept talking. "I swear Cole's gonna be the death of me yet," he went on. "Him and his damn fool ideas. He's just lucky that Comanche chief we ran into took a liking to him, or we'd a both been staked out and fed to the ants." He glanced over at Cole. "I swear, you could charm a rattlesnake if you had a mind." He turned to Bessie. "You know, that chief not only showed Cole how to tame a wild horse, but sent an escort with us all the way back to just the other side of the ridge there," and he nodded toward the hill behind the cabin.

Bessie's eyes widened. "You mean you brought Indians back with you?"

"Don't worry," Cole assured her. "They wouldn't ride all the way in with us. This is too close to Osage territory, and they said they have some scores to settle. They're already headed toward Three Forks and the Verdigris."

"And you let them?"

"There were almost a dozen of them. How was I going to stop them? Besides, I have to stay on friendly terms with them. There are too many horses running free out there for the taking."

Bessie shook her head. "Men!" she said disgustedly. "If you're not fightin' tryin' to prove how strong you are, you're schemin', tryin' to prove who's the smarter." She took a deep breath and shook her head. "I hope to goodness you won't rue the day you brought them Comanche here. That's all we need is more Indians stirrin' up trouble. There was a troop of soldiers through here the other day, said they'd been after some Osage who killed a settler and his family over near Mulberry Creek. Rumor is they were headin' west."

The laughter left Cole's eyes and he frowned. "You didn't

have any trouble while we were gone, did you?" he asked. "Mose didn't say anything when we rode in. He just seemed glad to see us."

"Nothing to speak of. Some Indians rode in one day while Mose was out huntin'. I grabbed that rifle you left with me and was waitin' in front of the door for 'em. Guess they was just hungry, though, 'cause after I had Helene bring some food out to them, they took off and never came back. Mose sat up almost all that night worryin' they might, but they didn't. Other than that, it's been quiet. Helene and I are gettin' ready to make a batch of soap, and everything's been goin' just fine. Fact is, by the time you wash up, I could probably have some food on the table for you."

"Now, that's what I call a homecomin'," Eli said, grinning.

Cole straightened, then realized Helene had been standing quietly just inside the door watching them. She was always so quiet, hovering in the background. Her large brown eyes had a haunted look and he often wondered if she had ever fully recovered from the shock of losing everyone but her mother in the steamboat explosion. It was almost as if she were living in the world without really being a part of it, and yet she seemed to know what was going on around her and occasionally joined in.

Cole smiled a greeting as he walked past Helene into the cabin, then pulled the pouch he carried on a leather thong beneath his shirt out and opened it, reaching in. He turned back, addressing the shy young girl.

"Here, Helene," he said as she moved away from the doorway. "This is for you. A young Indian girl made it, and the minute I saw it, I thought you might like it."

She stared at him, frowning skeptically.

"Go ahead, take it," he urged her. "It's just a necklace."

Helene took it from him, studying it curiously as she turned it over and over in her hands. The beads were in all different hues of pink and orange, each one carved with a special design.

"It's beautiful," she said hesitantly. "But I don't have any-place to wear such a pretty necklace."

"Wear it on your birthday." Cole smiled, trying to get her to smile back. "You'll be fourteen soon. That's a special occasion."

Her eyes suddenly sparkled and she looked up at him. "I will, won't I?" she said, as if the thought had never occurred to her before.

"Helene, you're precious," he said, laughing. "I bet you're

the only thirteen-year-old girl in the world who forgot she has to grow up.''

Helene flushed, her fingers caressing the carved beads. "Do you think maybe I could just wear them for a little while today?" she asked timidly.

Cole's eyes softened. "Wear them whenever you want. Today, tomorrow."

"Oh, no," she said very seriously. "After today I'll wear them only on special occasions. I don't want anything to happen to them. I'll keep them always," and she put them around her neck carefully, eyes shining as she fingered them.

"I think that's the first gift she ever got in her life," Bessie said as she watched Helene leave the cabin and go out into the sunshine, where she paraded back and forth, admiring the way the beads shone with the sun on them. "We never had any money for gifts, and I don't think her pa or brother would have thought of it anyway. She's really pleased, Cole."

"I worry about her sometimes," Cole said thoughtfully. "She's been through such a lot for a young girl, and living here, away from people her own age . . ."

"Don't worry, she and I are content enough," Bessie said, then turned to Eli. "And you, old man, if you intend to eat, you'd better get some of that dirt washed off or you won't sit down at my table."

"Old man, she says. Did you hear that, Cole?" Eli exclaimed. "I ain't more'n about ten years older'n she is, and she's always callin' me old man." He walked over and grabbed a towel and some soap and headed for the door. "You comin', Cole?" he barked. "Or are you some privileged character?"

Cole sauntered toward the door, watching the gleam in Eli's eyes as they settled for a brief moment on Bessie, before Eli went out; then a pang of regret washed over him. Oh, how he wished Heather were here so he could look at her like that and have her eyes dance back at him as Bessie's had just done with Eli. It had been over a month since her death. Would he never forget? And Case. How many times had he ached to hold them both. Well, that was past and he was still here, and there were things to get done, and he headed out the door behind Eli, following him to the spring to wash up after their long journey.

Bright and early the next morning, after spending an evening recounting their adventurous journey out onto the plains for the wild mustangs, telling Bessie, Helene, and Mose all the exciting details, Eli and Cole headed for the corral, with Mose beside them, ready to start the next phase of Cole's plan.

Although the big white stallion let Cole do almost anything with him, and treated Cole as a friend, Cole had never attempted to ride him. That was about to change.

Eli and Mose watched apprehensively as Cole entered the corral where the white stallion was nuzzling one of his mares. They had to admit he was beautiful. The animal threw his head back warily, then eyed Cole and nickered, identifying his friend.

"Well, big fella, are we ready to start?" Cole asked as he reached the stallion and laid a hand on his nose, patting it affectionately.

Eli put both arms on the top rail of the fence, leaned his head on them, then said, "Watch this, Mose. It's a wonder he don't get kilt," and both men watched as Cole took a rope from his waist, slipped it over the horse's head, then led him into the empty corral. Once inside, Cole turned all his attention to the horse, forgetting anything or anyone else was around.

He began talking to the big stallion, stroking him on the head and neck while he talked, then leaning forward, breathing into the horse's nostrils softly, while all the while his hands caressed the animal.

Eli and Mose watched the horse's withers tremble with response to the familiarity of Cole's nearness. At first, out on the plains when Cole had done this, the horse's two forefeet had been hobbled and a noose fastened around his underjaw, but now he no longer feared Cole's nearness, seeming to relish the attention he was getting.

As Cole's hands moved farther back onto the stallion's neck, his words being spoken directly into the animal's ear, Eli tensed. Cole's hands kept up their movement, stroking and petting as they continued to move farther and farther back on the animal, until now suddenly he was rubbing the animal's back with gentle, deft strokes.

The horse's ears twitched and he nickered nervously, shifting from one foot to the other, but he still held his ground as Cole continued talking and petting. Then, instead of just stroking, Cole leaned against the horse, letting him feel the familiar weight of a body against him, and all this time Cole kept up a low, pleasant chant, commending the stallion on his beauty and courage, as if the horse understood every word.

"Now comes the best part," Eli whispered to Mose, and as

both men stared, Cole quickly grasped the horse's mane and easily leaped onto his back, his long legs hugging the big stallion's sides.

The horse neighed, throwing his head back, and started rearing onto his hind legs, but as Cole kept talking and caressing his sleek white coat, he quickly settled down, although his nostrils flared and he shifted skittishly, pawing at the ground.

"He did it," Eli said, grinning eagerly.

Mose frowned. "He gonna do 'em all that way?"

"He sure as hell is."

"What about the saddles?"

Eli nodded toward the corral. "Watch." Within half an hour, using the same procedure, Cole was back on the horse again, a saddle beneath him, a bit with reins in the horse's mouth.

Cole patted the big stallion's head, then nudged him in the sides and rode him to the fence where Eli and Mose were still watching.

"Well, we're on our way, Eli," he said, pleased with himself.

Eli smiled, amazed at his young friend. "You win, Cole." But his eyes gazed out over the herd of horses in the two corrals, studying the dun-colored stallion riding herd over the mares that didn't belong to the white horse. He looked back at Cole. "That's still a lot of horseflesh, Cole," he said. "And they won't all be as easy as this."

Cole nodded. "At least it'll keep me busy," he said, then glanced at Mose. "Open the gate, Mose," he ordered. "I want to see what he'll do, given his head," and Mose opened the gate wide, Cole dug the big white stallion in the ribs and they took off, heading toward the far end of the valley.

When Cole returned from his ride, for the rest of the day his time was spent in the corrals, repeating over and over again the lessons the Comanche chief had taught him. Some of the mares tamed well, others fought him stubbornly, but by the end of the first week he knew it was going to be worth it, and each day that followed confirmed his earlier optimism. By the time April rolled around, he was certain they were going to beat the end-of-May deadline by weeks.

It was early afternoon the end of the first week in April. Cole had been busy all morning and had just finished eating lunch. Now he was on his way back to the corral. The weather had warmed, the day was hot, and he was shirtless, his body glistening a deep bronze under the same sun that made his hair shimmer an iridescent blue-black.

He had sent Mose on ahead to get one of the mares ready. Suddenly he glanced up, a movement in the hills toward the east catching his attention, and he squinted, stopping to shade his eyes against the early-afternoon sun.

"Mose! Come here," he called, and Mose tied the rope of the mare he was leading onto the rail fence, climbed it quickly, then dropped to the outside of the corral. "Grab the rifles!" Cole yelled. Mose reached down by the gate and snapped up two rifles that were leaning against the fence near it, then hurried to Cole on the run. He handed one to Cole; then both men walked slowly toward the end of the corral, rifles ready, waiting as the movement in the hills slowly became distinguishable.

Two people riding horseback were leading what looked like a strange menagerie down the side of the hill. There were at least four mules with what looked like a couple of sheep and a cow bringing up the rear. Some of the mules carried large crates; the others were bundled high with supplies.

Cole frowned as he watched; then suddenly he relaxed as Eli joined them.

"It's my supplies, Eli," Cole said, realizing what was going on. "I told Bradford to send someone out with them. Look," and he pointed. "There's the cow, sheep, and if my guess is right, those crates have chickens and geese in them."

Eli shook his head. "If that don't beat all," and as they watched the procession move closer, their rifles lowered.

For a few moments Cole forgot about the horses as he watched the people bringing the supplies he'd sent for, move down to the floor of the valley, and with them came the remembrance of the happiness he'd felt ordering them. The cow, sheep, everything had been for Heather and Case, to make their life better, and he had planned a garden so Heather could have the vegetables she liked so well.

He swallowed back the lump in his throat, forcing himself to put the memories behind him. He still needed everything. There were Bessie and Helene to think of, and he straightened, determined not to let the past interfere.

"Hello, there!" someone called, and Cole waved back, studying the tall figure on the horse that was leading the procession. Whoever the man was, he was wearing a floppy straw hat, with his legs dangling down at his horse's sides, showing he was a big man. His companion, riding farther back, toward the end of the mule train, helping guide the farm animals, was slighter of build. In fact, from where Cole and the others were standing, it looked like a young boy.

Cole stared, his green eyes deepening in color as he watched them approach; then suddenly a frown creased his forehead and he looked puzzled.

"The fellow in the lead, the one with the red beard," he said to Eli, who was standing next to him. "He looks familiar."

Eli shook his head. "Never seen him before."

"I have. Only where?"

The riders drew closer, and it wasn't until Zeke Baldridge took off his hat that Cole recognized him, only he couldn't remember his first name.

"Baldridge, that's who it is," exclaimed Cole as the big man slid from his horse and reached out to shake hands. "But I don't understand . . ."

"Who is Baldridge?" asked Eli as Cole shook hands with the husky young man, who was about his same age and height, but built more massively, with brown hair on his head, and on his chin, the most beautiful red beard Eli had ever seen.

"I stayed with the Baldridges on my way to see you a year ago New Year's Eve," explained Cole quickly. "But tell me," he asked Zeke, "what the hell are you doing out here, and with my supplies?"

"I guess I'm the one who should answer that," said a feminine voice from behind Zeke, and Cole stared in surprise as the other rider dismounted, removing her hat, letting a thick head of amber hair fall to her shoulders.

"Lily?" he gasped.

"Hello, Duke, or should I call you Cole?"

He shook his head, flabbergasted. "I don't understand . . ."

She took a deep breath, holding the old hat in front of her as if it gave her courage. "It's a rather long story," she began hesitantly.

"And a rather strange coincidence," he replied. "I'd never dreamed . . ."

She looked up at him, her brown eyes embarrassed. "It's not a coincidence," she said sheepishly. "It was deliberately planned."

Cole studied her curiously. "Go ahead, I'm listening."

"Well . . ." She paused, taking another deep breath. "Last summer a stranger came through like you did. His name was

Bernie Catlin, and he said he was headed for St. Lous to help his
uncle, who owned a feed and supply store. He stayed with us for
a while, and when it was time to leave, he asked me to go with
him. Bernie was a nice sort, he was from the South, like you,
and we got along pretty well, so I agreed to go with him, and we
were supposed to be married when we reached St. Louis.'' Lily
glanced over at her brother. ''Zeke came along to make sure
everything went like it was supposed to. You know how Papa
was. But by the time we reached St. Louis, Bernie was pretty
sick, so we had to wait to get married until he got better. Only
he didn't get better, he died about a month after we got there.
His uncle was nice, though, and let Zeke and me work at his
place, so we didn't have to go back home. I didn't want to go
back there. That's why, when that soldier from Fort Smith came
in and said he had an order for supplies to be sent out to Belle
Pointe, for a man named Duke Avery, I knew it just had to be
you. There couldn't be more'n one Duke Avery, so we talked
Bernie's uncle into lettin' us bring your things to you.'' She
flushed. ''So you see, it wasn't any coincidence. When I heard
your name, I told Zeke we had to come.''

Cole didn't know what to say. He stared at Lily. She had
changed. Her once plump body was almost lost in the men's
clothes she was wearing, and although the little-girl innocence
still glistened in her eyes, she had matured in the past year, and
in spite of the old clothes, she was very attractive, even with dirt
on her face.

''But why?'' he asked.

She straightened, hands tightening on the hat. ''I figured you
might be lonesome by now,'' she said truthfully. ''And there
was nothing for us in St. Louis.''

''But to come all the way out here on a whim . . .''

''It wasn't a whim. Zeke said you were going to need someone to plant the seed you ordered, and I figured you'd probably
need someone to take care of your house. Since you were still
out here in the wilderness, I figured you must have decided to
forget all about that girl you said you were running away from.''

''I didn't forget her,'' Cole said huskily.

''We found that out,'' said Zeke. ''Major Bradford told us all
about it when we reached Belle Pointe, but we figured as long as
we were this close, we'd come the rest of the way. After all, you
still need someone to help plant.'' He looked out over the
corrals. ''Looks like you got your hands full of horses right now.''

"And I can still help with the house," said Lily, smiling warmly. "The major said you had a housekeeper, but she could probably use some help."

Cole glanced over at the rustic cabin. "It isn't much of a house yet," he said, then caught himself. "But here, I haven't introduced you two." He turned back to Eli and Mose. "Eli, Mose, this is Zeke Baldridge and his sister Lily. Lily, Zeke, this is Eli Crawford, the man I was on my way to meet when I stopped by your place, and this"—he put an arm about Mose's shoulder—"this is Mose Wheatley. He sort of runs the place when I'm not around."

They shook hands all around, and Cole scratched his head as he began to walk down the line of mules, checking what was on them. He'd been right. There were crates of chickens and geese, bags and bundles, a plow, shovels, buckets, everything he had ordered, including bags of seed and gunpowder.

"Doesn't look like you forgot anything," he said.

Lily smiled. "We didn't. Fact is, you sent more'n enough money to pay for everything, so I added a few things you might be able to use, like some blankets, a kettle and pans, as well as some material for clothes."

"We make our own," Cole said. "Mose made a loom and spinning wheel and Bessie's learned how to make cloth out of almost anything she gets her hands on that even faintly resembles a fiber, but I thank you anyway."

Lily was watching Cole. He was still wearing the beard he'd worn when she'd first met him, but it was neatly clipped now and emphasized the blue-black sheen of his hair. Every bit as tall as she remembered, he walked with a catlike grace, muscles rippling across his broad back, buckskin pants tapering his slim waist. He was even better-looking than she remembered.

"Well, do we stay?" she asked after he'd checked over the supplies.

He frowned. "I can't pay you."

"Who said anything about pay?"

"I already have four to feed besides myself."

"Zeke knows how to hunt, and I don't eat much."

Cole glanced at the mules, then looked Lily and Zeke over thoughtfully. "I don't know where you're going to sleep. The cabin only has two bedrooms."

Lily flushed. "We don't mind sleeping on the floor."

Cole rubbed his chin. "We could probably use more help, but . . . What do you think, Eli?" he asked.

Eli shrugged. "I ain't much for gardenin' Cole," he offered. "And I don't think Mose cares much for it either, do you?"

Mose frowned. "I'd rather work with horses, Cole."

Cole patted one of the mules on the back. "For now, Mose can take you to the cabin and introduce you to Bessie and Helene," he said, unable to decide. "I'll let you know tonight. Right now, I've got some mares to break," and he motioned for Mose to take the entourage on up to the cabin.

Cole stood next to the rail fence watching Mose lead them away. Lily kept glancing back reluctantly.

"She's a pretty little gal," Eli said as he watched her sauntering along, absentmindedly herding the cow and sheep ahead of her.

"I hadn't noticed," said Cole, but he had. Maybe that's why he was having such a hard time deciding whether to let them stay. The past year had done well by Lily Baldridge. When he'd looked into her big brown eyes, watching the gold flecks dance in them, he remembered all too well that winter night a little over a year ago when she'd soothed the loneliness inside him, and a small voice kept telling him maybe she could do it again. Only he wasn't sure he wanted to let her, not just yet. Heather's death was still too new to him, the pain still festering, and he was so afraid trying to heal it too soon would only drive the pain deeper.

"You can't mourn her forever," Eli said as he watched Cole's face.

Cole straightened, anger at his thoughts and Eli's assumption bringing a quick response. "I think you'd better mind your own business, Eli," he said irritably, and stalked away, going back to his horses, where there wasn't time to brood about the past.

That evening, Cole made his decision. Lily and Zeke could stay. Lily would help Bessie and Helene, and Zeke would plow, plant, and tend the garden, as well as help hunt for game, and since circumstances were different now, the three women would have one bedroom, while the four men shared the other.

"And if you snore, Eli," Cole said as they sat around the dinner table that evening, "you're going to end up sleeping with the horses." Everyone laughed, and for the first time in weeks, Cole laughed with them, the memory of his loss eased somewhat by the coming of this young woman and her brother.

Zeke proved to be a veritable treasure. He handled the mules with expertise, whether plowing, hauling logs for a barn he'd decided should be built, or riding them, and he could tell a yarn as well as Eli, although Cole was certain most of his tales were pure fabrication. Besides being big in stature, he was bighearted, and his one wistful hope for the future was to go back to St. Louis someday and find himself a woman.

Unlike Eli, who was more of a loner, Zeke and Mose became close friends, and before long it was apparent that when Mose wasn't with the horses and Zeke wasn't in the garden, they were with each other, either hunting, or fishing, or working on the barn Zeke was determined to build.

The days moved on, the seeds in the garden sprouted, the plants grew, and every night Cole fell asleep exhausted, yet pleased at the headway he was making. And with each new day that passed, the valley was becoming more and more livable for him. Then slowly Cole began to realize why. Ever since her arrival, Lily had been subtly easing her way into his life. She was there in the morning when he woke up, helping Bessie with breakfast, her soft laughter warming the day; she brought his lunch to the corral in the afternoon and stayed while he ate, talking with him about any number of things; and by the end of the first week her presence was already being felt, so it was no surprise some weeks later when Cole found himself strolling with her one evening before bedtime, just the two of them.

Lily had made herself a dress out of some of the material she and Zeke had brought from St. Louis. It was a pink-and-white calico, very feminine and very nice, and as Cole glanced over at her, while they headed for the corral, he marveled again at the change in her. She wasn't as thin as most women, but on her it looked good. She was rounded and voluptuous, the kind of woman who looked all soft and warm.

"You're almost through breaking them, aren't you?" she asked as they reached the corral.

He put a hand on the top rail and looked out over the herd, feeling a pride in them he couldn't explain.

"Almost," he answered. "About another week's work and we'll be able to start toward Fort Smith."

"Then what?"

"I start all over again. There's a market for horses back east."

"That's why you came here?"

"That, and because I like it here." He straightened, looking off toward the far end of the valley.

"What was she like, Cole?" she asked after a long moment of silence.

He sighed. "Heather?"

"Yes."

"She was beautiful, fragile . . . If you don't mind, Lily, it hurts," he said softly.

She frowned. "I'm sorry. I thought maybe if you talked about it. I heard Mama say once that sometimes it's best to talk about things that hurt and bring them out in the open, then the hurt isn't so bad."

"I don't think this hurt will ever go away," he said bitterly. "What makes it even worse is it's all my fault."

"How can you say that?"

"Because it's true. She didn't belong here, and yet I made her come. I loved this valley so much that I blinded myself to the truth. I should have listened to Captain Brooks."

"Captain Brooks?"

"He was one of the soldiers we came up the Arkansas with. He saw what I couldn't see, and warned me that bringing her here was a mistake, only I didn't listen." Tears welled up in his eyes. "Now she's gone."

"You had no idea."

"I knew the wilderness could be cruel and dangerous."

Lily put her hand on his arm. "Cole, don't blame yourself, please. Eli told me what happened. You didn't know those men would follow you here."

He sighed. "But I knew Heather didn't belong, and I closed my eyes to it."

"I think you're being too hard on yourself. How can you be so sure she didn't belong? Just because she looked fragile . . . I may look strong and sturdy, Cole—Papa always said I was healthy stock—but if the same thing happened to me that happened to her, I'd be just as dead. It has nothing to do with belonging or not belonging, it has to do with circumstances. Your wife's death wasn't any more your fault than Bernie's death was mine. The only difference is you loved your wife. I didn't love Bernie."

Cole studied her face. How wise she was for her years. What was she, eighteen? Nineteen?

"I had a son, too, Lily," he said.

"I know. Eli told me."

"Seems Eli told you a great deal."

"I asked him." She looked up into his eyes. It was getting dark and his face was hard to see. "I came out here to find Duke Avery, but instead found Cole Dante. I think I like Duke Avery better, he was less complicated, not quite so hard on himself."

"Duke Avery was a fool," Cole said quickly. "If he'd had any brains, he'd never have left South Carolina."

"On the contrary, Cole Dante's the fool," she said softly. "If he had any brains, he'd know that the world doesn't have to end with one woman and one child."

Cole's eyes searched hers in the growing darkness, and a warmth coursed through him. He *was* a fool. Here was everything he needed to forget Heather, at least for a while. Someone to make him feel whole again.

He reached out and cupped her head in his hand. "Can you still the ache inside, Lily?" he asked gently. "Can you really make me forget, even for a little while?"

"I'd like to try."

He leaned down, his lips caressing her neck, the warm woman scent of her filling his nostrils, firing his loins. Then in one sweeping motion he drew her to him, his mouth covering hers, and kissed her long and hard until the bittersweet pain was gone, leaving a vibrant yearning in its wake.

He drew back, looking down at her, his eyes intense. "You're right, I've been a fool," he whispered softly, then sighed. "How would you like to go to Fort Smith with us?" he asked as he held her close.

"You need an extra hand with the horses?"

"I want you near me."

She stared up at him, her brown eyes steady on his. "Don't worry, I'll be here when you get back."

He shook his head. "I can't take that chance. You're coming with me."

"All right, I'll go with you," she whispered softly, and sighed as his arms tightened about her, and he kissed her again, this time with an urgency that was almost frightening.

For the next few days Cole and Lily spent more and more time together laughing and enjoying each other's company, and although Cole kissed her often and held her close, not once did he attempt to make love to her. Then at the end of the week, Cole, Eli, Zeke, and Lily left Cole's valley with fifty horses in tow, heading for Fort Smith, leaving only the white stallion behind, a move Eli knew was coming as he saw Cole become more attached to the animal with every passing day. Cole still rode his piebald mare, but the white stallion was becoming very special to him. He was a symbol of the valley perhaps, or a reminder of why he was there. Whatever it was, Eli knew Cole wasn't about to part with the animal, and it was no surprise when he was left behind.

It was supposed to take them four or five days to reach Belle Pointe, and their first night out they camped near a small stream, the night breeze bringing the scent of summer flowers with it. Lily was surprised to learn that summer flowers bloomed here in April and May instead of June and July like back in the Ohio Valley, and she loved flowers.

They had already eaten, and it was almost time to turn in. Lily was restless and had been all day. She stood up and walked along the stream away from where the men were talking, enjoying the peace and quiet of the night, stopping occasionally to pick a flower that was unable to escape the moonlight. Her thoughts wandered randomly, then finally settled on the reason for her unrest. Their first day had been a strange one. Cole had been wound like a spring, so afraid something would go wrong, but as the day wore on, he began to relax, although she still sensed a tension in him that was puzzling. He had his horses, they were all saddle-broken, he was delivering them three weeks early, and there was no reason for him to worry, yet something was wrong.

She sighed, then stiffened at a sound behind her.

"You shouldn't wander so far away," Cole said as he stepped from the shadows. She was wearing men's clothes again and once more looked lost in them. She sighed, relieved it was him, then studied him curiously. "What's wrong, Cole?" she asked.

He frowned. "You don't know?"

"Is it me?"

"It is and it isn't." He reached out slowly, almost reluctantly, pulling her into his arms. "I need you, Lily," he said huskily. "Yet I'm so afraid. I tried once before to forget her with other women, but it only made the wanting worse. I'm so afraid that'll happen again, and I don't want to hurt you."

"How could that hurt me?"

"Because I still love her, even though I know I'll never see her again." He reached up, running his hand through Lily's hair, watching the moon turning it to a pale golden brown. "I like you, Lily," he whispered softly. "You make me laugh when

I'm crying inside. You're warm and sweet, and I enjoy being with you but what I feel for you isn't love, I know that. It's what I'd feel toward any attractive woman under the circumstances, and that could hurt you. I told you last year, you're not the kind of woman a man can take lightly. You deserve love and marriage, and I'm not ready for marriage again. Not yet. Maybe never again, I don't know.''

"I'm not asking you to marry me, Cole," she answered. "I just want to be near you."

"That's just it." His eyes deepened passionately. "How can I keep you near, so close, and not touch you? I'm not a saint, Lily." His voice dropped to barely a whisper. "Right now I ache inside for what I had with Heather, and I know you can soothe it some and make life livable again for me, but I can't ask you to, knowing deep in my heart I'd only be using you as a substitute for her. I couldn't do that to you, don't you see, and it's driving me crazy."

She reached up and touched his lips with her fingertips. "Don't, Cole, please," she murmured. "Don't keep hurting yourself like this. If I give myself to you it'll be because I want to, not just because you need a woman. That night last winter, I begged you to make love to me and you refused, but you did give me something. You gave me a sweet taste of what it could be like, so when Bernie came along, I begged him to make love to me too, figuring this time it would be complete. He reminded me a little of you, with his dark hair and what Papa called his southern drawl, and I was hoping . . . But he wasn't like you. I thought it wouldn't matter that I didn't really love him, that there was no feeling when I was with him, but it did." She flushed as his eyes grew intense. "It happened in the barn the night before we left for St. Louis, and I hated it, Cole. He was nothing like you. There was no warmth, no tenderness. Only hurt and frustration. When it was over I felt so empty inside."

"And still you went with him?"

"I felt I owed it to him. Besides, I didn't want to stay in the middle of nowhere and I thought maybe in time it'd get better."

"Did it?"

"He never touched me again. We were with Zeke all the way to St. Louis, then Bernie got sick." Her hand touched Cole's neck, caressing it. "When Bernie died, I promised myself no one would ever touch me again unless I had the same feelings inside I had the night I was with you, and no one's made me feel that way till now, Cole. I feel all warm and giddy again, just like I did then.''

"I don't love you, Lily.''

"I know.''

"You can accept that?''

"I'm not a saint either, Cole,'' she whispered. "I'm willing to take my chances that you will someday. For now, let this be enough.''

Her lips were so close, her mouth inviting, and the feel of her body against him was like heady wine, stirring him. "I don't know . . .''

"Cole, let me try,'' she pleaded softly. "Let me take away the pain. I have enough love for both of us.''

Her eyes locked with his, her body yielding against him, and he couldn't fight it any longer. With an agonized groan, wrenched from deep inside him, he picked her up, cradling her in his arms, and went deeper into the woods along the stream until he found a place where the grass was soft, then gently laid her down.

Her body opened to him as he undressed her, the moonlight caressing her soft, rounded flesh, and as Cole's hands stroked and teased, his lips sipping at her mouth passionately, Lily felt her heart sing. This was what love was like, what it should be like, not that horrible mistake she had made with Bernie. This was heaven, and she reveled in it as Cole accepted her body as if it were a special gift just for him. And it was.

To Lily, she was giving Cole back his life, and with it went a part of her. Yet she never knew that as Cole moved over her, his long lean body covering hers, and entered her slowly, trying to savor the moment, to make it special for her, all he could see in his heart was Heather. And with every beat that pulsed through his body, throbbing in his loins as he brought her to pleasures she never dreamed existed, the ghost of Heather haunted him, mocking and taunting him until he wanted to cry out. Then, as he closed his eyes, trembling helplessly, climaxing deep within Lily, the battle was suddenly over and Cole knew he had lost when his release left him still wanting, and a sad, empty feeling gripped him.

He rolled off her, then held her close, trying to capture some of her warmth, to let it soothe him and take the empty feeling from him, and it did help some. She was soft and velvety in his arms, her flesh sensuous against his, and her lips, touching his throat lightly with feathery kisses, pleased him.

He sighed, knowing full well she was content, yet wanting to hear her say it. Instead she said, "I love you, Cole."

He tensed. If only he could lie to her and tell her what she wanted to hear, but he couldn't, not with the ghost of Heather haunting his every waking moment. His arms tightened about Lily and he reached up, stroking her hair. "Someday, maybe someday," he whispered softly, and tilted her head up until their lips met, and he kissed her again, long and hard, trying to purge himself from the past, which had brought him so much pain, and hoping this trip to Fort Smith was going to be the start of a new beginning.

15

Early morning was always the worst time for Heather, when she'd wake up shivering, with no one to cuddle up to. Although summer was well on its way, the nights were cool. She did have a thin blanket, which she usually ended up twisting out of somehow, so most of the time she woke up cold. This morning was no exception.

She glanced a few feet away to where Ian was still sleeping. He didn't even have a blanket, yet seemed to sleep so peacefully, and never complained about being cold. Early-morning mists were drifting up from the valley below, swirling about at the mouth of the cave, and now streaks of gold from the sun began to dance through them, making everything outside glitter and shine.

Heather sat up, then reached down and felt her leg. Today was the day he'd promised to take off the splints. It was still shadowed in the cave and she pulled herself about, leaning back against the rock wall, watching the last few embers of the fire glowing. She had lost track of how long they'd been here and how long it had been since she'd been kidnapped. At first it was easy to keep track, but after the miscarriage, and then her leg . . . She figured it must be almost May, or at least well into April. The woodland flowers were blooming already, and Cole had told her the flowers bloomed early here, like in South Carolina. Her mouth eased into a smile as she thought back to the afternoon a few days ago when Ian had gone hunting and come back with a bouquet of wildflowers for her. He had laughed about it, making sport of them, but she had seen the look in his eyes as he handed them to her, and heard the unmistakable tremor in his voice as he tried to pretend it was an afterthought on his part. She knew why he had brought them.

Each day with him was a battle for her. One she wished she could have avoided. If only he'd do something so she could hate him. Instead, he nursed her when she became fevered with an infection in her broken leg, spoon-fed her when she was unable to feed herself, made crutches for her to use so she could get around the cave, and treated her like a queen, without ever once yelling at her and blaming her for the predicament they were in. The only time he was ever angry with her was when she began to lose heart or wanted to give up, blaming herself for slipping and breaking her leg. Then he'd snap at her irritably. Most of the time, however, it was his uncanny good humor and warm companionship that made the day worth waking for.

Ian stirred, then turned onto his side facing Heather, and his eyelids fluttered. She watched them open slowly, an easy smile lifting the corners of his mouth. He took a deep breath, blinked, then stretched on the floor of the cave, his long muscular body taut against his clothes; then he sighed and sat up, running a hand through his tousled hair. It was growing long again. He rubbed his chin. The weather was getting a little warm for a beard, but he wasn't about to shave it off with a hunting knife. He found a few stray strands that had gotten too long, took the knife from its sheath, and whacked them off carefully. At least he could keep it trimmed; that wasn't too much of a job.

He glanced over at Heather, wondering how long she'd been awake. "I suppose you're hungry," he said as he slipped the knife back into its sheath.

"Not necessarily." She reached down, touching her leg. "I'm much more anxious to get these things off."

"Ah, yes, I did tell you we'd take them off today." He stood up slowly, stretching, and began stirring up the fire, throwing some more wood on. He'd built the fire near the mouth of the cave so the smoke would go out, and now he glanced outside. "Looks like it's going to be a pretty day." He turned back to her, then walked over, kneeling down beside her. "I wonder if it won't be too soon."

"You promised."

His eyes were glistening wickedly as they caught hers. "I've been known to break promises."

"Ian! Please, it's been so long."

She looked so vulnerable in the morning with her eyes heavy from sleep and wisps of curls framing her face. He had carved a comb of sorts for her from a piece of wood, and it worked quite well, but often during the night some of the hair would come loose from where the ribbon held it, and he always liked the way it made her look in the morning.

"All right," he said huskily. "But just because I take the splints off doesn't mean you're going to be able to get up and start walking right away."

"I know."

"Ready?" he asked.

She nodded expectantly, and he took a deep breath, then reached down and began untying the splints. After setting them aside and unwrapping the strips of buckskin that held the break in place, his fingers began carefully examining where the break had been, moving slowly back and forth on her leg and she watched him anxiously. The skin was pale and withered-looking from being wrapped for weeks.

"It looks weird," she said, watching him feel to make sure everything was all right.

"Don't worry," he assured her. "It'll be back to normal in no time."

She sighed. "Sometimes I don't think anything'll ever be back to normal again, including me."

He started to get up, then reached out for her hands. "Come on, time to try standing on it."

She faltered. "Right away? Can't I just get used to not having the splints on it for a little bit before I start walking on it?"

"I have to know if it's healed enough. If not, the splints have to go back on."

She reached up, letting him pull her to her feet.

"Keep your weight on your left leg until you're all the way up," he said as he reached out, an arm circling her waist to help her.

She leaned against him, then shifted all her weight on to her left foot before gingerly letting her right foot touch the ground.

"Easy," he cautioned. "Take it slow."

At first it hurt quite a bit when she stood on it, but after a few minutes the pain eased until the only time it hurt was when she walked, causing her to limp. She didn't like the limp, but was determined to get better, so for the rest of the day she exercised the leg and walked as much as Ian would let her, trying to build up the muscles again. That evening, content with the way the day had gone, she sat in front of the fire dreaming about home and the day they could leave, when suddenly she felt a strange sense of loss come over her, one she had no way of explaining.

Ian had decided to make a cane for her to use and was sitting across from her whittling, carving a fancy handle on it, and she had been watching him for some time. Now she continued to stare across the fire, her eyes still on him, and although she sensed he was aware she'd been studying him, neither of them spoke and it was so quiet all that could be heard were the crackling of the fire, the faint rasp as the hunting knife bit into the wood, and their soft breathing.

Suddenly Ian stopped whittling and looked up, across the fire, directly into Heather's eyes. He stared intently. Still neither of them spoke; then slowly Heather stood up, limped to the mouth of the cave, and stepped outside. The night was warm, but that wasn't why she was so flushed or why she was trembling inside.

She swallowed hard, hugging her arms against the darkness, and lifted her head, gazing at the stars overhead. They were so clear and bright, it almost looked like she could touch them. What a beautiful night. Somewhere down in the valley a wildcat screeched, and she shuddered.

"You're cold?" Ian asked from behind her.

She turned, startled. "I didn't hear you."

"Did I do something wrong?" he asked.

"No."

"Then what is it? Something's bothering you."

She shook her head. "I don't know."

"Don't you?"

"Ian!"

"Dammit, Heather," he blurted. "You know very well what's wrong. We've both been fighting it for weeks now."

"No!"

"Heather." He reached out, pulling her hard against him. "You know how I feel about you, how I've felt about you for a long time, and I think you care too, more than you want to admit."

She shook her head stubbornly. "It's the loneliness, being with you every day like this . . . that's all it is."

"Is it? Look at me and tell me you don't care."

She turned her head away.

"Heather look at me." He reached out, cupping her face with his hand, forcing her to face him, but she avoided his eyes. "Look at me," he demanded stubbornly, and bent his head so no matter where she looked, she'd have to look into his eyes.

She cried his name, murmuring it softly in protest; then their eyes met, and suddenly her voice was gone. She couldn't speak, could hardly breathe as she stared at him, feeling a surging warmth begin spreading through her, like heat flooding every nerve in her body.

"Now tell me you don't care," Ian whispered fervently.

She held her breath, her body quivering in his arms, then sighed. "It's wrong, Ian, all wrong," she said, her voice breaking. "What I'm feeling now has nothing to do with caring."

"Doesn't it? What does your heart tell you, Heather?" he asked, his arms still holding her close. "How will you tell your heart not to feel when we're forced to say good-bye?"

"No . . . no . . ."

His eyes softened. His hand was still holding her head, and he wiped a tear from her eye with his thumb. "Love isn't something we ask for, Heather," he said, trying to persuade her. "I didn't ask to love you. It's just something that's there, whether we want it to be or not, even when we try to pretend it isn't, like you've been doing for weeks now."

"It's not true . . ."

"Heather, sweet Heather." His hand moved to her chin, and he tilted her head up. "Maybe this will convince you." Slowly, reverently, his lips touched hers, softly sipping at them with a tenderness that made her ache inside, and all at once she knew he was right. Somehow, someway, she had grown to love him, and the realization only made it worse, because as he was kissing her, filling her with all the familiar sensations she'd felt in Cole's arms, she knew that in spite of him, in spite of everything, she still loved Cole, and it was frightening.

She'd never known anything like this could be possible. She loved Cole, and yet . . . did she really love Ian? It wasn't just desire and the need to feel a man's arms around her. Somehow she knew it was more than that.

She drew her lips from his and studied his face for a moment. The brown eyes, so expressive, so vibrantly alive, and the mouth, so soft, yet firm, and always so quick to smile. She reached up, running her fingertips across his beard, and she felt him tremble against her. His face was as intimately dear to her as Cole's, and she knew every inch of it. He was right. She did care. She cared too much, and it hurt.

"It's no good, Ian," she said after a few moments. "Yes, I care. I shouldn't, I know, only somehow I do, but that doesn't make it right. I love Cole, you know that, I'm his wife."

"I keep reminding myself of that every day," he said. "But it doesn't help."

There were tears in her eyes. "There can never be anything between us, Ian."

"There already is."

She felt defeated. "Hold me," she whispered softly. "For just a moment, hold me, Ian."

He held her close, burying his head in her soft hair, but when it was time to let go, he couldn't, and picked her up, cradling her in his arms as he carried her back into the cave. He laid her down gently on her blanket, and when she started to protest, his lips covered hers in a kiss that conquered the last vestige of strength she had left. Then, as his hands began to fumble with her buckskin shirt, she dredged up one last ounce of resistance and pushed him away, shaking her head, grabbing his hands, stopping him.

"No, Ian, please!" she begged. "I can't do this to Cole. Please, don't . . ."

Her fingers tightened on his hands, and he gazed down into her face. He wanted her so badly it hurt.

"What of me?" he pleaded helplessly. "Heather, I'm dying inside. Let me love you just once. Once to last a lifetime!" and he bent down, kissing her again, his lips caressing hers over and over, until she was on fire, her body aching for him, all thoughts of Cole vanishing under the spell of the love he was asking her to share with him. Then slowly, when he knew she was no longer fighting him, once more he reached down for the buckskin pants she wore, and stripped them from her.

His hands molded to the contours of her hips, and he marveled at her softness as they arched up, her need as great as his. There was surrender in her now, total, complete surrender, and Ian accepted it with a passion that frightened him. Never had he felt so close to a woman, so much a part of her, as he did at this moment. His hand circled her breast affectionately, then continued down, stroking her flesh, settling into the patch of curly red hair that hid the heart of her longing.

Then, as he felt her hands move beneath his shirt, sending shivers of desire through him, playing over his taut muscles, he wriggled free of his own clothes, and stretched out with her, his body savoring the touch of her flesh against his.

"You're so lovely," he murmured as he leaned over her. "So rarely sweet," and his head lowered, his lips nuzzling her neck, playing lightly on her skin, making pleasurable shocks run through her.

Heather's eyes closed and she held her breath, letting his lips assault the raging currents that tore through her body. It had been so long, and Ian knew exactly what to do.

His hands teased and tormented, his lips taking as well as giving, while he told her over and over again how much he loved her, and when his body finally covered her, and she felt him searching for her, she opened herself to him, then groaned ecstatically as he entered.

He moved in slowly, and she felt it through her whole body, each movement a delight, until he finally reached the center of her being; then he thrust hard, becoming one with her, and she wanted to crawl inside him. Heather clung to him desperately, wanting him, needing him, loving him; then, as he began to move in and out, giving her pleasures she had once thought only Cole could give her, seeking the love that he'd denied himself for so long, they were both lost in a world of bliss that clung for a brief moment on the edge of sanity before transporting them to a heaven all their own, where no one else existed but the two of them.

Heather moaned frantically, knowing the moment they had been waiting for was reaching them both at the same time, yet she couldn't stop, and twisted to and fro, caught in the frenzy of her release, hoping the sweet sensations flowing through her would never stop, trying to capture every precious moment as if it were the last, while Ian, deep inside, gloried in the aftermath of what for him had been a touch of heaven. Then he gazed down into her face, shadowed by the firelight. Her body was slowing its movements, and he watched her closely, marveling at how lovely she was even in the wild throes of passion; then slowly she trembled and stopped twisting, her body pressed to his as if she never wanted to let him go.

Heather sighed and opened her eyes.

"I love you," Ian whispered tenderly, and leaned down, kissing her softly, sealing the moment for them forever.

He lifted his head briefly, then dropped it down next to hers, rolled partway on his side, carrying her with him, and held her close in his arms.

Heather swallowed hard, her body still satiated with the love he'd given her; then suddenly tears welled up in her eyes.

"Heather?" he asked, his hand caressing her face.

"Don't let me go, not just yet," she murmured softly.

He kissed her again, his mouth lingering on hers for a long time, the feelings between them still so strong Heather trembled.

"Stay with me all night," Ian pleaded softly.

She sighed. "A night to remember?"

"For eternity," he said, and began kissing her again until she felt as though she had always belonged here in his arms. He made love to her again, more slowly this time, savoring every precious moment; then they fell asleep in each other's arms.

The next morning, dawn was just beginning to filter in among the trees in the valley when Heather felt the first cold chill touch her bare flesh. Her eyes opened slowly as the remembrance of last night came back to her, and she took a deep breath, staring at Ian's face close to hers. He was still sleeping peacefully, his breathing even. How handsome he looked, his face all tanned, hair like spun gold where the sun had streaked it.

For a long time she stared, trying to understand what was happening to her, then closed her eyes again, and suddenly thoughts of Cole began to invade her. Cole with his green eyes that always warmed her deep inside, Cole who was more dear to her than life itself, who taught her the meaning of love and shared his life with her, who gave her his son.

She opened her eyes again and stared at Ian. What of Ian? Oh, God! What was wrong?

Ian stirred slightly, and she slipped away, so as not to wake him, grabbed her clothes from where he'd set them, and quietly put them on, then limped to the mouth of the cave, breathing deeply, letting the fresh air fill her lungs, trying to find an answer for the hell her conscience was going through. There was none.

She stood for a long time looking out over the valley, tortured by thoughts of what she'd done. Adultery, that's what they called it back home. Adultery! And why? Why had she done it? Because Ian was here and Cole wasn't? No! Tears rolled down her cheeks. Because Ian was Ian! She bit her lip. If only she could hate him, but it was impossible, even now. She bit her lips and stifled a sob as she heard Ian stirring inside the cave; then suddenly he was behind her.

"Heather?" he asked, his hands circling her waist to pull her to him, but she stepped away from his grasp.

"No, don't touch me," she said through tears.

Ian flinched, his hands dropping to his sides. "I'm sorry, Heather," he said, his voice deep with emotion. "I didn't mean to hurt you."

She whirled to face him. He was dressed again, the sun peeping over the hill behind him touching his hair, highlighting it with gold, and he stood tall and straight, so like him, yet his eyes were troubled.

"It's over," she cried breathlessly as she stared at him. "You had your night."

"That's not the way I meant it."

"One night to remember, wasn't that it?"

"Heather, please . . ."

"One night to ruin my life."

He flinched. "I love you, Heather."

"So does my husband. At least he did. Oh, God, Ian, how can I face him now?" She shook her head, tears streaming down her cheeks. "How can I ask him to keep loving me after this?"

Ian wanted to answer, but what was there to say? He had listened to his heart last night instead of his head, forgetting for those few hours that you couldn't snatch happiness at someone else's expense without paying dearly for it. He loved her so much, and had wanted her so badly he'd forgotten there's always a morning after, a time when life has to be faced head-on.

He straightened, then stepped forward, taking her by the shoulders, holding her tightly so she couldn't move, his eyes boring into hers, silently cursing himself for the pain he was causing her.

"Heather, stop it right now," he said quietly, trying to soothe her. "What we did was wrong, yes, and we can't take it back, but it did have a meaning for both of us. I know that and you know that. Still, for all purposes, it never happened—do you understand?"

She shook her head. "But it did!"

"It was my fault. All mine, Heather," he exclaimed.

"Always the gentleman." She laughed bitterly. "I wish you

had raped me, Ian," she said. "Because then I wouldn't have to feel so guilty."

She burst into tears, breathless sobs wrenching their way from deep inside, and he pulled her into his arms, holding her close until the crying finally stopped; then he held her from him, his heart tortured by the pitifully lost look on her face.

"I said I was sorry, Heather, and I meant it," he explained quickly. "You say I'm being a gentleman. Far from it. I seduced you, Heather, as surely as God is my witness, but I also promise it'll never happen again, not unless you want it to. I asked you for one night, and you gave it to me, and I'll never forget it. Whether you will or not, I don't know, but I didn't want you hurt, and I know that I have hurt you, far worse than I could ever have imagined." He paused for a moment, making sure she was listening closely, then went on, even though his next words hurt. "I know you love Cole, and that's as it should be—he's your husband. I wish he wasn't there, I wish I had found you first, but that's not the way it is, so I'm forced to accept that. Now, you have to accept things the way they are. Don't tell him if you don't want to. I never will, you know that. Unless you tell him, he'll never know, but don't punish yourself for a moment of weakness, for something neither of us could control, and please don't hate me, Heather. I couldn't stand that."

She sniffed, swallowing hard, and stared at him, remembering the night she'd lost the baby, and how patient he'd been with her. And all the other things they'd shared together, and even though she knew the guilt would always be there haunting her, as well as the memory of her betrayal, she knew he was right. It did no good to brood, and they were both to blame, perhaps he a little more than she—that was debatable. For the next few days, until they broke camp again, neither of them spoke of what had happened, yet each read in the other's eyes the reason for its happening.

Heather was still limping, but very slightly, the day they finally left the cave and once more headed up the rocky hillside, avoiding the spot where she had fallen weeks before. She was using the cane Ian had made for her, more for confidence than anything else. The day after they left the cave, it rained off and on, forcing them to seek shelter and lose time, but the next day the sun came out again and they were able to move at a better pace.

One afternoon they frightened a herd of deer grazing at a

water hole, and a day or so later almost tangled with a mother bear and her cubs. The cubs were quite a good size already, and Heather, having never seen bear cubs, marveled at their antics as she and Ian watched them from a distance.

Things were going well between her and Ian once again, and although the painful guilt of what she had done still haunted her, Heather made up her mind to wait until she was with Cole again before deciding just what she was going to do about it. She was sure it would make her betrayal worse by keeping it from him, and yet the thought of losing him was more than she could bear.

They had been moving north for well over a week now after leaving the cave. She glanced over at Ian walking beside her as they made their way across a meadow deep in tall grasses that were now green and plush from spring rains and the hot, humid weather that had settled in. If only she could understand her feelings for him. Then she remembered something Cole had told her a long time ago about their Grandma Dicia. At one time she had thought her first husband was dead and married another man; then her first husband had shown up alive and she'd gone back to him. However, the way the story went, even though she still loved her first husband, she had never really stopped loving the man she had married when she thought he was dead, and Grandpa Roth, Heather's real grandfather, was the man. Later Grandma Dicia had married him again after her first husband really died, and there was never any question but that she loved him. She had loved both men at the same time. Could it be possible that she was like Grandma Dicia? That she loved both Cole and Ian? The thought was almost more than she could comprehend, yet there was no way she could deny she had feelings for Ian. He looked over at her and smiled, and she smiled back, realizing she had been staring at him again. She had to stop all this speculation; it was driving her crazy.

She was still using the cane, hefting it expertly as she avoided lumps in the uneven ground, but she was no longer wearing the torn buckskin pants she had been wearing when she fell. Ian had still had the extra pair he'd taken from the dead Indian when he'd confiscated the shirt for himself, and since he was still wearing his uniform pants and boots, he'd had no use for them, so she was wearing them now. They were a little bigger than the other pair she'd worn, but cut off to fit her short stature and gathered a little more at her waist, they were wearable.

Ian marveled at the fact that even with the baggy clothes, her hair topsy-turvy, and her face smudged, limping along with the cane, she still had the power to stir him, only he didn't let her know. God help him, he couldn't hurt her any more than he already had, even though every day spent with her was torture to him. The bond was still there between them. He knew it, and she knew it too, yet he forced himself to ignore the ache inside, trying to act like nothing had happened.

They were halfway across the meadow when she smiled back at him and he drew his eyes from her in self-defense, pretending to scan the sloping hillside up ahead so she wouldn't know how deeply just a smile from her affected him. Then suddenly, as his eyes swept the hillside, a movement caused him to hesitate, and he held up his hand, stopping her.

"Wait," he ordered, and Heather stopped, moving closer to him.

"What is it?"

"I'm not sure yet. Look," he pointed to a spot some distance away, where the line of trees on the hill thinned out, leaving a clearing.

They watched closely as a string of horses began moving into the clearing; then suddenly Ian drew in a quick breath.

"Soldiers!"

She frowned. "How can you be sure? They're so far away."

"I've been one long enough. I know how a soldier looks in the saddle." His hand was over his eyes, shading them from the sun as he watched the procession moving steadily down the hill. "I think they've spotted us, too," he said, and pointed to one of the men who had stopped and was pointing in their direction.

Ian raised an arm and waved slowly, then watched as one of the men seemed to be using a spyglass. A few seconds later, as Ian and Heather started hurrying toward the hillside, the men on horseback also increased their pace, coming down the rest of the hill at a slow canter.

Heather and Ian were half-running now, and her limp was more pronounced as he took her hand, trying to help her so she wouldn't trip. They reached the edge of the long meadow, and Ian cautioned her to wait. They caught their breath, watching the soldiers emerge from the thick stand of trees at the bottom of the hill.

The lead horse was reined to a halt, the other horses behind him following suit, and the soldier in command, Sergeant Joseph Turnbull from Fort Smith, stared incredulously at the two people standing in front of him at the edge of the meadow. Sergeant Turnbull had been at Arkansas Post with Major Bradford's men when Major Long and Captain Brooks had been there, and as he stared, he slowly recognized the captain, then was almost as certain he knew the identity of the woman with him.

"Captain Brooks?" he exclaimed as he dismounted and stepped toward him.

Ian took a deep breath, closing his eyes for a moment in silent prayer, then opened them again and greeted him.

"Thank God, Sergeant," he said, relieved. "I thought we were never going to see civilization again."

Sergeant Turnbull studied the captain's face briefly. He had lost weight and was wearing a scraggly beard and mustache, but it definitely was Brooks. And the woman . . . His eyes moved to Heather. She was deeply tanned; her red hair, although clean-looking, was messy and held back by a frayed ribbon, with curls lying damply on her forehead; and there was a dark smear on her left cheek. She too had lost weight from the last time he'd seen her, and she was limping noticeably.

"You're both supposed to be dead," the sergeant said in disbelief.

"I'm afraid we're very much alive, Sergeant," Ian answered. "And very glad to see you and your men."

"It is Mrs. Avery, isn't it, Captain?" the sergeant asked, still staring at Heather.

"Yes, it's Mrs. Avery." Ian frowned. "We've been traveling for weeks . . . months, actually." He eyed the sergeant curiously. "By the way, Sergeant, we've rather lost track of time. Could you tell us what month and day it is?"

"We're a little over two days out of Fort Smith, so it should be Wednesday, May 6," he answered.

Heather could hardly believe it. She had been kidnapped in January. The sergeant's words of a few moments ago penetrated her thoughts, and she studied him dubiously. "You said you thought we were dead?" she asked him.

He nodded. "I don't know too much about it, but from what I gather, your husband found some man who'd survived an Indian attack—I guess he was supposed to be one of the men who kidnapped you and your baby and the colored girl." He hesitated a second, watching her reaction, then went on. "Before he died, the man told Mr. Avery you'd been killed by the Indians along with all the others."

Heather thought back to that day months ago when she'd scared the Indian away with her hysterical laughter. She had stood looking at the bodies strewn about her, so sure none of them were still alive. But from what the sergeant was saying, one of them had been alive. She frowned. Who? Then she remembered why she'd been laughing. The only one not scalped was Rafe. Could he have survived? It seemed incredible.

"Do you remember the name of the man?" she asked.

He shook his head. "Don't know as I ever heard it."

"Oh."

Ian glanced at the men with the sergeant. Only five. "You know your way back to Belle Pointe?" he asked Turnbull.

"I wouldn't be out here if I didn't."

"Good." Ian ignored the hint of sarcasm in the man's voice. "Then we can ride to the fort with you. That is, if one of your men will double up so we can use a horse."

"Ian, I have to go to the valley," Heather interrupted.

He disagreed. "We're closer to Fort Smith."

"But Cole—"

"It'd be best to listen to the captain, ma'am," said Turnbull as he tried to decipher the look in Heather's eyes. "It'd take us four days to get to your valley, and the Indians have been up in arms lately. This way, you can go to the fort, Major Bradford can send word to your husband, and he can come for you there."

She looked into Ian's eyes, pleading. "I want to go home."

"I know." His eyes pleaded back with her silently. "Only first we go to Fort Smith."

There was no way she could change their minds. Ian turned to Turnbull. "A horse, Sergeant?" he asked.

"You can each ride with one of my men," he answered, but Ian shook his head.

"Mrs. Avery will ride with me, Sergeant," he demanded.

The sergeant wanted to argue the matter, but changed his mind and ordered two of his men to double up.

Ian picked Heather up and set her on the horse, then started to toss away her cane.

"No," she said quickly, then flushed. "I might still need it."

His eyes caught hers, and suddenly he understood. "You might at that," he said, then mounted behind her, the sergeant also mounting his horse, and they headed back up the hill on their way to Belle Pointe.

The first evening, they camped on the shore of a small lake;

the second, near a shallow stream. The weather stayed sunny during the day, and the nights were warm. They were scheduled to reach Fort Smith late in the afternoon or early evening on Saturday.

It was Friday evening. Heather sat watching the soldiers talk. Sometimes they'd eye her curiously, and she wondered what they were thinking; then she'd brush aside any doubts that they were being critical of her. After all, even if they were, it didn't matter. Nothing mattered except what Cole thought and how he was going to take the news that she was still alive.

She tried to think what it must have been like for him, learning she and Case were dead. If it had been the other way around, she'd have died inside. What had it done to him? Cole could be explosive at times, and quite emotional. It must have been a terrible blow. She closed her eyes and tried to remember his face as it was the last time she'd seen him, the morning he'd left for Belle Pointe with Eli. He'd been so proud, his slanted eyes and high cheekbones giving his dark features a majestic yet stern look that could never deny his heritage, and yet he was so gentle with those he loved. He and Case were her whole life then . . . now. She felt a movement beside her and opened her eyes as Ian sat down. "You were thinking about Cole?" he asked.

"Yes. And Case." She pulled her knees up, hugging them with her arms. "I was wondering what Cole will do when he finds out Case is still alive too." Her eyes fell before his gaze. "I've tried not to think about him myself," she said unsteadily. "But there are times I just can't help it. So many times I've wondered where he is, and if he's forgotten me already. Babies forget so quickly." She looked over at him. "You do think he's still alive, don't you?" she asked.

"I'm sure of it, only I wouldn't count on ever seeing him again. The odds are too great." He saw the tears in her eyes. "I wish it wasn't so, Heather," he said after a brief pause. "I'd give anything to be able to tell you otherwise, but let's face it, even if you went searching, the possibility of finding him is so remote. I told you that before."

She took a deep breath and nodded. "At least I'll still have Cole."

"Yes, you'll still have Cole." His voice was low, filled with emotion. "You've decided not to tell him."

"I don't know what I'm going to do. I'm so afraid he'll guess,

Ian.'' She stared into his eyes. "Feelings are so hard to hide sometimes, and I'm such a terrible liar.''

"Heather, if he does find out and doesn't understand, do you think you could ever be satisfied with second best?''

Her eyes softened. "Second best? You? Ian Brooks, don't ever think you're second best." She flushed. "I've been trying to make some sense out of this whole thing, Ian,'' she went on. "But it doesn't make any sense. I know I love Cole, and the thought of knowing I'll be seeing him again soon makes me ache inside with longing, and yet the thought of having to say good-bye to you . . . it hurts so terribly.''

"Don't worry, we won't have to say good-bye. Not for a while yet," he assured her. "I intend to stay until Cole comes for you, and your valley's at least four days' ride from the fort. Figuring both ways, that's at least a week, even if he rides fast.''

"And when he does come?''

"I'll play it whatever way you want, Heather.'' His voice lowered to barely a whisper. "I love you, and I want you to be happy. I wish it could be with me, but then maybe God knows more what he's doing than we think, because when I go back over the life I've lived, and look to what's ahead, I guess there isn't too much room in it for a wife and family. At least not one I could really share myself with. I'm always hunting for the end of some river or wanting to see what's over the next hill. I thrive on challenging the wilderness and finding out what's out there.'' His eyes warmed as they looked directly into hers. "I think I could give it all up for you, Heather—it'd be heaven to try,'' he went on. "But what if I couldn't? What if I was miserable staying in one place? Then I'd make you unhappy too. So you see, Cole is best for you. He loves the wilderness too—I could see that on our trip up the Arkansas—but he's content to live in it and carve his own place out of it. I'm too busy discovering it—that's why I was assigned to Major Long's outfit.''

She stared at him, knowing he was probably right. All their weeks together, he had never once said he was anxious to get to any one place. From what she'd learned of him, there was no place he called home, the way she called the valley home. He was like the wind, going wherever the moment led him.

"Is that why you never married?'' she asked.

"No." He sighed. "I never found anyone worth giving it all up for until now. Unfortunately, she belongs to someone else.''

"I'm sorry, Ian.''

"Don't be," he said, his voice deep with emotion. "I'm glad it happened. I think everyone should have at least one great love in his life, and if I should never love again, which I probably won't, I'll always have something to look back on."

"One night for eternity?" she said softly.

He nodded. "For eternity," he echoed, and as they stared at each other, remembering, Heather knew deep in her heart that she was going to miss Ian. And later, as she settled down for the night, she was glad they'd have at least a week at the fort before she was forced to put him out of her life forever. It was so little to ask.

16

Cole stood on the cliff at Belle Pointe, looking out over the river, remembering their trip up the Arkansas with regret. If he'd only stayed in Port Royal she'd still be alive, and so would Case. The ache was still there, although it had eased some, but it was so hard to forget.

He turned from his perusal of the river with its memories, and studied the fort that was slowly beginning to look like a fort instead of the jumble of log shelters it had been a few months back. They had even built a small corral for the horses, and he watched them milling about restlessly while some of the soldiers put finishing touches on the last-minute details. Major Bradford had explained yesterday afternoon when Cole, Eli, Zeke, and Lily rode in that he hadn't expected them so soon.

"In fact, I'd been wondering whether to expect you at all," he'd said sheepishly, and Cole smiled, remembering.

Bradford had been fascinated that Cole had come through on his contract, and three weeks early at that, but no amount of pleading would coax Cole to tell him how he'd done it.

Cole's smile broadened as he remembered the look on the major's face when they rode in, but now, his mission accomplished, Cole felt a restlessness hard to control. It was as if he were waiting for something, but what? The frown that had creased his forehead earlier returned.

The air was warm, not a breeze stirring as he began walking back toward one of the log shelters where some of the soldiers were congregated. It was Saturday night, and since there were no taverns, gaming houses, or other amusements, they'd often get together when not on duty and gamble, betting on anything and everything from the exact hour when the next patrol would be sighted coming in, or the minute the next boat would be spotted coming upriver, to grasshopper and beetle races. But tonight they were sitting around listening to one of the men entertain them on the zither, and the music filled the air, its sprightly tune helping pull Cole from his melancholy mood.

He began to whistle along with the tune, then suddenly stopped as he glanced a short distance away to see Lily headed toward him across what would later be the parade ground. She had brought the pink calico dress with her and was wearing it now, her long hair fastened atop her head with ribbons and combs. Except for some Indian squaws with the Osage, she was the only other woman at Belle Pointe, and when she'd ridden in the day before with Cole, Eli, and Zeke, all heads had turned. Everyone knew she and her brother had taken the supplies Cole had ordered from St. Louis out to Cole's valley, but the surprise was that she had accompanied Cole back to the fort, although there were a number of men who could understand the young widower letting her become a part of his life. There were few pretty girls in Arkansas County to choose from.

It was that time of evening when the sun had already gone over the horizon, but night shadows hadn't yet descended, and Lily smiled warmly as she reached Cole.

"Shall we dance?" she said as the music changed to a faster beat.

"Here?"

"Why not?" She glanced at the fairly even ground where soldiers had trampled the grass down. "It might be fun."

Cole straightened dramatically, as if they were at a grand ball, and held up his hands. "Madam?"

"Sir," she said, curtsying, then walked into his arms, and while the soldiers turned their attention from the zither player to the two people who had joined them, Lily and Cole began dancing about the small area. For a while the soldiers just kept tapping their feet and clapping in time to the music, but eventually the spontaneous gaiety of the couple dancing got to them, and one of the soldiers finally built up enough courage to cut in, then another and another, and before the dancing finally came to an end, Lily had danced with every one of them except the zither player, while Cole stood by frowning, a twinge of jealousy running through him every time any of the soldiers' warm smiles were answered by smiles from Lily.

"I think we should take a walk so you can cool off a little," he said as he retrieved her from her last dancing partner when the music ended.

Lily was laughing lightly as she fanned her face. "Thank you, kind sir," she told the soldier breathlessly, and he walked away, pleased, as Cole took her arm and they headed toward the river.

This time, instead of standing on the bluff, Cole led Lily down the hill to the water's edge, and they walked along the banks of the river slowly while she tried to catch her breath.

"Well, was it fun?" Cole asked.

She eyed him curiously. "Yes." She was still breathing heavily. "Only it would have been much more fun if I could have danced the whole dance with you."

He stopped beneath a huge cottonwood tree and whirled her about so she was leaning against it, then looked down into her eyes. "How did you know what I was thinking?"

"I know you better than you think, Cole," she answered. "You were jealous, weren't you?"

"I didn't like sharing you if that's what you mean." He reached out, pulling her into his arms. "Do you mind?"

Her breathing was still erratic, and being in Cole's arms didn't help any. "You know better than to ask," she said, half-whispering. "I'm glad you were jealous. It shows you care."

"You want that, don't you?"

"For you to care? I want you to love me someday, Cole, the way you loved her. I saw you before, standing on the bluff. . . . Memories are good, yes, but memories can't share the good and bad times or warm your bed."

He stared into her eyes, remembering last night. He'd slipped into the building where Major Bradford had told her she could sleep, and spent the night making love to her, and tonight he'd probably end up with her in his arms again. But he just wasn't ready to love. Not just yet, and he tried to tell himself the jealousy he'd felt when she'd smiled at the soldiers meant nothing. He was becoming possessive of her, that's all; it had nothing to do with caring. "Please be patient, Lily," he said slowly, hesitantly, then sighed. "Tonight?" he asked huskily.

"Yes, tonight," she answered softly, and his arms tightened

about her, his mouth covering hers as shadows began to settle in among the trees, finally bringing the darkness with them.

Suddenly Cole raised his head, his lips leaving hers reluctantly, and glanced toward the hill that led to the fort. A soldier was running down the hill, waving to get his attention, calling his name. Lily pulled away from him, flushing, hoping the soldier wouldn't notice now that it was practically dark out, and straightened her clothes; then Cole took her arm and they headed toward the soldier.

"Mr. Avery, I've been huntin' all over for you." The soldier was panting breathlessly when he reached them. Half the soldiers still called Cole Duke Avery, although word had gotten about that his name was really Cole Dante. Out here, however, no one seemed to care anymore. "Major Bradford sent me to tell you to come real quick, Mr. Avery," the soldier went on hurriedly. "It's your wife!"

"My wife?"

He nodded, still trying to catch his breath. "Sergeant Turnbull just got back with the patrol, and they have your wife and Captain Brooks from Major Long's outfit with 'em, and they're waitin' for you now at the major's quarters."

Cole stood motionless for a long time staring at the private, unable to believe what he was hearing; then suddenly he cried, "Oh, my God!" and grabbed Lily's hand, pulling her with him, heading back up toward the fort, while the soldier followed close at their heels.

Heather stood in Major Bradford's office, her heart in a turmoil. Someone had been playing music on a zither when they'd approached the fort. Gay, carefree music that carried on the night air and should have lifted her spirits, but hadn't, and she was glad it had stopped before they'd ridden onto the parade ground and across to the major's quarters. She should have been glad she was finally going to return home, but the thought of seeing Cole again had been frightening. And now Major Bradford said Cole was here. The major said he'd ridden in with a herd of horses yesterday afternoon. She thought she'd have at least a week more to decide whether to tell him about what had happened between her and Ian. Now . . . Her stomach tightened into a knot as she listened to Ian telling the major about running into the patrol.

She heard his words, yet they didn't really register as her thoughts wandered. Major Bradford had sent one of the men to find Cole, and she wondered how long it would take for him to come.

Suddenly there was a noise behind her and Heather's heart leaped into her throat. Ian whirled around sharply, and the major straightened behind his desk; then, as Heather slowly turned, gluing her eyes to the door, it burst open and Cole stepped in.

He stopped abruptly and stared hard at the woman standing before him. The lanterns in the major's office weren't any too bright, but there was no mistake. The woman staring back at him was dressed in dirty, sloppy old buckskins way too big for her, her curly red hair held back by a frayed ribbon, and she was so deeply tanned she looked more Indian than white, but there was no mistaking the eyes. They were bright and vivid, even in the flickering light from the lanterns on the wall, and were the most lovely shade of violet he'd ever seen. He'd know those eyes anywhere.

"Heather?" he gasped, his voice choked with emotion.

Heather continued to stare, her insides trembling with the upheaval they were going through. Cole looked exactly as he had the last time she'd seen him, and all her love for him suddenly welled up inside her, bringing with it a pain that was almost unbearable. She had to touch him, to feel him, to know he was real.

They started toward each other at the same moment; then Cole stopped, reaching out, grabbing her arms, worried. "You're limping."

Tears flooded her eyes. "Oh, Cole, hold me," she cried softly, and leaned toward him.

His arms enfolded her and he lifted her off the ground, holding her against him with such strength she was afraid for a moment he'd accidentally crush her, then slowly, gently, his arms eased, and although he held her off the ground, looking into her face tenderly, he no longer seemed afraid to let her go.

"You're really here?" he whispered softly, as if he couldn't believe it. "I'm not just dreaming?"

"No." She shook her head. "You're not dreaming, nor am I." Then suddenly he was kissing her deeply. A kiss filled with all the longing and yearning that had been tormenting him these past months.

When the kiss was finally over, and Cole realized there were questions to be asked and answers to be heard, he released her, setting her on the floor in front of him, for the first time becoming aware of Captain Brooks, who was staring at them intently.

Cole forgot that Lily was standing behind him, watching him greet his long-lost wife, and he stared back at Ian forcefully.

"You rode in together?" he asked after a brief silence in which he tried but was unable to read the look on Ian's face.

Ian took a deep breath. "We've been together for somewhere near three months," he answered. "If you're willing to listen . . ."

"Go ahead."

Cole stood with his arm about Heather.

"Maybe you'd better sit down," Ian said, motioning toward a bench against the side wall. "And the lady behind you, too. I imagine she's been wondering what this is all about."

Cole felt himself flush, embarrassed that he'd forgotten about Lily, and he turned quickly, facing her for the first time. Her face was pale, eyes bewildered, and for a moment he felt a spark of guilt sweep over him, then forced it from his mind stubbornly, not wanting anything to spoil this moment.

"Lily, I'd like you to meet my wife, Heather," he said. "Heather, this is Lily Baldridge."

Heather frowned as her eyes met Lily's and she saw tears there. "Who is Lily Baldridge?" she asked quietly.

She felt Cole stiffen beside her. "Lily and her brother brought some supplies out for us from St. Louis," he explained quickly. "Then she and her brother Zeke helped Eli and me bring the horses back to the fort."

Heather's frown deepened. That wasn't all there was to Lily Baldridge, and she knew it, but for now she said a meek hello and pulled away from Cole, walking over to sit on the bench Ian had mentioned.

Cole felt Heather's withdrawal, but said nothing. Instead he gestured for Lily to sit down next to Heather; then he sat down at Heather's other side and for the next few minutes Ian related events briefly as he knew them, letting Heather add her own part of the tale when it was called for. When they were through, a heavy silence seemed to hang over the room.

Heather felt Ian's eyes on her as he finished the story, but she didn't dare look at him, afraid Cole would see more than friendship in her glance.

Major Bradford was the first to break the silence. "You're to be commended, Captain Brooks," he said abruptly, realizing the situation was rather awkward for all concerned and that there seemed to be an undercurrent of something he couldn't quite put his finger on that was causing the silence. "Not many men would have been able to survive what you survived, and on top of everything else, from all indications, I'd say Cole Dante owes you for returning his wife to him in one piece."

"It was my pleasure," Ian said, and Cole frowned, staring hard at him.

While Ian had been talking, Cole suddenly realized that the Ian Brooks who was telling him all about the events of the past few months was far different from Captain Ian Brooks, second in command under Major Stephen H. Long, of the Topography Department of the Army. Captain Ian Brooks had been clean-shaven, crisply uniformed, and all spit and polish. The Ian Brooks who faced him now was a woodsman in every sense of the word. No wonder Major Long had told Cole more than once on their journey up the Arkansas that Captain Brooks was indispensable to his outfit. He wasn't just Army, he was more, much more.

Cole straightened, taking a deep breath. "You actually took care of Heather during her miscarriage?" he asked in surprise.

"That's right."

"And her leg?"

"It had to be set."

"I do owe you a great deal, Captain," Cole said. "I wish there were some way to repay you."

Ian drew his eyes from Cole's face and looked at Heather. "There is," he said. "I told you once your wife was too fragile and didn't belong out here, and you said you knew her better than I. You were right. She's a remarkable woman." He looked at Cole again as he spoke the last words: "And I ask you to accept my apology for doubting you."

Cole studied him for a few minutes, then nodded. "Apology accepted," he said, but added, "However, I wish I had listened to you, Captain. If so, none of this would have happened and there'd be no need for any apologies at all." He turned to Heather. "You said Palmer gave Case to some Comanche?" he asked.

"Harry said they were Comanche."

"Then they probably were." He thought for a moment. "I wonder . . . I know some Comanche."

"You're going to try to find him?" Ian asked.

Major Bradford shook his head. "That's impossible, Cole."

"I don't believe it is. If there's the slightest chance . . . Now that I know he's alive, how can anyone expect me not to try to find him?" He looked at Heather. She'd not only lost weight, but she'd lost the delicate aura that made her seem so fragile, and there was a strength about her that had been missing before. He addressed the major. "I'd like to talk to my wife alone, Major, if you don't mind. There's a great deal I'd like to go over with her."

Major Bradford stood up. "By all means."

Cole got to his feet and turned, holding his hand out for Heather, helping her to her feet, his eyes moving to the leg she was favoring. "Are you going to be all right?" he asked.

She nodded. "Yes."

He looked over at Ian one more time, studying him for a moment. There was something about the look on the man's face. It made Cole feel uneasy; then he glanced at Lily, still sitting on the bench, and he suddenly felt terrible, knowing how she must feel. His eyes silently asked for her forgiveness as he took Heather's hand and threaded it through her elbow.

"If you'll excuse us," he said awkwardly, then led Heather slowly to the door.

When the door was shut behind them, Ian turned to the major. "If you think you can find anything resembling a uniform for me, Major Bradford, sir," he suggested, "I'd sure like to clean up," and he rubbed his hand across his scraggly beard.

The major nodded, promising he'd have one of his men locate something, although he couldn't guarantee it'd have captain's bars; then Ian turned to Lily, still sitting on the bench, staring at the closed door, her face revealing far too much of the agony she was going through.

"Miss Baldridge, is there anything I can do?" he asked.

Lily shook her head. "No, Captain, there's nothing anyone can do," she said. "It's already been done," and she stood up, walked to the door, reached down to open it, then turned back, staring hard for a moment at Ian, her brown eyes close to tears. "Why did you have to bring her back?" she asked softly. "Why?" Then, without waiting for an answer, she left the major's office, closing the door slowly behind her.

Ian stared after her, his eyes glinting knowingly, and it was no surprise to him when Major Bradford said, "You know, Captain, I'm afraid Heather Dante's remarkable return from the dead isn't going to be the simple, uncomplicated homecoming I think she expected. Three months can be a long time, especially out here.''

Ian straightened, then took a deep breath. "You're right, there, Major," he replied. "Three months can be a very long time," and he walked out, leaving Major Bradford staring after him, a surprised look on his face.

Cole and Heather had run into Eli and Zeke a few minutes after leaving the major's office. And although Eli was ecstatic over Heather's return, rattling on about how pleased Bessie and Helene were going to be, and commenting on how glad Mose was going to be to hear Tildie wasn't dead after all, even though she was a captive of the Comanche along with Case, there was an undercurrent of wariness in Eli's enthusiasm, especially when Cole introduced Heather to Lily's brother Zeke.

"She's already met Lily," he said guardedly, and neither Eli nor Zeke made further comment.

Eli watched them walk away a few minutes later, Heather limping as she tried to keep up with Cole; then he glanced over at Zeke. "Better go find your sister, Zeke," he said. "I have a feeling she might be needing a good shoulder about now," and Zeke nodded knowingly.

Although neither man had made mention of it, both men knew Cole and Lily had become more than just friends.

Heather glanced over at Cole. "Where are we going?" she asked.

They were outside the area that was staked out for the walls of the fort, and Cole motioned up ahead to where she could barely see the vague outlines of a log shelter that had been erected. It was one of the shelters Major Long's men had put up, which the soldiers had used until Major Bradford's troops had begun actual work on the fort.

"Major Bradford lets us use them when we're at the fort," he said, taking her arm, helping her over some rough ground in the dark.

When they reached the place, he pulled a small wooden bench out of the shelter and had her sit down. Stars were already popping out all over the heavens, and Heather looked up at them, remembering all the nights she'd slept out under them, wondering if she'd ever see home again. Now . . .

"You know we have to talk," he said as he sat down beside her.

She felt her stomach tighten nervously. "I don't know what

more I can tell you," she offered. "You know the whole story. We told it all at the major's office."

He sighed. "Heather, you told us what happened. All right, you were kidnapped, they gave Case and Tildie to some Comanche, you were attacked by Indians and thought everyone was dead and started out on your own. You ran into Ian Brooks, escaped from Indians by hiding in a beaver dam, you had a miscarriage, then broke your leg, and finally met up with Sergeant Turnbull's patrol. That's fine as it goes, but you know as well as I do that there's more to it than that, Heather. You and the captain touched the basics. I want to hear the whole story."

"It's painful, Cole," she answered.

He took her hand. "I know, love," he said. "But I have to know it all."

She took a deep breath and started at the beginning, telling him about the kidnapping, going into detail about Carl's anger at not being able to marry her.

"Thank God the reverend was there to keep Carl from raping you," Cole commented when she told him of Carl's anger at finding her pregnant. "But what I can't understand is, why was the reverend there at all?"

"He had some distorted idea that he was saving me from a life of sin with you. He knew we were first cousins."

Cole shook his head and she went on telling him how, after the others were killed, she remembered all the things he'd told her back at Tonnerre and decided to try to get home by herself. "Then I ran into Ian, Captain Brooks," she said, trying to keep her voice steady as she told him of her first meeting with Ian. "At first glance I didn't recognize him with the beard and all, and like me, he looked rather scroungy, because he'd been on the run from some Cherokee, but . . . well, when I realized who he was, I was so thankful. For a minute I'd been afraid I'd gone from one bad situation to another and run into some trapper who wouldn't care whether I was white or Indian, just so I was a woman." She continued her story, although it was hard telling him about losing the baby.

"Ian never told me if he knew whether it had been a boy or girl," she said wistfully. "But I guess it wasn't really important."

"You mean the captain actually delivered the child for you?" Cole asked.

She flushed at the remembrance, but it was too dark for Cole to see it. However, the emotion in her voice revealed more than she realized. "Yes," she answered. "He took better care of me than Oleander did when Case was born, only it was too soon." He let her go on telling him about Ian's unselfish strength that had pulled her through the miscarriage, and his help searching for herbs so she'd heal, and finding the buckskins for her to wear. During all of it, Cole never said another word, just sat and listened. In fact, he listened quietly for a long time, making no more comments as she finished the rest of her story, trying to remember the details, leaving out only her indiscretion with Ian. Later, perhaps later I'll tell him, she thought as she told Cole about her leg healing, their leaving the cave, and the end of their journey when they ran into Sergeant Turnbull and the patrol. When she was finally finished, she sighed. "That's it," she said quietly.

Cole was still holding her hand, but there was something about the way he was holding it. He shifted positions on the bench, then dropped her hand and stood up.

"Cole?" she said, wondering what was the matter.

He turned to her. The suspicions that had begun to gnaw at him when he'd first seen Ian's flashing eyes in the major's office had taken deep roots while she'd been telling of her miscarriage, and now they were tormenting him unmercifully. He wanted to shove them aside, but couldn't. It was stupid to be jealous, he knew. The man had saved her life, yet . . . they had been together night and day for some three months, and he'd heard it in her voice. A strange quality when she spoke the man's name. He straightened.

"You make Captain Brooks sound like someone special," he snapped.

She hesitated, trying to choose her words, but it wasn't easy. "He is," she finally said. "He's a friend and he saved my life."

"That's all he is? A friend?"

"What more?"

"You were with him alone all this time," he answered. "He could be a great deal more by now."

"But he isn't."

"How do I know that?"

"Cole, please."

"You give yourself away, Heather," he accused bitterly. "Your voice when you mention his name, and your eyes . . . You think I'm blind? You never looked at him once the whole while we were in the major's office, did you? I could see what he was feeling." He knelt down in front of her and took her by the shoulders. The moon was just rising over the treetops and it fell on her face. "Heather, you're a rotten liar," he said. "You know that. You always have been, and you're lying now, you know you are. You should be laughing and happy to be back again, but you're not. There's a sadness in your eyes, and it cuts me deep inside because I have a horrible feeling it has something to do with him, and it's going to come between us."

"Never, Cole," she whispered softly. "You said you can tell when I'm lying. Am I lying when I say I love you? Because I do love you, Cole, I've always loved you, and I always will."

He stared at her, his heart listening to her words, and somehow he knew they were true. Still . . .

"Then why the sadness? Why the long face?"

"I don't know."

"You do know, only you won't say it, will you?"

"Say what?"

"That something happened between you and Brooks."

"Cole!"

"Say it, dammit," he cried helplessly. "He made love to you, didn't he? Or did he rape you? No!" He shook his head. "No, Brooks isn't the type to rape a woman. You let him, didn't you?"

"Please!"

"Didn't you?" he demanded.

She took a deep breath, her heart pounding. "Yes!" she finally yelled back at him, her voice barely a whisper. "Yes, yes, yes!"

His eyes hardened as he stared at her.

"I was lonely and he was good to me," she went on breathlessly. "He knew it was wrong, we both did, yet at the time it didn't seem to matter. All that mattered was that we were together."

Cole's hands dropped from her shoulders and he stood up, starting to walk away.

"Where are you going?" she asked.

"To find Brooks," he shot back, and kept right on going while she stared after him in dismay.

The clean soap and water had felt good to Ian, even though the water was cold, and now, as he finished getting the last of the beard shaved off, he stared into the tiny mirror on the wall, pleased with what he saw. He'd decided to keep the mustache,

but was going to have to have his hair cut again. He closed his
eyes for a minute, remembering the day he'd had Heather cut it
for him. Heather! He opened his eyes again and finished wiping
his face, wondering how things were going for her. For some
strange reason, he had a feeling Cole wasn't completely satisfied
with his telling of their adventure.

He set the towel down and reached for the army shirt one of
the men had brought for him, slipping it on, beginning to button
it. Suddenly the door burst open and Cole stood on the threshold,
eyes wild with rage.

"You bastard!" he yelled furiously.

Ian tensed just in time, as Cole lunged at him, his fist just
missing Ian's chin, as Ian leaned his head back.

"Now, wait a minute, Cole! What the hell's the matter with
you?" Ian cried as he caught Cole's arms, using every ounce of
strength to hold him off.

"You know what's wrong," Cole yelled, and Ian's jaw set
hard.

"She told you?"

"She told me!" Cole twisted free and stared at him. "I'm
going to kill you, Ian Brooks!"

Ian's eyes narrowed. "Why?"

"Why? You cuckolded me, you son of a bitch. Heather's my
wife, not yours."

"Then what about Lily?"

"Lily?"

"Yes, Lily. Where does she fit into your life, Cole, or had
you forgotten about the lady?"

Cole stared at him, dumbfounded. "What do you know about
Lily?"

Ian straightened, finishing buttoning his shirt as he talked,
alert to Cole's still-simmering temper. "According to people
who should know, I hear you're sleeping with her regularly."

Cole's eyes flashed. "Who told you?"

"The lady herself."

"Lily?"

"She and I had a little talk. She's in love with you."

"Damn you," Cole said angrily. "You had no right."

"I know. But I had a feeling when she followed you into the
office, and I thought maybe it might be wise to learn if I was
right, just in case Heather needed some leverage."

"Lily has nothing to do with Heather. I thought Heather was dead. Heather knew I was alive, and there's a difference."

"Is there?" Ian asked. "Heather wasn't here, and you were attracted to Lily. I realize if you knew Heather was still alive you undoubtedly wouldn't have touched Lily. But you see, you had other people around to help if you needed it, and you didn't have to spend every waking moment with Lily. So even if you had known Heather was alive, you'd have had a chance." He took a deep breath. "Heather had no chance. She knew you were alive, yes, but being together day after day, people just naturally become close." His eyes hardened. "She made one mistake, Cole," he said. "One night when she forgot she was your wife."

"And I'm supposed to forgive and forget, I suppose?"

"She's not a saint, Cole, she's a woman."

"And you're a bastard!" said Cole, once more swinging at Ian, the unexpected blow connecting with Ian's chin.

As Ian flew backward, Cole pressed the advantage, but wasn't quick enough, and Ian grappled with him, trying to push him off.

Suddenly the door flew open again, and Heather rushed in. Her limp had slowed her, and she had lost Cole in the darkness; then it had taken her a while to discover where Ian was. She stood for a moment staring at the two men grappling with each other, flickering light from a wall sconce in the small room at the back of the soldiers' quarters throwing them into relief.

She let out a cry and ran over, pulling on Cole, trying to pull him off.

"Stop it!" she yelled, tugging at his shoulders and pounding on him. "Stop it, Cole!"

Cole tried to throw Heather off, while still trying to grab for Ian's throat, and Ian was doing his best to keep him from it, neither of them realizing Heather was the one trying to break them up.

Cole swung his arm back, pushing against whoever was pulling on him, and unknowingly he caught Heather under the chin, flinging her backward.

As she flew through the air, she let out a shriek, then hit against the door, landing in a sitting position. She was furious, anger raging in her like a wildcat, and she screamed at the two men, who suddenly began to realize they weren't alone.

Cole heard Heather shriek, and it cut through him like a knife.

His hold on Ian eased, and he whirled around, both of them extricating themselves from each other slowly as she yelled at them, pulling herself slowly to her feet.

"I said stop it!" she screamed, infuriated. "Stop fighting, both of you!"

"What are you doing here?" asked Cole.

"Trying to stop you from killing Ian."

"Why shouldn't I kill him?"

"Because I love him!"

Cole's eyes widened. "You what?"

"I love you both," Heather cried through tears. "I wanted to tell you, Cole. I don't know how or why, but I can't let you hurt him, and I don't want you hurt either."

Cole couldn't believe what he was hearing. "You can't love us both," he said defiantly.

Her chin lifted. "Why not?" She stared at both of them stubbornly, then looked at Cole. "If Grandma Dicia could love your grandfather and my grandfather both at the same time, why can't I love both of you?"

"But Grandma Dicia . . . You can't compare yourself with her."

"I'm her granddaughter." Her eyes were flashing. "I didn't ask to fall in love with Ian, Cole, but he's so . . . so . . . well, anyway, I didn't ask to fall in love with you either, but I did, and when I did, I married DeWitt, or have you forgotten?"

"How could I?"

"Then let's act like sane adults," she said, calming some. "I know what I did hurt you, Cole," she said her voice trembling. "But your Lily hurts me too. I know you thought I was dead, but the hurt isn't any easier to take. I said I love Ian, and I do, but I don't intend to leave you to be with him. There's a strange bond between him and me, but it's not as strong as the one between you and me. Maybe I don't really love Ian, maybe I only care for him in some special way because of what we've been through together—I don't know, but I do love you, and it's more than just caring." She paused to take a breath. "Now, I came back to be with you," she said, looking at Cole. "I'm sorry for being weak and giving in to feelings I know I shouldn't even have had. If you can't forgive me, then I've lost. But if I can forgive you for Lily, I think it's unfair to condemn me for Ian. It's your choice, Cole—I'm still yours if you want me."

Cole stared at her, unable to answer, his mouth dry, insides burning.

"When you make up your mind, let me know," she said, her eyes threatening tears, and turned, walking out, leaving both of them staring after her.

Cole watched her leave, his green eyes intense, mouth rigid.

"She means it, Cole," Ian said as he turned to Cole. "She doesn't want me. She came back to the man she loves."

"But you'd take her if I don't?"

"Take her? I'd cherish her for the rest of her life."

"Knowing she loves me?"

"You forget, she loves me too."

"And it wouldn't bother you?"

Ian frowned. "The only way it would bother me is if you decided to be our next-door neighbor. Other than that, no, it wouldn't bother me, because I know that Heather's one moment of weakness with me isn't an everyday thing, and you should know that too. But she doesn't want me, Cole, not really. Like she said, we shared a time together, and it was special, but she came back to you. I just hope you don't make the wrong decision," and he tucked his shirt in, grabbed a hat that had been hanging on a hook near the door, and left, leaving Cole standing in the room all by himself.

Heather was walking slowly, picking her way along in the darkness, stepping over split logs, trying to make her way back to the shelter where Cole said he was staying while he was here. Suddenly she stopped, listening, then turned. Someone was coming toward her in the darkness.

"Heather?" It was Lily.

"Yes," answered Heather, making sure there was no trace of tears on her face.

"I hope you don't mind," Lily said. "I have to talk to you."

Heather unconsciously reached up to primp her hair into place, forgetting for a moment that it would do no good even if it wasn't too dark for anyone to see. Lily was standing in the moonlight, and for a second Heather wanted to scream at the thought that Cole had held her in his arms. Instead she braced herself.

"What is it?" she asked.

"I don't know what Cole has told you about me," she answered. "But . . . oh, I feel so awkward," she suddenly blurted.

Heather felt sorry for her. "You love him, don't you?"

Lily nodded.

"I'm sorry, Lily. You see, I love him too."

"I just wanted you to know," Lily said. "He never stopped loving you, ever, and I don't think he ever would have, although I was hoping."

Heather sighed. "Thank you, Lily."

"Don't thank me," Lily said. "The only reason I'm telling you this is because I want you to say good-bye to Cole for me. I couldn't face him, not now. Zeke and I are taking the keelboat downriver in the morning."

"Where will you go?"

She shrugged. "Who knows? New Orleans or back east. Someplace where I can start all over again and maybe find someone else." She took a deep breath. "You will say good-bye to him for me, won't you?" she asked.

Heather could tell she'd been crying. "Don't you think it'd be better if you said good-bye yourself?"

"How can I, when it hurts so much?"

"It'll hurt worse if you don't, believe me."

Heather knew what it was like to lose someone you loved, besides, she had to be fair to Cole. What if he didn't want to say good-bye to Lily? "He's back in the soldiers' quarters," Heather told her. "Go see him, Lily. Let him be the one to tell you it's over."

Lily stared at her for a minute, trying to see Heather's face in the darkness, but couldn't. Then she turned without saying any more and headed toward the soldiers' quarters.

"You're taking quite a chance, aren't you?" Ian said from the shadows to the left of where Lily had been standing. He'd been hidden beneath rafters that would someday be part of one of the fort's blockhouses. "What if he asks her to stay?"

"Then I lose." Heather inhaled sharply. "I don't want to lose, Ian," she whispered. "Oh, God, I do love him."

"I know." Ian stepped close and reached out, cupping her head in his hand. "Don't worry, you won't lose him," he said. "He just needs time to fight the demons. It's hard to have to accept the bitter in order to attain the sweet. And you *are* sweet, Heather. My dear, sweet Heather."

"Ian!"

"It's true," he said softly. "But don't worry, I won't cause you any more trouble. All I want to do is say good-bye."

She studied his face. He looked so different without the beard, with only the mustache and his hair smoothed back. She reached out, touching his cheek, then put her hand over his where it cupped her head. His hand was strong and warm.

"Don't say good-bye, please, Ian," she begged. "Not yet. What if you're wrong? What if Cole doesn't want me anymore?"

"Then come to me." His eyes searched hers. "Major Bradford is giving me a horse to use and I'll be leaving in the morning, riding cross-country to Belle Fontaine near St. Louis. If Cole doesn't come to you tonight, then come to me by dawn tomorrow and I'll take you with me."

"You'd do that, wouldn't you?" she said.

"Try me." He sighed. "Now, come on." He released her head and took her arm. "Let me walk you back to the shelter, but first I have something for you." He'd kept his left hand hidden the whole while they'd been talking; now he lifted it and handed her cane to her. "The major gave me this earlier," he said. "I grabbed it when I left the soldiers' quarters. I think you wanted it. Am I right?"

Tears welled up in her eyes as she took it from him, running her hands over the carved handle. It was the only remembrance she'd have of him. "Thank you," she whispered softly. "Yes, I do want to keep it." She wiped the tears away, then put the tip of the cane on the ground, leaning on it.

"Shall we go, Captain?" she asked, and they headed for the shelter, avoiding the few soldiers still wandering about.

When they reached it, Ian took her arm again, turning her to face him. "For my sake I hope he doesn't come," he whispered softly. "But in case he does . . ." He leaned down, drew her to him, and kissed her deeply, letting his lips linger on hers longer than usual. "Good-bye, sweet Heather," he murmured softly. "I'll never forget you," and he turned, disappearing into the darkness, leaving her standing alone, leaning on the cane.

Heather held her breath, still feeling the warmth of his lips on hers, then exhaled, turning slowly, and limped to the shelter to wait for Cole.

Eli and Zeke came and went, instructing her to tell Cole they'd see him in the morning, and still she waited.

It was late. Eli had built a fire nearby while he was there, and she lay wrapped in a blanket, staring at the flames, wondering how her life had gotten so messed up. It seemed as if nothing ever went the way it was supposed to for her, and now Cole. Would he come, and if he didn't, what of Ian? Would she have the courage to meet him in the morning? Oh, God, don't let me have to make that decision, she prayed.

The flames in the fire burned lower, and a hushed quiet settled over the fort. Still Cole didn't come.

It must have been well past midnight when she heard the footsteps. At first she wasn't sure it was Cole, and backed as far into the blanket as she could; then he stepped into the firelight and she saw his tall, lean frame. He stood by the fire for a long time, staring into it; then she saw him straighten and he walked over to the shelter. He ducked inside, dropped down on the blanket beside her, and leaned close.

"Heather?" he whispered hesitantly.

She stirred, and rolled over on her back, looking up at him. "Cole?"

"I understand, love," he said simply, his voice breaking. "It isn't the easiest thing to live with, but I do understand."

"Oh, Cole," she murmured breathlessly. "I thought you didn't love me anymore, that you didn't want me."

"Not want you? Heather, I died inside when I thought I'd never see you again." He gazed down at her, watching the dim firelight reflecting in her eyes. "I love you so damn much."

"And I hurt you so terribly." She reached up and touched his face, running her hand over his clipped beard. "Forgive me, Cole, I didn't mean to hurt you," she said. "You're my whole life, my reason for living."

"And Ian Brooks?"

"Ian is . . . I don't really know, Cole. He's one of those things that can't be explained, and I wish he'd never happened, but he did. I have feelings for him I know I shouldn't have, just as I imagine you have feelings for Lily that can't be explained away by using reason."

"Why did you send her to me tonight?" he asked.

"So she could say good-bye."

"What if I'd wanted her to stay?"

"Then I'd have lost the dearest thing I have left, your love." She took his hand and held it close against her breast. "I'm sorry, Cole," she whispered softly. "I'm sorry for DeWitt, and Carl, and Ian, and all the other things I did wrong and can't change, but through it all I've never stopped loving you, you know that. You're my first love, the most important person in my life, and all I can do is ask you to forgive me for being less than perfect, and to take me back. I need you, I love you with all my heart.''

Cole leaned closer, his eyes searching hers. They were filled with tears. He bent down, kissing the tears away, then kissed her lips.

"Don't cry, love," he whispered softly.

"But I've made so many mistakes. I almost lost you, and I lost our unborn child and our son."

"Don't worry, we'll find him, love."

"And if we don't?"

"We will! In the meantime, love, we'll make more babies so he'll have a family to come home to."

"Oh, Cole!"

He kissed her again, slowly, sensuously, and Heather felt the stirrings that had begun inside her when she'd seen him again for the first time in the major's office, begin to creep through her again, gradually at first, then flooding over her like waves devouring a ship, inch by inch, reaching into every part of her that could feel, wildly, ecstatically, surging through her until she felt as if she was on fire. Her lips tingled as she answered him back, and Cole groaned from deep within.

"I want you, Heather. I need you, love," he murmured against her lips, and his hand began fumbling with her buckskin shirt.

She grabbed it, stopping him.

"I'm so dirty, Cole," she whispered breathlessly. "We've been traveling for days and days."

He stared at her in surprise, then frowned. "What a fool I've been," he said. "You didn't even have a chance to clean up." His hand moved to her face, and he brushed a curl from her cheek, his eyes gleaming expectantly. "Come," he whispered, and stood up, grabbing her hand, pulling her up with him, letting the blankets drop to their feet.

"Where are we going?" she asked, but he only shook his head, cautioning her to be quiet.

He led her down the hill to the river's edge, then along its banks until they were far enough away from the fort, where only the moonlight could reach them; then he took both her hands in his and drew her to him.

"Do you remember?" he asked huskily.

She took a deep breath. "How could I forget?" and as she exhaled, trembling, he reached down, stripping the buckskin

shirt from her. She sighed with longing as the rest of her clothes
fell to the ground, and when they were both naked, only the
moonlight covering them, he took her hand and led her down to
the water.

It was cool yet, in May, but not cold enough to put out the fire
that raged within them both, and as they slipped into the water,
she shivered. Not from the cold, but from his touch.

"Cole, that old medicine man was right," she said, suddenly
remembering, and he frowned. She reached up, her arms circling
his neck as she melted against him. "Don't you remember the
Indian's dream?" she asked breathlessly. "You were in danger,
just like he said, not just from Carl, but from me. You said it
was only an old man's dream, but it wasn't, Cole. All of it came
true, and I almost lost you. You told me he said only my love for
you would save us, and it has. It brought me home, it made you
forgive me."

His arms closed around her. "It was just an old man's dream,
Heather," he said quietly, but she shook her head.

"No, Cole, not just an old man's dream, it was a prophecy,
and now it's over."

"Is it?" he asked, remembering too the old man's dream.
"We still have to find Case."

Pain filled her eyes and he wished he hadn't reminded her. His
arms tightened about her. "Don't, Heather, please don't. Forget
what I just said," he pleaded anxiously. "For now, forget
everything but that I love you," and as he kissed her, carrying
her with him to the edge of the sandbar, and making love to her
as the waters flowed over them, for the first time in months
Heather's heart felt free. This was where she belonged, in Cole's
arms, and she let his love surround her, smother her, devour her
until she was one with him and all the agony of what lay behind
as well as anticipation of what lay ahead was unimportant. For
them there was no tomorrow, only now, and life was good
again.

Lizette

17

Bain stood in the library and stared out the window into the backyard, where Lizette, her mother, Rebel Dante, and Grandma Dicia were playing with the twins. Braxton and Blythe were close to six months old already, and it hardly seemed possible that so much time could have gone by. He watched the afternoon sun highlighting Lizette's dark hair as she sat on the quilt with Braxton in her lap. She was even more lovely than the first time he'd laid eyes on her, and he shuddered to think he'd almost lost her. That's why he was so apprehensive now.

Business trips to Charleston, Savannah, or Philadelphia were one thing. He glanced at the message in his hand, frowning. This was a summons from Washington and had nothing to do with business. What would he tell Lizette? The frown deepened. And what did Washington want with him? The war had been over for three years. Why, all of a sudden, the urgent communiqué?

He shoved the message back into the pocket of his dark blue frock coat, straightened his cravat, and decided to join the ladies, ignoring for at least a few minutes the word "urgent" that was used more than once in the message.

Out in the yard, Lizette ran her hand atop her young son's head, the fine baby hair like silk between her fingers. Both Braxton and Blythe had blond hair like their grandmother and gray eyes like their father, with the tawny complexion of their mother, who was part Indian. It was a rare combination, and with the deep dimples that dented their cheeks when they smiled, Lizette was certain they were the two most beautiful children who'd ever been born.

Many parents still kept their children in swaddling clothes for their first year, and gave them little freedom to move and grow, but Lizette had listened too long to Grandma Dicia, who'd raised her children in the wilderness, and now she was glad she had as she watched Blythe trying to crawl forward on her stomach so she could reach a rattle her grandmother was waving in front of her.

The twins were lively, and Lizette was glad her slave Pretty had stayed to help her with them, even though Lizette had signed the papers giving Pretty her freedom long before the twins were born. It would have been almost impossible for her to handle the two of them by herself and run the house too. But things had worked out fine, and as she glanced up to see Bain leave the house, heading toward them across the lawn, her heart swelled with love for him.

"Well, what are you doing home so early?" she asked, greeting him with a smile.

He nodded hello to his mother-in-law and Grandma Dicia, then leaned down and kissed Lizette lightly on the lips. "Since I'm my own boss, I figured it was too pretty a day to work," he answered. "So I'm procrastinating."

Grandma Dicia laughed. "I think you've been around Roth too long," she mused, her violet eyes twinkling.

Bain winked at her. He was terribly fond of his wife's grandmother. Her name wasn't really Dicia, it was Loedicia, Loedicia Chapman, and she was married to Roth Chapman, a strapping man, still good-looking at almost seventy, with white hair and warm dark eyes. He was an ex-congressman and a man with integrity. A rarity in government these days, so it seemed. Loedicia was a small woman, still showing the delicate beauty she'd handed down to her daughter and granddaughter, her silver hair, with dark streaks still running through it, making her appear fragile. But there was nothing fragile about her. She could still ride and shoot if the necessity arose.

Dicia smiled at her granddaughter's husband. Lizette had certainly picked a handsome man to marry, she thought, what with his flashing gray eyes and russet hair. His clipped beard was darker and had a little more black in it than his hair, making him appear rugged. She liked Bain, even if he and Lizette had had a bit of trouble in the beginning. No one had seemed to know what had happened between them, but now, ever since the night Cole and Heather had sailed away and almost taken Liz with them, there seemed to be a new understanding between the young couple. Loedicia was pleased.

"I know you haven't heard the latest, Bain," Loedicia said as she looked up at him from where she sat beside Lizette on the quilt. "We came to tell Liz about the letter Rebel and Beau got from Cole."

"She's alive, Bain," Lizette said hurriedly. "Cole sent the

letter from Fort Smith before they left to go back to the valley, and Heather isn't dead.''

Bain knelt down beside Lizette and reached out, letting Braxton wrap his hand around one of his fingers. He looked at his mother-in-law. ''But the letter you received earlier . . . it said she'd been killed by Indians.''

''It was all a mistake,'' Rebel said happily. ''It's a rather long story. Only one sad thing, though, the baby. He and Heather's girl Tildie were traded to some Indians, and God knows where he is. They're both heartbroken about it, but Cole said he and Heather are planning to go looking for him as soon as they can make arrangements to leave the valley.''

''I hope they find him,'' Bain said thoughtfully. ''It's a big place out there.''

''That's right, you have been there, haven't you?'' she said.

''He's been to St. Louis, too,'' offered Lizette.

''And a few other places.'' Bain took Braxton from her and bounced him on his knee. ''Afraid I've never been up the Arkansas, though.''

Loedicia was wearing a watch on a chain about her neck, and she checked the time. ''Gracious, Reb, dear, we should really be getting back,'' she exclaimed. ''As it is, we'll be late for dinner.'' She looked at Lizette. ''Your father and mother are dining with us tonight at the Château, dear . . . why don't you come too.'' She glanced from one to the other. ''You both could come and bring the babies and Pretty. It's a lovely afternoon for a ride. I'm sure they'd enjoy it. And you could stay overnight. We'd love to have you. Your Uncle Heath and Aunt Darcy had to go to Washington, so the place has been rather empty.''

Bain saw Lizette's eyes light up and hated having to disappoint her. ''I'm afraid we can't tonight, Grandma Dicia,'' he said. ''I have some important matters to take care of—''

''Oh, Bain, can't they wait?'' Lizette begged. ''We've been away so little the past few months.''

He stared at her intently; then, ''Not tonight,'' he said. ''But I'll tell you what I'll do. If it's all right with Grandma Dicia, I'll send you, Pretty, and the twins to the Château early tomorrow morning and you can spend a week there if you like. How's that?''

Lizette's green eyes darkened. ''A week?'' she said hesitantly.

He tried to be nonchalant. ''I have to go to Charleston on business,'' he said, hating to lie to her like this. ''And I thought if you were at the Château with everyone, you wouldn't miss me as much.''

"You were just there two weeks ago," she complained. "Can't they handle whatever it is without you this time?''

He glanced down at Braxton, the baby's pudgy body feeling so comfortable in his hands. "It can't be helped, Liz," he answered. "That's why I came home early. I thought maybe it'd be nice to spend a quiet evening with you before I go.''

Lizette flushed. She knew what Bain's quiet evening was going to consist of.

Loedicia and Rebel exchanged furtive glances. "Bain's right, Liz," Rebel said, agreeing with him. "Come up tomorrow, after he's gone. Your father and I'll still be there. He and Grandpa Roth are doing something at the cotton mill, some newfangled idea, so we're staying for a couple of days, and I'm sure they'd both love to see you and the children.''

Lizette glanced down at Blythe and Braxton, then to her husband's face, searching his eyes. "All right," she said quietly, turning once more to her grandmother. "I think maybe that would be nice. It gets pretty lonely when he's gone.''

Which is too often, thought Loedicia. It was too bad Bain hadn't become involved in business closer to home, but then, he'd been a wanderer for a long time before settling down to raise a family. Still, it was a shame. Maybe when the children were older Lizette could go with him occasionally. She'd probably like that.

"Are you coming, Mother?" Rebel asked as she stood up, smoothing the skirt of her pale pink dress and setting a straw bonnet back onto her head, since they'd be riding in the open carriage.

Bain had set the baby back down and helped Rebel to her feet; now he held his hand out to help Loedicia.

"Gracious, I'm not that decrepit yet," she said, smiling impishly. "But I guess it is rather nice to know the handsome young men think I'm still somewhat of a lady." She thanked Bain, and brushed a few stray strands of grass from the skirt of her watered silk dress. It was deep crimson with a tight bodice and lace inserts in the billowing sleeves and skirt. Loedicia rarely wore pale colors. Most of her clothes were vivid greens, blues, purples, and reds, and she was proud of the fact that she could wear them and look well in them. "They keep me feeling young," she'd told Lizette once, a long time ago.

Bain called for Pretty to come watch the babies, and after the usual kisses and hugs by their doting grandmothers, the children were left in Pretty's care, while Bain and Lizette walked Rebel and Loedicia out to the drive, where their carriage waited.

Lizette watched the carriage, driven by Grandma Dicia's faithful old servant Jacob, move down the drive, turn to the right, and disappear from sight; then she turned to Bain.

"What time do you have to leave?" she asked.

He took her arm, and they headed toward the house. "Early, I'll be sailing this time. The *Dragonfly*'s in port and it's quicker than going overland."

She sighed. "I wish you didn't have to go."

He didn't answer right away, but put his arm about her as they walked. When they reached the foyer, he stopped, turning her to face him. "I hope you don't think I like leaving you, Liz," he said, watching her eyes closely. "If I had my way, we'd never be separated again."

Her arms moved up about his neck, and she melted against him. "Take me with you, Bain," she whispered fervently. "I don't have to go to the Château. Pretty can take the twins up. Grandma Dicia and mother would have a great time with them."

He shook his head.

"Please," she pleaded. "We haven't been away alone together since . . ." She flushed remembering the horrible circumstances of her first and only trip on the *Dragonfly*, when she thought Bain hated her and was marrying her only to give his brother's bastard child she was carrying a name. "I'm sorry, Bain. I didn't mean to remind you . . . I just think it would be nice to have you all to myself."

"You're sharing me with someone?" he asked.

"This house, your business, the children, your family." Her eyes softened. "It'd be so nice just the two of us."

"I can't take you with me this time, Liz," he said, then pulled her closer against him, kissing her deeply, sensuously. His lips lingered on hers longer than usual; then he reluctantly drew them away. "Have you forgotten, you're still nursing the twins," he reminded her. "And there's no way you could have everything you'd need ready by morning."

"All I needed last time was the clothes on my back."

"And the twins?"

She sighed, her eyes falling before his steady gaze. "You're right, of course," she said, the seductive warmth gone from her voice; then suddenly her chin tilted up stubbornly, and she looked him straight in the eyes. "But I swear, Bain Kolter, that somehow, some way, I'm going to wean Brax and Blythe, either that, or find a wet nurse somewhere, or two if I have to, and the next time you have to leave, I'm going with you."

He laughed lightly. "Can I count on that?"

"Oh, Bain."

"I mean it," he said, gazing down at her as he held her close. "While I'm gone, I want you to work on weaning the twins and getting the things you need ready, and when I get back, as soon as you think we can get away, we'll leave on the *Dragonfly*, just the two of us. How does that sound?"

"You promise?"

"I promise."

She eyed him skeptically. "You won't change your mind?"

"Now, why would I do that?" His eyes saddened. "Haven't I convinced you yet how much I love you, Liz?" he asked. "Do I have to give you my soul as well as my heart?"

She reached up, touching his face. "Don't ever stop loving me, Bain," she whispered softly. "I don't think I could stand it."

He kissed her again; then, "I have to go down to the docks to tell Captain Holley to have the *Dragonfly* ready to sail in the morning," he said. "When I get back, we'll have the whole evening all to ourselves, and I intend to make the most of it."

She smiled. "I'll be waiting."

He released her and reached for his hat behind him on the hall tree.

"Isn't it wonderful about Cole?" she said as she watched him. "I felt terrible when he wrote that Heather was dead. Not just for him, but for me too. You know how close we were. More like sisters than cousins."

"Your brother's a lucky man, Liz," Bain said, putting the hat on his head at a rakish angle. "And I'm lucky too, to have you. Now, let me get going so I can get back in time to show you just how lucky," and he kissed her again, then left.

Lizette watched her husband walk down the flagstone walk that led to the drive, unhitch his horse from the hitching post where he'd left it when he came home, and head down the drive; then she shut the front door of the stone house where they had been living since returning from their elopement a year ago last spring, and she hummed softly to herself, pleased with the way her life had turned out as she headed toward the backyard again to help Pretty with the twins.

The next morning, after a night of love that almost frightened Liz with its intensity, she kissed Bain a reluctant good-bye; then she and Pretty packed up the things they needed and left for the Château, her grandparents' plantation on the Broad River at Port Royal, where she'd keep herself busy until Bain's return.

As the *Dragonfly*'s sails unfurled and Bain watched the crew casting off, he felt a tension grip him. It was the kind of uncertainty that fills a man before going into battle, and once more he took the message from the pocket of his frock coat and read it. If only he could have been honest about it with Liz, but the message specifically said to tell absolutely no one he was headed for Washington, not even family.

He shoved it back in his pocket again. Well, he'd know soon enough what it was all about, and he gripped the rail, watching Beaufort being left behind as the ship's sails caught in the wind, moving them farther out into Port Royal Sound, heading toward the open sea. Suddenly he had a premonition that he wasn't ever going to see Beaufort again. He stared out across the water for a long time, then sighed, brushing aside the weird feeling as nothing more than the natural feelings of a man who was going to be terribly lonely without his family, and he turned, looking up at the early-morning sun as it turned the sky to gold; then he straightened, bracing himself against the morning breeze, and went to find Captain Holley, to tell him, now that they'd set sail, to change his course from Charleston to Baltimore.

It had been a long time since Bain had been in Washington, and as he rode down New York Avenue toward the President's house on Pennsylvania Avenue, he marveled that so much had been restored already since the British had burned it. It had been four years since that tragic night, and although there wasn't too much more to do, he had heard it'd probably be another year before things were completely back to normal.

He studied the White House as he rode by, unconsciously maneuvering his Morgan horse Amigo past a couple of carriages, then reined up for a minute to let some people cross the street in front of him. The pause gave him a chance to look around. Someday he was going to bring Liz to the capital. She'd really enjoy the excitement that always seemed to be going on.

Suddenly he tensed, listening, drawing his eyes from the buildings, searching the carriages and people's faces as he nudged

Amigo and began to move on again. For a split second he'd sworn he heard someone call his name. All he'd need would be for someone to recognize him, although the only one he really felt he'd have to worry about was his brother Stuart, and Stuart should be in Columbia, since the Senate wasn't due to convene yet.

He forgot about the incident quickly as he reached the next intersection and turned right onto Connecticut Avenue. His instructions were to sail one of his ships to Baltimore, entering the harbor after dark; then he was to ride to Washington alone and meet at an address on Connecticut Avenue, talking to no one on the way unless it was an absolute necessity. He had done all that, and now, a short time later, after traveling a few more blocks, he reined up in front of a brick house, its simple lines blending in with the surrounding neighborhood, making it very inconspicuous.

He was met at the door by a tall black man who ushered him to a room at the back of the house, where he was instructed to make himself comfortable and someone would be with him shortly.

Bain had given the servant his hat and now he stood examining the room. It looked like a library, with a desk at one end, a fireplace on the far wall, and windows on each side of the fireplace letting in a slight breeze that helped little to cool things off. Washington in July could be sweltering, and although it wasn't as hot as it could have been, Bain could feel the sweat dampening his shirt, and he unbuttoned his frock coat as he moved closer to the windows, hoping to feel some of the air.

An hour later he was still waiting, refurbished some by a glass of cool ale and an assurance from the servant who brought it, the same one who had opened the door for him, that someone would be with him shortly.

He was just going to finish the last few drops of ale he'd been nursing along slowly when the door opened abruptly, and Bain stared in disbelief at the man who entered. He'd never met President James Monroe personally, but had seen him from afar when he'd been Secretary of War, and had seen enough paintings and drawings of him since his election to recognize him in person.

"Mr. Kolter, don't look so dumbfounded," the President said as he motioned toward a couple of overstuffed chairs in front of the cold fireplace. "Have a seat, and would you like some more ale?"

Bain shook his head. "No, thank you, sir, Mr. President," he said, still flustered by the President's unexpected appearance. Bain held up the mug. "I still have a few drops left."

"Yes, I guess you do." The President sat down in one of the chairs and Bain sat in the other; then James Monroe studied the young man before him. He was about twenty-seven if he remembered the statistics in the file right, had proved himself well during the war, was Senator Stuart Kolter's younger brother, and seemed to have all the qualifications that were needed. "You probably wonder what this is all about," he said, watching Bain's reactions closely. "My informants have spoken well of you."

"Yes, sir," Bain said, his shock at meeting the President in these strange surroundings finally over. He chided himself silently for losing his composure, something that rarely ever happened. It had been a natural reaction, however, since he'd been expecting someone else.

"I know you thought you'd be meeting Sam," the President explained. "But I felt it was the only way of getting to see you without anyone knowing of our meeting, except Sam of course, although he has no idea as yet why we're meeting. I'll tell him later, when and if we come to an agreement."

Bain stared at the President, puzzled, wondering what the hell this whole thing was all about. Bain had worked with Sam Hewitt during the war when he'd been blockade running, and had done a number of other jobs for him that were over and above what were normally expected of someone who wasn't really part of the official War Department. He hadn't minded at all. After all, it was his country too, and there were times he felt what he was doing was just as important as or even more important than joining one of the branches of the service. Sam Hewitt had been an old friend and he was one of the highest men in naval intelligence, answering only to the Secretary of War; it was unthinkable that what the President had to say couldn't be shared with Sam from the start.

"Why are we meeting, sir?" asked Bain, straightening more self-assuredly in his chair.

The President's eyes grew intense. "I understand you own some holdings in Mexico, Mr. Kolter," he said. "Am I right?"

"Yes, sir. I own two copper mines in what they call Texas."

"Where in Texas?"

"One's about thirty miles northwest of an island known as

Galvez Island. The other is farther south, not far from the San Antonio River. But may I ask how you happen to know, sir?"

"Evidently you mentioned it at one time to Sam or one of his colleagues, and it managed to get onto your file."

"My file?"

The President smiled. "You have no idea Sam has a file on you?"

"I guessed, but didn't think it was that extensive."

"It's a little out of date, I'm afraid," James Monroe said. "I believe the last entry on it was about two years ago. You did some work for him back in 1816?"

"That's right. When it was over, I decided to head home for a while."

"You still have your ships?" he asked.

"Yes sir. The *Dragonfly*'s in Baltimore waiting for me. The other two are out to sea."

"But you do have one at your disposal, right?"

Bain straightened in the chair, his hands tightening about the mug still in his hand. "Sir, is it presumptuous of me to ask just what this is all about?"

"It's a rather sticky situation, Mr. Kolter," he answered. "You've heard of Jean Lafitte?"

"I've met the man, yes, sir."

"You know him personally?"

"We've met."

"Under what circumstances?"

"When I was running the British blockades in New Orleans, I had to have a safe place to bring my cargoes ashore where the British wouldn't bother me. Lafitte helped a few times. Although I disliked working with the man, it was a necessity at the time, and I fought side by side with some of his men during the actual battle."

President Monroe stroked his chin thoughtfully, then leaned back in his chair. "Did you part friends?"

Bain shrugged. "I guess. We never had words, if that's what you mean."

"It is." The President was pleased. "Do you know how well he knows you, Mr. Kolter?" he asked.

Bain frowned. "I doubt he knows much at all about me, except that I captained the *Dragonfly*."

"Good." The President's eyes narrowed shrewdly. "How

would you like to meet Mr. Lafitte again, Mr. Kolter?" he asked.

Bain's frown deepened. "I don't understand."

"Undoubtedly." The President cleared his throat, straightening as he leaned closer to Bain. "As you probably know, Jean Lafitte and his brother Pierre were pardoned for their crimes of piracy right after the end of the war, in payment for their help in New Orleans against the British. However, it seems the Lafitte brothers are determined to live dishonest lives. Rumor has it that the Lafittes have taken over the island of Galvez off the coast of Texas and are up to their old tricks, operating a haven for any cutthroat willing to throw in with them, and American vessels unfortunately are, more often than not, the main targets of these pirates, since the waters adjacent to the island are plied mostly by Americans." He paused, taking a deep breath. "I've sent two men into the territory already to see what they could learn. Neither man has been heard from since. I can only assume they're both dead." He stood up and paced to one of the windows and back, then stood looking down at Bain. "Mr. Kolter, I need someone to take their place, and I'd like you to be that someone."

Bain stared at him, the enormity of what the President was asking him sinking in. "Why don't you just ask the Spanish government in Mexico to check on it for you?"

"The Spanish won't cooperate. I've tried. I sent an open delegation to the Spanish in that area. They learned nothing Mr. Lafitte didn't want them to know. As it is, the Spanish are hostile because of the mess over Amelia Island and Jackson's blunder. They know we want the Florida territories and they guard the northern boundary of Mexican territory, what you referred to as Texas, with an iron hand. Any American caught in Texas territory without a damn good reason—and it better not be for military or trade purposes—is either thrown in jail or escorted out of the territory with little ceremony."

"I see." Bain grew thoughtful. "What makes you think I could succeed when the other two men you sent failed?"

"Your file and your record." His eyes were steady on Bain. "The men who were sent before had never been to the territory. They were easterners who had learned their Spanish in embassy ballrooms and their sailing on the Potomac. Besides that, their faces were too familiar here in Washington, and Lafitte has spies everywhere. His brother Pierre is a regular visitor to the capital. I should have known better than to send them. This time, I intend to do it right. You, Mr. Kolter, have the qualifications I need. You speak Spanish, fluently from what I'm told. You've been in and out of Mexico a number of times. In fact, you have Mexicans managing your mines for you, am I right?''

Bain nodded. ''Yes, sir.''

''And before the war you were a bit of a rapscallion, known to bend the rules of honesty now and then in order to further your ambitions. Right?''

''You mean because I won my first ship as payment of a gaming debt?''

''No, Mr. Kolter, because you wanted that ship so badly you let a man bet on what you knew was a sure thing, knowing there was no possible way for the other man to win the bet.'' The President's eyes twinkled slightly. ''Most people consider a bet something with an even chance for either side to win. I wouldn't say you were exactly dishonest, my young friend,'' he said, ''but you must admit you did have an advantage.''

''I always called it making the most of an opportunity.''

''Good,'' said the President, then smiled. ''You'll make an excellent pirate, if you need to go that far, and your family's already used to your being gone, so your parents won't even miss you, and the people in Beaufort will think nothing of the fact that you're gone again.''

Bain tensed. ''What of my wife, sir?'' he asked abruptly.

President Monroe was startled. ''Your wife? The file didn't say anything about a wife.''

''I married Lizette Dante a year ago last spring, sir, and we now have twins, a boy and a girl almost six months old.''

The President stared at him for a moment, then straightened and walked to one of the windows, staring out at the warm afternoon sunshine. Bain watched him curiously as the President stood motionless for a long time, then turned, walking back to sit down in the chair he'd been sitting in earlier. He leaned back, staring at the empty fireplace, then took a deep breath and turned to Bain.

''I'd still like you to go, Mr. Kolter,'' he said firmly. ''May I call you Bain?''

''Yes, sir.''

''I know what I'm asking is hard, Bain,'' he said. ''But I don't know where else to turn. We're losing too many ships too close to home. If Lafitte is behind it, as the rumors say, then we have to figure a way to stop him, and the only way is to have someone on the inside. That someone has to be you.''

This time it was Bain's turn to pace the floor. He stood up, set the empty mug on a stand next to the chair where he'd been sitting, and walked to the same window, staring out. What should he do? There were so many questions still left unanswered. He turned and faced the President.

''Who, besides you and me, will know where I am and what I'm doing?'' he asked.

''Only Sam.''

''Then I'd really be on my own.''

''In a manner of speaking. If anything were to go wrong, I couldn't give you any help officially. Officially you'd be just another American in trouble. But I could try to help unofficially, if need be.''

''I see.'' He bit his lip, cogitating; then, ''I couldn't even tell my wife where I'm going?'' he asked.

''Not even your wife.''

''You don't know Lizette. She'd raise hell from Beaufort to Charleston. I'd have to tell her something.''

''You have other business interests. Tell her you have to check on one of them, but don't mention going to Mexican territory.''

''But wouldn't it be logical for me to check on the mines?''

''Check on the mines, yes, but happily married men with families don't take up with pirates, and if you should have to become one, it'll be better if she doesn't know where you are. If anyone discovers you're married and that your wife thinks you're somewhere else, you can pretend your marriage isn't the happy life you expected it to be. It's happened before. But the less your wife knows, the better your chances are of returning alive.''

''I think you've forgotten another thing, sir,'' Bain said. ''What about my brother? When Bain Kolter arrives on Galvez Island, somebody's sure to discover that Senator Stuart Kolter has a brother with the same name. The whole scheme would be shot to hell.''

''I've already thought of that.'' He looked at Bain curiously. ''I understand you and your brother aren't any too close. Am I right?''

Bain winced at the memories the President's statement conjured up. ''I guess you could say that.''

''All right, then, if you do have to join Lafitte's band of

cutthroats to get what we're looking for, what would your brother's reaction be if he learned of it?''

Bain nodded knowingly. ''I see what you mean.'' His eyes hardened. ''He always did think I was irresponsible and would no doubt think it was a typical thing for me to do.''

''Exactly. So you see, we'll be covered there. The point is, Bain, that you're a natural to send in. Even if you don't actually become a pirate, just the fact that you could get into Lafitte's confidence would be a help. We have to have some sort of proof. Otherwise, if we go in to clean him out and he's warned ahead of time, or if he convinces the Spanish authorities that his operation there is a legitimate one, then the Spanish could use an incident like that to say we were trying to provoke a war by invading their territory, and we'd have another mess on our hands.'' His fist came down on the arm of the chair. ''I need proof that what he's doing is piracy. Will you do it?''

''How soon do you need an answer?''

''That's just the trouble. I need it now.''

Bain stared at the President, trying to think of a way out. There was none. How did one refuse the man? But leaving Lizette and the twins . . . For a regular business trip, yes, but what if he didn't come back? There was always that possibility. Yet someone had to do it, and President Monroe was right, he had the qualifications. Damn! He hadn't wanted to go back to Texas. In fact, he'd been thinking of selling the mines. Now . . .

He took a deep breath, then made his decision. ''All right, I'll go,'' he said. ''How soon?''

''Now. When you leave here, don't stop to talk to anyone in the city, but head straight for Baltimore and your ship.''

''What about my crew?'' asked Bain. ''I'll have to confide in them.''

''You can tell them where you're headed, but tread easily with them. Don't take anyone you can't trust. But if I remember right, Sam said the crews of all your ships were handpicked by you, so I'm hoping you'll know how to handle them.''

Bain sighed. ''I think I can manage the crew once they know. They're used to my intrigues. The one who worries me most is my wife. How do I convince her that I have to go away again?''

''Don't,'' he said as he stood up and stretched a bit. ''When you leave here, go straight to Mexico. Send her a message saying you've been delayed.''

Bain shook his head. ''That's asking too much, sir,'' he said.

"No, when I leave here, I'll head home first. But don't worry, I'll be in Texas before the month's out."

President Monroe held out his hand. "Shall we shake on it?" he asked.

Bain shook his hand reluctantly. "I hope to God I can be of help, sir," he said quietly.

The President stared at him. "Just get back with the proof I need, written documents, eyewitnesses to what's been going on. Anything to give me a reason to go in there or at least arrest the men who sail the ships he sends out. And also, keep your eyes open, Bain, and let me know what the Spanish are thinking. See if you can find out how badly they want to hold on to Texas territory while you're at it. Who knows, someday that knowledge might be important too. A lot of people have been talking about Texas. There's a lot of land out there." The President started toward the door. "By the way, just in case either of the other two men I sent down there is still around, the password is 'wines of summer' and the countersign is 'a rose in winter.' Can you remember that?"

"I'll make it a point."

"Then, good luck."

"Oh, sir!" Bain stopped him. "If I have to contact you . . . how do I go about it?"

"I'm sorry. I forgot. You'll reach me through Sam, and how you get your messages to Sam will be up to you, but you'll use your old code name, Domino. He has orders to deliver your messages directly to me."

Bain sighed. "Then I guess that's all, sir."

"I want to thank you, Bain," the President said. "I know it won't be easy, but believe me, what you're doing is important, not only to me but also to every American who sails the seas. One word of caution. Remember, the brothers Lafitte may look like gentlemen and act civilized at times, but they can be deadly."

"I'll remember."

"Good. Then again, I wish you luck. Good-bye, my friend."

"Mr. President . . ." Bain nodded as President James Monroe left the room.

Half an hour later, after being let out by the servant who'd ushered him into the library, Bain was on his way back to Baltimore, where the *Dragonfly* lay at anchor. His mind ran back over the events of the afternoon and he kept telling himself he hadn't been dreaming. If he'd been handed this assignment two, three years ago he'd have jumped at the chance to do it. It was the kind of adventure you could tell your grandchildren. If you lived through it, that is. Grandchildren. The twins and Lizette! He didn't want to leave them. It was bad enough when he was gone for more than a week, and a job like this could take months, and he'd promised to take her with him the next time. Well, she'd just have to understand. He knew Lafitte well enough to know that if President Monroe was right, he'd have to be stopped. Yes, Lizette was going to have to understand, and he urged his horse a little harder as the afternoon sun began to lower on the horizon, and he hoped he'd make Baltimore before midnight.

18

Lizette and Bain stood alone in the library at the Château, just the two of them. Her face was flushed from anger, green eyes flashing dangerously. Bain had sailed the *Dragonfly* into the sound, up the Broad River, and dropped anchor at the pier behind Lizette's grandparents' plantation, arriving less than an hour ago, and now, already, he was telling her he'd be weighing anchor again at dawn.

"But you promised!" she cried furiously. "You said we'd sail together."

"I know what I said," he agreed. "But sometimes promises have to be broken."

"Why? We've been working all week, and the twins are almost weaned. Why can't I at least go with you?"

"Because you can't. There are just some things . . . It wouldn't be practical."

"Who cares about being practical? So a forge blew up. I'm sure it didn't blow up the whole city of Pittsburgh."

"No, but even if you were there, I wouldn't be able to spend any time with you."

"We'd be together on the ship."

"It's out of the question, Liz. I'm sorry."

"You're sorry? I'm beginning to wonder. What is it, Bain? Have you decided I'm not worth it? Is that why you're always gone, why you won't take me with you?"

"You know better than that."

"Do I?" She stared at his handsome face, a tiny shred of fear beginning to gnaw its way into her thoughts. "What did you do, discover someone else out there and decide your brother's castoff mistress wasn't really what you wanted after all?" she cried.

"Liz, you're going too far."

"Am I? How far is too far?" She felt lost and defeated. "You treated me like this once before, Bain, remember?" she reminded him. "You loved me, yes. Every night you loved me, but when morning came you acted as if I wasn't even around. Haven't I paid for my mistakes yet? Is that why you won't take me, or is it because I might get in the way? Who is she, Bain?"

"Liz, for God's sake, will you stop this nonsense? There's no one else."

"Then take me with you."

"I can't!"

"You won't!"

"All right, then, won't," he yelled. "But there are damn good reasons why I won't. Reasons you wouldn't understand, but reasons that make it impossible to take you this time. I know I promised, and I hate having to break that promise, but I have no choice, believe me. Maybe someday you'll understand. But I swear to you, Liz, there's no other woman. You can accuse me all you want, but I won't change my mind. I wish I could take you with me, but I can't. Not now, not this time."

"Not ever!"

"I didn't say that. I will keep my promise to you. We will go away together, but not this time. I just can't take you with me this time."

"Why?"

He shook his head. If he didn't love her so damn much, he'd turn her over his knee. He stared at her, his gray eyes solemn. This could be the last time he'd ever see her if things went wrong, and here they were fighting. His eyes wandered over her voluptuous figure poured into the green silk she was wearing. He loved to look at her. Liz always looked like her clothes fit her a little too well, and she was forever worrying about her weight, but he didn't care. He loved her padded curves and the sensuous feel of her soft flesh when he made love to her, and suddenly he couldn't keep his hands off her. He reached out and pulled her into his arms, his eyes searching her face.

"Liz, please," he begged huskily. "Don't let's quarrel. Everything has been so right with us for so long now. Don't let the past cloud your heart and make us both miserable. Please, have faith in me. If I could take you, if I could see any possible way of taking you, I would. There's no other woman, and there never will be, you know that.'' His eyes saddened. "I told you a long time ago I married you because I loved you. I wouldn't have come back to Beaufort if I hadn't loved you.''

"Then why, Bain? Why can't I sail with you?'' she said.

He took a deep breath, his eyes troubled. "Just believe me, it's impossible,'' he whispered, then kissed her, his lips lingering on hers for a long time, as if he couldn't get enough of her. And that night, after a late meal with only her grandparents, since her mother and father had already returned to their plantation, Tonnerre, the day before, Lizette and Bain played with the twins for a while, then retired to one of the upstairs bedrooms, where Bain made love to her with a gentle tenderness that left her weak and satiated.

It was almost dawn. Bain lay staring at the window, watching the first faint streaks of light play against the curtains, and instinctively his arms tightened about Lizette. She was sleeping half on her stomach, half on her side, with her face buried against his jawline, her even breathing tickling the side of his cheek. It felt warm and pleasurable. If only he could tell her the truth. Yet he knew it was impossible. Too much was at stake.

Lizette stirred as his arms tightened, and she snuggled closer to him.

"Liz?'' he whispered. "I hate to wake you, but I have to leave soon.''

Her lips caressed his neck just below the clipped beard, and he trembled.

"I don't want you to go,'' she murmured.

"And I don't want to go.'' He rolled her onto her back, staring down into her face. Her eyes were heavy with sleep, her dark curly hair tousled. He reached out, burying his hand in the curls. They were soft, like silk. "I'll miss you,'' he said, then saw the look in her eyes change. "But don't ask again, please, my love,'' he went on. "The answer would have to be the same as it was last night.''

"How long will you be gone?''

"I don't know.'' His fingers ran through the curls, then traced her jawline, trailing down, running back and forth across the flesh, touching it lightly. "We'll have to rebuild—that means plans have to be drawn up and changes made here and there. A month, maybe two.''

"So long?"

"I know. I don't like it either, but life isn't always what we like.''

She reached up and touched his lips. "Then love me again,'' she whispered breathlessly. "So I have something to keep with me until you get back.''

He leaned down and kissed her, then let his lips trail to her breasts, full and inviting. Liz moaned softly as his mouth covered her left breast; then his eyes caught hers, and he lifted his lips, kissing the tip of her taut nipple.

"I thought you said you were weaning them.''

She flushed. "I am, only the milk just doesn't seem to want to stop.''

He kissed her again and she tasted the faint trace of milk on his lips. "I'm sorry, Bain,'' she said as he drew his mouth from hers.

He smiled, licking his lips. "Why, for tasting like a mother?'' His voice lowered, the smile softening. "Don't ever apologize to me for being a woman, Liz,'' he said. "I waited long enough for you to grow up, and I don't mind at all sharing you with the twins. Only there's one part of you I won't share with anyone, ever,'' and as his mouth descended on hers again, he moved over her, pulling her to him, his love for her helping to take away some of the pain he knew she'd feel when he was gone, and her love for him reminding him of what he had to come back to. He had to come back not only for her but also for himself, because to him life without Liz wasn't worth living.

She was willful, stubborn, and ornery at times, but as he kissed her and loved her, feeling her surrendering to him completely, her body arching to meet him with all the fire and passion that was only hers to give, he knew deep in his heart this was the last time he'd ever leave her. When he got back, he'd sell everything that wasn't in Beaufort so he'd never have to go away again. This was the last time. The next time he sailed, she'd be with him, and with that decision made, he plunged deep inside her, bringing them both to a moment in time that neither would ever forget.

"I love you, Liz,'' he whispered softly seconds later as the first rays of sunshine streamed through the window.

She stared up at him, trembling, her body basking in the

aftermath of his lovemaking. "I love you too," she gasped breathlessly, and as he kissed her again, suddenly a strange sadness seemed to engulf her. A sadness she couldn't explain, and it was still with her later as she stood on the pier at the back of the Château, with her grandparents at her side, saying good-bye to Bain, then tried to get the twins to wave to him as he waited at the rail of the *Dragonfly*, letting Captain Holley cast off and weigh anchor, wind filling the ship's sails, carrying it into midstream.

As the ship increased its speed, heading farther and farther downriver, Bain couldn't take his eyes from Lizette. He stood watching until she was only a small speck in the distance, then prayed for her safekeeping, thankful for one thing. Grandma Dicia and Grandpa Roth had insisted she stay with them while he was gone. At least that helped. With everything else, he didn't want to have to be worrying about his family. Her grandparents both loved the twins, and Liz liked it at the Château. It would be good for them there, and with them safe and sound, he was free to concentrate fully on the job ahead. As he turned from the rail, no longer able to see the pier or the woman who waited for him, he began to go over the plan he'd decided on while sailing down from Baltimore, and the first thing on the agenda when they reached the open sea was to let the crew in on the job that lay ahead of them.

The *Dragonfly* caught good weather most of the way, and now, as they neared the Texas coastline, Bain felt the tension beginning to build inside him. It had been two years since he'd been to the mines to make sure everything was all right. The money from it had arrived regularly three times a year by courier, and the letter from Señor Hernández that always accompanied the money gave him a full rundown on the previous month's operations, so he hadn't worried much about them. Profits had fallen off some in the past year, however, so he had decided to use that fact as an excuse for suddenly arriving unannounced to look things over.

It was a hot day, the last week in July, when Bain stood on the deck of the *Dragonfly* beneath a beautiful blue summer sky filled with tufted clouds and stared off toward the west. He could faintly make out a break in the horizon, but the sun was so bright, even squinting didn't help. He reached for his spyglass.

Suddenly a sharp cry rang down from the crow's nest. "Sail

ho!'' and Bain glanced up, then looked in the direction where the crewman was pointing.

The spyglass went to his eye, and he took a deep breath as the sails of a ship rode the horizon directly in his sights. She was still too far away to identify the flag she was flying, but he was certain it would have nothing to do with the sympathies of her crew. He was too close to Galvez Island for it not to be one of Lafitte's cohorts.

"Sound the alarm!" he yelled to one of the men, and within minutes the deck was bustling with men.

Although the *Dragonfly* was basically a merchantman, because of the precarious life her owner often led, she was equipped with thirty twelve-pounders, fifteen hidden behind camouflaged gunports on each side, and four twenty-four-pounders, two fore and two aft, concealed beneath canvas. They probably weren't as many as the ship bearing down on them carried, but since the *Dragonfly* had been built for running instead of fighting, Bain had learned to compensate.

He watched the other brig bearing down on them, no doubt in his mind now that she was patrolling the coast to prevent strangers from reaching the island. He glanced at Captain Holley, who'd stepped up beside him. The captain wasn't as tall as Bain, but he was brawny and muscular, with side whiskers that carried some gray in them, attesting to the fact that he was well into his forties. He had been with the ship when Bain first became owner and had liked Bain from the start. He was frowning now as he watched the distant ship on the horizon.

"Tell the helmsman to stay steady on the course," Bain said. "She's bigger than we are, but right now that gives us the advantage." He looked up at the clouds, watching them for a second as they changed form, billowing across the sky. "If the wind stays with us, I think we can beat her to the island."

"I hope you're right," Captain Holley answered. "I have a feeling Lafitte's friends don't waste much time talking," and he turned, heading for the wheel to give the order.

Bain raised the spyglass again and searched the coastline this time. They were making good time, and the land, which a short time ago had been only a blur between water and sky, was now taking on form. Galvez Island was long, its northern tip the entrance to Galveston Bay. If Lafitte was here, the northern end of the island was the logical place for him to be, since it would be hard for any ship to leave or enter the bay without his knowledge, and that's where they were headed.

He swung the spyglass about again, centering on their pursuer. The other ship had gained ground, but not enough.

"Sail ho," yelled the man in the crow's nest again, and pointed ahead toward the island.

Bain cursed softly as he caught sight of another ship moving in from the north. Well, he'd have to bluff it and hope they were willing to talk before starting anything. They could probably blow him out of the water if they had a mind.

He told Captain Holley to cut sail, and by the time the other two ships came into range, the *Dragonfly* was bobbing gently on the water, its crew still half-hidden, waiting.

"Ho, there, the ship," yelled a voice as the vessel that had been chasing them drew close enough so Bain could see the faces of her crew. She didn't look any too friendly. "Who are you and where are you bound?"

"The *Dragonfly*, from the Carolinas, bound for Galveston Bay," Bain called back, straining his voice.

"Why?"

Bain tensed. "Who wants to know?"

"Captain Billie Byrd and his crew, of the *Sea Hawk!*"

Bain felt the tension ease from his body some. What luck. "Billie Byrd? Not the Billie Byrd who sailed for Lafitte out of Barataria?"

The voice came back quickly this time. "The same!"

"Then might I ask what you want to stop an old friend for? It's Bain Kolter, Billie," he yelled. "We shared a few trying times together, if you'll jog your memory."

"Kolter?" Captain Billie Byrd leaned as far over the rail as he could to get a better look, and Bain straightened tall so there'd be no mistake. "What the hell are you doin' in these waters, Kolter?" he asked.

"I have business north of Galveston Bay that needs tending, but I could ask the same of you. Don't tell me you're back to your old tricks?"

Captain Byrd smiled. "Here comes another old friend," he yelled, and pointed.

Bain glanced to his left and watched a huge three-masted brigantine begin taking in sail as she slowed, then rode the water quietly, directly in the *Dragonfly*'s path. Bain didn't recognize the ship and used his spyglass, quickly reading the name. The

Golden Rose. That meant the man sailing her was Captain Lewis French, or Frenchie as his comrades called him. He too had been with Lafitte at Barataria.

"If you're after my cargo, Billie, all I have is enough for me and the crew," Bain yelled across to the other ship.

Billie straightened. "What makes you think I want what's in your hold?"

"Well, you sure as hell stopped me for some reason." Bain leaned out a little farther over the rail and cupped his hand around his mouth so he didn't have to yell quite so loud. "All I want to do is drop anchor in Galveston Bay and go about my business."

Captain Byrd stared across the water at the handsome young captain of the *Dragonfly*. Bain Kolter was a hard man, if he remembered right, and a hell of a fighter, taking chances most men would consider foolish, yet he always seemed to come out on top. Byrd had fought beside Kolter more than once during the battle at New Orleans and knew the man was anything but a coward. Byrd's eyes looked over Bain's ship. It was small for a three-master, but the lines were sleek. She'd been used for blockade running and could no doubt outrun both the *Sea Hawk* and the *Golden Rose*, even with a full cargo, but it was obvious the way she sat the water that her holds weren't full.

Kolter said he had business north of Galveston Bay. Well, maybe Lafitte would be interested in that business.

"We'll follow you into Galvez Island," he yelled across to Bain, then turned, instructing one of his men to signal the *Golden Rose* that they were heading in to port.

Bain sighed, relieved, as he waved, acknowledging that he heard, then addressed Captain Holley, who was once more at his side. "Well, it looks like we'll be getting in all right. Now let's just hope we can get out again when the time comes."

Captain Holley frowned. "Amen!"

A short time later, with the *Sea Hawk* on one side of her and the *Golden Rose* on the other, the *Dragonfly* dropped anchor off the shore of Galvez Island in Galveston Bay. The last time Bain had been here, he'd anchored at the western end near where the Trinity River empties into the bay, and the place had been practically deserted, only a few native fishermen about.

Now it was as if a small village had suddenly sprung up on the island, and as he watched the crew lower the longboat over the side, he stared at all the houses. Directly in the center of them was one house that seemed to command the whole area. It was painted bright red, and on their way in, as Bain squinted in the sun, he could make out the muzzle of cannon pointing seaward from the second floor. There was only one man who'd live in such a monstrosity, and Bain was certain he knew who it would be.

When he reached the shore, setting foot on land for the first time, Captain Billie Byrd was already there to greet him.

"Looks like things have gone well for you the past few years," Billie said as he shook Bain's hand.

Bain smiled. "They could be better, I suppose." He studied Billie Byrd. The man had changed little. His hair, once red, was streaked with gray, his eyes icy blue in a face weathered and wrinkled from the sun. A deep scar marred his chin from his thick bottom lip to where side whiskers began, and a red mustache adorned his upper lip. His nose was rather large and the bicorne hat he wore with its bright green ostrich plume made it look all the larger, as well as contrasting with the rest of his unusual outfit, which consisted of black boots, brown fatigue pantaloons, white linen shirt, and what was left of a gilt-buttoned officer's uniform. Most of the men with him were as haphazardly thrown together, contrasting greatly with the neat appearance of Bain's crew.

Bain finished his perusal of the captain and turned his eyes inward toward the houses, where a bustle of people were coming to life. "What's all this?" he asked, playing ignorant. "The last time I was here, there was hardly a soul about."

Billie grinned. "That was last time. Come along," he said, and turned, heading up the beach directly toward the red house. "You men stay here," he ordered Bain's crew.

Bain nodded. "I'll be back shortly," he said, and winked furtively at one of his men, who quickly blinked both eyes, acknowledging the silent message.

"I don't know what the hell you're up to, Billie," Bain said as they reached the red house and were ushered inside by a servant who looked like he'd be just as at home with a cutlass in his hand as a tea tray.

"You'll see," said Billie as the servant disappeared down a long hall, coming back a few minutes later with an invitation for them to go right on in.

While they were approaching the house, and now while standing inside, Bain made a mental picture of the place. It was like a strong fortress, the walls thick, windows placed at strategic points. Lafitte was intending to stay. And it had to be his residence. The furniture, everything, was too elaborate. The man commanded an expensive life-style.

His answer was quick in coming when Billie led him through an arched doorway into a spacious living room but Bain pretended surprise.

"Lafitte?" he questioned, acting every bit as surprised as Jean Lafitte expected him to be. "Good Lord, what are you doing here?"

Jean Lafitte stared at Bain Kolter. It had been almost four years since he'd seen the man, but he'd recognize him anywhere. He'd always been a little jealous of Kolter. Kolter still had his youth and good looks, whereas Lafitte was pushing forty, an age young women found less attractive, and he remembered a certain young lady back in New Orleans shortly after the battle, when things had quieted down and the city was starting to get back to normal. It wasn't until Kolter had left New Orleans that the young lady had finally consented to let Lafitte escort her about town.

His eyes narrowed slightly. "The shoe is on the other foot, Mr. Kolter," Jean said, unsmiling. "The question is, what are you doing here?"

"I happen to have business in Texas," he said. "I come here every so often to check on things."

"What things?"

"It's none of your business, really, Lafitte," he answered. "But I happen to own a copper mine northwest of here about thirty miles or so, and I usually come every two to three years to make sure everything's all right. It's been a little over two years now since I've been here, and because profits seem to be falling off, I came to find out why."

"That wouldn't happen to be the Caballito del Diablo mine, would it?" Lafitte asked.

"That's right. In English, the Dragonfly, the same as my ship. You know of it?" Bain asked.

Lafitte was sitting down and he leaned back in his satin-upholstered chair. "I should have remembered the name of your ship, Kolter, then perhaps I'd have realized," he said. "I've not only heard of it, but since the ore is now being shipped from Galveston Bay instead of sent overland to San Antonio de Bexar and on down to Saltillo, that could be why your profits are falling short. You see, I control the shipping from Galveston Bay, and safe passage through the gulf can be costly.''

Bain eyed him skeptically. ''You're the one cutting into my profits?''

''Let's say I'm ensuring your shipments' safe passage.''

''How long ago did they start shipping the ore?''

Lafitte shrugged. ''Shortly after my arrival. It's faster that way.''

Bain would have liked to smash the man in the face. For all of his supposed charm and manners, he was no better than Billie Byrd, who stood beside Bain. Only Billie didn't hide his dishonesty under a cloak of respectability like Lafitte attempted to do.

''I see.'' Suddenly he forced a grin. ''Well, that settles it, then,'' he said. ''I came down here prepared to sell, and you've given me a good reason to go through with it. I like a fast dollar and a fast turnover in my investments, but I don't like paying tribute.''

''Tribute? Is that what you call it?'' Lafitte was dressed in a fancy frock coat with ruffled shirt, and he straightened his cravat leisurely as he crossed his legs. The shine on his boots caught the sun as it shone in one of the parlor windows. ''I trade in goods, Kolter,'' he said, pretending congeniality. ''I buy your ore, then it's my responsibility to see it reaches its destination. Naturally, I can't pay full price.''

''And I presume your shipments get through, when others don't.''

''My ships are armed.''

''So I noticed.'' Bain straightened, frowning. ''If you're buying the ore and shipping it out, then why hasn't your name ever appeared on the manifests sent to me?''

''I'm a silent partner,'' Lafitte answered boldly. ''You see, I hate having to hunt for markets and all that. So everything is left the way you arranged it, only from the time the ore leaves Galveston Bay, the money for it goes into my coffers.''

''Surely you haven't built this whole town with money from my mine?'' Bain said.

Lafitte smiled, one of his rare smiles. ''I have a few other engaging enterprises,'' he answered.

''Fast money?'' Bain asked.

''You're interested?''

''Let's put it this way,'' Bain said, feeling him out. ''I'm going to have to sell my mine at a loss, no doubt, and since you're the reason, I think you should give me a chance to make up for it.''

Lafitte's dark eyes narrowed shrewdly. ''What's on your mind?''

Bain eyed Billie, then glanced about the room. ''I know damn well, what with Billie here, and Frenchie out there, and who knows how many more old friends of yours from Barataria around, that you're doing more than buying and selling honest goods,'' he told Lafitte, then took a deep breath. ''I was hoping to sell the mine at a profit because things haven't been going too well lately, but having to lose a good deal of my investment . . . I need money. As much as I can get, and as fast as I can get it.''

''I thought you said things were going all right,'' Billie said.

''They were,'' Bain said. ''When I thought I could still make a profit off the mine. However, with it losing money . . .''

''What do you propose?'' Lafitte asked again.

''I want you to let me in on what's going on here, Lafitte,'' he said forcefully. ''I've got a ship. I admit it isn't as well armed perhaps as the *Golden Rose* or the *Sea Hawk*, but it can outmaneuver anything you've got afloat.''

''Just what kind of an operation do you think I have here?'' asked Lafitte.

''The same kind you had at Barataria.''

''When did you decide that?''

''When I walked in here and saw you sitting in that chair.'' Bain's gray eyes darkened. ''Jean Lafitte doesn't do anything unless there's a profit in it, and with men like Billie here, and Frenchie, there's only one kind of profit, the easy kind.''

''Nothing comes easy,'' Lafitte said quickly.

''That's just an old saying,'' said Bain. ''I'm sick and tired of working my fool head off and getting nowhere, while your men make more in one haul than I make all year.''

Lafitte studied Bain for a long time. ''How do I know I can trust you?'' he asked.

''You don't. Not any more than you know you can trust Billie here. Look''—he tried to sound desperate—''I need money, and I don't care how I get it.''

''What about your men?''

''I can control my men.''

''If they don't want to go along with you?''

''They will. They've been complaining for ages because I haven't been able to pay them. I keep promising, but a few already jumped ship at the last port.''

"I don't know." Lafitte was hesitant. For some reason he wasn't sure about Bain Kolter. But then, he couldn't actually be sure about any of the men. If Kolter couldn't be trusted, it'd be better to keep him here, where he could keep an eye on him. He had worked for the American government once, blockade running, but that was in wartime. Still . . . "All right, Mr. Kolter," Lafitte said reluctantly. "We'll try you." He stood up and walked to the windows, throwing them open to let in the scent of oleanders that blended with the sea breeze. "Welcome, Mr. Kolter," and Bain felt a sudden coldness run through him, raising gooseflesh as Jean Lafitte's dark eyes caught his and held.

19

It took Bain a little over two weeks to ride out to the mine and check on things, leaving his ship and crew back at Galvez Island to ensure his return, then ride down to San Antonio de Bexar and confront Señor Hernández, who was supposed to be managing both mines. The man was terribly upset. In the first place, the mine up north was starting to peter out, and now, with Lafitte and his men forcing them to sell the copper ore through them, things weren't going well.

"Haven't you complained to the governor?" Bain asked in Spanish as he and Hernández sat at Hernández's table enjoying a glass of wine after dinner.

"*Sí,*" Juan Hernández answered. "But Governor Martínez is down here and Señor Lafitte is at Galveston Bay. He has convinced not only the governor but almost everyone else that his business is legitimate. Besides," Hernández said furtively, "Jean Lafitte hates the Spanish, and there are those in Mexico, including myself, who are working toward independence for Mexico. The more Spanish ships Lafitte's men take out of commission, the closer the day is when we will be in a position to achieve that independence. So Martínez and the rest pretend to close their eyes."

Bain had guessed as much. Lafitte was known to hate the Spanish and it was the only logical reason he hadn't been sent running from Galveston Bay. Mexico was quiet now, but the rumblings of insurrection that had started years before had never died. Just three years ago when America was trouncing the hell out of the British, the Spanish were squelching another uprising here in Mexico. Bain gazed at Hernández sympathetically. Maybe one of these days the Mexicans would succeed in breaking the yoke of Spain, but right now Bain's only interest was in getting rid of the mines.

It took him and Señor Hernández three days to find a buyer for both mines who was willing to let Señor Hernández buy in as a partner, and now Bain was back at Galvez Island—Campeche, as Lafitte called his new possession. Bain was living on board ship, an arrangement he preferred at the moment, and he stood at the rail now, looking down into the longboat that had just rowed alongside. It was late afternoon and he was surprised to see Billie Byrd.

"You're wanted at Maison Rouge," Billie called from the longboat, and Bain tensed, wondering if this was finally it.

"I'll be right with you," Bain yelled back, and went down to his cabin to slip into a frock coat and grab his hat. He'd been back from his trip inland for three days already and was getting restless.

Half an hour later, Jean Lafitte was greeting him again in the red house known throughout Campeche as Maison Rouge.

"Sit down, Mr. Kolter. Or is it all right to call you Bain?" he asked.

"Bain will do," Bain said as he sat in the brocade chair Lafitte offered him.

"My men told me you got back the other day," he said. "Did you manage to sell the mine?"

"I had to go to San Antonio de Bexar, but it turned out well. Not as much money as I wanted, but at least I don't have to worry about losing the whole thing anymore."

"Good. Since that's settled, I suppose you're ready for action." Lafitte glanced over at Billie, then back to Bain. "You're welcome to leave and try your hand at your new trade anytime you want now, Mr. Kolter," he said. "But there's one stipulation. Captain Byrd goes with you the first time out."

Bain's eyes shifted from Lafitte to Billie Byrd, then back to Lafitte. "Why?" he asked.

"I'll be honest with you, Bain," he answered. "I don't trust you. Not yet. You were a government man once . . ."

"You mean because I was running the blockades? Hell, I was

making a profit off everything I brought in. Government be damned. I was working for me.''

"That may well be," Lafitte said. "But until I'm satisfied you're not here for some ulterior motive . . . I don't care when you leave, where you go, or how much you bring back, just make sure the *Sea Hawk*'s alongside when you sail out."

Bain shrugged, his gray eyes intense. "Then I'll leave in the morning," he said. "If the captain can be ready by then. When I was in San Antonio de Bexar, I heard from a reliable source that the *San Gabriel* is due in Mexico City soon with a full cargo, including some gold bullion. If I play my cards right, I think I can intercept her."

"The *San Gabriel*'s a pretty big ship. You'll do well having the *Sea Hawk* with you."

"It isn't always might that wins, Lafitte," Bain said arrogantly. "Sometimes its brains that count, so just make sure Billie here remembers one thing: I'm going to command this venture. We do it my way or not at all. Is that understood?"

Lafitte's eyes narrowed. "What do you have in mind?"

"Never mind what I have in mind. Just make sure he knows his place."

Lafitte looked at Captain Billie Byrd. "Let him take it, Billie," he said. "Do it the way he says and don't interfere unless he asks you to."

Billie stared at Bain. "There's only one way to take a ship, Jean," he said. "Kill the crew, take the cargo, and scuttle it."

"His way, Billie!"

Billie Byrd didn't like taking orders from someone else, but he didn't like crossing Lafitte either. "All right, his way," he conceded. "But it had better work."

"It will," Bain assured him. "You see, I've got a good crew, hard to replace, and I don't like risking my men when there's no need. Now, if we're leaving tomorrow, I'd better get things ready. There's a lot to be done before morning. Coming, Billie?" he asked, and they left Lafitte standing in the parlor of his fancy house, wondering if he was doing the right thing by letting this impulsive young man join his fold. He shrugged, his long, lean frame straightening importantly. Well, he'd soon find out just what kind of a man Bain Kolter really was, that's for sure, and he followed the two men on outside and watched them walk down to their ships.

The next morning, as the sun burst forth on the horizon,

turning the sea to a golden pink that melted into the pale blue sky, the *Dragonfly* sailed out of Galveston Bay with the *Sea Hawk* in her wake, and Bain Kolter embarked on his new career as a pirate.

Lizette was restless as she rode along the bridle path at the Château, letting her palomino Diablo pick his own way. She paid little attention to where she was going. It didn't much matter. She was so worried. Bain had been gone for over two months and not a word from him. Some of the leaves were turning already, and she sighed. What if something had happened to him? The sea lanes were full of pirates, and even though the *Dragonfly* was armed, she wasn't a fighting ship. If only he'd come home.

A bird flew onto a branch nearby, and she craned her neck, watching it for a few minutes, then straightened in the saddle and brushed a leaf off the skirt of her deep violet riding habit. It was one she'd had before she'd married Bain, and it was a little tight in the waist, even though Pretty had let it out some. She pulled on the reins, turning Diablo back toward the house. She couldn't ride to the pond. Not now. There were too many memories there, and she patted Diablo's neck, remembering the day she and Bain had raced to the willow and back. That was the day she knew she was falling in love with him but wouldn't admit it even to herself.

As she rode back to the house, she thought over everything that had happened in her life so far, and thanked God it had turned out the way it had after such a disastrous start. She had Bain and the twins. Now, if he'd only come home.

She rode out of the woods and down the lane past the slave quarters, following the dusty road across the back of the Château, past the dock, and on to the stables.

"Your mother's stopped by. She's in with your grandmother," Jacob said as he helped her from the horse, then took the reins.

Lizette thanked him and walked to the house, entering by the side door.

"Your mama and grandma's in the parlor," said Mattie as Lizette started through the kitchen. Then the big black woman slapped Lizette's hand lightly as Lizette reached for a small pastry on the table where she had set them to cool. "Fetch off! That ain't no way to lose them pounds you put on, honey," Mattie admonished sternly. "Land sakes, you wants to look nice when that fella of yours comes back, don'tcha?"

Lizette made a face at her. "It's a good thing you've been around so long, Mattie," she said, pretending to be upset with the old servant for reminding her, "or I'd tell Grandpa Roth to find someone else to do the cooking."

Mattie chuckled. "Lordy, child, you'd miss old Mattie's cookin' and you knows it," Mattie said. "But don't you worry none, I'll make it up to you at dinner tonight."

"You'd better," said Lizette, and waved a warning finger at Mattie as she left the kitchen and headed for the parlor.

Lizette was taking her hat off just outside the parlor door, ready to enter, when she stopped suddenly, cocking her head, catching a word here and there from the other room. Her hands slowed their movements as she pulled the hatpin from the plumed riding hat while she listened intently.

"But how do I tell her?" her mother was saying from inside the room, and Grandma Dicia's voice sounded worried as she answered.

"I don't know, dear, but we're going to have to. If we don't, the next time she rides into Port Royal or Beaufort she'll find out on her own, and who knows how she might react."

"But what if it isn't true?" Rebel's heart was torn. "What if the reports are wrong?" Her voice changed pitch nervously. "After all, Mother, it seems to be only hearsay."

"With everyone talking about it?" Loedicia shook her head, then straightened suddenly as Lizette stepped into the room.

Lizette stared at her grandmother curiously. "What is it? What's wrong?" Lizette asked, her knees beginning to tremble.

Rebel looked at her daughter and flushed nervously.

"Well?" Lizette asked again.

"Come in, sit down, Liz," Loedicia said quickly, but Lizette didn't move.

Her knuckles were white as she gripped the hat in her hand. She glanced from her mother to her grandmother, then back to her mother again. "It's about Bain, isn't it?" she guessed, and her face went white. "He's . . . he's dead?"

"Oh, no, Liz," Rebel said quickly. "Good heavens no, he's not dead."

Loedicia stepped over and put an arm about Lizette's waist, forcing her granddaughter to move farther into the room. "It's nothing like that," she explained hurriedly, hoping to relieve

Lizette's mind. "In fact, we aren't even sure there's anything wrong. It's only rumor, you understand."

Lizette pulled away from her grandmother. "What rumor?"

The two older women exchanged glances.

"They're saying Bain is wanted for piracy," Rebel said unsteadily. "That he's turned pirate and joined Jean Lafitte."

Lizette stared at her mother, dumbfounded for a moment; then, "That's a lie!" she cried. Tears sprang to her eyes, turning them a deep green. It wasn't true. It couldn't be true. A deep gnawing pain settled in her breastbone. "It isn't true, Mother," she gasped. "Bain would never . . ." She shook her head. "He couldn't!"

Loedicia made her sit on the sofa, then sat down beside her, taking the hat from Lizette's hands, setting it aside. She took Lizette's hands in hers. They were cold.

"Liz, it may not be true," she reminded her. "Just because people say it, doesn't make it so. Your grandfather's over at the mill. When he gets back, I'll ask him to go see some of his old friends in Congress to find out if they know anything. They always know the latest news. And in the meantime, we'll go see the Kolters. I'm sure if anything's happened, Rand and Madeline would know."

Lizette's heart was beating rapidly and her hands shook. "He wouldn't do that, Grandma," she said softly, tears clinging to her lashes. "Not Bain."

"Don't worry, we'll find out what it's all about," Rebel said as she came over and gazed down at her daughter, marveling at how much Lizette looked like her grandmother. Now she hoped to God that if the rumors were true, Lizette would have the same courage Grandma Dicia possessed. If not, she hated to think what might happen. Rebel reached out her hands. "Let's go upstairs, and I'll help you change, Liz," she urged her, "while Grandma Dicia tells my driver to bring my carriage around to the front door. Then we'll go see Bain's parents. Like Grandma Dicia said, Rand and Madeline should know something."

Lizette reached out and took her mother's hand, letting her help her from the sofa and lead her from the room. As they started up the stairs, in the foyer, Pretty was on her way down carrying the twins. She had one in each arm, and Lizette kissed them, hugging each absentmindedly, new tears replacing the ones that had been there before, and their pudgy little arms hugged her back.

"Get one of the other girls to help you with them, Pretty," Lizette said, sniffing back tears. "They're getting to be too much for you to handle alone."

Pretty stared at Lizette, then frowned, her eyes questioning as she turned to Rebel.

"We're going away this afternoon, Pretty," Rebel said, realizing Lizette was in no condition to try explaining things. "I know Lizette was planning to take the children for a ride in the pony cart with you. But something important's come up." She reached out and put her hand on the black girl's arm, squeezing it affectionately. "We'll explain it all to you later, but for now, have a couple of the girls go with you. Just take good care of them," and she looked at each of her grandchildren in turn, then followed Lizette, and they went on upstairs.

The ride into Beaufort was the longest Lizette ever remembered having to take. It seemed like they'd never get there. The initial shock she had suffered was replaced now by a bitter anger, and she was determined to learn what she could. She was wearing her rose taffeta pelisse over a pink silk afternoon dress, and although the October air was cool, perspiration was making her embroidered bodice cling to her damply, and she could feel the moist warmth of it beneath her arms.

They were using her mother's carriage to go back to Beaufort. Rebel had just returned from shopping there and had taken one of the larger carriages when she'd left Tonnerre that morning so she could bring back her purchases. Now her packages had been taken into the house at the Château until they returned, and Lizette sat next to her mother, while Grandma Dicia sat on the seat opposite them as they rode along.

"Don't worry, dear," Loedicia said as she saw the troubled look on Lizette's face. "One way or another we'll get to the bottom of all this."

"I know, Grandma," Lizette answered, determined. She studied Loedicia's face. Her grandmother was wearing a bright blue dress and bonnet that gave her violet eyes a gentian hue and highlighted the gray in her hair. "You don't believe it, do you?" Lizette asked. "You know what he's like, Grandma Dicia," she went on. "Bain could never do anything like that. You and mother have both known him for years."

Rebel reached over and took her daughter's hands, and Loedicia tried to smile reassuringly. "I'm sure it's a mistake," she said. "Just don't you start fretting until we learn the facts."

But they learned very little from Rand and Madeline Kolter. No more than the rest of Beaufort knew. It seemed someone had returned from Charleston and told someone else that the Charleston newspapers had carried the story of a Spanish ship that was attacked by pirates. Strangely, the crew had been found floating in longboats, but the ship, with its cargo, which included a small fortune in gold, had been lost, and every member of the rescued crew said the name of the ship that had accosted them was the *Dragonfly*; and although, when the pirate ship was letting out sail, her crew was laughingly calling their leader Captain Gallant, because of his courteous behavior during the ordeal, more than one crew member, including the captain of the *San Gabriel*, had heard the pirate leader's men call him Captain Kolter.

Lizette was heartsick.

"Maybe the *Dragonfly* was captured by pirates and someone is posing as Bain," she said that evening as she stood in the parlor window and stared out at the front drive. Then she whirled around. "I'll prove it's not Bain," she suddenly said, her eyes flashing angrily. "I'm going to the ironworks in Pittsburgh, and when I prove he's there rebuilding the forge that blew up, everyone'll be sorry they started all this nonsense, you'll see."

"Liz, you can't go to Pittsburgh," Loedicia said. "What about the babies?"

"They're weaned now, and . . . can't I leave them here?"

"But you can't go alone."

"I'll talk to your father," Roth told Lizette quickly, then addressed Loedicia. "Beau and I will go with her."

Loedicia finally agreed, and they left two days later. But the trip only proved more damning. Not only hadn't any of the forges blown for the past five years at the Kolter Iron Works, but no one had heard from Bain Kolter since his last visit in the spring, and Lizette left Pittsburgh feeling empty inside.

Lizette, her father, Beau Dante, and Grandpa Roth arrived back at the Château a few days before Christmas, tired and discouraged. Lizette felt as if she were about to explode. While they were traveling, trying to prove Bain's innocence, the pirate whom even the newspapers were starting to refer to as Captain Gallant had struck two more times, and a crewman on one of the ships was certain he had recognized the man in charge, identifying him as Bain Kolter.

Lizette was in a turmoil. She still hadn't heard from Bain, and his silence was only more discouraging. Why? she kept asking herself. If it was Bain, why would he suddenly change so, and if it wasn't Bain, if it was someone masquerading as her husband, where was Bain?

Christmas Day was strained at the Château. Aunt Darcy and Uncle Heath were back from a trip to Columbia to see Darcy's Aunt Nell, who had moved back to the capital of South Carolina after Heather and Cole had sailed away on the *Interlude,* and Lizette's parents came down from Tonnerre to spend the day with them. But even though Grandma Dicia and Grandpa Roth tried to make everything pleasant, a tension seemed to permeate everything, and Lizette found herself fighting back tears too many times to count.

Even Braxton and Blythe seemed to sense friction in the atmosphere, and Pretty had her hands full all day trying to keep them amused and content.

The day after Christmas, Lizette's patience finally got the better of her. There were numerous parties and balls over the holiday season. She had declined all except one. Christmas was on Friday this year, and the day after, Saturday, December 26, her brother-in-law, Senator Stuart Kolter, who was home from his duties in Washington for the holidays, and his wife, Julia, were celebrating at their home, the Summit. It was a lovely house on the outskirts of Beaufort. He had bought the place shortly after his election because Julia wanted to move back home from Columbia. It was the only gathering Lizette felt safe attending without Bain, because she knew all the Kolters would be there, but mostly Stuart, and she had to talk to Stuart.

Her grandparents were pleased she had accepted at least one invitation, but now the time had come, and Lizette was nervous. Her hand was trembling slightly, although she tried not to show it as the footman helped her and the others from the carriage and they moved toward the door of the huge brick and frame home that nestled in the rolling hills surrounding Beaufort, the ornate wrought-iron fencing and elaborate landscaping setting it apart from other houses in the area. It had been a long time since she'd set foot in Stuart's home without Bain beside her to help dispel the memories that lingered here, and she wasn't quite sure how she was going to be able to fight them without him to give her courage. Yet she had to.

But once inside, with the music and laughter drowning out most of the conversation, and stares from the least tactful guests making her flush each time their eyes met, there wasn't really time to remember the past. Not at the moment. There was only time to try to live down the present, and that was hard enough in itself.

Lizette stood in the foyer, feeling all eyes on her, and straightened her dress nervously. She had gained weight again since the news had come about Bain, and Pretty had helped her make a new dress for tonight because she didn't want to wear one of her old ones that had been let out. It was bad enough feeling like a stuffed goose without having her clothes show where the seams used to be.

The dress she wore was a delicate peach with lace inserts gracing the huge puffed sleeves, and lace and ribbon decorating the full skirt that was a number of layers of gauze glistening with tiny crystal beads, with the same beads also adorning the bodice, so one had the impression she was engulfed in a shimmering glow, as if her dress were sprinkled with diamonds. Her hair, piled atop her head and adorned with small strings of the same beads and delicate lace, contrasted remarkably with her mother's blond beauty.

Rebel in green satin, Beau in black velvet, and her grandparents both dressed in deep burgundy made a rainbow of color behind Lizette, framing her as she headed toward the back of the house, to where the senator and his wife were receiving guests, and for a brief moment, strange memories began to wash over her. She took a deep breath, blinking her eyes, brushing them aside. This was 1818, she told herself angrily, not 1816. Stuart's your brother-in-law now, not your lover. Remember that. Two years ago was the same as a century ago. Leave it in the past.

It had been a long time since Stuart had seen Lizette. He had purposely made himself scarce since she had married his brother. In fact, since last year at Christmas, when she and Bain had joined the Kolter family at his parents' home for dinner, it was the first time he'd seen her. The time before that had been when she'd met him at the crumbling old building near the Château where they used to rendezvous and begged him to take a letter from Heather to the governor to secure a pardon for her brother Cole. He had known she was going to be here tonight, and the thought had kept him in a state of unrest all day. He knew she'd heard the stories about Bain, and he wondered how she was handling it.

Now, as he stood in the receiving line, greeting newly arrived guests, he suddenly felt a strange tingle run through him, settling

with a painful thud in the pit of his stomach as he turned from
the gentleman he'd just greeted and saw Lizette walking toward
him down the hall.

Julia, standing at his side in a dress of pale green gauze with a
sprig of artificial flowers gracing her small bosom, tugged at the
sleeve of Stuart's dark green frock coat and leaned close, on
tiptoes, hoping to reach to his ear so he could hear, then covered
her mouth with her hand as she said, "Oh, dear, and she's
gained weight again, poor thing." She hoped Stuart had heard,
and leaned a little closer. "I certainly can understand why Bain
left her. Why, the girl hasn't taken care of herself at all, and
she's probably blaming it all on having twins." Then, as Lizette
came within hearing distance, Julia's hand dropped, and she smiled.

"Liz, so glad you could make it," she said, her pale blue eyes
greeting her sister-in-law enthusiastically.

Stuart was trying to compose himself from the shock he'd felt
at the sight of Liz, looking more beautiful than ever, and also
from the shock of hearing Julia's unforgiving sarcasm. He knew
she wasn't purposely being cruel to Liz; in fact Julia had always
tried to be nice to Liz. The only thing was, Julia, who was
actually too thin, had always been critical of people she considered fat. And to Julia, Lizette would probably always look fat.
To Stuart she was so lovely he was almost speechless.

"Liz, I'm glad you came," he said gently, recovering his
voice, taking her hand. He looked into her eyes, and for a
moment he thought he saw tears. "We wish you had been at
Mother's and Father's yesterday," he went on, trying to make
small talk to make her feel more comfortable. "The twins would
have had a lovely time."

She smiled hesitantly. "We just stayed at the Château."

"Mother said that's where you were staying," he said, then
dropped her hand reluctantly as he greeted Rebel, Beau, Loedicia,
and Roth. The moment was over so quickly, and Lizette slowly
melted into the crowd in the drawing room.

The evening wasn't going well at all. At least not for Lizette.
She felt so out of place. Everyone here had heard about Bain,
and she knew by the way they were treating her that they were
pitying her. She didn't want pity. She didn't need pity. What she
wanted were answers. Grandpa Roth's friends in Congress had
been unable to help, and now she was desperate.

She gazed about the room, her eyes falling on Stuart, who at
the moment was alone and heading for a door at the other end of

the room that she knew led to another part of the house. She glanced around quickly. For the first time all evening, no one was watching her, and she moved across the room quickly, threading her way inconspicuously through the crowd, reaching the door at the same moment he did. Her hand touched his arm.

Stuart had purposely avoided Lizette all evening. Now suddenly he found himself gazing into her eyes, her hand on his arm, his own blue eyes shining with a depth of passion he hoped didn't show.

"I have to talk to you, Stuart," Liz said, trying to ignore the fact that Stuart's resemblance to Bain was making it difficult for her to completely forget the past and the part he'd played in it.

He tensed. "Meet me in the conservatory, by the orchids," he whispered softly. "Do you remember where they are?"

"I think so." Her hand dropped. "Right now?"

"Right now," he said briskly, and continued on through the doorway, leaving her staring after him.

She straightened, taking a deep breath, and turned, making her way back across the room to where the back wall was covered with floor-to-ceiling draperies of burnished gold. As unobtrusively as she could, Lizette found the opening in the draperies and reached behind them, searching until she found the handle to the French doors. Then, making certain she wasn't noticed, she swung one of the French doors out, opening it into the conservatory, then slipped behind the draperies and on out through the French door, closing it quietly behind her.

She stood for a moment, breathing deeply, taking in the sweet scent of the flowers that filled the air, while she gazed overhead at the stars visible through the glass that separated the conservatory from the outside world. The place was filled with so many memories.

Her hands left the door latch and she walked slowly along the rows of flowers, trying to distinguish them in the darkness. Then suddenly she stopped.

He was standing in the faint light that was beaming down from the sliver of a moon overhead, and she caught her breath. He was so like Bain. The way he held his head, his dark wavy hair that shone russet in the sunlight but deepened to a golden amber with the moonlight on it, and the clipped beard and mustache. The resemblance was uncanny. Even the stance was all too familiar. Stuart and Bain could almost pass for twins, only Stuart was older, his eyes a brilliant blue.

"Well?" he asked when she reached him.

She shook her head. "You have to help me, Stuart," she pleaded anxiously. "You have to help me find out what's going on."

He stared at her, his eyes filled with pain. "Isn't it obvious, Liz?" he said softly. "I told you a long time ago that Bain was no good. That he was irresponsible and would break your heart." He frowned. "I was hoping . . . For a while I thought maybe he was really going to settle down. . . . Don't ask me what happened, because I don't know."

"You don't mean it," she cried, her voice trembling as she tried to keep it to a whisper. "I was hoping you'd tell me it wasn't true, that it's all a mistake."

"I wish I could. There's no mistake, Liz," he said. "And the damnedest thing is that he's left witnesses all over the place. From the reports that are coming back, he supposedly takes his plunder with hardly a shot being fired. They say that he makes his ship look like it's already been plundered and left to drift helplessly with a few wounded survivors on deck. Since the *Dragonfly*'s not quite as big as most pirate ships, the ruse usually works. That's why they're calling him Captain Gallant. I guess he overdoes the gentlemanly courtesy when relieving the passengers and crew of their valuables and cargo, especially any ladies that might be on board. Oh, he's smart, he is." His eyes were troubled as he looked at her. "I guess he just wasn't the sort to settle down."

"That's not true," Liz said tearfully. "Something's wrong, Stuart, I know it is," she cried softly. "Bain isn't like that. You don't know him like I do. He'd never leave me, and he loves the twins. He'd never leave Braxton and Blythe to rob ships and kill people. That's not Bain."

Stuart studied her face in the moonlight. She believed what she was saying, but women didn't always know their husbands' secret thoughts. Look at Julia. She'd swear to anyone that she knew her husband's every thought, that there wasn't anything she didn't know about him. Some people were so easy to deceive, but Liz? She wasn't as naive or as self-centered as Julia.

"What do you want me to do?" he asked.

She sighed. "I don't know if there's anything you can do, but there ought to be a way to find out if anyone knows where Bain is. Maybe, if it is him, I could talk to him and find out why he's doing this. But if it's someone pretending to be him, we'd find that out too." Tears flooded her eyes. "He said he was going to Pittsburgh to rebuild a forge that blew up, and the next thing I know, people are telling me he's become a pirate. I can't believe it and I won't," she said, sniffling, trying to hold back the tears. "I love him so!"

Instinctively Stuart's arms went out to her, and he pulled her close, cradling her head against his chest. "Go ahead and cry," he offered tenderly. "I know how you feel. It hurts to lose someone you love."

"Oh, Stuart, I'm sorry," she said, and pushed her head from his chest. "I shouldn't have asked for your help."

"Who better to ask?" he said. "I'll see what I can do. Mind you, I can't promise anything, but maybe I can hire someone to investigate and find him for you. You know, in a way I have a stake in this too, Liz," he went on. "He took you away from me, just when I needed you the most, and by hell, I think for that alone I deserve an answer, along with you. I'll help you, Liz, all I can, but for God's sake don't let Julia or the others know. They may not understand, and it would be rather hard for me to explain."

She started to wipe her eyes, and he handed her his handkerchief.

"I'm returning to Washington in a few days," he said. "If I find out anything, I'll let you know."

"How?"

"Don't worry. You're my sister-in-law now, remember? I don't think anyone will question it if Senator Kolter sends a letter to Mrs. Bain Kolter, the Château, Port Royal, South Carolina."

"Thank you, Stuart," she said, wiping her nose and handing him back his handkerchief.

He turned to leave, then frowned. "I know one thing, Liz," he said bitterly as he faced her. "If what they say about Bain turns out to be true, if he has deserted you and become a pirate, you won't ever have to worry about ridding yourself of him, because if I ever get hold of him, I'll kill him with my bare hands," and this time he did go, leaving her standing alone in the conservatory staring after him with tears still in her eyes.

20

It was close to dawn. Bain had wakened with his head aching about an hour earlier and was having a hard time getting back to sleep. He stared at the ceiling of the small house at Campeche he now shared with his men. He'd been here some eight months already and it wasn't until a few days ago that he'd finally discovered something he could use as proof against Lafitte. The only trouble was, it was neatly entrenched behind the walls of Maison Rouge. Jean Lafitte was a meticulous businessman, and Bain had suspected for a long time that he kept books on all the transactions at Campeche, so there was no chance for anyone to cheat him. Now he was certain of it.

He turned over on the feather mattress he'd taken from the captain's bed when they'd taken the *San Gabriel*. He hated this life, but if he had to live it, which at the moment was a necessity, he'd rather make life miserable for the Spanish than anyone else. He had too many friends in Mexico the Spanish government had treated badly, so it didn't bother his conscience too much when he took their ships, but oh how he wished he was home.

He sighed, holding his head in his hands, rubbing the temples. If only Liz were here, she'd take the pain from his head—her fingers were like magic—and she'd take the ache from his body too. He closed his eyes, trying not to think of her, wondering if she'd heard about him and what she might be thinking. God, don't let her hate him. If only he could write to her, let her know he still loved her so damn much. If only he could let her know how much he missed her and the twins.

The gray light of dawn made its way slowly into his room and he sat up. He knew what had done this to him. It was that god-awful bottle Billie had passed to him last night. Three swigs, that's all he'd had. He never had more than three, but that was enough last night. Never again, he told himself. Not that stuff. He could do without women until he got home to Liz, and he could do without tequila too.

He left the bed, went to the washstand, and cleaned up, the cold water helping relieve the ache behind his eyes. But it wasn't until after he'd put some food in his stomach that Bain finally began to feel better.

He sat at the table in the small kitchen a short while later and glanced over at Captain Holley, who was more of a first mate on this trip than anything else.

"How much longer?" the captain asked.

Bain shook his head. "I'm not sure, but I know what you're thinking. The men are getting restless. I realize that, and I want to get out of here as badly as they do. That's why I was up early, and I think I've made up my mind on what I'm going to do, only I'm going to need help."

Bain had told his men they were on a special assignment, no questions asked. The less they knew, the less chance of talking too much when they got drunk. Now he needed their help. There were close to a thousand men, maybe more, at Campeche. That meant the risk of being caught was doubled. One factor in their favor. Lafitte's house, affectionately called Maison Rouge, faced the open sea rather than the inland harbor, and the *Dragonfly* had speed. There were only two problems: getting his hands on Lafitte's business ledgers and getting them aboard the ship.

He was working by himself now, without having Billie Byrd breathing down his neck all the time, and could come and go as he pleased, and he was pretty sure the idea he'd been mulling over this morning would work. He tested it on Captain Holley.

"I know where all the patrols are, and when," he said eagerly as he finished telling him the plan. "And I know where I can get the gunpowder. All we need is the time, and then I'll need about four men to help with the last part of it."

Holley eyed him reluctantly. "If you don't mind, I think you'd better use younger men than me, Bain, for the last part," he said. "I'll man the ship, like always, but I'm getting a little too old for all the rough stuff. I've been faking ever since we got here, and I cringe every time we board ship, because, Lord, take it, I don't think I could fight my way through a pack of seaweed anymore."

Bain smiled. "Don't worry, old friend," he said. "I want you at the helm. I wouldn't trust it to anyone else."

Captain Holley sighed. "I know which men you should use," he said. "And I'll make sure they're briefed. When do we leave?"

"Tomorrow morning. By tomorrow night the moon'll be gone. Billie Byrd's leaving this morning. Three left yesterday, and the

Sea Mist is due any day now. I'd rather leave before she gets here, because I hear tell Pierre Lafitte should be on her, heading back from the States. I'll feel better if we're gone before Lafitte's brother arrives.''

"You think he'd cause trouble?"

Bain shrugged. "Just a feeling I have. Now, go bring the men."

The next morning, Bain once more said good-bye to Lafitte and the *Dragonfly* weighed anchor and moved off with the tide, as it had so often now over the past few months, only this time it was different. After moving out to sea, making everyone at Campeche think they were headed out into the gulf, the *Dragonfly* veered north; then, avoiding the ships Bain knew were patrolling the coastline, they sailed inland, anchoring in a small cove, out of sight from the sea. Once anchored, Bain set to work on the first part of his plan. He had always brought Amigo with him no matter where he sailed, and now the horse was put over the side, Bain helped get him out of the water, then mounted and rode him all the way to the old copper mine and back, bringing with him three Mexicans, three horses, and four kegs of gunpowder gladly given to him by the foreman at the mine.

They were met at the cove by the longboat, and by evening, when darkness began to descend and the *Dragonfly* slipped away from the cove again, Bain and his crew had everything ready for their night's work.

It was one o'clock in the morning. The sky was pitch black, the sea rolling in gently onto the beach at Galvez Island when the *Dragonfly* cut sail and drifted in close to the shore just down the coast from Campeche. It was so dark, in fact, that for a second Bain had a hard time even keeping Amigo in his sight as they rowed toward shore, the horse struggling at the end of a lead rope swimming behind. Even when they reached the shore, it was like working in a black fog, and the cool mists that swirled around them weren't helping. Bain held the stallion's reins, while the men who had rowed the longboat in helped him load the fireworks they'd made that afternoon onto Amigo's back. The horse was skittish under the strange load, the smell of the gunpowder making him jittery, but with Bain talking gently, he soon calmed down; then Bain, with the four crewmen following, set off, leading Amigo toward the encampment that was slowly becoming a good-sized village.

They had to work fast, and Bain thanked God, all the while

they were laying out the fireworks at strategic places around the island, for letting him spend enough time in the Far East to learn how it was done. The Chinese had it down to an art, and although the fireworks he and his men had made couldn't be compared to what he had witnessed in the Orient, he was certain it would work. All he wanted was something that would explode.

When the last explosive was planted, he told one of the men to start counting to five hundred, light all the fuses and candles, then hightail it back to the beach, taking Amigo with him. The other three, Bain took with him, heading back toward the edge of the village to wait. It seemed like an eternity.

Jean Lafitte was snoring peacefully, dreaming he was crawling through piles and piles of gold and jewels, when the first explosion went off and he practically fell out of bed reaching for his breeches, then stumbled in the dark, pulling them up, while downstairs the guard at the front craned his neck, trying to see what had happened. Before the guard could settle on a definite cause, there was another explosion closer than the last, followed by what sounded like shots, and within minutes the whole place was in pandemonium.

Bain and the three men with him had moved forward with the first explosion, dodging in and out of yards in the darkness, yelling to everyone, and making it sound even worse, and by the time the second explosion went off, they had reached Maison Rouge and were hiding in some bushes near the front entrance, ready for the next part of the plan. When the second explosion went off and the guard at the front door moved away from it, trying to see what was going on, Bain and two of the men slipped past him behind the wall that surrounded Maison Rouge, and hugging close against it, moved around the side, gaining entrance to the building through a window in one of the side rooms.

Bain knew right where he was going, even in the dark. While confusion reigned outside, he pried open the drawer where Lafitte kept his accounts, stuffed two large ledgers into a bag he was carrying, then moved back to the window, where the men waited, and all three left the house.

By the time they reached the front of Maison Rouge again and joined the fourth man waiting on watch in the bushes, everyone including Lafitte was at the back of the house still trying to figure out what was going on.

Lafitte's first thought was that the Spanish had found his

,hideout or that the Americans were bombarding him from the sea. It was so dark, though, that it was hard to tell what was happening. When he finally did establish a semblance of order again and realized what it was all about, it was too late. Bain and his four crewmen were climbing into their longboat, Bain was leading Amigo back into the water, and they were on their way back to the ship.

Once they were aboard, the *Dragonfly*'s sails were unfurled, and in the wee hours of the morning she pulled away from Campeche, this time heading in the direction she was supposed to have gone earlier that morning, out into the gulf, while behind her, Lafitte, realizing he'd been duped, caught a brief glimpse of a ship sneaking away when the light from one of the explosions lit the sky, and although he had no idea whose ship it was, and wouldn't know until much later, he ordered Frenchie out with the *Golden Rose*.

At first Bain thought he'd been mistaken, but the next morning, as the first faint rays of dawn began to lighten the horizon in the east, he knew he hadn't. Somehow Lafitte had seen them slip away and had sent a ship after them.

For the next few days the *Dragonfly* managed to stay well ahead of the *Golden Rose*, but no matter what ploy Bain used to lose the other ship, it didn't work. They had even doused all the lights and tried to slip away in the darkness, but the *Golden Rose* was still there when the sun came up in the morning. For a while he had even thought of stopping in New Orleans or Mobile, but that was wishful thinking. By now the *Dragonfly* was an outlaw ship and the authorities, knowing nothing about his mission, might have him and his crew hung before they could even raise a protest, so the *Dragonfly* kept on its course. He was heading for Port Royal and the Broad River. Once at the Château, he was certain he could make his way to Washington without being caught by any of Lafitte's men. His only problem would be the American authorities, but if he sailed in at night, shaved off his beard and mustache . . . It was the only thing he could think of. He couldn't even sail the *Dragonfly* into Baltimore anymore. Not now, not with a price on his head.

A week passed. The weather stayed balmy and the *Golden Rose* stayed in their wake, sometimes getting dangerously close. Then suddenly, early one evening, the wind began to change. Bain was the first to feel it as he stood on deck, shirt sleeves rolled up, the wind ruffling his hair. He held his head high, smelling the air, feeling the slight temperature drop against his face and arms. His eyes moved to the horizon ahead of them, searching the sky, and already he could see it. Low gray clouds that looked like part of the water were starting to roll in, mixing with the billowing white clouds that had hung in the sky all day.

"We're in for a storm, Holley," he said to the man beside him.

Captain Holley squinted, scrutinizing the same darkening sky. "Aye," he agreed. "I just hope it's bad enough to help us lose our company, but not bad enough to cause us undue trouble."

Bain frowned. "We should be nearing the southern tip of Florida soon," he said. "I hope we can get through the keys and up the coast before she blows in too hard."

The captain grabbed the rail and leaned forward, studying the sky as it began to darken more, the wind, already filling the sails, beginning to pick up momentum. He felt the salty spray, like a fine mist, caress his face. They were standing in the bow and he glanced down, watching the sea foam as the *Dragonfly* cut the waves that were starting to swell.

"I don't think we're going to make it, Bain," he commented briskly. "I'd say within the hour, maybe less, we'll be worrying more about the weather than those bastards behind us."

Captain Holley was almost right, but the storm took a little longer to build up momentum than he had predicted. As the sun sank in the west and the sky deepened, purple streaks slashing across the pink and crimson sunset, the storm surrounded them with wailing winds, and the night sky as it drove the purple sunset from the heavens brought with it black clouds that hung low, rumbling ominous warnings. Occasionally lightning shattered the clouds, turning the world around them into a weird illusion, then darkening again. And finally, after more than an hour of warning, the rain began. Huge drops spattered intermittently against Bain's face at first, only to be quickly replaced by a downpour that soon brought pounding waves with it, and high winds that tore at the sails ferociously, trying to rip them from their rigging.

Hours after the storm had first hit, Bain still stood on the deck, trying to keep his balance. For the first time in his long years of sailing, he was worried. He'd been in a dozen storms before, but there was something frightening about this one. They'd been buffeted about like this for what seemed like an eternity. It was as if the storm had grabbed them and just didn't want to let go. The gale winds were fierce, driving the rain against his face, stinging it viciously as he hung on to a guy rope, making his way to Captain Holley, who was at the helm trying to control the floundering ship. Bain always strung ropes in strategic places about the deck during storms, ever since a seaman had washed overboard some years before because there'd been nothing to hang on to. Now he was glad he had, as the wind and rain drove into him, and his hands tightened on the rope.

"Do you think she'll hold, Holley?" he shouted.

The captain shook his head. "Don't know. We've already lost half the sail and some rigging." He tried to hold the wheel steady, but even the strength in his brawny arms couldn't hold it against the raging storm. The wheel slipped a few degrees before he managed to get it under control again; then, as lightning streaked through the rain from the dark clouds swirling overhead in the night sky, his eyes widened.

"Land!" he yelled at Bain, trying to be heard above the shrieking wind.

Bain turned slightly, still holding the rope, and stared into the darkness ahead of them as Captain Holley fought the wheel, trying to turn the ship. Another streak of lightning flashed, and Bain saw it too. The mainland of Florida? One of the islands in the keys? There was no way of knowing, since they'd been blown off course hours ago.

"I'll take it!" Bain yelled, reaching a hand toward the wheel.

"I can't let go." Holley was fighting the wheel as hard as he could.

Suddenly there was a loud crunch and Bain felt the deck beneath him shudder. "We're aground," he yelled.

"Damn!" Holley swung the wheel around, hoping the sudden turn of the rudder, combined with the swirling water, would cut her loose, but instead, she only creaked and groaned, rocking back and forth.

Once more lightning lit the horizon. Bain frowned, staring at the land, still some hundred or so yards away. If the land was out there, what were they hung up on? Some of the crew had been out on the deck, trying to keep the sails and rigging intact. Now one of them reached Bain.

"It's rocks," he yelled, trying to be heard above the wind.

Bain swore, then made his way to the side of the ship and leaned over the rail, staring down at the dark jagged rocks protruding from the water, part of them hidden beneath the splintered hull of the *Dragonfly*.

"Tell Captain Holley I'm going to check below," he told the seaman, then headed for his cabin, while the crewman went back toward the wheel.

Belowdecks, the rest of the crew were trying to keep their heads as best they could. Water was pouring into the hold from gaping holes in the ship's side, and there was no possible way they could repair it.

"At least we'll have time to abandon ship," Bain said as he inspected the damage. "She won't be sinking, hung up on the rocks like this. The only thing we have to do now is pray the wind and waves don't smash up the rest of her before the storm dies down."

He grabbed one of the crew, a man who'd been with him for years.

"Go tell Captain Holley to leave the wheel and come down here," he ordered quickly, and felt the ship rock slightly beneath his feet, a few more slabs of wood wrenched from her hull. If this kept up, they might have to leave her sooner than he'd anticipated, and he dreaded the thought of trying to put a long-boat over the side against those waves.

A short time later, when Captain Holley reached Bain's cabin, there was no reason to knock. The door was open and Bain was trying to salvage as much as he could from the desk built into the wall beneath the windows.

"She's breaking up, Bain," Holley said hurriedly. "But the storm's beginning to blow itself out. The wind has tamed some, and I think if we can hold off long enough, and leave at the last minute, we can make it in the longboats."

Bain shoved the desk drawer shut. He was holding two pack-ets in his hand, along with the logbook. He handed the logbook to Holley. The two packets were wrapped in oiled paper to keep them from getting wet, and he tucked them in the crook of his arm, holding them against his midsection as he headed out the door, Holley following close behind.

Suddenly he stopped, cursing, as a loud, frightened whinny echoed above the creaking and grinding of the ship. He turned back to the captain.

"Take these above deck," he yelled, handing him the packets. "I'm going after Amigo."

"Don't be a fool, Bain," said Holley. "You can't get him out of the sail room with the ship listing so badly. He'll break a leg, if he doesn't fall on you first.''

Bain shook his head. ''I have to try,'' and he disappeared down the passageway while Captain Holley clenched his jaws angrily and headed above deck.

As Captain Holley reached the deck, he stopped abruptly, looking about, pinpointing the men ready with the longboats. The rain had let up some, and so had the wind, but it was still battering waves against the side of the ship, and with each wave he cringed.

''Goddammit, come on, Bain!'' he roared as he heard man and horse behind him on the stairs leading to the deck, and a few anxious minutes later, Amigo's head emerged, eyes wild with terror as the full force of the rain hit him.

''Ahhh! Wait!'' screamed Bain, as the horse made a savage leap and bolted onto the deck. Only his scream of protest was lost on the animal, as horse and master plummeted across the deck into one of the guy ropes and came to an abrupt halt, Bain landing on his backside.

Amigo was still wearing a halter, and Bain had wrapped the reins about his fist to secure them. Now, as he gained his feet, trying to keep the horse from sprawling on the slippery deck, and trying to keep from falling again himself, he released the reins. He patted Amigo's neck hurriedly, trying to quiet him some, assuring him he'd make it to shore, when suddenly there was a streak of lightning and a loud crack directly above him, so loud it could easily be heard above the storm. He looked up, not knowing what to expect, and was just in time to see the top of the mizzenmast heading right for him.

Holley screamed at the top of his lungs, but there was no time for Bain to move, and with a sickening thud the tangled wreckage knocked Bain to the deck, pinning him beneath rope, pulleys, and splintered wood.

Holley called to some of the men, who left the longboats, grabbed the guy lines that were still fastened, and made their way to where Bain lay. His head was bleeding, there was a hole in his right shoulder with a huge chunk of wood from the mizzenmast protruding like a spear, and the rest of the mast was across his legs. Amigo too had been hit, although not as badly, but even at that, he was beneath part of the rigging, trying to get to his feet and throw the wreckage off.

It was still raining, but the wind had let up some, and the

men, not waiting for Holley's orders, bent down, grabbed the heavy mast in unison, and lifted it from Bain and the horse, throwing it aside, watching as it slid across the slanted deck and cracked against the rail.

As one of the men helped Amigo to his feet, Holley knelt next to Bain, holding on to the guy rope with one hand and keeping the ledgers and logbook close against him with the other, using his knee to keep Bain from slipping as the ship began to list even more.

"Get to the boat," Bain gasped breathlessly as he realized his legs wouldn't move. His eyes fell on the packets in Holley's arms. "Those papers have to get to Washington."

"You're coming with us," Holley said quickly.

Bain shook his head, the rain making it hard for him to keep his eyes open. His body felt like it was on fire, and it was getting hard to breathe.

"Find Sam Hewitt," he ordered, hoping to be heard above the wind. "Tell him . . . tell him Domino sent you, tell him you have to see the President." He stopped for a minute to catch his breath. "Tell the President . . ." He reached out hesitantly and took Holley's arm. "Tell him 'the wines of summer.' He'll answer about 'a rose in winter.' Then give them to him," and he laid his hand on the packets.

"No, Bain, you'll go with us," Holley insisted.

Bain swallowed, turning his head, trying to keep the rain from filling his mouth. "Go!" he yelled as he heard a loud shuddering moan belowdeck. "Dammit, Holley, don't let it be for nothing."

Captain Holley stared at Bain, then glanced at the men hanging on to the ropes, trying to steady themselves so they could pick Bain up. The ship gave another lurch, tilting even more, and once more Amigo hit the deck, but this time, unable to get his footing with the slippery deck at too unsteady an angle, he whinnied frantically and slid to the rail, then fell over the side into the raging waters far below.

Bain heard Amigo's frantic cry, and he wanted to scream. Amigo, Liz, the twins—he was never going to see them again. Suddenly he remembered the empty feeling he'd had the day he'd left to answer the urgent message from Washington. His eyes flooded with tears, but Captain Holley wouldn't have seen them even if it hadn't been dark, as Bain's tears mingled with the rain.

Lightning was still playing about the sky as Bain once more

looked up at Captain Holley. "Go, damn you, Holley," he ordered, trying to muster enough strength to sound gruff and convincing. "Tell him I did my part, the rest is up to him."

There were tears in the captain's eyes, only Bain couldn't see them either. "I can't leave you," he cried angrily.

"You have to." Bain put his hand on the captain's arm. "Go, please. There isn't much time." Bain swallowed back the agony that was making everything hazy. "Please, Holley, remember, 'wines of summer' and 'a rose in winter.' Now, go," and his hand fell from Holley's arm.

Captain Holley hesitated, but only for a moment. In the light from the spattering of lightning that was still penetrating the storm, he glanced down and saw Bain's body slacken and grow still. He cursed, then called Bain's name softly. There was no response. There was nothing he could do. Swearing softly to himself, he hugged the packets against his chest, said good-bye to his friend and employer, then ordered the men to the longboats to cast off while there was still time.

As the last longboat hit the waves and was cut loose with the crew of the *Dragonfly* aboard, none of them knew that up on the deck of the ship Bain lay with his eyes open again, feeling his body beginning to slide slowly across the deck. His head was aching, his legs all but useless, but his arms were free, and as he neared the side of the ship, just before being washed overboard as the ship broke in two, he grabbed the air, fighting all the way to the water before starting to sink beneath the deadly waves.

Bain gulped a huge mouthful of air, then held his breath as long as he could. When it felt as if his lungs were about to burst, he began to let the air out, at the same time arching his arms upward, and he reached the surface just in time.

He gulped what air he could, and for a second thought he was going to go under again, then suddenly felt a sleek solid mass bumping against him. It was Amigo. The horse was winded but keeping his head above water. Bain grabbed the stallion's mane and hung on; then, as the waves began to diminish, making it easier for the longboats to row clear of the rocks and the doomed ship, Bain, half-conscious, his brain and body working on instinct alone, watched the rest of the *Dragonfly* sink to its watery grave, and just before passing out, struggled onto the back of his faithful stallion, wound the reins around and around both wrists so he wouldn't fall off, and leaned forward, resting his bleeding head on Amigo's straggly mane.

Amigo, although terribly shaken, seemed to sense what was happening, and he began swimming with determination now, by instinct alone, the burden on his back familiar to him. He let his body drift with every wave, and every wave that broke washed him closer toward shore. He passed the rocks and moved inland, swimming on toward the beach, an inborn need to survive taxing every muscle in his long sleek body. When his hooves finally touched the gravelly bottom beneath the waves, he stumbled momentarily, but it didn't stop him. Undaunted, the weary horse caught his footing, kept going, and minutes later emerged from the water onto the beach, where he plodded on until he reached a cluster of trees; then finally he stopped and stood wearily beneath their sheltering branches, whinnying sadly, throwing his head toward the night sky that was finally starting to clear itself from the crippling storm, trying to rouse the unconscious man who was still tied to his back. When there was no answer, he lowered his head and stood motionless, listening, then nickered low as all he heard were the pounding waves and the faint voices of the crew of the *Dragonfly* as their longboats drifted farther and farther out to sea, where two days later, unbeknownst to the horse and his master, they were found by an American warship, all of them still alive.

21

Lizette stood in the bedroom of the stone house she and Bain had shared since returning from their elopement. She was staring at the bed, her green eyes misty with tears, the shock still numbing her powers of belief as it had the day they had told her. It just didn't seem possible that Bain could be dead. One day she'd been told he was a pirate, then out of a clear blue sky they'd suddenly told her he was dead. When and how? Strange that no one seemed to have the answers.

One rumor claimed he was hung, another said his crew mutinied, another said he was killed trying to seize a Spanish ship, and still another stated that he'd gone down with his ship in a storm. Who was right? The only word she had was a short letter written to her father by Stuart, telling him to tell her he was dead and that the authorities had confirmed it. No reason, no explanation.

Her father had ridden down from Tonnerre Tuesday morning to tell her. That was a week ago, and still she had a hard time accepting it.

She closed her eyes and took a deep breath, fighting back tears. He had died without even an explanation, without any good-byes. If only there were some way . . . She opened her eyes and turned, straightening stubbornly. She wasn't going to cry again. She had cried all the way into Beaufort. Her eyes settled on her image in the mirror.

"Lizette Dante Kolter," she said to herself. "Fat, ugly Lizette!" Is that why Bain left? She'd gained a few pounds since the twins were born. But he always said he didn't care and laughed at the way she worried over her weight.

Damn! Her fist hit the dresser, rattling the bottles of cologne on it. It just wasn't right. He was dead. All right, she'd accept that, but what she wouldn't accept was the fact that nobody seemed to know how he had died. She stared at herself in the mirror, studying the way the riding habit fit her. It was black velvet with satin collar and cuffs, and with the fancy satin hat that matched sitting atop her dark curls, she looked every bit as womanly as other men's wives. Maybe that was the trouble. She was too ordinary. She sighed, shaking her head. If only there were some answers.

She probably shouldn't have ridden into Beaufort today. There were too many memories here at the house, but then, she had to give the servants their new orders. With Bain gone, she was going to close down the house. Grandma Dicia had asked her to stay at the Château. For a while it would probably be the best thing, so for now the slaves, including the groom, would stay at the Château with her. Mattie could do with some help in the kitchen, and Jacob would welcome another hand in the stables.

She straightened, taking one last look at the room where she and Bain had shared their love, then opened the door and left, going downstairs to make sure everyone knew what to do.

"We'll expect you at the Château by tomorrow evening," she told the three slaves who stood quietly listening. "Make sure the furniture's covered with dustcovers, and don't leave any food about. And make sure everything's locked tight."

When they had assured her everything she'd asked would be done, she finally made one last tour of the rooms, then hurried outside to the mounting block near the stable, climbed into the saddle, and headed Diablo down the drive and toward Port Royal, tears once more rimming her eyes.

It was late afternoon when Lizette rode up the drive to the Château, and for a second her heart skipped a beat as she saw the sails of a ship at the pier in back of the house. She spurred Diablo into a gallop, then reined in, disappointed as she recognized Grandpa Roth's ship, the *Interlude*. He had sailed to Charleston on a business trip and been gone when the news of Bain's death had arrived, and she wondered if he'd been shocked when Grandma Dicia told him. But then, he'd probably read about it in the Charleston newspapers. After all, Bain had become quite notorious.

She was surprised to find her grandfather waiting for her when she stepped into the parlor, a troubled look on his face and an envelope in his hand.

Roth had seen Lizette heading up the drive, and his heart went out to her. She looked so much like Loedicia had looked when she was young. He had gone to his desk, unlocked the drawer, and taken out the letter he'd had hidden there for so long. Now he handed it to her, after greeting her with a kiss on the cheek.

"What is it?" she asked as she handed her grandmother the fancy satin hat she'd taken off on the way in.

Loedicia set Lizette's hat down on a nearby stand. "Roth said Bain gave it to him the morning he sailed," she explained as Lizette stared at the letter.

"He told me if anything happened, if he didn't come back, I should give it to you," added Roth.

Lizette frowned. All that was on the front of it was her name. Her hands trembled as she opened it.

"Maybe you'd rather we not be here when you read it," Loedicia suggested, but Lizette shook her head.

"No, please stay, Grandma." Her voice was unsteady. "I might need you."

She slipped the letter from its envelope, unfolded it, and began silently reading.

My darling Lizette,

Your grandfather has been kind enough to promise to keep this letter and give it to you in case anything should happen to me, so I know since you're reading it that you will have learned of my death. I wish I could have told you where I went and why, but I could not. I was sworn to secrecy by powers greater than you or I, and not to adhere to the command of the one who sent me would have been no less than treason.

You may hear many things of me, my love, some of them painful to believe. They are not true, no matter what people say. Things are not always what they seem. I did not desert you and the children. I love you dearly, and knowing that I will not be at your side to share your life as I had planned makes my heart ache. Right now I wish I could hold you in my arms and tell you all, but much depends on my silence, even after I am dead.

Know only that I loved you with all my heart, and leaving you and the children, not knowing whether I would return or not, was the hardest thing I've ever had to do. Forgive me, Liz, and remember me with love, for you shall live in my heart through all eternity.

Your loving husband,
Bain

She could hardly see the last words for the tears that clung to her lashes. "Here," she said, handing it to her grandmother.

Loedicia was hesitant. "Are you sure you want me to read it, dear?" she asked.

"Read it aloud, Grandma," she answered softly.

Loedicia stared at her for a moment, then began to read. When she finished, the room was silent; then Lizette, who had walked to the window to stare out while Loedicia was reading, whirled about to face them.

"I knew," she said, tears streaming down her cheeks. "I knew he loved me." Then her knees buckled, and she grabbed the arm of an overstuffed chair, lowering herself quickly. She looked up at her grandparents, who had come quickly to her aid. "Everyone's so quick to accuse," she said tearfully. "He wasn't a pirate, I know he wasn't, you read it. He said things aren't always what they seem." She reached up and grabbed Loedicia's hand. "Grandma, while you were reading, I decided there's something I have to do," she said anxiously. "If you and Grandfather will let me leave the twins here while I'm gone, or maybe Mother would let them stay at Tonnerre, I'm going to go to Washington. You read what he said. I know it won't be easy, but I have a feeling Bain was working for the government. Why else would he say that to refuse would have been treason?" Her jaw set stubbornly. "I intend to clear his name, Grandma, and find out why he died."

"That's quite a task," Roth said as he reached over and took the letter from Loedicia, studying it for a minute. "I don't know, Liz." He frowned. "I know Washington. You won't get any help. In fact, they'll probably try to hinder you all the way."

"I don't care. I have to go, Grandpa," she insisted. "I can't bring the children up thinking their father was a criminal."

"But to go to Washington, dear," Loedicia pleaded. "Where would you stay? And you couldn't go alone."

"Why not?"

Loedicia stared at her for a few minutes, then smiled knowingly. "Just like me, aren't you?" she said. "A mind of your own."

"Grandma, if Bain gave his life for his country . . . I have to go. His father was at the house the other day and went through the papers in his study. I have the money, Grandma. Bain had businesses all over. That's why I knew the rumors against him were so ridiculous. He didn't have to steal to make money. Mr. Kolter said Bain left more than enough money for us to live on. There are hotels in Washington, aren't there? Or rooming houses. Surely there's somewhere I could stay."

"The senator," Loedicia said suddenly, and Lizette stared at her in surprise. "Your brother-in-law, Liz," Loedicia explained. "He has a home in Washington as well as the one here in Beaufort. I'm sure he'd have no objections. Stuart's a nice sort . . ."

Lizette opened her mouth to protest, then stopped abruptly, continuing to stare at her grandmother. Stuart did have a house in Washington. She'd never seen it, since she'd never been to Washington, but he had talked about it a number of times. There was only one problem, though. Stuart! But maybe he knew someplace she could stay. After all, he knew a great many people in Washington. Surely one of them would welcome a paying guest for a short while.

"What is it, dear?" asked Loedicia, seeing the strange look on her granddaughter's face.

"You've just given me an idea," Lizette said thoughtfully. "Felicia and Alex are getting married this Saturday, and I'm sure Stuart will be home for his sister's wedding. I don't necessarily want to stay at his place, but I'm sure he'd know where I could stay."

"You've decided to go to the wedding, then?" Loedicia asked.

"Don't worry, I'll wear black, Grandma," Lizette assured her. "But Felicia is my best friend, even if I can't stand Alex Benedict." She shook her head. "God in heaven, I don't know what she sees in him except his money and the fact that she's almost twenty and afraid she'll end up a spinster."

"Maybe she really loves him," suggested Roth.

Lizette smiled. "Maybe she does at that, Grandpa," she said. "I guess if we all loved the same kind of person, we'd be fighting all the time over who gets whom. I only hope she'll be happy." She straightened in the chair, composing herself a little better, and Roth handed her letter back to her. "Thank you, Grandpa," she said, and glanced down at it a moment before returning it to the envelope that was still in her other hand. "This is one letter I don't want to lose." Then she stood up, picked up the little hat off the stand where Loedicia had set it, fastened it back on her head, tucked the letter into the bodice of her riding habit, and excused herself, announcing that she was going to ride upriver to Tonnerre to tell her parents about it.

"I'll find Pretty and the twins and give them a kiss before I leave," she said quickly, then waved halfheartedly as she left the room.

"I bet she'll cry all the way there," Loedicia said as she stared after her.

Roth sighed. "I hope so. Maybe it'll take away some of the pain." He put his arm about Loedicia's waist and pulled her close against him, gazing down into her face. "She reminds me of you," he whispered softly. "I just hope she has your strength."

Loedicia stared up into his dark eyes, proud of the love this man had given her over the years and hoping there were many more years to come. She turned into his arms, her own arms lifting, circling his neck, and ran her hand into his snow-white hair, remembering when it was as dark as his eyes. "Who said I was strong?" she said tremulously. "Without your love to make me live again, darling, when Quinn died, I'd have died too, I know I would. She loved Bain terribly, Roth," she went on. "I only hope, now with him gone, she can find someone to fill her heart again."

He stared down into her violet eyes. "Don't worry, she will, my love," he whispered softly. "She's too much like her grandmother," and he pulled her close, kissing her passionately as the sound of Diablo's hooves galloping down the drive echoed in through the open window.

It was Saturday, May 1, and Lizette was nervous as she stepped from the carriage, then made her way with her grandparents and parents into her in-laws' beautiful brick home to attend Felicia's wedding. Her sister-in-law, Felicia Kolter, was being married in the lovely gardens that stretched out beyond the terrace at the back of the house in Beaufort. How many times Lizette and Felicia had played there when they were younger, and how many times they had told their parents they were going to picnic in the summerhouse in the middle of the gardens, then had stolen away to watch a cockfight or get into some other equally wicked mischief.

As she stepped into the gardens now, hoping none of the guests already gathered there would notice her, Lizette felt a tremor run through her. There were also other memories here. Memories of Stuart and Bain. Oh, how she wished she could forget. She gazed about at all the people. She felt strange in her black silk, since almost everyone else was wearing pastel summer frocks. But she was a widow now, and respectable widows wore mourning clothes.

She watched as her mother-in-law approached, beaming delightedly at all of them. Madeline Kolter was an attractive woman with dark amber hair, a warm smile, and was one of Lizette's mother's best friends. She greeted everyone, then took Lizette's hands.

"Oh, Lizette, I'm so glad you came," she said affectionately. "Felicia feels so badly because you aren't able to be her matron of honor now, and I was so afraid you might be too upset to come. She'd have been terribly disappointed."

"I wouldn't miss it for the world, Mother Kolter," Lizette replied. "But I didn't think it proper to be part of the wedding party."

"Well, you can come sit with the family, at least."

Chairs and benches were set out on the lawn beside the garden, and Lizette glanced over to the first row of seats, reserved for the bride's family. Stuart, Julia, and their two children were sitting there already, with the children, a boy and girl, sitting between their parents. Julia was talking to a woman who had stopped to say hello, but Stuart's eyes were on Lizette, and she flushed.

"I really think it best I sit with my family, Mother Kolter," she answered.

"But we're still your family, dear," Madeline said. "You're still a Kolter."

"I know." She bit her lip self-consciously. "Only, under the circumstances, I think today I'd like to remember I'm also a Dante, just for a little while."

Madeline kissed her on the cheek. "Whatever you want, dear," she said, then suggested they all sit down, since it was almost time for the ceremony.

Lizette followed her parents and grandparents to a bench about midway in the crowd, then sat down, looking about uncomfortably. She probably shouldn't have come, but it was the only way she could think of to see Stuart without being obvious. Her green eyes raked over her in-laws as she watched them greeting the rest of the guests. She was trying to be nice to them. She'd always liked the Kolters, but like everyone else, they'd believed the stories about Bain, and although she knew Madeline and Rand Kolter loved their son, they felt he had disgraced them, and were doing a very good job of pretending nothing had happened, so her presence here today was probably embarrassing for them, even though they treated her decently. She watched her father-in-law stop to talk to someone for a moment before going into the house to join the bride for the traditional wedding march.

Rand Kolter was a proud man, and both his sons had inherited much of his looks. Bain had his same gray eyes, and both had his thick wavy hair that shone a golden russet in the sun. But the years had added a few extra pounds on Rand, although he was still attractive for his age. Since he was a barrister, he was handling all the legal matters concerning Bain's death, and both Rand and Madeline made it plain to her that they didn't blame her for Bain's behavior, but as far as Bain was concerned, he had ceased being their son when he deserted her and turned to piracy.

A few minutes later the small string orchestra struck up the wedding march, but Lizette saw little of the ceremony. Her thoughts were wandering over so many things, and later, after the ceremony was over, when everyone was milling about, congratulating the bride and groom, after she had given them her best wishes, she slipped away, farther into the gardens, to get away from the whispering she knew was going on, and before she realized it, she was at the summerhouse. She sighed and moved toward it along the flagstone walk, then stepped inside. The smell from the wisteria that covered the roof was strong here, filling the air and making her melancholy, but it was cool in the summerhouse and the day was warm. She walked over and sat down on the bench that circled the inside of it, then took a deep breath, trying to put herself in a better mood. She'd been trying to talk to Stuart ever since the ceremony ended, but every time she started to approach him, someone else would get there first. In a way, she supposed it was silly to insist on talking to him privately, but she didn't want anyone else to know why she was so set on clearing Bain's name. She'd sworn her family to secrecy about the letter, at least until she felt the time was right, because there were too many people who'd think it was all just a ploy to vindicate Bain now that he was dead. Some people might even think she had written the letter herself to make things look better.

She leaned back against one of the posts that supported the roof, drew her legs from the floor, tucking them beneath her, and curled up, putting her arm on the rail, then rested her head on her arm so she could look out toward the back of the gardens. Music from the band entertaining the guests as they enjoyed themselves eating and talking floated back to her on the afternoon breeze, an she felt a twinge of regret, wishing she could have had a big elaborate wedding like Felicia and all their other friends. Even Heather had been married in a beautiful white dress once, with all the fancy trimmings. Of course, she had married DeWitt Palmer, a man she grew to hate, but still the wedding had been a fancy one, not like Lizette's hurried ceremony on board the *Dragonfly* in the middle of the night, with a bunch of bawdy sailors gawking at her. It would have been so nice if Bain could have seen her in a real wedding gown. She was so engrossed in her daydreaming, she didn't hear the footsteps until Stuart spoke.

" 'O, my love is like a red, red rose,' " he began softly as he slowly walked toward her. " 'That's newly sprung in June. O, my love is like the melody that's sweetly played in tune! As fair art thou, my bonnie lass, so deep in love am I. And I will love thee still, my dear, till all the seas go dry.' "

He stopped directly in front of her and she lifted her head, staring at him. It was as if time stood still. He was wearing a coat of deep crimson, with buff breeches, and she had to force herself to remember three years had gone by since she'd last heard him quote Robert Burns.

He went on, his voice deep and rich, his eyes boring into hers. " 'Till all the seas go dry, my dear, and the rocks melt with the sun. I will love thee still, my dear, while the sand of life shall run. And fare thee well, my only love, and fare thee well a while! And I will come again, my dear, tho it were ten thousand miles.' " His voice trembled as he finished, and neither of them said anything for a long time. Then Lizette flushed.

"You remembered," she murmured softly.

"How could I ever forget?"

Her hands dropped to her lap and her eyes followed them, watching her fingers toy with the silken folds of her beaded reticule. "Don't make things worse, Stuart," she said unsteadily, then composed herself, shaking off some of the old memories, and faced him again. Her eyes held pain. "I'm glad you came. I wanted to talk to you," she said, changing the subject. "Before you wrote to my father telling him of Bain's death, you said you hadn't heard anything," she went on. "Are you sure, Stuart?"

"You think I wouldn't have told you?"

"I don't know. You and Bain . . . I know the animosity between you was mostly because of me, but you always did think he was a bit of a wastrel."

"Not a wastrel," Stuart corrected. "He was an irresponsible wanderer who took what he wanted and never worried about the consequences."

"That's not true!"

"Isn't it? Oh, I don't doubt he loved you, Liz, in his own special way. In fact, I know he did, but it wasn't enough. He was too used to being responsible only to himself. Having a wife and children was too confining. He tried, Lord knows I think he tried, but it just wasn't in him to settle down in one place with one woman."

Lizette straightened on the bench, put her feet on the floor again, and held her head up stubbornly. "You didn't know Bain at all, Stuart," she replied. "You only saw what you wanted to see."

"I saw my brother break your heart."

"But he didn't, not really. You see, I was right, Stuart," she said proudly. "He didn't leave me, not because he wanted to, not because there was nothing here for him anymore. He didn't even want to go. Here," and she reached into the small beaded bag in her lap and took out the letter Bain had left with Roth. "Read this," she said, her voice breaking. "Then tell me Bain isn't worth my tears."

Stuart took the envelope from her hesitantly and stared for a minute at her name on the outside, then opened it and unfolded the letter. Lizette watched his face while he read it, her own filled with anticipation.

"Where did you get this?" he asked when he'd finished.

"Grandpa Roth gave it to me. Bain gave it to him to give to me the morning he left, in case he didn't come back alive."

Stuart frowned as he read the letter again more slowly. "According to this . . ."

"According to that, he was on some sort of mission. He had to be. Why else would he refer to not going as treason?" Her face was suddenly animated, eyes alive with hope. "Stuart, Bain had to have been working for the government. That would explain everything." She eyed him curiously. "By the way, how did you learn he was dead?"

He stared at her, his frown deepening, trying to remember back to a few weeks before, when he'd been given the news. The second session of Congress had ended March 3, and he'd stayed in Washington some weeks longer than he'd planned, getting caught up on a few things he had to do, then left for Columbia the twenty-third of April, and arrived in Beaufort yesterday, just in time for his sister's wedding.

"Sam, Sam Hewitt," he said thoughtfully as he went over the events of that unsettling day. "He's the one who told me."

"Who is Sam Hewitt?"

"He's with the Navy Department."

"Did he say how he knew?"

He shook his head. "Just that it had been confirmed. Bain had gone down with his ship in a storm off the Florida keys."

"Who confirmed it?"

"I don't know."

"Weren't there any survivors at all?"

"I don't know." Stuart stared at her curiously. "Liz, I didn't even think to ask those questions. I just took his word for everything. After all, he's official Navy and I was upset enough about hearing he was dead and knowing what it was going to do to you."

She stood up. "Stuart, if his death was confirmed, there had to be survivors, or a body, and since there was no body to ship home . . . How about Captain Holley and the rest of the crew? What happened to them? How many went down with the ship?''

"Hey, wait a minute. That's too many questions."

"I know," she answered. "And I want the answers to them. That's one of the reasons I decided to come today, even though I'm in mourning." She gazed into his eyes intently. "Stuart, I want to go to Washington," she said anxiously. "I have to clear Bain's name. He was no more a pirate than you or I, not really, and I can't have the twins growing up thinking he was. I wanted to ask you if you know of anyone who wouldn't mind a house guest for a while. I'd pay my way. Bain left me well taken care of, but I think, since I'd be there alone, it'd be best if I stayed with a family or at a rooming house, rather than a hotel."

He took a deep breath as he studied her face. "You're sure you want to do this?" he asked. "It could get messy, and again, you might not find out a damn thing."

"I have to," she insisted. "I'm not going to have people whispering pityingly behind my back for the rest of my life."

He nodded. "All right, if you're determined to go." He paused a moment, then went on, his voice deepening. "You can stay at my place."

"Oh, no . . ."

"Liz, I won't be there," he said quickly. "The session was over March 3 and we're not due to convene again until December."

"But what if you had to be in Washington for some reason? And what would people say?"

"They'd say I let my brother's widow use my house while she tried to console herself over his death." His eyes softened. "Liz, they know nothing about you and me, so there'd be no reason for them to wonder or become suspicious. The only one we'd have to worry about is Father, but when I explain it to him and tell him I won't be there, I don't think he'll say too much."

"Maybe you'd better not tell him."

"Why?"

"Because he and your mother believe all the lies about Bain, just like you did, and he might say something to someone else. Stuart, I don't want anyone to know about the letter Bain sent me until his name is cleared. They might say I wrote it myself or something, just trying to make people think it wasn't true."

"I see." He studied her face intently. "Liz, how do you intend to accomplish anything in Washington?" he asked. "You don't know anyone there."

"I'm going to start out by seeing your Mr. Sam Hewitt."

"Then I think I'd better give you a little more help," he said. "There's a man, his name is Jeffrey Magee. He was an old classmate of mine from school and he's also a barrister, but he just loves a challenge. He's the one who was originally trying to find out anything he could about Bain."

"But if he couldn't come up with anything in all those months, how can he help me now?"

"He did learn a few things, Liz," he answered. "It's just that I'm afraid what he did learn wasn't very helpful. However, after reading this, it may give him some incentive to dig further into this whole mess."

He gave the letter back to her. "Only I wish you could just forget," he said. "The rest of the world doesn't seem to care one way or another about whether Bain's innocent or not."

"Well, I do. And so do your parents, Stuart. Someday your mother and father, and you too, you'll all thank me when you can all hold your heads up and tell the world Bain was a hero, not a traitor."

"I hope so, Liz," he said. "Only I'm afraid you're going to be opening a great big hornet's nest, and you're the one liable to get stung."

"Then that's my problem, but I have to do it. I can't sit back and ignore it. Besides, what could happen to me just because I ask a few questions?"

"You may be right, but if you need help, you know where to find me."

She nodded. "Thank you."

"Now," he said. "Maybe we'd better join the others before everyone decides to slip off to the summerhouse," and he took her arm, ushering her out of the summerhouse after she put the letter back in her reticule for safekeeping.

22

Spring in Washington could be extremely warm. It was late in the morning. Lizette had arrived the night before, going directly to the small house Stuart owned near the edge of town. She hadn't told her parents she was going to stay at Stuart's, she had only told them he had found a place for her to stay. Her mother and Madeline Kolter were too close to take a chance, because if her mother-in-law discovered she was staying at Stuart's, she might tell Rand Kolter, and Bain's father was the only one who knew the whole truth about her affair with Stuart and her marriage to Bain. She didn't want him causing problems.

She stretched in the bed, then sat up. She had arrived rather late last night, tired and weary from the long overland ride from South Carolina, and had been so anxious to get some rest, she hadn't even taken time to look around. Now she studied the room carefully.

Stuart kept a small staff at the house, so it was always ready for him or his family at a moment's notice, in case he was called to Washington. After reading the letter of introduction Stuart had given her, the housekeeper had led her here. Lizette assumed it was where guests usually stayed. It was a pretty room, simply furnished with crimson draperies, a Persian rug, and the usual ornate furniture, including a huge armoire on the inside wall where she could keep all the black dresses she'd brought with her.

She hated wearing black. It was so boring, and there was so little you could do with it. She stared across the room to where they'd put the trunks. "Well, might as well get on with it," she whispered softly to herself, and left the bed, slipping into a wrapper, then choosing a dress from the trunks to have pressed for the day.

The first item on her agenda after a light breakfast was to locate Jeffrey Magee, which was harder than she had imagined. Stuart had given her the address of his office. He wasn't there. Nor was he at his residence. She had taken a public coach from Port Royal and was using Stuart's driver and carriage while she was in the city. The driver was a young black named Archibald, who happened to know Mr. Magee.

"If you's really bound to find him, ma'am, I think I knows where he mights be," he said as he helped her into the carriage in front of Jeffrey Magee's unpretentious home.

"Where would that be?" she asked as she seated herself back in the carriage.

"There's an ale house a few blocks away where he usually congregates this time of day. He just mights be there." He smiled. "I knows you can't go in no ale house, ma'am," he suggested. "But I can go in and fetch him if'n you want."

"Splendid," she said, more determined than ever. "On to the ale house, Archibald."

Half an hour later, Jeffrey Magee was standing outside his favorite ale house beside a small carriage, being informally introduced to Mrs. Bain Kolter.

"This here's the lady," Archibald told him.

Jeffrey Magee was somewhat surprised. He had met Bain Kolter a few times and often wondered what kind of woman had managed to get her hands on him. Lizette Kolter was a delightful surprise, and so young. She barely looked out of her teens. She was a bit plump for his taste, which was another surprise. He'd have imagined that a man like Kolter, one the women all fawned over, would pick a woman of more slender proportions. Ah, well.

"Mrs. Kolter?" he greeted. "Stuart's driver said you were looking for me. I'm Jeffrey Magee."

She shook his hand. "Lizette Kolter," she said. "Yes, I am looking for you. Is there anywhere we can talk?"

Jeff nodded. "We could have Archie drive around a bit."

"Sounds fine."

He went to the other side of the carriage and climbed in; then Lizette nodded to the driver. As the carriage started forward, she glanced over at him. He was in his mid-thirties, with light brown hair, a big full mustache, and brown eyes that had studied her closely while she introduced herself. He wasn't quite as tall as Bain or Stuart, but gave the impression of being taller because of his brawny build that was stretching the seams on a green frock coat and buff breeches. He had set a beaver hat atop his head when he sat down, and it made him look much more distinguished. Her first impression of him when he strolled out of the ale house was that he looked more like a fighter than a barrister.

"Well, Mrs. Kolter?" he asked as they rode along.

"I want to know what you found out about my husband," she said. "Stuart said there were a few things—"

"Not enough, I'm afraid, although I do know he was in Washington last July, shortly before Stuart said he'd left Port Royal. I saw him myself, riding down Pennsylvania Avenue, but when I called to him, I guess he didn't hear, and kept right on going."

"That proves it, then," she said eagerly, and reached in her reticule for the letter, but before giving it to him, she made him promise to tell no one about it.

"This is his handwriting?" he asked after reading it.

She nodded. "So you see, Mr. Magee, something's going on that isn't right. If Bain was sent on some secret mission, he should be exonerated from charges of piracy."

Jeff shook his head. "Even if you're right," he said, "the government will never go along with it."

"But he's dead. Why should it matter now whether anyone learns the truth or not?"

"That's not how they work."

"Well, it's how I work. Everyone thinks my husband deserted me. I intend to prove he didn't."

"And you want my help?"

"Stuart said you would."

He glanced over at her. She was wearing black, right down to her black satin bonnet, and it framed her face, making her eyes shine a brilliant green.

"He knows me too well," he said, and smiled. "Anything for the poor maiden in distress." Then he grew serious. "How can I help?"

"How do I go about getting an appointment to see Mr. Sam Hewitt?"

"Sam? Hmmm! Now, that won't be easy." He rubbed his chin, frowning. "But I'll try."

And he did try. All the next week he tried, and the week after that. When he did manage to get her an appointment, it would be canceled at the last minute; then he'd have to start all over again.

Finally, after being left waiting in the man's outer office for the fourth time and being told an emergency had come up and the appointment would have to be canceled again, Lizette stormed out in a fury. Later that evening, she faced Jeff in the library at Stuart's home.

"What am I going to do, Jeff?" she asked angrily. "I have to see him. Which way does he go to the office? Where does he live? I'll do anything for just five minutes with the man."

Jeff sighed. "I told you it wouldn't be easy."

"He's purposely avoiding me."

"You know that, and I know that, but he'd never admit it."

She was pacing the floor, the skirt of her black cotton dress swishing crisply as she walked. Suddenly she stopped, staring at him impatiently. "I have to see him, Jeff," she said stubbornly.

Jeff sat thoughtfully for a minute, trying to think of something. "Aha," he suddenly said, and she eyed him curiously. "There's only one way I know of that you'll be able to see him without him suspecting anything ahead of time."

"And . . . ?"

"Next Sunday's the Fourth of July, and there's going to be a presidential ball Saturday night. Everyone who is anyone will be there, including Mr. Sam Hewitt and his wife."

"Oh, grand. How does that help me?"

"You wouldn't be averse to attending, would you?"

"With you?"

"Afraid I'm not invited. And even if I were, I don't think Celia would understand if I left her home and went dancing with another lady. Especially one so young and lovely."

Lizette smiled, pleased with his answer. "Neither would I," she said. "I like your wife, Jeff, even if she does think I'm as notorious as my husband was supposed to have been."

He grinned. "Celia means well, she just isn't quite as broad-minded as I am."

"All right, so it isn't you," she said. "Whom do I go with?"

"How about your brother-in-law?"

"Stuart? He's not in Washington."

"He will be by the Fourth."

"How do you know?"

"Because he sent a message on ahead, saying he'd like to stay at our place, and if that wasn't possible, I'm to make reservations for him at one of the hotels. He was afraid it might look rather strange if he stayed here, with you in the house."

"Then he isn't bringing Julia with him?"

"Evidently not." Jeff was sitting at Stuart's desk and leaned back casually. "I know you're still in mourning, Lizette," he said. "But I think between the two of us, he'll agree to take you."

"If he doesn't?"

"Then I'll have to find someone else."

"Really, Jeff, I have to know one way or the other," she said. "I can't just wear any old dress to something like that."

"You find a dress," he answered confidently, "and I'll guarantee you an escort."

She eyed him dubiously. "You're sure Stuart was invited?"

"Positive."

"All right, I'll trust you," she said. "Now, where's the best place for me to find a fancy dress in Washington?"

He wrote down the names of a few places his wife frequented,

then left, and for the next couple of days Lizette searched
frantically for something appropriate, finally discovering a lovely
black lace with small puff sleeves, high waist, and low neckline,
perfect to show off her diamond necklace and earrings, with
black feathers to decorate her hair. And if the evening was cool,
she had her black velvet cape to wear.

She was eager for Saturday evening to get here so she could
meet the elusive Mr. Sam Hewitt, but skeptical about going to
the ball with Stuart, and was secretly hoping he'd say no so Jeff
would have to find someone else. But on Friday evening a
message arrived, informing her Stuart was staying at the Magees'
and would be picking her up Saturday evening at eight. She was
ready when he arrived.

Stuart had been worried about Lizette being in Washington all
by herself, even though he knew Jeff would help keep an eye on
her, because he knew how headstrong she could be at times. So
it was no surprise to him when the letter from Sam Hewitt
arrived telling him she was making a pest of herself, and wasn't
there something he could do. When he'd arrived at Jeff's house
on Friday and been told what she was planning for the next
evening, there was no question that he wouldn't take her to the
ball. If Julia didn't understand, he'd worry about that when the
time came, but for now . . . It was obvious if Hewitt had been
avoiding Lizette so far, he was going to be quite upset when he
ran into her there, so maybe he could talk her out of going. If
not, at least he'd be there to see she didn't do anything rash. He
was frowning as he followed his housekeeper toward the parlor,
where Lizette was waiting.

Lizette was nervous. In the first place, widows in mourning
weren't supposed to attend balls, civic functions, or any other
public doings, and certainly not with a married man, even a
brother-in-law, but she had to go. One way or another, she was
going to find out why Sam Hewitt was avoiding her. She had
been pacing the floor, and now stopped as she heard the housekeeper talking to someone in the hall; then she stiffened as
Stuart stepped into the room.

Stuart stopped just inside the room, staring at her. On the way
over, he had a mild suspicion she might have been foolish
enough to buy a flamboyant dress to wear tonight, especially
after Jeff had told him he'd given her the names of some of the
best shops in the capital, but now, as he stared at her, he realized
she didn't need bright colors to make her look beautiful. All she

had to do was be herself. The black lace dress with black satin underskirts was the perfect complement to her dark hair and tawny flesh, and the small black lacy plumes in her hair made her even more sensuous.

"You look lovely," was all he could say.

She blushed, then straightened, trying to ignore the look in his eyes. "Hello, Stuart, what brought you to Washington?"

"You," he said, and saw the question forming on her lips. "I told you they weren't going to like your asking questions," he explained as he strolled farther into the room.

"They asked you to stop me?"

"They asked me to see if I could do anything about it."

"Well, you can't!"

He stopped directly in front of her. "I figured as much."

"Then why did you come?"

"To make sure you don't get into more trouble than you can handle." He studied her closely. "Why don't you forget about the ball tonight, Liz," he said. "We could go somewhere else."

"No."

"Liz, be reasonable."

"If you don't take me, Stuart," she warned, "I'll go alone if I have to and sneak in. I'm not giving up."

"All right, we'll go," he conceded reluctantly. "But remember, this is a presidential party, not one of Port Royal's homey little soirees."

"What is that supposed to mean?"

He took her arm and began ushering her from the room. "It means that when and if you get a chance to talk to Sam Hewitt, you're to go easy," he said as they headed toward the foyer. "Remember, these people don't care a fig about Lizette Kolter's personal problems. They've got the whole country's problems to worry about, and they aren't going to be sympathetic to your pleas. I just don't want you making a scene with half the world watching." He looked worried as he took her black cape from the housekeeper and set it on her shoulders. "You do have a tendency to pay little attention to convention, my dear sister-in-law," he said. "I'd hate for you to do anything embarrassing."

Her eyes flashed. "Don't tempt me, Stuart," she said testily, and he suddenly had the strangest premonition that tonight was going to be a night he'd never forget.

"Shall we?" he asked as he held his arm out for her to take while he brushed aside the notion that he should rip the cloak from her shoulders and insist they stay home. She took his arm, he accepted his hat from the housekeeper, opened the door for Lizette, and escorted her down the front walk to where the carriage waited, then gave their destination to Archie, who was driving.

The President's house was all aglow when they arrived, with carriages coming and going, footmen and lackeys bustling about, and lanterns strung along the drive with flags displayed everywhere.

Lizette's stomach was full of butterflies as their carriage waited in line for them to be let off. Her cheeks were flushed and she was nervously clenching and unclenching the black beaded evening bag in her lap. However, unlike the other guests, she wasn't excited at the prospect of meeting the President, Vice-President, senators, congressmen, and other government officials, nor did the thought of seeing all the foreign dignitaries in their costumed splendor thrill her. Her only thoughts were that she was finally going to meet the elusive Mr. Sam Hewitt in person, and she tried to rehearse silently what she was going to say to him. She knew what she'd like to say to him, but glanced over at Stuart, remembering his warning.

Stuart was watching the driver in anticipation of reaching the front walk, and she studied him furtively, realizing they were going to make a striking couple. His black frock coat was velvet, the black cravat adorning his lace ruffled shirt was of the finest silk, and his buff pantaloons were covering Wellington boots that gleamed with a high shine. As a couple, they complemented each other beautifully. She frowned. If only he didn't look so much like Bain. He glanced over at her and she felt a tug at her heart.

"Are you ready for your plunge into Washington society?" he asked.

"As ready as I'll ever be," she replied, and took a deep breath, trying to ignore the feelings Stuart was stirring inside her, as the carriage stopped and Archie climbed down.

Unfortunately, the presidential ballroom was one of the last things to be restored after the war, and as they stood in the receiving line just inside the ballroom, Lizette could see that even now it wasn't finished.

Its plastered walls were still unpainted, and raw timbers showed here and there, but the people arriving didn't seem to mind. It was decorated with floral arrangements, and a huge American flag was displayed behind the stage where the orchestra was playing. Lizette thought it was quite impressive as she finally forced her thoughts from her anticipated encounter with Sam Hewitt and paid attention to her surroundings, relinquishing Stuart's arm so he could present her to the President and Mrs. Monroe.

"My sister-in-law, Mrs. Bain Kolter, Mr. President," he said after shaking hands with James Monroe himself, and Lizette stared at this tall, thin man, the blush on her face revealing the slight discomfort she wished she wasn't feeling.

For a brief moment James Monroe hesitated, then slowly reached for her hand. "Mrs. Kolter?" he questioned as if he wasn't certain he'd heard right. "Mrs. Bain Kolter?"

"Yes, sir," she answered, her voice unsteady. "My name's Lizette."

"I see." He was still holding her hand, and for a moment . . . "You look vaguely familiar, Mrs. Kolter, Lizette," he said thoughtfully. "Have we ever met?"

"No, sir, but I believe you met my parents once, years ago in France," she said. "People say I resemble my mother a great deal, except her hair is very blond."

"Your parents are . . . ?"

"Rebel and Beau Dante." Her smile was stilted. "At that time, my father was privateering for the French and was known as Captain Thunder," she explained self-consciously.

"Ah, yes," said the President, nodding. "I vaguely remember the incident." Then he looked directly into her eyes, his own intense, and his mouth grew firm. "Let me extend my condolences to you, my dear, in all ways," he went on. "I know it was painful enough for you to learn of your husband's treasonable actions. His death at this time must make the blow all the harder to take. I hope you're able to manage?"

"Thank you, sir, I'm managing quite well," she answered.

"Good." He looked relieved, then said, "Let me introduce you to Mrs. Monroe," and Lizette turned to the first lady.

The preliminaries were over quickly, and Stuart escorted her the rest of the way into the ballroom, quite aware that more than one head was turning his way. He accepted the reactions with mixed emotions. Many of the people here knew Julia, since he'd been in politics so many years, and it was understandable that until they learned who Lizette was, they were going to regard her entrance on his arm with raised eyebrows. What he didn't realize was, many of them already knew who she was and knew she was staying at his town house, and her reputation of being the widow of the notorious Captain Gallant had preceded her into the ballroom.

"Would you like some punch?" he asked.

She nodded, and he escorted her to the buffet table, where servants were busy pouring punch and handing out tea cakes.

"Nothing to eat," she cautioned him, and his expression told her he understood.

They moved toward the side of the ballroom and stood for a long time sipping the punch, while Lizette surveyed the room. Now she knew what Stuart meant when he had cautioned her about half the world watching. There were men and women from all over. Ambassadors, royalty, military men. Most wore their native costumes, and many carried titles. It was strange to see them mingling with the American politicians, for there were some Americans from the newer states and territories who were obviously not at home in Washington society. For a while it was amusing just to watch.

She drained her goblet, then turned to Stuart as the orchestra began playing a waltz. He was partway behind her, but close at her elbow. She handed him her empty goblet and he set it on the table beside him, followed quickly by his own; then his eyes caught hers as she glanced at him over her shoulder.

"Stuart, dance with me," she whispered so no one else would hear.

He frowned. "Widows in mourning aren't supposed to dance."

"I don't care."

His eyes hardened. "Liz, so many people are watching. I didn't realize we'd create such a stir." He flushed uncomfortably. "I can already hear the whispering. If you start dancing . . ."

"What will happen, the roof cave in?" She sighed. "Stuart, please . . . I'm not the one who died, Bain did. I want to feel alive again." Her eyes clung to his, and he knew he was lost. "Please, Stuart, dance with me," she pleaded.

"Oh, what the hell," he mumbled under his breath, and put his arm about her waist, ushering her onto the dance floor. "They're already crucifying you, what's one more nail?" and he swung her about, into his arms, and they joined the whirling couples on the floor.

For a while Lizette forgot all about why she was at the ball. The music and laughter, Stuart's graceful dancing, and the memories of all they had once meant to each other were like a balm to her aching heart. Stuart cared, she could see it in his eyes. In spite of his anger with her, and his insistance on propriety, he still cared, and for a while it helped. Then the music came to an end.

He stared into her eyes as the last note sounded. She had a faraway look on her face.

"Lizette?" he asked, worried.

She blinked, and drew herself away, slowly taking her hand from his, her breathing a little unsteady, then straightened, looking about as if suddenly coming back to reality.

"I'm all right," she said softly as his hand dropped from her waist. "I was just remembering things I shouldn't remember." She reached up, fussing with the neckline on her dress, then made sure all her curls were still in place. "Now, Senator Kolter," she said as she turned, beginning to look over the crowd, "which one is Mr. Sam Hewitt?"

Stuart moved closer to her. "Can't you just forget it, Liz?" he asked.

Her eyes sparked. "You know I can't."

"Let me look," he said reluctantly, and his eyes began to search the room for the man Lizette was so determined to meet. "I'm not going to point," he said as they moved away from the dance floor. "But if you'll look over near the door." She followed the direction of his eyes. "See the clean-shaven man with the thick head of black hair and rather deep-set eyes? That's Secretary of War John Calhoun. The man talking to him is Sam Hewitt."

Lizette felt a surge of energy begin to flood her as she stared at the man she'd been trying to talk with for well over a month. His hair was quite dark and very curly, with thick side whiskers that stopped at the end of the jawline, leaving his chin bare, and from where they were standing, he didn't look too tall, perhaps because of the paunch that was visibly pushing against his blue frock coat and the way his shoulders drooped.

"I want an introduction, Stuart," she said as she stared at the man.

"What are you going to do?"

"I'm not certain," she answered vaguely. "But one thing is sure. He's looking this way, and if Mr. Calhoun tells him who I am, and he goes back through that door again, I'll never get to see him. Please, Stuart . . ."

Stuart knew he was a damn fool, but he also knew Liz. If she thought Hewitt was leaving the ball, she'd be just as likely to chase after him as stand here and watch him leave. Figuring it was the better of two evils, Stuart held out his arm for her to take, and began making his way across the room, introducing her casually to people on the way, so they wouldn't look too obvious.

Sam Hewitt saw Stuart Kolter heading toward him with his sister-in-law on his arm, and cursed softly to himself. Damn the man anyway. He'd written, telling him to come get her out of his hair, not bring her here. What the hell did he think he was doing? Any other place, and he'd just leave, but it wasn't proper to walk out on the President. His jaw clenched with rage, and his eyes were blazing as he stood his ground. All right, if she insisted on meddling, he'd make it worth her while. Nothing, not even the man's wife, was going to jeopardize the country's security. He braced himself for what lay ahead, and finally met the Widow Kolter head-on.

Stuart was tense, his stomach constricting nervously as he greeted Calhoun and Hewitt, then introduced Lizette.

Sam Hewitt's eyes were an unusual contrast to his dark hair. They were pale blue, so pale they looked as if they'd been bleached in the sun, giving him a weird appearance, and as they shook hands, Lizette almost felt as if he could look right through her.

"Mrs. Kolter, I heard you were in Washington," he said, pretending a warmth he didn't feel.

"I imagine you did, sir," she countered sharply. "Since I've made a number of appointments to see you at your office, and they were all canceled at the last minute."

"Oh, dear, I am sorry," he offered, forcing himself to be polite. "But I'm afraid things are rather hectic here. It seems there's always some crisis."

"Oh, I can understand crises, Mr. Hewitt," she said, bristling irritably. "I've had a number of them myself recently . . . in fact, that's exactly what I was anxious to talk to you about." She took a deep breath, then plunged right in. "I understand you're the one who told Stuart that my husband was dead, is that right?" she asked.

He hadn't expected her to be so blunt, and she saw his mouth twitch. "That's right," he answered. "And I extend my condolences, Mrs. Kolter. I imagine the whole incident is painful to you."

"It's painful, all right, Mr. Hewitt," she snapped. "Th

whole episode is quite painful, that's why I'd like to ask you how you happened to learn of my husband's death."

"Since he was a pirate, and our Navy keeps close track of such matters," he answered, "the commuiqué regarding his death was received at our naval headquarters."

"From where?"

"From the Spanish authorities in Florida."

"Who brought it to you?"

"My dear young woman," he said, "I have absolutely no idea who the gentleman was who brought the message. It could have been any one of a number of couriers. Who brought it didn't seem important. The important matter was that the message was received."

"What I'm trying to get at, sir," she went on, refusing to be intimidated, "is who, with the Spanish authorities, signed the document telling of Bain's death? Surely, if he were lost with his ship in a storm, as I've been led to believe, there had to be an eyewitness to confirm it, otherwise it's merely speculation."

Sam didn't like the way the conversation was going. His eyes hardened. "The Spanish government confirmed his death," he answered. "Perhaps you'd better take the matter up with them."

"No, perhaps you'd better take the matter up with them," she said curtly. "And there's another matter you might try to learn something about while you're at it, Mr. Hewitt," she went on. "I have reason to believe my husband, far from being the pirate he was accused of being, was on a special mission of some sort for the American government. What that mission was, and why he had to pose as a pirate in order to accomplish it, is what has me puzzled. However, I do know since I've been in Washington the past few weeks there have been a number of stories about ships being attacked and little being done about it. I've even heard the name Jean Lafitte mentioned in a few conversations. Mr. Hewitt, what part did my husband play in all this?"

"Your husband was a pirate, Mrs. Kolter," he answered stubbornly. "I feel sorry for you, and equally embarrassed for the good senator here, because Stuart's done much for this country. But don't try to make your husband into a hero, ma'am," he went on. "He was a pirate, and as such, if caught, would have hung on a gallows along with his men."

"No," she argued. "He was not a pirate. I know he wasn't. You see, he left me a letter in case he didn't return, and I intend to find out what it's all about."

"A letter?" Sam asked, surprised. This was the first he'd heard of a letter.

"That's right, Mr. Hewitt. Bain left a letter saying he hadn't deserted me, and that although he couldn't tell why he left or what he was doing, he warned me not to believe anything bad I might hear about him. I don't, Mr. Hewitt. If my husband died for loyalty to this country, then I think he deserves the recognition." Her voice rose slightly, as anger at Sam Hewitt's seeming indifference regarding Bain made her seethe inside. "And I think it's despicable that a government like ours, one based on the will of the people, should treat one of its people so shabbily."

"Please, Mrs. Kolter, there's no need to be upset," John Calhoun interrupted. "I'm sure Sam didn't mean to be tactless regarding your husband, but you must admit you have nothing to base your assumptions on."

"I have my letter!"

"A letter anyone could have written, including you, madam," Sam accused, trying to keep himself under control.

"That's not fair, Sam," remarked Stuart, jumping to Lizette's defense.

"You call this fair?" Sam asked angrily. "To be accused of maligning your brother's name? Your sister-in-law goes too far, Stuart," he retorted.

"I want to know who saw my husband die," Lizette said, trying to keep her voice down. "And why he had to die." Her eyes were blazing. "He wasn't out there because he wanted to be, he was out there because he was sent out there. I want to know who sent him. All I ask is that he be given credit for what he did. That he won't have died with the world thinking he was a pirate, because he wasn't."

"Get her out of here, Stuart," Sam ordered half under his breath, but already people were staring at them.

"That's it, go ahead," she fumed. "Try to get rid of me. Try to shut me up, but I'll tell you, Mr. Hewitt," she stated angrily, "I won't give up. Bain died because someone sent him out there to die, and I intend to find out who it was and why. I intend to clear Bain's name, whether anyone likes it or not."

Stuart took Lizette's arm. "Calm down, Liz," he whispered, but her anger was already in full bloom.

"Calm down—that's all I ever hear. Calm down," she angrily half-whispered. "Well, I'm tired of calming down, Stuart, and

I'm tired of being ignored and given the runaround. Somebody in Washington knows why Bain did what he did, why he wasn't even allowed to tell me, and dammit, I want to know too.''

Hewitt and Calhoun both stared at her dumbfounded.

"Nice ladies don't use profanity, Liz," Stuart warned through rigid teeth.

"So I'm not a nice lady," she blurted furiously as she stared at the two shocked men. "I'm the widow of that horrible pirate, Captain Gallant, remember? No one wants to talk to me, no one wants to give me any answers. Well, I'll tell you"—she addressed Sam Hewitt rather than John Calhoun—"I'm going to find out what's going on if I have to stay here forever. I want to know who saw my husband die. Why he was there in the first place. What his mission was. What happened to his men. If they all supposedly went down with the ship, then how does anyone know it ever happened? I want answers, Mr. Hewitt, and I'll get them any way I can, do you understand?''

"Perfectly," he said, his eyes hard, his face like chiseled granite. "Only let me warn you, Mrs. Kolter." He lowered his voice so only Lizette, Stuart, and Calhoun could hear. "You cause too big a stir, and you'll find yourself very unwelcome in Washington.''

"I already have, Mr. Hewitt," she answered bitterly. "The only one who's welcomed me here is Stuart, but then, you wouldn't understand that, would you? You see, Stuart knows me, he knows Bain wrote that letter, and he knows why I know Bain wouldn't desert me to become a pirate, and I think he wants answers too, but you see, he's a senator, and being a politician, he's more diplomatic than I am. He asked me not to come, even warned me it'd be useless, but I don't take advice very well.''

"Well, take some now," Sam said, interrupting her. "Go home, Mrs. Kolter. You're only going to end up in a mess of trouble.''

"Threats, Mr. Hewitt?" she asked, then glanced at John Calhoun. "You heard him, Mr. Calhoun," she said. "Tell me, as Secretary of War, what department handles foreign intrigue, secret missions, and that sort of thing?''

John Calhoun's deep-set eyes were agitated. "That, Mrs. Kolter," he said defensively, "is none of your business.''

"That's what I thought you'd say. Well, I intend to make it my business if I have to turn Washington upside down to do it.''

"Go home, Mrs. Kolter," Hewitt said again, but she shook her head, her eyes narrowing shrewdly.

"Not on your life, Mr. Hewitt," she answered stubbornly, then turned to Stuart. He was angry with her, and she knew it, but at the moment she didn't care. "Thank you, Stuart," she said, trying to suppress the anger that still seethed inside her. "Thank you for at least giving me a chance, and now that my talk with Mr. Hewitt is over, I do believe I'm thirsty again." She wound her arm through his and smiled at him, a smile he knew was strained. "If you don't mind, I'd love some more punch."

Stuart laid his hand over hers on his arm, excused the two of them, and led her away toward the buffet table, while Sam Hewitt and John Calhoun stared after them and some of the other guests who'd been within earshot of the conversation began whispering furtively.

"Something's going to have to be done about that woman, John," Sam said forcefully. "Before she causes any more problems."

"Aye," John Calhoun said, nodding. "But what?"

Neither of them had an answer.

23

Lizette's knees were trembling as she let Stuart lead her toward the buffet table, and she had to force her hand to stay steady while she sipped the cool punch.

"I hope you're satisfied," Stuart murmured under his breath as he pretended to sip his own punch.

She fought back tears. "Are you?" she asked.

"No, but that doesn't mean anything can be done about it." He held the goblet in his hands, his fingers tightening on it as he stared at her. "You heard them, especially Sam. Liz, if, like Bain's letter said, he was on some special mission, they aren't going to tell you, and how do you intend to find out?"

"I don't know. But I've got to do something."

"You can. Right now, you can dance with me again," he suggested. "There's nothing more you can do tonight, so as long as we're here, and as long as you've got the whole place whispering about you anyway, you might as well enjoy yourself."

"You don't think I should go home?"

"I'd love to take you home," he said, his voice vibrant with emotion. "Only it's early yet, and I might not want to leave. No, Liz." He took a deep breath. "I think it's safer for both of us if we stay and try to enjoy the ball."

"Then that's what we'll do," she said quietly, and handed him her empty goblet to put back on the table, and once more they joined the other guests on the dance floor.

Stuart was glad they had stayed at the ball in spite of the fact that he knew, since Lizette's untimely conversation with Sam Hewitt, they had quickly become the topic of conversation all over the ballroom. Ignoring the fact, however, he even introduced her to a number of people, and voiced his approval when she accepted a few offers to dance, although he silently admitted to himself he felt a pang of jealousy, watching her in other men's arms.

Close to midnight, when the dancing was over, everyone gathered outside on the back lawn to watch a display of fireworks create a thrillingly colorful panorama against the night sky. When they were over, hats, capes, and walking canes were once more distributed, guests bid farewell to the President, and the carriages began their long procession to pick up their owners. Lizette and Stuart stood to one side on the walk waiting for Archie to bring their carriage around.

"Did you enjoy yourself?" Stuart asked Lizette as he gazed over at her, watching the flickering lantern light play across her face.

She looked up at him and smiled sadly. "Too much," she answered hesitantly, then frowned. "Stuart, Julia's going to be upset, isn't she?" she asked.

"I don't know. I imagine it all depends on the circumstances. If I tell her I escorted you rather than letting you attend with just anyone, because you had to talk to Mr. Hewitt . . ."

"In other words, the truth."

"That's right. If I tell her, I don't think she'll be too angry. But if she hears about our evening out from the viewpoint of someone else here tonight, I don't think she'll be too understanding."

"But we haven't done anything."

"Haven't we? Liz, for you, just coming here was the height of impropriety. You're supposed to be in mourning for a year, remember?"

"Well, Bain's been gone almost a year, did they figure that?

It'll be a year the end of this month since he sailed away on the *Dragonfly*. A year's a long time, Stuart.''

"I know. I guess that's why I can understand how you feel." He started to say something else, but was interrupted.

"Excuse me, Senator Kolter?"

He turned to see a young man in perhaps his mid-twenties, with sandy hair, his hat in his hand, and a pair of spectacles perched on his nose.

"Something I can do for you?" Stuart asked.

"I'm with a local newspaper," the young man said hurriedly. "I hope you'll forgive me, Senator," he went on. "But is it true the lady with you is the widow of your brother, the pirate known as Captain Gallant?"

Stuart's eyes hardened. "I'd rather not discuss it, if you don't mind," he said.

"I'm sorry, sir, I'm not being malicious," the young man apologized. "In fact, I'll agree my facts have come my way through rumor and what I've heard while mingling with the crowd leaving the ballroom, but I'm asking because I'm on Mrs. Kolter's side. If it's true she has a letter stating her husband's innocence, I think it should be brought to light. What better way to make the government sit up and take notice?"

Stuart started to protest again, but Lizette stopped him.

"No, wait, Stuart," she said anxiously. "He may be right. Maybe that's what we need."

"Our names in the paper?"

"No, someone to do a story about Bain. All the newspapers ever knew about him was what the government told them or what they already believed to be the truth. If we could make people aware that Bain was working for his country . . ." She studied the young man for a minute. "Would you print the truth?" she asked.

"Certainly, ma'am," he answered.

Stuart shook his head. "You're playing with fire, Liz," he said, but he could already see she'd made up her mind, and it was no surprise to him when she made arrangements for the young man to come to the house Monday afternoon for an interview.

"You really think that's going to help?" he asked when the young man left.

She took his arm as she saw Archie bringing the carriage around, and they began walking toward it.

"I'll try almost anything, short of sleeping with Sam Hewitt," she said softly, but a few minutes later, as their carriage rolled down the drive, neither was aware that behind them the young man she had set up the appointment with was in deep conversation with two men who had stepped out of the shadows and accosted him.

Monday afternoon Lizette paced the floor in the library and stopped occasionally to glance at the grandfather clock on the far wall, frowning. She had distinctly told the young man one o'clock, and it was one-forty-five already. She walked to the window and stared out, trying to take her mind off the fact that he wasn't here yet. She thought back to Saturday night.

Now that it was over, she suddenly wondered where she'd gotten the nerve to talk to Sam Hewitt as she had. She blushed. No wonder Stuart was embarrassed. Dear Stuart. What would she have done without him? But the poor man was beside himself, and she hoped she hadn't jeopardized his career too much by coming here.

Stuart! She stared out into the gardens for a long time, not really seeing them; she was seeing Stuart. Stuart and Bain! Where did one end and the other begin? Now that Bain was lost to her forever, was she going to do the same thing she had done before? God forbid! She wouldn't let it happen again, ever. She couldn't, and she turned from the window, shaking herself back to reality, remembering the polite way they'd said good-bye Saturday night, and again last night, when he'd left after having dinner with her. That's the way it was going to stay. She'd make certain of that, and she glanced at the clock again. Two o'clock, and the young man wasn't here yet. Well, she'd soon find out why.

Luckily she remembered the name of the newspaper the young man said he worked for, and forty-five minutes later she was walking into the newspaper office, the odor of wet ink filling her nostrils. But her trip was for nothing. Not only was the young man not there, but the man in the office said he'd been called out of town suddenly, and in answer to her question about setting up a new appointment, the man informed her the newspaper wasn't interested, after all, in any news of the late Bain Kolter.

"It isn't fair," she told Stuart later that evening as they strolled in the gardens at the back of the house. "I went to every newspaper in the city, and none of them are interested. Not one. I know someone must have gotten to them before I did, and they must have threatened that young man, Stuart," she exclaimed angrily. "How can they get away with that?"

"I told you, Liz." He shook his head. "What they don't want you to know, you'll never learn. Not here in the capital, anyway."

She frowned. "What do you mean?"

"That's why I came over tonight," he said as they reached the small gazebo at the end of the walk. "Shall we sit down?"

She sat down, tucking the skirt of her black silk dress close to her legs. "Go ahead," she urged him.

He sat beside her. It was not quite dark yet, and he could still see her face clearly, but deep shadows were moving into the gazebo quickly with the evening breeze.

"Remember I told you Jeff went to his wife's home in Baltimore to celebrate the fourth with her parents?" he asked.

She nodded.

"He arrived back late last evening with some surprising news." He looked pleased. "One of Bain's other ships, the *Raven*, was in Baltimore. Jeff knew the ship was Bain's and took a chance the crew might know something."

"And . . . ?"

"They didn't, but, Liz, think it over. If you owned three ships and suddenly decided to become a pirate, would you use only one of those ships, or would you use all three?" he asked.

She frowned. "I'd use all three."

"Exactly, but Bain didn't. The other two ships, the *Raven* and the *Sparrow*, have been doing exactly what they've been doing ever since the war's end, carrying trade goods between here and Europe."

"You mean the crews didn't know about Bain?" she asked.

"They knew about it, but Captain Wilcox of the *Raven* said they were told by Bain's office in Charleston to carry on as if nothing were wrong."

"That seems strange."

"That's what I thought, so I've sent Jeff to Charleston to see if there's anything the men there can tell him."

"That'll take weeks."

"It's better than letting you waste time trying to get information from the Navy Department."

"Don't you know anyone besides Hewitt who works there?" she asked.

"I know a lot of people who work there, but none of them would tell us anything. Besides, if he was on a secret mission, it's logical that few men in Washington know about it. It's done as a precaution.''

"I can't just sit here waiting for Jeff to get back.''

He straightened self-consciously. "I thought perhaps you'd let me show you the town,'' he said hopefully. "I know you've been here for almost two months, but I know there are things you haven't seen and places you'd like to go.''

She glanced at him abruptly, her mind running over his suggestion. "Do you think that's wise?''

"Why not? People are already talking, and you staying closed up at the house isn't going to make them stop. After all, you are my brother's wife.''

"Widow,'' she corrected. "There's a difference, Stuart, and Julia might not understand.''

"Julia will believe what I tell her, which will be the truth. She knew nothing of what happened before, Liz,'' he said. "There's no reason for her to even begin to suspect anything's wrong.''

"I don't want it to be wrong either, Stuart,'' she said, coming to grips with the situation. "What we did before . . . what I caused you to do . . . I could have hurt her so badly. I know what it's like to be a wife now, Stuart,'' she went on. "I know how I'd have felt if I discovered Bain hadn't been faithful to me after we were married.'' She shook her head. "I was young and foolish then, thinking I could take what I wanted without anyone getting hurt. Unfortunately, I hurt myself the most.''

"I'm sorry, Liz. I never wanted to hurt you, you know that.''

She reached out, taking his hand. "You didn't hurt me. You gave me love,'' she said. "I hurt myself, but now when I think of how Julia could have been hurt too . . . I can't let that happen again, Stuart,'' she said emotionally. "We have to stay friends, and only friends. Can we do it?''

"We can try.'' He held her hand, squeezing it affectionately. "If I get out of line, don't hesitate to tell me. Is it a bargain?''

She looked into his face, shadowed in the early twilight. She should say no, but every instinct inside her warred with her answer. Stuart was all she had to hang on to, even as a friend. She sighed.

"It's a bargain,'' she whispered softly, promising herself it was a bargain she couldn't afford not to keep.

"Good.'' He smiled. "Then tomorrow I'll pick you up about one and we'll start with the Senate Building, where I work.''

For the next two weeks Lizette almost forgot why she was in

Washington. During that time she received a letter from Grandma Dicia telling her how much the twins were growing, and a letter from her parents wanting to know if she had learned anything. She answered both promptly, but still didn't tell them she was staying at Stuart's town house, nor that Stuart was showing her the sights. Again, she was afraid Rand Kolter might find out and think she and Stuart had become lovers again.

As she finished the letters and got them ready to drop off at the post, she sat for a minute at the desk in Stuart's library, going over her reason for not wanting Rand to know she was seeing Stuart. Was her fear of Rand finding out the real reason, or was it that she almost felt as if they were lovers again?

She trembled at the thought. Bain was dead, and she missed him terribly. Was it possible she was doing it again? The brothers were so much alike, and she'd been having such a good time these past few days. They talked and laughed together, each often anticipating what the other would say. It was almost as it had been before between them. The only thing missing was the physical bond of lovemaking, and there were times when she wished they could share that too, yet knew to do so would court disaster, and she thought back to the nights she'd cried herself to sleep because of the loneliness and yearning need inside her.

She held the letters out in front of her and shook her head vigorously. No, that wasn't why she didn't tell anyone. It wasn't the same as being lovers, it was just the old guilt surfacing, trying to ruin her happiness. She was lonely, that was all, and when she cried herself to sleep, it was because she missed Bain, not because she couldn't have Stuart. She had been happy these past few days, and if it took Stuart to help her to adjust to Bain's death, then she'd borrow him for a while, as a friend. She left the library to go post the letters.

By the time Jeff returned from Charleston, Lizette was thoroughly acquainted with the city of Washington, including the buildings that had been restored since the war, and the new ones going up.

"I didn't learn too much," Jeff told them as they sat over a light luncheon at Stuart's place. "Bain did stop there, though, evidently after he left here last year, because the dates coincide. His instructions were that no matter what they might hear, or what might happen, they were to carry on as always." He looked over at Lizette while reaching for a biscuit. "Your father-in-law was there and gone already, over a month before me," he went on. "He told them to keep going on as they had been and that he was handling things for you, since you were the new owner but knew nothing about business."

"I guess I'll have to learn," she said. Jeff and Stuart exchanged quick glances. "Well, I can," she exclaimed. "I think a lot of women could, if the men would let them."

Stuart grinned. "Can you imagine what my brother was up against, Jeff?" he said.

Jeff studied Lizette for a minute, then nodded. "Aye, I can imagine," he said. "But I'll bet his life wasn't dull."

"Which reminds me," said Stuart. "Life wasn't dull around here either. We had an intruder the other evening. Liz and I went to the theater, and while we were out, somebody went through the whole house, tied up the servants . . . I think they were looking for Bain's letter."

"Did you report it?"

"Naturally, but the men were masked and nothing was missing. The authorities didn't do much."

Lizette was ready to add something, when they were suddenly interrupted by the housekeeper.

She was a thin woman in her mid-fifties, with gray hair pulled back severely into a bun and sharp features that reminded Lizette of one of her old teachers from boarding school. Only she liked Stuart's housekeeper; she hadn't liked her teacher.

"Excuse me, Senator," the housekeeper said, "but there's a man outside says he has to talk to you. It's about your brother and is extremely important."

All three exchanged glances. "Bring him in," Stuart said as he set his napkin on the table.

"What do you suppose he wants?" asked Jeff.

Stuart shrugged. "Who knows? But we'll soon find out," and he glanced toward the doorway.

The man the housekeeper was bringing in was plainly dressed, his frock coat of gray broadcloth, looking quite out of date with knee breeches that ended with buttons at the top of his dusty boots. In his hand he was clutching a gray felt hat.

Stuart stood up, greeted the man cordially, while shaking hands, then introduced him to Lizette and Jeff. Jeff also stood to shake the man's hand, then sat back down.

"Will you sit down, Mr. Glazer," Stuart asked, but the man declined. "All right, then, what is it you came about?" Stuart sat back down and waited for the man to talk.

"I'm not from Washington, Senator Kolter," the man began in a slow, easy drawl. "I live in Charlottesville." He paused nervously.

"What does that have to do with my brother?"

"Well, I got a brother what was a sailor on your brother's ship, the *Dragonfly*, during the war, but he was wounded during the Battle of New Orleans and couldn't sail no more. We was both originally from Pittsburgh, but since our parents is dead, instead of goin' to a home he didn't have no more, he come to live with me and the missus." He took a deep breath, but none of them interrupted, and he went on. "To make a long story short, my brother knows Captain Holley from the *Dragonfly* as well as he knows me, and he knows your brother lets him run the ship, even when he's aboard, though your brother can sail her as well as Holley. But what I'm gettin' at is, my brother said he saw Captain Holley in Charlottesville only a short time back and since all hands were supposed to have gone down with the ship, including your brother, he thought maybe you might like to know about it." He paused a second, glancing over to Lizette, then back to Stuart. "You see, since Charlottesville's the President's hometown, we keep up pretty well on the latest news, and one of our citizens was at the ball here over the Fourth and heard tell that you and your sister-in-law, meanin' you, Mrs. Kolter, that the two of you could use any information anybody had about the late Mr. Kolter because you think there was somethin' wrong, and that he wasn't no pirate."

Lizette was leaning forward, not missing a word, while both Jeff and Stuart's eyes were glued to the man.

"You came all the way from Charlottesville to tell me this?" Stuart asked.

Mr. Glazer nodded. "My brother's a stubborn cuss," he said. "He insisted right from the start that there was somethin' wrong. He kept tellin' me every time our local newspaper had any stories about your brother bein' a pirate. 'Tom,' he'd say. 'Tom, that man wouldn't no more turn pirate than I would.' That's why, when he saw Cap'n Holley, he told me if I didn't come tell you, he'd never speak to me agin."

Stuart wanted to believe the man. "When was the last time he saw Captain Holley?" he asked.

"That's just it," Mr. Glazer said, frowning. "He's seen him twice. Once some time back, then about two weeks ago."

"What was he doing?"

"Ridin' through town on a horse both times."

"Hmmm!" Stuart looked over to Jeff. "What do you make of it?"

"I think somebody should go to Charlottesville."

Stuart nodded. "Right."

"I'm going too," said Lizette, and they looked at her in surprise. "If you think I'm staying here, you're sadly mistaken," she told Stuart. "Bain was my husband and I have a right to go."

"Afraid I can't go," Jeff said quickly. "I do have a law practice to take care of, and I spent enough time in Charleston to throw me back a spell, but I sure as hell would like to go. Sounds like it might prove interesting."

Before the afternoon was over, all arrangements had been made. Mr. Glazer invited Lizette and the senator to accompany him back to Charlottesville, and Stuart graciously accepted, insisting, however, that he would pay for any overnight lodgings for the man, as well as reimbursing him for coming to Washington in the first place. Mr. Glazer wavered at first over accepting recompense for what his brother considered a duty, but eventually reconsidered. They would leave first thing in the morning, since it was some hundred miles to Charlottesville, and they'd ride horseback instead of taking a carriage, because there was no direct road to Charlottesville that could safely accommodate a carriage once they turned off the turnpike. The turnpike went straight through to Richmond.

Stuart insisted Mr. Glazer stay here at the house overnight rather than at an inn, then figured as long as he and Lizette wouldn't be alone in the house, he too would spend the night so they could get an early start. So later that afternoon he brought most of his things to the house from the Magees', and the next morning, as the sun streamed up over the capital, turning the buildings to a golden glow behind them, Lizette, Stuart, and Mr. Glazer, with two packhorses in tow, carrying Lizette and Stuart's few pieces of baggage, crossed the Potomac River into Virginia, headed for Charlottesville.

The trip took almost five days, but the weather was good, so no one complained. When they reached Charlottesville, Stuart acquired rooms for himself and Lizette at a small inn, where he hoped they'd be inconspicuous; then they joined Mr. Glazer and his family for dinner.

The Glazers were a quiet family, with four children, Mrs.

Glazer, her husband's brother, Charles, and Mr. Glazer sharing a small but neat home at the edge of town, where Mr. Glazer grew tobacco and a few other crops, as well as working at his trade of harnessmaker.

"That's where Charles comes in handy," he told Lizette and Stuart on their way out to his place. "We both know the trade, and since his leg's gone to above the knee where he can't walk, he does much of the leatherwork while I look after the fields."

Lizette liked Charles Glazer. Perhaps because he'd thought so much of Bain, but the man seemed honest, straightforward, and anxious to help any way he could. However, there wasn't too much more he could tell them that his brother hadn't already told them. Now it was a matter of trying to locate the man they'd come so far to see, and they returned to the inn that evening, determined the trip wouldn't be for nothing.

During the next few days, however, Stuart began to think perhaps the sailor had been wrong, because although they asked all over Charlottesville, not mentioning last names, using only descriptions, no one remembered seeing a man who looked like Captain Holley.

They had been in Charlottesville almost a week, and Stuart was about ready to give up, but Lizette was being stubborn.

"Just a few more days, Stuart," she begged. "We have to be sure."

They were sitting in the dining room of the inn where they were staying, enjoying a breakfast of honey, wheatcakes, and fresh fruit. The weather was extremely hot, and Lizette was dressed in a black gauze dress with short puff sleeves, a square neck, and black satin ribbons banding the high waist and trailing down the front of her skirt. Her dark curls were pinned atop her head on the sides, with a cascade of ringlets falling to the nape of her neck, and she was wearing small onyx earrings, but no other jewelry. Even with the thin material of her dress she was already uncomfortably warm, and she glanced across the table at Stuart, who, she imagined, was sweltering in a pale blue frock coat, which, although silk, was worn over a long-sleeved shirt, the matching cravat tied snugly beneath a ruffled shirt collar.

"So where do we go? Where do we look now?" he asked. "Liz, we've been all over."

"Please, Stuart?"

"All right. Maybe one more look around."

They finished eating, then began to wander about the small town. Lizette had put on her black silk bonnet before leaving the inn, and by late afternoon, with the heat from the sun beating down on them, perspiration began to trickle from the ties beneath her chin, as well as dampening her hair.

"Now, that's the sort of chapeau I should be wearing," she said as they reached a milliner's shop and she caught sight of one of the new style hats, directly from Paris. It was black gauze, the wide brim decorated along the edge with a delicate lace ruffle, and the crown surrounded with black satin roses. There was no tie beneath the chin, but a jeweled hatpin to keep it secured to the hair. "I'm beginning to abhor bonnets. Especially in this heat."

She turned to Stuart and was about ready to say something else about the hat when two young boys burst from the doorway of an ale house next to the milliner's shop, one of them bumping into Stuart.

" 'Scuse me, sir," the boy said hurriedly. "Didn't mean no harm. I didn't slop no ale on you, did I?"

Stuart glanced at the small bucket of ale in the boy's hand, then examined his clothes. "No harm done," he said.

"Oh, good. I'd hate to think I spoiled them fine clothes."

"Quit jawin', Luke," the other boy piped in. "Doc and the captain said they wanted the ale cold. You go spendin' all your time apologizin', and it's gonna be warm for sure by the time they gets it."

"It ain't neither," said the boy with the ale. "Besides, they's payin' me for gettin' it for 'em this time, not you."

"But you promised to share. That's why I said I'd help." The other boy was also carrying a small bucket of ale.

"I won't if you keep on naggin' me." The boy nodded his head to Lizette and Stuart. "Glad none got on you, sir," he went on as he started walking away. "Sorry I was so clumsy, but Robbie here was arguin' over who should go out the door first. Sorry, sir," and both boys began crossing the dusty road.

Stuart was frowning. He watched the boys start down the other side of the street; then suddenly, as Lizette started to turn back to the milliner's window again, he grabbed her about the waist and began ushering her away in the same direction the two boys were going.

"Stuart . . . ?"

"Just walk, but not too fast, and pretend we're casually talking," he said quickly.

She tripped on the hem of her dress and he caught her.

"This is ridiculous!" she exclaimed.

"One of those boys said they were getting ale for Doc and the captain," he explained quickly as he released her, watching her straightening her clothes. "I thought it might be wise to check."

She stared at him, the implication sinking in. "That's right, he did." She glanced down the street. The boys were no longer in sight. "Where did they go?"

"Around the corner. Come on," and this time when he took her arm, she hurried along beside him without complaining.

When they reached the corner, after dodging a number of people who stared at them curiously, they were just in time to see the boys round another corner farther down. Once more they hurried, trying to keep up, and this time Lizette held her skirt up so they could go even faster. They had been on the main street when the boys almost ran into Stuart; now they were on a side street that was almost deserted. There were a few children playing about, and some women on the way to market, but few other people.

They followed the boys for four more blocks, hurrying every time they disappeared around a corner, then slowing down so they wouldn't look obvious when the boys were in sight in case they happened to look back. But the boys didn't seem interested in whether someone might be following. They were more interested in stealing sips from the ale buckets now and then. Finally they disappeared into a building at the end of a street near the edge of town.

Lizette and Stuart stopped near the front of the building and stared up at the sign. There were three names on it. One name was "Michael Bastion, Doctor of Medicine."

"Doc?" Stuart said, and glanced at Lizette.

"Sounds logical."

Stuart reached for the doorknob. Again the two boys burst out of the doorway, this time hitting Stuart with the door.

"Hey, it's the gent from before," Robbie said.

Luke stared up at Stuart, then frowned. "Was you following us, mister?" he asked. "You said I didn't get no ale on you."

"You didn't," Stuart said. "But you did hit me with the door just now."

"Sorry, sir," Luke said quickly.

Stuart smiled. "It's all right. But there is something I'd like to know. The ale—did you buy it for Dr. Bastion?"

"How'd you know?" Luke asked.

"He's an old friend," Stuart lied. "I haven't seen him for a number of years. I didn't know he was still around. Is his office still the same place?"

"Yes, sir, on the right at the end of the hall."

Stuart thanked the boy, then opened the door, ushering Lizette inside. The boys watched for a few moments, then took off running back toward the main street of town—to spend their money, no doubt, thought Stuart.

The hallway was dark and untidy, the only light coming from a window at the end of the hall, plus another window in the door behind them. Stuart's hand was at Lizette's waist as he ushered her down the hallway to the last door.

"Ready?" he asked.

She took a deep breath, then nodded, and Stuart opened the door. A small bell above the door tinkled when they entered, and a voice called from the back.

"Office hours are over for the day! If it's an emergency, sit down and I'll be right there. If not, I'll hear the bell ring again."

Lizette glanced back over her shoulder to Stuart.

"It's an emergency," Stuart called out, and he and Lizette stood waiting.

Dr. Bastion was in his mid-forties. There was frost at his temples, with a bald head above the frosted fringe, and his dark eyes looked over the top of a pair of spectacles that sat on his freckled nose. He poked his head out the inner door first, then stepped out, eyeing Lizette and Stuart curiously. He studied them for a minute.

"I thought you said it was an emergency," he said.

"It is," answered Stuart. "We have to talk to your visitor."

"What visitor?"

Stuart had anticipated the man's answer. "The one drinking the other bucket of ale the boys brought," he said. "I know the captain's here, doctor," he went on. "Either you take me in there to see him or I'll go in on my own."

Dr. Bastion straightened belligerently. "You're mistaken, sir," he said. "There's no one in the other room."

"Doctor, I have to speak to the captain," Lizette insisted.

"And we don't want any trouble," added Stuart.

Michael Bastion's eyes narrowed. "What kind of trouble?"

"I happen to be Senator Kolter," Stuart explained curtly. "My brother Bain Kolter was accused of piracy and supposedly went down with his ship off the coast of Florida. If I'm not mistaken, the man in your office could possibly be a man who is supposed to have died with him. Now, either I meet him and see if he is the man I'm looking for, or I'll be forced to call the authorities. The decision's yours."

The door to the inner office suddenly opened. "You wanted me?" Captain Holley asked, and Lizette gasped as Dr. Bastion began to protest. "It's all right, Michael," the captain said. "I don't want to cause you trouble."

Lizette couldn't take her eyes off Captain Holley. It had been a chance, only a vague chance.

Stuart had met the captain only a few times, but there was no mistaking him. "You know why we're here, Holley?" he asked.

The captain nodded. "I know why you *think* you're here," he said. "But I'm afraid you're out of luck. I didn't sail with Bain when he became a pirate."

"You're lying," Lizette cut in. "You were with him when he left the Château, and you were with the ship when it went down."

"Mrs. Kolter, please," he insisted. "I don't know anything."

"Then why have you been hiding?" Stuart asked.

"I haven't."

"What do you call it?"

"I gave up sailing," Holley said. "That's all."

Stuart took a deep breath. "When did you leave the ship?"

"When I discovered what Bain had in mind. I didn't relish the thought of ending up at the end of a rope."

"How did you get here?"

"Really, Senator," Holley said. "I made him let me off the ship in St. Augustine, then took another ship north."

"And you just happened to end up in Charlottesville. Which happens to be the hometown of President James Monroe. How convenient." Things were finally beginning to make sense to Stuart. "You have been staying at Ash Lawn, right?"

Captain Holley's eyes grew wary. "What does it matter where I've been staying?"

"It matters a great deal. Am I right? You've been staying at Ash Lawn?"

"I'm working at Ash Lawn, yes."

"Since when?"

"Look, Senator, I happened to come here after I left Bain, and I just happen to have gotten a job at Ash Lawn. That's all there is to it."

"I see."

Lizette started to say something, but Stuart put a hand on her arm, stopping her. "It won't do any good, Liz," he said. "Like Bain, he's been told to keep his mouth shut."

"But he was Bain's friend."

"I'm sorry, Mrs. Kolter," Holley said. "I wish I was able to tell you more, but as I said, I wasn't with him."

Stuart knew there was no use pushing Holley further. He'd never change his story. "That's it, Liz," he said. "I'm afraid our stay in Charlottesville is over."

"He has to tell us!"

"He has. He's told us all he's going to tell us." Stuart took her arm. "We might as well go."

She stared at the captain, her eyes searching his face for some sign that he might be willing to change his mind. His mouth was set in a firm line, lips compressed tightly, and although his eyes held a spark of remorse, she knew Stuart was right.

"I'll never forgive you for this, Captain Holley," she said, her voice breaking, then let Stuart lead her from the room, the tiny bell tinkling softly behind them.

Dr. Bastion watched the couple leave, then turned to his newfound friend. He'd met the captain some months ago when he'd been called to Ash Lawn to treat him for a minor ailment. "You could have helped them, couldn't you?" he asked curiously.

Captain Holley's eyes were misty with tears as he stared at the closed door. "Not unless I wanted to jeopardize the lives of a lot of people, Michael," he said, then turned, starting back toward the inside office. "Now, let's get back to our ale."

There was nothing more to keep Lizette and Stuart in Charlottesville, so that evening they said good-bye to the Glazers and the next morning started back for Washington. This time it was just the two of them, each leading a packhorse. The road was dusty, as it had been earlier, but for some reason the dust and inconvenience had been easier for Lizette to take the first time. Perhaps because her spirits had been high in hopes of finding answers to all her questions. Now the heat made her uncomfortable, the constant riding made her weary, and by the time they found a place to spend the night, she was in a testy mood.

The place wasn't any too luxurious. From the looks of the taproom and the condition of the building, it might have been built before the revolution, and probably had. Although it was fairly clean, the rooms were small, the bedding worn, and she hoped to God there weren't any bugs. They had avoided this inn on the way down, but it had been getting too dark and Stuart wasn't sure how far they'd have to travel to reach another.

"Do you suppose someone in this despicable place could manage to heat some water and find me a tub?" Lizette asked Stuart as they headed for their rooms at the end of the long narrow upstairs hall.

"I'm sure they'll accommodate us," he answered, and they did, for a fee.

The tub they brought Lizette was a wooden one, the water not too hot, and the towels, although clean, were a dingy gray. And on top of everything else, she had to put her same riding habit back on after brushing the dust off, because it would be too much to unpack the small trunks the packhorses were carrying.

It was a black watered silk with a removable spencer of black velvet that she left in her room when they went downstairs to eat. She hoped it would be a little cooler. But the evening was as warm as the day had been, and her riding dress had long full sleeves and a high ruffled collar. The inn was crowded, the faint odor of sweaty bodies dulling her appetite, and she gladly welcomed Stuart's suggestion that they step outside after dinner.

She took his arm and let him lead her to a side door the owner said opened onto a walk that led to a small garden out back. She breathed deeply as she stepped outside, then choked, covering her nose quickly as she realized the walk led past a pigsty, barn, and privy first, before reaching the garden.

"I'm sorry, Liz," Stuart apologized as they hurried past the buildings in the darkness. "When he said garden, I never dreamed. . . ."

She chuckled, her hand still over her nose as they reached the end of the walk. Suddenly it all seemed so funny. "Your beautiful garden, Senator?" she said, gesturing toward an open area to their left, and now Stuart too saw the humor in it.

It was hard to make out at first because the moon hadn't quite cleared the trees yet, but the garden was only a few straggly flowers scattered here and there, neatly weeded, but almost dried up from lack of water, with a narrow gravel walk down the center and a wooden slab bench at the end of the walk.

"Shall we?" Stuart asked as they stared at the pathetic-looking garden. "At least it's away from the smells."

"Maybe we wouldn't have to stop at the bench," she said as she started down the path. "See there, beyond," and she pointed. "I'm sure that's a hay field, some trees, and what looks like a rail fence."

Lizette was right. She held his arm as they made their way across the field, dodging stacks of hay that had already been cut and bundled together; then she straightened, smelling clean air again as they reached the trees and fence. The moon was out full now, and Lizette sighed.

"I like this," she said softly. "For a minute it almost makes me forget."

Stuart stared at her. She was leaning back against the fence, her arms over the top rail, gazing up at the moon, and he inhaled sharply. "Liz, what happens now?" he asked, watching her closely.

"I don't know. I suppose I should give up and go back home. I miss the twins terribly, but I just can't." She looked over at him. It had been so hot Stuart hadn't bothered to put his frock coat back on after he'd cleaned up, and he had also left his shirt open, with no cravat at the throat. For a long time she'd been steeling herself from intimate moments like this, forcing herself to ignore the attraction he held for her, but it had been so hard because he always reminded her so much of Bain. Tonight, for some reason, it seemed even worse, and she felt a warm glow spread through her that she was unable to stifle. She untwined her arms from the fence. "Do you think it's wrong for me to stay, Stuart?" she asked, her voice strained.

His eyes softened. "For you or me?"

"That's not what I meant."

"Isn't it?" His voice deepened. "Are you sure?"

She avoided his eyes. "No, I guess I'm not sure, not really."

"I didn't think so." She was still leaning back against the split-rail fence and he put his hands out, his fingers tingling at the touch of her as he pulled her gently to him. "Liz, be honest with yourself," he whispered huskily. "These past weeks, it's almost like it used to be with us, and you know it."

"But it shouldn't be, don't you see. We don't have the right." She shook her head. "Stuart, it's all wrong."

"Wrong for me to love you?"

"Yes."

"Then tell my heart it's wrong," he whispered tenderly. "Liz, I've tried, Lord knows I've tried, but all the good intentions in the world can't change the way I feel about you. I love you, Liz, I always have."

"No. . . ."

"You can deny it all you want, but it won't change a thing."

She leaned her head forward, resting her forehead on his chest, not daring to look up at him. It wasn't fair. She missed Bain so terribly, and Stuart was so like him. If only Bain were alive, she could wait for him to ease the ache inside her. But Bain was gone, and with his death all promise of fulfillment vanished, leaving her empty and alone.

Stuart's arms felt good, the musky smell of him taunting her recklessly. She wanted to brush her lips against his bare chest and warm her soul with him as she once had. The memories were sweet, yet she was filled with pain because she knew it shouldn't be. She turned her head, resting her cheek against his chest, feeling the curling hairs against her flesh.

"Stuart, I can't do this to you, not again," she finally answered. "I can't let you be a substitute for what I had with Bain. It wouldn't be fair to you."

He inhaled, then reached down, cupping her chin in his hand, forcing her head up so there was no way she could avoid his eyes.

"You think I'd be a substitute?" he asked, and shook his head. "Liz, look at me, look hard." She was staring up at him, her green eyes heavy with passion. "I've never been a substitute for Bain with you, Liz, even then, and I think you know it. I don't deny he and I are all wrapped up together in your heart—I can understand that, and accept it. But when we made love, Liz, it was me you gave yourself to, not Bain, and that I know deep down inside. And it'll be me you give yourself to again, not Bain, you'll see," and with those words, his mouth covered hers, lightly at first, then deepening as he held her close against him.

Lizette was lost. His lips on hers brought a flood, like liquid fire invading every nerve in her body, spreading through her and over her until she moaned with rapture. Then, as the tip of his tongue danced lightly against her lips, they parted slowly, receiving him, letting him explore the sweet corners of her mouth. She wanted to crawl inside him and become a part of him. To feel the naked nearness of his body against her own, and know the exquisite rush of love she knew could be hers for the taking. Her arms twined about his neck, her body pressed to his, and for the first time in months she freed her emotions, letting them fill her and devour her body, her loins throbbing with desire.

Stuart's tongue withdrew slowly, then insistently his lips played at the corners of her mouth, trailing down her throat, and nibbling at her ear before returning to her mouth, and sipping at it again, as if he couldn't get enough of her.

"Liz, my lovely, Liz," he murmured breathlessly between kisses. "It's been so long."

Suddenly she drew back. Her arms had been about his neck. They dropped to his chest and she pushed herself from him, trembling.

"What . . . ?"

Her face was flushed, her voice unsteady. "No, Stuart, I can't!" she cried helplessly, and he stared at her.

His breathing was shallow, his chest heaving erratically. "Liz?"

"I can't do this to Julia, not again," she cried breathlessly. "She didn't find out the last time, but it was such a chance we took, and I can't take that chance again, Stuart. What if I got pregnant like before? There is no Bain to cover our mistake this time. This time there'd be no way out for us, no way at all." There were tears in her eyes and they rolled down her cheeks. "I know how I felt when I thought Bain was making love to someone else. It hurts so much, Stuart, and nearly tore me up inside. I can't take the chance of doing that to Julia. If she found out, I'd die inside. For all of her indifference, she does love you."

The glazed passion veiling his eyes slowly lifted, and he gazed down at her, his body trembling. "God help me, I don't know if I can let you go again, Liz," he groaned.

She touched his face, her hand warm above the clipped beard, then let her fingers touch his lips. "Stuart, we have to use our heads," she whispered tearfully. "It'd be such a joy to let you take me—make no mistake about that—and right now I could so easily give in because it's been so long. But we don't dare. As long as Julia's there between us . . . Stuart, I can't be that selfish, not anymore."

"What will you do? You can't deny yourself forever."

"I'll find someone else who's free."

"While I watch from afar?" He took her face between his hands, his eyes searching hers. "I can't do it, Liz," he whispered passionately. "There's no way I can pretend you don't exist."

"Then don't," she whispered tremulously. "Tonight, Stuart, I feel alive again for the first time in months." She put her hands on his, where he held her face. "And all because of you, I won't deny that. And knowing that you care means so much. All I ask is that you don't demand more from me than I can give, or tempt me beyond my bounds of self-control. If it gets too rough and you can't stay away, then come to me, I won't deny you, but don't expect what we had before . . . I just can't, it's too risky for us both."

He sighed, his hands sliding down her body, and he held her close. "Do you know how hard that's going to be?" he whispered softly.

She inhaled. "Not as hard as never seeing you again."

He shook his head. "Oh, God, don't say that, Liz," he whispered softly, and held her tight, hoping this would be enough. And later that evening, while Lizette cried herself to sleep in her lonely room, Stuart stared at the ceiling in his room, awake half the night, wondering if he was strong enough to face the days ahead, yet knowing that for her sake, he had to.

24

Breezes drifting onto the veranda of the rambling two-story frame house were hot, but with the humidity high, they cooled Bain's forehead as he lay on the lounge. He stared at the blue sky, streaked with a few wispy clouds, and frowned, trying to will his brain to remember. Some things came easily, others didn't come at all, and he'd been accosted every day by a hazy mass of memories that tried to find substance, but more often than not were as elusive as the winds that had been blowing the night they'd found him.

He glanced over across the veranda to where Elena was arranging flowers in a small vase. Elena with her dark hair and dark eyes, always hovering close by. She was a lovely young woman, her tawny flesh reminding him of someone, but who?

"It was a dark stormy night when we found you," she had

told him in Spanish when he had finally been able to hold a tight grip on reality.

His legs had been injured, his chest penetrated by a sharp chunk of wood, he'd swallowed a great deal of water, and to their surprise he was on the back of a sleek black horse. They had found the horse wandering down the road with him tied to its back by the reins. Part of it he could remember. What he couldn't remember was how he got there, where he came from, or who he was. The only name he could remember was Domino. No last name, just Domino. So that's what they called him.

He stretched, feeling the pull of his muscles, then sat up a little straighter on the lounge.

"Ah, I see you woke from your nap," Elena said in Spanish as she walked over.

He answered her back in Spanish. "How long was I asleep?"

Her dark eyes sparkled. "Not long enough. You need all the rest you can get."

He watched her set the vase of flowers on the stand beside the lounge. Elena de Córdoba was perhaps twenty, not beautiful, but with a hauntingly unusual face characterized by an aquiline nose and broad mouth, her full lips rather sensuous. Although she wasn't too tall, the skirt of her red silk dress hid long graceful legs below wide hips, and above her tiny waist her small bosom was almost lost in the tucks and folds of the low-cut bodice. Her hair, waist-length when hanging loose, was twisted and pinned at the nape of her neck and held on the side by jeweled tortoiseshell combs.

She and her family had been nursing him for months now, and he knew it was getting closer to the day he'd be able to walk without needing the canes her father had had one of the servants make for him. He was thankful for their help, but embarrassed by it. Especially since he had no idea where he might go once he was well.

"You had a bad dream, Domino?" she asked.

He nodded. "The usual demons and such."

"Perhaps one day they will bring back your memory."

"Perhaps."

"And maybe there will be a lady in it?"

"If there is?"

"I shall hate her!"

"Why?"

"Because she would have you." She blushed. "I shouldn't say such things, I know, but I can't help feeling them."

"I'm sorry, Elena." He took her hand. "I like you very much. There are times . . . your dark hair, lovely skin . . . I feel strange inside, as if it should mean something to me, then suddenly it's gone."

She squeezed his hand, her dark eyes searching his. "Perhaps someday they will mean something," she said softly. "In the meantime, I thought you might like to know, we're having visitors for a few days."

"Anyone you think I might know?"

"I doubt it. It's a friend of my father's from St. Augustine. He usually comes every year at this time for a visit, just to keep in touch. I think at one time he was quite smitten with Tía Isabella," she explained. "But his family had already betrothed him to his present wife." She released Bain's hand and returned to the vase, fussing with a couple of the flowers. "His name is Don Hernando de Vaca."

"You're right, I don't think I know him."

She smiled. "You're teasing, but come." She handed him the canes that were resting against the table. "It's time to exercise the legs."

He took a deep breath, swinging his legs to the floor, then stood up, using the canes for support. The wound in his shoulder had healed quickly, leaving only a scar; his legs had not fared as well. Although badly bruised, they hadn't seemed to be broken, but the muscles were severely injured and every day Elena or her aunt, Tía Isabella, would force him to walk to the beach and back, at least three or four times. Then every morning and every evening, Elena's thirteen-year-old brother, Mario, would also exercise Bain's legs by lifting them and manipulating them. Elena's father, Luis de Córdoba, said he had once known of a cripple who was helped in such a manner, and it was working. Each day Bain felt his legs getting a little stronger.

He followed Elena from the veranda, down the flagstone walk, placing the canes carefully, his walk clumsy but improving. When they reached the beach, she let him put the canes aside, kick off the sandals he was wearing, roll his breeches up past his knees, and lie with his legs in the water, letting the waves lap against them.

He had discovered, after coming to in a bed in one of Don Luis's guest rooms, that the hacienda was built on a long strip of land almost like an island, near the western tip of Florida just west of the keys, with mangrove swamps between them and the mainland. The land had been given to Don Luis years before by the Spanish government at the request of the king for favors granted. Since Don Luis was the youngest son of a baron, with no hope of ever gaining the title, he accepted the grant and moved his family here, where he built his hacienda, which he called Barlovento, meaning windward, living off money sent from abroad and enjoying the life of a wealthy landowner.

"There are not many who can boast of owning what is almost an island," he told Bain when Bain was well enough to listen. "I enjoy it here, and the land seems to enjoy our presence, for it's been good to us."

Bain lay on the beach now, staring off toward the horizon, the feel of the warm ocean water pleasant as it caressed his legs.

"You look worried," Elena called to him. She was sitting on a piece of driftwood a few feet from him, in the shade of a tree.

"I was wondering," he said, squinting in the sun. "Don't you ever leave Barlovento? I've been here somewhere near five months already, and so have you."

"If I wanted, I'd leave," she replied. "But where would I go? I've been to the mainland. It's not that much different than here, except there are more people."

"You aren't curious about the world?"

"I'm curious about you, Domino," she answered. "You have the look of a countryman, you speak our language, yet your eyes say you are not Spanish. No Spaniard has eyes as gray as yours. Where are you from, why were you tied to a horse that was walking down the road in such an isolated place, and how did you get hurt?"

"I too am curious about me," he said frankly. "Perhaps someday we'll have the answer."

She frowned. "I am almost frightened of it."

He stared at her. The sun was so bright it was hard to see her in the shadows, but he knew she was watching him closely. She wanted him to love her. He had known this for a long time. From the very start he had felt her turn toward him, and had tried to discourage it, although he didn't know why. There was something excitingly alive about her. She walked with a catlike grace and her smile was quite alarming, but try as he might, to feel anything other than a physical attraction for her was impossible.

If he left tomorrow, he knew he could easily say good-bye and not look back. There had to be a reason.

"We said we wouldn't talk of it," he warned her.

The frown faded. "Then we shall talk of other things," and she told him all she could about their expected guests.

The arrival of Don Hernando de Vaca, Señora Consuelo de Vaca, and their entourage was a disrupting influence at Barlovento. Since there was no way to build a road through the swamps, anyone coming to and from Barlovento had to come by sea, and with rocks on the eastern shore making it unsafe for any ship to approach, the ship bringing the de Vacas was to anchor off the western shore, opposite the hacienda, and they'd be rowed to the beach in longboats.

Bain sat on the veranda the next afternoon and watched the visitors arrive. No wonder they came only once a year. Even once a year looked like too often, what with the trunks and hatboxes and complaints from Señora de Vaca as she was carried from the longboat and set ashore. Her shrill voice was easily heard up at the house when they set her on her feet in the sand, complaining how hard it was to walk in, then screaming at her personal maid for not being more attentive, and yelling at one of the sailors who almost dropped a small chest as he lifted it from the boat.

Señora de Vaca was in her mid-forties, her dark hair streaked with gray, her dark eyes set a little too far apart to be attractive, and her nose slightly blunt on the end, with a small mouth that was often pursed tightly in disapproval. Her husband was quite different. He was a striking man of extraordinary height, with graying hair that waved and curled to his collar, and a set of broad shoulders that surprised Bain with their strength, for Don Hernando de Vaca was lean, not brawny, his face handsome for a man of his years. He seemed to be an easygoing man who paid little attention to his wife's complaints, merely smiling at her and saying, "Yes, dear," then doing as he pleased. His nose was a little large and classic, with a slight bend to it, but it fitted perfectly with his heavy mustache and warm smile, and he treated the manservant who followed him ashore with a gentle respect.

He seemed such an opposite to Luis de Córdoba, who was short and heavyset with a round face he kept clean-shaven, and a volatile temper that often got him in trouble with his daughter and widowed sister, who had come to be hostess at her brother's house some years before. Tía Isabella was much like her brother, only not quite as plump, and her dark hair was prematurely gray. Her face too was round, but huge dimples dented her cheeks, and her dark eyes were always filled with warmth and interest.

She was sitting on the vernada now with Bain, and they watched Mario run down to help his father and Elena greet his old friend.

"You're not going to meet them?" Bain asked her.

She shook her head. "I dislike walking on the sand too, Señor Domino," she said, then he remembered Elena telling him about her aunt and their guest, and he understood as he saw her eyes settle on the tall man who was already heading up the flagstone walk toward the house.

When the visitors reached the veranda, the greetings were enthusiastic; then Luis introduced them to Bain, explaining in the brief introduction that Bain had been ill.

"Domino?" Don Hernando questioned as he leaned over, shaking Bain's hand. "No family name?"

"None I'm aware of, señor," Bain answered. "I'm afraid the accident that incapacitated me has also left me with a rather skimpy memory of the past."

Señor de Vaca frowned, seriously concerned. "I'm sorry, Señor Domino," he said thoughtfully, then turned to his friend. "But, Luis, I have such news. When was the last you were near a city?" he asked.

Luis shrugged. "Who knows? I go so little."

"And the boats passing haven't stopped to tell you?"

"Tell me what?"

"The United States has made a pact with our country." He put a hand on Luis's shoulder. "You are no longer a Spaniard, my friend, but an American now."

Luis's mouth fell. "You are fooling this old man, Hernando," he said.

Hernando shook his head. "Why do you think I left St. Augustine? I am too much the Spaniard to stay." His mouth became grim. "The Spanish minister, Señor Onis, has finally come up with boundaries both countries agreed on, and as of February the Florida territories belong to the United States."

"February? That was months ago."

"*Sí.* It's taken me all this while to get my affairs in order."

"You're really leaving?" Luis shook his head in disbelief. "But you have lived here for years. Your children were born here."

"I know." Hernando nodded. "But my children are back in Spain now." He took a deep breath. "I would like you to go back with me, old friend," he suggested as he glanced over, watching the man carry the last of the trunks into the house.

"Leave here?" Luis glanced at Elena. She looked fearful. "What would I do back in Barcelona?" he asked, and saw relief in her eyes. "No, my friend, I've been here too long. I'll stay."

"There's talk some of the grants won't be honored."

"There're always rumors. But come, before we get too engrossed in talk, you both must be tired." He gestured toward the house.

Tía Isabella stood up and led the way inside, with Consuelo and Hernando close behind, followed by Luis and Mario.

Bain studied Elena closely. "You had no idea Florida had changed hands?" he asked.

"How would we know?" She walked over and handed him his canes. "We see no one month after month."

He stood up. "The beach again?" he asked.

"Guests or no guests, your legs have to heal." She was wearing a dress of gold silk with ruffles along the bottom and gold lace ruffles decorating the bodice. "We'll go take a look at the ship that brought them. It won't be here long," she said.

"How will they get to Spain?"

"The ship will go on to New Orleans, then stop on its way back to pick them up again."

They started down the flagstone walk. Suddenly Bain stopped, staring at the sailors rowing the longboat back to the ship, anchored some three to four hundred feet offshore. He scowled, squinting. There was something familiar about the scene that jogged his memory, and for a moment he could see another ship, only it was dark and he was leading Amigo.

"Amigo," he whispered absentmindedly.

Elena looked over at him. "Yes?"

"The horse I was tied to. His name is Amigo," he answered incredulously.

Her eyes widened. "You're sure?"

"I'm positive." He straightened, his eyes glued to the ship. "It was dark, there were men in the longboat, and everything was blowing up."

"You were hurt?" she asked.

He shook his head. "No . . . I remember sailing . . ." He closed his eyes, then opened them again slowly and continued making his way to the beach, where he stood in the sand staring out to sea. "If only more would come," he said helplessly.

They watched the longboat reach the ship and the men start climbing aboard.

"Nothing more?" she asked.

"Nothing more." He straightened, and put all of his weight on his legs, lifting the canes from the sand. For a second they were wobbly; then with difficulty he managed to stand erect and steady. "There! Now to walk," he said, determined.

She touched his arm. "Not yet, you're not ready."

"When will I be?" He looked down at her. "I may not do too well at first, but I have to start sometime. I have to see if I can."

"And if you can't?"

"I'll let you pick me up."

Her hand dropped from his arm, and she stepped back, watching him closely. For a minute he just stood there; then he threw his canes aside and straightened stubbornly. The afternoon sun shone on his hair, deepening the russet highlights, and beads of perspiration stood out on his forehead, then ran down into his clipped beard. His mouth twisted anxiously and he licked his lips; then, summoning all his strength, he lifted his right foot, dragged it forward in the sand, and exhaled. A few seconds later, his left foot followed.

It was awkward at first, and painful, but with each step it became a little easier.

He reached the edge of the water and stopped. "Elena!" he called.

She was at his side in seconds. "I'm here."

He put an arm around her shoulder and hugged her to him. "Help me back to the house."

"But your canes?"

"I won't need them anymore."

Her arm went about his waist and she helped him slowly turn. His decision hadn't been an easy one because his legs were still weak, but somehow he knew the canes were becoming too much of a crutch to depend on. If he expected his legs to get strong again, they had to do it on their own. With each step, he became more determined, and by the time they were halfway up the flagstone walk, he was leaning on her less and less, and the slow, tiring shuffle had become a steady, stumbling gait.

"Shall we show Father?" she asked when they reached the veranda.

"Why not?" he answered cheerfully, and let her lead him into the house.

The next morning when Bain woke in the downstairs guest room, it was barely dawn. He started to move, then flinched. The muscles in his legs were sore. He gritted his teeth and moved anyway, throwing back the sheet that covered him, then forced his right leg off the bed, pulling it up, bending it to his chest.

"Mmm . . ." It hurt, but the leg had moved of its own volition. He lowered it slowly, then repeated the process with the other leg. For some minutes he kept at it, then suddenly stopped, staring at the ceiling.

"Amigo," he whispered softly, remembering his revelation of the night before, then sat up in bed, anxiously calling for Paco, the houseboy, or Rosa, the housekeeper. Anyone close enough to hear.

"Something you want?" Mario asked as he stuck his head in the door.

He might have known. Mario was usually the only one around this early. "My boots," Bain said anxiously. "Where are they?"

"You can't wear your boots, Señor Domino," the young boy said as his dark eyes studied Bain, who was pulling his breeches on as he sat on the edge of the bed.

"You find them, I'll put them on," Bain said, and Mario shook his head of curly black hair.

"You are stubborn, señor. One day you walk, now you think you can wear boots."

"Mario, the boots," Bain insisted, and Mario laughed as he left the room, but some five minutes later came back with a pair of black top boots. Even though they'd been shined, there were creases of wear in them. They were a little tight at first, but soon felt comfortable, and Mario watched Bain intently as Bain stood up and tested them.

"Now what do you do, señor?" he asked.

Bain glanced over at the lively young man with the ready grin and flashing dark eyes. He too looked like he was ready for riding.

"I let you lead me down to the stables," he answered.

Mario eyed him curiously. "You intend to ride?"

"Why not?"

"You can barely walk."

"All the more reason to ride." Bain frowned. "My horse is still here, isn't he?"

"*Sí.*"

"Then I'll ride him."

Mario shrugged. "It's your neck, señor. Come," and he walked over, letting Bain lean on him, although the support wasn't as necessary as Bain had thought. The stables were only a short distance from the house, and once there, Bain waited while Mario saddled Amigo, then saddled a horse for himself and helped Bain onto Amigo's back.

"You're going with me?" Bain asked.

Mario nodded. "I'd better. If you got into trouble, Father'd skin me alive."

Bain patted Amigo's sleek neck, the familiar feel of the horse comfortable beneath him, and Amigo, after nickering loudly at the sight of his master after all these months, threw up his head and whinnied, pleased at the touch of familiar hands, while Bain sat on his back stroking him. If only Bain had thought of the horse before this, it might have helped him. But it wasn't until the flash of memory had alerted him that he realized the horse wasn't just any horse, but a significant part of his life.

"What did you call him?" Mario asked as they rode from the stables onto a gravel path that led toward the back of the horse. They headed into the sun as it broke through the early-morning mists rolling in from the swamps.

"His name's Amigo," Bain answered. "But don't ask me how I know."

Mario watched Domino out of the corner of his eyes. He was remembering. Was that good or bad? It would require watching.

The path they were following moved inland farther, toward groves of trees that edged the swamps, and Bain reined Amigo away, heading out across a field toward the far end of the spit of land. He felt little like tangling with mangroves and alligators this early in the morning. Flowers were abundant everywhere, and as they neared the road that traversed the island, colorful birds played noisily in the trees. Bain reined in abruptly and stared ahead of him at the road where it crossed over the field, heading southward. It was lined with huge trees hung heavy with Spanish moss.

"The Château," he whispered softly in English.

Mario's ears perked up. "*Qué?*"

"The Château! My wife's grandmother lives at the Château." Bain's eyes widened. "Oh, my God!"

"Domino?"

"No, Bain!" he yelled, still in English. "Not Domino, Mario, Bain." Then suddenly, as quickly as he remembered, a warning deep inside closed his lips, and he stared for a minute without uttering a sound. He knew who he was, and in a flood of recognition, one memory piling on top of another, Bain suddenly saw the whole thing laid out before him. He was Bain Kolter, Captain Gallant, pirate, secret agent, father, and husband. He closed his eyes and Elena's face floated before him. At least for a moment he thought it was Elena. But no . . . The skin was the same tawny velvet, the hair dark as ebony, but the eyes were like fiery emeralds, the hair a mass of tight curls, the nose small and tapered, lips full and rich, and he knew now why he could never love Elena. Lizette was his life, his love, and he wanted to cry out for the pain that coursed through him at the thought of her.

It was frightening and overwhelming all at the same time, and Bain shuddered.

"Domino, are you all right?" Mario asked again.

This time Bain didn't correct him. For the moment it was better the boy believed him to be an injured Spaniard.

Bain nudged his horse in the ribs as he reined him about. "I think we'd better go back to the house, Mario," he said thoughtfully, in Spanish this time. "I don't want to overdo it," and he was conscious all the way back to the stables of Mario staring at him curiously, probably wondering why he had suddenly cut his ride short and why he had been shouting in English.

The household was abuzz with activity by the time they returned, and although Elena was upset at first that he'd been riding, she soon agreed that perhaps it would help, so much so that every morning she began to accompany him on his ride, using the excuse that she had to get away from the de Vacas.

"Don Hernando is a jewel," she said one morning about a week after their arrival. "But if I hear Doña Consuelo scream at her girl one more time, I think I shall scream myself."

She and Bain were riding along the tree-lined road, the smell of the swamps some distance to the left, mingling with the fresh salt air from the sea. Elena watched him closely as they rode along. There had been a distinct change in him lately, and she tried to remember when she'd first noticed it. The day the de Vacas arrived? It seemed to have started then. Before, he had seemed indifferent as far as recovering was concerned, and took little interest in the things around him. Occasionally there were

moments he'd remember, but what he remembered never seemed
to excite him or make a difference in his life, until the day the de
Vacas arrived. Now, suddenly, the past few days, it was as if he
couldn't exercise enough. As if life held meaning for him again.

"I thought you liked the de Vacas," he challenged.

She smiled. "Like most people, I appreciate Señor de Vaca
much more than his wife." Her smile faded wistfully. "Wouldn't
it have been marvelous if he and Tía Isabella could have married?
What a pair they would have made." She sighed. "Even after all
these years, I think they are still very much in love. He can't
fool me. He uses my father's friendship as an excuse to see her.
I saw them in the garden the other evening, then the other day I
happened to overhear them talking outside the parlor window.
I'm only glad his wife was still taking her siesta upstairs."

"Eavesdropping, Elena?" He laughed. "Shame on you!"

She eyed him, smiling mischievously. "I guess you haven't
kept me busy enough," she said playfully. "I have to find
excitement somewhere," and she spurred her horse faster, putting him into a loping gallop, and Bain watched her leaving him
behind for a minute before spurring Amigo to catch up.

By this time they had reached the end of the road, where it led
down to a grove of trees and a small beach with jagged rocks
jutting out of the water beyond it. The spit of land Barlovento
was built on was somewhere near ten miles long and about three
or four miles wide, and today was the first day Bain had ridden
to the end of the road. They maneuvered their horses through the
grove of trees and onto the small beach, then dismounted, and
Bain stared transfixed at the rocks in the water, where he now
knew the *Dragonfly* had met her fate.

"Why didn't you tell me, Domino?" Elena suddenly asked
from close behind him.

He shoved the memories aside, turned, and looked down at
her. "Tell you what?"

"That your memory's come back."

He stared into her brown eyes. She was wearing a brilliant
blue riding dress and matching plumed hat that clashed with her
dark hair and made her eyes all the darker. They looked stormy
and troubled.

"What makes you think that?" he asked.

"You." She frowned. "You've changed, Domino."

"Changed? Because I can almost walk without stumbling?"

"Because you're reluctant when I hold your hand, and your eyes don't talk to me anymore."

"Don't be ridiculous, Elena. You're imagining things."

"No, I know." She shook her head unhappily. "I said I would hate her, and I do, but I knew someday it might come."

"Elena, please, you're wrong."

"Don't lie to me," she said angrily. "Please, I'm not a child . . . I'm a woman, and a woman knows when a man's heart is somewhere else. Why do you think Señora de Vaca is such a shrew?"

He stared at her, puzzling over what to do. By now Captain Holley would have given Lafitte's ledgers to the President—that is, if he and the rest of the crew had been rescued—and there should be no need for his silence. But what if things hadn't gone right? What if Captain Holley hadn't reached the President, or if he had, what if the ledgers weren't enough and Monroe still had to play cat and mouse with Lafitte? Don Hernando had mentioned some men being hung in New Orleans on piracy charges recently. Had the ledgers helped in their conviction? If only he knew what was going on in the outside world. Barlovento was so isolated.

"Elena . . . what can I tell you?"

"The truth," she answered. "All I want is the truth, Domino. I may not like it, but I can live with it." She reached out. His shirt was open at the throat and she touched the front of it, then rested her hands on his chest. "Who is she, Domino?" she asked softly.

He inhaled, then sighed. "My wife. Her name's Lizette."

"French?"

"No, a mixture of French, English, and Indian. By now she thinks I'm dead."

"You love her?"

"With all my heart."

"There are children?"

"Twins."

She nodded. "Yes, you would have twins. When you do things, you do them right." She reached up, touching his face. "I was hoping . . ."

"I'm sorry."

Her hand dropped, resting over where she knew the scar was on his right shoulder. "When will you leave?"

"I don't know."

"The ship returns for the de Vacas in a few days."

"I know."

"You'll be on it?"

"And go to Spain?"

"I'm sure they'd drop you somewhere along the coast so you could catch another ship for home."

"I doubt it. They'd have to go too far up the coast, it'd be out of their way."

"I hope so," she said. "Then you'll have to stay all the longer."

"I can't stay forever."

"You may have to, once the de Vacas leave. Another ship isn't expected for months."

He turned, gazing back out to sea, to the rocks and the horizon beyond. "Elena, I couldn't go with the de Vacas, even if I wanted," he said, making a quick decision.

"Why?"

He turned back, looking deep into her eyes. "I can trust you?"

"With your life."

"That's what I'm doing." He had no other choice. "Elena, I'm a wanted man," he confessed reluctantly. "I'm wanted for piracy by the British, the Spanish, and the Americans. I don't dare leave here on a Spanish ship or any other kind of ship. All I'd need is for one person to recognize me and I'd hang from the nearest yardarm, like those pirates Don Hernando was talking about in New Orleans."

She was staring at him in surprise. "You? A pirate?"

"For all purposes, yes."

She laughed, a low throaty laugh filled with warmth, and the knowledge of something she knew, that he didn't. "And all the time we were being so careful," she said. "So you wouldn't get suspicious."

"Suspicious?"

"*Sí*, Mario swore you were a government agent sent to spy on us, and Father was sure you were a nobleman heading for the courts in Mexico."

"What does that have to do with me being suspicious?" he asked. "Suspicious of what?"

She studied him for a long moment. "Now I must trust you with *my* life," she said. "Remember when Father told you he lives off the moneys from back home?"

"Yes."

"They aren't enough to live on, Domino," she said. "In fact, there are times when no moneys ever come." She blushed, embarrassed at having him know. "We live partly off the salvage of ships like the one you must have been on. Only your ship was a puzzle to us. We never found any cargo, and no survivors except you."

He had suspected something was going on, yet they all seemed so far removed from the cutthroats that usually preyed on the coastal shores. "If there had been more survivors . . . ?" he asked.

"Each man has his price at the slave markets in the Caribbean," she answered matter-of-factly.

And he'd been worried about telling her. "But I've seen no ships come or go." He was puzzled.

"We have a few small boats at the edge of the swamps, and there is one ship, but she doesn't land here. There's a cove up the coast that can be reached by a trail through the swamps. It's a two-day journey, but worth it. The sailors come down here whenever the ship comes in, take what we have, carry on a few other transactions, then return to the cove."

"Why don't they just anchor off the shore like the de Vacas' ship did?"

"Too much chance to be seen." Her flush deepened. "Father would be mortified if anyone found out. You see, the men he deals with are wanted men, as you are, and unfortunately, one is my brother."

"An older brother?"

"*Sí*, he's about your age. The ship is his. It was originally outfitted as a privateer by a group of insurgents, but when he realized they were letting him do all the work and taking the rewards themselves, he decided the balance of power was in the wrong hands and took the ship over for himself."

"The name of your brother's ship?" Bain asked warily.

"*La Piranha*," she answered. "You've heard of it?"

He'd heard of the ship, all right. Who hadn't? Sancho de Córdoba. He should have put two and two together. Emilio Sancho de Córdoba, or Sancho el Sangriento, Sancho the Bloody, as he was often called by those who had come in contact with him, was one of the few men who refused to tie in with the Lafittes, preferring to trade in the Caribbean and the Tortugas. He not only hated Frenchmen, but was known to be even crueler if confronted with men of the nobility, whether French, English, or Spanish. His cruelty was known far and wide. Bain wasn't sure whether he was pleased by this new turn of events or not. He was glad the man wasn't one of Lafitte's cohorts—but did he have to be one of the most savage pirates on the seas?

"Yes, I've heard of your brother," he said after a few thoughtful moments. He stared at her hard. "All this is financed by your brother's piracy?"

She frowned. "At first Father was so against it. But when the money from Spain began to dwindle . . . we had to live." Her eyes faltered self-consciously. "Besides, I don't think he could ever disown Sancho. My brother is a delight to Father, in spite of his profession."

"He comes often?"

"Once or twice a month. Many times we have nothing for him except supplies for the ship, but he always shares with us."

"When is he due again?"

Her eyes darkened. "I'm telling you so much," she said. "And you've told me so little." She straightend, watching him closely. "I'm still calling you Domino."

"My name's Bain Kolter," he answered.

"Where are you from?"

"The Carolinas. At least that's where my family is."

"Your wife knows of your piracy?"

"If you don't mind, that's one subject I'd rather not discuss," he said, hoping she'd go along with him. "I'm afraid I'm going to have a great deal of explaining to do to Lizette."

"She doesn't approve?"

"We've never discussed it . . . but tell me," he said, changing the subject, "how did you know my memory had come back?"

"A number of things. For one, Mario said you were yelling something in what he thought was English the other day. Then, there's the way you've been acting."

"It's so different?"

"It's as if you have a purpose now."

"I do."

"Your wife?"

"Among other things."

Elena tried to reconcile herself to the fact that he was married. It was so hard.

"You say you're a pirate?" She frowned. "Mario was so sure you were a special agent sent here to spy on us."

"Why would he think that?"

"Because there was no sign of you having been on any ship. Usually we can hear the ships breaking up, but the storm was exceptionally bad that night. Father and I told him anything left afloat was probably swept out to sea, but he's been worried ever since you've been here."

"What of your brother Sancho? Did he know I was here?"

"He knew."

"And did nothing about it?"

"You had been here almost a month by the time he learned of it. By then . . ." She flushed. "I'm afraid I'd already become attached to you. We had no idea who you were, but since you had no memories anyway, I made him promise not to do anything, on the chance that things would turn out all right. After all, I meet so few men here."

"You made him?"

"Why should that surprise you? Sancho would do anything for me."

Bain chuckled. "Do you know what they call your brother in the outside world?" he asked incredulously.

"No."

"Sancho the Bloody."

"They couldn't."

"He's a pirate, Elena."

"So are you."

"I, my dear, was known as Captain Gallant."

"You never killed anyone?"

"I didn't say that. But what I do say is that if you told anyone else you made Sancho de Córdoba do something, they'd think you were insane. Nobody makes him do anything he doesn't want to do."

"You make him sound terrible."

"Let's just say he isn't a man I'm anxious to meet."

"Under the circumstances, you don't have much choice, do you?"

"I guess I don't. So what do you do, Elena?" His eyes bored into hers. "Keep me a prisoner on your island, or talk your brother into taking me home?"

Tears welled up in her eyes. "You can't go!"

"I have to."

She reached up, touching the side of his face, her hand caressing his short beard, then dropping to stroke his neck sensuously. "Why?" she pleaded. "Your wife thinks you're dead, you said so yourself. Let her go on thinking it. We could be so happy here, you and I. Father's getting old, and until Mario's big enough, he'll need someone to look after things. No one would ever have to know who you really are, not even Sancho."

"You have it all thought out, haven't you?"

"I love you!"

"Then let me go. For my sake, and yours, Elena, let me leave Barlovento." He inhaled sharply. "It wouldn't work, don't you see? I like you, yes. You're a beautiful woman, but my heart isn't here."

"It could be." She pressed close to him and reached out, pulling his arms around her, so she was within their circle. "You could love me, I know you could." Her arms went about his neck. "I can give you what she gave you ten times over, I know I can," she went on, her voice husky with emotion. "I'd do anything to make you happy, Domino . . . anything."

"Then let me go!" It was a half-whisper, wrung from deep within.

Instead she pulled his head down until his mouth touched hers, and Bain trembled at the passion assaulting him. Her lips were warm and vibrant, her tongue playing against his teeth tempestuously as her body molded to him. It would be so easy to relax and let himself go, to still the ache that was surging inside him, but there was something wrong. He wanted to lose himself in her kiss—it had been so long since his lips had given love— and he groaned at the thought of fulfilling the need to be a man again, yet even though his arms tightened around her and his mouth answered hers with a passion of its own, it just wasn't the same.

Slowly, deliberately, he pulled his head up as the desire within him diminished, to be replaced by a quiet affection, the kind one would have for a friend.

"You see," he whispered, his voice breaking. "It wouldn't work. When I open my eyes, she's not there."

"I told you I would hate her," she cried passionately, then reached up, holding his head between both her hands. "It isn't fair."

"I know."

"I have to let you go?" She shook her head, then let her hands drop and hung her head. "I don't know if I can." She took a deep breath, straightening, and slowly raised her head. Her eyes were shut, and she exhaled, then opened them. "I will ask Sancho," she said, her voice breaking. "He will do this for me."

"When?"

"Soon." She turned from him and walked to her horse, leading him to the path from where he'd been grazing with Amigo. Bain walked over and helped her into the saddle, then whistled softly for Amigo. The horse raised his head and sauntered over so Bain could grab the reins. He glanced up at Elena. She was staring at him, her eyes misty with tears.

"I'm sorry, Elena," he offered.

She shook her head. "Don't be, it's not your fault," she said. "They warned me," and she nudged her horse, heading up away from the grove of trees and the beach. Bain mounted and followed, catching up to her.

"He's not due in for almost two weeks or more," she said when he reached her.

He frowned.

"Don't worry," she assured him. "We can reach him. I said you could go, and you will," and with that she dug her horse in the ribs, putting him into a full gallop, heading toward the house, while Bain lit out after her, hoping she was right about her brother doing anything she asked. If not, he was dead for sure this time.

25

One week later, the day after the de Vacas departed, Bain, with Mario leading the way, and Elena insisting she go along, climbed into one of the small boats hidden behind Barlovento and headed out into the swamps.

"So this is where you always disappeared to," Bain said to Mario as they paddled away from the shore.

Mario grinned. "I have friends in the swamps," he answered. "They teach me all kinds of things."

"The Indians," Elena explained. "There are a number of them around here, and Mario's made friends with them all."

"That way they leave Sancho alone," he said.

Elena and Bain had told Luis and Mario about Bain's recovery only minutes after the ship with the de Vacas on it had sailed away. At first Luis was terribly upset because he knew Elena was in love with Bain, but at his daughter's insistence, he agreed to let her try to talk Sancho into taking Bain home.

"He has a wife and a family," she said stubbornly, trying to pretend his leaving didn't matter. "He deserves to see them. If it doesn't work out, he's welcome to come back."

Now, as Bain stared at Elena sitting in the other end of the boat, he wondered what she was thinking.

Elena was wearing more casual clothes than she usually wore. They were clothes he had seen on the servants at Barlovento. A long dark green skirt, a white blouse that was often falling off one shoulder, bare legs, and leather sandals, with her hair in a long thick braid down the back. Was she hoping he'd change his mind at the last minute? He wondered.

As they left Barlovento behind and moved deeper into the swamps, Bain took time to look around. Trees heavy with Spanish moss grew out of the water, some attached to clumps o saw grass, others with their roots, like fingers, stretched below the murky surface, holding them up. Vegetation was thick, heavy vines and flowers choking what small patches of ground there were above the waterline, and the air was heavy with insects.

Bain swatted a mosquito away from his face as the boat glided past a cluster of twisted mangrove trees. An alligator slid from concealment on a bank opposite them, and Elena's eyes followed him warily as he swam behind the boat.

"No matter how many times I see them, I still can't get used to them," she said, her eyes staying on the alligator until he decided to find different prey and swam to a new sandbar to wait.

They had left Barlovento shortly after dawn, when the mists were still heavy above the water, and as the day progressed, the mists were replaced by sweltering heat that hung low, fermenting the dense vegetation and filling their nostrils with the pungent smells of rotting plant life. Before long, the trees closed in overhead, and birds screamed at them raucously, while the water rippled now and then, broken by the antics of some wild animal.

A sense of complete isolation seemed to grip Bain, the deeper they went. The only sounds were the calls of the birds, the faint dip of the paddles in the water, and an occasional growl or roar from an alligator or shrill screech from some wild animal in trouble.

"How do you know your way through this maze, Mario?" Bain asked as Mario's paddle once more maneuvered the small boat around a bend and into a tributary that forked to the left.

"Practice," he said. "I've been to the cove so many times, I could probably go through here in the dark."

Bain had to agree with him. All day they wound their way through a maze of waterways, sometimes gliding beneath a canopy of low branches that seemed to reach out, trying to snag anything that managed to get too close. Then, at other times, the open sky would break through and the sun beat down on them, blistering hot, the water deeper, with fewer trees to obstruct their path. Occasionally, and much to Bain's surprise, a few of Mario's friends would make an appearance, their striped and brilliantly trimmed hand-woven clothes colorful against the green surroundings. Mario would wave and call to them, and they'd smile and wave back, their dark eyes curiously watching until the trio was out of sight again.

Bain asked Mario about them a few times, but he seemed reluctant to reveal anything constructive, except that they didn't care much for strangers. Bain was a little disappointed. They looked like an interesting people, but he didn't press the boy. Right now he was more interested in getting through the swamps alive. Especially since the waters were infested with poisonous snakes and alligators.

As the afternoon wore on, he began to wonder where they'd stop at nightfall. Their only stops so far had been to relieve themselves whenever necessary on some patch of high ground where there were trees or bushes to hide behind. They had even eaten while moving through the water earlier in the day.

To his surprise, when nighttime came, they were neatly ensconced in an old Indian hut built on stilts above the water, their boat tied up at the bottom of the ladder they'd used to climb up into the place. Mario had brought a whale-oil hurricane lantern they'd lit with a flint, and before settling down for the night, they shared a loaf of bread, some cheese, fruit, and a flask of warm lemonade.

"I wanted to bring a bottle of wine," Elena said. "But knowing Mario, he'd probably drink too much and end up getting us lost tomorrow."

"It's just as well," Bain said. "As hot as it is, the wine

would only make us hotter.'' He looked about the hut. The sides were made of sturdy saplings covered with woven saw grass, the roof thatched with saw grass, and floor made of split logs covered with reed mats. It was dusty and dirty, with mold and mildew in the corners, but dry, and as soon as the sun went down, Mario and Elena let woven mats down over the door and windows to keep out the mosquitoes and other insects. Bain had noticed other huts just like this one surrounding the one they were in, and assumed they were a regular stopover on the way to the cove.

The hut was about eight feet square, and Elena spread blankets on the floor for them before turning the wick of the whale-oil lamp down low.

''We can't blow it all the way out,'' she said as she set it in the far corner. ''It helps keep animals away. The swamps are full of creatures looking for a dry place to sleep.''

She walked over, sat on the blanket between Mario and Bain, and leaned against the side of the hut. She stared at the lantern, aware that Mario was curling up on his blanket and turning his back to them.

''Good night,'' Mario said as he yawned. ''Don't talk too loud, you'll keep me awake.''

Bain too was leaning against the wall of the hut, and he wondered how Mario was going to be able to sleep in this heat. It wouldn't be so bad if they could leave the windows free of the mats, but he'd rather put up with the heat than the bugs.

''You never did say, how will you get in touch with your brother?'' Bain asked. ''You said he wasn't due at the cove for weeks yet.''

''We build a fire on the hill overlooking the cove, keep it going, then wait.''

''How long will it take?''

''Two, maybe three days, sometimes longer.''

''Do you know where Sancho stays?''

''If he's not out with the ship, he stays up the coast in an inlet, but I don't know just where.'' She glanced over at him. ''You'd better get some sleep. Tomorrow's going to be as bad as today was, and it won't get any cooler tonight.''

He was watching her closely. ''What about you?''

''I don't know if I can sleep.''

''I didn't mean to hurt you.''

''I know that.''

"Then will you try to sleep?"

Her eyes begged him. "May I sleep on your shoulder?"

"Elena . . ."

"Please, Domino. I'll only sleep. . . ."

He felt the sweat from the heat dampening his flesh all over. What would it hurt to let her ease the pain some? It was too hot for anything else anyway, and besides, with Mario so close . . . He took a deep breath, then stretched out on the blanket and lifted his arm, nodding to her. Her eyes lit up, and in seconds she was stretched out beside him, her head on his shoulder.

"I'll be good, Domino," she whispered softly.

He sighed. "Good night, Elena."

"Good night."

It was some time before Bain was able to fall asleep.

The next morning Mario woke them as the first faint rays of dawn crept through the cracks of the mats, and after a breakfast of more cheese and bread, they were soon on their way again. Elena was right, today was as bad as yesterday as they paddled through endless swampland, covering miles of waterways thick with steaming vegetation decaying in the heat. Wild birds sometimes scattered from the trees above, hitting into each other in their frightened flight, while still others stood solitary, like the long-legged egrets, defying the intruders to make them move. It was a strange world, and at times frightening in its sheer loneliness.

Then finally, as the afternoon sun began to lower to the edge of the horizon, Bain noticed the water was getting deeper, the air not so heavy, and the trees were thinning out. The moss, hanging heavy on them earlier, was now like thin threads, letting the light shine through. A little over an hour later, the small boat broke from the watery trail out into a larger body of water, and Mario smiled. They had reached the cove.

Bain glanced up as the boat moved farther into the lagoon, and he studied the land on either side. The hills surrounding the cove were high, a perfect place to conceal a ship from the outside world, with a natural harbor to sail into.

Mario maneuvered their boat to the inland shore, beaching it near the mouth of the cove on a sandbar that wasn't more than twenty feet long.

"Farther down from the sandbar is where they drop anchor," he said, then pointed to a small hill on their left, overlooking the ocean. "That's where we'll build the fire. Come on."

They made sure the boat was secure, hefted the supplies they'd brought with them, and headed for the hill, reaching the top shortly before dark. Much to Bain's surprise, there was a pile of wood there already, concealed by some vines, but ready to burn, and some of it was already stacked, ready to light.

"What if another ship answers your signal?" Bain asked as he watched Mario trying to light the kindling with his flints, while Elena started going through their supplies.

"Then we douse the fire with sand."

Bain looked around. Again Mario was right. Most of the hill was rich earth, with trees and grass clinging to it, but the spot where the fire was set up was a sandy stretch with clumps of saw grass and a few yucca plants sprouting out of it. The fire could be kicked out in minutes.

By the time Mario had the fire going, it was so dark Bain could barely see the cove below them.

"We just stay here?" he asked curiously.

Elena laughed. "You didn't see the hut?" she asked in surprise.

He looked around, but it was too dark to see anything other than what the fire illuminated. "No."

She took his hand. "Come, I'll show you."

While Mario had been working on the fire, Elena had lit the hurricane lantern they had used the night before; now she turned the wick higher and held it up as she looked about. She found her bearings quickly and started off toward some trees, pulling him after her as she hurried along.

No wonder he hadn't seen the hut. As she held the lantern high, he could see it now, nestled between some bushes, the construction the same as the one last night, but not on stilts, and with a dirt floor.

"We don't use it much unless it rains," she said, and he could understand why.

It was beautiful here on the hill with the smell of the fresh gulf water and warm breezes that blew up from the cove.

Elena turned and stared at the fire as the flames grew even brighter, lighting up the sky.

"Now we wait," she said softly, and Bain felt the gooseflesh rise on his arms.

Yes, we wait, he thought, but for what?

Three days later, they were still waiting, with no sign of Sancho's ship. The fire had been going both day and night and they were running out of food as well as running low on wood.

June Lund Shiplett

The wood could be replaced from the abundance of trees near the cove, but it wasn't so easy to replenish the food. It was close to midnight and Elena and Bain were both watching, as they had every night so far.

"We have enough for three, maybe four more days on the hill," Elena said as they sat near the edge of the sandy hill, looking out to sea. "Then I'm afraid we'll have to go back."

"You'd like that, wouldn't you?" he said. They'd become close these past few nights, closer than he had intended, as they sat and talked and watched out to sea.

She shrugged. "Would it be so bad?" She bit back a curse. "I wish I had never met you, Domino," she cried.

"For God's sake, Elena," he asked, "what would you have me do?"

"Make love to me."

"I can't."

"You won't!"

"All right, then, I won't!"

She fell back on the sand, staring up at the star-filled sky. "You love her that much?"

"Yes."

"You can give nothing to me?"

"There's nothing to give."

"I think there is." She sat up and moved closer to him, her eyes studying his profile in the firelight. "I don't ask for it all, Domino," she whispered softly into his ear. "I don't ask that you stay here with me, but if I could just have a little . . ." She touched his arm, feeling the muscles moving beneath her fingers. "She'll have you for the rest of her life. Can't I have just one moment?"

"You don't know what you ask."

"Yes, I do."

"No, you don't!" He turned to her, gazing into her shadowed face, the light playing softly on her hair. "If I gave you that moment, just that one moment, Elena, I'd no longer have my soul, do you understand?" He swallowed hard. "Lizette's my life, I've loved her with my heart, and my body, and to share that moment with you . . . You're lovely, Elena, and any man would gladly welcome your arms, as I would, if I were free. But to give you what belongs to Liz . . ." He shook his head sadly. "I can't, I just can't!"

"Oh, Domino!" She laid her head on his shoulder, burying

her face hard against him, her breathing erratic, and he knew
he'd let things go too far. She was young, inexperienced, unable
to stop what she'd started, and he knew she was fighting it hard.
She trembled against him, then moaned softly, her body quivering.
"Domino!"

He had to do something, anything, to help her; he couldn't let
her go on like this. Yet what could he do without sacrificing the
love that was Lizette's, and Lizette's alone? His arms went about
her and he held her close, then laid her back in the sand. Her
arms reached for him, her body yearning, and she cried his name
again.

"This is the only moment I can give you," he whispered
softly, and with that his hand moved down her body, while his
mouth covered hers, and he kissed her long and hard, sipping at
her mouth passionately, until a few minutes later she shuddered,
then lay still.

He raised his head slowly and gazed down into her face.
"Elena . . . ?" he whispered softly.

She sighed. "I love you!"

"No, please," he begged. "You don't love me, no." He sat
back up and reached his hand out for her to take, pulling her into
a sitting position again as they had been before. "That's not
love, Elena," he explained, his voice a little unsteady. "That's
something else. It's the way love starts sometimes, the way it
can feel, but love is more than that. Love is wanting someone so
badly no one else will do. It's sharing the good and the bad, and
losing a part of yourself when they're gone. What you feel, what
you felt tonight, is only the beginning of what love can be, and
someday you'll meet someone who will show you the rest of it."

She shook her head, her eyes shining. "Thank you for my
moment," she whispered softly. "It wasn't hers, and it will
always be mine." She drew her eyes from his face and gazed out
to sea; then suddenly her face lit up.

"Sancho!" she cried breathlessly, pointing into the night.
"It's the signal, it's Sancho!" and before Bain could say anything more, she scrambled to her feet and ran back toward the
hut to wake Mario and tell him Sancho was coming.

Bain watched as she hurried away. Out here, dressed like she
was, legs bare and hair let down, Elena seemed different. She
lost the graceful airs of a lady and was more like a wild urchin,
free and unrestrained. Like a young filly with no reins to guide
her. He frowned, feeling the stirrings of the arousal she'd dredged

from deep within him beginning to subside. Strange, he thought. Before Lizette, he could never have resisted such blatant seduction. Now . . . it seemed so easy. All he had to do was think of Lizette's dark hair, green eyes, and voluptuous body, and other women paled before her, even Elena.

He stood up slowly, stretching, and drew his eyes away from the hut, looking seaward to where lights were blinking, signaling an answer they'd been waiting for.

A short while later, Bain stood at the edge of the water, watching the ship sail silently into the cove and drop anchor some fifty feet from shore. Elena was on one side of him, and Mario on the other; still his insides were twisted into knots. The thought of death had never bothered him before, until he'd come so close to it. Now . . . it was so permanent, and he prayed to God Elena's faith in her brother was justified.

There was a sliver of a moon hanging low in the sky amid the stars, and he watched them lower a boat over the side, then climb in, rowing toward shore. Elena was holding the hurricane lantern, and she stepped forward, down toward the edge as the longboat hit the sandbar, a man in the bow jumping out to greet her.

"Little sister, what is it?" Sancho asked as he stared at her anxious face. "Not Father?"

She shook her head. "No, not Father."

He grabbed her then, and she held the lantern awkwardly, keeping it from hitting him as he hugged and kissed her, and she hugged him back. He released her as Mario came forward; then he reached out, ruffling his young brother's hair and hugging him as well.

"What is it, then?" he asked, and hesitated, then stood motionless as he caught sight of Bain standing a few feet away.

Bain couldn't see Sancho's face yet. All he could see was a man's frame, tall and broad, the clothes a mixture of military and civilian, with a cutlass at his side, and a broad hat.

"Well, what have we here?" Sancho asked as he stood with his arm about Mario and stared at Bain.

Elena hurried toward Bain, the lantern held high. "It's Domino," she answered quickly, her voice vibrant with emotion. "Only he isn't Domino. He knows who he is now."

"And . . . ?"

"I want you to take him home, Sancho," she pleaded anxiously. "Please, for me, take him home?"

Her brother walked slowly toward Bain, his arm dropping from Mario's shoulder to rest on the hilt of his sword. "I thought you wanted him for yourself," he said roughly.

"I did," she agreed. "As long as he was Domino." She straightened, confronting her brother's question with an answer she knew he'd respect. "But he isn't anymore. He's Bain Kolter, with a wife, and I refuse to share him with her memory."

"Why don't I just kill him, then?"

"No!" She reached out, grabbing her brother's arm, and now Bain could see Sancho's face clearly in the light from the lantern. It was hard and tanned, handsomely chiseled, the cheekbones prominent above a bushy beard and mustache, with a deep scar puckering the flesh on the right temple close to his eye. Elena had told Bain Sancho looked more like their dead mother, and he knew she had to be right, for he looked nothing like Luis. His nose was aquiline like Elena's and he had the same crooked smile that often crossed Mario's face.

"I don't want him dead," Elena said sharply. "And you won't kill him, either."

"Bain, did you say?" asked Sancho, suddenly grabbing the name, putting a significance to it. He snatched the lantern from Elena and held it up, studying Bain's face.

Bain offered his hand. "Bain Kolter, Captain Gallant, at your service," he said boldly, and Sancho laughed.

"By God, it is!" His dark eyes widened, and his laughter was deep, throaty. He shook Bain's hand, then turned, calling to the men who'd rowed in with him, who were standing quietly next to the longboat. "You hear that, men?" he asked jovially. "I always did want to meet the bastard who put one over on Lafitte. I only wish to hell you'd killed the son of a bitch for us," he said, addressing Bain.

"You heard about it?" Bain asked.

"Heard about it? By God, Lafitte was fit to be tied. Tried to keep it quiet, he did, but you know how men talk, especially that mealymouthed Frenchman who sails the *Golden Rose*." He grinned broadly. "It was all the talk a few months back." His eyes hardened, the grin fading. "But what's this Elena says? You leaving her?"

"I have no choice."

"The world thinks you're dead."

"I know I'm not."

Sancho looked at Elena. "Is that why you signaled?"

"Yes. He wants to go home, Sancho, and you're the only one who can take him."

"Well, now, that's something I'm going to have to think about, little sister," he said. He looked at Bain. "Where's home?"

"Port Royal, South Carolina."

"Hmmm . . ." Sancho stared at him suspiciously. "What's to stop you from bringing the authorities back here?" he asked skeptically. "This is part of the United States now, and they'd give a fat reward for the capture of Sancho de Córdoba, not to mention learning about Barlovento. What guarantee do I have we wouldn't all end up swinging from a rope?"

"My word."

"Your word?" He sneered. "Lafitte took you at your word."

"Lafitte's a greedy fool. He tried to cheat me."

"That's not what he claims."

"No?"

"He told his men you were a government agent."

"Because I tried to steal his ledgers? Hell, I wanted proof he'd been cheating us, that's all. Unfortunately, my plan didn't work."

"He says it did."

"He said I got his ledgers?"

"So the boys say."

"Then they're the fools," Bain said confidently. "With them thinking his ledgers are gone, Lafitte's in the clear. There's no way the men can prove he was cheating them."

"You say he still has the ledgers?" Sancho asked.

"All I got away with was blowing up his magazine and a few storage sheds," Bain lied. "The ledgers are still hidden somewhere in Maison Rouge. If I had gotten them, you think I'd have run?" he asked calmly. "I'd have waited for the *Golden Rose*, showed Frenchie the ledgers proving Lafitte was cheating us, and we'd have sailed back into Campeche and torn it apart." Bain straightened. "No man risks his life for the crumbs," he said angrily. "If I go down, I go down for the biggest share of the cake."

Sancho studied Bain closely. "Now you want to go home?" he asked thoughtfully.

"What else is there?"

Sancho motioned with his head toward his sister. "There's Elena."

Bain glanced at Elena. What if she suddenly changed her mind? Her eyes were devouring him, and he saw her lips quiver slightly.

"I have a wife," Bain said, his voice deepening. "Elena knows why I can't stay."

Sancho gazed at his sister. She was staring at Kolter with her heart in her eyes, and he cursed silently to himself. Damn the man! Damn him!

"You sure you want this, Elena?" he asked. "I could kill him for hurting you."

"No," she cried, her voice breaking. "I said before, you won't hurt him. I want your promise on that." She looked into Bain's eyes, trying to be strong. "He hasn't hurt me. I've hurt myself. He's given me all he can give."

"No babies, I hope," Sancho said angrily. "For that I would kill him."

"No, no babies," Bain said. "Your sister still has her virtue, Captain, don't worry about that. What she doesn't have, I'm sorry to say, is my love."

Sancho straightened, then looked at Mario, who'd been quietly listening. "And what of you, little brother?" he asked. "You think I should take Kolter home?"

Mario sighed. "*Sí*," he said. "That's why we brought him here. The longer he stays, the worse it is for Elena."

Sancho took a deep breath. "I'm outnumbered, señor," he said to Bain. "All right, I will trust you with our lives. For Elena, and only for Elena, I will take you home, but if the day ever comes when I discover you've betrayed us, I'll hunt you to the ends of the earth and roast you on a spit, understand?"

Bain nodded. "*Sí*." He knew Sancho meant every word, and the pirate's dark eyes confirmed it. "There is one thing more, though," Bain said rather hesitantly.

"He has a horse, Sancho," Elena cut in. "It's not just a horse, but a special horse, and I told him I'd ask if you could stop by the house and get him."

"Stop by the house? You have butterflies in your brain?"

"Please, Sancho," she begged. "If we left now, and all sail on the *Piranha*, we could reach Barlovento before dawn. You could drop Mario and me off so we wouldn't have to go back through the swamps, and pick up the horse at the same time."

"You have it all thought out, don't you, little sister?" he said. She smiled affectionately, and Bain marveled that she could

be so casually loving to a man whose eyes flashed so dangerously and who looked so unlovable that Bain wondered how he
could truly be her brother. In spite of the tender way he was
treating his sister and brother, there was a ruthless cruelty apparent in Sancho de Córdoba's every movement, and Bain knew he was
a man few people crossed and lived to tell of it.

As Elena said, though, he'd do anything for her, and Bain had
to admit she was right. They made sure the fire on the hill was
completely out, gathered everything together, including the small
boat and paddles they'd used to reach the cove, then boarded the
Piranha, sailing silently out of the inland harbor and down the
coast, reaching Barlovento while the moon still hung low in the
sky. It had taken them two days through the swamps to go the
same distance it took the *Piranha* only hours to go by sea, and it
was near breaking dawn by the time Bain stood on the beach
holding the reins on Amigo, ready to take him out to the ship.
Sancho and four of his men had ridden to shore with Mario,
Elena, and Bain, and Elena woke her father so he'd know what
was going on, and so he could see his son. The two men had
looked so strange together to Bain. He was used to seeing sons
who looked like their fathers, like him and Stuart. It was odd to
see a father and son so unlike each other, who, in spite of it,
seemed to have an affection and tenderness so strong. Because it
was apparent Luis de Córdoba thought the world of Sancho, as
he did his two other children.

Sancho, Luis, and Mario were near the flagstone walk still
talking, Sancho's men were already in the boat waiting, and
Bain took the opportunity to say good-bye to Elena.

"I wish it could have been different, Elena," he said. "You
know that."

She nodded. "It isn't your fault. I found you too late, that's
all. But it still hurts."

He reached down and took her hand, pulling her into his arms.
"Why don't you leave here, Elena?" he whispered softly. "There
are men out there just waiting for someone like you to come
along."

"I wouldn't know where to go."

"Go anywhere. St. Augustine, New Orleans, New York.
What does it matter where? It's dangerous for you here, you
know that."

"You're not going to tell?"

"No, I won't tell, not a soul."

"Then I'll die here of old age."

He shook his head. "You deserve better than Barlovento," he said. "You deserve a home and children."

"Yours?"

"You're a hard woman to resist, Elena de Córdoba," he whispered huskily. "But I have no choice, we both know that. I can't control my heart, anymore than you can control yours. I only hope someday, someone else will come along who can give you what's not mine to give." He inhaled sharply. It wouldn't hurt to say good-bye the way it should be said, he thought. It was the least he could do for all she'd done for him. His legs were still a little weak, and as he held her close, he felt her melt against him. "In the meantime," he murmured, his mouth inches from hers, "keep this in your heart to remember me by," and he kissed her tenderly, lovingly, giving her as much of himself as he could, without losing himself completely. "Good-bye, Elena," he said against her lips.

"Good-bye, Domino," and her lips clung to his again for a brief moment as she heard Sancho approaching.

"Come on, Kolter," Sancho said gruffly. "Leave her, or love her, you can't have it both ways."

Bain tore himself from Elena's embrace, grabbed Amigo's reins again, and followed Sancho, climbing into the longboat. Sancho's men shoved off, and with Amigo in tow, swimming behind, they rowed out to the ship, and the last Bain saw of Elena, once Amigo was brought aboard, was her lone figure, still wearing the dirty clothes she'd put on days before, waving to him from the beach as the first rays of the sun came up over Barlovento. But that's not the way Bain would remember her. He'd always remember her wearing her fancy clothes, sedate and ladylike, nursing him back to health, and making him a man again.

The trip to the Château was without incident, except for the usual bouts with the weather. Elena had made Sancho promise, on pain of death, not to attack anything afloat until after they'd dropped Bain off. Surprisingly, he kept to his promise, affording Bain an unusual insight into the man.

His crew was something else, however, and after meeting them, Bain knew why the man was so ruthless. He had to be, to command such merciless men, and Bain thanked God Sancho de Córdoba was so fond of Elena.

All during the trip, Bain walked the deck of the *Piranha*,

strengthening his legs even more. They still bothered him at times, and he knew he still wasn't walking as freely as he once did, and he hoped by the time he reached Port Royal there'd be no sign of his having been injured. It was almost a useless hope, however, because he still felt so clumsy at times.

It was late afternoon. Bain stood on the deck of the *Piranha* and watched the sun sinking low on the horizon. Earlier in the day, they had hauled in the sails so they could drift aimlessly some two to three miles off the Hilton Head, where they hoped they wouldn't be discovered. They were waiting for nightfall. Their plan was a simple one. They'd slip past the Hilton Head into Port Royal Sound, and up the Broad River sometime between midnight and dawn. Since Bain was a strong swimmer, they'd pull in as close to shore as possible, downriver a short distance from the Château, where Bain and Amigo would be put over the side, and man and animal would swim ashore while the *Piranha* sailed back down the river and out to sea again.

Bain wished they could tie up at the pier behind the Château, but it would be too risky. If the *Interlude* was already there, the *Piranha* would too easily be seen; if not, there was still too much chance someone from the plantation might spot them, and he'd promised Elena that Sancho wouldn't run into any trouble.

Bain was nervous, his eyes scanning the horizon. As the afternoon wore on, the sun slid behind a cloud, and he frowned. The sky turned gray, then darkened, and soon the shadows of night dimmed the world around him. He ate lightly that evening, then was back on the deck again, watching and waiting.

Shortly before midnight it began to rain, a light misty rain that clung to everything like a heavy dew. Bain checked the ocean around them as a fog began to gather above the water; then suddenly the word went up, the rigging creaked, and the slap of the sails filling caught on the night air. They began to move.

"I didn't count on the rain," Sancho said as he walked up to Bain. "You know your way in, I hope."

"Like the back of my hand."

"Good, then you can stay by the helmsman. I don't want to get beached and end up hanging because I did my sister a favor."

"You love Elena, don't you, Captain?" Bain asked as they headed toward the wheel.

"Naturally, she's kin."

"Then for her sake, take her away from that island, de

Córdoba," Bain said. "Take her somewhere so she can find someone to love her, where she can lead a normal life and have a husband and children."

"You telling me what to do?"

"No." Bain stopped and looked at Sancho's vague figure next to him, unable to see the man's face. "I'm asking you to do your sister another favor. Give her a chance in life. Don't let her end up alone, or worse yet, in prison if anything should go wrong. Let's face it. With Florida an American territory now, chances are they'll make a stronger effort to rid the seas of men like you and me—that's why I've made up my mind to quit. Don't let her get caught in it. Take her away from Barlevento, let her be free."

Sancho stared at Bain, his eyes hard, mouth tightening stubbornly. He wasn't used to taking orders, and he didn't like being told. "I suggest you keep your mind on getting us past the Hilton Head, Señor Kolter," he said, refusing to answer. "I'll do with my sister as I wish," and he turned, heading belowdecks to go to his cabin.

Bain cursed as the man walked away. Stubborn jackass, he thought. Well, he had tried, and he took position beside the helmsman to wait for the first sight of land that would tell him he was close to home.

It was pitch dark as the *Piranha* moved stealthily through the water, passing moored ships, working her way into the sound. They were challenged once by a ship heading out through the fog, and Bain called back in English, telling him a story about being an American ship headed to pick up a cargo at Tonnerre.

"What if that happens on the way out?" asked Sancho as Bain went back to the wheel. "I don't speak English too good."

"Then I suggest maybe you see if one of your men does," Bain said. "I doubt if it'll happen again, but you never know."

They passed the southern end of Port Royal and began inching up the Broad River.

"Rumor is, Teach and his men spent time here," Bain said as they kept their eyes on the riverbank.

Sancho studied the terrain. "I wouldn't doubt it." He turned to Bain. "You live here?"

"My wife's grandparents do. My home's a short distance away in Beaufort. But you couldn't get close enough there without being challenged. Here we've got clear sailing right up the river.'' Bain glanced up at the rigging. ''You can cut sail,'' he said anxiously. ''We're almost there.''

The rain had stopped shortly after the fog rolled in, and now the fog too was lifting, but slowly, and they had moved in as close to the riverbank as possible. The sails were furled, anchor dropped, and Bain stood near the boarding ropes watching the men fasten the sling about Amigo's middle, readying him to be lowered over the side. He touched the stallion's velvety nose, reassuring him softly, as he always did before hoisting him over the side. The men were just finishing securing the last hooks.

''Well, Captain,'' Bain said as he extended his hand, able to see Sancho a little better now in the dark, since there was no rain, and little fog anymore to hinder his vision. ''I thank you for all you've done.''

Sancho grabbed his hand, shook it, then released it abruptly. ''I guess you're welcome,'' he said briskly, unused to using niceties with people. ''But don't thank me, thank Elena. If it weren't for her, I'd have run you through. I don't have much feelings for a man who can take a girl's heart like you took hers, then leave her. But I promised her, and I keep my promises.''

''Then thank her for me,'' Bain said, and headed for the side of the ship.

''Remember, Señor Kolter,'' Sancho reminded him as Bain grabbed the boarding rope to swing himself over the rail. ''I'm trusting you. Our lives are in your hands, and so is Barlovento.''

''I keep my promises, too,'' Bain said quickly, then climbed over the side and began scrambling down the ropes, while the men hoisted Amigo into the air, lowering him overboard.

Bain was partway down when he heard his name being called from above.

''Señor Kolter?'' It was Sancho.

''Captain?''

''About Elena,'' Sancho called, his voice low so it wouldn't carry too far. ''I'll think about what you said earlier. Maybe you're right.''

''I am,'' Bain answered.

''We'll see. Now,'' Sancho said hurriedly, ''go with God, my sister's friend, and I'll tell her you reached home safely.''

''Thank you, Captain,'' Bain said. ''For everything,'' and he went the rest of the way down the boarding ropes, into the water, where he reached Amigo and freed him from the sling. Then, as the *Piranha* weighed anchor, her sails unfurling again to the night breeze, Bain struck out swimming, with Amigo close at his side, toward the banks of the Broad River.

Bain was winded when he pulled himself from the water, then helped Amigo onto the grassy bank. He gazed back out to the river. It was so dark he could barely make out the silhouette of the *Piranha*'s sails as she disappeared downstream. The night was quiet, so quiet. He stood still, listening. Crickets called, a bull frog grumbled nearby, and somewhere a night heron clucked raucously to its mate.

Bain was holding the reins to Amigo's halter, and he leaned forward, resting his head for a moment against the horse's head, then whispered.

"Well, what do we do now, old friend?" he said, talking freely in English again for the first time in months. "Wake them up? Or wait till morning?"

Amigo nickered softly.

"I agree," Bain said anxiously. "Tonight it is," and he leaped carefully onto the stallion, no longer having the strength he once had for such antics, straightened himself firmly on the horse's back, and they headed upstream along the banks of the river toward the Château.

Loedicia had been restless most of the night. The rain and fog earlier had left things muggy, and now there didn't seem to be a breath of air stirring. She was just turning over again, trying to fall back to sleep, when she heard the knock.

"Miz Dicia?" Mattie called softly from the hallway. "Mistuh Roth?"

Loedicia inhaled sharply, rubbed a hand over her eyes, then slipped slowly from the bed, moving to the door.

"What is it, Mattie?" she asked, opening the door a crack. She was half-asleep, her body clammy with perspiration, night-gown damp and stuck to her legs.

"You gotta come, Miz Dicia," Mattie whispered hoarsely. "You ain't gonna believe it. It's Mistuh Bain."

Loedicia stood for a moment, not moving. She stared into the darkness of the room. "What do you mean, it's Mr. Bain?" she asked, half-asleep. "What about Mr. Bain?"

"He's here, ma'am," Mattie said fearfully. "I don'ts believe it myself. But he's down in my kitchen right now, wet and drippin' and waitin' for Miss Lizzie."

"Oh, my God!" Loedicia couldn't believe her ears. For a

second she was frozen to the spot; then quickly she shook her head clear and raced to the bed, grabbing a wrapper on the way. "Roth!" she yelled, half-whispering excitedly, shaking him, scaring him half to death before his head cleared. "It's Bain," she said, then jumped up from the bed again, tying the sash on her wrapper, and threw him his robe. "Come on, we've got to go downstairs."

Roth fumbled with his robe as he slipped from the bed, a bit dazed yet, but letting her words sink in.

"Bain?" he asked hesitantly. "You did say Bain?"

"That's what Mattie said," and in minutes they were at the door, then following their old servant downstairs to the kitchen.

Mattie went in first, then held the door for them.

Bain was by the far counter with his back to them, staring out the window when he heard the door open, and he turned quickly.

"Liz?" he blurted, expecting his wife, then stopped motionless, staring at her grandparents.

Loedicia shook her head, her hand covering her mouth, and Roth grabbed her around the waist to make sure she wouldn't sink to the floor.

It was Bain, all right. His clothes were wet, and dirty, hair disheveled, and he had lost a little weight. "Good Lord," Roth exclaimed breathlessly. "For a minute I thought you were a ghost."

"Hardly," Bain said, then frowned. "Where's Liz?"

"She's not here."

"She's at her parents'?"

Roth shook his head. "They've gone to Boston with Aunt Darcy and Uncle Heath. Lizette's in Washington." He was still in a mild state of shock, as was Dicia; then suddenly he came to his senses. "What the hell . . . where . . . ? We thought you were dead," Roth said, bewildered. "How did you get here?"

Bain flushed, realizing the Chapmans were upset, and understanding why. "I'm sorry," he apologized. "I should have waited until morning."

"No," Roth said quickly as he ushered Loedicia farther into the room so she could sit at the table. "I'm glad you came tonight. But what I don't understand is . . . you're supposed to be dead!"

"I almost was." Bain moved to the table and stood staring at them both. "We were in a storm off the coast of Florida," he explained hurriedly. "When I came to, I was being taken care of by a Spanish family, but I had no idea who I was until just a few weeks ago." He addressed Roth. "You said Lizette's in Washington?"

"When we thought you were dead, I gave her your letter. She went to Washington, insisting she was going to clear your name."

"The twins?"

"They're here."

Loedicia finally managed to compose herself. "Wait till you see them, Bain," she said eagerly. "They're walking all over, and starting to put words together."

Bain took a deep breath, and suddenly there were tears in his eyes. "I was hoping . . . that is . . . Liz . . . ?"

"Wait till she finds out, Bain," Loedicia interrupted, knowing he was hurting inside at the disappointment. "She was simply devastated."

"I can imagine."

"But here," Loedicia went on, finally pulling herself together. "You're wet and tired. Mattie'll fix you something to eat, you can clean up and get some rest." She motioned to Mattie, who shuffled off toward the larder to see what she could find. "Liz closed the house in Beaufort. But your clothes are all there. We'll send Jacob in to get some for you, and in the meantime, we'll decide what's to be done."

"I'm going to Liz," Bain said stubbornly.

Roth nodded. "Yes, I agree, I think that's best, but for now, I think maybe you'd better sit down, you look rather tired."

"It's my legs," Bain said reluctantly. "They still aren't what they should be. I'm afraid I was hurt when the ship went down." He sat on the chair Roth offered him, then studied them both. "I didn't mean to scare you," he said after a few moments. "But I thought Lizette would be here."

"What happened, Bain?" Loedicia finally had the courage to ask.

He paused, choosing the words carefully. "I'm sorry," he answered, unable yet to tell the truth. "I just can't say. Not yet. All I ask is that you take me to Liz. She's in Washington . . . That's good, because that's where all the answers are. Please, trust me."

Loedicia felt Roth's hands at her shoulders and she leaned her head back, looking up at him. "Roth?" she asked.

He took a deep breath, remembering the letter, then sighed. "All right, Bain, we'll trust you," he said confidently. "You want to see Liz, we'll take you to her. We'll all leave in the morning,'' and true to his word, late the next morning, after Bain had cleaned up and gotten some rest, with a strong wind to carry them, Roth's ship the *Interlude* slipped from her moorings and moved out into the Broad River, lazily catching the current, then picking up speed as her sails began to unfurl.

On board her, standing near the rail, Roth turned to Loedicia, who was holding Blythe in her arms, cuddling the toddler close.

"We are doing the right thing, aren't we, Dicia?'' he asked thoughtfully as he studied their great-grandchild's smiling face.

Loedicia's violet eyes warmed, her gray curls whipping in the wind as she looked at him and smiled. "What do you think?'' she asked lovingly. "Look at them, darling, just look at them. Bain's no more a pirate than you or I,'' and as they both glanced toward the wheel, watching Captain Casey maneuver the ship into full stream, Bain, standing next to the captain, his small son in his arms, hugged the child to him, then glanced toward Roth and Loedicia, his heart in his eyes. Grandma Dicia reminded him so much of Liz.

Soon, Bain thought anxiously as he stared at them, soon I'll be with you, Lizette, and everything'll be all right. I'll have my whole family with me. He felt his heart sing as he drew his eyes from his wife's grandparents, lifted Braxton high onto his shoulders so they could both watch the sails catch the wind, and the ship cut the water, heading toward the sound and on out to sea.

26

It was early afternoon when Lizette and Stuart finally rode into Washington, returning from Charlottesville, Virginia. Their clothes were dusty, they were tired and hungry, and Lizette was still peeved over Captain Holley's silence.

"I told you it'd be rough,'' Stuart said as they rode up the drive and stopped their horses in front of the carriage house and barns. "The government knows what they're doing when they pick their men.'' He dismounted and walked over, helping her down.

"I wish I knew what I was doing,'' she said wearily. "Sometimes I think I was insane to think I could fight them.''

Her feet were on the ground and he stood looking down at her. "Ready to concede?" he asked.

Her jaw tightened stubbornly. "No!"

"I didn't think so."

The groom came out of the stables and Stuart gave him orders to bring in their trunks, then take care of the horses.

He took Lizette's arm and they walked toward the back of the house, then through the garden, talking casually about the trip, entering by the French doors that opened into the parlor. Suddenly they both stopped, staring. In the center of the room, with one hand resting on the back of an overstuffed chair, the other held firmly at her side, was Julia. She was staring back at them, unsmiling.

"Hello, Stuart," she said crisply.

He caught himself quickly, trying to bridge their awkward surprise. "Julia! Good heavens, when did you arrive? Why didn't you let me know?"

"Isn't it obvious?" she answered, ignoring Lizette. "If I'd warned you ahead of time, there'd have been no reason to come."

"What do you mean?"

"Oh, come Stuart. I admit I've been naive," she said. "But not anymore. It doesn't take a thunderbolt to jolt me out of my complacency."

Lizette tried to think of something to say, but couldn't.

"I had expected to catch the two of you here at the house," Julia went on bitterly. "But that's just as well. Instead, I arrive and find out you went on a holiday together."

"A holiday?" Lizette finally found her voice. "A holiday?" she yelled at her sister-in-law. "Do I look like I've been on a holiday?" and she held out her dusty skirt, then wiped the dirt and grime from the road off her face. "Stuart was thoughtful enough to take me to Charlottesville, to hunt for Captain Holley," she went on. "That's where we were."

Julia straightened, her pale blue eyes sparking dangerously, the red silk dress she wore making her seem quite formidable. "I suppose it was thoughtfulness on his part to let you stay in our home with him?" she asked. "And for taking you to the Fourth of July ball, and for escorting you all over town, making a laughingstock of me?"

"Julia, for God's sake," Stuart cut in. "You've been listening to gossip."

"I've been listening to my friends," she retorted. "How do you think I felt, getting letters from people dropping sly hints about my husband's indiscretions and asking if it's true she's really his brother's widow? Believe me, Stuart," she said angrily, "it wasn't enjoyable for me."

"And you listened to all of it," he said, trying to make it sound unimportant. "You didn't wait to ask. You just jumped to conclusions, expecting the worst."

"I wanted to see for myself, and now I've seen."

"What did you see?" He gestured to his clothes. "Do we look like we've been enjoying ourselves? Lizette's been trying to clear Bain's name."

"She's been living here."

"I had to have someplace to stay!"

"With my husband?"

"He hasn't been here. He's been at Jeff's."

"Julia, be reasonable," Stuart pleaded. "What will the servants think?"

"They already think what I know."

"What do you know?"

"I know you two have been having an affair."

"Nonsense!" Stuart tried to stay calm. "Julia, Liz is my brother's widow, nothing more. We're friends, and as such I've been trying to help her prove he wasn't a pirate."

"Then you're a fool, Stuart. The whole world, including your parents, knew what he was."

"No," Lizette cried. "That's not true. Bain left me a letter." Lizette began to rummage around in her reticule. "Here," she said, handing Julia the letter Bain had written to her. "Read it, Julia, and you'll know why Stuart's been helping me."

Julia stared at Lizette for a minute, then looked down at the envelope Lizette had thrust into her hand.

"It's from Bain," Lizette explained. "Grandpa Roth gave it to me when we learned Bain was dead."

Julia fingered the envelope hesitantly, then finally opened it and took out the letter. Her expression didn't change as she read it, and Lizette waited expectantly.

"You see," Stuart said when Julia looked up from the letter, "all I've been doing is trying to help Lizette prove that Bain was on some sort of secret mission for the government."

"Then why didn't you tell me?"

"I was planning to."

"When? At a time like now, when you had to?"

"You wouldn't have understood," Lizette said helplessly. "Nobody understands except Stuart. I wouldn't let him tell you because I didn't think you'd let him help me. Everybody else was so quick to think Bain guilty, including you."

"And yet, now you want me to believe he's innocent?" Julia sneered. "You must really think me the fool."

"It's true, Julia," Stuart said, straightening stubbornly. "You can ask Jeff."

"I have."

"Then you know the truth."

"I know men cover for their friends," she said angrily. "Naturally, he'd stick by you."

"Julia, this is ridiculous," Stuart insisted. "There's nothing between Liz and me."

"Good, because I want her out of this house."

Stuart shook his head. "You don't mean that."

"I do," she said savagely. "I don't care where she goes. To a hotel, the street, back to Beaufort for all I care. But I want her out!" Her chin tilted stubbornly. "I have an appointment at the dressmaker's this afternoon," she said curtly. "I'll be gone for several hours. When I get back, I want her gone."

She started to walk away, but Stuart grabbed her arm. "Julia, this is insane," he said angrily. "She's your sister-in-law. What will people say?"

"It's what they're already saying that counts, Stuart," she answered. "And I don't like what they're saying." She glanced back at Lizette, suddenly realizing how voluptuously sensual she was in spite of her tight clothes and thick waistline; then she looked back directly into her husband's eyes. "You swear there's nothing between you, and she tried to deny it, but it's not as easy as that, Stuart. I've seen you look at her, your eyes caressing her, and I've seen her answer you back more than once. Even when Bain was alive, there seemed to be a silent communication between the two of you at family dinners and the like. As if . . ." She stopped for a moment, and her eyes hardened defensively. "I just know I didn't like it, and I don't like what's been going on here. Maybe your friends have mistresses, Stuart, but I won't have it. You'll move her out of this house."

"I won't stop helping her," he said.

"You will!"

"I won't. Bain was my brother, and something's not right.

Whether you believe it or not is your problem, but I won't desert her now. Lizette needs help, and by God, I'll keep helping her.''

"Fine, then help her," she yelled angrily, and her eyes blazed. "Go ahead, help her. But if you go to a party, you'll escort me, and if you go for a walk, you'll take me, and if you go to the theater, you'll take me, is that understood?''

"Perfectly," he answered.

"And remember what I said, I want her out of here!" she finished, and turned quickly, leaving the room, calling to the housekeeper to order her carriage while she went to get her hat, parasol, gloves, and reticule to go to the dressmaker's.

Lizette stared after her, then looked at Stuart, who was also staring after his wife.

"Oh, Stuart, I'm sorry," she said unhappily. "I get you into more trouble.''

"No," he said, shaking his head, then turning to face her. "There's no trouble, really. I can handle Julia.''

"How?''

"By doing what she says." His eyes caught hers and held. "You'll have to leave here, Liz," he said.

"Where will I go?''

"There's a nice hotel. It's not the best, but the rooms are clean, the help adequate.''

Her eyes were glistening with tears of frustration and anger. "I wish I had slept with you now," she said bitterly. "I'm being accused of it anyway.''

"No, you don't," he said warmly. "Because then she'd have been right." He sighed. "It's bad enough her words were close to the truth. For her sake, I wish I could change how I feel, Liz, but I can't." He straightened uncomfortably. "All I can do is try to make the best of it, and for now that means finding someplace else for you to stay.''

"Maybe I should go home.''

"Not yet," he said. "I've got a new idea. I'll tell you on the way to the hotel. For now, I'll call the servants. I think we'd both better change before leaving. We look rather bedraggled.''

They left the parlor, passing Julia on the way as she came downstairs ready to leave the house.

"Remember, Stuart," she said haughtily, "I want her out!" and she kept on going through the foyer, slamming the front door behind her.

The Mackgowan Hotel was far from being fancy, but Lizette

was glad they had a vacant suite of two rooms for her. It was closer to the center of things and to the river, and Stuart assured her that if she wanted to go anywhere, she wouldn't have to worry. There was a livery near the hotel and he'd see to it her needs were met.

"If you want to go out, just let the manager know. But don't go out alone too much," he cautioned her. "It's not always safe. Especially not after dark."

"I know, I'm to sit here and stagnate," she answered helplessly. "I hope your new idea works, Stuart. I'd like to get this whole thing over and get on with my life."

He smiled, taking her hand. "Trust me, everything'll work out." He pulled her into his arms. They were alone now. The servants were still back at the house packing her trunks to be sent over later, and the young man who'd brought them up to the rooms had left. "If there's anything else you need, don't hesitate to let me know."

"She was really mad, Stuart," Lizette said unhappily. "What if she causes you trouble?"

"She won't." His eyes met hers. "She likes being a senator's wife as much as I like being a senator."

"Why did he have to die, Stuart?" she cried softly. "Why? I need him so!"

His hand cupped her face and he kissed her, his lips vibrant, alive, their warmth soothing the hurt deep inside her, and Lizette clung to him.

Finally, "Go," she whispered softly against his mouth. "For God's sake, go, please, Stuart," she begged. "Before I forget all my promises to myself and do what I vowed I wouldn't do!"

He kissed her again quickly, then took a deep breath, his hands easing from around her, and he grabbed his hat off a hook near the door.

"I'll see you tomorrow," he said abruptly, and walked out, leaving her staring after him, tears flooding her eyes.

"Damn you, Bain," she whispered tearfully as she watched the door shut behind Stuart. "Damn you for leaving me alone again. You had no right to die," and she turned from the door, stumbled to the bedroom, unable to see for the tears, and fell on the bed, rolling into a ball, hugging the pillow, and cried until there were no tears left.

*   *   *

Julia was like a finely wound spring, and Stuart knew it, as they dressed that evening to go to the President's mansion—the White House, as people had begun referring to it some years back, although the name wasn't used officially. He had left Lizette at the hotel, stopped off to see Jeff, then come home and gone through the mail that had piled up since he'd been gone.

Julia had said very little to him since his return to the house. She'd been resting when he got back, so the servants said. He'd taken advantage of the fact and let her rest, hoping when she woke up she'd have calmed down some. But Julia had had too many days to build up her anger. It would take more to appease her than moving Lizette out of the house.

Stuart stared at her now as she fussed in front of the mirror with her hair, and he tried hard not to compare her to Liz, to see her in her own perspective. If only she wasn't so damn thin. She wasn't emaciated or anything, but for years he'd been wishing she had a little more flesh on her bones. It'd be different if she couldn't help it, he'd love her anyway, but she hadn't been this thin when he'd married her. She was just right then, although she always talked about being too fat. Sometimes he felt she was refusing to put on weight just to prove he should love her regardless, and it irritated him. She glanced up at him in the mirror, watching him stare at her. Her cheekbones were so prominent that the hollows in her cheeks made her face look longer than it was, and her collarbones above the low-cut bodice of her lavender dress stuck out atrociously, causing the amethyst lavaliere she wore to lie in the hollow between them.

"Is something wrong?" she asked, jolting him out of his daydreaming.

"No." He flushed. "I was just thinking . . . you look lovely tonight," and she did.

Her hair was curled and coiffed just so, very becoming on her, the dress was a beautiful concoction of lace and gauze, with flowers embroidered all over it, and her jewelry not too overpowering, with amethyst stones at her earlobes. Except for the fact that her dress was purposely tucked and folded, anyone seeing her would never know her bosom was so small. She was pretty in her own way, and he should be grateful. He was, really. That was the whole trouble. He liked Julia. Julie, as he called her during their intimate moments together. She was pleasant enough to talk to, she understood enough about his job not to complain about the hours and his time away from home, she ran a household well, and except for the fact that she was deathly afraid of getting pregnant again, she'd always seemed to enjoy his lovemaking, and he'd been content, until Liz came into his life. But Liz never had belonged to him, and Julia had. He'd married her years ago when he hadn't yet learned the difference between love and friendly affection.

Julia watched Stuart closely, then turned to face him. "You think telling me I look nice tonight is going to make me forget?" she asked stiffly.

"You didn't like the compliment?"

"Not when I know you were comparing me to her."

Stuart slipped his watch from his pocket. "We'd better go," he said, checking the time. "The President detests tardiness," and he dismissed her comment unanswered, opening the door so they could go downstairs to get their wraps.

There were numerous dinners and teas in Washington, tonight's no different from most, except tonight there would be fewer people. It was a small dinner party; therefore wives were invited. Many of the senators and congressmen never brought their wives to Washington. So most dinner parties were for the men alone, while the women had teas and drawing rooms earlier in the day. Tonight's dinner required the men to bring ladies, since Mrs. Monroe would be in attendance.

Stuart had found the invitation with the mail on the desk shortly before he and Lizette left for the hotel, and he'd been pleased with it, sending a response to the White House immediately on his return to the house, with his apologies for the late acceptance, explaining he'd been out of town. He was anxious to talk to the President, and this would save making a special appointment.

Only a few guests had yet to arrive when Julia and Stuart were ushered in and announced, and Stuart could feel the distinct change in the atmosphere only moments after being presented. Most of the people knew Julia, and those who didn't had evidently been warned ahead of time she was coming, because it seemed everyone was being overly nice to her. Even Mrs. Monroe, who normally was rather distant, was more sympathetic than usual, as was her daughter Eliza, who lived at the White House with her husband, George, who was also in attendance. More than once, as the evening wore on, Stuart had the distinct impression he was quietly yet systematically being censured, not only by James Monroe but also by his fellow senators, for what they undoubtedly believed was a liaison with his widowed sister-in-law. Although not a word was mentioned, the atmosphere when he was around was certainly strained.

It wasn't until the men retired to another room for the usual smoke and glass of wine that Stuart was able to talk to the President without a dozen ears listening. And thankfully, Sam Hewitt was absent this evening.

Stuart walked over to the President. "Excuse me, but may I have a private word with you, sir?" he began as he joined Monroe in a quiet corner of the room, while the others were arguing over an issue that would be coming up for a vote in the fall.

The President had watched Stuart heading his way, and now he eyed him candidly. "It all depends on what it's about," he answered.

Stuart straightened, his fingertips caressing the glass of wine in his hands. "I think you know what it's about, sir," he said, his voice deepening. "Lizette and I found Captain Holley in Charlottesville, Virginia."

Monroe's composure faltered, but only for a moment.

"What's going on, sir?" Stuart went on stubbornly as he caught recognition in the President's eyes. "We know he's working for you at Ash Lawn. It was a good way to keep him hidden, I'll agree, but you should've known you couldn't hide him forever."

"You think a great deal of your brother's widow, don't you, Stuart?" the President said, ignoring Stuart's statement.

"What does that have to do with anything?"

"Just answer the question. Do you or don't you like her?"

"Certainly I like her," he answered. "I've known her since she was a little girl, and I think she deserves more than what she's being given, if that's what you mean."

"That's not what I meant, and you know it," the President said. His eyes narrowed suspiciously. "I'm sorry, Stuart. I'm afraid your conduct with her since she arrived here has been anything but brotherly."

"To hell with my conduct, if you'll excuse the expression, sir," Stuart blurted angrily. "But don't threaten to censure me to take pressure off the facts, especially since you're involved."

"No one's threatening or censuring you."

"Not officially, maybe, but don't underestimate me, sir, I know how to read between the lines."

"Good, then maybe you'll take some advice and not ask so many ridiculous questions. Forget it, Stuart. Leave it alone." His face was grim. "And you can be thankful your wife arrived when she did, Stuart, or you might not be getting off so easy."

"You don't intend to tell me anything, do you, sir?" Stuart said bitterly. "You're simply ignoring the fact that I even mentioned Holley."

"I'm sorry, Stuart," the President answered. "My lips are sealed. If—and mind you, I only say *if*—Bain Kolter has done anything to make this country proud of him, then I'm sure someday he'll receive recognition for it. But at the moment, Senator, the fact is, your brother died with a price on his head. Now, I suggest you forget you ever had a brother."

"And his widow?"

"I suggest you forget her too. She could be your undoing," and he stared at Stuart hard for a moment; then, "Shall we join the others, Stuart?" he asked casually, and left Stuart standing alone as he walked across the room, entering into the heated conversation going on.

President or no President, Stuart wanted to throttle the man, because Stuart knew he'd guessed right. Monroe was one who'd sent Bain away; he had to be. It was too coincidental. Well, fine, there were more men on that ship besides Holley. He'd hunt to the ends of the earth if he had to in order to find one of them who couldn't be intimidated by Hewitt and his men.

For the rest of the evening Stuart made it a point to act as if nothing was wrong, although beneath his calm exterior he was seething. It wasn't until they were in the carriage on the way home that he was able to let his true feelings show, and unfortunately Julia received the brunt of much of his anger.

"Here I thought you seemed to be enjoying yourself," she said as she glanced at him. He was sitting next to her, staring straight ahead, scowling.

"I was," he snapped.

"You don't sound like it."

"Maybe I have things on my mind."

"What things?"

"You wouldn't understand."

"I might. After all, we've discussed politics before."

"It has nothing to do with politics."

"Oh." She stiffened, suddenly realizing what he meant. "I'd

certainly like to know what she has to do with our having dinner at the White House," she said.

"I was hoping Monroe would tell me what's going on," he answered irritably. "Why else do you think I accepted the invitation? I just got back from Charlottesville. I'm tired, nothing's gone right. If I hadn't thought I could learn something tonight, I'd be home getting some rest."

Tears threatened Julia's eyes, and she turned away.

"I'm sorry, Julia," he said, realizing he'd hurt her. "It's just that nobody will say anything, and it's frustrating."

"There's probably nothing to say."

"But there is, and they're trying to cover it up. Liz has a right to be upset."

"If you don't mind, Stuart, I'd rather not discuss it," she said. "There are more pleasant things to talk about." She held her head up, pretending nonchalance. "Did you notice Mrs. Monroe's dress?" she asked superficially. "Eliza said it was from that Parisian woman who's becoming all the rage. And she was so pleased I decided to come for a while. I guess I should come to Washington more often, but the social whirl can become terribly exhausting."

He listened to her raving on about the food and the other wives who were pleased she'd be in town, and he wished to God he'd stayed home tonight. At least if he had, maybe he could have convinced Julia he wasn't about to run off with his brother's widow. Although he did have a few reckless moments when the thought was tempting.

By the time they arrived home, he was up to his ears with Paris fashions, rich cuisine, the latest in furniture, as well as a number of other equally mundane topics Julia always seemed to find interesting.

Two lamps were lit on the dresser when they reached the bedroom. Stuart followed Julia inside and quickly began unfastening his shirt collar and cravat. It was quite late and he'd told the servants not to wait up when he and Julie left earlier. Now he was glad, because he was in no mood to have them puttering about underfoot. The only one who'd met them at the door was the housekeeper, and she retired quickly, informing him the bed was turned down and their things set out.

He stood for a minute, watching as Julie sauntered to the window and stood looking out. The night was hot and the open window an enticing invitation. He slipped off his frock coat, tossed it, with his cravat, on a chair, and walked over, standing beside her. She hadn't started undressing yet.

"You're not tired?" he asked.

"A little."

He reached out and began unfastening the hooks at the back of her dress. He felt her tense, but continued, then reached up, fumbling for the pins in her hair.

She looked back over her shoulder. "What are you doing?" she asked.

He hesitated, then touched the back of her neck, letting his hand slide to her shoulder, and pulled her back against him. "I'm glad you came," he whispered against her ear. "It's been too long."

She pulled away and turned. "You're serious, aren't you?" she said. Her hands were on his chest, holding him back, and she stared up at him. "You honestly expect me to let you touch me, as if nothing's happened, don't you?"

He frowned. "I thought you wanted to be with me."

"I came to keep you from making a fool of yourself."

His eyes hardened. "Are you telling me I'm not welcome in your bed?"

She wanted to cry. "I don't know. All I know is I cringe at the thought of sharing you with her."

"I told you . . . we both told you, we haven't slept together."

"It doesn't always happen in a bed!"

"For God's sake, Julia. If I'd been doing it with Liz, would I need you now so desperately? And I do need you, feel!" He pulled her hard against him, letting her feel his arousal. He couldn't tell her why he really needed her so badly. That the torment of being with Liz and unable to release his pent-up emotions had been almost unbearable. But Julia was his wife. He had a right to touch her and let her try to soothe the ache inside him. "Is this the body of a man who's been giving himself to another woman?" he asked angrily.

"Then why?" she asked. "Why didn't you tell me what you were doing?"

"Would you have understood?"

"I'd have tried."

"Like you tried today? You listened with your ears closed, Julia. Bain was my brother and he has two children who're going to grow up thinking their father was a criminal unless somebody does something about it, and I'm in a position to try."

"At my expense?"

"Because I'm seen about town with Liz?"

"Yes, and because she was living in this house. Stuart, how can you expect me not to wonder, when everyone's talking about it?"

"Julia, don't."

"I can't help it. You went away with her, just the two of you. How do I know what happened between you?" She sighed. "I was watching when you rode up the drive this afternoon, Stuart. I saw you help her from her horse, the way you looked at her."

"You condemn me for a look?"

"It was the way you looked." She pushed him away, remembering. "You wanted her, Stuart. I know you did, and I wondered how many times you'd looked at her like that while you were gone, and how many times that look led to more."

"I told you it didn't."

"But that doesn't help me, don't you see? I want to believe it, but I can't!"

"You can!"

"I don't know. Maybe in time."

"I don't have time." He pulled her close. "I need you, Julie . . ."

She turned her head from his kiss. "No!"

She was so close, her hair touching his lips, the faint scent of lavender, familiar to him, tantalizing him, reminding him that he could lose himself in her arms.

"Julie, please . . ." he begged, his lips brushing her ear. "Don't do this to us, please."

"I can't help it."

"You can if you want to." He leaned down, his lips caressing her neck, and she trembled. "Let me love you, Julie, don't turn from me."

"On one condition," she whispered breathlessly.

His lips froze, and he held his breath. "What's that?"

"You never see her again."

He tensed, then slowly raised his head and stared at her, "Oh, no, Julie. We don't bargain with it."

"This time we do."

"So that's the way it is, is it? I see." His eyes hardened, and she felt his arm tighten about her. "All right, you want to bargain, I'll show you what kind of a bargain you'll get. Either I join you in our bed on my terms, and they don't include never seeing Liz again, or I'll do what you've been accusing me of doing, and join Liz in her bed on her terms, and I'm sure they won't be as hard to keep as yours.''

"You wouldn't!"

"Try me." His eyes bored into hers. "Well, Julie, do you really love me, or am I just a possession to show to the world? Which is it? My terms, or yours?"

She couldn't think straight. How could she give herself to him, knowing? But what if he hadn't? And what if he had? She loved him so. What would she do without him? And yet the thought of him with Liz! She wanted to scream.

"Well, I guess I have your answer, don't I?" he said when she was silent for so long, and his arms dropped reluctantly. He started to leave, but she called him back.

"Stuart! No, wait . . ." she cried breathlessly.

He was reaching for his coat on the chair, and straightened, then turned.

"Don't go," she whispered, her voice breaking. "What would I do without you?"

He stared at her hard for a minute, then walked slowly toward her, his voice unsteady. "Don't ever try to use it as a weapon like that against me again, Julie," he warned bitterly. "Love isn't something you bargain with. It's there to be shared."

"I know that." Her eyes were misty. "I love you, Stuart, you know I do," she cried, her hand touching his face. "It's just that I'm so afraid of losing you. Hold me, Stuart," she pleaded tearfully. "Hold me and make it right again," and this time when he took her in his arms, she melted against him, turning her mouth up to meet his, hoping she could keep on pretending like this, telling herself over and over as he kissed her and made love to her, then fell asleep with her in his arms, that there was no one named Lizette, that for now, for a little while, she didn't even exist.

But the next morning she was there again between them as Julia watched Stuart leave the house. He said he had business to attend to, but somehow she knew what that business was. He was going to see Liz, she just knew it. He was going to see her to tell her about his meeting with the President last night, and as she watched him mount his horse and ride down the drive, she only hoped that's all he was going to her for, and the gnawing suspicions began again.

Stuart hadn't told Julia he was going to see Liz, although he figured she guessed it. But for some reason, he couldn't bring himself to mention her name. Maybe because he felt she'd been upset enough. Or maybe because he didn't want to have to start answering questions again. Whatever the reason, he felt safer just telling her he was going out on business.

Lizette was still nibbling on breakfast when he arrived, and she offered him some tea, which he accepted readily.

"Then we're right back where we started, aren't we?" she said angrily after he'd told her about his talk with Monroe.

Stuart looked dismayed. "In a way, but he forgets. Holley wasn't the only one on the *Dragonfly* with Bain. I'm going to see Jeff when I leave here. I want him to send a man back to Charlottesville to see Charles Glazer. He should be able to give us the names of some of the men who sailed with Bain, and where they're from. If we can find just one who'll talk, the government will have to come up with something."

"That's what we thought when we found Holley."

"But Holley wouldn't talk."

She toyed with the spoon in her teacup, staring across the table at him. "Is everything all right otherwise?" she asked.

"You mean Julia?"

"You look troubled."

He gazed into her eyes. "They're trying to censure me, Liz," he said huskily. "Not officially, but I've been in Washington long enough to know what's going on."

"I'm sorry, Stuart."

"It's not your fault. Besides, I can live through it, as long as it doesn't get too messy."

"Can it hurt you politically?"

"Not unless it became official, and that would have to be done after we convene in December, from the floor. I guess I'm just mad more than anything else. Monroe and Hewitt are using the gossip about us as a threat to make me quit trying to learn the truth about Bain, and it sticks in my craw."

"Maybe you'd better quit helping me, then," she said. "I've hurt you enough, Stuart. I don't want your career ruined because of me."

"It won't be. December's a long way off."

"And it could take months to find the men who sailed with Bain."

He took her hand, squeezing it. "I don't intend to desert you, now. We'll just be more careful, that's all. We won't ask any more questions until we get more facts.''

"And we don't see each other anymore.''

"I didn't say that.''

"You should have.'' She pulled her hand from his. "Stuart, this is no good,'' she said. "You saw what it's done to Julia . . . and it isn't helping either of us. You have Julia to ease you over the bad times if you need her. I have no one.''

He reached for her hand again, but she wouldn't let him take it. She stood up. "I'm going to go home, Stuart,'' she decided quickly. "I've made enough mess out of my life. I don't have to keep playing the fool.''

"Liz, no,'' he whispered as he left the table and confronted her, holding her gently by the shoulders. "Not yet, please . . . you have nothing to go back for.''

"I have nothing here. Not even you.''

"You'll always have my heart, and you know it.''

"Can I make love to your heart? Can I tell the world it's mine? No . . .'' There were tears in her eyes. "Stuart, I thought I could be content with your arms, to be held and just loved once in a while, but I don't think I can, and I won't come between you and Julia. I've made things bad enough for the two of you. I don't want to hurt her worse than she's already been hurt.''

"When will you go?''

"As soon as I can.''

"Will you just wait until Jeff's man comes back from seeing Glazer? Just to see if we have a reason for hoping?''

"I shouldn't.''

"It'd be only a little over a week. Surely you can wait that long.'' His eyes softened. "Please, Liz.''

"All right, but there's no future in it for either of us, Stuart, we both know it, so I want to stick strictly to business, because I can't go on hurting like this.''

He stared at her hard. "Not even a good-bye kiss?''

"They're the worst of all.'' She sniffed, trying to hold back the tears. "I'm a woman, Stuart, and I know what I'm giving up, so don't tempt me, please.''

He reached up, cupping her head in his hand. "I know you're right, Liz, but it's hard to take.'' His voice broke with emotion as he looked deep into her eyes. "All right, for your sake I'll stay away unless it's business, and when I do come, I'll try to behave

myself, but I can't promise, Liz. I love you too damn much."
He kissed her lightly on the lips. "If only you were mine."

"But I'm not," she murmured breathlessly. "That's just the
trouble." Her lips were trembling and he kissed her again, this
time long and soft, losing himself in the feel of her mouth on
his, her body melting against him.

"I'm sorry Liz," he sighed as he drew his lips from hers.
"But I had to have one last kiss to remember."

"Stuart, go!" she gasped breathlessly, and he released her,
grabbed his hat, and started for the door.

"I'll be in touch," he said huskily, and walked out, leaving
her staring at the door he'd closed behind him.

It was done, and all for the best, she knew, yet it was so hard
to do. She straightened stubbornly, fought back tears, and made
up her mind. There were other men in Washington, dozens of
them. Let's see, what was the name of the gentleman she'd met
in church last Sunday? The one the minister had introduced her
to. She'd run into him in the lobby last evening and they'd talked
some. He was young, rather nice-looking.

She walked over to the stand beside the door where she'd set
the mail she'd brought from Stuart's with her yesterday afternoon,
and picked up an envelope, staring at it. It was from the same
gentleman and it had arrived early this morning by messenger.
She hadn't bothered to read it, but had just set it on top of the
mail. Now she opened it in desperation, hoping it would be what
she wanted it to be. She was right. It was an invitation to go
riding in the afternoon, then to dinner in the evening. Why not?
she asked herself, then argued over her answer before finally
giving in. Bain was dead, she couldn't have Stuart, so she might
as well, and she sat down at the breakfast table, tears of unhappi-
ness blurring the words as she wrote the man a note, accepting
his invitation.

The gentleman's name was Richard Roget. He was somewhere in his late twenties, nice enough, but a bit of a braggart,
and she was sure the only reason he'd sent the invitation was her
reputation. It seemed to be important to him to be able to tell his
friends he'd wined and dined the notorious widow of the late
Captain Gallant. He hardly talked about anything else all evening,
except once, when he mentioned the senator, asking her if she
was invited to the birthday party his wife was planning for him
the next evening.

"I haven't been invited," he said, tossing his head of thick blond hair from the side of his face. His brown eyes, set in a very square face, stared across the table at her while they ate at one of the local inns.

It was the first she had heard of the party, but since she was afraid he'd ask her to go somewhere with him again tomorrow, she said she wasn't invited, but already had plans for the next day, so it didn't matter.

That evening, after being escorted to her room and having to fight off some uncalled-for advances from him, Lizette was relieved, and vowed she'd rather go out alone than tackle another Richard Roget. So that ended that.

The next evening, Lizette sat alone in her room, looking out the window, watching the traffic down below. Her rooms were at the front of the hotel, giving full view of the busy street. It wasn't quite dark. She'd been reading Bain's letter again, as she often did when she was upset. Even though it hurt, the words were a comfort—just knowing he had cared.

She watched the carriages going by, and the people walking, and with the window open, she listened to the sounds. She wasn't a part of it, not really. She missed the twins, and Grandma Dicia and Grandpa Roth and the Château and Tonnerre. So many times she'd think of the lonely days and nights ahead of her and wonder if it was worth it, then become angry with herself for even doubting whether it was. Anything was worth clearing Bain's name.

A breeze blew in at the window, carrying the faint scent of flowers with it from across the road, and she began to feel restless. It was Friday evening, and everyone would be out and about. She'd been in her room all day and it was so hot. Stuart had warned her not to go out alone, but she couldn't stay here all the time. Besides, she'd have a driver for the carriage. It wouldn't be like she was alone.

She folded the letter, quickly tucked it into the front of her bodice, grabbed a bonnet and her reticule, and as the shadows of night crept into her room, she left, closing the door and locking it behind her.

Two hours later, her carriage, along with its driver, left a mile back with a broken wheel and a lame horse, Lizette hurried along the dark road, heading back toward the city and her hotel. She probably should have been frightened, but she wasn't. Instead she was angry. It was dark, she was sweltering in the heat, and her feet hurt in her fancy heeled shoes. If one more thing went wrong in her life . . .

She heard a carriage rumbling somewhere in the distance behind her. Good. Maybe this one would stop. None of the others had. They probably thought she was a robber, since highwaymen were known to frequent isolated roads. It was her own fault, really. She should have had the driver stay in the city instead of driving along the river, but she'd been homesick, and driving along the Potomac was as close as she could come to seeing the Broad River again.

She moved to the side of the dirt road to be out of the way of the carriages, and stumbled over a stone.

"One more thing!" she mumbled under her breath, then turned as the carriage behind her began to slow down. "Thank God," she sighed, relieved, and headed toward it.

The carriage turned out to be a small buggy with two men in it, and she stopped as she neared it, suddenly realizing the danger she could be in. She stared apprehensively. They were dressed like gentlemen, from what she could see in the dark, with high beaver hats and ruffled shirts.

"Well, what have we here?" the man driving said as he pulled on the reins, stopping the one-horse buggy.

"Could you do me a favor, sirs?" she asked, staying a far distance from the buggy. "Could you go to the home of Senator Kolter, I'll give you his address, and tell him to come pick me up. My carriage broke its wheel and I have to get back to the hotel."

"Senator Kolter?" said the man next to the driver, and he quickly stepped from the carriage as he continued talking. "Then you'd have to be Lizette Kolter, right?"

She began backing away. "Who are you?" she gasped.

"It's her, Tim," the driver yelled. "Grab it and let's get out of here."

Lizette didn't wait for any explanations. She picked up her skirts, whirled about, and began to run, with the tall one named Tim at her heels. But she was no match for his long strides, and he was at her in no time, grabbing her arm, yanking her back. Lizette swung a fist in his face, and he cursed. Her shoe connected with his shin and he spluttered something obscene as the man in the buggy holding the reins yelled.

"What the hell's keeping you? Just grab it!"

The man named Tim reached for the reticule hanging from

Lizette's wrist, but she elbowed him in the stomach, then reached up, scratching his face.

"Damn you!" he yelled furiously as her nails dug into his face. "Let go!"

The more he tugged at her reticule, the harder she fought, until suddenly his hand slapped across her face and Lizette's head swam dizzily, her ears ringing. Her head was clearing quickly, and she wasn't about to give in. Again, mustering up enough strength, she began to pummel him with all her might. This time, he used his fist, and when Lizette felt it connect with her jaw, she thought her world had ended.

This time her legs did give out, and she went down on her knees, holding her head in her hands.

"Grab it, quick!" the man in the buggy yelled as he drove up beside them, and while she was on her knees nursing her jaw, he reached down, grabbed the reticule, ripped it off her wrist, and ran to the buggy.

Lizette's head was clear now as she knelt in the road, only she felt sick as she watched them rummaging around in her reticule. Then suddenly it dawned on her what they wanted. Her hand covered her bosom and she felt under the edge of the bodice. The letter was still there, but if they didn't find it in her reticule . . .

Quickly, yet quietly, she moved into a crouch and began backing off the road into the woods. When she was certain she was far enough away, she took off running, dodging from tree to tree, yet keeping the stretch of road in sight. Suddenly she heard shouts behind her and knew she had been missed.

"Probably got it on her somewhere!" she heard one yell.

"Do you see her anywhere?"

"Hell, no!"

She stopped for a minute and crouched behind some bushes, holding her breath.

"No use hunting her," the one named Tim was saying as he walked along, peering into the woods. "Dark as pitch in there."

He walked right past Lizette, only ten feet away, and didn't even know it.

"Get in, then," the man driving the buggy said. "We'd better get out of here. I think I hear someone coming."

The man named Tim threw Lizette's reticule aside, climbed back in the buggy, and they were on their way, passing a carriage heading toward them.

Lizette peered from the bushes, watching the running lights from both the carriage and the buggy disappear at both ends of the road, then let out a sigh of relief. When she was certain no one else was in sight, she left her hiding place, salvaged her reticule where it lay in the road, then straightened, brushing the dirt from her clothes. Well, she couldn't stand here all night, and with a show of strength she hadn't thought she had left, she began trudging down the road again, determined not to stop any more carriages for a ride. She'd make it to where she was going on her own, even if her knees were wobbling.

27

Stuart had been completely surprised by the birthday party Julia had planned for him, more so because many of their Washington friends came as well as a number of his colleagues, and he was hoping it was their way of letting him know they didn't believe the gossip. There was no sign of censuring tonight, only the usual tall tales, politics, and friendly chatter.

Julia was flitting about in a pale yellow silk, discussing the children, the weather, recipes, and the latest fashions, pleased with the turnout and proud of her ability as a hostess. Her house wasn't as big as some, but the main drawing room was large enough to accommodate a good many people.

After a lovely dinner everyone retired to the drawing room, where the women sat around talking, and Stuart had tables set up so the men could play cards.

The evening was going well. Stuart won a few hands, lost a few, and thankfully the conversation stayed fairly neutral. They had just finished a hand, and Stuart leaned back in his chair. He was sitting near the door and heard the clock in the hall strike ten-thirty.

"It's your deal," Jeff said from beside him, handing him the cards.

He started to shuffle, when the housekeeper came in. She made her way to the table and nodded slightly.

"Sorry to interrupt, Senator," she said, flushing. "But it's urgent. May I see you in the hall?"

"It can't wait?"

"No, sir," she said, trying to sound calmer than she felt.

Stuart handed the cards to Jeff. "Deal me out of this hand. I'll be right back," he said, and followed her from the room. "What is it?" he asked when they reached the hall.

"You'd better go to the parlor, sir," she said hurriedly. "It's Mrs. Kolter."

"My wife?"

"No . . . no . . ." She shook her head. "The other one."

"Lizette?"

"Yes, sir."

He frowned. "She's here?"

"Yes, sir, and she's hurt."

"My God." He hurried down the hall, leaving the housekeeper behind.

He stopped for a second as he burst into the small parlor, then stared at Lizette, lying on the sofa.

Her clothes were filthy, her hair disheveled, and her face was dirty and streaked with tears. She started to sit up when she saw him, but he hurried toward her and made her stay like she was, propped against the pillows on the arm of the gold brocade sofa.

"Good Lord, what happened?" he asked in disbelief as he looked at her face.

She sniffed, then wiped a hand across her nose, streaking her face all the more. "They tried to get the letter," she said wearily. "But I wouldn't let them."

"Who's they?"

"I don't know." She shook her head. "Two men. But I scratched and kicked . . . anyway, it wasn't in my reticule, it was here," and she patted her bodice.

He was kneeling on one knee beside her, and reached out, touching her face. "You're hurt."

Her hand covered his. "You mean the chin? That's where he slugged me."

"He what?"

"Look." She moved her head slightly so he could see the left side of her mouth. "He split my lip."

"My God!" He stood up and went to the door of the parlor, looking for the housekeeper, then came back to the sofa. "Wait here, I'll get the housekeeper to have the carriage brought around and take you home."

"But your party."

"To hell with the party." He reached out and plumped the pillows up behind her head. "I'll be right back."

Stuart purposely avoided Julia. He found the housekeeper giving instructions to one of the girls serving punch to the guests and instructed her to have Archie bring the carriage to the side door.

"Sir, the guests' carriages are all blocking the drive," she said. "Archie wouldn't be able to get ours out of the carriage house."

"That's right." He rubbed a hand across his chin, smoothing his clipped beard, and frowned. "And she's in no condition to ride a horse." He thought for a minute. "I have an idea," he suddenly said. "Go pull the covers back on the bed in the guest room and I'll bring her right up."

"You're sure, sir?" the housekeeper asked.

"I'm very sure," Stuart answered, then headed back to the parlor.

Lizette was still on the sofa.

"Can you stand?" he asked, reaching out a hand.

"I hope you didn't think you were going to carry me," she said, taking his hand, letting him pull her to her feet, but her knees buckled and he caught her.

"I think I'd better," he said quickly.

He lifted her, cradling her in his arms.

"Stuart, don't be ridiculous, I'm too heavy," she protested, but he refused to listen.

"Nonsense, just put your arms about my neck."

She took a deep breath, did as he asked, then frowned as he headed toward the hallway instead of the French doors.

"Where are you going?" she asked, puzzled. "I thought you were taking me home."

"I can't," he answered. "Too many carriages in the way. Besides, you're in no condition to travel." He stopped, ready to step into the hallway. "You're going to the guest room," he said.

"Stuart, I can't."

"You can. Now, just be quiet and let me handle it, and don't make a sound."

He turned his back to the door and leaned his head back, peering into the hall. It was empty. The drawing room was at the far end of the house beyond the library, and they could hear people talking and laughing.

"Well, here goes," he said, then took a deep breath and started toward the stairs.

The stairs were at the far end of the small foyer and curved about disappearing into the upstairs with a graceful flourish, the bottom half with an open railing, so he could be seen by anyone in the foyer or walking down the long hall. Lizette thought he'd never reach them, but he did, and started up them as fast as he could, carrying her. Which wasn't too fast, really, because as much as he said it was nothing, Lizette knew she was no lightweight. He was almost out of sight around the curve and she was just about ready to whisper "We made it," when they heard Julia's voice from behind them. Stuart stopped for a moment, listening to her call his name, then kept on going, not stopping until he reached the guest room, where he set Lizette down on the bed.

"Just what do you think you're doing?" Julia asked as she hurried into the room behind him.

Stuart turned to face her. "Lizette's been hurt," he answered hurriedly. "She was in no condition to go on to her hotel, so I thought it best to bring her up here."

"Well, she's not staying."

"She is."

"I won't have it!"

"Stuart, it's all right," Lizette said, her words not as distinct because of her swollen lip. "Maybe someone can take me home."

"You're in no condition to go anywhere."

"Please, I don't want to cause trouble."

Julia laughed bitterly. "You don't want to cause trouble? You're nothing but trouble," she cried. "Why did you come here when I have a house full of guests?"

"I didn't know where to go!"

"I told you she's been hurt," Stuart said angrily. "Can't you see that?"

"I don't care if she's been beaten within an inch of her life," Julia walked toward the dresser, then turned to face Stuart again. "I told you before, and it still goes. I won't have her under my roof!"

"Be reasonable, Julia," Stuart began as he walked over to her. "What harm can it do for her to stay one night?"

Stuart's back was to Lizette as he began arguing with Julia, and neither of them saw Lizette push herself up from the bed and stand up, steadying herself apprehensively, using the nightstand by the bed to lean on, until she could stand alone. Then, when she was sure her legs would hold her, she headed for the door, their heated argument drowning out her footsteps on the Persian rug.

She couldn't stay. Not with Julia resenting her so. Maybe Jeff was downstairs. Maybe he'd take her home. Her eyes were swimming with tears as she reached the stairs. She had to get away. Away from Stuart and Julia and the terrible ache in her head.

Suddenly she heard Stuart's voice behind her. "Liz . . . oh, my God, no!" he yelled, but it was too late, she had already started down the stairs, and as she tried to put weight on her leg, it crumpled beneath her and she felt herself hurtling through the air.

Stuart stood at the top of the stairs, with Julia standing beside him, and he watched as Lizette seemed to half-float, half-bounce the length of the stairs, her muffled shriek echoing after her until she lay in a hump just beyond the curve, almost at the bottom.

"Liz!" Stuart took the steps two and three at a time, reaching Lizette before most of the guests realized anything had happened. "Liz, darling, please," Stuart pleaded softly as he dropped to the stairs beside her and picked her up, cradling her in his arms. "Liz, open your eyes." There were tears in his own eyes, and without realizing what he was doing, he leaned down and kissed her tenderly. "Liz, speak to me, please . . ." he pleaded.

Julia stood on the steps where the stairs curved and watched Stuart pleading with Lizette to open her eyes, then watched him kiss her, and her face went white. For a moment she didn't want to believe it, yet she couldn't deny it, and she suddenly felt sick. Then, as people began streaming out of the drawing room, wondering what was going on, she fought hard, managing to compose herself, and slowly moved down to where Lizette lay cradled in Stuart's arms.

Lizette stared up at Stuart, her face flushed, eyes filled with tears. "I'm sorry, Stuart," she whispered breathlessly. "I didn't mean to cause more trouble."

"Shhh," he said gently, relieved she was able to talk. He'd forgotten himself for a brief moment, then realized where he was and who was around, and by the time the first guest reached him, he was completely in control again. "Can you move?" he asked fearfully, trying not to listen to the whispering around him.

She sighed. "I don't know. Let me try." Gingerly, slowly at first, Lizette moved one arm, then the other, then one leg and the other; then Stuart helped her sit up.

"I'm lucky, I guess," she said as she sat on the step, tired, dirty, and disheveled; then she glanced up and saw Jeff in the crowd, standing next to his wife, Celia. "I was looking for you, Jeff," she said hurriedly. "I was hoping maybe you and Celia could take me home."

"Me?" Jeff smiled, then glanced at his wife. She was a small blond woman with big blue eyes and teeth that protruded slightly, with big dimples in her cheeks, and the dress she was wearing was the brightest red Lizette had ever seen. "Ceil?" Jeff asked.

"Why not?" she said, then shrugged, murmuring softly to herself. "It might prove interesting," and she moved up a step or two, addressing Stuart. "Maybe Jeff should carry her out," she said helpfully, and Stuart smiled, grateful for her suggestion.

"Maybe he'd better, at that," he answered, then watched along with his guests as Jeff picked Lizette up and carried her outside to the carriage.

While Jeff made sure Lizette was seated all right in the carriage, the rest of the guests began leaving too, and Stuart was glad, although in a way he wished he could explain what had happened. He tried a couple of times, but no one seemed interested, shrugging it off with remarks such as: "Great party, Stu," and "Sorry you didn't win more at cards, old man," and, "Thanks for inviting us, Senator," and a dozen other comments, none of which he wanted to hear. It would have been good if just one person had blurted out, "What the hell happened here, anyway?" but they didn't, and as Stuart watched the last carriage disappear down the drive, he breathed a sigh.

Julia was standing in front of him at the door and he watched her close it slowly.

"I'm sorry your party was spoiled," he apologized softly. "Really I am."

"I know," she said flatly. She was still numb inside. It was one thing to suspect, another to actually see.

"Do you really, Julie?" he asked desperately. "Do you know that I do care, in spite of what you think?"

"I guess," she said.

"That's all you can say, I guess?"

She turned to face him, her face pale, her eyes filled with pain. "Stuart, I saw you kiss her," she said slowly, her voice breaking tearfully. "Now, please, if you don't mind, I'd like to go to bed," and she brushed by him, leaving him in the foyer staring after her, his eyes suddenly beginning to mist with tears because he hadn't even realized he'd done it.

Lizette didn't go back to the hotel from Stuart's house that Friday night, August 6. Instead, after hearing her story, Celia insisted they take her home, and after a much-needed bath and a good night's sleep, she arrived back at her hotel the next afternoon, to rest her bruised body, protect her letter, and wait for the man Jeff had sent to Charlottesville to arrive back in Washington with some news for them.

It was a steamy morning when the *Interlude* sailed into the harbor at Baltimore with Bain standing on her deck, watching the familiar skyline come into view.

"What have you decided?" Roth asked from beside him.

Bain sighed. "I have to go alone, Grandpa Roth," he said firmly. "It's the only way."

"What if someone recognizes you before you reach Liz?"

"No one will. If anyone was looking for me, maybe, yes. But for all purposes, Bain Kolter's dead. I think I can make it."

"I wish you luck."

Bain smiled. He needed it. He needed all the luck he could get, but he didn't want Liz's grandfather to know he was worried, and as soon as the ship tied up and the gangplank was down, he put on some old clothes and a nondescript hat, kissed the twins good-bye, promising to bring back Mommy, then led Amigo off the ship and headed for the capital. It was a good thirty miles or more of dusty road, and Bain normally dreaded the long ride, but today he was in high spirits, just glad to be alive again. At least that's how he felt now that he knew who he was and where he was going.

It was late afternoon, Saturday, August 7, 1819, when Bain rode back into Washington, past the White House, and turned into Connecticut Avenue, stopping in front of the house he had visited the last time he was here.

At first he'd planned to go directly to Liz, but the more he thought about it, the more he felt he couldn't go to her until she was able to know the truth, and he couldn't tell her the truth until he learned it all himself. So here he was, staring at Sam Hewitt's house, ready to plunge into the man's life again, and probably scare the hell out of him.

A few minutes later Bain stood in the library where he'd stood a year ago, staring out the same window. It hadn't changed much. He'd changed, but the garden hadn't.

Suddenly the door opened behind him and he whirled around, facing Sam Hewitt, who was staring at him in disbelief. Sam's face was a pasty white, his pale blue eyes like agates.

"My God, it's you!" he exclaimed as he slowly shut the door behind him. "When Luther said a man named Domino was here . . . I never dreamed . . . I thought it was Holley wanting something."

"Then he made it?"

"Yes . . . yes . . ." Sam shook his head. "I still don't believe it. You're supposed to be dead. Where the hell have you been? What happened?"

"Maybe you'd better sit down," Bain said as he realized Sam was really distraught.

"No, that . . . I'll be all right," Sam replied shakily. "But damn, I thought I was seeing a ghost."

"It's a long story, Sam, too long to waste telling twice, so I was hoping you could take me to Monroe without too much fuss."

Sam had forced his heart to stop pounding, and made his knees quit their nonsense, now that he knew Bain was truly flesh and blood, and he straightened, his mind beginning to sift and sort out events of the past few weeks.

"I don't think I should take you to him," he said, thinking it over for a minute. "I'd rather have him come here, like before. He's going to have to explain a lot, and it's best he do it here, before anyone realizes you're back. Look . . ." He walked over and stood staring at Bain's clothes. "You've ridden a long way. Why don't I call one of the servants and have him set out a tub for you upstairs? He can dust your clothes off, and clean them up for you, and you can take a bath while you wait for me to locate the President. It's Saturday night, and it may take a few hours."

"I hope not," Bain said. "I know Liz is in Washington, and I'm anxious to see her."

Sam frowned and Bain caught the hesitation in his eyes at the mention of Liz's name.

"She's still here, isn't she?" he asked.

"Yes, she's still here," Sam answered.

"Then why the look?"

"What look?"

"Come on, Sam. I've worked with you too long not to know when something's bothering you."

"Wait for Monroe, Bain," Sam suggested diplomatically. "He'll give you all the answers. Now, come on, he'll be here by the time you get the dust washed off."

But he wasn't. An hour after his bath was over, Bain sat in the library drinking a cup of hot tea, still waiting. At least he felt refreshed. Sam's suggestion he clean up had been a good one, and he'd even taken time to trim his beard a bit, but now he was restless, and more anxious than ever to see Lizette.

Suddenly the door opened, and once more he was face to face with the President, but this time he was facing a man who was completely at a loss.

"At first I thought Sam had lost his mind," Monroe said, his voice unsteady. "But when he insisted . . ." He stepped farther into the room. It was getting late and evening shadows were already creeping into the corners. He stared at Bain. "I don't know what to say, except, how . . . ? What. . . . ?"

"Maybe we'd both better sit down, sir," Bain suggested.

"Yes. I guess that would be best."

They sat on the chairs they'd used the last time they'd talked together, and Bain began to tell him the events of the past year, trying not to leave anything out.

"So here I am," he finally said, warning Monroe in those four words that something was going to have to be done, then adding, "And first of all, I want to know, sir, since I got the proof you needed, why is Lafitte still at Campeche?"

The President flushed, his face reddening. "I'm so sorry, Bain," he said, visibly shaken. "I might as well tell you the whole truth and get it over with."

Bain straightened in his chair. "I'm listening."

"When I sent you to Lafitte's camp, Bain, I thought it would be a simple matter of proving the man guilty and getting rid of him," he began. "Unfortunately, things don't always go the way we want them to. You, of all people, should know that. Shortly after you left, Spain decided to negotiate for the Florida territories. Good and fine. I was pleased. Negotiations are over now and we've ratified the treaty. However, Spain hasn't ratified it as yet. It's over there waiting, and if we were to push our way into Campeche, they could refuse to sign. For all purposes, Florida's already ours, but technically she's still not officially ratified." He studied Bain for a minute. "But the worst is that a man named James Long has decided he didn't like the treaty we signed, so he gathered himself a small army of about three hundred men and stormed into Texas territory by way of Nacogdoches, setting up what he calls an independent republic. And he's already sent men down to negotiate with Lafitte, promising to make him governor of the territory when he takes over if Lafitte will give him a hand. The whole thing's a mess, and the United States is right in the middle." He took a deep breath. "Spain's hollering, Mexico's hollering. There are some Europeans who've moved in with Lafitte the past couple of months, high-ranking muckety-muck, and they're hollering for Spain to keep her nose out or they'll call on their friends for help, then all of Europe will be in on it. Bain"—he looked at him, his eyes intense—"I don't dare touch Lafitte right now. The most we can do is what we've been doing. If we happen to catch one of the men we know is written up in those ledgers you stole, we can prove he was dealing in stolen goods and have him hung, that's about all. But I can't go into Campeche."

Bain couldn't believe it. "Then it was all for nothing?" he asked incredulously.

"I'm afraid so. At least right now. Eventually, if Lafitte's still going strong when this whole thing is settled with Long, those ledgers and your men's testimony can be used, but at the moment it's all worthless. I'm sorry. It's my fault for getting you into this thing, but how was I to know. . . . ?"

Bain wished he could cry. Everything, his months away from Liz, the lies, almost losing his life. All of it for nothing! He set the teacup he'd been holding down and put both hands on his legs, rubbing the thighs with his palms. Almost crippled, and for what? So a few measly pirates would hang if they could catch them, while Lafitte sat back and laughed at the world?

"I know how you feel, Bain, and I can't blame you," the President said. "I only wish there was some way I could make it up to you."

"There is," Bain finally said, and he faced the President squarely. "You can clear my name so I can go back to my wife and family, so I can live again."

The President was anxious. "How?"

"I don't know how, sir," Bain said bitterly. "But I do know this." His voice lowered emotionally. "I did what you asked. I risked my life, my home and family, everything that was dear to me, so you could have your proof against Lafitte, and you got it.

If you could have run him out of Galvez Island I'd have been recognized as a hero for my work, and everyone would be proud of what I'd done. The fact that you can't touch him has nothing to do with my part of it. I fulfilled my part of the bargain, and now I want to go home, but I can't go out that door with a price on my head.''

Monroe knew that Bain was right, but what could he do? With Bain dead, there'd been no problem—all they had to do was keep their mouths shut and wait until the whole thing in Texas was thrashed out; then, if and when sometime in the future they were able to use the evidence Bain had stolen from Lafitte, it wouldn't matter if the world knew what they'd done. Lafitte would be gone, they could tell the world Bain had actually been a hero instead of a pirate, and everything would be all right. However, Bain wasn't dead, he was very much alive, and to have to tell the world now that the United States had sent a spy into Mexican territory to get evidence against a man the Mexicans were calling a friend . . .

Monroe cursed silently to himself. What more could go wrong?

"Sir?" Bain asked, uneasy about the President's silence.

"I'm trying to think, Bain," he said. "I'm at a loss."

"I want to go home, sir," Bain said unhappily. "I want to see my wife, and take her home, and I have to tell people something."

"I know, I know." Monroe nodded, trying to think. He leaned back in his chair and studied Bain for a long time. Bain had risked so much, and yet he and Sam had risked nothing except a few doubtful looks from their colleagues when Bain's wife and the senator began prying. Bain's wife! The President flushed self-consciously, thinking about all the gossip. Was she still waiting for her husband, or had Bain lost her as well as his reputation? My God, what had he done to the young man? And all he'd wanted was to stop Lafitte. Nothing seemed to be going right.

He straightened, then leaned forward, making a decision he hoped he could live with, without having to explain too much.

"Your name will be cleared, Bain," he promised firmly. "I'll see to that, but we'll make no mention of Lafitte. Nor do I want you to mention him. The United States will acknowledge that you were working under orders directly from the Navy Department, to infiltrate pirate shipping in order to help the United States track down and convict those men caught in American waters who were claiming to be legal privateers but who were actually using their ships for piracy. I'll work it out with Sam tonight and make sure the newspapers put out a special edition tomorrow, with the story on the front pages. If anyone says anything, I'll just pretend I didn't know anything about it, and if we all keep rather vague, the whole matter should die down in no time. You know how it is in Washington.''

"My name will be cleared.''

"I promise. By morning everyone will know that Bain Kolter is not only alive, but was never a pirate.''

"Thank God!'' Bain took a deep breath, relieved, then sighed as he gazed toward the window. It was almost dark outside already. "I guess I'd better find Liz, now,'' he said. "I have a lot of explaining to do. Do you know where she's staying, sir?'' he asked.

Monroe's eyes grew wary. "I'm not sure. She was at Stuart's house, but I think, with Julia arriving, she went to one of the hotels. I don't know which one.''

Bain stared at him for a long hard minute, a knot suddenly beginning to tighten in the pit of his stomach. "Stuart's house?'' he asked.

"You were right when you said your wife would protest, Bain,'' he answered. "She raised such a fuss that Sam wrote asking Stuart to come and get her out of our hair. Which reminds me. Did you leave her a letter, Bain?''

"I had to leave her something, in case I didn't come back. I couldn't let her think I'd deserted her.''

"Well, that's over and done,'' he replied quickly. "But I have to tell you, it was almost our undoing.''

"I'm sorry, sir,'' Bain apologized. "But she is my wife, and I do love her.''

"Yes, I know.'' The President stood up, and Bain followed suit. "Now, I suggest you go find her, Bain, while I have a few words with Sam. I'm afraid it's going to take a lot of maneuvering on our part to set things straight again. But don't worry, it'll all work out. I'm just terribly sorry you went through so much for nothing.''

"So am I,'' Bain said bitterly. "Good-bye sir,'' and he shook the President's hand, then left the room, telling the servant on the way to the door that the President was still in the library and wanted to see Mr. Hewitt.

A short time later, Bain reined off the main road and moved slowly up the drive of Stuart's house, stopping near the side door.

He dismounted and looked around. It was barely dark and he could still see everything quite clearly, although lights were already on in the house. This was going to be hard. There was no easy way to approach people without scaring them when they thought you were the last person they'd ever see alive again. He tied his horse to the hitching post, then straightened his shoulders. Well, the only way was the direct approach, like with Sam. He strolled up the walk and knocked at the front door.

A few minutes later he stood in the small parlor off the foyer waiting for Julia to come downstairs. He assumed Stuart wasn't home, since the housekeeper had mistaken him for Stuart when she'd first opened the door. It wasn't until he'd stepped into the light that she'd recognized him and almost fainted. However, he'd managed to keep her on her feet and help her over the initial shock, then told her to warn Julia so she'd know what to expect when she came downstairs.

He was standing by the French doors that opened into the garden, staring outside into the warm night, when he heard a slight noise behind, and turned. Julia was in the doorway, staring at him, a strange look on her face.

He frowned. There were dark circles beneath her eyes, and she looked sad. Her face was pale, the gray dress she wore making her look gaunt, as if she'd been sick.

"Julia?" he said affectionately as he walked over to her, taking her hands.

"I didn't believe it," she said, half-whispering. "When she told me, I thought I was still dreaming and it was part of the nightmare."

He studied her face. "What is it, Julia? What's wrong?" he asked.

"Is it really you?" she murmured, staring at him incredulously. "You're really alive?"

"I'm really here." Bain stared at her hard. Julia had always been on the thin side, but tonight it wasn't just that. She looked terrible, and he was concerned. "Maybe you'd better sit down," he suggested, leading her toward the sofa.

"I don't believe it," she said again as she sat down, not taking her eyes from him. "All day I've been wishing . . . and then tonight, when he left. . . ."

"When who left? Stuart?"

She nodded.

"Where is he, Julia?" Bain asked. "Where is Stuart?"

"You don't know, do you?" she said, her voice breaking. "No, you wouldn't know." A sob wrenched from deep inside her. "He's with her, Bain. He went to her. I know he did!"

Bain felt the jolting impact of her words and his jaw tightened angrily. "He went to her?" he asked hesitantly.

"To Lizette! Your wife," she sobbed. "He's having an affair with Lizette!"

"No! God no!"

"I didn't want to believe it either," she cried helplessly. "But after last night . . ." She sniffed, trying to stop crying. "He swore he hasn't slept with her, but he's lying, I know he is. I saw him kiss her, and they'd been alone here in the house all that time. I knew what was going on . . . all the gossip . . . and now he's with her. I know he went to her."

"Where is she, Julia?" he asked.

"At the Mackgowan Hotel."

"You're sure."

"I'm sure."

He straightened thoughtfully, staring at her hard for a minute, then headed for the door.

"Where are you going?" she asked hesitantly.

He turned, his gray eyes dark and stormy with rage. "To the Mackgowan Hotel," he answered furiously, and walked out, slamming the front door behind him.

28

Lizette was still lying in bed when Stuart arrived, and he insisted she climb back in after unlocking the door for him. Last night had been like a nightmare and she'd been thankful to Jeff and Ceil for their help, and for bringing her home today. She limped back to the bed and climbed in, wrapper and all, pulling up the covers.

Stuart stood for a long time watching her. Even with her lip cut and the bruise on the side of her chin, she looked so lovely. Her dark curls were tousled all over her head, and her green eyes were so alive. He felt a tightening in his chest that hurt.

"How do you feel today?" he asked as he watched her settle against the pillows.

"Sore." She made a face. "I never had so many bruises before in my life."

"You could have been killed."

"But I wasn't."

He walked over and motioned for her to move over, then sat on the edge of the bed. He knew it wasn't the gentlemanly thing to do, nor was it proper for him to even be with her here alone, but he and Liz were too close to let propriety stand in the way.

"We have to talk, Liz," he said softly.

She studied his face. "It's Julia, isn't it?"

He nodded. "She saw me kiss you last night."

She sank back into the pillows. "Oh, Stuart. I'm sorry."

"The worst part is, I didn't remember kissing you. I did it without thinking." He reached out and took her hand, holding it tight. "You were right the other day, Liz," he said huskily. "I can't do this to Julia. If you could see her." He took a deep breath. "Before, it was just anger and suspicion, but since last night, all she needed was to see me kissing you, to believe the worst, and nothing I said seemed to make any difference. It's like she's dead inside."

Liz sat up straighter on the bed. "Stuart, what can I say?" she said, her voice breaking. "If I could change last night, I would . . . I didn't know."

"It's not your fault. It's mine," he answered. "I thought I could have you both, but life doesn't work that way." He took her hand, lifting it to his lips, and kissed her palm. "I love you, Liz, I'll always love you," he whispered softly. "But there's a bond between Julia and me. One I can't explain. Maybe because of the children, or because we've been together so many years." He flushed. "I guess I do love her in a way . . . not like it is with us. But I do care, and I can't stand seeing her like this. If she'd only yell at me like she did at first, maybe I could take it, but she doesn't. She doesn't do anything. She just walks around with tears in her eyes. If I talk, she answers. I kiss her and there's no response." He was still holding her hand and caressed her fingers tenderly. "I came to say good-bye, Liz," he said, his voice breaking. "Clearing Bain's name isn't worth killing Julia in the process. I've already talked to Jeff and he said he'd help you. I'm going to take her back to Beaufort and try to make her forget, and try to forget myself, and hope it isn't too late. It's the only thing I know to do."

Their eyes met. "I'm glad, Stuart," she said painfully. It hurt to lose him. "You're too much like Bain for me not to want you, and I know it isn't right. So as soon as his name is cleared, I'm going to take the children and go away somewhere, so I can forget I ever loved him."

"Will you?" he asked helplessly.

She shook her head. "No, just like I'll never really forget you."

He smiled wistfully. "A kiss, Liz. Just one kiss," he said. "To say good-bye."

She leaned toward him and he reached out, holding her face in his hands.

"Good-bye, love," he whispered softly, then his lips were on hers, warming her deep down inside for the last time. Stuart trembled. He was saying good-bye. It was over and he had to go on. The kiss was long and passionate; then, as he reluctantly drew his lips from hers, their eyes met and neither of them spoke for a moment, until finally she broke the silence.

"Good-bye," she whispered breathlessly.

Stuart straightened, still staring down at her, then turned abruptly and left, closing the door firmly behind him.

He stood in the hall for a long time, fighting the urge to go back, then thought of Julia and what it would do to her if he did, and with a strength he didn't know he had, tears threatening his eyes, he started for the lobby, knowing life would never be the same again.

Outside the hotel, it was dark as Bain dismounted and tied his horse to the hitching post. He stood for a minute gazing around. No one was paying the least bit of attention to him. Good. Because he didn't want to be stopped now. He patted his horse on the nose, turned and headed for the door of the hotel, then stopped inside and suddenly froze. Descending the stairs at the far end of the lobby and coming directly toward him was Stuart. He was handsomely dressed in a brown silk frock coat, ruffled shirt, buff pants tucked into top boots, and carrying a beaver hat. Bain's breath caught at the sight of his brother, and all the anger he'd been nursing on the way to the hotel exploded.

Stuart didn't see Bain at first, his eyes were too full of tears; then suddenly he caught a glimpse. A russet beard, familiar stance. Stuart stopped and blinked his eyes, then slowly moved toward the man who was dressed in a seaman's blue coat, white shirt open at the throat, and black pants tucked into top boots. He was wearing an old sailor hat and was standing just inside the door. Stuart's face went white.

"Bain?" he blurted incredulously.

Bain stood tall and erect, his eyes falling on his brother's face.

"My God! It *is* you!" Stuart gasped, astonished, and Bain tensed.

"Where is she, Stuart?" he asked angrily.

For a minute Stuart was at a loss for words. Now suddenly he came to life. "Good Lord, Bain, where've you been? What happened? What are you doing here?" he asked all at once.

Bain shook his head. "Never mind that, where's my wife?"

Stuart frowned. "Christ's sake, Bain. We thought you were dead!" he countered. "You can't just walk in out of nowhere without even an explanation."

"I'll explain to Liz."

"You can't!"

"What? See my wife?"

"Walk in on her without any warning. What do you want to do, Bain, kill her?"

"I should kill you!"

"For what?"

Bain's eyes were blazing and both men were so engrossed in what was happening that neither of them realized a few people in the lobby were watching.

"You did it to me again, didn't you?" Bain said recklessly. "You couldn't keep your hands off her."

"Who told you that?"

"Julia!"

"Julia doesn't know what she's talking about. I've been trying to help Liz clear your name, that's all."

"That's all?" Bain grabbed the front of Stuart's shirt. "I don't need your lies, Stuart, I can do without them," he said. "In fact I can do without you, too. You cuckolded me again, didn't you? My own damn brother, but I'll make you pay for it this time." He threw Stuart from him, his mind made up once and for all. "Tomorrow at dawn, Stuart, you know where, and you choose the weapons."

Stuart winced. "I don't want to fight you, Bain," he pleaded.

"Well, I want to fight you. I want to get you out of my hair, out of my wife's bed, and out of my life. Now, choose your weapons!"

Stuart still shook his head. "No, Bain, I won't."

"Then I'll choose. It'll be pistols, Stu . . . pistols, do you understand? Now, will you find yourself a second and meet me there, or are you going to prove to all of Washington you're a coward as well as a bastard?''

Stuart stared at Bain long and hard. There was no way he was going to change his brother's mind. Bain thought he'd made love to Liz again, and all the explanations in the world weren't going to make him believe otherwise. He straightened the front of his shirt and squared off, facing Bain reluctantly.

"If that's really how you want to settle it."

"It is." Bain frowned. "Now, where is she?"

"Suite ten at the top of the stairs."

Bain started past Stuart, who grabbed his arm. "Wait," Stuart said through clenched teeth. "Before you go to her, remember, Bain, she thought you were dead. That she'd never see you again." His eyes narrowed. "If I find out you've taken any of your rage out on her, I'll make sure I don't miss tomorrow, do you understand?"

Bain stared back at him, his own eyes blazing. "Is that all?"

Stuart let go, and Bain headed for the stairs.

"Is that the senator's brother?" one of the men in the lobby asked the man next to him.

The other man frowned. "Hell, no, it's probably a cousin or something. The senator's brother's dead, or didn't you know?"

Stuart heard the two men as he watched Bain disappear up the stairs, and again the impact hit him. Bain was alive! Where had he come from, and how? He turned quickly and left, heading for Jeff's house.

Lizette was still sitting on the bed, staring toward the door Stuart had closed only a few minutes before. She had a straight view of it from her bedroom, and knew she should get up and lock it, but her legs were still trembling. She didn't want to say good-bye to Stuart, not really. Bain was gone forever, but as long as Stuart was close, Bain's death wasn't as much of a reality. Now, suddenly, she felt the same emptiness inside she'd felt when Bain had first died, before Stuart had come back into her heart again. It was such a horribly lonely feeling. Her eyes filled with tears.

It was dark out already, and she glanced toward the lamp beside the bed. It was the only one lit in the whole suite. The sitting room was already deep in shadows, and getting darker by the minute. She sighed and wiped the tears from her eyes, remembering last night. She'd better lock the door and light the lamps.

She moved stiffly, her muscles aching as she left the bed, grabbed the flint, and went into the sitting room. Faint light from the window made shadows play about the room, and it was scary, reminding her of her long walk to Stuart's last night, dodging barking dogs, and ducking shadows. She lifted the flint, took the chimney off the lamp, and was just ready to light it when she heard the loud click of the doorknob. She froze, heart pounding, knees trembling. The door was still unlocked.

Quickly she set the flint and chimney down, and grabbed a vase from a stand, then moved over to the door, carefully flattening herself against the wall.

The door began to open, slowly at first, then more deftly, and Bain stepped a few feet into the dark room.

Lizette saw the familiar figure silhouetted in the light from the bedroom, and her heart did a turn. Oh, Lord, Stuart looked so much like Bain. But what was he doing back? Had he forgotten something or changed his mind?

"Stuart?" she asked hesitantly as she lowered the vase she'd been planning to hit him with.

Bain turned, and something—the way he held his head, a vague sense of . . . Lizette stared, unable to speak. It wasn't Stuart. Instinctively she knew it wasn't, and yet it couldn't be. . . .

"Bain?" she gasped breathlessly.

"Liz!"

That voice. That familiar voice, deep, loving. Only one person spoke her name like that. But it couldn't be—he was dead! The room slowly began to spin, her heart started pounding, and as he took a step toward her, Lizette inhaled sharply, and everything suddenly went blank.

Bain caught her before she hit the floor, but the vase crashed, shattering. He swung her into his arms, cradling her against him, kicked the door to the hallway shut, and headed toward her bedroom, where the light was on. When he reached the bed, he laid her down gently, her head on the pillows, then sat beside her on the edge of the bed.

Lizette's mind was foggy and she felt strangely disoriented. Slowly, frantically, the vague memory of Bain calling her name registered amid the swirling darkness, and she opened her eyes hesitantly.

She hadn't been wrong . . . yet, was she dreaming? "Bain?" she murmured, half-disbelieving.

He was staring down at her, studying the dark bruise on her chin and cut lip. "I didn't mean to frighten you," he said huskily. "But there was no other way."

She was still skeptical. Was he real or an apparition? She reached up, touching his face, then looked into his gray eyes. He was real.

"Oh, Bain!" she cried ecstatically, and pulled his head down, looking deep into his eyes for such a long time, drinking in the wonder of seeing him again. Then slowly their lips met in a lingering kiss that seared its way to her heart.

Bain answered her lips desperately. He'd waited so long. His anger and all thoughts of Stuart, were suddenly forgotten in the violent emotions that tore through him. This was Liz, his love, his life.

He raised his head, gazing down at her, drinking in her voluptuous beauty, his hand touching her shoulder, the fingers trailing down to cover her breast.

Lizette sighed, whispering his name over and over again, until she was mesmerized with her need for him, the loneliness that had gripped her only a short time before suddenly replaced by a wonder beyond compare.

"I thought I'd never see you again, or touch you, or kiss you," she whispered passionately. "Oh, Bain, tell me I'm not dreaming, that I won't wake up and find it isn't true."

He stroked her hair, winding a curl around his finger, then lowered his head to her ear. "You're not dreaming, Liz," he murmured softly. "I'm here, truly here," and he kissed her neck, savoring the feel of her flesh beneath his lips, his hands beginning to explore her body, finding all the familiar hills and valleys that always kindled his desire and brought him pleasure.

"How? What happened?" she asked as his lips explored her throat, dipping down into the valley between her breasts where the ruffles from her wrapper and nightgown hindered their further progress.

"Later, darling," he answered dreamily, his mind only on loving her. "We'll have time for explanations later." He raised up and gazed down into her eyes once more, marveling in their languid beauty and the vibrant yearning they transmitted to him. "Right now, it's been so long, I want only to lose myself in you and live again," and as his mouth took hers once more, Liz forgot all the painful, aching months apart. They were together again, and it was all that mattered, and seconds later, as they shed their clothes and he slid in next to her, she even forgot about the bruises that marked her body, and why they were there, reveling only in the moment, while Bain made love to her, and she returned his love, bringing them both a wild rapture that swept over them like a raging storm, leaving them spent and breathless in its wake.

Afterward she lay in his arms for a long time while he told her where he'd been, and why, treading lightly over his stay at Barlovento, and making her promise not to mention Lafitte's name to anyone.

"The President doesn't know I'm telling you the whole truth, Liz," he said as he held her close. "The rest of the world will know nothing about Lafitte, they'll only know that I was pretending to be a pirate as an agent for the government."

"What's so special about Lafitte?" she asked, her cheek resting against his shoulder.

"He's not an ordinary man, Liz," he explained. "He's shrewd and cunning, and right now, if Monroe were to admit he'd sent a spy into his camp, it could have tragic repercussions. From what the President's told me, there's a mess going on in Texas right now, and the United States is trying to keep the lid from blowing off the whole thing."

"Politics?" she asked.

"Nasty politics."

"That's why he didn't want me asking questions." She cuddled closer against his shoulder. "I remember when I first got to Washington, they were all up in arms about some American who was causing trouble in Texas."

"James Long," Bain answered. "He's still there and he's set up his own republic. Right now he's trying to get Lafitte to help him. Monroe's been worried that if the Spanish learned I'd been to Lafitte's camp as an American agent, they'd think the United States was backing Long. When the news of my death arrived, it was just what they needed to be able to keep the whole thing quiet until something's settled down there one way or another. Then you had to show up asking questions."

"Why didn't they just tell me? I'd have kept quiet about it if they'd asked."

"I guess they thought it was too much of a risk. They didn't know you that well, Liz, and you were so determined to clear my name."

"Well, they didn't have to get so rough," she said angrily,

and sat up, showing him her split lip and explaining about her bruised chin as she told him about the events of the night before.

He started to get mad, but she suddenly laughed. "Don't blame them too much, darling," she said, running her hand playfully across his chest. "I guess it was partly my fault too. All they did was try to grab my reticule, thinking your letter was in it. I'm the one who started fighting." She flushed sheepishly. "And you know how stubborn I can be."

He smiled, cupping her head with his hand. "Such a vixen." He looked into her eyes, his own vibrant and intense. "Liz, did you really think you could clear my name?" he asked curiously.

"We were trying."

"We?"

"Stuart and I." She felt him tense. "Bain, no," she whispered softly. "It's not like before. It never could be. I'm your wife now."

"You thought I was dead."

"Julia wasn't."

"You didn't care before."

She stared at him apprehensively. "That was before, Bain, this is now," she said. "Stuart was just helping me, that's all."

"Is that why Julia's so upset?" he asked, his jaw tightening as he stared at her. "Because Stuart's helping you?"

"You saw Julia?"

"Before coming here." His eyes darkened. "She looks terrible, Liz, and it isn't because you and Stuart are just friends, either. What happened between you, Liz?" he asked, anger clearly showing on his face.

"Nothing."

"He visits in your hotel room while you're in bed, and you tell me nothing?"

"You saw Stuart?"

"I saw him leave, yes."

"It isn't what you think, Bain," she said quickly. "Please, there's nothing between us."

"Don't lie, Liz. I won't listen to lies," he demanded. "You thought I was dead and he was so handy!"

"That's not how it was!"

"Then how was it?"

Her eyes smoldered. "It was terrible without you," she cried helplessly. "I felt lost, alone . . . he's so like you, Bain. It was like having you with me again. But nothing happened."

"No words of love? No assignations?"

"Bain, don't do this to us, please," she begged. "Don't spoil your homecoming."

His eyes bored into hers. He wanted to believe her, but how could he? The thought of her with Stuart brought an ache to his heart, because he loved her so terribly much. Sometimes it frightened him the way he loved her. Even now, knowing she'd turned to Stuart for the love he hadn't been here to give her, didn't dampen his love for her. He wanted her more than ever, to prove to her and to himself that their love far eclipsed anything she could have had with Stuart.

His hand was still in her hair and he pulled her head toward him, his eyes searching her face, then lowering to the twin mounds of flesh gracing her tawny body. He remembered it all so well, and had dreamed of it all so often, ever since his memory had returned. Yet he knew that one wrong word and she'd turn from him, her temper as furiously wild as an untamed cat. He couldn't take that. Not now, when he'd just found her again.

His eyes grew intense as they rose from her full breasts. "My homecoming?" he asked her breathlessly.

"Your homecoming," she murmured softly, and he pulled her close to him, shoving his anger at Stuart aside for the moment, holding her close in his arms again, taking her once more to the blissful world of love they'd both been without for so long. And later, as she curled up beside him and fell asleep, her body satiated from her complete surrender, Liz forgot all about Stuart and the accusations. But Bain didn't, and as the wee hours of the morning rolled around, and he knew dawn lay close around the corner, he slipped from the bed, leaving her sound asleep, put on his clothes, and left the rooms, closing the door quietly behind him.

The first faint streaks of dawn were beginning to break over the city, sending splinters of light through the bedroom windows as Lizette stirred in the large wooden bed. Her eyes felt as if they had sand in them, and with them still shut, she sighed, remembering last night. She opened them slowly and reached out, expecting to feel Bain beside her; instead, she frowned at the empty side of the bed.

"Bain?" she called.

There was no answer. She blinked her eyes again in the shadowy room, and pushed up onto her elbows, trying to see into the sitting room.

"Bain?" This time she called a little louder.

Still no answer.

Her frown deepened, her stomach tightening apprehensively. "Could I have dreamed it?" she whispered aloud to herself, then realized she was naked, and the remembrance of his body taking hers was too real, too vivid.

"Bain?" she called again, this time louder, and she slipped from the bed, grabbed her nightgown, pulling it over her head, then put on her black satin wrapper. She went into the sitting room. He wasn't there. But where?

She was pulling the sash tighter on her wrapper when there was a knock on the door. Bain? But why would he knock? She moved to the door, pressing her head against it.

"Who's there?" she asked hesitantly.

"It's Julia!"

Julia? Lizette shook her head, perplexed as she opened the door.

"Where's Bain?" Julia asked hurriedly as she rushed in, kicking aside shards of the broken vase still underfoot on the floor as she entered.

Lizette stared in wonder at the dark circles under Julia's eyes, and at her paleness, made even worse by the scarlet dress she was wearing. Julia's blue eyes were darting about the room anxiously.

"What do you mean, where is he?" Lizette asked as she stared at her sister-in-law. "That's what I'd like to know."

Julia let out a cry, her hand covering her mouth. "Oh, God, I'm too late."

"For what?" Lizette demanded, and Julia looked at her dumbfounded.

"You don't know, do you?" she asked.

"Know what? For heaven's sake, Julia . . ."

"Last night Bain challenged Stuart to a duel, and all because of you," Julia answered desperately. "Because you and Stuart are lovers. . . ."

"Oh, no . . . God, no!" Lizette cried.

"I thought I could stop Bain." Tears filled Julia's eyes. "It's too late . . . too late . . ."

"Where?" Lizette asked, grabbing Julia by the shoulders. "Where have they gone?"

"By the river. A place by the river . . ." Julia stared at her, tears streaming down her face. "You'll never get there in time."

"I can try." Lizette ran to the armoire in the bedroom, grabbed a dress, took off her nightclothes, hurried into her underclothes, then pulled on a black cotton dress, buttoning it up the front. It took only seconds more to put on her shoes, grab her bonnet and reticule, and head for the door. She didn't even bother to comb her hair.

"Are you coming?" she asked Julia as she threw the door open. Julia stood staring as if in a trance. Lizette grabbed her arm. "Good Lord, I can't leave you here," she yelled, and she hurried her into the hall, slamming the door behind them, and began dragging Julia down the hall.

"Do you have a buggy?" she asked Julia as she hurried her through the lobby.

Julia nodded. "I had Archie bring me."

"Good."

When they reached the carriage, Lizette wasted no time. It took her less than two minutes to learn from Archie where the brothers might have gone, and in no time they were heading toward the river, the sun at their backs.

Lizette was scared, but didn't want to show it because of Julia. If anything happened to either one . . . what would they do? If only Bain had told her, she might have talked him out of it. Damn him anyway! Tears threatened Lizette's eyes, but she fought them back.

"Can't we go faster, Archie?" she yelled.

He shook his head. "Not 'lessen you want to end up in the road."

As it was, she and Julia were holding the sides of the carriage as hard as they could while Archie careened through the streets that were practically deserted so early on a Sunday morning.

"It's just up ahead," Archie called back as they rode along the river. Lizette leaned over, trying to see. She recognized Amigo beside a closed carriage pulled off to the side of the road in a field, and a few horses stood nearby.

"Oh, God, I hope we're not too late," she began praying, when suddenly a shot filled the air and her heart stopped.

As the carriage slid to a stop, another shot rang out, and as Lizette's feet hit the grass, she stood transfixed, staring into the clearing ahead, where two men were standing facing each other. One was Bain, the other Stuart. Both their pistols were smoking, and as she and Julia watched in horror, the pistol dropped from Stuart's hand and he crumpled to the ground, then lay still.

Julia screamed, and tears gathered in Lizette's eyes. Bain had killed Stuart! Lizette stared straight ahead, her eyes on Bain, her heart constricting inside her, and she began to walk toward him, across the field, ignoring a few men who were standing around, and the doctor who was heading for Stuart, with Julia right behind him.

"You had to do it, didn't you?" she accused as she reached Bain, and his head turned in her direction, seeing her for the first time. "Why?" she asked tearfully, but he didn't answer, only stared at her. "He was your brother!" she shouted.

"You think I don't know that!" he yelled back, his voice breaking, and there were tears in his eyes. "You know why? I can't stand sharing you!"

"You never had to, I was always yours, Bain."

"For how long? As long as I'm in sight, but the minute my back's turned, you're in his arms again."

"No, always," she cried hysterically. "I was always yours. But not now! Not like this. You killed Stuart, and I can't forgive you for that. He never hurt you, not intentionally, Bain. All he did was love me and try to help me pick up the pieces when you were no longer there."

Tears rolled down her cheeks. "Why did you have to kill him?"

"For you! I did it for you!"

"No!" she cried angrily. "You did it for you, because you were jealous, and I hate you, Bain! I never want to see you again," and she covered her face with her hands, sobbing as Julia wailed from somewhere behind her.

Bain stared at Lizette, and suddenly he felt sick. The gravity of what he'd done suddenly hit him. He'd killed his brother! His own flesh and blood, and for what? For the love of a woman who'd betrayed him. A woman who was crying now, not because he had killed someone, not because of the hurt that was grinding away inside him over what he'd done, but because Stuart was dead. She was crying because Stuart was dead!

Tears filled Bain's eyes, and he dropped the dueling pistol at her feet in the grass; then, without saying a word, he turned from her, walked across the field to Amigo, mounted his stallion, and rode toward town, Julia's wailing sobs and Lizette's muffled cries ringing in his ears.

Lizette stood for a long time, trying to stop the tears, her heart hurting from the pain. Stuart . . . and Bain. What had she done to them? God, what had she done? She raised her head, staring at the sun-filled morning sky, watching a bird riding the air currents, and prayed.

"God, please, forgive me!" she pleaded aloud, her voice breaking on a sob. "Don't let this happen, please, don't! Let it all be a mistake, God, please!" and suddenly a shout went up behind her, and she whirled around.

"He's alive," Julia was shrieking hysterically. "Please, doctor, don't let him die. He's alive!"

Lizette stared, then wiped the tears from her eyes as she walked slowly toward Julia and the men gathered around Stuart, who was still on the ground.

"He's alive, Liz," Jeff said as she reached them, and Lizette glanced at him incredulously.

"Alive? Stuart's alive?"

"Yes."

She moved closer and stood behind Julia, who was on her knees on the grass, wiping Stuart's face with a handkerchief.

She saw the doctor tuck a cloth under his shirt, on the left side, a few inches above the middle of his chest; then the doctor stood up, motioning for his carriage.

"Doctor?" she asked anxiously.

"I think he'll live, ma'am," he said quickly. "But I'll have to get him home to bed before I'll really know for sure."

She nodded, dazed, and watched as the doctor's carriage was brought over. They made a stretcher, then lifted Stuart in, and Julia rode in the closed carriage with Stuart, while Jeff rode to Stuart's house in the other carriage with Lizette, his and Stuart's horses tied on behind.

Jeff didn't say much all the way to the house, nor did Lizette. They only stared at the early-morning traffic, both seemingly lost in thought. When they reached the house, Lizette watched them carry Stuart in, Julia at his side; then she and Jeff made their way to the parlor to wait.

"Do you think he'll be all right?" Lizette finally asked Jeff, breaking the silence that seemed to hang over them since they'd watched the men put Stuart on the stretcher.

He nodded. "The doctor knows what he's doing."

"But what if he dies? It's all my fault."

"Your fault? No, Liz. Stuart's a grown man. What he's done is his own doing, make no mistake there. It's no more your fault the man loves you than it is your fault he's breathing. You don't control his mind or his heart. None of us controls our minds or hearts. There are many kinds of love, Liz, and some people just make it easier to love them. You didn't make him love you. It's just something that happened."

"But you don't understand, Jeff," she said tearfully. "He doesn't love me, not really. Not the way Bain does. Stuart's heart's so big . . . maybe he does feel something for me, maybe he always will, I don't know, but he loves Julia. I know he does. Last night he came to tell me he couldn't help me anymore. You know that, and you know why. He kissed me once, and Julia saw him, and it tore him up inside to see what it did to her. Stuart loves her, Jeff, and I only hope she knows it."

"She does," Julia said from the doorway, and Lizette whirled around. Julia's face was grave, but the color was back, and her eyes were shining. "He wants to see you, Liz," she said, tears glistening in her eyes. "And Jeff too."

"Julia, I'm sorry," Lizette said unhappily.

Julia swallowed hard, then straightened. "I'll take you to him," she said, and led the way upstairs.

Stuart was lying on the bed, his chest bare, a bandage on the left side of it. When they walked in, the doctor stepped away.

"He's all right?" Lizette asked.

"I'm fine," Stuart answered, his voice a little unsteady, and she stared at him in surprise. "Bain's always been a lousy shot, Liz," he said, half-smiling.

She started to cry.

"None of that," he said, wincing as he coughed a little. "It smarts some, but I'll live."

"He could have killed you."

The smile left Stuart's face. "Yes, he could have, Liz," he said seriously. "And would have, too, if he'd been a better shot. But it's over now, all of it, and I think you'd better find him, and somehow convince him that I don't want his wife." He reached out and took Julia's hand. "I have one of my own, whom I love very much."

"Thank you, Stuart," she said gratefully. "Oh, God, I'm so glad you're still alive."

"You're glad?" he exclaimed, making a face as he tried to move a little. "I'm the one who's really glad. Now, go, find him, tell him you love him, and put things right again. You both deserve it."

She stood for a minute, staring at Stuart and Julia. "Oh,

Lord,'' she cried, suddenly remembering. ''I don't know where he is!''

Stuart looked at Jeff. ''Well?'' he asked. ''Can you help her this time?''

Jeff grinned. ''I'll try.'' He started for the door. ''Liz?''

''I'm coming.'' She looked once more at Julia, then to Stuart. ''Thank you, for everything,'' she said quickly, then turned and left the room, following Jeff on outside, where Jeff gave Archie orders to hitch up a carriage.

''Where to?'' she asked as they got in.

''Archie knows all the places,'' he answered. ''If he's in town, we'll find him.''

But they didn't, and it was close to noon when they accidentally discovered he'd left for Baltimore.

''I should have thought of that,'' Lizette yelled out through the crack in her bedroom door a short while later while she put on a riding habit. Jeff was waiting for her in the other room. They had sent Archie off to Stuart's to get a horse for Lizette, and now they were getting ready to leave for Baltimore. ''When Bain came back last night, he told me my grandparents were in Baltimore with Grandpa's ship the *Interlude*,'' she went on. ''I should have realized he'd go there.''

She came out of the bedroom and Jeff looked at her and smiled. ''I meant to tell you before, that was a nice thing you did at Stuart's earlier,'' he said.

She eyed him curiously. ''What's that?''

''Telling me, in front of Julia, that Stuart really loves her, not you. How did you know she'd walked in when she did?''

Lizette flushed. ''I saw her reflection in the mirror over the fireplace and I was hoping she hadn't heard everything you'd said before she came in. I guess she didn't.''

''I think you saved her life.''

''No, Stuart saved her life. He does care, Jeff,'' she said solemnly. ''Maybe not the same, it's hard to say. How do you judge the years that form a bond between people? But he does care.''

''You didn't have to do it, though, Liz, and that was the important thing. Many women wouldn't care anything for Julia's feelings. Most brag about all the men who love them.''

''Not me, Jeff,'' she answered firmly. ''There's only one man I truly love, and only one man I want to love, and if we don't get on those horses and leave for Baltimore right away, I might lose him again for good, and I couldn't stand that.''

Before leaving, they made one more stop at Jeff's house to tell Ceil, who had just arrived home from church, that Jeff was escorting her to Baltimore, and to their surprise, Ceil had a special Sunday-morning edition of one of the local papers with a headline exonerating Bain and informing everyone there was no longer a price on his head. It said he had been working for the government and was also very much alive. There was a great deal to the story, but Lizette didn't take time to read it all. All she could think about was getting to Baltimore and finding Bain before she lost him again.

Jeff tucked one of the papers into his pocket and kissed Celia good-bye; then they mounted their horses and headed northeast, leaving the city of Washington behind.

Bain arrived in Baltimore early that same afternoon. He was tired, unhappy, and wishing he had really gone down with the *Dragonfly*. Nothing in his life seemed to be going right anymore. Nothing. Even after leaving Liz behind, he knew he still loved her. He'd always loved her, and there was no way he could change how he felt. But he'd loved Stuart, too. They hadn't always gotten along, brothers never did, but they'd never really been enemies, not until Liz came into their lives.

He felt embarrassed, the way the tears didn't want to stop. But you couldn't kill your brother without hating yourself and mourning the loss, and he'd cried for almost the whole thirty miles. Was it any wonder Lizette's grandparents knew right away something was wrong?

He stepped off the gangplank onto the deck of the *Interlude*, handing Amigo's reins to one of the men, then stared at Grandma Dicia and Grandpa Roth, trying to think of something to say.

"The twins?" he asked first, realizing they weren't about.

"Pretty has them taking a nap."

"Oh."

"Where's Liz, Bain?" Loedicia asked.

His eyes filled with tears again, but he bit them back. "She's not coming," he managed to say unsteadily.

Loedicia frowned. "Why not?"

He straightened, trying to compose himself. "May I talk to you both alone, down in your cabin, Grandpa Roth?" he asked, nodding toward Lizette's grandfather.

Roth glanced at Loedicia, then led the way, and they went belowdecks, where Bain told them everything right from the beginning, including Lizette's affair with Stuart a few years before, when Bain had ended up marrying Lizette to give Stuart's child a name, only to have her lose the baby shortly after the wedding, and get pregnant right away with the twins.

"She never wanted you to know," he said sadly. "And neither did I, but I feel you have to know now, to understand," and he told them the rest of the story, right up to date.

"I shot my brother, Grandma Dicia," he said angrily. "I didn't care that he was my brother at the time. All I cared about was that he'd taken advantage of her loneliness again, and I hated him for it. And now he's dead."

Loedicia and Roth both stared at him for a minute; then Loedicia reached across the table where they were sitting and took his hands.

"Bain, don't, please," she begged helplessly, wishing she could change things. "You've punished yourself enough."

"Have I?" he asked. "God help me, I wonder if I'll ever stop punishing myself. He didn't want to meet me, and I made him. I called him a coward and a bastard." His jaw tightened stubbornly. "I'm the coward, not him. I was too much of a coward to admit to myself I was afraid Liz loved him more than she loved me." He shook his head. "She said she'd never forgive me, and I don't blame her."

"What do you plan to do now?" Roth asked, seeing the pain in his eyes.

Bain shook his head. "I don't know . . . there's the twins . . . I love them, they're part of me. I can't leave them. But she doesn't want me. Not anymore, not after what I've done. She'll never forgive me. Besides, I've killed a United States Senator. The law won't look kindly on that."

"It was a fair duel," Roth reminded him.

Bain sighed disgustedly. "Why . . . why didn't I just let things be? Why did I have to act like a fool?"

"We all do foolish things at times," Roth said, trying to help him ease the pain some.

"My parents will never understand—how can they? I don't even understand myself."

"Sail home with us, Bain," Roth suggested. "Maybe by then you'll know what to do."

Bain's eyes darkened. "No! Oh, I don't know." He shook his head. "Right now I wish I'd never come back."

"Spend the rest of the day with the children," Loedicia said, her heart going out to him. "We won't leave until morning, and maybe you can decide by then."

He looked at them both. "Thank you for not condeming me," he said sadly. "I'm not proud of what I've done, but there's no way I can undo it, and that's what hurts."

"Sleep on it," said Roth. "We're in no hurry."

Bain thanked them, and left the cabin as they all heard Pretty in one of the other cabins, with the twins, who were starting to wake up from their nap, and Bain spent the rest of the day with Braxton and Blythe, trying to bring a little happiness back into a day he knew he'd remember through all eternity.

It was almost dusk when Lizette and Jeff, tired and dirty, rode into Baltimore and headed for the docks. Their horses were winded from being pushed too hard, and Lizette leaned over, patting her mount's neck.

"Only a little farther, fella," she said, trying to catch her breath as they galloped down the street. "We're almost there," and a short time later they turned a corner and reined up, staring at the ships lined up at the wharf.

"Which one's the *Interlude?*" Jeff asked as they slowed to a walk and began moving down the long line of ships.

They maneuvered in and out among sailors and carts, while Lizette studied the ships, the steady clop of their horses' hooves on the wooden wharf echoing behind them. Suddenly Lizette reined up and pointed.

"There!" she said firmly. It was barely light enough to see the figurehead, but the name was clear.

Jeff dismounted, then helped her down.

"I'll wait for you here," he said quickly, but she shook her head.

"You will not. You were kind enough to come with me so I didn't have to come alone. You can come on board and get something to eat. You're as hungry as I am, and since I made you ride right through, instead of stopping at an inn to eat, it's the least we can do."

He shrugged. "What do we do with the horses?"

"Tie them up somewhere?"

He found a hitching post next to one of the buildings, tied the horses, and they headed toward the gangplank.

"Well, this is it," she said as they went up it, and minutes later, she stood on the deck of the *Interlude* facing her grandparents.

"Where is he?" she asked after quickly explaining to them that everything was all right.

Roth nodded belowdecks. "He's helping Pretty with the twins, and I wish you luck."

Lizette took a deep breath, brushed the dirt from her skirt, straightened her hat, and squared her shoulders. "I think I need it," she said unsteadily, and headed toward the door that led belowdecks. But before she could reach it, it suddenly opened and she stopped abruptly as Bain stepped through.

He stared at her, eyes widening. "Liz?" he asked hesitantly. He could barely make her figure out in the darkness.

"Bain!"

He moved toward her, closing the door slowly behind him. "What are you doing here?" he asked, his voice raw with emotion.

She sighed. "I came to tell you I love you."

"It's too late, Liz," he replied. "I killed my brother, or have you forgotten so soon?"

"No, I didn't forget," she said stubbornly. "But he didn't die, Bain. Stuart's still alive." She moved toward him, hoping to see his face, but it had gotten too dark. "He told me you're a terrible shot," she said, her voice breaking. "And I'm glad."

"He said that?"

"He did, and he also told me to tell you he doesn't need your wife, Bain, because he has one of his own whom he loves very much."

"Liz, don't—"

"It's the truth, Bain." She gazed up at him, her heart in her eyes, and her voice lowered so only he could hear. "I never slept with him, Bain," she whispered urgently. "I'll admit, being with him was like keeping a part of you with me, even though I thought you were dead. And I'll admit his resemblance to you was hard for me to deal with, especially loving you like I do, but I never gave myself to him, Bain, please believe me, darling, I didn't."

He stared at her, letting her words sink in. "I want to believe you, Liz," he said. "But it's so hard. You're so lovely, and I know how much you need love, and how much he loves you."

"Yes, I guess he does," she answered unhappily. "But I don't think he can help it, any more than I can help loving you, or you loving me. That's my fault from before, Bain, and I can't change that, I'm sorry. But he does love Julia, too, in a way he can't love me, and that's the way it should be.''

"You believe that, don't you?"

"Yes," she said, feeling she was right.

He reached out and touched her face, unable to see her eyes in the darkness. He sighed. "Liz, I've been such a stupid fool," he said. "Can you forgive me?"

"Why do you think I came?"

"Is Stuart really bad?"

She shook her head. "No, just a shoulder wound."

Bain laughed softly, suddenly seeing the irony of it. "You know, I am a terrible shot." He chuckled. "Thank God!" he said, and sighed, relieved. "I could have killed him."

"Yes, you could. And something else," she said. "A paper came out this morning, all Washington's talking about it. You're free, Bain. The President kept his promise and now everyone knows you were never a pirate."

"You mean I can really go home?" he asked incredulously. "It's really true?"

"It's really true," she assured him happily, and he reached out, pulling her to him, hugging her close.

"Good news, eh, Bain?" Roth called over as they all saw Bain holding Lizette in his arms.

"The best!" he shouted at the top of his lungs so all the world could hear. "Stuart's alive, there's no price on my head, and I have my Liz back again," and he swung her up, cradling her in his arms, his heart singing for joy for the first time in months, and as they all watched, he disappeared belowdecks, carrying her with him, both laughing, as she lost her bonnet in the doorway.

He made his way to the small cabin they'd be sharing and laid her on the narrow bunk, able to see her face now for the first time in the light from the lantern on the wall.

"Now, tell me again," he whispered softly as he bent over her. "Tell me everything, Liz. Tell me you love me and forgive me, while I can see it in your eyes and know it's in your heart."

She reached up, touching his face, aware of the shadows beneath his eyes from the tears she knew he'd shed for all he thought he'd lost, and she told him once more that he hadn't lost it, that Stuart was still alive and he and Julia were still together, and she loved him with all her heart.

"And now I want to go home, darling," she whispered softly

as he stretched out on the bunk beside her. Her arms twined
about his neck. "I want to go back to our house in Beaufort with
you and the twins, and never set foot in Washington again."

"What about your clothes?" he asked as his lips brushed her
ear, his hands beginning to loosen the front of her riding habit.
"I saw tons of clothes in the armoire in your hotel room. Don't
you want to go back and get them?"

"Never," she sighed ecstatically as he began to make love to
her in earnest. "I'll go naked all the way to Beaufort if I have to.
Besides," she said dreamily as she lay close in his arms, "I
don't need those clothes anymore, Bain, they're black and terrible,
and they're mourning clothes. I'm not a widow anymore, you
know." She sighed. "My love's come home," and as his lips
found hers, making everything between them right again, up on
deck Captain Casey took Jeff to the galley for something to eat,
while Loedicia and Roth stood together by the rail.

Roth's arms were around Loedicia, and as she leaned back
against him, watching the moon come up from behind them to
bathe the city in its soft glow, her thoughts began to wander back
to the letter they'd received from Cole some weeks before Bain's
return, telling them that in spite of the fact that Heather's broken
leg had left her with a limp, they had left the valley and were now
in Comanche territory searching for the baby. And she thought
back over all the heartbreak the past few months had held for
Lizette, and as Roth's arms tightened about her, she wondered,
as she had so often before, why life always seemed to bring her
family the bitter before giving them the sweet.

Epilogue

Early in the year 1821, with James Long's aborted attempt to take over Texas crushed by Spain the year before, the United States, enraged over Jean Lafitte's continuing piracy, and ignoring the fact that he was in Spanish territory because they had written proof to back their claims, dispatched the brigantine *Enterprise,* under the command of Lieutenant Lawrence Kearny, to rout the pirates at Galveston Bay. And after quickly contemplating the situation, Jean Lafitte, knowing to stand up against an American man-of-war would be futile, quietly accepted his fate, burned down Campeche, and sailed away, spending his last years on the Spanish Main, where he and his brother Pierre were lost to history and legend.

About the Author

The granddaughter of an old-time vaudevillian, Mrs. Shiplett was born and raised in Ohio. She is married and lives in the city of Mentor-on-the-Lake. She has four daughters and several grandchildren and enjoys living an active outdoor life.